SD에듀

독학사
2단계

─ 영어영문학과 ─

19세기 영미소설

SD에듀
(주)시대고시기획

머리말

학위를 얻는 데 시간과 장소는 더 이상 제약이 되지 않습니다. 대입 전형을 거치지 않아도 '학점은행제'를 통해 학사학위를 취득할 수 있기 때문입니다. 그중 독학학위제도는 고등학교 졸업자이거나 이와 동등 이상의 학력을 가지고 있는 사람들에게 효율적인 학점 인정 및 학사학위 취득의 기회를 줍니다.

학습을 통한 개인의 자아실현 도구이자 자신의 실력을 인정받을 수 있는 스펙으로서의 독학사는 짧은 기간 안에 학사학위를 취득할 수 있는 가장 빠른 지름길로 많은 수험생들의 선택을 받고 있습니다.

독학학위취득시험은 1단계 교양과정 인정시험, 2단계 전공기초과정 인정시험, 3단계 전공심화과정 인정시험, 4단계 학위취득 종합시험의 1~4단계 시험으로 이루어집니다. 4단계까지의 과정을 통과한 자에 한해 학사학위 취득이 가능하고, 이는 대학에서 취득한 학위와 동등한 지위를 갖습니다.

이 책은 독학사 시험에 응시하는 수험생들이 단기간에 효과적인 학습을 할 수 있도록 다음과 같이 구성하였습니다.

01 단원 개요
핵심이론을 학습하기에 앞서 각 단원에서 파악해야 할 중점과 학습목표를 정리하여 수록하였습니다.

02 핵심이론
다년간 출제된 독학학위제 평가영역을 철저히 분석하여 시험에 꼭 출제되는 내용을 '핵심이론'으로 선별하여 수록하였으며, 중요도 체크 및 이론 안의 '더 알아두기'를 통해 심화 학습과 학습 내용 정리를 효율적으로 할 수 있게 하였습니다.

03 실전예상문제
해당 출제영역에 맞는 핵심포인트를 분석하여 구성한 '실전예상문제'를 수록하였습니다.

04 최종모의고사
최신출제유형을 반영한 '최종모의고사(2회분)'를 통해 자신의 실력을 점검해볼 수 있으며, 실제 시험에 임하듯이 시간을 재고 풀어본다면 시험장에서의 실수를 줄일 수 있을 것입니다.

19세기 영미소설은 우리가 주변에서 익히 보고 들어왔던 대표적인 영미소설이 주로 해당됩니다. 당대의 경제적·정치적·사회적 변화의 과정과 반응이 다양하게 내용을 이루고 있으며 19세기는 소설의 시대라고 할 만큼 19세기에 성취한 소설 장르의 결실은 매우 특별하다고 볼 수 있습니다. 전공자의 입장에서 본다면, 19세기 영미소설에 대한 내용 전개의 피상적인 지식의 습득에서 머물기보다는 작가별 다양한 창조적 특성과 등장인물들의 묘사, 소설의 전개가 당대의 사회적 변화를 얼마나 반영하고 있는지에 대한 심도 있는 분석이 필요합니다.

편저자 드림

BDES

독학학위제 소개

독학학위제란?

「독학에 의한 학위취득에 관한 법률」에 의거하여 국가에서 시행하는 시험에 합격한 사람에게 학사학위를 수여하는 제도

- ✓ 고등학교 졸업 이상의 학력을 가진 사람이면 누구나 응시 가능
- ✓ 대학교를 다니지 않아도 스스로 공부해서 학위취득 가능
- ✓ 일과 학습의 병행이 가능하여 시간과 비용 최소화
- ✓ 언제, 어디서나 학습이 가능한 평생학습시대의 자아실현을 위한 제도
- ✓ 학위취득시험은 4개의 과정(교양, 전공기초, 전공심화, 학위취득 종합시험)으로 이루어져 있으며 각 과정별 시험을 모두 거쳐 학위취득 종합시험에 합격하면 학사학위 취득

독학학위제 전공 분야 (11개 전공)

국어 국문학 | 영어 영문학 | 심리학 | 경영학 | 법학 | 행정학

컴퓨터 공학 | 가정학 | 유아 교육학 | 정보 통신학 | 간호학

※ 유아교육학 및 정보통신학 전공: 3, 4과정만 개설
※ 간호학 전공: 4과정만 개설
※ 중어중문학, 수학, 농학 전공: 폐지 전공으로 기존에 해당 전공 학적 보유자에 한하여 응시 가능

※ SD에듀는 현재 4개 학과(심리학과, 경영학과, 컴퓨터공학과, 간호학과) 개설 완료
※ 2개 학과(국어국문학과, 영어영문학과) 개설 진행 중

독학학위제 시험안내

과정별 응시자격

단계	과정	응시자격	과정(과목) 시험 면제 요건
1	교양	고등학교 졸업 이상 학력 소지자	• 대학(교)에서 각 학년 수료 및 일정 학점 취득 • 학점은행제 일정 학점 인정 • 국가기술자격법에 따른 자격 취득 • 교육부령에 따른 각종 시험 합격 • 면제지정기관 이수 등
2	전공기초		
3	전공심화		

4	학위취득	• 1~3과정 합격 및 면제
		• 대학에서 동일 전공으로 3년 이상 수료
		  (3년제의 경우 졸업) 또는 105학점 이상 취득
		• 학점은행제 동일 전공 105학점 이상 인정
		  (전공 28학점 포함) ➡ 22.1.1. 시행
		• 외국에서 15년 이상의 학교교육과정 수료
			없음(반드시 응시)

응시 방법 및 응시료

• 접수 방법: 온라인으로만 가능
• 제출 서류: 응시자격 증빙 서류 등 자세한 내용은 홈페이지 참조
• 응시료: 20,400원

독학학위제 시험 범위

• 시험과목별 평가 영역 범위에서 대학 전공자에게 요구되는 수준으로 출제
• 시험 범위 및 예시문항은 독학학위제 홈페이지(bdes.nile.or.kr) ➡ 학습정보 ➡ 과목별 평가영역에서 확인

문항 수 및 배점

과정	일반 과목			예외 과목		
	객관식	주관식	합계	객관식	주관식	합계
교양, 전공기초 (1~2과정)	40문항×2.5점 =100점	–	40문항 100점	25문항×4점 =100점	–	25문항 100점
전공심화, 학위취득 (3~4과정)	24문항×2.5점 =60점	4문항×10점 =40점	28문항 100점	15문항×4점 =60점	5문항×8점 =40점	20문항 100점

※ 2017년도부터 교양과정 인정시험 및 전공기초과정 인정시험은 객관식 문항으로만 출제

합격 기준

■ 1~3과정(교양, 전공기초, 전공심화) 시험

단계	과정	합격 기준	유의 사항
1	교양	매 과목 60점 이상 득점을 합격으로 하고, 과목 합격 인정(합격 여부만 결정)	5과목 합격
2	전공기초		6과목 이상 합격
3	전공심화		

■ 4과정(학위취득) 시험: 총점 합격제 또는 과목별 합격제 선택

구분	합격 기준	유의 사항
총점 합격제	• 총점(600점)의 60% 이상 득점(360점) • 과목 낙제 없음	• 6과목 모두 신규 응시 • 기존 합격 과목 불인정
과목별 합격제	• 매 과목 100점 만점으로 하여 전 과목(교양 2, 전공 4) 60점 이상 득점	• 기존 합격 과목 재응시 불가 • 1과목이라도 60점 미만 득점하면 불합격

시험 일정

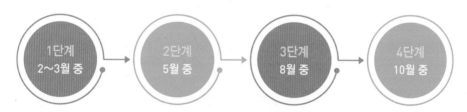

■ 영어영문학과 2단계 시험 과목 및 시험 시간표

구분(교시별)	시간	시험 과목명
1교시	09:00~10:40(100분)	영어학개론, 영국문학개관
2교시	11:10~12:50(100분)	중급영어, 19세기 영미소설
중식 12:50~13:40(50분)		
3교시	14:00~15:40(100분)	영미희곡Ⅰ, 영어음성학
4교시	16:10~17:50(100분)	영문법, 19세기 영미시

※ 시험 일정 및 세부사항은 반드시 독학학위제 홈페이지(bdes.nile.or.kr)를 통해 확인하시기 바랍니다.

※ SD에듀에서 개설되었거나 개설 예정인 과목은 빨간색으로 표시했습니다.

독학학위제 과정

1단계
교양과정 01

대학의 교양과정을 이수한
사람이 일반적으로 갖추어야 할
학력 수준 평가

2단계
02 **전공기초**

각 전공영역의 학문을 연구하기
위하여 각 학문 계열에서 공통적으로
필요한 지식과 기술 평가

3단계
전공심화 03

각 전공영역에서의 보다
심화된 전문 지식과 기술 평가

4단계
04 **학위취득**

학위를 취득한 사람이
일반적으로 갖추어야 할 소양 및
전문 지식과 기술을 종합적으로 평가

GUIDE

독학학위제 출제방향

국가평생교육진흥원에서 고시한 과목별 평가영역에 준거하여 출제하되, 특정한 영역이나 분야가 지나치게 중시되거나 경시되지 않도록 한다.

교양과정 인정시험 및 전공기초과정 인정시험의 시험방법은 객관식(4지택1형)으로 한다.

단편적 지식의 암기로 풀 수 있는 문항의 출제는 지양하고, 이해력·적용력·분석력 등 폭넓고 고차원적인 능력을 측정하는 문항을 위주로 한다.

독학자들의 취업 비율이 높은 점을 감안하여, 과목의 특성상 가능한 경우에는 학문적이고 이론적인 문항뿐만 아니라 실무적인 문항도 출제한다.

교양과정 인정시험(1과정)은 대학 교양교재에서 공통적으로 다루고 있는 기본적이고 핵심적인 내용을 출제하되, 교양과정 범위를 넘는 전문적이거나 지엽적인 내용의 출제는 지양한다.

이설(異說)이 많은 내용의 출제는 지양하고 보편적이고 정설화된 내용에 근거하여 출제하며, 그럴 수 없는 경우에는 해당 학자의 성명이나 학파를 명시한다.

전공기초과정 인정시험(2과정)은 각 전공영역의 학문을 연구하기 위하여 각 학문 계열에서 공통적으로 필요한 지식과 기술을 평가한다.

전공심화과정 인정시험(3과정)은 각 전공영역에 관하여 보다 심화된 전문적인 지식과 기술을 평가한다.

학위취득 종합시험(4과정)은 시험의 최종 과정으로서 학위를 취득한 자가 일반적으로 갖추어야 할 소양 및 전문지식과 기술을 종합적으로 평가한다.

전공심화과정 인정시험 및 학위취득 종합시험의 시험방법은 객관식(4지택1형)과 주관식(80자 내외의 서술형)으로 하되, 과목의 특성에 따라 다소 융통성 있게 출제한다.

독학학위제 단계별 학습법

1단계 평가영역에 기반을 둔 이론 공부!

독학학위제에서 발표한 평가영역에 기반을 두어 효율적으로 이론 공부를 해야 합니다. 각 장별로 정리된 '핵심이론'을 통해 핵심적인 개념을 파악합니다. 모든 내용을 다 암기하는 것이 아니라, 포괄적으로 이해한 후 핵심내용을 파악하여 이 부분을 확실히 알고 넘어가야 합니다.

2단계 시험 경향 및 문제 유형 파악!

독학사 시험 문제는 지금까지 출제된 유형에서 크게 벗어나지 않는 범위에서 비슷한 유형으로 줄곧 출제되고 있습니다. 본서에 수록된 이론을 충실히 학습한 후 문제의 유형과 출제의도를 파악하는 데 집중하도록 합니다. 교재에 수록된 문제는 시험 유형의 가장 핵심적인 부분이 반영된 문항들이므로 실제 시험에서 어떠한 유형이 출제되는지에 대한 감을 잡을 수 있을 것입니다.

3단계 '실전예상문제'를 통한 효과적인 대비!

독학사 시험 문제는 비슷한 유형들이 반복되어 출제되므로 다양한 문제를 풀어 보는 것이 필수적입니다. 각 단원의 끝에 수록된 '실전예상문제'를 통해 단원별 내용을 제대로 학습했는지 꼼꼼하게 확인하고, 실력점검을 합니다. 이때 부족한 부분은 따로 체크해 두고 복습할 때 중점적으로 공부하는 것도 좋은 학습 전략입니다.

4단계 복습을 통한 학습 마무리!

이론 공부를 하면서, 혹은 문제를 풀어 보면서 헷갈리고 이해하기 어려운 부분은 따로 체크해 두는 것이 좋습니다. 중요 개념은 반복학습을 통해 놓치지 않고 확실하게 익히고 넘어가야 합니다. 마무리 단계에서는 '최종모의고사'를 통해 실전연습을 할 수 있도록 합니다.

COMMENT

합격수기

> 저는 학사편입 제도를 이용하기 위해 2~4단계를 순차로 응시했고 한 번에 합격했습니다.
> 아슬아슬한 점수라서 부끄럽지만 독학사는 자료가 부족해서 부족하나마 후기를 쓰는 것이 도움이 될까 하여
> 제 합격전략을 정리하여 알려 드립니다.

#1. 교재와 전공서적을 가까이에!

학사학위취득은 본래 4년을 기본으로 합니다. 독학사는 이를 1년으로 단축하는 것을 목표로 하는 시험이라 실제 시험도 변별력을 높이는 몇 문제를 제외한다면 기본이 되는 중요한 이론 위주로 출제됩니다. SD에듀의 독학사 시리즈 역시 이에 맞추어 중요한 내용이 일목요연하게 압축ㆍ정리되어 있습니다. 빠르게 훑어보기 좋지만 내가 목표로 한 전공에 대해 자세히 알고 싶다면 전공서적과 함께 공부하는 것이 좋습니다. 교재와 전공서적을 함께 보면서 교재에 전공서적 내용을 정리하여 단권화하면 시험이 임박했을 때 교재 한 권으로도 자신 있게 시험을 치를 수 있습니다.

#2. 시간확인은 필수!

쉬운 문제는 금방 넘어가지만 지문이 길거나 어렵고 헷갈리는 문제도 있고, OMR 카드에 마킹까지 해야 하니 실제로 주어진 시간은 더 짧습니다. 1번에 어려운 문제가 있다고 해서 시간을 많이 허비하면 쉽게 풀 수 있는 마지막 문제들을 놓칠 수 있습니다. 문제 푸는 속도도 느려지니 집중력도 떨어집니다. 그래서 어차피 배점은 같으니 아는 문제를 최대한 많이 맞히는 것을 목표로 했습니다.
① 어려운 문제는 빠르게 넘기면서 문제를 끝까지 다 풀고 ② 확실한 답부터 우선 마킹한 후 ③ 다시 시험지로 돌아가 건너뛴 문제들을 다시 풀었습니다. 확실히 시간을 재고 문제를 많이 풀어봐야 실전에 도움이 되는 것 같습니다.

#3. 문제풀이의 반복!

여느 시험과 마찬가지로 문제는 많이 풀어볼수록 좋습니다. 이론을 공부한 후 실전예상문제를 풀다보니 부족한 부분이 어딘지 확인할 수 있었고, 공부한 이론이 시험에 어떤 식으로 출제될지 예상할 수 있었습니다. 그렇게 부족한 부분을 보충해가며 문제유형을 파악하면 이론을 복습할 때도 어떤 부분을 중점적으로 암기해야 할지 알 수 있습니다. 이론 공부가 어느 정도 마무리되었을 때 시계를 준비하고 최종모의고사를 풀었습니다. 실제 시험 시간을 생각하면서 예행연습을 하니 시험 당일에는 덜 긴장할 수 있었습니다.

> 학위취득을 위해 오늘도 열심히 학습하시는 동지 여러분에게도 합격의 영광이 있으시길 기원하면서 이만 줄입니다.

이 책의 구성과 특징

01

제**2**장 Jane Austen
- 『Pride and Prejudice』

제1편 19세기 일

단원 **개요**

핵심이론을 학습하기에 앞서 각 단원에서
파악해야 할 중점과 학습목표를
수록하였습니다.

> Elizabeth의 결혼이 비록 신분상승적인 결혼이긴 하지만, 그 과정에는 Elizabeth와 Darcy가 공통되는 어진 혼적이 있다. 두 사람의 결혼은 서로의 단점을 극복하고 상대의 본질적인 자질에 대한 확실한 존중에 기초한 결혼이라고 해석할 수 있다. 또한 Elizabeth가 성장하는 인물이라는 사실이 중요하다. 소설은 남성을 주인공으로 하여 주인공의 정신적·육체적 성장과정을 그린 것이 대부분이었다. Austen의 소설에서는 변화하고 발전된 여성이 등장한다.

출제 경향 및 수험 대책

> 이 소설은 사랑과 결혼이 주요 플롯(Plot)이지만 작가가 낭만적으로 결혼을 그리기보다는 날카로운 현실 인식을 바로 당대 사회를 비판하고 있음을 염두에 두어야 한다. 다양한 등장인물들의 결혼 과정을 그리면서 각 인물들의 이들 그들의 특징 및 성격을 묻는 문제에 대한 대비가 요구된다.

제1절 작가의 생애

Jane Austen(1775~1817)은 1775년 12월 16일 영국의 남부 지역 햄프셔(Hampshire)주의 스
(Steventon)이라는 마을에서 영국 성공회 교구 목사인 아버지 조지 오스틴(George Austen)과 어
산드라 리(Cassandra Leigh) 사이에서 태어났다. Austen 가문은 젠트리(gentry) 계급에 속하며,
여덟 남매 중 일곱째 아이였다. Jane의 오빠들은 목사, 해군 등이 되었지만, 그 당시의 시대적 관습
딸들은 직업을 갖지 않고 친지를 방문한 경우를 제외하고는 집에 머물러 있었다. Jane은 아주 어렸을
니 Cassandra와 함께 작은 기숙학교를 다녔지만 11세 이후에는 집에서 교육을 받았다. 그들은 피아노
법과 이태리어, 프랑스어 등의 외국어를 익혔고 역사를 배웠다. 또한 문학에도 관심이 깊어 Shakesp
Milton 외에도 18세기의 소설가, 수필가 및 시인들에 대한 깊은 지식을 갖게 되었다.

02

핵심**이론**

독학사 시험의 출제 경향에 맞춰 시행처의
평가영역을 바탕으로 과년도 출제문제와
이론을 빅데이터 방식에 맞게 선별하여
가장 최신의 이론과 문제를 시험에
출제되는 영역 위주로 정리하였습니다.

제1편 19세기 일

제**1**장 19세기 영국소설과
빅토리아조 문학의 개관

제1절 19세기 영국소설

영문학사에서 소설(novel) 장르는 시(poetry)나 희곡(drama)보다 비교적 늦은 시기인 18세기 초에
다고 볼 수 있다. 18세기에 풍자 소설(satire), 감상주의 소설(sentimental novel), 고딕 로맨스(Gothic ro
등과 같은 다양한 형태로 형성된 영국소설은 19세기에 들어와서 '소설의 시대', 19세기 영국의 '리
소설'로 전성기를 맞이한다. 이 시대의 영국소설은 영어의 활력과 가능성이 최고의 상태로 발현되
가와 대중 사이에 활발한 교류와 소통이 이루어진다는 점에서 전체 영국 문학의 역사에서도 큰
지닌다.
19세기 영국소설의 특징을 간단히 요약하거나 일반화하는 것은 어렵다. 물론 이 시기의 소설은 대
실주의적인 특징을 지니고, 개인과 사회의 유기적인 관계를 다루며, 단일하고 통일적인 구성보다는
이고 복합적인 구조를 갖는다고 말할 수 있다.
이 시기의 영국소설을 규정하는 용어인 'Realism 소설'에 대해서도 추가적인 설명이 필요하다. 일
로 영어의 'Realism'은 사실주의로 번역된다. 사실주의는 말 그대로 당대의 현실을 있는 그대로 세
정확하게 재현한다는 의미를 담고 있다. 18세기 소설이 전대의 문학적 전통주의와 구별되는 가장
도 바로 이 사실주의적인 특성이었고, 이것은 당시로서는 상당한 의의를 지니는 문학사적인 변화였
러나 19세기 영국소설의 리얼리즘은 18세기 영국소설보다 더 폭넓은 개념을 가지고 있다. 현실에
단순한 묘사와 복제를 넘어서 '현실에 대한 올바른 인식', 그리고 그것에 바탕을 둔 실천이 소설에
다. 이는 '현실주의'라고 부를 수 있는 문학적 입장이 그 안에 복합적으로 녹아들어 있기 때문이
19세기 리얼리즘 소설의 진수는 George Eliot과 Charles Dickens 그리고 1870년대 이후에 주로 ㅋ
동을 한 Thomas Hardy의 작품에서 찾을 수 있다. 이외에도 주요 작가로는 William Makepeace Tha

03

제2편 19세기 C

제 **2** 편 | 실전예상문제

해설 & 정답

제 2 장 | Edgar Alan Poe – 「*The Black Cat*」

01 다음 중 Edgar Allan Poe의 작품이 <u>아닌</u> 것은?

① 「*Ligeia*」
② 「*The Fall of the House of the Usher*」
③ 「*The Murders in the Rue Morgue*」
④ 「*Wessex Tales*」

01 총 5편으로 이뤄진
Tales(1888)는 T
작품이다.

02 Edgar Allan Poe에 대한 설명으로 옳지 <u>않은</u> 것은?

① 시의 경우에는 100줄 정도의 길이가 적당하다고 하였다.
② 소설은 앉은 자리에서 독파할 수 있는 분량이 적당하다고 하였다.
③ 아름다운 여성의 죽음이야말로 가장 소설적인 소재라고 설정하기도 하였다.
④ 작품의 단일성 확득을 위해 치밀하게 언어 사용을 규제하였다.

02 아름다운 여성의 죽
시적인 소재라고 설

실전예상문제

독학사 시험의 경향에 맞춰 전 영역의 문제를 새롭게 구성하고 지극히 지엽적인 문제나 쉬운 문제를 배제하여 학습자가 해당 교과정에서 필수로 알아야 할 내용을 문제로 정리하였습니다. 풍부한 해설을 추가하여 이해를 쉽게 하고 문제를 통해 이론의 학습내용을 반추하여 실제시험에 대비할 수 있도록 구성하였습니다.

최종모의고사

'핵심이론'을 공부하고, '실전예상문제'를 풀어보았다면 이제 남은 것은 실전 감각 기르기와 최종 점검입니다. '최종모의고사 (총 2회분)'를 실제 시험처럼 시간을 두고 풀어보고, 정답과 해설을 통해 복습한다면 좋은 결과가 있을 것입니다.

04

독학사 영어영문학과 2단계
제 **1** 회 | **최종모의고사** | 19세기 영미소설

제한시간 : 50분 | 시작 ___시 ___분 ~ 종료 ___시 ___분

➡ 정답 및 해설

01 Jane Austen에 대한 설명으로 옳지 <u>않은</u> 것은?

① 1775년 영국의 햄프셔의 Steventon에서 태어났다.
② 활발한 사회생활을 했으며 글 쓰는 것 외에도 그녀의 생을 가족에게 애정을 쏟았다.
③ 젊은 시절에는 무도회와 파티에서 많은 남성들의 관심을 받기도 하였다.
④ 27세가 될 무렵 햄프셔의 부유한 지주와 결혼하여 행복한 가정을 꾸몄다.

02 「*Pride and Prejudice*」에 관한 설명으로 옳은 것은?

① Mr. Bennet은 자진하여 딸들을 데리고 Netherfield의 무도회에 갔다.
② Darcy와 Wickham은 어렸을 때부터 친한 친구이다.
③ Elizabeth는 Pemberley에 가서 Darcy를 찾기 위해 애쓴다.
④ Darcy는 Wickham으로 인해 곤경에 빠진 Lydia를 도와준다.

목차

제 **1** 편

19세기 영국소설

www.sdedu.co.kr

I wish you the best of luck

독학사 영어영문학과 2단계

제 1 장 19세기 영국소설과 빅토리아조 문학의 개관

제 1 절 19세기 영국소설

영문학사에서 소설(novel) 장르는 시(poetry)나 희곡(drama)보다 비교적 늦은 시기인 18세기 초에 등장했다고 볼 수 있다. 18세기에 풍자 소설(satire), 감상주의 소설(sentimental novel), 고딕 로맨스(Gothic romance) 등과 같은 다양한 형태로 형성된 영국소설은 19세기에 들어와서 '소설의 시대', 19세기 영국의 '리얼리즘 소설'로 전성기를 맞이한다. 이 시대의 영국소설은 영어의 활력과 가능성이 최고의 상태로 발현되고, 작가와 대중 사이에 활발한 교류와 소통이 이루어진다는 점에서 전체 영국 문학의 역사에서도 큰 의미를 지닌다.

19세기 영국소설의 특징을 간단히 요약하거나 일반화하는 것은 어렵다. 물론 이 시기의 소설은 대체로 사실주의적인 특징을 지니고, 개인과 사회의 유기적인 관계를 다루며, 단일하고 통일적인 구성보다는 다층적이고 복합적인 구조를 갖는다고 말할 수 있다.

이 시기의 영국소설을 규정하는 용어인 'Realism 소설'에 대해서도 추가적인 설명이 필요하다. 일반적으로 영어의 'Realism'은 사실주의로 번역된다. 사실주의는 말 그대로 당대의 현실을 있는 그대로 세밀하고 정확하게 재현한다는 의미를 담고 있다. 18세기 소설이 전대의 문학적 전통주의와 구별되는 가장 큰 특징도 바로 이 사실주의적인 특성이었고, 이것은 당시로서는 상당한 의의를 지니는 문학사적인 변화였다. 그러나 19세기 영국소설의 리얼리즘은 18세기 영국소설보다 더 폭넓은 개념을 가지고 있다. 현실에 대한 단순한 묘사와 복제를 넘어서 '현실에 대한 올바른 인식', 그리고 그것에 바탕을 둔 실천이 소설에 담겨있다. 이는 '현실주의'라고 부를 수 있는 문학적 입장이 그 안에 복합적으로 녹아들어 있기 때문이다.

19세기 리얼리즘 소설의 진수는 George Eliot과 Charles Dickens 그리고 1870년대 이후에 주로 작품 활동을 한 Thomas Hardy의 작품에서 찾을 수 있다. 이외에도 주요 작가로는 William Makepeace Thackeray가 있다.

19세기 영국소설의 리얼리즘을 논하기에 앞서 19세기 초에 전환기적 작가인 '스코틀랜드 문학의 대부'인 Sir Walter Scott과 Jane Austen의 작품 세계를 살펴볼 필요가 있다.

1 Sir Walter Scott(1771~1832)

Sir Walter Scott은 영국소설사의 '역사소설'(the historical novel) 장르에서 큰 위상을 차지하고 있는 인물이다. 그의 작품은 중세부터 근세에 이르는 시대를 배경으로 하고 있다. 그는 소설에서 특히 자신의 고향인 스코틀랜드(Scotland)를 소재로 다루고 있다. Scott은 1814년 「*Waverly*」를 발표하면서 소설가의 길로 들어섰는데, 그의 역사소설은 Waverley Novels로 불린다. 그는 「*The Heart of Mid-Lothian*」(1818),

「Ivanhoe」(1819) 등 30여 편에 이르는 장편 역사소설을 발표하였다. 중세를 배경으로 한 그의 작품들은 낭만주의의 특성인 도피주의적인 성향을 지니고 있지만, 18세기 특히 스코틀랜드를 배경으로 한 일부 작품은 농부들의 삶과 애환을 사실주의적으로 묘사하는 데 부분적으로 성공했다는 평가를 받기도 한다. 타고난 이야기꾼으로 평가받고 있는 Scott은 당대에 상당한 대중적인 인기를 누렸고, 유럽대륙에서도 인기 작가로서 많은 독자층을 확보하고 있었다.

Scott이 활동하였던 19세기 초를 영문학사에서는 낭만주의(Romanticism) 시대라고 한다. William Wordsworth, Samuel Taylor Coleridge, Percy Bysshe Shelley, John Keats 등 뛰어난 서정 시인들이 활동한 '시의 시대'가 바로 이 낭만주의 시대였다. 이러한 면에서 Scott에게 '낭만주의 소설가'라는 이름을 붙일 수 있는데, 낭만주의가 가진 특유의 열정과 감수성은 Scott과 거의 같은 시기에 활동하였던 작가인 Jane Austen의 소설에도 부분적으로 반영된다.

2 Jane Austen(1775~1817)

Jane Austen은 시기적으로는 낭만주의에 속해 있음에도 불구하고 Austen의 소설사적 시대 구분은 그리 간단하지 않다. 프랑스 혁명(1789~1799)과 낭만주의를 비롯하여 당시 유럽 대륙을 휩쓸었던 정치・사회적 격변에 대해서 Jane Austen은 무심한 편이었다. 또한 그녀가 소설에서 궁극적으로 지향하는 가치와 정서는 여전히 18세기의 이성주의와 합리주의에 가깝다. 그러므로 Austen은 18세기와 19세기 전환기의 작가라고 할 수 있다.

이전까지의 영국소설, 즉 Daniel Defoe의 자전적 서술이나 Samuel Richardson의 서간체 양식, Henry Fielding의 피카레스크(picaresque)적 잔재 그리고 Laurence Sterne의 형식적 실험 등과 같은 18세기 주요 작가들의 소설적인 성취는 새로운 장르가 나타날 때 볼 수 있는 자의식의 표출로 이해할 수 있다. 그런데 Austen의 소설은 위에서 언급한 새로운 장르가 지니는 생소함에 머물지 않고 소설의 형식적 정형성을 구축하고 있음을 볼 수 있다. Austen이 소설에서 담고 있는 정교한 플롯 설정과 심리 묘사, 대화의 적절한 균형, 전형적이면서도 개성강한 인물의 창조와 사실주의적인 묘사에 기초한 진지한 현실 인식 등과 같은 Austen 소설의 특징들은 이전의 소설들과 일정한 차이를 보이며 이후 소설 양식의 발전에 하나의 모델을 제시하고 있다는 평가를 받고 있다. 그런 점에서 영국소설의 '위대한 전통'(the Great Tradition)을 주창한 비평가 F. R. Leavis가 George Eliot, Charles Dickens, Henry James, Joseph Conrad, D. H. Lawrence로 이어지는 전통의 앞자리에 Austen을 놓은 것은 충분히 설득력을 지닌다.

제 2 절 빅토리아 시대 소설(1832~1900)

영문학사에서 19세기는 크게 19세기 초의 낭만주의 시기와 이후의 빅토리아 시대(the Victorian era, 빅토리아 여왕 재위기간, 1837~1901)로 나누어진다. 낭만주의 시기가 '시의 시대'였다면 낭만주의의 대가

Walter Scott이 사망한 해인 1832년부터 이어지는 빅토리아 시대는 '소설의 시대'이다. 18세기 Daniel Defoe, Samuel Richardson, Henry Fielding 등에 의하여 소설 장르의 전개 과정을 보인 영국소설은 Jane Austen과 Walter Scott에 와서 심화와 확대 과정을 거쳐 Brontë 자매와 Charles Dickens, William Makepeace Thackeray, George Eliot, Thomas Hardy 등에 이르러 전성기를 맞이한다.

1 빅토리아 시대 문학의 특징

(1) 일차적으로는 당대에 일어난 경제적·정치적·사회적 변화의 기록이자 반응이다.

(2) 희곡 영역을 제외한 모든 다양한 장르에서 풍성한 결실을 성취했다.

(3) 빅토리아 시대를 '소설의 시대'라 할 정도로 소설 문학의 성취는 특별했다.

(4) 소설 창작이 양적으로 가장 왕성했고 소설가와 독자, 대중과 긴밀한 관계 형성이 되었다.

2 대표작가

(1) Charles Dickens(1812~1870)

Dickens는 빅토리아 시대에 가장 널리 알려진 작가로서 사회 비판 및 항거의 기풍이 그의 전 작품에서 흐르고 있다. 그는 중산층의 일상생활을 소설에서 다루고 있는데, 특히 산업 팽창에 따른 지나친 사회악과 사회 불의에 항거하는 개인들, 가난한 사람들의 투쟁을 매우 생생하게 묘사했다. Dickens는 낙관주의와 진보에 대한 신념을 가지고 있으면서도, 당대의 산업 제도에서 유래하는 빈민층의 생활을 리얼하게 묘사하였는데, 거기에서 낭만주의적 요소와 사실주의적 요소가 혼합되어 있다.

Dickens가 26세에 발표했던 「*Oliver Twist*」(1838)는 당시 베스트셀러에 오를 만큼 폭발적인 인기를 얻었던 작품으로, 고아 소년 Oliver를 통하여 빈부격차에서 오는 영국의 부조리한 사회와 모순을 사실적으로 묘사한 작품이다. 「*David Copperfield*」(1849~1850)는 그의 자서전적인 작품으로 전체적인 구성이 조화롭게 균형이 잡혀있는 걸작이다.

(2) William Makepeace Thackeray(1811~1863)

잡지 등에 글을 기고하며 작가 활동을 시작한 Thackeray는 결혼 후 아내의 우울증과 많은 부양가족 때문에 고생을 했지만 역경을 딛고 대작가로 성장하였다. 그의 대표작 「*Vanity Fair*」(1848)는 '허영의 시장'으로 번역되는데, 이 제목은 영국 기독교 문학의 고전인 John Bunyan의 「*The Pilgrim's Progress*」(1678)에서 따온 것이다. 제목에서도 알 수 있듯이 이 작품은 1813년부터 제1차 선거법 개정(1832) 후인 1833년까지의 영국 사회를 배경으로 하여 두 여주인공 Becky Sharp와 Amelia Sedley 를 통해 신흥 중산 계급의 천박함 및 상류 계급의 물질 만능주의와 부패한 생활상을 생생하게 그린 사회 비판 소설이다.

(3) Charlotte Brontë(1816~1855)

Emily Brontë의 언니인 Charlotte Brontë는 그녀의 소설 「Jane Eyre」(1847)에서 주인공 Jane을 통하여 중간계층의 여성이 감내해야 했던 고민과 역경을 생생하게 보여준다. Roe Head 기숙학교 졸업 후 가정의 경제적 어려움 때문에 교사로 일해야 했던 작가 자신의 경험이 주인공 Jane의 이력 속에 그대로 반영되어 있다. 이러한 점에서 이 소설은 리얼리즘 소설로도 상당한 시대적 의미를 갖고 있다. 당대의 여성은 마땅한 결혼 상대를 찾지 못하거나 경제적으로 활동하려면 (가정)교사 자리를 찾거나 독신으로 늙어가는 수밖에 없었다. 중간계층 여성의 직업과 일에 대한 현실적 반영이 담긴 이 작품은 이른바 '집안의 천사'(the angel in the house)로 중산층 여성의 역할에 한계를 지우던 빅토리아 사회의 가부장적인 가치관에 대한 도전이라는 점에서 Charlotte의 여성적 입장에 담겨있다.

중간계층 여성의 일과 직업뿐만 아니라 사랑 또한 이 소설의 중요한 주제이다. Rochester와 John의 청혼에 쉽게 응하지 않는 Jane의 태도는 남녀 간의 사랑에서도 수동적인 역할에 머물지 않는 독립심의 표현이다. 그녀는 Rochester를 진심으로 사랑하고 있었지만 Rochester의 사랑은 여성을 소유하는 형태이기에 Jane은 그것이 자신의 독립에 장애가 된다고 보았고 이러한 이유로 그와의 결혼을 거부한다. 하지만 그들의 결혼이 가능하게 되었던 것은 Rochester가 다락방에 숨겨왔던 그의 첫째 아내 Bertha가 죽고, Jane이 스스로 경제적인 독립을 할 수 있는 시점이 되었을 때이다. Jane은 Rochester와 동등한 상태 혹은 그를 돌봐주고 보호하는 입장이 되었을 때 비로소 결혼에 동의한다.

Jane Eyre는 여성 작가에 대한 당대 독자들이 가진 편견으로부터 벗어나기 위하여 Currer Bell이라는 필명으로 이 소설을 출판하였고 엄청난 성공을 거두었다. Jane의 당당하고 독립적인 태도 때문에 독자들은 이 소설의 작가를 남성으로 추측하기도 하였다. 이 같은 Jane의 독립심과 삶을 대하는 열정적인 태도는 Charlotte Brontë가 낭만주의 시인들과 그 시대로부터 적지 않은 영향을 받았음을 의미한다. 또한 다락방의 광인 또는 유령, 숨겨진 비밀, 끔찍한 사건, 공포감 등은 고딕소설의 흔적이다. 고아 소녀가 힘겨운 어린 시절을 이겨내고 마침내 일과 사랑을 성취하여 독립적인 성인으로 성장해 나가기까지의 정신적·심리적 성장과정을 다루고 있다는 점에서 성장소설(Bildungsroman)의 특징도 지닌다.

(4) Emily Brontë(1818~1848)

Emily Brontë의 「Wuthering Heights」(1847)는 Catherine과 Heathcliff의 운명적인 사랑을 그린 비극이다. 폭풍이 휘몰아치는 음산한 언덕 위를 야생마처럼 뛰어 놀던 소년과 소녀의 모습이 그려지면서 Catherine을 향한 Heathcliff의 사랑과 집착에 상당한 낭만성이 부여되어 있다. Wuthering Heights를 떠난 지 3년 만에 신사가 되어서 돌아온 Heathcliff가 악마의 화신이 된 듯 집요하게 Catherine의 오빠 Hindley와 Catherine의 남편 Edgar를 파멸시키는 복수의 과정은 Catherine을 향한 Heathcliff의 사랑에 대한 이미지를 강하게 그린다. 이와 같은 로맨스적인 분위기는 이 작품이 가진 중요한 특징이다. 이 점에서 이 소설은 역사적으로 인접한 고딕소설과 낭만주의의 흔적을 지닌다.

그러나 이 소설의 낭만적 요소와는 대조적으로 작품의 주요 줄거리를 이루고 있는 Heathcliff의 복수는 당대의 복잡한 상속법 규정을 이용하고 있다는 점에서 작가의 현실에 대한 지식의 수준이 높았다는 것을 알 수 있다. 즉, 「Wuthering Heights」는 현실에 굳건히 뿌리내린 작품이기도 하다.

이중 화자를 이용하고 있는 이 작품의 서술 구조 또한 이 소설이 지닌 특이한 이야기에 대한 신뢰성과 현실성을 부여하는 적절한 장치이다. 작품의 1차 화자인 Lockwood는 번잡한 도시를 떠나 시골에 온 이방인으로, Earnshaw가(家)의 하녀[나중에는 Linton가(家)의 하녀] Nelly Dean으로부터 두 집안과

Heathcliff 사이에 얽힌 이야기를 전해 듣고 이것을 독자들에게 다시 전달한다. 이 과정에서 바깥세상의 일반적 삶의 방식을 지닌 1차 화자와 이 소설의 주요 인물들과 오랫동안 함께 해온 2차 화자인 Nelly Dean의 진술은 소설의 강렬하고 기이한 이야기의 어조와 분위기를 한 단계 누그러뜨림으로써 독자들에게 수용 가능한 형태로 바꾸어 놓는다. 특히 간헐적으로 이어지는 Nelly의 서술은 괴팍하고 악마적인 인물로 보이는 Heathcliff의 성격과 행동에 개연성을 부여하는 중요한 역할을 한다.

이야기의 중심에는 언덕 위에 있는 저택 Wuthering Heights와 두 주인공 Catherine과 Heathcliff가 그 저택에서 함께 보낸 유년시절이 있다. 신분의 계층 차이가 있는 두 인물이 거실에서 함께 어울릴 수 있었고, 폭풍이 휘몰아치던 언덕을 마구 뛰어 놀았던 유년의 경험은 당대의 역사적 배경에서 큰 의미를 지닌다. Mr. Earnshaw가 살아온 Wuthering Heights는 중세 이래 꾸준히 이어져 온 자작농 (yeoman)의 전통과 맞닿아 있고, Thrushcross Grange는 그보다 좀 더 세련된 지주 계층, 즉 젠트리 (gentry)를 대표하는 것으로 이해되기 때문이다. 작품의 시대적 배경인 1770년 이후의 30년은 산업 혁명이 고조되었던 시기였고, 이러한 점에서 Emily Brontë가 설정한 소설의 배경은 사회의 변화와 계층 간의 갈등구조를 반영한다.

제 **2** 장 Jane Austen
- 「*Pride and Prejudice*」

단원개요

Elizabeth의 결혼이 비록 신분상승적인 결혼이긴 하지만, 그 과정에는 Elizabeth와 Darcy가 동등하게 다루어진 흔적이 있다. 두 사람의 결혼은 서로의 단점을 극복하고 상대의 본질적인 자질에 대한 확실한 이해와 존중에 기초한 결혼이라고 해석할 수 있다. 또한 Elizabeth가 성장하는 인물이라는 사실이 중요하다. 18세기 소설은 남성을 주인공으로 하여 주인공의 정신적·육체적 성장과정을 그린 것이 대부분이었다. 그러나 Austen의 소설에서는 변화하고 발전된 여성이 등장한다.

출제 경향 및 수험 대책

이 소설은 사랑과 결혼이 주요 플롯(Plot)이지만 작가가 낭만적으로 결혼을 그리기보다는 날카로운 현실 인식을 바탕으로 당대 사회를 비판하고 있음을 염두에 두어야 한다. 다양한 등장인물들의 결혼 과정을 그리면서 각 인물들의 이름과 그들의 특징 및 성격을 묻는 문제들이 대한 대비가 요구된다.

제 **1** 절 작가의 생애

Jane Austen(1775~1817)은 1775년 12월 16일 영국의 남부 지역 햄프셔(Hampshire)주의 스티븐턴(Steventon)이라는 마을에서 영국 성공회 교구 목사인 아버지 조지 오스틴(George Austen)과 어머니 카산드라 리(Cassandra Leigh) 사이에서 태어났다. Austen 가문은 젠트리(gentry) 계급에 속하며, Jane은 여덟 남매 중 일곱째 아이였다. Jane의 오빠들은 목사, 해군 등이 되었지만, 그 당시의 시대적 관습에 따라 딸들은 직업을 갖지 않고 친지를 방문한 경우를 제외하고는 집에 머물러 있었다. Jane은 아주 어렸을 때 언니 Cassandra와 함께 작은 기숙학교를 다녔지만 11세 이후에는 집에서 교육을 받았다. 그들은 피아노 치는 법과 이태리어, 프랑스어 등의 외국어를 익혔고 역사를 배웠다. 또한 문학에도 관심이 깊어 Shakespeare와 Milton 외에도 18세기의 소설가, 수필가 및 시인들에 대한 깊은 지식을 갖게 되었다.

Jane은 출생 이후부터 25년간을 스티븐턴의 목사관에서 보냈다. 그 후 1801년 아버지의 목사직 퇴임 후 부모와 언니와 함께 배스(Bath)로 이사했는데 Jane은 배스의 화려하고 시끌벅적한 분위기와 생활을 좋아하지 않은 것으로 알려져 있다. 그로부터 4년 뒤인 1805년에 아버지가 돌아가시자 그 후 3년간을 항구도시인 사우샘프턴(Southampton)에서 지내다가 그녀의 어머니, 언니와 함께 오빠 에드워드 나이트(Edward Knight) 소유의 햄프셔주 초턴(Chawton)의 작은 시골집에 정착했다. Jane은 이 집의 거실에서 주요 작품들의 최종 원고를 작성하였으며, 죽기 몇 개월 전까지 이곳에서 살았다. Jane과 Cassandra 두 자매는 서로에게 헌신적이었으며 오늘날 우리가 알고 있는 Jane의 생애와 사상 중 많은 부분은 Jane이 Cassandra에게 보낸 편지에서 알 수 있다. Jane은 27세가 될 무렵 옥스퍼드 출신이자 부유한 상속인인 해리스 비그위더(Harris Bigg-Wither)가 청혼하여 받아들였으나, 그 다음날 약혼을 취소하였다. 이후 그녀는 자신의 언니와 함께 평생을 미혼으로 지냈지만 글을 쓰는 것 외에도 가족과 친척들에게 애정을 쏟으며 가깝게 지냈다. 1816년 그녀의 건강이 악화되기 시작하였고, 1817년 5월에 Jane은 치료를 위해 언니 카산드라와 함께 윈체스터(Winchester)로 갔다. 같은 해 7월 18일 그녀는 41세의 생을 마감하고 윈체스터 사원에 묻혔다.

🔔 더 알아두기 🔍

Jane Austen의 주요작품
- 「*Sense and Sensibility*」(1811)
- 「*Pride and Prejudice*」(1813)
- 「*Mansfield Park*」(1814)
- 「*Emma*」(1816)
- 「*Northanger Abbey*」(1818)
- 「*Persuasion*」(1818)

제 2 절 작품 세계

1 시대적 배경

Jane Austen이 살았던 시기(1775~1817)는 세계사에 있어서도 큰 혼란의 시기였다. 1789년에 일어났던 프랑스 혁명은 주변의 많은 나라에 영향을 주면서 이와 비슷한 혁명 운동을 야기했다. 아일랜드(Ireland)에서의 반란 진압, 아일랜드를 대영제국의 일부로 만드는 1800년 연합법(Acts of Union, 1800)의 체결과 인도에서의 마라타(Mahratta) 전쟁(1817~1818), 미국의 독립 전쟁(1775~1783) 등으로 영국은 세계 곳곳에서 여러 나라와 교전하고 있었다.

2 경제적 배경

영국은 외국과의 교전상태를 유지하면서 급격한 변화를 겪었고, 농업 경제에서 산업 경제로 바뀌었다. 때때로 영국은 나폴레옹의 지배를 받던 유럽 전체로부터 고립되기도 하였는데, 이 결과로 영국의 곡물 가격이 계속 상승하여 가난한 사람들은 많은 고통을 받았다. 이러한 사회적 혼란과 갈등은 민중들로 하여금 혁명적 사상에 관심과 지지를 갖게 하였고, 이와 동시에 기독교에서도 신앙 부흥운동이 일어났다. John Wesley의 감리교(Methodism) 창시가 그것인데, 이것은 절박한 서민들에게 주는 영혼 구원의 메시지였다.

3 정치적 배경

Austen이 살던 시기의 영국은 정치적으로 '리젠시 시대'(the Regency, 1811~1820)라고 불리는 섭정 시대였다. 1760년 이래 영국을 통치하였던 조지 3세(George III)가 병으로 정신 착란을 일으키자, 1789년 섭정 황태자 법안(the Regency Bill, 1789)이 통과되어, 그의 큰아들 조지 4세(George IV, the Prince Regent)가 왕을 대신할 통치자가 되어 섭정(regent) 시대가 되었다. 그러나 조지 4세는 정치적으로 능숙하지 못했다.

Austen의 편지에서는 이와 같은 당대의 국제적·국내적 상황에 대한 세세한 정보가 들어있다. 해군인 그녀의 오빠와 동생은 나폴레옹 전쟁에 참전 중이었고, 친구의 친척들 중에는 인도, 미국과의 전쟁, 서인도 제도에 연관되어 있거나 프랑스 혁명에서 사망한 사람들도 있었으며, 이러한 사건들은 그녀의 편지 속에 자세히 쓰여 있다. 그러나 그녀의 소설은 이러한 당대의 국제적·국내적 정치와 사회의 혼란스러운 상황을 거의 반영하고 있지 않다. Austen은 자신의 소설에서 역사 기록이나 그 당시 유행하던 풍습을 서술하도록 의도하지 않았기 때문이다. 그녀는 나폴레옹 전쟁 시기에 소설을 집필하면서도 그 사건에 대하여 언급하지 않았다는 이유로 비판을 받기도 하지만, 이러한 큰 사건에 대한 그녀의 침묵은 Austen의 집필 태도를 그대로 반영하고 있다고 볼 수 있다. 즉, 역사적으로 아무리 중요한 것이라고 하더라도 자신의 소설의 특수 영역인 영국 시골 마을의 일상생활에 별로 영향을 미치지 않는 그러한 사건들을 자신의 소설에서 언급하려 하지 않았다.

4 신고전주의적 문체

Jane Austen의 작품은 18세기의 형식을 존중하는 신고전주의와 감정을 중시하는 19세기 낭만주의 사이에 있다. 즉, '이성의 시대'가 '감성의 시대'로 바뀌는 시점에 있다. 그러나 그녀는 특정한 어떤 유파의 작가군에 속하지는 않았다.

Jane Austen의 문체는 18세기 중엽 문예 전성기의 시인과 산문 작가들의 문체에 훨씬 가깝다. 비록 Austen은 Robert Burns(1759~1796), Walter Scott(1771~1832), Lord Byron(1788~1824)과 같은 동시대 낭만주의 시인들의 작품들을 읽었지만, 그녀의 작품 내용과 문체는 Alexander Pope(1688~1744)와 같은 전 시대의 시인들, 가령 Joseph Addison(1672~1719)이나 Samuel Johnson(1709~1784)과 같은 18세기 수필가나 비평가들의 문체와 비슷하다. 이들이 표방하던 신고전주의적 문학에 대한 견해는 안정된 규칙, 즉 질서와 균형이 있어야 하며 무엇보다도 이성이 열정을 통제해야 한다는 것에 기반을 두고 있으며 이는 Austen이 가지고 있었던 신조였다. 그들 문체에 나타난 형식에 대한 존중, 균형 있는 문장들, 질서정연한 논제의 순서 등은 Austen의 산문 속에서도 볼 수 있다. 또한 그들의 작품에 나타난 중용에 대한 옹호, 도덕성, 풍자적인 초연함 역시 그녀의 작품 속에 반영되어 있다.

제 3 절   Jane Austen 소설의 특징

1   고딕 로맨스, 지역소설, 풍속소설

Horace Walpole(1717~1719)의 「*The Castle of Otranto*」에 의하여 영국에 소개된 고딕 로맨스, 지역소설, 풍속소설이 유행하게 되었으며 여성작가들이 이를 발전시켰다. 이 소설들은 인기는 많았으나 지나치게 감상적이었기 때문에 종종 품위가 없고 부자연스러운 상황이 그려지기도 하였고, 소설 속의 여주인공들은 거친 시련을 겪으며 격렬한 감정을 표현하였다. 고딕소설은 외딴 지역의 중세 시대를 배경으로 하면서 성과 폐허를 등장시켰다. 대부분의 줄거리는 매우 비현실적이고 환상적이었으며 작가들은 독자들에게 흥분과 공포를 느끼게 하려고 노력했다.

2   고딕소설과 그 관례들을 조롱

Jane Austen은 「*Northanger Abbey*」를 통해 고딕소설과 그 관례들을 조롱했다. 다른 작가들이 스코틀랜드(Scotland)나 웨일즈(Wales), 아일랜드의 예절과 풍습을 보존한 것처럼 Austen 역시 영국 시골의 예절과 습관들을 정확하고 세세한 것까지 묘사하고 사회생활에 대해 꼼꼼하게 조사를 했다는 점은 풍속소설과 연결된다.

3   객관적인 시선으로 집필

자신이 잘 아는 소재를 객관적인 시선으로 집필하였다. Austen은 섬세한 묘사로 18세기 영국의 우아함과 편안한 삶을 묘사한다. 소설 속 인물의 가치관 역시 그녀가 속한 젠트리(Gentry) 계급의 전형적인 가치관을 지닌 인물들로서 평범한 삶을 살아가는 보통의 사람들, 즉 젠트리 계급의 사람들에 대한 사실적인 묘사에 집중한다.

4   중류층 주인공 종요 ★★★

(1) 당시는 귀족과 중상류층, 상업에 종사하는 사람들 사이의 경계선이 희미해지던 시기였으며 Austen 소설의 중심인물들이 속한 계급은 대부분 중류층이었다.

(2) 출신, 돈, 토지에 의하여 계급이 분명해지는 사회상을 보여준다. 이를 바꾸려면 위험을 각오하여야 한다는 사실을 소설을 통해 묘사하고 있다. Austen 작품의 주요 인물들은 대부분 가족과 사회 안에서의

전통적인 삶의 양식을 선택한다. 여기서 전통적 삶의 양식이란 가족, 친구, 지인, 윗사람들, 아랫사람들에게 취해야 한다고 기대되는 행동양식이다.

5 여성의식 중요 ★★★

(1) 보수적인 사회에서 활동한 여성작가라는 점만으로도 진보적 여성의식을 보여주고 있다. 대부분의 여주인공이 자신보다 신분이 높거나 재산이 많은 남성과 결혼하는 구성이고, 여성의 결혼은 경제적 조건 하에서 이루어질 수밖에 없는 상황을 그린다. 이러한 구성은 잠재력 있는 여성조차도 결혼 이외에는 대안이 없는 당시 사회현실에 대한 묵시적 비판이라 볼 수 있다.

(2) 여성의 성장과정을 묘사한다. 여성 인물은 실수를 저지른 후 일련의 성숙과정을 거쳐 도덕적으로 올바른 선택을 한다. 여성은 이성적인 존재이며 올바른 교육에 의해 개선될 수 있음을 담고 있다.

6 사회에 대한 비판

(1) 당시 영국 사회의 많은 결점들, 가령 위선·물질 만능주의·허례허식 등에 대한 강한 비판을 담고 있다. Austen이 집필한 소설에는 어리석고 이기적이며 악의에 찬 사람들 사이에서도 도덕적인 성실성을 고수하는 동시에 자신들을 사회의 요구에서 벗어나지 않도록 애쓰는 인물들이 등장한다.

(2) 인물들은 자신의 잘못된 판단으로 인하여 좌절, 갈등, 실수의 과정을 겪지만, 마침내 성숙한 성인인 동시에 사회의 믿음직한 구성원이 된다. 자아와 사회의 요구를 조화시키려는 계속적인 시도는 낙관주의와 연결된다.

제 4 절 Jane Austen 작품의 공통주제

1 세대 간의 갈등

소설 속에서 부모나 부모를 대신하는 인물들은 대체적으로 자녀의 성장에 별로 영향을 미치지 못하거나 해로운 영향을 미치는 인물로 묘사된다. 부모의 무능력이나 주인공들에게 주어진 환경 때문에 주인공들은 스스로 인생을 헤쳐 나가야 한다. 이러한 역경에도 불구하고 각 소설의 젊은 주인공들은 더 나은 성격의 인물로 거듭난다. 이러한 결말은 사회 갱신에 대한 작가의 긍정적인 시각을 반영하고 있다.

2 이상적인 사회

(1) Austen은 개인의 사적인 삶과 공적인 삶의 일치를 중요시했기 때문에 소설 속 장소와 인물들의 관계를 자신의 믿음을 입증하는 수단으로 사용한다. 가령, 소설 속 저택이나 토지는 소유주의 도덕적 역량과 사회적 책임감의 표상으로 묘사하였는데, 이는 곧 내적 가치의 반영이자 전해져 내려오는 것을 유지하고 발전시키는 능력의 반영이다.

(2) 소설의 결말에서 각 저택의 운명은 소유주의 운명과 밀접한 관련성을 가진다. 책임감과 도덕성이 강한 인물들은 조상으로부터 물려받은 집을 지키지만, 무책임하고 약한 인물들의 저택은 타인의 소유가 된다. Austen은 이러한 연관성을 소설을 통해 확립시키면서 개인의 공적인 삶과 사적인 삶 사이의 조화로운 관계를 기반으로 한 이상적인 사회에 대한 견해를 드러낸다.

3 등장인물들의 태도와 사회적인 행동의 표현 방식

Austen의 소설에서 사회는 좋은 예법을 지키고 필요한 사회적인 의식을 잘 행하는 개인의 능력을 통하여 유지된다. 내적인 도덕성과 올바른 사회적 예절의 외적 준수를 결합하여 전체적인 인간관계를 향상시키고, 이는 더 나은 사회가 되도록 만든다고 보고 있다.

4 결혼 종요 ★★★

(1) Austen의 소설 모두가 주인공의 행복한 결혼으로 결말짓는다. Austen의 소설에서 점잖은 가문의 여인은 오직 결혼을 통해서만 사회에서의 올바른 위치와 역할을 얻을 수 있었다.

(2) 사회적인 차원에서, 결혼이라는 제도를 통해 지적이며 책임감 있는 두 개인의 결합으로 이루어지는 사회는 이전보다 도덕적으로 더 건전하고 좋은 세상이 될 것이라고 보고 있다. 이러한 궁극적 목표를 위해서 각 개인은 자각의 과정과 자신의 잘못을 수정하는 여러 단계를 거쳐야만 성숙한 인격체가 된다.

(3) 남녀 주인공의 결혼과 같은 이상적인 결합과 대조되는 전혀 다른 종류의 결혼생활이 많이 제시되어 소설의 전개를 더욱 복잡하고 모호하게 만든다. Austen 소설 곳곳에 부정적인 결혼의 예시들이 있는 이유는 결혼에 대한 상반된 작가의 견해를 나타내는 듯이 보이지만 훌륭한 지성을 지닌 남녀가 결혼할 때 더 나은 사회로 나아간다는 긍정적인 결말의 의도와 연결된다.

제 5 절 줄거리

베넷 부인(Mrs. Bennet)은 허포드샤이어(Herfordshire)주의 작은 동네에 찰스 빙리(Charles Bingley)가 네더필드 파크(Netherfield Park)로 이사를 온다는 소식을 듣고 자신의 딸들을 그에게 소개시켜주기 위해 남편을 설득하여 Netherfield로 간다. 무도회에서 Charles Bingley와 Bennet가(家)의 첫째 딸 Jane이 서로 무언가를 느끼는 한편, Bingley의 친구 Darcy는 Elizabeth에 대하여 좋지 않은 말을 하고 그것을 Elizabeth가 듣게 된다. Jane은 Bingley의 동생인 Caroline Bingley의 초대를 받아 Netherfield에 가는데 그 와중에 비가 와서 감기에 걸린다. 감기 때문에 Jane이 며칠간 집으로 돌아갈 수 없게 되자 Elizabeth는 걱정이 되어 언니가 있는 Netherfield로 간다.

Darcy는 일전에 자신이 무시했던 Elizabeth가 사실은 굉장히 매력적인 여성임을 느끼고 그녀에게 호감을 가진다. 그러나 Caroline은 옷을 더럽힌 채로 찾아온 Elizabeth를 무시하고 험담하며 자신이 좋아하는 Darcy에게 Elizabeth에 대한 좋지 않은 이미지를 심어주려고 노력한다.

Bingley와 Jane의 사랑은 점점 깊어가고, Mrs. Bennet은 Bingley가 Jane에게 청혼할 것이라 확신하며 아무데서나 이 사실을 떠들고 다니면서 Darcy와 Caroline에게 안 좋은 이미지를 준다. Jane의 동생들 또한 어리석고 허영심이 많은데, Kitty와 Lydia는 항상 장교들을 보기 위해 Meryton에 놀러가고 Mary Bennet은 똑똑한 척을 하며 나서기를 좋아한다. 어느 날 동생들과 Meryton에 놀러간 Elizabeth는 잘생긴 Wickham이라는 군인을 만나 그에게 호감을 느낀다. 그러나 그때 우연히 마주친 Darcy와 Wickham이 서로를 좋지 않은 눈빛으로 보는 것에 Elizabeth는 놀라고 그 이유를 Wickham에게 묻자 Wickham은 자신의 경제적 권리를 Darcy가 박탈했으며 그 이유로 인하여 자신이 지금 가난한 군인에 머물러 있다고 말한다. Elizabeth는 이 말을 듣고 Darcy에 대해 더욱 안 좋은 편견을 갖게 된다.

Bennet가(家)의 딸들은 당시의 법에 따라 아버지의 유산을 상속받을 수 없고, 유산은 먼 친척인 Collins에게 상속되는데, 어느 날 불쑥 Collins가 찾아온다. 그는 아주 정중하게 행동하지만 높은 위치에 있는 사람에게만 아첨하는 속물근성을 지닌 목사이다. 그의 진짜 목적은 Bennet가(家)의 딸들 중 자신의 신붓감을 찾는 것이다. 그는 처음 Jane에게 눈독을 들이지만 Jane이 약혼할 것이라는 Mrs. Bennet의 말에 포기하고, Elizabeth에게 청혼하지만 똑똑한 Elizabeth는 그의 청혼을 거절한다. 그래도 포기하지 않던 Collins는 Elizabeth의 친구인 Charlotte에게 청혼을 하고 그녀는 청혼을 받아들인다. Elizabeth는 친구가 속물이자 허영심 있는 Collins와 결혼한다고 하자 걱정하지만, Charlotte은 노처녀로 늙어죽을 바에는 차라리 빨리 안정된 가정을 꾸리는 것이 낫다고 한다.

한편, Bingley가 갑자기 런던으로 떠나버리고 그의 동생 Caroline은 Jane에게 오빠가 Netherfield로 돌아갈 마음이 없다고 말한다. 상심한 Jane은 런던의 중산층이 사는 지역에 있는 이모 Mrs. Gardiner댁으로 가고, Elizabeth도 Charlotte의 집으로 놀러간다. Charlotte의 집은 Darcy의 이모인 Lady Catherine de Bourgh의 집과 매우 가깝고 Collins는 Lady Catherine과 개인적인 친분이 있어 Lady Catherine의 집에 모두 같이 초대받는다. 그곳에서 Elizabeth는 다시 Darcy와 그의 친지 한 사람을 만난다. Lady Catherine은 아주 오만하고 자기주장이 강한 사람이다. Elizabeth는 그녀에게 공손하지만 단호한 태도로 반대의견도 내면서 바르게 행동한다. 그러던 어느 날 Darcy의 친지와 산책을 하던 중 그녀는 Darcy가 Jane과 Bingley의 사랑을 깨뜨려 버린 것을 알게 된다. 화가 난 Elizabeth는 Lady Catherine의 초대도 거절하고 혼자 집에 오는데 놀랍게도 Darcy가 그녀를 찾아와 불쑥 청혼을 한다. 그의 청혼은 열렬한 것이었으나 Elizabeth는 그가 오만하며 그녀의 가족을 무시한 행동이라고 판단한다. Elizabeth는 청혼을 거절하고 언니 Jane과 Bingley의 일, 그리고 Wickham의 일을 말하며 어떤 일이 있어도 그의 청혼을 받아들일 수 없다고 말한다. Darcy는 충격을 받아 떠났다가, 다음날 아침 다시 Elizabeth를 찾아와 한 통의 편지를 건넨다. 그 편지에는 Elizabeth의 말에 대한 그의 해명이 적혀 있었는데, Jane과 Bingley의 일은 Jane의 동생들, Mrs. Bennet의 어리석음과 집안의 차이, 그리고 Jane이 Bingley에게 그리 큰 애정을 가지고 있지 않은 것 같아 반대했다는 것이었으며, Wickham의 일은 그가 이미 많은 돈을 자신에게서 받았고, 게다가 그가 Darcy의 동생 Georgiana에게 접근해 동생을 잃을 뻔했다는 말이었다. 이 편지를 읽은 Elizabeth는 크게 동요하지만 큰 상황의 변화는 오지 않는다. Elizabeth는 집으로 돌아가고 집에서는 군부대가 이동한다고 난리가 난다. Bennet가(家)의 막내 Lydia는 친구의 초대로 그곳으로 며칠 놀러가기로 한다. Kitty는 그런 동생을 부러워하고 Elizabeth는 이모와 함께 Darcy의 고향 Derbyshire로 여행을 떠난다. Darcy의 저택인 Pemberley에 가지 않겠다고 Elizabeth는 결심하지만, 궁금하기도 하고 Darcy가 집에 없다는 사실에 망설이다 결국 Pemberley 구경에 나선다. Pemberley는 굉장히 아름다운 저택이며, 그 집의 하인은 Darcy에 대한 칭찬을 침이 마르도록 하고 그 이야기를 들은 Elizabeth는 Darcy가 자신이 생각한 것만큼 나쁜 사람이 아니라는 것을 느낀다. 그리고 그녀가 Pemberley를 막 떠나려고 하는 순간 Darcy를 만나게 되고 그녀는 부끄러움에 어쩔 줄 모른다. 그녀에게 아주 친절하게 대하는 Darcy를 보며 Elizabeth는 그가 달라진 것을 느낀다. 그러던 중 Jane에게서 갑자기 편지 한 통이 날아오고 마침 Darcy가 Elizabeth를 찾아온다. 편지의 내용은 Lydia가 Wickham과 도망갔다는 것이었고, 이 사실에 충격을 받은 Elizabeth를 Darcy가 따뜻하게 위로해준다. 그리고 곧 Darcy는 떠나고 Elizabeth는 이모부 내외와 함께 여행을 마치고 집으로 돌아간다. 그녀가 집으로 돌아와 보니 어머니는 앓아눕고 아버지는 Lydia를 찾으러 런던으로 갔지만 그들을 찾지 못하고 돌아왔다. 그리고는 얼마 지나지 않아 Lydia를 찾았다는 편지가 왔는데 그 둘은 결혼하여 북부로 가서 살게 된다는 것이었다. Lydia와 Wickham은 북부로 가기 전 집을 방문했는데 Lydia는 여전히 철이 없었고, Wickham은 뻔뻔하기 그지없었다. Lydia는 자신의 결혼식에 Darcy가 왔었다는 말을 실수로 하게 되고, 그것을 궁금하게 여긴 Elizabeth는 이모에게 편지를 써 Darcy가 Wickham을 설득하여 Lydia와 결혼하게 하고 비용도 다 대주었다는 사실을 알게 된다. Darcy를 다시 보게 된 그녀는 자신의 마음이 이미 그에게 가고 있다는 사실을 깨닫게 된다. 마을에는 Bingley가 Netherfield로 돌아온다는 소문이 돈다. Mrs. Bennet은 다시 야단을 피우고, Jane은 태연한 척 하지만 마음은 크게 동요한다. Bingley가 Netherfield로 돌아와 Bennet가(家)에 인사를 하러 오고 Darcy 역시 함께 온다. 그리고 얼마 지나지 않아 Bingley는 Jane에게 청혼하고, 그녀도 기쁜 마음으로 청혼을 받아들인다.

행복한 가운데 갑자기 Lady Catherine이 찾아온다. 그녀는 Elizabeth에게 Darcy와 약혼했다는 소문의 진상에 대해 묻고, Elizabeth는 약혼은 하지 않았지만 약혼하지 않겠다는 약속은 못한다고 말한다. 이 이야기를 듣게 된 Darcy는 Elizabeth가 자신에게 마음이 있다는 사실을 눈치 채고 그녀를 찾아가 청혼한다. Elizabeth는 그의 청혼을 받아들이고, Darcy는 Mr. Bennet에게 결혼 승낙을 받는다. 그렇게 Elizabeth는 Pemberley에서 살게 되고 Bingley는 Pemberley와 가까운 곳에 집을 마련하여 살게 된다.

제 6 절 작품의 주제

1 예법

인간관계에서 예법(good manners)의 중요성을 강조하지만 그것이 과도할 때에는 가차 없이 조소를 던진다.

2 오만과 편견 중요 ★★

Elizabeth가 첫 인상(first impressions)부터 Darcy에게 갖게 된 편견(prejudice)과 오만함(pride)을 극복하고, Darcy가 보다 낮은 신분의 Elizabeth에 대해 가졌던 편견과 오만함을 극복하여 둘은 결혼에 성공한다.

3 사회적 관습

한 개인이 사회에 편입되어 공동체와 조화를 이루는 과정을 보여준다. 공동체와의 조화는 개인이 사회적 관습(social conventions)을 따를 때 가능해지며, 이때 도덕성이 강조된다.

4 인간관계

모든 종류의 인간관계를 제시한다(부부, 형제자매, 우정의 관계 등).

5 결혼 상대의 선택

「*Pride and Prejudice*」의 중심 주제는 Jane Austen의 다른 소설에서와 마찬가지로 결혼 상대의 선택이다. 특히 결혼 전 두 사람이 극복해야 하는 난점들에 관한 것으로, 주인공 Elizabeth와 Darcy는 그들이 서로에게 적합한 반려자가 되기 위해서 그들 자신의 '오만과 편견'을 이해하고 극복해야 하는 것이다. 이 소설에서 Austen은 결혼을 광범위하게 다루고 있으며, 개인의 도덕적 자질과 결혼의 종류 사이의 관련성을 뚜렷하게 드러낸다.

6 결혼의 예

(1) 베넷 부부(the Bennets) : 실패한 결혼의 예

(2) 가디너스 부부(the Gardiners) : 성공한 결혼의 예

(3) Lydia와 Wickham : 성급한 열정으로 이루어진 결혼의 예

(4) Charlotte와 Collins : 경제적인 현실에 의한 결혼의 예

(5) Jane과 Bingley : 비슷한 성격에 의한 결혼의 예

(6) Elizabeth와 Darcy : 대조적 성격으로 서로를 보완해주는 결혼의 예

제 7 절 등장인물

1 Elizabeth Bennet 중요 ★★

강한 자아와 뚜렷한 가치관을 지닌 여주인공이다. Bennet가(家)의 둘째 딸로 21세 정도이다. Collins와 같이 허영에 찬 사람의 청혼을 거부할 만큼 자존심과 진실한 자아를 가지고 있으며, 다른 자매들보다 정확한 판단력과 지성을 지니고 있다. 하지만 그녀의 지나친 지성과 판단력이 Darcy에 대한 편견을 불러일으키는 원인이 되기도 한다.

2 Fitzwilliam Darcy

28세의 남자 주인공이다. 과묵하여 다른 사람들에게 오만하다는 첫인상을 주지만, 사려 깊고 진중하며 신사적이다. Darcy는 Elizabeth가 자신보다 신분이 낮음에도 춤을 추자는 자신의 제안을 거절하고, 부유한 자신에게 아첨을 하며 다가오는 비굴한 사람들과는 달리 자신에게 당당히 맞서는 그녀를 높이 평가한다. 동시에 그는 그녀의 그런 모습에 감명 받아 결혼을 결심하게 된다.

3 Charles Bingley

부유한 신사로 Darcy의 친구이지만 그와 많은 면에서 대조적인 모습을 보인다. 낙천적이고 사교적인 성격의 소유자이며, Jane Bennet의 미모에 반하여 신분 차이에 연연하지 않고 그녀와 결혼한다.

4 Mr. Bennet

Bennet가(家)의 아버지로, 위트와 학식을 갖춘 시골의 젠트리(gentry) 계급의 신사이다. 아내인 Mrs. Bennet과 대조적인 성격으로 결혼생활에 크게 재미를 못 느끼는 인물이지만, 냉소적인 태도로 작품의 희극적인 면에 기여한다. 다섯 딸들 중 Elizabeth를 가장 아낀다.

5 Mrs. Bennet

Bennet가(家)의 어머니로 호들갑스러운 면모가 있으며 우둔한 편이다. 딸들을 부유한 남성에게 시집보내려는 목표를 가지고 있으며 소설에서 웃음을 자아내는 역할을 한다.

6 Jane Bennet

Bennet가(家)의 장녀이자 Elizabeth의 언니다. 20대 초반의 그녀는 굉장한 미인이며 심성 또한 아름답다.

7 Catherine (Kitty) Bennet

Bennet가(家)의 셋째 딸로 Lydia와 마찬가지로 남자들에게 관심이 많다.

8 Mary Bennet

Bennet가(家)의 넷째 딸로 조용하고 독서를 좋아한다.

9 Lydia Bennet

Bennet가(家)의 다섯째, 즉 막내딸로 노는 것을 좋아하는 성격이다. 발랄함이 매력적이며, George Wickham과 성급한 결혼을 한다.

10 George Wickham

잘생긴 군인으로 Darcy의 아버지 Mr. Darcy의 대자(代子)이며, 어릴 적 Darcy와 함께 자랐다. Darcy의 동생인 Georgiana의 재산을 노리고 그녀와 달아나려고 한 적이 있으며, 큰 유산 상속을 받을 Mary King에게도 경제적 이유로 청혼하려고 하는 난봉꾼(rake)으로 신사답지 못한 인물로 그려진다.

11 Caroline Bingley(Miss Bingley)

Charles Bingley의 여동생으로 Darcy와의 결혼을 통한 신분 상승을 노려보지만, Darcy가 결혼 상대자로 Elizabeth를 선택하자 그녀의 계획은 수포로 돌아간다. 자신보다 낮은 Elizabeth의 신분을 경멸하는 속물적 성격의 소유자이다.

12 Reverend William Collins(Mr. Collins)

Mr. Bennet의 먼 친척으로 Bennet가(家)의 유산 추정 상속인이다. Austen이 당시의 사회상을 유머러스하게 비꼬는 대상으로 삼은 인물로, 과시적이고 속물적이며 위선적이다.

13 Lady Catherine de Bourgh

Darcy의 이모이자 재산이 많은 귀족이다. 권위적이고 우월 의식이 있으며, 코믹한 인물로 남의 일에 참견하기를 좋아한다. 딸 Anne de Bourgh를 Darcy와 결혼시키길 원하지만 Darcy가 오히려 신분이 낮은 Elizabeth와 결혼하려 하자 반대한다. Collins 목사의 후원자이기도 하다.

14 Mrs. Phillips

Mrs. Bennet의 여동생이자 Bennet가(家) 자매들의 이모이다.

15 Mr. and Mrs. Gardiner

Mr. Gardiner는 Mrs. Bennet의 남동생으로, Bennet가(家) 자매들의 외삼촌이다. Mrs. Gardiner는 Mrs. Bennet의 올케이자 Bennet가(家) 자매들의 외숙모이다. 두 사람은 작품 속에 등장하는 속물들과는 정반대인 인물들이다.

제 8 절 작품의 구조(Plot)와 시점

1 구조

(1) 주요 plot

작품의 구조는 시간의 순서에 따라 사건들이 소설 전체에 흐르며, 주요 플롯과 부차적인 세 개의 플롯이 상호 보완 작용을 하고 있다. 주요 플롯은 Darcy의 오만함(pride)과 Elizabeth의 편견(prejudice)의 갈등이다.

(2) 세 개의 sub-plot

① Charles Bingley가 Jane Bennet에게 끌림과 둘의 관계에 Darcy가 개입이 되는 것
② Wickham과 Darcy 가족과의 얽힘과 갈등 관계
③ Charlotte Lucas와 Reverend William Collins의 결혼

2 시점(Point of View)

3인칭 전지적 화자(third-person omniscient narrator) 시점, 즉 외부 관찰자에 의한 객관적인 관찰 시점이다. 때때로 인용 부호 없이 인물의 생각이나 말이 서술자의 말과 겹쳐지는 자유 간접 화법(free indirect discourse)이 사용되므로 인물들의 말인지 서술자의 말인지를 구분하기 어려울 때가 있다. 등장인물들의 사고 과정과 감정을 탐색할 때는 작가의 주관적 생각이 개입되어 있다.

제 9 절 Text

Chapter 1

It is a truth universally acknowledged, that a single man in possession of a good fortune, must be in want of a wife.

However little known the feelings or views of such a man may be on his first entering a neighbourhood, this truth is so well fixed in the minds of the surrounding families, that he is considered the rightful property of some one or other of their daughters.

"My dear Mr. Bennet", said his lady to him one day, "have you heard that Netherfield Park is let[1] at last?"

Mr. Bennet replied that he had not.

"But it is", returned she; "for Mrs. Long has just been here, and she told me all about it."

Mr. Bennet made no answer.

"Do you not want to know who has taken it?" cried his wife impatiently.

"You want to tell me, and I have no objection to hearing it."

This was invitation enough[2].

"Why, my dear, you must know, Mrs. Long says that Netherfield is taken by a young man of large fortune from the north of England; that he came down on Monday in a chaise and four[3] to see the place, and was so much delighted with before Michaelmas[4], and some of his servants are to be in the house by the end of next week."

"What is his name?"

"Bingley."

"Is he married or single?"

"Oh! Single, my dear, to be sure! A single man of large fortune; four or five thousand a year. What a fine thing for our girls!"

"How so? How can it affect them?"

"My dear Mr. Bennet", replied his wife, "how can you be so tiresome! You must know that I am thinking of his marrying one of them."

"Is that his design in settling here?"

"Design! Nonsense, how can you talk so! But it is very likely that he may fall in love with one of them, and therefore you must visit him as soon as he comes.

"I see no occasion for that. You and the girls may go, or you may send them by themselves, which perhaps will be still better, for as you are as handsome as any of them, Mr. Bingley may

---

1) is let : 세 들어올 사람이 생기다
2) This was invitation enough (for her to speak) : 이것은 어서 말해달라는 것과 마찬가지였다.
3) 사두마차. 네 마리의 말이 끄는 마차
4) Michaelmas : (기독교에서) 성 미카엘 축일(9월 29일)

like you the best of the party5)."

"My dear, you flatter me. I certainly have had my share of beauty, but I do not pretend to be anything extraordinary now. When a woman has five grown-up daughters, she ought to give over6) thinking of her own beauty."

"In such cases, a woman has not often much beauty to think of."

"But, my dear, you must indeed go and see Mr. Bingley when he comes into the neighbourhood."

"It is more than I engage for7), I assure you."

"But consider your daughters. Only think what an establishment8) it would be for one of them. Sir William and Lady Lucas are determined to go, merely on that account, for in general, you know, they visit no newcomers. Indeed you must go, for it will be impossible for us to visit him if you do not."

"You are over-scrupulous9), surely. I dare say Mr. Bingley will be very glad to see you; and I will send a few lines by you to assure him of my hearty consent to his marrying whichever he chooses of the girls; though I must throw in a good word for my little Lizzy."

"I desire you will do no such thing. Lizzy is not a bit better than the others; and I am sure she is not half so handsome as Jane, nor half so good humoured as Lydia. But you are always giving her the preference."

"They have none of them much to recommend them, replied he; "they are all silly and ignorant like other girls; but Lizzy10) has something more of quickness than her sisters."

"Mr. Bennet, how can you abuse your own children in such a way? You take delight in vexing me. You have no compassion for my poor nerves11)."

"You mistake me, my dear. I have a high respect for your nerves. They are my old friends. I have heard you mention them with consideration these last twenty years at least."

"Ah! you do not know what I suffer."

"But I hope you will get over it, and live to see many young men of four thousand a year come into the neighbourhood."

"It will be no use to us, if twenty such should come, since you will not visit them."

"Depend upon it12), my dear, that when there are twenty, I will visit them all."

Mr. Bennet was so odd a mixture of quick parts13), sarcastic humour, reserve, and caprice, that the experience of three-and-twenty years had been insufficient to make his wife understand his character Her mind was less difficult to develop. She was a woman of mean understanding14), little

---

5) the party : 일행
6) give over : 단념하다
7) It is more than I engage for : 나는 그런 것을 약속할 수 없소.
8) an establishment : 결혼해서 자리를 잡는 것
9) over-scrupulous : 지나치게 까다로운
10) Lizzy : Elizabeth의 약칭
11) poor nerves : 약한 신경
12) Depend upon it : 염려하지 마요.
13) quick parts : 머리 회전이 빠름
14) mean understanding : 이해력이 부족한

information, and uncertain temper. When she was discontented, she fancied herself nervous. The business of her life was to get her daughters married; its solace was visiting and news.

Chapter 2

Mr. Bennet was among the earliest of those who waited on[15] Mr. Bingley. He had always intended to visit him, though to the last always assuring his wife that he should not go; and till the evening after the visit was paid she had no knowledge of it. It was then disclosed in the following manner. Observing his second daughter employed in trimming a hat, he suddenly addressed her with:

"I hope Mr. Bingley will like it, Lizzy."

"We are not in a way to know[16] what Mr. Bingley likes", said her mother resentfully, "since we are not to visit."

"But you forget, mamma", said Elizabeth, that we shall meet him at the assemblies, and that Mrs. Long promised to introduce him."

"I do not believe Mrs. Long will do any such thing. She has two nieces of her own. She is a selfish, hypocritical woman, and I have no opinion of her."

"No more have I", said Mr. Bennet; "and I am glad to find that you do not depend on her serving you[17]."

Mrs. Bennet deigned not to make any reply, but, unable to contain herself, began scolding one of her daughters.

"Don't keep coughing so, Kitty, for Heaven's sake! Have a little compassion on my nerves. You tear them to pieces."

"Kitty has no discretion in her coughs", said her father; "she times them ill[18]."

"I do not cough for my own amusement," replied Kitty fretfully[19].

"When is your next ball to be, Lizzy?"

"To-morrow fortnight[20]."

"Aye, so it is," cried her mother, "and Mrs. Long does not come back till the day before; so it will be impossible for her to introduce him, for she will not know him herself."

"Then, my dear, you may have the advantage of your friend, and introduce Mr. Bingley to her."

"Impossible, Mr. Bennet, impossible, when I am not acquainted with him myself; how can you be so teasing?"

---

15) waited on : 방문했다
16) We are not in a way to know : 우리는 알 수가 없다.
17) serving you : Mrs. Long이 Mr. Bingley에게 소개해 주는 수고
18) times them ill : 기침의 타이밍이 나빴다(them = cough)
19) fretfully : 짜증을 내며
20) fortnight : 2주 후

"I honour your circumspection21). A fortnight's acquaintance is certainly very little. One cannot know what a man really is by the end of a fortnight. But if we do not venture somebody else will22); and after all, Mrs. Long and her nieces must stand their chance; and, therefore, as she will think it an act of kindness, if you decline the office23), I will take it on myself."

The girls stared at their father. Mrs. Bennet said only, "Nonsense, nonsense!"

"What can be the meaning of that emphatic exclamation?" cried he. "Do you consider the forms of introduction, and the stress that is laid on them24) as nonsense? I cannot quite agree with you there. What say you, Mary? For you are a young lady of deep reflection, I know, and read great books and make extracts."

Mary wished to say something sensible, but knew not how25).

"While Mary is adjusting her idea, he continued, "let us return to Mr. Bingley."

"I am sick of Mr. Bingley," cried his wife.

"I am sorry to hear that; but why did not you tell me that before? If I had known as much this morning, I certainly would not have called on him. It is very unlucky; but as I have actually paid the visit, we cannot escape the acquaintance now."

The astonishment of the ladies was just what he wished; that26) of Mrs. Bennet perhaps surpassing the rest; though, when the first tumult of joy was over, she began to declare that it was what she had expected all the while27).

"How good it was in you, my dear Mr. Bennet! But I knew I should persuade you at last. I was sure you loved your girls too well to neglect such an acquaintance. Well, how pleased I am! and it is such a good joke, too, that you should have gone this morning and never said a word about it till now."

"Now, Kitty, you may cough as much as you choose," said Mr. Bennet; and, as he spoke, he left the room, fatigued with the raptures28) of his wife.

"What an excellent father you have, girls!" said she, when the door was shut. "I do not know how you will ever make him amends for his kindness; or me, either, for that matter. At our time of life it29) is not so pleasant, I can tell you, to be making new acquaintances every day; but for your sakes, we would do anything. Lydia, my love, though you are the youngest, I dare say Mr. Bingley will dance with you at the next ball."

"Oh!" said Lydia stoutly, "I am not afraid; for though I am the youngest, I'm the tallest."

The rest of the evening was spent in conjecturing30) how soon he would return Mr. Bennet's visit,

---

21) circumspection : 신중함
22) somebody else will : somebody else will (venture to introduce Mr. Bingly)
23) the office : 소개하는 역할
24) the stress that is laid on them : 소개하는 형식을 중시하는 것
25) knew not how : did not know how to
26) that : The astonishment
27) it was what she had expected all the while : Mr. Bennet이 가족들 몰래 Mr. Bingley를 찾아간 것은 그렇게 되리라고 줄곧 기대했던 일이었다.
28) rapture : 환희
29) At our time of life it : 날마다 새 사람을 만나는 것
30) conjecturing : 추측하다

and determining when they should ask him to dinner.

Chapter 3

NOT all that Mrs. Bennet, however, with the assistance of her five daughters, could ask on the subject, was sufficient to draw from her husband any satisfactory description of Mr. Bingley. They attacked him in various ways; with barefaced[31] questions, ingenious suppositions, and distant surmises[32]; but he eluded[33] the skill of them all, and they were at last obliged to accept the second-hand intelligence of their neighbour, Lady Lucas. Her report was highly favourable. Sir William had been delighted with him. He was quite young, wonderfully handsome, extremely agreeable, and, to crown the whole[34], he meant to be at the next assembly with a large party. Nothing could be more delightful! To be fond of dancing was a certain step towards falling in love; and very lively hopes of Mr. Bingley's heart were entertained[35].

"If I can but see one of my daughters happily settled at Netherfield", said Mrs. Bennet to her husband, "and all the others equally well married, I shall have nothing to wish for."

In a few days Mr. Bingley returned Mr. Bennet's visit, and sat about ten minutes with him in his library. He had entertained hopes of being admitted to a sight[36] of the young ladies, of whose beauty he had heard much; but he saw only the father. The ladies were somewhat more fortunate, for they had the advantage of ascertaining[37] from an upper window that he wore a blue coat, and rode a black horse.

An invitation to dinner was soon afterwards dispatched[38]; and already had Mrs. Bennet planned the courses that were to do credit to her housekeeping, when an answer arrived which deferred it all. Mr. Bingley was obliged to be in town the following day, and, consequently, unable to accept the honour of their invitation, etc. Mrs. Bennet was quite disconcerted[39]. She could not imagine what business he could have in town so soon after his arrival in Hertfordshire; and she began to fear that he might be always flying about from one place to another, and never settled at Netherfield as he ought to be. Lady Lucas quieted her fears a little by starting the idea of his being gone to London only to get a large party for the ball; and a report soon followed that Mr. Bingley was to bring twelve ladies and seven gentlemen with him to the assembly. The girls grieved over such a number of ladies, but were comforted the day before the ball by hearing, that instead of twelve he brought only six with him from London, his five sisters and a cousin. And when the party entered

---

31) barefaced : 노골적인
32) surmise : 추측, 억측
33) elude : 피하다
34) to crown the whole : 게다가
35) very lively hopes of Mr. Bingley's heart were entertained : 모두들 Mr. Bingley의 마음을 사로잡아 보겠다는 희망을 품게 되었다.
36) being admitted to a sight : 볼 수 있다는
37) for they had the advantage of ascertaining ~ : ~을 확인할 기회가 있었기 때문에
38) dispatch : (편지 등을) 보내다
39) disconcerted : 당황한

the assembly room it consisted of only five altogether; Mr. Bingley, his two sisters, the husband of the eldest, and another young man.

Mr. Bingley was good looking and gentlemanlike; he had a pleasant countenance, and easy, unaffected manners. His sisters were fine women, with an air of decided fashion. His brother-in-law, Mr. Hurst, merely looked the gentleman; but his friend Mr. Darcy soon drew the attention of the room by his fine, tall person, handsome features, noble mien, and the report which was in general circulation within five minutes after his entrance, of his having ten thousand a year. The gentlemen pronounced him to be a fine figure of a man, the ladies declared he was much handsomer than Mr. Bingley, and he was looked at with great admiration for about half the evening, till his manners gave a disgust which turned the tide of his popularity; for he was discovered to be proud; to be above his company, and above being pleased[40]; and not all his large estate in Derbyshire[41] could then save him from having a most forbidding, disagreeable countenance, and being unworthy to be compared with his friend.

Mr. Bingley had soon made himself acquainted with all the principal people in the room; he was lively and unreserved, danced every dance, was angry that the ball closed so early, and talked of giving one himself at Netherfield. Such amiable qualities must speak for themselves[42]. What a contrast between him and his friend! Mr. Darcy danced only once with Mrs. Hurst[43] and once with Miss Bingley, declined being introduced to any other lady, and spent the rest of the evening in walking about the room, speaking occasionally to one of his own party. His character was decided. He was the proudest, most disagreeable man in the world, and everybody hoped that he would never come there again. Amongst the most violent against him was Mrs. Bennet, whose dislike of his general behaviour was sharpened into particular resentment by his having slighted[44] one of her daughters.

Elizabeth Bennet had been obliged, by the scarcity of gentlemen, to sit down[45] for two dances; and during part of that time, Mr. Darcy had been standing near enough for her to hear a conversation between him and Mr. Bingley, who came from the dance for a few minutes, to press[46] his friend to join it.

"Come, Darcy," said he, "I must have you dance. I hate to see you standing about by yourself in this stupid manner. You had much better dance."

"I certainly shall not. You know how I detest it, unless I am particularly acquainted with my partner. At such an assembly as this it would be insupportable[47]. Your sisters are engaged, and there is not another woman in the room whom it would not be a punishment to me to stand up

---

40) above being pleased : 함께 있는 사람들을 깔보며 그들과 즐기려 하지 않는 것
41) Derbyshire : 영국 잉글랜드 중부에 있는 카운티(county)
42) speak for themselves : 자명하다
43) Mrs. Hurst : Mr. Bingley의 누나, Miss Bingley는 그의 누이동생
44) slight : 무시하다
45) sit down : (춤을 출 상대가 없어서) 앉아 있다
46) press : 졸라대다
47) insupportable : 참을 수 없는

with."

"I would not be so fastidious[48] as you are," cried Mr. Bingley, "for a kingdom[49]! Upon my honour, I never met with so many pleasant girls in my life as I have this evening; and there are several of them you see uncommonly pretty."

"You are dancing with the only handsome girl in the room," said Mr. Darcy, looking at the eldest Miss Bennet.

"Oh! She is the most beautiful creature I ever beheld I But there is one of her sisters sitting down just behind you, who is very pretty, and I dare say very agreeable. Do let me ask my partner to introduce you."

"Which do you mean?" and turning round he looked for a moment at Elizabeth, ill catching her eye, he withdrew his own and coldly said: "She is tolerable, but not handsome enough to tempt me; I am in no humour at present to give consequence[50] to young ladies who are slighted by other men. You had better return to your partner and enjoy her smiles, for you are wasting your time with me."

Mr. Bingley followed his advice. Mr. Darcy walked off; and Elizabeth remained with no very cordial feelings toward him. She told the story, however, with great spirit among her friends; for she had a lively, playful disposition, which delighted in anything ridiculous.

The evening altogether passed off pleasantly to the whole family. Mrs. Bennet had seen her eldest daughter much admired by the Netherfield party. Mr. Bingley had danced with her twice, and she had been distinguished by his sisters. Jane was as much gratified by this as her mother could be, though in a quieter way. Elizabeth felt Jane's pleasure. Mary had heard herself mentioned to Miss Bingley as the most accomplished[51] girl in the neighbourhood; and Catherine and Lydia had been fortunate enough never to be without partners, which was all that they had yet learnt to care for at a ball[52]. They returned, therefore, in good spirits to Longbourn, the village where they lived, and of which they were the principal inhabitants. They found Mr. Bennet still up. With a book he was regardless of time; and on the present occasion he had a good deal of curiosity as to the event of an evening which had raised such splendid expectations. He had rather hoped that his wife's views on the stranger would be disappointed; but he soon found out that he had a different story to hear.

"Oh! my dear Mr. Bennet," as she entered the room, "we have had a most delightful evening, a most excellent ball. I wish you had been there. Jane was so admired, nothing could be like it. Everybody said how well she looked; and Mr. Bingley thought her quite beautiful, and danced with her twice! Only think of that, my dear; he actually danced with her twice! and she was the only creature in the room that he asked a second time. First of all, he asked Miss Lucas. I was so vexed to see him stand up with her! But, however, he did not admire her at all; indeed, nobody can, you know; and he seemed quite struck with Jane as she was going down the dance[53]. So he inquired

---

48) fastidious : 까다로운
49) for a kingdom : 나라면 왕국을 준다 해도 자네처럼 까다롭게 굴지 않겠다.
50) give consequence : 함께 춤을 춤으로써 상대 여성에 대한 중요성을 더해주다.
51) accomplished : 교양이 있는
52) which was all that they had yet learnt to care for at a ball : 무도회에서 신경 쓸 것은 춤의 상대가 있기만 하면 되는 것이었다.
53) going down the dance : 춤의 여러 동작을 하는 것

who she was, and got introduced, and asked her for the two next. Then the two third he danced with Miss King, and the two fourth with Maria Lucas, and the two fifth with Jane again, and the two sixth with Lizzy, and the Boulanger[54] —"

"If he had had any compassion for me", cried her husband impatiently, he would not have danced half so much! For God's sake, say no more of his partners. Oh that he had sprained his ankle in the first dance!"

"Oh! my dear," continued Mrs. Bennet, "I am quite delighted with him. He is so excessively handsome! And his sisters are charming women. I never in my life saw anything more elegant than their dresses. I dare say the lace upon Mrs. Hurst's gown —"

Here she was interrupted again. Mr. Bennet protested against any description of finery[55]. She was therefore obliged to seek another branch of the subject, and related, with much bitterness of spirit and some exaggeration, the shocking rudeness of Mr. Darcy.

"But I can assure you," she added, hat Lizzy does not lose much by not suiting his fancy[56]; for he is a most disagreeable, horrid man, not at all worth pleasing. So high and so conceited that there was no enduring him! He walked here, and he walked there, fancying himself so very great! Not handsome enough to dance with[57]! I wish you had been there, my dear, to have given him one of your set-downs[58]. I quite detest the man."

---

54) Boulanger : 네 사람이 한 조가 되어 서로 마주 보며 추는 프랑스 춤인 카드릴의 5단
55) finery : 화려한 옷
56) suiting his fancy : 그의 마음에 드는 것
57) Not handsome enough to dance with : 같이 춤출 만큼 멋지지 않다니.
58) set-down : 기죽이기, 질책

제3장 Emily Brontë – 「Wuthering Heights」

단원개요

「Wuthering Heights」는 소설의 Narrator가 이야기를 듣는 장면이라는 독특한 이중적 구조와 고딕소설의 분위기, 강렬하고 극단적인 인물들의 성격묘사로 폭발적인 에너지를 담고 있다. 「Wuthering Heights」는 신비롭고 환상적인 낭만주의적 분위기에 현실과 영혼의 세계를 사실성 있게 묘사하여, 사랑과 증오라는 인간의 내면적 본질을 심도 있게 탐구한 작품이다. 특히 빅토리아 시대 당시의 작품들에서는 찾아볼 수 없었던 복잡하고 치밀한 구성은 그 시대를 훨씬 앞선 것이었다.

출제 경향 및 수험 대책

각 등장인물 간의 갈등구조를 파악하고 소설에서 등장하는 각 인물들의 특징을 파악하며 이야기의 흐름을 이해할 필요가 있다. Catherine과 Heathcliff의 갈등과 사랑은 이루어지지 못한 사랑의 한계에서 벗어나 당대의 산업과 문화적 변화의 맥락에서 이해해야 하며 대립되는 사회적 경험을 축으로 모든 행동과 갈등이 발생하고 있음을 염두에 두어야 한다. 또한 18세기 말 젠트리(Gentry) 여성의 위치와 연관 지어 작품을 분석할 필요가 있다.

제1절 작가의 생애

Emily Brontë(필명 Ellis Bell, 1818~1848)는 아일랜드 출신 영국 성공회 목사인 Patrick Brontë와 그의 아내 Maria Branwell 사이에서 1남 5녀 중 넷째 딸로 태어났다. Emily가 세 살이 되던 해 어머니가 암으로 사망하자 이모 Elizabeth Branwell이 여섯 명의 아이들을 키우기 위하여 웨스트요크셔(West Yorkshire)주의 작은 마을 하워스(Haworth)의 목사관(Haworth Parsonage)으로 이사 와서 함께 살았다. 이곳의 한쪽은 요크셔(Yorkshire)의 황량한 황무지이고, 다른 쪽에는 교구의 무덤이 존재했는데, 바로 Brontë 자매의 문학적 상상력의 바탕이 되는 곳이라고 할 수 있다.

Emily가 여섯 살이 되던 해에 목사 자녀들을 위한 Cowan Bridge school에 입학하여, 이미 그 학교에 다니고 있던 언니들, 즉 첫째 언니 Maria, 둘째 언니 Elizabeth, 그리고 셋째 언니 Charlotte과 함께 학교 생활을 하게 된다. 하지만 학교에 장티푸스가 유행하자 자매들은 집으로 돌아오고 1825년 Maria와 Elizabeth가 폐결핵으로 사망한다(이 질병은 나중에 어린 동생 Anne의 목숨도 가져가게 된다). Emily, Charlotte, Anne 세 자매는 황량한 황무지에 둘러싸인 척박한 요크셔 목사관의 고독하고 외로운 생활 속에서 시 쓰기에 열중하여 필명을 사용해 시집 『Poems by Currer, Ellis, and Acton Bell』을 1846년에 출판하기도 했다. 이 작품들은 대중적으로 성공하지 못했지만 이후 Charlotte은 소설가로 성공한다.

Emily는 Cowan Bridge School을 다니던 시절과, Charlotte이 교사로 재직하던 Roe Head Girls' School에 재학하다 곧 향수병으로 돌아온 이력, 20세에 웨스트요크셔주의 도시 할리팩스(Halifax)에 있는 여학교 Law Hill School에서 잠시 교사 생활을 한 것을 제외하고는 황량한 요크셔의 목사관에서 외부와 거의 단절된 생활을 하며, 주변을 산책하는 취미와 더불어 자기 자신만의 문학세계를 구축하며 작품 집필로 일생을 보냈다. 그녀는 언니 Charlotte Brontë와는 달리 독신으로 살았고, 몇 편의 시와 29세에 출판한 유일한 대작 「*Wuthering Heights*」(1847)를 남기고 1848년 30세가 되던 해에 세상을 떠났다.
「*Wuthering Heights*」는 신비롭고 환상적인 낭만주의적 분위기에 현실과 영혼의 세계를 사실성 있게 묘사하여, 사랑과 증오라는 인간의 내면적 본질을 심도 있게 탐구한 훌륭한 작품이다. 특히 빅토리아 시대 당시의 작품들에서는 찾아 볼 수 없었던 복잡하고 치밀한 구성은 그 시대를 훨씬 앞선 것이었다.

제 2 절 　작품 세계

1 「*Wuthering Heights*」의 의미

「*Wuthering Heights*」는 신비롭고 환상적인 낭만주의적 분위기에 현실과 영혼의 세계를 사실성 있게 묘사하여 사랑과 증오라는 인간의 내면 본질을 심도 있게 탐구한 작품이다. 이 소설은 당시 빅토리아 시대의 작품들에서는 찾아볼 수 없었던 복잡하고 치밀한 구성을 가진다. '폭풍의 언덕'이라는 제목으로 알려진 「*Wuthering Heights*」는 소설 속 저택의 이름인데, 'Wuthering'은 소설의 배경인 영국 북부 지방에서 쓰이는 '세찬 폭풍우에 고스란히 노출된 상태'를 의미하는 영국 사투리이다. 소설에서 'Wuthering Heights'가 폭풍우에 노출된 언덕에 위치해 있음을 암시하기 때문에 이러한 근거로 본 소설을 '폭풍의 언덕'으로 번역하는 것이 가능하다. 'Wuthering'이라는 형용사는 소설의 핵심을 표현함으로써 폭풍우가 몰아치는 가운데 개들이 울부짖는 소설 속 분위기를 함축적으로 지닌 단어라 할 수 있다.

2 시대적 배경

빅토리아조 소설은 빅토리아조의 사회, 문화, 역사적인 상황 등과 연관성 있게 논해야 한다. 그런데 Emily Brontë는 예외적인 경우에 속한다. 그녀의 작품인 「*Wuthering Heights*」는 시대적인 틀에 맞지 않는 변종에 속한다고 할 수 있다. 이 소설은 빅토리아조에 속한 작품이라기보다는 William Blake나 John Keats의 시(時) 정신과 맥이 닿아있는 낭만주의적인 작품이라고 보는 것이 바람직하다. 그러나 「*Wuthering Heights*」가 출판되었던 1847년에는 Blake나 Keats가 직접적으로 표현했던 낭만주의적인 감정과 분위기가 이미 그 정점에 도달한 후였기 때문에 Emily Brontë의 작품세계는 당대의 흐름과 거리가 있다. 즉, 그녀는 '혁명적인 정신적 에너지를 방출하기 위하여' 천국과 지옥의 가치관을 뒤집어 버렸고, 그것이 당시의 시대적인 정황이나 시대정신과 간극이 있었다는 것이다. 당시는 Charles Dickens의 시대였고 George Eliot의 시대였다.
이러한 관점에서 「*Wuthering Heights*」를 보면 이 소설이 당시에 '불유쾌'(disagreeable)하고 '악마적'(diabolical)이라는 비판을 받았던 것—그러나 이러한 악평은 오히려 이 소설에 대한 관심과 인기를 증가시켰다—은 충분히 이해할 수 있다. 구체적으로 소설의 주요 등장인물인 Catherine과 Heathcliff, 특히 Heathcliff가 소설에서 표현하는 악마적인 에너지는 당대에서 용납될 수 없었다. 그러나 무엇보다도 이러한 사회적인 상황에서 과감하게 표현할 수 있었다는 데에 Emily Brontë의 위대성이 있다. Emily Brontë 는 William Blake나 John Keats가 표현했던 것처럼 열정을 직접 전달할 수 있는 길을 영국소설사에 터놓았다. 그러나 이것이 빅토리아조의 작가들에게 곧바로 이어진 것은 아니었다. 빅토리아조의 소설들은 Emily Brontë의 텍스트에 녹아들어 있는 폭발적인 에너지를 수용하기에는 책임감, 도덕성, 진지함을 너무 강조했다. Emily Brontë가 소설에서 표현했던 것은 시간을 건너 Thomas Hardy와 D. H. Lawrence, Joseph Conrad로 이어졌다고 할 수 있다. Catherine이 표현했던 사랑의 강도와 복잡성은 Thomas Hardy 의 'Tess' 또는 'Eustacia', Lawrence의 'Gurdrun' 또는 'Ursula'와 같은 인물로 이어진다.

3 산업사회와 「*Wuthering Heights*」

「*Wuthering Heights*」는 1840년대 초에 쓰였으나 작품의 배경은 1771년부터 1802년이다. 특히 이 작품이 1801년에 끝나는 것은 특별한 사회적 의미를 지닌다. 이 시기는 가부장적 가족에 기초한 과거의 거친 농경 문화가 빅토리아 시대의 계급의식을 만들어낼 여러 사회적 문화적 변화에 도전받고 길들여지는 시기인 것이다. Catherine과 Heathcliff의 갈등과 사랑은 이러한 문화적 변화의 맥락에서 이해해야 하며, 특히 Catherine의 선택은 직접적으로는 18세기 말 젠트리(Gentry) 여성의 모순적 위치와 연관 지어 읽을 필요가 있다.

Q. D. Leavis와 Arnold Kettle은 「*Wuthering Heights*」를 사회 계급과 경제적인 측면에서 접근하는데 이 것은 Heathcliff의 소외와 경제적인 문제가 맞물려 있는 점에 논의의 초점을 맞추고 있기 때문이다. Heathcliff의 악마적인 행동이 설득력과 개연성을 지니고 있는 것은 그를 다른 인물들로부터 분리시켜 소외된 인간으로 처리하면서 그 소외가 표방하는 심리적인 에너지와 성적 에너지가 Catherine의 결혼 이후에는 경제적인 에너지로 대치되는 상황을 적나라하게 묘사한 작가의 테크닉에 힘입고 있는데, 결국 사랑의 문제가 자연스럽게 경제적인 문제와 섞이는 것이다. Heathcliff가 Earnshaw가(家)와 Linton가(家) 소유의 모든 재산을 차지해 나가는 과정은 어떤 리얼리즘 소설보다도 정확하게 그려져 있다.

이 소설이 쓰인 것은 1840년대였고 출판된 시기는 1847년이었으며, 이 소설의 배경은 1771년에서 1802 년까지의 약 32년간이다. Charles Percy Sanger에 따르면 Emily Brontë는 당시의 법률적 문제들을 소상히 파악하고 있었으며, 그것에 입각하여 Heathcliff가 모든 재산을 획득하는 방식을 치밀하게 기술하였다고 한다. 그러나 이 소설은 돈이나 재산에 관한 문제 등 산업사회의 문제점을 직접적으로 드러내고 있지는 않다. Emily Brontë는 산업사회와 동떨어진 황야에서 살았던 작가였다. Catherine과 Heathcliff가 Linton 가(家)의 저택을 처음 들여다보고 느끼고 반응하는 것 자체가 바로 그들 나름의 '사회적 경험'이라고 할 수 있다. 「*Wuthering Heights*」는 바로 이러한 두 사람의 대립되는 사회적 경험을 축으로 모든 행동이 벌어지고 규정되는 소설이라고 볼 수 있다. 비록 「*Wuthering Heights*」가 직접적으로 산업사회를 형상화하여 보여주고 있지는 않지만, 두 사람의 '사회적 경험'을 통하여 당시의 사회적 현실을 보여주고 있다.

4 고딕소설과 리얼리즘 중요 ★★

고딕소설은 주로 중세 시대의 음산한 성곽을 배경으로 하고 음침한 풍경 같은 데서 일어날 법한 신비와 공포를 다루며, 지하 감옥·비밀 통로·유령이 출몰하는 낡은 저택에서 일어나는 이야기나 으스스한 초자연 현상들을 다룬다. 「Wuthering Heights」의 배경은 사회와 동떨어진 황량하고 거친 초지가 있는 요크셔이며, 그 중심에는 비밀스럽고 음침한 Wuthering Heights 저택이 있다. Mr. Lockwood는 가정부 Nelly Dean을 통해 Wuthering Heights와 Thrushcross Grange를 둘러싼 비밀스럽고 신비스러운 이야기를 들으며, 초자연적 존재인 Catherine의 유령을 마주하기도 한다.

「Wuthering Heights」는 사회적 현실과 완전히 동떨어져 있는 로맨스가 아니다. 그리고 바로 이러한 점이 이 작품의 강점이다. 「Wuthering Heights」는 한편으로는 낭만주의적인 속성을 갖고 있고, 다른 한편으로는 빅토리아조 리얼리즘 소설의 속성을 갖고 있다. 따라서 이 작품은 고딕소설과 리얼리즘의 중간쯤에 위치하고 있다고 할 수 있다.

제 3 절 줄거리

소설은 1801년경에 Lockwood라는 한 신사가 도시에서부터 은거할 땅을 찾아 이 황야로 들어와 Thrushcross 저택을 빌리고 Wuthering Height라고 불리는 저택을 방문하는 데서 시작한다. 그는 Earnshaw 가문과 Linton 두 집안의 3대에 걸친 역사를 아는 늙은 가정부 Ellen(Nelly) Dean에게서 이야기를 듣는다.

30년 전, Wuthering Heights 저택의 주인 Earnshaw는 여행 중에 길에서 어린 고아를 하나 데려와 Heathcliff라고 부르며 자신의 딸 Catherine과 아들 Hindley와 함께 키운다. Catherine은 어려서부터 Heathcliff를 좋아하여 사이좋게 지내지만, Hindley는 Heathcliff를 싫어한다. Heathcliff가 온 지 2년도 채 안 되어 Catherine과 Hindley의 어머니는 병으로 세상을 떠났고, 그 후 Hindley는 Heathcliff를 더욱 미워하며 아버지의 애정과 자기의 권리를 가로챈 나쁜 존재로 생각하기 시작한다.

어느 덧 시간이 흘러 Hindley는 대학에 입학하여 기숙사로 가게 되었고, Catherine의 아버지는 몸이 점점 쇠약해져서 건강을 회복하지 못하고 Hindley가 대학교 3학년이 되던 해에 10월의 어느 날 세상을 떠나게 된다. 장례를 치르기 위해 돌아온 Hindley는 아내인 Frances를 함께 데리고 돌아와 모두를 놀라게 한다. 부친이 죽자 Hindley는 노골적으로 Heathcliff를 증오하고 학대하기 시작한다. Hindley의 아내 Frances는 가구와 그 외의 모든 것은 마음에 들어 하지만 장례식 준비 및 조문을 오는 모든 사람들을 싫어했다. Frances는 좀 야윈 편이고 얼굴에 활기가 넘치기는 했지만 계단을 오를 때면 늘 숨차하고 조그만 소리에도 깜짝 놀라곤 했다. Hindley는 부인인 Frances가 하자는 것이면 무엇이든 들어주었다. 그러나 Hindley는 Heathcliff가 목사로부터 배우고 있던 공부마저 못 하게 하고 힘든 일만 시키며 Heathcliff가 하인과 다름없는 생활을 하게 한다. 그러나 Heathcliff는 이런 상황을 별로 신경 쓰지 않았다. 그 이유는 Catherine이 Heathcliff에게 자신이 배운 것을 가르쳐 주고 밭에서 같이 일을 하거나 놀아주기도 했기 때문이다. 둘은 교회도 부지런히 다녔고 둘만 있으면 늘 즐거웠다.

어느 날 저녁, 떠들었다는 이유로 쫓겨나서 들판을 달리던 Heathcliff와 Catherine은 우연히 Thrushcross Grange의 대지주인 Linton의 저택에 접근했다가 도둑으로 몰려 봉변을 당한다. 개에게 물린 Catherine은 그 집에서 치료를 받게 되면서 Linton 가문의 아들 Edgar Linton과 친해지게 되고, 이를 알게 된 Heathcliff는 좌절하게 된다. Catherine의 오빠인 Hindley 부부 사이에 아이가 태어나고 그 아이를 출산한 Frances가 아이를 낳은 지 일주일 만에 죽자, Hindley는 갈수록 술과 도박으로 타락하며 난폭해졌고, Heathcliff에 대한 학대는 나날이 심해진다. Heathcliff는 복수를 꿈꾸게 된다. 열다섯 살이 된 Catherine은 아름다운 아가씨가 되고 Edgar Linton의 청혼을 받는다. Catherine은 Heathcliff와의 사이에서 결혼에 대한 고민을 하면서 가정부인 Nelly에게 근본도 모르는 Heathcliff와는 결혼할 수 없다는 이야기를 하던 중 Heathcliff가 그 내용을 우연히 듣고 성급하게 떠난다. 그러나 사실 Catherine은 가정부인 Nelly에게 곧바로 그 말을 부정하고 Heathcliff에 대한 사랑을 고백했었다.

그 후 3년이 지나 Catherine은 결국 Edgar Linton과 결혼하게 된다. 그럭저럭 결혼생활에 안정을 찾아가며 지내던 몇 년 후 Heathcliff는 그 전과 완전히 다른 신사가 되어 돌아온다. 돈도 많이 벌고 교양 있는 신사가 되었지만 사실 Heathcliff는 자신을 학대한 Hindley와 사랑하는 Catherine을 빼앗은 Edgar에 대한 복수심으로 불타고 있었다. 그는 도박으로 Hindley를 파멸시켜 Wuthering Heights를 빼앗은 뒤 Hindley Earnshaw의 아들 Hareton Earnshaw에게 자기가 받은 학대를 그대로 행한다. Hareton의 용모는 여느 귀공자의 모습처럼 자라나게 되지만 무식하고 거칠다. 그 후 Heathcliff는 Edgar Linton의 동생 Isabella Linton을 유혹해 결혼한 후 그녀를 학대한다. 그녀는 Heathcliff가 자신의 집안에 복수를 위해 결혼한 것을 깨닫고 자신을 학대하는 Heathcliff로부터 피해 집을 나간 후 런던에서 아들을 낳는다.

Heathcliff를 사랑했던 Catherine은 그 충격으로 7달 만에 딸을 낳다가 죽고 병약한 Edgar도 딸 Cathy를 기르다가 죽는다. Isabella가 죽으면서 Edgar가 데려다 키우려던 Heathcliff의 아들 Linton Heathcliff는 아버지 Heathcliff의 손에서 병약하게 성장한다. Heathcliff는 아들 Linton에게도 아버지로서 자식에게 느끼는 사랑을 느끼지 못하고 오로지 자기의 복수와 야망의 도구로 이용하려는 의도를 품는다. Edgar가 죽자 Edgar와 Catherine의 딸인 Cathy Linton을 감금시키고 강제로 Linton Heathcliff와 결혼시킨다. 강제로 결혼시켜 아들이 없는 Edgar의 저택 Thrushcross Grange까지 자기 손에 넣고 Edgar의 모든 재산을 몰수한다.

병약하게 자란 Linton Heathcliff는 Cathy에게 병간호만 시키다가 결국 세상을 떠난다. Cathy는 남편인 Linton Heathcliff가 죽은 후에도 Heathcliff의 손에서 벗어나지 못한다. 죽은 Linton Heathcliff의 아내로서의 임무를 수행하면서 Heathcliff의 수모를 견디고 돈 한 푼 없이 Wuthering Heights에서 살아간다. 한편, Heathcliff는 Catherine의 환영 속에서 정신이 점차 이상해져간다. Heathcliff는 결국 눈도 감지 못한 채 복수와 야망으로 얼룩진 생을 마감했으며, Cathy와 Hareton은 Heathcliff의 장례를 치르고 난 후 결혼을 한다. 이들은 Heathcliff가 죽고 나서 유령을 보았다는 사람이 많아지자 Wuthering Heights를 버리고 Thrushcross Grange의 Linton가로 옮겨가게 된다. Mr. Lockwood는 아쉬운 듯 달을 쳐다보면서 돌아서는 Hareton과 Cathy의 모습을 보면서, 그 옛날 Heathcliff와 Catherine Earnshaw도 이렇게 달을 쳐다보았을까라고 생각하며 Wuthering Heights와 작별하게 된다.

제 4 절 작품의 주제

1 사랑

1부는 Heathcliff와 Catherine의 못다 한 사랑이, 2부에서는 Young Catherine(Cathy)과 Hareton의 화합적인 관계가 다뤄진다. 「Wuthering Heights」의 큰 주제는 남녀 간의 사랑에 관한 것이라고 할 수 있지만 그 사랑은 단순히 개인적인 애환의 차원이 아니라 경제적인 차원까지 포함하는 광범위한 성격을 지닌다.

2 복수와 반항

작품이 끝나기 직전까지 Heathcliff는 자신을 타락하게 한 사람들에게 복수를 행한다. 돈 한 푼 없이 버림받은 Heathcliff는 압제자들을 응징하며, 그의 복수는 다소 폭력적이다. Hindley가 Heathcliff에게 행했던 물리적 폭력과 그에 대한 보복으로 Hindley의 아들 Hareton을 대하는 Heathcliff의 태도는 가학적이어서, 출판 당시 잔학성(cruelty)과 잔인함(inhumanity) 때문에 비판을 받기도 했다. Heathcliff의 복수와 반역은 사실 상위 계층에 대한 복수이기도 하다. 미천한 고아 신분과 경제적 소외에서 탈피해 재산을 축적해나가는 Heathcliff는 자신을 괴롭히던 상위 계층에게 반역하는 것이다.

3 대조적인 삶의 방식과 갈등 중요 ★★

Wuthering Heights에서의 자유롭고 광란적인 삶과 Thrushcross Grange의 평온한 삶의 방식이 서로 대립하고 갈등한다. 문명과는 담을 쌓고 황야에 무방비 상태로 존재하는 Wuthering Heights는 자연 친화적인 반면에, 계곡에 안전하게 자리 잡고 있는 문명의 저택이라고 할 수 있는 Thrushcross Grange는 교양 있는 문명사회에 가깝다. Thrushcross Grange는 '선'(善)과 '천국'으로 비유되지만 Wuthering Heights는 '악'(惡)과 '지옥'으로 비유된다. 작가는 두 저택을 대조하면서 자연과 문명, 이상과 현실, 경제적 소외와 사회적 계급 문제를 형상화한다.

제 5 절 등장인물

본 소설의 등장인물들은 크게 두 가지의 성격으로 나뉜다.

> • Wuthering Heights형(型) : 강인하고 정열적이며 격렬한 인간형
> • Thrushcross Grange형(型) : 수동적이고 교양적이며 조용한 인간형

1 Heathcliff

Mr. Earnshaw가 데려온 고아로, Earnshaw 집안의 저택인 Wuthering Heights에서 고아이자 천한 신분이라는 이유로 Hindley와 Edgar Linton에게, 특히 Hindley로부터 온갖 핍박과 학대를 받는다. 그로부터 3~4년 뒤 성공한 영국 신사가 되어 돌아온 그는 Hindley를 비롯하여 자신을 업신여기고 핍박한 모든 사람들에게 처참할 정도의 복수를 행한다. 그 가운데서도 Catherine에게만은 애정을 느끼며 자신의 진실한 사랑을 준다. 그러나 그는 Edgar와 결혼한 Catherine의 이중적인 행동 때문에 그녀와의 사랑을 이루지 못한다. 그는 Catherine이 죽은 후에도 그녀의 무덤 근처 벌판을 헤매며 사랑하는 그녀의 영혼과 하나가 되고자 한다. Heathcliff는 핍박 속에서 성장하며, 교양이라는 울타리 속에 속박되지 않고, 인간의 내면에 자리하는 증오의 본질을 적나라하게 드러내는 복수와 집념의 인간형으로 변한다.

2 Catherine Earnshaw(결혼 후 Catherine Linton)

Mr. Earnshaw의 딸이자 Hindley Earnshaw의 여동생으로, 정열적이고 순수한 감정으로 Heathcliff와 애정을 나누지만, 두 사람 사이의 신분상 장벽을 이유로 Heathcliff를 버리고 Edgar Linton과 결혼한다. 그러나 Edgar와의 결혼 후에도 Heathcliff를 잊지 못하는 Catherine의 이중적인 태도는 Heathcliff와 Edgar Linton의 갈등을 더욱 증폭시키고, 나아가 양쪽 집안, Wuthering Heights와 Thrushcross Grange를 혼돈 속으로 빠트리는 결과를 낳는다. Catherine은 Heathcliff와 황야를 맨발로 헤매는가 하면, 귀부인의 모습도 보여주는 등 두 가지의 속성을 지닌 여주인공이다.

3 Hindley Earnshaw

Earnshaw 집안의 아들이자 Catherine의 오빠이다. Heathcliff를 무자비하게 짓밟는 가해자이면서 동시에 자신의 아버지로부터 박해받는 피해자이다. 거칠면서도 심약한 성격이며, Heathcliff가 행하는 복수의 첫 번째 희생자이다. Heathcliff의 유인책에 빠져 도박과 마약 등으로 폐인이 되어 결국 파멸한다.

4 Edgar Linton

Thrushcross Grange 저택의 주인으로, Isabella Linton의 오빠이자 Catherine Linton의 남편이다. 겁쟁이로 보이기도 하나, 귀족적이고 신사적이며 세련된 기품이 흐르는 교양적 측면이 더 강하다. Catherine Earnshaw와 결혼 후에는 집에서 착한 아버지로서의 역할을 충실히 해나가지만, 그녀와의 결혼 이후 Heathcliff가 벌이는 복수극에 휘말려 비극을 맞는다. Heathcliff가 악(惡)이라면 Edgar Linton은 선(善)으로 대변된다.

5 Isabella Linton

Edgar Linton의 여동생으로, Heathcliff의 유혹에 빠져 그와 결혼한다. Heathcliff가 자신의 집안에 복수를 하기 위해 자신과 결혼한 것을 깨닫고 Wuthering Heights를 떠난다. 아들인 Linton Heathcliff가 12살이 되던 해에 죽고 만다.

6 Hareton Earnshaw

Hindley의 아들로, 거칠게 자라 용감하기는 하나 나쁜 기질을 가졌다. Heathcliff는 Hindley를 향한 반감과 복수로 Hareton에게 교육의 기회를 제공하지 않아 Hareton은 글자를 읽지 못하며, 학대받으며 자란다. Hareton은 Hindley가 죽은 후, Heathcliff에게 억류되어 Wuthering Heights에서 그의 하인으로서 부당한 대우를 받으며 살아간다. Hareton은 Wuthering Heights에서 함께 생활하는 Mrs. Catherine Heathcliff (Cathy)와 갈등을 반복하다가 극적인 화해 후 결국 두 사람은 결혼한다. Hareton을 무시하던 Cathy가 그에게 책 읽는 법을 알려주고 도와주는 장면은 유년시절 Heathcliff와 Catherine의 모습과 유사하다.

7 Linton Heathcliff

Heathcliff와 Isabella Linton 사이에서 태어난 아들이다. 사촌인 Cathy(Catherine Linton)과 결혼한다. 병적인 성격을 가지고 있고 버릇이 없으며 이기적이고 가학적 성격을 지니고 있다.

8 (Young) Catherine (Cathy) Linton – 첫 번째 결혼 후 Catherine Heathcliff(Mrs. Heathcliff)

Edgar Linton과 Catherine Earnshaw 사이에서 태어난 딸로, 동명인 어머니 Catherine과 구분하기 위해 Young Catherine 혹은 Cathy라고 불린다. 그녀는 Wuthering Heights를 파멸시킨 후 Linton가(家)의 재산까지 손에 넣으려는 Heathcliff에 의하여 그의 아들 Linton Heathcliff와 강제로 결혼해 Mrs. Heathcliff가 된다. Linton Heathcliff가 죽자 미망인이 된 그녀는 Wuthering Heights에서 Heathcliff와 Hareton Earnshaw와 함께 살게 된다. Hareton과 자주 싸우고 대립하지만, Heathcliff의 사망 후에는 Hareton Earnshaw와 결혼한다.

9 Frances Earnshaw

Hindley Earnshaw의 아내이다. 조금 정신병적인 증세를 보이는 우둔하고 무식한 여인이다. Hareton Earnshaw를 낳고 바로 죽는다.

10 Joshep, Zillah

Wuthering Heights에서 시중을 드는 하인들이다. Earnshaw 집안사람들이 주인으로 있었을 때부터 집 주인이 Heathcliff로 바뀐 뒤에도 계속 하인으로 일하면서 남아있다.

11 Narrators : Mr Lockwood, Nelly Dean 중요 ★★★

(1) Mr. Lockwood

Frame-narrator로 객관적인 시점을 제공한다. Thrushcross Grange 저택에 세 들어 살다가 Wuthering Heights에 관한 숨겨진 모든 의문을 풀기 위해 가정부 Nelly(Ellen) Dean에게 이야기를 서술하도록 질문을 던지고, 자신의 생각 또한 서술하는 인물이다.

(2) Nelly(Ellen) Dean

원래 Earnshaw가(家)의 저택인 Wuthering Heights의 가정부였으나 Catherine Earnshaw가 Edgar Linton과 결혼하자 그녀를 보살피기 위해 Thrushcross Grange의 가정부로 거처를 옮긴다. Mr. Lockwood가 Thrushcross Grange에 세를 든 후에는 그의 가정부로도 시중을 든다. 포근한 모성애로 Catherine 모녀를 돌보기도 하고, 재치와 포용력을 가지고 있어 다른 등장인물들 간의 갈등을 조율하기도 한다. 또한 다른 서술자인 Mr. Lockwood가 그녀에게 질문을 하면 그녀는 지난날의 이야기를 그에게 말해준다.

제 6 절 작품의 구조(Plot)와 시점 및 기법

1 구조

(1) 삶의 비극을 2대에 걸쳐 다룸 중요 ★★

본 소설에서는 등장인물들의 삶의 비극을 2대에 걸쳐 다루고 있다. 1대는 Catherine Linton이 죽을 때까지이고, 2대는 Heathcliff의 아들인 Linton Heathcliff와 Catherine의 딸인 Cathy Linton이 결혼을 하면서 시작한다. 두 세대가 전체적인 소설에서 각각 절반을 차지하며 대조되는 두 가문의 아이들이(2대) 결혼하여 짝을 이루는 전개이다.

(2) 두 명의 서술자 중요 ★★

당대의 소설에서 일반적으로 쓰이던 전지적 작가 시점의 서술자가 아니다. 특이하게도 등장인물들에 의하여 회상하고 지난날을 서술하는 형식으로 전개된다. 1801년 Thrushcross Grange에 살고자 세를 들어 온 Mr. Lockwood가 Wuthering Heights에 방문한 뒤, Thrushcross Grange와 Wuthering Heights 저택의 두 집안에 걸친 내력에 대해 의문을 품고 자신의 가정부인 Nelly Dean에게 두 집안에 대한 사연을 묻고 듣는 형식이다.

독자는 Heathcliff와 Catherine의 격정적인 사랑을 두 화자의 눈을 통하여 보게 된다. Mr. Lockwood 와 Nelly Dean은 Heathcliff나 Catherine이 대변하는 윤리적·사회적·도덕적인 차원과 동떨어진 별 개의 세계를 정상적이고 관습적이며 평범한 시각으로 독자에게 제공한다. 본 소설에서 등장하는 두 명의 화자를 통해 Wuthering Heights에서 벌어지는 믿기 힘든 일들을 독자들이 믿을 수 있게 하는 역할을 한다. Heathcliff와 Catherine의 세계는 무의식적인 아이들의 세계이고, Mr. Lockwood와 Nelly Dean의 세계는 성인이자 현실적인 의식의 세계라고 할 수 있다. Nelly Dean은 자신이 해야 할 일이 무엇인지 알고, 그것을 스스로 처신하는 극히 현실적인 가정부이며, Mr. Lockwood는 초연하 고 절제 있게 사물을 바라볼 수 있는 시선을 가진 도시인의 모습을 지니고 있다.

2 시점

(1) 다중시점

Nelly Dean과 Mr. Lockwood가 중심 화자이다.

(2) 액자식 구성 중요 ★★

Nelly Dean이 주로 서술하는 이야기에 Frame-narrator인 Mr. Lockwood가 일종의 틀(frame)을 부여 한다. Mr. Lockwood와 Nelly Dean이 가장 많은 서술을 하고 있으며, 이 두 인물이 가장 정상적인 인물임을 드러내고 있다. 그 외 Catherine, Heathcliff, Isabella, Cathy, Zillah 등의 서술도 포함한다.

(3) 기타

서술자들은 모두 Heathcliff와 Catherine의 정열을 이해하지 못한다. 다만, 독자들만이 이것을 파악할 수 있는 구조이다.

3 기법

(1) 작가의 자기 반영

「*Wuthering Heights*」의 특징으로 자기 반영적인 테크닉을 들 수 있다. Emily Brontë는 따뜻함보다 치열함을, 안정보다 정신적 자유를 택했던 작가였다. Charlotte Brontë(「*Jane Eyre*」의 작가)가 Emily Brontë를 가리켜 "남자보다 강하고 아이보다 단순하다."라고 한 말은 그녀의 성격뿐 아니라 예술적인 성향까지 폭넓게 암시하고 있다. 혁명적이라고 할 만큼 순수한 어떤 것을 치열하게 추구하고자 하였던 Emily Brontë의 철학은 이 작품에 잘 나타나 있다.

(2) 자연과 초자연적 이미지

Emily Brontë가 즐겨 쓰는 이미지로는 자연(동물, 식물, 불, 토지, 날씨 등)과 초자연물(천사, 악마, 천국, 지옥 등)이 있다.

(3) 통제된 강렬한 감정

다른 작가들의 소설과는 달리 「*Wuthering Heights*」에 나오는 대화는 대화라기보다 서로 다른 적대적인 감정을 단순히 내비치고 있는 것 같은 인상을 준다. 이것은 Emily Brontë의 치열함을 고스란히 보여준다. Heathcliff와 Catherine의 사랑의 대화마저 대화가 아닌 폭력에 가깝다. 이처럼 「*Wuthering Heights*」는 강렬한 감정이 강력하게 통제되어 있는 소설이다.

제 7 절 Text

Chapter 1

1801 — I have just returned from a visit to my landlord — the solitary neighbour that I shall be troubled with. This is certainly a beautiful country! In all England, I do not believe that I could have fixed on a situation[1] so completely removed[2] from the stir of society. A perfect misanthropist's[3] Heaven — and Mr. Heathcliff and I are such a suitable pair to divide the desolation between us. A capital fellow![4] He little[5] imagined how my heart warmed towards him when I beheld his black eyes withdraw so suspiciously under their brows, as I rode up, and when his fingers sheltered themselves, with a jealous[6] resolution[7], still further in his waistcoat, as I announced my

---

1) situation : 장소
2) removed : 동떨어진, 먼
3) misanthropist : 사람을 싫어하는 사람, 염세가
4) capital fellow : 멋진 사람
5) little : 전혀 ~ 않다
6) jealous : 경계를 게을리 하지 않는
7) resolution : 결단력

name.

"Mr. Heathcliff?" I said.

A nod was the answer.

"Mr. Lockwood, your new tenant[8], sir. I do myself the honour of calling as soon as possible after my arrival, to express the hope that I have not inconvenienced you by my perseverance[9] in soliciting[10] the occupation of Thrushcross Grange: I heard yesterday you had had some thoughts — "

"Thrushcross Grange is my own, sir," he interrupted, wincing[11]. "I should not allow any one to inconvenience me, if I could hinder it — walk in!"

The "walk in" was uttered with closed teeth, and expressed the sentiment, "Go to the Deuce:"[12] even the gate over which he leant manifested[13] no sympathizing movement to the words; and I think that circumstance determined me to accept the invitation: I felt interested in a man who seemed more exaggeratedly[14] reserved than myself.

When he saw my horse's breast fairly pushing the barrier, he did put out his hand to unchain it, and then sullenly preceded me up the causeway[15], calling, as we entered the court, — "Joseph, take Mr. Lockwood's horse; and bring up some wine."

"Here we have the whole establishment of domestics[16], I suppose," was the reflection suggested by this compound order. "No wonder the grass grows up between the flags[17], and cattle are the only hedge[18] — cutters."

Joseph was an elderly, nay, an old man: very old, perhaps, though hale[19] and sinewy[20]. 'The Lord help us!' he soliloquized[21] in an undertone of peevish displeasure, while relieving me of my horse: looking, meantime, in my face so sourly that I charitably conjectured he must have need of divine aid to digest his dinner, and his pious[22] ejaculation[23] had no reference to my unexpected advent.

Wuthering Heights is the name of Mr. Heathcliff's dwelling. 'Wuthering' being a significant provincial adjective, descriptive of the atmospheric tumult[24] to which its station is exposed in

---

8) tenant : 세든 사람
9) perseverance : 고집
10) solicit : 졸라대다
11) wince : 주춤하다
12) Go to the Deuce : 꺼져 버려라
13) manifest : 표시하다
14) exaggeratedly : 심하게
15) causeway : 포장한 길
16) domestic : 하인
17) flag : 포석, (길에) 까는 돌
18) hedge : 생나무 울타리
19) hale : 정정한
20) sinewy : 건장한
21) soliloquize : 혼잣말하다
22) pious : 경건한
23) ejaculation : 부르짖음
24) tumult : 혼란

stormy weather. Pure, bracing ventilation[25] they must have up there at all times, indeed: one may guess the power of the north wind blowing over the edge, by the excessive slant of a few stunted[26] firs at the end of the house; and by a range of gaunt thorns all stretching their limbs one way, as if craving alms[27] of the sun. Happily, the architect had foresight to build it strong: the narrow windows are deeply set in the wall, and the corners defended with large jutting stones.

Before passing the threshold, I paused to admire a quantity of grotesque carving lavished over the front, and especially about the principal door; above which, among a wilderness of crumbling griffins[28] and shameless little boys, I detected the date '1500', and the name 'Hareton Earnshaw'. I would have made a few comments, and requested a short history of the place from the surly[29] owner; but his attitude at the door appeared to demand my speedy entrance, or complete departure, and I had no desire to aggravate[30] his impatience previous to[31] inspecting the penetralium[32].

One stop brought us into the family sitting-room[33], without any introductory lobby or passage: they call it here 'the house' pre-eminently[34]. It includes kitchen and parlour, generally; but I believe at Wuthering Heights the kitchen is forced to retreat altogether into another quarter: at least I distinguished a chatter of tongues, and a clatter of culinary utensils[35], deep within; and I observed no signs of roasting, boiling, or baking, about the huge fireplace; nor any glitter of copper saucepans and tin cullenders[36] on the walls. One end, indeed, reflected splendidly both light and heat from ranks of immense pewter[37] dishes, interspersed with silver jugs and tankards[38], towering row after row, on a vast oak dresser, to the very roof. The latter had never been underdrawn: its entire anatomy[39] lay bare to an inquiring eye, except where a frame of wood laden with[40] oatcakes[41] and clusters of legs of beef, mutton, and ham, concealed it. Above the chimney were sundry[42] villainous old guns, and a couple of horse-pistols[43]: and, by way of ornament, three gaudily-painted canisters[44] disposed along its ledge. The floor was of smooth white stone; the chairs, high-backed, primitive structures, painted green: one or two heavy black ones lurking in the shade. In an arch

---

25) ventilation : (공기의) 환기
26) stunt : 제대로 자라지 못한
27) alms : 자비
28) griffin : 그리핀(머리와 날개는 독수리, 몸은 사자인 괴물)
29) surly : 무뚝뚝한
30) aggravate : 악화시키다
31) previous to : ~에 앞서
32) penetralium : 내부, 깊숙한 안채
33) sitting room : 거실
34) pre-eminently : 특별히
35) culinary utensils : 부엌 도구
36) cullender : 체(소쿠리), 여과기
37) pewter : 백랍(주석과 납 등의 합금)
38) tankard : 손잡이가 달린 큰 컵
39) anatomy : 구조
40) laden with : ~이 놓인
41) oat cake : 귀리로 만든 비스킷
42) sundry : 여러 가지의
43) horse-pistol : 대형권총, 말안장에 다는 권총
44) canister : 깡통

under the dresser, reposed a huge, liver-coloured bitch[45] pointer[46], surrounded by a swarm of squealing[47] puppies; and other dogs haunted other recesses.

The apartment and furniture would have been nothing extraordinary as belonging to a homely[48], northern farmer, with a stubborn countenance, and stalwart[49] limbs set out[50] to advantage in knee-breeches[51] and gaiters[52]. Such an individual seated in his arm-chair, his mug of ale frothing[53] on the round table before him, is to be seen in any circuit of five or six miles among these hills, if you go at the right time after dinner. But Mr. Heathcliff forms a singular contrast to his abode[54] and style of living. He is a dark-skinned gipsy in aspect, in dress and manners a gentleman: that is, as much a gentleman as many a country squire: rather slovenly, perhaps, yet not looking amiss with his negligence, because he has an erect and handsome figure; and rather morose[55]. Possibly, some people might suspect him of a degree of underbred[56] pride; I have a sympathetic chord within that tells me it is nothing of the sort: I know, by instinct, his reserve springs from an aversion[57] to showy displays of feeling — to manifestations of mutual kindliness. He'll love and hate equally under cover, and esteem it a species of impertinence[58] to be loved or hated again. No, I'm running on too fast: I bestow my own attributes overliberally on him. Mr. Heathcliff may have entirely dissimilar reasons for keeping his hand out of the way when he meets a would-be[59] acquaintance, to those which actuate[60] me. Let me hope my constitution[61] is almost peculiar: my dear mother used to say I should never have a comfortable home; and only last summer I proved myself perfectly unworthy of[62] one.

While enjoying a month of fine weather at the sea-coast, I was thrown into the company of a most fascinating creature: a real goddess in my eyes, as long as she took no notice of me. I 'never told my love' vocally[63] still, if looks have language, the merest idiot might have guessed I was over head and ears[64] she understood me at last, and looked a return — the sweetest of all imaginable looks. And what did I do? I confess it with shame — shrunk icily into myself, like a snail; at every

---

45) bitch : 암캐
46) pointer : 포인터(사냥개로 많이 쓰이는 개 품종의 하나)
47) squeal : 낑낑거리다
48) homely : 소박한
49) stalwart : 억센
50) set out : 돋보이게 하다
51) knee-breeches : 반바지
52) gaiter : 각반, 각반 모양의 목 긴 구두
53) froth : 거품이 일다
54) abode : 거주지, 집
55) morose : 침울한
56) underbred : 비천한
57) aversion : 혐오감
58) impertinence : 부적절
59) would-be : 장래의, ~이 되려고 하는
60) actuate : (특정한) 행동을 하게 하다
61) constitution : 성질
62) unworthy of : ~에 적합하지 않은
63) vocally : 말로
64) over head and ears : 제정신이 아닌

glance retired colder and farther; till finally the poor innocent was led to doubt her own senses, and, overwhelmed with confusion at her supposed mistake, persuaded her mamma to decamp. By this curious turn of disposition I have gained the reputation of deliberate[65] heartlessness; how undeserved[66], I alone can appreciate.

I took a seat at the end of the hearthstone opposite that towards which my landlord advanced, and filled up an interval of silence by attempting to caress the canine[67] mother, who had left her nursery, and was sneaking wolfishly to the back of my legs, her lip curled up, and her white teeth watering for a snatch[68]. My caress provoked a long, guttural[69] gnarl[70].

"You'd better let the dog alone," growled Mr. Heathcliff in unison[71], checking fiercer demonstrations with a punch of his foot. "She's not accustomed to be spoiled — not kept for a pet." Then, striding to a side door, he shouted again, "Joseph!"

Joseph mumbled[72] indistinctly in the depths of the cellar, but gave no intimation[73] of ascending; so his master dived down to him, leaving me vis-á-vis[74] the ruffianly[75] bitch and a pair of grim shaggy[76] sheep-dogs, who shared with her a jealous guardianship over all my movements. Not anxious to come in contact with[77] their fangs[78], I sat still; but, imagining they would scarcely understand tacit[79] insults, I unfortunately indulged in winking and making faces[80] at the trio, and some turn of my physiognom[81] so irritated madam[82], that she suddenly broke into a fury and leapt on my knees. I flung her back, and hastened to interpose[83] the table between us. This proceeding aroused the whole hive[84]: half-a-dozen four-footed fiends, of various sizes and ages, issued from hidden dens to the common centre. I felt my heels and coat-laps peculiar subjects of assault; and parrying[85] off the larger combatants[86] as effectually as I could[87] with the poker, I was constrained to[88] demand, aloud, assistance from some of the household in re-establishing peace.

---

65) deliberate : 고의의, 계획적인
66) undeserved : 당치 않은
67) canine : 개의, 개와 같은
68) snatch : 달려들기
69) guttural : 목구멍에서 나오는
70) gnarl : 으르렁거리다
71) in unison : 제창으로, 일치하여
72) mumble : 중얼중얼하다
73) intimation : 암시, 통달
74) vis-á-vis : 마주 대하여
75) ruffianly : 흉포한
76) shaggy : 덥수룩한
77) come in contact with : ~와 접촉하다
78) fang : 송곳니
79) tacit : 무언의
80) make face : 인상을 찌푸리다
81) physiognomy : 인상, 얼굴
82) madam : 소설에선 암캐를 지칭
83) interpose : 사이에 놓다
84) hive : 벌 떼(소설에선 개떼들을 지칭)
85) parry : 쳐내다, 막다
86) combatant : 전투원
87) as ~ could : 최대한 효과적으로
88) be constrained to : 부득이 ~하다

Mr. Heathcliff and his man climbed the cellar steps with vexatious[89] phlegm[90]: I don't think they moved one second faster than usual, though the hearth was an absolute tempest of worrying and yelping. Happily, an inhabitant of the kitchen made more dispatch[91]: a lusty dame, with tucked-up[92] gown, bare arms, and fire-flushed cheeks, rushed into the midst of us flourishing a frying-pan: and used that weapon, and her tongue, to such purpose, that the storm subsided[93] magically, and she only remained, heaving like a sea after a high wind, when her master entered on the scene. "What the devil[94] is the matter?" he asked, eyeing me in a manner that I could ill endure, after this inhospitable treatment.

"What the devil, indeed!" I muttered. "The herd of possessed[95] swine could have had no worse spirits in them than those animals of yours, sir. You might as well leave a stranger with a brood of tigers!"

"They won't meddle[96] with persons who touch nothing," he remarked, putting the bottle before me, and restoring the displaced table. "The dogs do right to be vigilant[97]. Take a glass of wine?"

"No, thank you."

"Not bitten, are you?"

"If I had been, I would have set my signet[98] on the biter."

Heathcliff's countenance relaxed into a grin[99].

"Come, come," he said, "you are flurried[100], Mr. Lockwood. Here, take a little wine. Guests are so exceedingly rare in this house that I and my dogs, I am willing to own, hardly know how to receive them. Your health[101], sir?"

I bowed and returned the pledge[102]; beginning to perceive that it would be foolish to sit sulking for the misbehaviour of a pack of curs[103]; besides, I felt loth to yield the fellow further amusement at my expense[104]; since his humour took that turn. He — probably swayed by prudential[105] consideration of the folly[106] of offending a good tenant — relaxed a little in the laconic[107] style of chipping off his pronouns and auxiliary verbs, and introduced what he supposed would be a

---

89) vexatious : 짜증스러운
90) phlegm : 가래
91) dispatch : 급파(사람을 더 불러왔다는 의미로 쓰인다)
92) tucked-up : (소매를) 걷어 올린
93) subside : 가라앉다
94) What the devil : 도대체
95) possessed : 미친
96) meddle : 간섭하다
97) vigilant : 경계하고 있는
98) signet : 도장, 자국
99) grin : 싱긋 웃음
100) flurried : 당황한
101) Your health : (To) your health(건강을 기원합니다)
102) pledge : 축배
103) cur : (성질 사나운) 똥개
104) at my expense : 나를 희생하여
105) prudential : 신중한
106) folly : 어리석음
107) laconic : 간결한

subject of interest to me, — a discourse on the advantages and disadvantages of my present place of retirement. I found him very intelligent on the topics we touched; and before I went home, I was encouraged so far as to volunteer another visit tomorrow. He evidently wished no repetition of my intrusion. I shall go, notwithstanding[108]. It is astonishing how sociable I feel myself compared with him.

Chapter 2

YESTERDAY afternoon set in misty and cold. I had half a mind to spend it by my study fire, instead of wading through[109] heath and mud to Wuthering Heights. On coming up from dinner, however, (N.B.)[110] — I dine between twelve and one o'clock; the housekeeper, a matronly[111] lady, taken as a fixture[112] along with the house, could not, or would not, comprehend my request that I might be served at five[113], on mounting the stairs with this lazy intention, and stepping into the room, I saw a servant-girl on her knees surrounded by brushes and coal-scuttles[114], and raising an infernal dust as she extinguished the flames with heaps of cinders[115]. This spectacle drove me back immediately; I took my hat, and, after a four-miles' walk, arrived at Heathcliff's garden-gate just in time to escape the first feathery flakes of a snow-shower.

On that bleak hill-top the earth was hard with a black frost, and the air made me shiver through every limb. Being unable to remove the chain, I jumped over, and, running up the flagged causeway bordered with straggling[116] gooseberry-bushes, knocked vainly for admittance, till my knuckles tingled[117] and the dogs howled.

"Wretched[118] inmates[119]!" I ejaculated, mentally, "you deserve perpetual isolation from your species for your churlish[120] inhospitality. At least, I would not keep my door barred in the day-time. I don't care — I will get in!" So resolved, I grasped the latch and shook it vehemently[121]. Vinegar-faced[122] Joseph projected his head from a round window of the barn.

"What are ye for?" he shouted. "T' maister's down i' t' fowld[123]. Go round by th' end o' t'

---

108) notwithstanding : 그럼에도 불구하고
109) wade through : 걸어서 건너다
110) N.B. : 주의(nota bene : 글에서 중요한 정보 앞에 붙이는 표시)
111) matronly : 품위 있는
112) fixture : 늘 붙어 있는 사람, 터줏대감
113) 영국 남부(런던) 출신인 Lockwood가 저녁을 5시에 먹는다는 요구사항은 일반적으로 저녁을 더 일찍 먹는 북부 지방 사람인 Nelly에겐 낯선 일이다.
114) coal-scuttles : 석탄통
115) cinder : 탄 재, 뜬 숯
116) straggling : 흩어져 있는
117) tingle : 얼얼하다
118) wretched : 고약한
119) inmate : 집안사람, 동거인
120) churlish : 심술궂은
121) vehemently : 세차게
122) Vinegar-faced : 찡그린 얼굴의
123) t' fowld : the fold, 습곡, (산언덕 사이의) 움푹한 곳

laith[124]), if ye went to spake to him."

"Is there nobody inside to open the door?" I hallooed[125]), responsively.

"There's nobbut[126]) t' missis; and shoo'll not oppen 't an[127]) ye mak'yer flaysome[128]) dins[129]) till neeght."

"Why? Cannot you tell her who I am, eh, Joseph?"

"Nor-ne me![130]) I'll hae no hea wi't," muttered the head, vanishing.

The snow began to drive thickly. I seized the handle to essay another trial; when a young man without coat, and shouldering a pitchfork[131]), appeared in the yard behind. He hailed me to follow him, and, after marching through a wash-house, and a paved area containing a coal — shed, pump, and pigeon-cote[132]), we at length arrived in the huge, warm, cheerful apartment, where I was formerly received. It glowed delightfully in the radiance[133]) of an immense[134]) fire, compounded of coal, peat[135]), and wood; and ear the table, laid for a plentiful evening meal, I was pleased to observe the 'miss is,' an individual whose existence I had never previously suspected. I bowed and waited, thinking she would bid me take a seat. She looked at me, leaning back in her chair, and remained motionless and mute.

"Rough weather[136])!" I remarked. 'I'm afraid, Mrs. Heathcliff, the door must bear the consequence of your servants' leisure attendance: I had hard work to make them hear me.'

She never opened her mouth. I stared — she stared also: at any rate[137]), she kept her eyes on me in a cool, regardless manner, exceedingly embarrassing and disagreeable.

"Sit down," said the young man, gruffly[138]). "He'll be in soon."

I obeyed; and hemmed, and called the villain Juno, who deigned[139]), at this second interview, to move the extreme tip of her tail[140]), in token of[141]) owning my acquaintance.

"A beautiful animal!" I commenced again. "Do you intend parting with the little ones, madam?"

"They are not mine," said the amiable[142]) hostess, more repellingly[143]) than Heathcliff himself

---

124) o' t' laith : of the barn, 헛간의
125) halloo : "이봐!"라고 소리쳐서 남의 주의를 끌다
126) There's nobbut : There's only
127) an : (even) if : ～하더라도
128) flaysome : frightful, 무서운
129) din : 소음
130) Nor-ne me! : Not I!
131) pitchfork : 쇠갈퀴
132) pigeon-cote : 비둘기 집
133) radiance : 빛남
134) immense : 큼직한
135) peat : (연료용) 이탄
136) rough weather : 악천후(험악한 날씨네요!)
137) at any rate : 하여튼
138) gruffly : 통명스럽게
139) deign : 황송하게도 ～하여 주시다
140) move ～ tail : 꼬리를 조금 움직이다
141) in token of : ～의 표시로
142) amiable : 정감 있는
143) repellingly : 통명스럽게

could have replied.

"Ah, your favourites are among these?" I continued, turning to an obscure[144] cushion full of something like cats.

"A strange choice of favourites!" she observed scornfully[145].

Unluckily, it was a heap of dead rabbits. I hemmed[146] once more, and drew closer to the hearth, repeating my comment on the wildness of the evening.

"You should not have come out[147]," she said, rising and reaching from the chimney-piece[148] two of the painted canisters.

Her position before was sheltered from the light; now, I had a distinct view of her whole figure and countenance. She was slender[149], and apparently scarcely past girlhood: an admirable form, and the most exquisite little face that I have ever had the pleasure of beholding; small features, very fair; flaxen[150] ringlets[151], or rather golden, hanging loose on her delicate neck; and eyes, had they been agreeable[152] in expression, that would have been irresistible: fortunately for my susceptible heart, the only sentiment they evinced[153] hovered between scorn and a kind of desperation, singularly unnatural to be detected there. The canisters were almost out of her reach; I made a motion to aid her; she turned upon me as a miser[154] might turn if any one attempted to assist him in counting his gold.

"I don't want your help," she snapped[155]; "I can get them for myself."

"I beg your pardon!" I hastened to reply.

"Were you asked to tea?" she demanded, tying an apron over her neat black frock, and standing with a spoonful of the leaf poised over the pot.

"I shall be glad to have a cup," I answered.

"Were you asked?" she repeated.

"No;" I said, half smiling. "You are the proper person to ask me,"

She flung the tea back, spoon and all, and resumed her chair in a pet; her forehead corrugated[156], and her red under-lip pushed out, like a child's ready to cry.

Meanwhile, the young man had slung[157] on to his person[158] a decidedly[159] shabby upper

---

144) obscure : 한눈에 잘 띄지 않는
145) scornfully : 비웃는 듯이
146) hem : 에헴 하다, 헛기침하다
147) should ~ out : 나오지 말았어야 했다
148) chimney-piece : 화덕 선반
149) slender : 호리호리한
150) flaxen : 아마(황갈색) 빛의
151) ringlet : 곱슬머리
152) had they been agreeable : 그것들이 상냥했더라면
153) evince : 명시하다, 증명하다
154) miser : 구두쇠
155) snap : 쏘아붙이다
156) corrugated : 주름 잡힌
157) slung : (sling의 과거형) 걸치다
158) person : 몸
159) decidedly : 분명히, 아주

garment, and, erecting himself before the blaze, looked down on me from the corner of his eyes, for all the world[160] as if there were some mortal feud[161] unavenged between us. I began to doubt whether he were a servant or not: his dress and speech were both rude, entirely devoid of[162] the superiority observable in Mr. and Mrs. Heathcliff; his thick brown curls were rough and uncultivated, his whiskers[163] encroached bearishly over his cheeks, and his hands were embrowned like those of a common labourer: still his bearing was free, almost haughty[164], and he showed none of a domestic's assiduity[165] in attending on the lady of the house. In the absence of clear proofs of his condition[166], I deemed it best to[167] abstain[168] from noticing his curious conduct; and, five minutes afterwards, the entrance of Heathcliff relieved me, in some measure, from my uncomfortable state.

"You see, sir, I am come, according to promise!" I exclaimed, assuming the cheerful; "and I fear I shall be weather-bound[169] for half an hour, if you can afford me shelter during that space."

"Half an hour?" he said, shaking the white flakes from his clothes; "I wonder you should select the thick of a snowstorm to ramble about[170] in. Do you know that you run a risk of being lost in the marshes[171]? People familiar with these moors often miss their road on such evenings; and I can tell you there is no chance of a change at present."

"Perhaps I can get a guide among your lads, and he might stay at the Grange till morning — could you spare[172] me one?"

"No, I could not."

"Oh, indeed! Well, then, I must trust to my own sagacity[173]."

"Umph[174]!"

"Are you going to mak' th' tea?" demanded he of the shabby coat, shifting his ferocious[175] gaze from me to the young lady.

"Is he to have any?" she asked, appealing to Heathcliff.

"Get it ready, will you?" was the answer, uttered so savagely[176] that I started[177]. The tone in which the words were said revealed a genuine bad nature. I no longer felt inclined to call Heathcliff

---

160) for all the world : 무슨 일이 있더라도
161) feud : 원한
162) devoid of : ～이 없는
163) whiskers : 구레나룻
164) haughty : 거만한
165) assiduity : 부지런함
166) condition : 신분
167) deem ～ to : ～이 최선이라고 생각하다
168) abstain : 그만두다
169) weather-bound : 악천후, 비바람에 갇힌
170) ramble about : 산책하다
171) marsh : 습지
172) spare : 나누어 주다, 빌려 주다
173) sagacity : 기민함, 현명
174) umph : Humph(흥! 의심 혹은 경멸 등을 나타내는 소리)
175) ferocious : 사나운
176) savagely : 거칠게
177) start : 움찔하다

a capital fellow. When the preparations were finished, he invited me with — "Now, sir, bring forward your chair." And we all, including the rustic[178] youth, drew round the table: an austere[179] silence prevailing while we discussed our meal.

I thought, if I had caused the cloud, it was my duty to make an effort to dispel[180] it. They could not every day sit so grim and taciturn[181] and it was impossible, however ill-tempered they might be, that the universal scowl[182] they wore was their everyday countenance[183].

"It is strange," I began, in the interval of swallowing one cup of tea and receiving another — "it is strange how custom can mould our tastes and ideas: many could not imagine the existence of happiness in a life of such complete exile from the world as you spend, Mr. Heathcliff; yet I'll venture to say, that, surrounded by your family, and with your amiable lady as the presiding genius[184] over your home and heart — "

"My amiable lady!" he interrupted, with an almost diabolical[185] sneer on his face. "Where is she — my amiable lady?"

"Mrs. Heathcliff, your wife, I mean."

"Well, yes — OH, you would intimate that her spirit has taken the post of ministering angel[186], and guards the fortunes of Wuthering Heights, even when her body is gone. Is that it?"

Perceiving myself in a blunder[187], I attempted to correct it. I might have seen there was too great a disparity[188] between the ages of the parties to make it likely that they were man and wife[189]. One was about forty: a period of mental vigour at which men seldom cherish the delusion of being married for love by girls: that dream is reserved for the solace[190] of our declining years. The other did not look seventeen.

Then it flashed on me — "The clown at my elbow, who is drinking his tea out of a basin and eating his bread with unwashed hands, may be her husband: Heathcliff junior, of course. Here is the consequence of being buried alive[191]: she has thrown herself away upon that boor[192] from sheer ignorance that better individuals existed! A sad pity — I must beware[193] how I cause her to regret her choice." The last reflection may seem conceited[194]; it was not. My neighbour struck me as

---

178) rustic : 촌티 나는
179) austere : 엄한, 딱딱한
180) dispel : 없애다
181) taciturn : 과묵한
182) scowl : 찌푸린 얼굴, 성난 얼굴
183) it was ~ countenance : ~는 불가능하였다
184) genius : 수호신
185) diabolical : 악마 같은
186) ministering angel : 구원의 천사
187) blunder : 큰 실수
188) disparity : 불균형
189) to make ~ wife : 그들을 부부라고 하기에는
190) solace : 위안
191) the consequence of being buried alive : 생매장 당한 결과
192) boor : 천박한 사람
193) beware : 조심하다
194) conceited : 잘난 체하는

bordering on repulsive[195]); I knew, through experience, that I was tolerably attractive.

"Mrs. Heathcliff is my daughter-in-law," said Heathcliff, corroborating[196]) my surmise[197]). He turned, as he spoke, a peculiar look in her direction: a look of hatred; unless he has a most perverse[198]) set of facial muscles that will not, like those of other people, interpret the language of his soul.

"Ah, certainly — I see now: you are the favoured possessor of the beneficent[199]) fairy," I remarked, turning to my neighbour.

This was worse than before: the youth grew crimson, and clenched his fist, with every appearance of a meditated[200]) assault[201]). But he seemed to recollect himself[202]) presently, and smothered the storm in a brutal curse, muttered on my behalf[203]): which, however, I took care not to notice.

"Unhappy in your conjectures[204]), sir," observed my host; "we neither of us have the privilege of owning your good fairy; her mate is dead. I said she was my daughter-in-law, therefore, she must have married my son."

"And this young man is — "

"Not my son, assuredly[205])."

Heathcliff smiled again, as if it were rather too bold a jest[206]) to attribute the paternity of that bear to him.[207])

"My name is Hareton Earnshaw," growled the other; "and I'd counsel[208]) you to respect it!"

"I've shown no disrespect," was my reply, laughing internally at the dignity with which he announced himself.

He fixed his eye on me longer than I cared to return the stare, for fear[209]) I might be tempted either to box his ears or render my hilarity[210]) audible. I began to feel unmistakably out of place[211]) in that pleasant family circle. The dismal[212]) spiritual atmosphere overcame, and more than neutralized[213]) the glowing physical comforts round me; and I resolved to be cautious how I ventured[214]) under those rafters[215]) a third time.

---

195) bordering on repulsive : 거의 혐오감을 일으키는
196) corroborate : 확실하게 하다
197) surmise : 추측
198) perverse : 별난, 그릇된
199) beneficent : 인자한
200) meditated : 계획된
201) assault : 강습
202) recollect oneself : 진정하다
203) on my behalf : 나를 위하여, 대신하여
204) conjecture : 추측
205) assuredly : 확실히, 의심 없이
206) too bold a jest : 지나친 농담
207) attribute ~ to : ~을 -에게 속하게 하다
208) counsel : 충고하다
209) for fear (that) ~ : ~하게 될까봐
210) hilarity : 환희, 즐겁게 놀기
211) feel out of place : 그 자리에 어울리지 않는 위화감을 느끼다
212) dismal : 음울한
213) neutralized : 상쇄시키다
214) venture : 조심스럽게 말하다
215) rafter : 서까래(그 집 안에서는 다음 방문부터는 말을 조심해야겠다는 의미)

The business of eating being concluded, and no one uttering a word of sociable conversation, I approached a window to examine the weather. A sorrowful sight I saw: dark night coming down prematurely[216], and sky and hills mingled in one bitter whirl of wind and suffocating[217] snow.

"I don't think it possible for me to get home now without a guide," I could not help exclaiming. "The roads will be buried already; and, if they were bare, I could scarcely distinguish a foot in advance."

"Hareton, drive those dozen sheep into the barn porch. They'll be covered if left in the fold all night: and put a plank before them," said Heathcliff.

"How must I do?" I continued, with rising irritation[218].

There was no reply to my question; and on looking round I saw only Joseph bringing in a pail of porridge[219] for the dogs, and Mrs. Heathcliff leaning over the fire, diverting[220] herself with burning a bundle of matches which had fallen from the chimney-piece as she restored the tea canister to its place. The former[221], when he had deposited[222] his burden, took a critical survey of the room, and in cracked tones grated out[223]: "Aw wonder how yah can fashion to[224] stand thear i' idleness un war[225], when all on 'em's goan out! Bud yah're a nowt[226], and it's no use talking — yah'll niver mend o'yer ill ways, but goa raight to t' divil, like yer mother afore ye![227]"

I imagined, for a moment, that this piece of eloquence[228] was addressed to me; and, sufficiently[229] enraged, stepped towards the aged rascal[230] with an intention of kicking him out of the door. Mrs. Heathcliff, however, checked me by her answer.

"You scandalous[231] old hypocrite[232]!" she replied. "Are you not afraid of being carried away bodily[233], whenever you mention the devil's name? I warn you to refrain[234] from provoking[235] me, or I'll ask your abduction[236] as a special favour. Stop! look here, Joseph," she continued, taking a long, dark book from a shelf; "I'll show you how far I've progressed in the Black Art[237]: I shall

---

216) prematurely : 너무 이르게
217) suffocating : 숨 막히는
218) irritation : 짜증
219) porridge : 죽
220) divert : 기분을 전환시키다
221) the former : 전자(여기선 Joseph을 지칭)
222) deposit : 놓다
223) in ~ out : 귀에 거슬리는 쉰 소리를 냈다
224) fashion to : bear to, have the face to, 뻔뻔하게 ~을 하다
225) un war : and worse, 게다가
226) a nowt : a useless creature, 쓸모없는 존재
227) but ~ ye! : 그냥 에미하고 같이 퍼뜩 죽어라(Joseph이 Mrs. Heathcliff, 즉 Cathy에게 하는 말이다)
228) eloquence : 웅변
229) sufficiently : 충분히, 몹시
230) rascal : 악한
231) scandalous : 고약한
232) hypocrite : 위선자
233) bodily : 송두리째
234) refrain : 삼가다
235) provoke : 성나게 하다
236) abduction : 유괴
237) Black Art : 마법

soon be competent[238] to make a clear house of it. The red cow didn't die by chance[239]; and your rheumatism can hardly be reckoned[240] among providential[241] visitations!"

"Oh, wicked, wicked!" gasped the elder; "may the Lord deliver[242] us from evil!"

"No, reprobate[243]! you are a castaway[244] — be off, or I'll hurt you seriously! I'll have you all modelled in wax and clay; and the first who passes the limits I fix shall — I'll not say what he shall be done to — but, you'll see! Go, I'm looking at you!"

The little witch put a mock malignity[245] into her beautiful eyes, and Joseph, trembling with sincere horror, hurried out, praying, and ejaculating "wicked" as he went. I thought her conduct must be prompted by a species of dreary fun; and, now that we were alone, I endeavoured to interest her in my distress[246].

"Mrs. Heathcliff," I said earnestly, "you must excuse me for troubling you. I presume, because, with that face, I'm sure you cannot help being good-hearted. Do point out some landmarks by which I may know my way home: I have no more idea how to get there than you would have how to get to London!"

"Take the road you came," she answered, ensconcing herself in[247] a chair, with a candle, and the long book open before her. "It is brief advice, but as sound as I can give."

"Then, if you hear of me being discovered dead in a bog or a pit full of snow, your conscience won't whisper that it is partly your fault?"

"How so? I cannot escort[248] you. They wouldn't let me go to the end of the garden wall."

"You! I should be sorry to ask you to cross the threshold, for my convenience, on such a night," I cried. "I want you to tell me my way, not to show it: or else to persuade Mr. Heathcliff to give me a guide."

"Who? There is himself, Earnshaw, Zillah, Joseph and I. Which would you have?"

"Are there no boys at the farm?"

"No; those are all."

"Then, it follows that I am compelled to stay."

"That you may settle with[249] your host. I have nothing to do with[250] it."

"I hope it will be a lesson to you to make no more rash[251] journeys on these hills," cried

---

238) competent : 유능한
239) by chance : 우연히
240) reckon : 간주하다
241) providential : 신의
242) deliver : 구출하다
243) reprobate : 타락한 사람
244) castaway : 버림받은 사람
245) malignity : 악의
246) I endeavoured to interest her in my distress : 나는 그녀가 나의 고충에 관심을 가지게 하려고 애썼다.
247) ensconce oneself in : 편히 앉다
248) escort : 동행하다, 바래다주다
249) settle with : 상의하다
250) have nothing to do with : 상관이 없다
251) rash : 경솔한

Heathcliff's stern voice from the kitchen entrance. "As to staying here, I don't keep accommodations[252] for visitors: you must share a bed with Hareton or Joseph, if you do."

"I can sleep on a chair in this room," I replied.

"No, no! A stranger is a stranger, be he rich or poor, it will not suit me to permit any one the range of the place while I am off guard[253]" said the unmannerly wretch.

With this insult, my patience was at an end[254]. I uttered an expression of disgust[255], and pushed past him into the yard, running against Earnshaw in my haste. It was so dark that I could not see the means of exit; and, as I wandered round, I heard another specimen[256] of their civil behaviour amongst each other. At first the young man appeared about to befriend me.

"I'll go with him as far as the park," he said.

"You'll go with him to hell!" exclaimed his master, or whatever relation he bore[257].

"And who is to look after the horses, eh?"

"A man's life is of more consequence[258] than one evening's neglect of the horses: somebody must go," murmured Mrs. Heathcliff, more kindly than I expected.

"Not at your command!" retorted Hareton. "If you set store on him, you'd better be quiet."

"Then I hope his ghost will haunt you; and I hope Mr. Heathcliff will never get another tenant till the Grange is a ruin." she answered, sharply.

"Hearken[259], hearken, shoo's cursing on 'em!" muttered Joseph, towards whom I had been steering.

He sat within earshot[260], milking the cows by the light of a lantern, which I seized unceremoniously[261], and, calling out that I would send it back on the morrow[262], rushed to the nearest postern[263].

"Maister, maister, he's staling t' lanthern!" shouted the ancient, pursuing my retreat.

"Hey, Gnasher! Hey, dog! Hey Wolf, holld him, holld him!"

On opening the little door, two hairy monsters flew at my throat, bearing me down, and extinguishing the light; while a mingled guffaw[264] from Heathcliff and Hareton, put the copestone[265] on my rage and humiliation[266]. Fortunately, the beasts seemed more bent on stretching their paws and yawning and flourishing their tails, than devouring me alive; but they would suffer no

---

252) accommodations : 숙박시설
253) while I am off guard : 내가 보고 있지 않을 때
254) be at an end : 다하다
255) disgust : 넌더리, 혐오감
256) specimen : 표본
257) whatever ~ bore : (Heathcliff가 Hareton과 주인-하인 관계가 아닌) 어떤 관계를 가졌든지 간에
258) of (more) consequence : (더) 중요한
259) Hearken : 들어 보세요
260) within earshot : 부르면 들리는 곳에
261) unceremoniously : 격식을 차리지 않고
262) on the morrow : 다음날
263) postern : 뒷문
264) guffaw : 큰 웃음
265) copestone : 절정, 극치
266) humiliation : 모욕감

resurrection[267]), and I was forced to lie till their malignant[268]) masters pleased to deliver me: then, hatless and trembling with wrath, I ordered the miscreants[269]) to let me out — on their peril to keep me one minute longer — with several incoherent threats of retaliation[270]) that, in their indefinite depth of virulency[271]), smacked of[272]) King Lear.

The vehemence[273]) of my agitation brought on a copious[274]) bleeding at the nose, and still Heathcliff laughed, and still I scolded. I don't know what would have concluded the scene, had there not been one person at hand rather more rational than myself, and more benevolent[275]) than my entertainer. This was Zillah, the stout housewife; who at length[276]) issued forth[277]) to enquire into the nature of the uproar. She thought that some of them had been laying violent hands on me; and, not daring to attack her master, she turned her vocal artillery[278]) against the younger scoundrel[279]).

"Well, Mr. Earnshaw," she cried, "I wonder what you'll have agait[280]) next? Are we going to murder folk on our very doorstones? I see this house will never do for me — look at t' poor lad, he's fair choking! Wisht, wisht! you mun'n't go on so[281]). Come in, and I'n cure that: there now, hold ye still."

With these words she suddenly splashed a pint of icy water down my neck, and pulled me into the kitchen. Mr. Heathcliff followed, his accidental merriment[282]) expiring quickly in his habitual moroseness[283]).

I was sick exceedingly, and dizzy, and faint; and thus compelled perforce[284]) to accept lodgings under his roof. He told Zillah to give me a glass of brandy, and then passed on to the inner room; while she condoled[285]) with me on my sorry predicament, and having obeyed his orders, whereby I was somewhat revived, ushered[286]) me to bed.

---

267) resurrection : 부활
268) malignant : 악랄한
269) miscreant : 악한
270) retaliation : 보복
271) virulency : 악의, 신랄함
272) smack of : ~의 기미가 있다
273) vehemence : 격렬함
274) copious : 심한
275) benevolent : 인정 많은
276) at length : 마침내
277) issued forth : 나오다
278) artillery : 대포, 무기
279) scoundrel : 악당, 불한당
280) agait : on hand, afoot, 계획 중인
281) you mun'n't go on so : 계속 그런 식으로 지내면 안 돼요.
282) merriment : 웃으며 즐기기
283) moroseness : 까다로움, 침울함
284) perforce : 어쩔 수 없이
285) condole : 위로하다
286) usher : 안내하다

제 4 장 Charles Dickens
- 「*Great Expectations*」

단원개요

Charles Dickens는 당대 리얼리즘 소설의 가장 뛰어난 성취와 결합되어 있다. 강한 개성을 지닌 다양한 계층의 인물들, 전형적인 악한들과 천사와 같은 주인공들, 유머와 당대 사회의 신랄한 묘사, 범죄물과 미스테리가 얽힌 복잡한 플롯으로 독자들의 흥미를 지속적으로 이끄는 작가이다. Charles Dickens는 당대 사회에 대한 근본적인 비판을 제기함으로써 단순한 관찰자의 수준에서 벗어나 적극적인 참여자의 태도도 보여준다.

출제 경향 및 수험 대책

예민하고 자의식이 강한 핍(Pip)이 일련의 복잡한 사건들을 거치면서 순진한 소년에서 속물로, 그리고 다시 진정한 신사로 거듭나는 과정을 통해 작가가 보여주고자 하는 진정한 신사의 이미지의 모습을 파악할 필요가 있다. 소설에서 등장하는 여러 형태의 신사들을 만나면서 당대 사회에서 통용되는 신사와 디킨슨이 제시하는 당대의 신사의 이념을 뒤집는 과정을 파악해야 한다.

제 1 절 작가의 생애

찰스 디킨스(Charles Dickens, 필명 Boz, 1812~1870)는 빅토리아조 당대에서 현재에 이르기까지 대중적 인기를 얻고 있는 작가이다. 그는 소박한 평민이나 교양 있는 사람들, 빈민이나 여왕을 막론하고 누구에게나 호소력을 지니고 있었기 때문에 생전에도 폭넓은 인기를 누렸다. 그는 8남매 중 장남이었다. 영국 남부의 군항인 햄프셔(Hamphsire)주 포츠머스(Portsmouth)에서 태어났다. 그의 아버지 John Dickens는 영국 해군 경리국에서 근무하는 하급 관리였지만, 금전관념이 희박하고 많은 식구들을 부양할 정도가 안 되는 낮은 임금 때문에 빚을 갚지 못해 투옥된 일도 있었다. 이러한 이유로 Charles Dickens는 소년시절부터 빈곤의 고통을 겪었으며 학교에도 거의 다니지 못하고 12세부터 공장에 나가서 일을 해야 했다.

19세기 전반의 영국 대도시에서는 자본주의 번영의 이면인 심각한 빈곤 및 어린이와 부녀자들의 열악한 노동 조건이 사회 전반을 어둡게 했다. 이러한 사회의 모순과 부정을 직접 체험한 디킨스는 빈곤의 늪에서 벗어나려고 필사적으로 노력하면서, 15세경에 변호사 사무소의 사환, 법원 속기사를 거친 끝에 신문기자가 되어 의회에 관한 기사를 쓰게 되었다. 그는 소년시절부터 고전문학을 탐독하면서 일찍부터 문학에 눈을 떴고, 기자생활을 하면서 경험한 많은 여행이 풍부한 관찰과 식견에 도움을 주었다.

1833년 그는 어느 잡지에 단편을 투고하여 채택된 데 힘입어 계속해서 단편소설 등을 여러 잡지에 발표하였고, 1836년 이들을 모은 『*Sketches by Boz*』가 출판되어 24세에 신진작가로 화려하게 문단에 데뷔했다. 다음 해에 완결한 장편 소설 「*The Pickwick Papers*」(1837)는 네 명의 인물이 여행하는 도중에 곳곳에서 우스꽝스러운 사건을 일으키는 단순한 줄거리였으나, 그의 뛰어난 유머로 폭발적인 인기를 얻었고, 다음 작품인 「*Oliver Twist*」(1838)도 베스트셀러가 되어 작가적 지위가 확립되었다.

그 뒤 영국과 미국의 각계각층 독자들의 호응에 보답하여 「*Nicholas Nickleby*」(1839), 「*The Old Curiosity Shop*」(1841), 「*A Christmas Carol*」(1843) 등 중·장편 소설을 연이어 발표하였다. 그는 몸소 체험으로 알게 된 사회 밑바닥 서민들의 생활상과 그들의 애환을 생생하게 묘사함과 동시에 세상의 부정과 모순을 용감하게 지적하면서도 유머를 섞어 비판한 하여 인기를 얻었는데, 그의 소설에 영향을 받아 어린이에 대한 학대와 재판의 비능률이 개선되기도 했다.

1850년에 완결한 자전적인 작품 「*David Copperfield*」를 쓸 무렵부터 작품의 특징이 조금씩 변하여 그의 후기 특성이 두드러진다. 다음 작품인 「*Bleak House*」(1853)가 그 좋은 예로, 이전의 작품처럼 주인공 한 사람의 성장과 체험을 중심으로 사회 각층을 폭넓게 바라보는 이른바 파노라마적인 사회 소설로 다가갔다. 작품에서는 개인의 삶을 가로막는 해결이 불가능한 사회체제의 벽에 가로막혀, 디킨스의 유머도 쓴웃음으로 바뀌고, 무력감과 좌절감이 전편에 흐르게 되었다. 그러나 그의 창작력은 쇠퇴하지 않았고, 공장 파업을 다룬 「*Hard Times*」(1854), 어두운 사회 소설인 「*Little Dorrit*」(1857), 프랑스 혁명을 다룬 「*A Tale of Two Cities*」(1859), 다소 자전적인 「*Great Expectations*」(1861) 등의 장편 외에 많은 단편과 수필을 썼다. 디킨스는 잡지사의 경영과 편집, 자선사업 참여, 연극 상연, 자작 공개낭독, 각지로의 여행 등 쉴 새 없이 활동을 계속하여 건강을 잃었으나 쉬려 하지 않았다. 또한 1858년에는 아내와 별거하는 등 정신적 고통도 겹쳐 1870년 추리소설 풍의 수수께끼로 가득 찬 「*The Mystery of Edwin Drood*」를 미완성으로 남긴 채 세상을 떠났다.

디킨스는 전 세계 각계각층의 애도 속에 문인 최고의 영예인 웨스트민스터 사원에 안장되었다. 죽은 뒤 그의 소설은 1세기에 걸쳐 각 나라말로 옮겨져 셰익스피어와 함께 영국 문학을 대표하는 작가로 인정받고 있다.

> **더 알아두기**
>
> **Charles Dickens의 주요 작품**
> - 「*The Posthumous Papers of the Pickwick Club*」(*The Pickwick Papers*)(1836)
> - 「*Oliver Twist*」(1839)
> - 「*A Christmas Carol*」(1843)
> - 「*David Copperfield*」(1850)
> - 「*Bleak House*」(1853)
> - 「*Hard Times*」(1854)
> - 「*Little Dorrit*」(1857)
> - 「*A Tale of Two Cities*」(1859)
> - 「*Great Expectations*」(1861)

제 2 절 작품 세계

1 소설의 제목 중요 ★

「*Great Expectations*」를 국내에서는 '위대한 유산'이라고 옮기고 있다. 그런데 이 제목은 작품의 내용을 제대로 파악한 번역이라고 하기는 어렵다. 'Great Expectations'의 뜻을 정확히 풀이하면 '막대한 또는 대단한 유산 상속에 대한 기대'라고 할 수 있다. 실제로 작품 속에서 Pip은 이 유산을 물려받지 못했으며, 다만 유산 상속에 대한 기대 속에서 젊은 시절을 보냈을 뿐이다. 따라서 '유산'이라는 책의 제목의 의미는 '유산 상속에 대한 Pip의 기대'라고 이해하는 것이 적합하다.

2 1인칭 서술

「*Great Expectations*」는 1인칭 화자의 소설로서 Pip이 보다 성숙된 시점에서 잘못된 환상을 쫓던 자신의 젊은 시절을 반성하며 회고하는 형식으로 화자의 문체가 유기적이고 일관되게 작품 전체를 통합하고 있다. 「*Great Expectations*」에는 디킨스의 또 다른 1인칭 소설인 「*David Copperfield*」에서 보이는 서술자의 자기 연민이나 근거 없는 편견 따위가 거의 없다. 자신의 옛 환상을 다시 되살리며 강한 노스탤지어를 느끼지만 한편으로는 그 진상을 명확히 비판하는 주인공 Pip의 서술은 젊음을 그리워하면서도 현실을 인정하는 성숙한 면모가 절실히 드러난다. 자신의 젊은 시절의 꿈과 오류, 환상이 자기 자신의 일부분이지만, 거기에 안주하거나 탐닉할 수 없는 객관적 현실의 논리와 이를 돌아보는 성숙한 화자의 문체가 작품에서 사용된다.

3 기대와 환상

이 소설이 주목하는 기대와 환상은 외딴 시골에서 하층민으로 일하며 살아갈 운명인 주인공 Pip이 신사가 되어 런던에 가서 멋지게 살아보려는 기대와 욕심, 그리고 이러한 욕심이 생기게 만드는 촉매제이자 환상의 상징인 Estella에 대한 Pip의 짝사랑이다. 이 모든 것은 Pip의 'Satis House'의 출입에서부터 시작한다. Satis House라는 이름은 '만족의 집'이라는 뜻인데, Satis House는 Pip에게 자신의 본래 모습에 대한 깊은 불만을 심어주고, 고향에서는 대장장이인 매형의 집에서 사는 것을 형벌로 느끼도록 만든다. 즉, Pip은 현실에 대한 불만에 시달리며 환상의 세계로 가려는 마음에 사로잡힌다.

그러나 Dickens는 스크루지(Scrooge)와 귀신 이야기도 서슴없이 책으로 냈던 작가였던 만큼 글의 소재와 전개에 전혀 주저하지 않는 대중적 작가였다. 그래서 갑자기 Pip에게 뜻밖의 돈이 생기게 한 후, Pip이 그의 환상의 하나인 런던에 가서 멋지게 사는 꿈을 실현할 수 있게 해준다. 그러나 「*Great Expectations*」에서 Dickens는 궁극적으로는 환상에서 깨어나야 함을 강조한다. 결국 Pip이 믿었던 그 돈은 Miss Havisham이 물려주는 재산이 아니었다. Dickens는 그 돈의 이면에 깔린 범죄와 음모를 들추어낸다.

4 유산(돈)의 역할 중요 ★★

Pip은 신사 수업을 받는 과정에서 속물이 될 수 있었지만, 그 이전에 대장장이인 매형 Joe의 집에서 살 때부터 이어져 온 인간적인 성실함과 진실함을 잃어버린 것은 아니다. 애초에 Pip이 Magwitch에게 약속대로 물품을 갖다 준 데에 대한 보답으로 재산을 물려받을 뻔했다는 점을 고려하면 그가 인생을 바꿀 수 있었던 것도 그의 성실함 때문이라고 할 수 있다. 또한 그가 런던생활 중의 신사 수업에서 편견과 좁은 시야에서 벗어나 보다 성숙한 인물로 변모한 것도 사실이다. Magwitch의 돈은 결국 Pip을 '신사'답게 변하게 한 후 사라지므로 Pip이 여생을 속물로서 살게 하는 것을 방지하는 적절한 교육적 조치가 된 것이다. 그 교육이 헛되지 않았음을 우리는 Magwitch가 위기에 처했을 때 알게 된다. Pip이 신사로서 여생을 보내게 해줄 돈이 사라질 때 그는 의리를 저버리지 않는 진정한 신사다움을 보여주기 때문이다.

작가는 진정한 신사다움이 물려받은 많은 재산에서 나오는 것이 아니라 인간적 신의를 지키고 남을 배반하지 않는 성실함에서 오는 것임을 강조한다. 고생 끝에 유산을 물려받아 여생을 편안하게 보내게 되는 「Oliver Twist」나 젊은 시절 노력 끝에 인기 작가로 넉넉한 여생을 사는 「David Copperfield」와 비교해 볼 때 「Great Expectations」는 초기 Dickens와는 다른 관점에서 유산 문제를 다룬다.

5 물질 만능주의 비판 중요 ★★

「Great Expectations」는 당시에 만연했던 물질 만능주의를 고발한 작품이다. 가난한 소년 Pip이 막대한 유산을 받아서 하류층에서 상류층으로 자신의 신분을 상승시키고자 하는 욕망을 갖지만 '막대한 유산'의 실체에 대한 허망함을 느낀다. Pip은 자신에게 참된 인간상을 일깨워 준 매형 Joe Gargery의 진정한 사랑이 다름 아닌 '막대한 유산'이었다는 사실을 깨닫게 된다. 디킨스 작품의 특징은 자신이 직접 체험하고 느낀 사회의 부정함과 모순들을 생생하게 묘사하면서도 동시에 유머를 잃지 않았다는 데 있다.

6 식민지적 배경과 작품의 한계

「Great Expectations」를 보는 시각은 이 소설의 중요한 배경을 형성하는 식민지적 상황의 문제에 주목한다. 만약 Magwitch가 본국에서 감옥생활을 했다면 Pip에게 물려줄 돈을 벌었을 리가 없고 이 소설의 이야기는 현실성이 없었을 것이다. Magwitch가 억울하게 누명을 쓰기는 했어도 그가 큰돈을 벌 수 있는 식민지로 갈 수 있었다는 점에서 이 소설은 식민지의 혜택을 그리고 있다. 작가는 식민지 상황을 Pip의 환상과 그 운명을 추적하는 데 이용만 할 뿐 그것에 대해 진지하게 반성하는 데는 이르지 못한다. 「Great Expectations」에서는 성숙한 Pip이 돈을 벌어서 걱정 없이 살게 되는 장소도 영국 밖의 또 다른 식민지 지역이므로 이 소설은 식민지에 대한 견해의 한계를 지니고 있다.

제 3 절   줄거리

주인공 Pip은 시골 대장간에 사는 가난한 소년이다. 그는 부모가 없는 고아로 누나의 손에 의해 길러진다. Pip은 대장장이인 매형 Joe 밑에서 견습공을 하며 함께 산다. 매형 Joe는 온화한 성격의 소유자이고, 그의 누나는 폭력을 일삼는 거친 성격을 가졌다.

어느 날 Pip이 돌아가신 부모님 묘지 앞에서 울고 있을 때 두 명의 탈옥수를 만난다. 이들은 사기꾼 Compeyson과 Magwitch였다. Pip은 그들로부터 협박을 받아 그들에게 음식을 주고 사슬을 끊을 수 있는 도구를 대장간에서 훔쳐다주었다. 결국 Compeyson과 Magwitch는 다시 잡히지만 탈옥수 Magwitch는 자신을 도와 준 Pip이 곤경에 처하지 않도록 자신이 먹을 것을 훔쳤다고 말한다. 외딴 마을에서 살기 때문에 다른 사회를 전혀 접할 수가 없었던 Pip에게 이 사건은 그의 최초의 외부인과의 접촉이었다.

한편, Pip이 사는 마을의 부자인 Miss Havisham은 그 동네의 은둔자로 수십 년 동안 그녀를 본 사람은 아무도 없었다. 그녀는 자기의 어린 양녀와 놀아 줄 소년을 찾던 중 Pip을 그 상대로 선택한다. 그녀는 햇빛을 피하고 바깥 세계와 완전히 차단된 생활을 하고 있으며, 방 안의 공기는 곰팡내가 날 정도였다. 또한 결혼식 날에 신랑으로부터 배신당한 과거로 인해 언제나 신부의 드레스를 입고 지낸다. Miss Havisham의 양녀인 아름다운 Estella에게 Pip은 한 눈에 반하지만 그녀는 Pip의 기대와는 달리 그를 무시한다. 이런 그녀의 태도를 통해 Pip은 자신이 비천한 노동자에 지나지 않는다는 것을 알게 된다. 자기 자신에 대해서뿐만 아니라 자신의 집과 직업, 그리고 자신을 지금까지 돌보아 준 친절한 매형에게까지 불만과 혐오를 품게 된다.

몇 년 후 청년이 된 Pip은 매형 Joe와 함께 간 술집에서 변호사 Jaggers를 만난다. 그는 Pip이 막대한 양의 유산을 물려받을 것이며 이것을 위해 런던에서 신사 교육을 받아야 한다고 한다. 누군가 Pip의 후견인이 되어 신분상승을 현실로 만들어 준다는 것이다. 꿈만 같은 현실에 Pip은 후견인의 정체에 대해 막연하게 Miss Havisham이 그의 후견인일 것으로 생각하고 Jaggers를 따라 런던에 도착한다.

런던에 도착한 Pip은 돈이 생기자 허영을 부리며 속물적인 인간이 되어가고, 매형이 그를 찾아와도 반갑게 맞이하지 않는다. Pip은 런던에서의 생활에서 단 한 번도 행복한 시간을 갖지 못하지만, 여전히 Estella의 주위를 맴돌며 그녀와 평생 함께 지낼 것이라는 환상에 사로잡혀 있다. Estella는 매력적인 여성이지만 그녀도 Pip과 마찬가지로 비천하고 형편없는 집안 출신이었다. 그녀의 아버지는 Pip이 늪지대에서 만났던 죄수이며, 어머니는 집안의 가정부였다. 더군다나 Estella 자신도 신경쇠약에 걸린 여인의 손에서 어린 시절을 보냈다. Pip은 그런 Estella를 위해 '신사'가 되고 싶다고 한다. 그러나 Estella는 어리석은 신사들이 모이는 '숲속의 방울새' 그룹 중에서도 가장 둔한 인물인 Drummle과 결혼한다.

한편, Pip에게 막대한 유산을 물려준 사람은 Miss Havisham이 아니라 Pip이 늪지대에서 도와주었던 죄수로 밝혀진다. 바로 그 죄수가 Magwitch이며, Pip을 매부의 대장간에서 끄집어내어 허망한 희망의 사회에서 살도록 해 놓은 장본인이다. 그는 자신이 Pip을 신사로 만들어 놓았다고 자랑한다. 그러나 Pip은 죄수 Magwitch가 바라는 것과 같은 신사가 되지는 못한다. Magwitch는 자신이 만든 신사를 보고 싶은 갈망 때문에 갖은 고생 끝에 Pip을 찾아오지만, Pip은 그가 싫게만 느껴진다. 단지, 고통 받는 사람에 대한 동정의 감정만을 느낄 뿐이다. Magwitch를 몰래 탈출시키려는 시도는 실패로 끝나고 Magwitch는 심한 상처를 입고 다시 체포된다. 상처 입은 죄수의 침대 옆에서 Pip은 비로소 진정한 신사가 되어 가기 시작한다. Magwitch는 유죄 판결을 받고 사형을 선고받았으나, 사형 집행이 되기 전에 죽는다. 또한 그의 중죄로 인하여 전 재산이 국가에 몰수당한다. Pip이 물려받기로 되었던 유산은 흔적도 없이 사라지고 오히려 그는 큰 빚을 지고 만다. 또한 그 동안 흥청망청 시간을 보낸 탓으로 특별한 기술이나 직업도 없는 형편이 되고 만다.

Pip이 오랜 방황 끝에 고향으로 돌아왔을 때, 누나가 죽은 후 매형 Joe가 재혼한 Biddly와의 사이에서 낳은 아이를 Pip이라고 이름 지은 것이, 다름 아닌 자신에 대한 매형 Joe와 Biddly의 사랑의 표시임을 알게 된다. Pip은 매형에게서 위대하고 진실된 인간의 모습을 보게 된다. Pip은 몇 년간 Herbert Pocket과 외국에서 무역을 하다 영국으로 돌아온다. 자신에게 용서를 구한 Miss Havisham은 죽고, 폐허가 된 Satis House의 정원에서 Pip은 Estella를 만난다. Estella의 남편 Drummle은 좋지 않은 남편이었으며, 그는 죽고 Estella의 냉담함은 사라졌다. Pip과 Estella는 서로 손을 잡는다. Pip은 Estella와 영원히 함께할 것이라는 느낌을 받는다.

제 4 절 작품의 주제

1 막대한 유산

아이러니하게도 Pip이 기대했던 모든 것은 사라져 버린다. Pip은 자신이 물려받을 유산이 Miss Havisham 의 유산이라고 기대했지만, 사실 탈옥수 Magwitch의 계획이라는 사실을 알게 된다.

2 돈 중요 ★

돈은 이 작품에서 미묘한 가치를 지닌다. 돈은 Herbert Pocket을 돕고, Pip을 감옥에 가지 않도록 해주기도 하지만 위험한 요소를 지닌 대상이다. 돈은 가난했던 Pip이 런던으로 가서 신사수업을 받는 데 도움이 되지만, 그를 속물로 만들기도 한다. 아이러니하게도 Pip을 신사로 만드는 돈은 Magwitch가 신대륙(호주)에서 불법으로 취득한 돈이기도 하다. 디킨스는 돈이라는 주제를 통해 진정한 신사는 재산이 아닌 인간적인 신의를 지키고 타인에 대한 믿음을 지키며 성실하게 사는 모습을 통해 이룰 수 있는 것임을 보여주고 있다.

3 노동의 가치

Joe Gargery처럼 성실하고 열심히 노력한 대가로 얻은 돈은 결코 비난받지 않는다. 반면에 한순간에 우연히 물려받는 유산은 쉽게 사라질 수 있다. Pip은 기대했던 타인의 유산이 아닌 자신이 성실히 일을 하며 번 돈으로 생계를 유지한다.

4 가족 관계

고아와 양자, 보호인의 관계로 가득한 이 작품은 부모와 자식 간의 실패한 관계를 묘사한다. 고아인 Pip은 폭력적인 누나 Mrs. Gargery(Mrs. Joe)에 의해 양육되지만, 매형 Joe Gargery의 사랑을 받으며 자라고 그 의미를 뒤늦게 깨닫는다. 고아였던 Estella는 남성에 대한 복수의 도구로서 Miss Havisham의 양녀로 양육되지만, 진정한 사랑을 배우게 되며, Magwitch가 그녀의 친부라는 사실이 밝혀진다.

5 인간의 유대관계

작품 속 많은 등장인물들이 인간관계에서 소외되어 있는데, 결과는 정신질환과 비참함뿐이다. 대표적으로 Miss Havisham은 결혼식이 무효가 된 이후 외부와의 접촉을 끊고 양녀 Estella를 통해 남성들에게 복수하려 한다. Pip은 여러 인물들과 관계를 맺으며 성장하고 돈의 관계보다 사랑의 관계가 더욱 중요함을 깨닫는다.

6 선과 악

작품 곳곳에 선과 악의 대결이 등장하지만 선악은 이분법적으로 분리될 수 없기 때문에 서로 혼재된 모습을 보인다.

7 신사(gentleman)의 본질 중요 ★

진정한 신사란 물질적인 풍요로움이나 인위적인 교육, 대외적으로 드러나는 태도에서 만들어지는 것이 아니라 인간에게 따뜻한 사랑을 가질 때 비로소 완성된다. 진정한 신사는 다름 아닌 대장장이 Joe Gargery라는 점을 Pip은 뒤늦게 깨닫는다.

제 5 절 등장인물

1 Pip(Philip Pirrip)

작품 속의 화자이며 주인공이자 작가의 목소리를 대변하는 인물이다. 결점이 많은 인간이 성숙한 인격을 형성해 나간다는 점에서 작가 자신의 모습과도 비슷하며, 부끄러운 일과 두려움 등을 모두 고백한다. Pip

은 가난한 고아로 성장하며, 사랑하는 Estella와 함께하기 위해서는 반드시 신분 상승을 해야 한다는 강박 관념에 사로잡혀 있던 어느 날, 누군가로부터 상당한 유산을 받을 것이라는 소식을 듣고, 매형 Joe Gargery를 촌뜨기라며 거들떠보지도 않는 허영에 가득 찬 신사가 되어버린다. Pip은 자신을 도와준 사람이 막대한 재산을 가지고 있다고 믿었던 Miss Havisham이 아니라 탈옥수 Magwitch라는 사실이 드러나자, '막대한 재산의 상속자'로서의 꿈을 접는다. 그리고 바로 Joe Gargery의 마음과 진실한 애정을 깨닫고 다시 예전의 순수성을 되찾는다.

소년기의 Pip은 강압적인 누나의 성격 때문에 불행한 시절을 보냈고, Miss Havisham의 유산을 상속받아 신분 상승을 이루어 보겠다는 야심을 갖기도 했으며, 일방적으로 Estella를 사랑하다가 좌절감을 맛보기도 했다. 그러나 Pip은 이러한 유혹과 좌절, 정신적 방황을 경험하면서 점점 사람들에 대한 애정의 깊이를 깨닫게 되고, 이성과 사랑을 되찾아가는 인물로 그려진다.

2 Joe Gargery

Pip의 매형이다. Pip이 정신적인 구심점이라면, Joe는 도덕적이고 실천적인 구심점이라고 할 수 있다. Pip은 선량해지고자 애를 쓰지만, Joe는 천성이 선량하다. 비록 그는 대장장이(blacksmith)지만 내면에는 진정한 '신사'만이 가질 수 있는 온화한 심성이 넘쳐흐르고 있다. 그는 영원한 Pip의 보호자로서 촌스럽다며 자신을 멀리하고 떠난 Pip이 런던에서 Magwitch와 Estella, 그리고 빚과 열병으로 고생하며 인생의 고비에 서 있었을 때, 그에게 다가가 그를 보살펴 주며 빚을 갚아주는 진정한 신사의 참모습을 지닌 인간상을 보여준다. 이렇게 Joe는 Pip에게 위대하고 진실한 참인간상을 보여주게 되고, 비로소 Pip은 '위대한 유산'을 물려받게 되는 것이다.

3 Abel Magwitch

탈옥수(convict)로서 Pip에게 위협적인 존재로 다가온다. 삶을 위해 원시적인 투쟁을 벌이며, 인간의 악한 심성을 상징한다. 어둡고 폭우가 치는 밤에만 나타나서 동물에 비유되기도 하지만, 선량한 면도 있어서 다시 체포되었을 때 Pip을 보호하기 위해 거짓말도 한다. 자신이 탈옥했을 때 먹을 것을 가져다준 고마움으로 Pip에게 많은 재산을 주어 그를 신사로 만들어 준 사람이다. 탈출을 감행하다가 붙잡힌 감옥 안에서 마지막으로 Pip의 모습을 보며 평온한 마음으로 숨을 거둔다. 자신의 정체를 숨기기 위하여 Provice라는 가명도 쓴다. Molly와의 사실상 혼인관계에서 Estella를 낳은 Estella의 친부이다.

4 Miss Havisham

때로는 미치광이 같은 모습을 보이지만, 제정신일 때는 탐욕스러운 친척들에게 포위된 피해자 같다. Pip에게 상속 재산과 사랑에 너무 기대지 말라는 경고를 하는 역할을 한다. 결혼식 당일 아침에 당대 최고의 사기꾼인 Compeyson에게 사기 결혼에 휘말린 이후, 세상과 담을 쌓고 평생 동안 결혼 예복을 입고 살아가며 남성들을 저주하며 복수의 대상으로 삼는다. 그녀는 자신의 양녀 Estella를 야비하고 어리석은 Bentley Drummle과 결혼하도록 유도하여, Estella를 진심으로 사랑하는 Pip과 그 이외의 구혼자들에게 마음의 상처를 안겨준다. 그녀의 바람대로 Pip은 마음에 커다란 상처를 입지만, 자신의 불행을 그녀에게 돌리지 않는 그의 모습에 감동을 받아, 자신이 Pip에게 유산을 상속한 증여자인 척한 사실에 양심의 가책을 느끼고 회한의 눈물로 Pip에게 용서를 구하기도 한다.

5 Estella

Miss Havisham의 양녀이자 유일한 말벗으로, 남성들에게 상처를 주는 냉담한 여성으로 양육된다. Pip의 사회적인 신분이 비천하다는 이유로 Pip에게 여왕처럼 군림하며, 그에게 수치감을 안겨준다. 그러나 이에 아랑곳하지 않고 그녀의 아름다움에 이끌린 Pip은 계속 그녀에게 그의 진실한 사랑을 보인다. 그러던 중 그녀는 Miss Havisham의 계획으로 인해 Bentley Drummle과 결혼한다. 그러나 그녀의 결혼생활은 실패하고, 결국 Pip의 순수한 사랑을 받아들여 다시는 헤어지지 않기를 바라며 Pip의 영원한 여인으로 남는다.

6 Herbert Pocket

Miss Havisham의 조카로, 그녀의 저택 Satis House에서 Pip과 우연히 싸움을 벌인 어린 신사이다. 신분 상승을 한 Pip과 런던에서 우연히 재회하며 둘은 친한 친구가 된다. Pip과는 나이가 비슷한 친구로, 서로 인생의 협력자가 된다.

7 Mrs. Gargery(Mrs. Joe)

동생 Pip과 남편 Joe Gargery에게 조금의 애정도 보이지 않는 포악하고 강압적인 성격의 소유자이다. 이런 그녀의 성격은 Pip의 성장과정에 정서적으로 나쁜 영향을 미쳐 Pip의 성격을 왜곡시킨다.

8 Biddy

어린 시절 Pip의 공부를 가르쳐준 학교 친구이자 초등학교 선생님이다. Mrs. Joe가 다쳤을 때 Joe의 집안 사람들을 돌봐주다가 Mrs. Joe가 죽은 이후 Joe와 결혼한다.

9 Compeyson

Miss Havisham의 결혼식 날에 신부를 배반하고 나타나지 않은 남자이다. 좋은 교육을 받은 인물이지만 심성이 악한 사기꾼이다. Abel Magwitch와 같은 범법자로 그를 죽이려고 하다가 도리어 자신이 그와의 결투 끝에 죽는다.

10 Dolge Orlick

Joe Gargery의 대장간 조수로 있다가 나중에는 Miss Havisham의 저택 문지기가 된다. 다른 모든 등장인물에게 사악한 모습으로만 비추어지는 전형적인 악인이다. Mrs. Joe를 공격한 인물이며, Pip을 죽이려고도 한다.

11 Bentley Drummle

Matthew Pocket으로부터 가르침을 받는 Pip의 동료 중 한 사람이다. 우둔하고 퉁명스러운 성격의 소유자로, Estella와 사랑이 없는 결혼을 하고 몇 년 후 죽는다.

12 Mr. Jaggers

탈옥수 Abel Magwitch의 증여 재산을 익명으로 Pip에게 전달해주는 임무를 맡고 있는 변호사이다. Miss Havisham의 변호사이기도 하며, 형사 전문 변호사이다.

13 Wemmick

Jaggers 변호사 사무실의 서기로서 사무적인 일에 익숙한 성격이지만 집에서는 쾌활한 모습도 보인다. Pip의 친구로 Pip이 하는 일에는 몸을 사리지 않는 적극성을 보인다.

14 Startop

Pip과 Bentley Drummle과 함께 Matthew Pocket으로부터 가르침을 받는 학생 중 한 명으로 부드러우면서도 세심한 성격의 인물이다.

15 (Uncle) Pumblechook

Joe의 친척으로 Pip과 Miss Havisham의 첫 만남을 주도하는 인물이다. 고물상의 주인으로 돈에 집착하며, Pip이 신사가 되는 데 있어 자신이 Pip의 첫 후원자라고 주장한다.

16 Molly

Abel Magwitch와 사실상의 혼인 관계에서 Estella를 낳는다. Mr. Jaggers의 가정부이다.

제 6 절　작품의 구조(Plot)와 시점 및 기법

1 구조

총 3부(Volume)로 구성되어 있다.

(1) Volume Ⅰ(Chapter 1~19)

Pip의 소년시절의 내용이다. 소년의 눈으로 보고 있기 때문에 환상과 비논리가 섞여 있다.

(2) Volume Ⅱ(Chapter 20~39)

런던에서 Pip의 청년시절이다. 그의 변화의 과정이 이루어지며, 사회 풍자와 경제적 문제 등이 등장한다.

(3) Volume Ⅲ(Chapter 40~59)

Pip은 일을 하며 사회의 적극적인 참여자가 된다. 추리 소설과 같은 장면이 많이 나온다.

2 시점

1인칭 화자시점으로 서술되고 있다. 사춘기에 접어들었을 때 Pip은 자신의 어린 시절을 비판적인 눈으로 돌아보며 스스로를 '그'라고 언급하고 있다. Pip이 직접 보지 못한 부분은 Biddly를 통해 묘사하는데, 35장의 Mrs. Gargery의 죽음, 42장의 Abel Magwich의 행동 등이 그 예이다.

3 기법

다양하게 변모하는 서술기법으로 소설이 전개된다. 우스꽝스러운 과장법, 풍자, 중후한 어조와 비극적이고 엄숙한 어조 등이 많이 쓰인다.

제 7 절 Text

Chapter 39(Vol. II. Ch. XX)

I was three-and-twenty years of age. Not another word had I heard to enlighten me on the subject of my expectations, and my twenty-third birthday was a week gone. We[1] had left Barnard's Inn[2] more than a year, and lived in the Temple[3]. Our chambers were in Garden court, down by the river.

Mr. Pocket and I had for some time parted company[4] as to our original relations, though we continued on the best terms. Notwithstanding my inability to settle to anything — which I hope arose out of the restless and incomplete tenure[5] on which I held my means — I had a taste for reading, and read regularly so many hours a day. That matter of Herbert's[6] was still progressing, and everything with me was as I have brought it down[7] to the close of the last preceding chapter.

Business had taken Herbert on a journey to Marseilles. I was alone, and had a dull sense of being alone. Dispirited and anxious, long hoping that tomorrow or next week would clear my way, and long disappointed, I sadly missed the cheerful face and ready response[8] of my friend.

It was wretched[9] weather; stormy and wet, stormy and wet; mud, mud, mud, deep in all the streets. Day after day, a vast heavy veil[10] had been driving over London from the East, and it drove still, as if in the East there were an eternity of cloud and wind. So furious had been the gusts[11] that high buildings in town had had the lead[12] stripped off their roofs; and in the country, trees

---

1) We : 이 소설의 시점은 1인칭 화자이자 주인공인 Pip이 과거를 회상하는 시점이다. 변호사 Jaggers가 하라는 대로 Pip은 런던에 도착하던 때부터 Miss Havisham의 친척인 Herbert Pocket과 같은 방에서 함께 지낸다.
2) Barnard's Inn : Pip이 런던으로 와서 머물렀던 곳으로, 원래는 Gray's Inn에 부속된 건물이었다.
3) the Temple : The four great Inns of Court - Innre Temple, Middle Temple, Lincoln's Inn and Gray's Inn possess the sole right of admitting persons to practice as barristers. Garden court is one of many courts within the Temple's precincts. The construction of the Victorian Embankment(1862) had robbed the Temple of direct access to the river which it certainly has here. Garden court itself was rebuilt in 1830.
4) part company : ~와 갈라지다, 의견을 다르게 하다
5) tenure : (부동산, 지위, 직분 등의) 보유
6) That matter of Herbert's : Pip은 사업자금이 없어 고생하고 있던 Herbert를 돕기 위해 자신의 수입 중 일부를 그에게 몰래 투자하려는 계획을 세우고 있었다.
7) bring it down : (기록, 이야기 등을) ~까지 계속하다
8) ready response : 즉각적인 응답(Herbert의 언제든지 반응해 주는 상냥한 태도)
9) wretched : detestable, 혐오할 만한, 몹시 싫은
10) a vast heavy veil : a vast heavy veil of cloud and wind(구름과 바람이 엄청 많은 것처럼)
11) gust : 세찬 바람, 돌풍
12) the lead : (지붕을 일 때 쓰는) 함석

had been torn up, and sails of windmills carried away; and gloomy accounts[13] had come in from the coast of shipwreck and death. Violent blasts of rain[14] had accompanied these rages of wind, and the day just closed[15] as I sat down to read had been the worst of all.

Alterations have been made in that part of the Temple since that time, and it has not now so lonely a character as it had then, nor is it so exposed to the river. We lived at the top of the last house, and the wind rushing up the river shook the house that night, like discharges of cannon[16], or breakings of a sea. When the rain came with it and dashed against the windows, I thought, raising my eyes to them as they rocked, that I might have fancied myself in a storm-beaten lighthouse. Occasionally, the smoke came rolling down the chimney as though it could not bear to go out into such a night; and when I set the doors open and looked down the staircase[17], the staircase lamps were blown out[18]; and when I shaded my face with my hands[19] and looked through the black windows (opening them ever so little was out of the question[20] in the teeth of[21] such wind and rain), I saw that the lamps in the court were blown out, and that the lamps on the bridges and the shore were shuddering, and that the coal fires in barges[22] on the river were being carried away before the wind like red-hot splashes[23] in the rain. I read with my watch upon the table, purposing to close my book at eleven o'clock. As I shut it, Saint Paul's, and all the many church-clocks in the City — some leading, some accompanying, some following — struck that hour. The sound was curiously flawed by the wind[24]; and I was listening, and thinking how the wind assailed and tore it, when I heard a footstep on the stair.

What nervous folly made me start,[25] and awfully connect it with the footstep of my dead sister[26], matters not[27]. It was past in a moment, and I listened again, and heard the footstep stumble in coming on. Remembering then, that the staircase lights were blown out, I took up my reading-lamp and went out to the stair-head[28]. Whoever was below had stopped on seeing my lamp[29], for all was quiet.

"There is some one down there, is there not?" I called out, looking down.

---

13) gloomy accounts : 우울한 소문
14) Violent blasts of rain : 굉장한 폭우
15) the day just closed : 이제 막 저문 하루
16) discharges of cannon : 대포의 발포
17) staircase : 계단
18) blow out : (불을) 끄다, 꺼지다
19) shaded my face with my hands : (어둠 속을 들여다보기 위해) 두 손으로 얼굴을 가렸다.
20) out of the question : impossible
21) in the teeth of : ~에 대항하여, 을 무릅쓰고
22) barge : 바지선(운하, 강 등에서 사람과 화물을 싣고 다니는 바닥이 납작한 배)
23) splash : 물방울
24) The sound was curiously flawed by the wind : 묘하게도 종소리가 바람소리 때문에 변질되었다(Magwitch의 방문이 Pip의 조용하고 안락했던 일상을 바꾸어 버리는 이후의 전개를 생각하면 문장은 상징적인 의미를 지닌다).
25) What nervous folly made me start : 불안한 중에 어리석게도 얼마나 놀랐는지. / start : (놀람, 공포 따위로) 깜짝 놀라다
26) my dead sister : Pip을 구박하던 누나 Mrs. Gargery는 Pip이 고향을 떠나기 전 어떤 괴한의 습격을 받고 앓아눕게 되고, Pip이 런던에 온 후 한참 지나서 사망한다.
27) matters not = does not matter : 중요하지 않다
28) the stair-head : 층계의 꼭대기
29) on seeing my lamp : 내 등불을 보자마자

"Yes," said a voice from the darkness beneath.

"What floor do you want?"

"The top. Mr. Pip."

"That is my name — There is nothing the matter?30)"

"Nothing the matter," returned the voice. And the man came on.

I stood with my lamp held out over the stair-rail, and he came slowly within its light. It was a shaded lamp31), to shine upon a book, and its circle of light was very contracted; so that he was in it for a mere instant, and then out of it. In the instant, I had seen a face that was strange to me, looking up with an incomprehensible air of being touched and pleased by the sight of me32).

Moving the lamp as the man moved, I made out that he was substantially33) dressed, but roughly, like a voyager by sea. That he had long iron-grey34) hair. That his age was about sixty. That he was a muscular man, strong on his legs, and that he was browned and hardened by exposure to weather35). As he ascended the last stair or two, and the light of my lamp included us both, I saw, with a stupid kind of amazement, that he was holding out both his hands to me.

"Pray36) what is your business?" I asked him.

"My business?" he repeated, pausing. "Ah! Yes. I will explain my business, by your leave37)."

"Do you wish to come in?"

"Yes," he replied, "I wish to come in, Master38)."

I had asked him the question inhospitably enough39), for I resented the sort of bright and gratified recognition that still shone in his face. I resented it, because it seemed to imply that he expected me to respond to it. But, I took him into the room I had just left, and, having set the lamp on the table, asked him as civilly as I could, to explain himself.

He looked about him with the strangest air — an air of wondering pleasure, as if he had some part in the things he admired40) — and he pulled off a rough outer coat, and his hat. Then, I saw that his head was furrowed and bald, and that the long iron-grey hair grew only on its sides. But I saw nothing that in the least explained him41). On the contrary, I saw him next moment once more holding out both his hands to me.

"What do you mean?" said I, half suspecting him to be mad.

He stopped in his looking at me, and slowly rubbed his right hand over his head.

---

30) There is nothing the matter? : (그에게) 무슨 일 있습니까?
31) a shaded lamp : 갓을 씌워놓은 등불
32) with an incomprehensible air ∼ by the sight of me : 나를 보고 감격스러워하며 기뻐하는 이해하기 어려운 태도로
33) substantially : 든든하게, 충분히
34) iron-grey : 철회색(약간 녹색을 띠고 있는 광택 있는 회색)
35) browned and hardened by exposure to weather : 야외활동을 오래하여 거무스름하고 단단한
36) Pray : Please(I pray you의 간략한 형태)
37) by your leave : with you leave(미안하지만, 실례지만)
38) Master : ∼님. 하인 등이 주인집의 젊은 자제를 부를 때 사용하는 말
39) inhospitably enough : 굉장히 무뚝뚝하게
40) as if he had some part in the things he admired : 자신이 놀라워하고 있는 것들에 자기가 어느 정도 관여한 것처럼
41) I saw nothing that in the least explained him : 그에 대해 알 수 있는 것은 아무것도 발견하지 못하였다.

"It's disapinting[42]) to a man," he said, in a coarse broken voice[43]), "arter[44]) having looked for'ard[45]) so distant, and come so fur[46]); but you're not to blame for that[47]) — neither on us[48]) is to blame for that. I'll speak in half a minute. Give me half a minute, please."

He sat down on a chair that stood before the fire, and covered his forehead with his large brown veinous[49]) hands. I looked at him attentively then, and recoiled[50]) a little from him; but I did not know him.

"There' s no one nighs[51])," said he, looking over his shoulder; "is there?"

"Why do you, a stranger coming into my rooms at this time of the night, ask that question?" said I.

"You're a games[52]) one," he returned, shaking his head at me with a deliberate affection, at once most unintelligible and most exasperating; "I'm glad you've grow'd[53]) up, a game one! But don't catch hold of[54]) me. You'd be sorry[55]) arterwards[56]) to have done it."

I relinquished[57]) the intention he had detected, for I knew him! Even yet, I could not recall a single feature, but I knew him! If[58]) the wind and the rain had driven away the intervening years[59]), had scattered all the intervening objects, had swept us to the churchyard where we first stood face to face on such different levels[60]), I could not have known my convict[61]) more distinctly than I knew him now as he sat in the chair before the fire. No need to take a file from his pocket and show it to me; no need to take the handkerchief from his neck and twist it round his head; no need to hug himself with both his arms, and take a shivering turn across the room, looking back at me for recognition. I knew him before he gave me one of those aids, though, a moment before, I had not been conscious of remotely[62]) suspecting his identity.

He came back to where I stood, and again held out both his hands. Not knowing what to do for,

---

42) disapinting : disappointing[교육을 제대로 받지 못한 Magwitch는 broken English를 사용한다. Pip의 표준어법과 대조를 이루며 그를 신사(gentleman)로 만들려는 Magwitch의 염원이 부각된다]

43) in a coarse broken voice : 거칠면서도 충격을 받은 목소리로

44) arter : after

45) look for'ard : look forward(기대하다)

46) fur : far

47) you're not to blame for that : 그건 자네의 잘못이 아닐세.

48) neither on us : neither of us

49) veinous : 힘줄이 튀어나온

50) recoil : 뒷걸음질 치다, 주춤하다

51) nigh : [고어] near

52) game : 용기 있는

53) grow'd : grown

54) catch hold of : ~을 이해하다, 파악하다

55) be sorry (for) : 후회하다

56) arterwards : afterwards

57) relinquish : 포기하다

58) If : Even if

59) the intervening years : 소년 Pip은 7살로 추정되기 때문에 이 기간은 약 16년에 해당한다. 이 작품의 서술 시점은 Pip이 34세인 때로 설정되어 있다.

60) the churchyard where we first stood face to face on such different levels : 우리가 그렇게 다른 높이에서 서로 얼굴을 마주하고 서 있었던 교회당의 묘지(이 작품의 제1장에서 Pip은 교회당의 부모님 묘지 옆에서 탈옥수 Magwitch에게 붙잡혀 협박당한다. different levels라고 한 이유는 그때 그가 Pip을 거꾸로 세우기도 하고 묘석 위에 올려놓기도 하며 위험했던 것에 대한 언급으로, 다른 한편으로는 두 사람의 위치가 지금과는 정반대였다는 것에 대한 지적이다)

61) convict : 죄수(어린 Pip은 공포심에 Magwitch의 탈옥을 도와주었기 때문에 그를 my convict라고 지칭한다)

62) remotely : 희미하게, 어렴풋이

in my astonishment I had lost my self-possession[63]) — I reluctantly gave him my hands. He grasped them heartily, raised them to his lips, kissed them, and still held them.

"You acted noble, my boy," said he. "Noble, Pip! And I have never forgot it!"

At a change in his manner as if he were even going to embrace me,[64]) I laid a hand upon his breast and put him away.

"Stay!" said I. "Keep off! If you are grateful to me for what I did when I was a little child, I hope you have shown your gratitude by mending[65]) your way of life[66]). If you have come here to thank me, it was not necessary. Still, however you have found me out, there must be something good in the feeling that has brought you here, and I will not repulse[67]) you; but surely you must understand that — I — "

My attention was so attracted by the singularity of his fixed look at me[68]) that the words died away on my tongue[69]).

"You was a saying," he observed[70]), when we had confronted one another in silence "that surely I must understand. What, surely must I understand?"

"That I cannot wish to renew that chance intercourse[71]) with you of long ago, under these different circumstances. I am glad to believe you have repented and recovered yourself. I am glad to tell you so. I am glad that, thinking I deserve to be thanked, you have come to thank me. But our ways are different ways, none the less. You are wet, and you look weary. Will you drink something before you go?"

He had replaced his neckerchief loosely, and had stood, keenly observant of me[72]), biting a long end of it[73]). "I think," he answered, still with the end at his mouth and still observant of me, "that I will drink (I thank you) afore[74]) I go."

There was a tray ready on a side-table. I brought it to the table near the fire, and asked him what he would have? He touched one of the bottles without looking at it or speaking, and I made him some hot rum-and-water[75]). I tried to keep my hand steady while I did so, but his look at me as he leaned back in his chair with the long draggled[76]) end of his neckerchief between his teeth — evidently forgotten[77]) — made my hand very difficult to master. When at last I put the glass to him,

---

63) self-possession : 침착, 냉정
64) At a change in his manner as if he were even going to embrace me : 심지어 나를 껴안기라도 하려는 것처럼 그의 태도가 바뀌는 것을 보고
65) by mending : 고치며, 개선하며
66) way of life : 삶의 방식
67) repulse : rebuff, refuse(거절하다)
68) by the singularity of his fixed look at me : 나를 뚫어지게 쳐다보는 그의 묘한 표정에
69) that ~ tongue : that-on the tip of my tongue 내 혀끝에서 단어들이 사라져 버리고 말았다.
70) observe : 말하다
71) that chance intercourse : 그 우연한 교제
72) keenly observant of me : 나를 예리하게 살펴보곤
73) it : his neckerchief
74) afore : [고어] before
75) rum-and-water : 물탄 럼주[독한 술인 럼주를 묽게 하기 위해 물을 섞은 일종의 칵테일로서 오랜 항해에 지친 선원들이 주로 마셨다고 한다. 일명 그로그(grog)라고 하는데, '휘청거리는' 의미의 groggy라는 단어가 여기에서 유래되었다]
76) draggled : 질질 끌린, 더러운
77) evidently forgotten : 목도리를 입에 물고 있으면서도 잊고 있었다는 의미

I saw with amazement that his eyes were full of tears.

Up to this time I had remained standing, not to disguise that I wished him gone. But I was softened[78] by the softened aspect of the man, and felt a touch of reproach[79]. "I hope," said I, hurriedly putting something into a glass for myself, and drawving a chair to the table, "that you will not think I spoke harshly to you just now. I had no intention of doing it, and I am sorry for it if I did. I wish you well, and happy!"

As I put my glass to my lips, he glanced with surprise at the end of his neckerchief, dropping from his mouth when he opened it, and stretched out his hand. I gave him mine, and then he drank, and drew his sleeve across his eyes and forehead.

"How are you living?" I asked him.

"I've been a sheep-farmer, stock-breeder[80], other trades[81] besides, away in the New World[82]," said he, "many a thousand mile of stormy water off from this."

"I hope you have done well?"

"I've done wonderfully well. There's others went out alonger me as has done well too,[83] but no man has done nigh as well as me. I'm famous for it."

"I am glad to hear it."

"I hope to hear you say so, my dear boy."

Without stopping to try to understand those words or the tone in which they were spoken, I turned off to a point that had just come into my mind.

"Have you ever seen a messenger you once sent to me[84]," I inquired, "since he undertook that trust[85]?"

"Never set eyes upon him.[86] I warn't likely to it.[87]"

"He came faithfully, and he brought me the two one-pound notes. I was a poor boy then, as you know, and to a poor boy they were a little fortune. But, like you, I have done well since,[88] and you must let me pay them back. You can put them to some other poor boy's use." I took out my purse.

He watched me as I laid my purse upon the table and opened it, and he watched me as I separated two one-pound notes from its contents. They were clean and new, and I spread them out and handed

---

78) soften : 누그러지게 하다, 누그러지다
79) a touch of reproach : 자책감
80) stock-breeder : 목축업자 / stock : livestock(가축)
81) trades : occupations, 직업
82) away in the New World : 멀리 신대륙에서(Magwitch는 호주로 유배를 갔다가 몰래 돌아온 것으로 되어 있다)
83) There's others went out alonger me as has done well too : 나와 같이 나가서 성공한 사람들이 있어요. / alonger : with
84) a messenger you once sent to me : 당신이 언젠가 내게 보냈던 심부름 꾼[Miss Havisham의 집을 드나들기 시작한 지 얼마 후에 Pip은 마을의 술집에서 매형 Joe와 함께 낯선 사람을 만나게 되는데, Pip을 특히 유심히 바라보던 그는 Pip에게 두 장의 1파운드짜리 지폐에 1실링을 싸서 준다. 그가 자신의 럼주를 줄(file)로 저어 마시는 것을 보고 Pip은 그 줄이 바로 자신이 탈옥수 Magwitch에게 주었던 매형의 대장간에 있던 줄임을 알아차린다. Pip은 이것으로 인해 두려움에 사로잡히지만, 이 사건은 후에 Pip이 물려받는 유산이 Magwitch와 관련된 것임을 암시하는 복선이라고 할 수 있다]
85) since he undertook that trust : 그가 그 책임을 맡은 뒤로
86) Never set eyes upon him : 그를 보지 못했다. / set eyes upon(on) : ～을 보다
87) I warn't likely to it : 그럴 수 없었다. / warn't : wasn't
88) I have done well since : (당신과 마찬가지로) 나도 그 뒤 성공했습니다[자신이 많은 양의 유산을 물려받게 되었다는 사실을 가리킨다. 그러나 Magwitch만이 그 유산의 비밀을 알고 있을 뿐 독자들도 이 시점에서는 그 사실을 알 수 없다).

them over to him. Still watching me, he laid them one upon the other, folded them long-wise[89], gave them a twist, set fire to[90] them at the lamp, and dropped the ashes into the tray.

"May I make so bold[91]," he said then, with a smile that was like a frown, and with a frown that was like a smile, "as ask you how you have done well, since you and me was out on them lone shivering marshes[92])?"

"How?"

"Ah!"

He emptied his glass, got up, and stood at the side of the fire, with his heavy brown hand on the mantelshelf[93]. He put a foot up to the bars, to dry and warm it, and the wet boot began to steam; but, he neither looked at it, nor at the fire, but steadily looked at me. It was only now that I began to tremble.

When my lips had parted, and had shaped some words that were without sound, I forced myself to tell him (though I could not do it distinctly), that I had been chosen to succeed to some property.

"Might a mere warmint ask what property?[94])" said he.

I faltered[95], "I don't know."

"Might a mere warmint ask whose property?" said he.

I faltered again, "I don't know."

"Could I make a guess, I wonder," said the Convict, "at your income since you come of age[96]! As to the first figure now. Five?"

With my heart beating like a heavy hammer of disordered action, I rose out of my chair, and stood with my hand upon the back of it, looking wildly at him.

"Concerning a guardian," he went on. "There ought to have been some guardian, or such-like, whiles you was a minor[97]. Some lawyer, maybe. As to the first letter of that lawyer's name now. Would it be J?"

All the truth of my position came flashing on me,[98] and its disappointments, dangers, disgraces, consequences of all kinds, rushed in such a multitude that I was borne down by them[99] and had to struggle for every breath I drew.

"Put it,[100]" he resumed, "as the employer of that lawyer whose name begun with a J, and might

---

89) long-wise : lengthwise(세로로, 길게)

90) set fire to : ~에 불을 붙이다

91) make so bold as : make bold to(감히 ~하다)

92) them lone shivering marshes : the lone shivering marshes(이러한 자리에 the 대신 them을 쓰는 것은 제대로 교육을 받지 못한 사람들의 습관적 오류이다). 춥고 오싹한 습지

93) the mantelshelf : 벽난로 선반

94) Might a mere warmint ask what property? : 나같이 형편없는 놈이 누구의 재산인지 물어봐도 되겠소? / warmint : vermin, 해충 (사회의) 해충, 악당, 망나니

95) falter : 목소리가 흔들리다, 머뭇거리다

96) come of age : 성년이 되다(이 당시에 법적인 성년은 21세가 기준이었다. 2년 전 Pip이 성년이 되던 날 Jaggers 변호사는 그를 불러 성년이 되었으니 이제 스스로 유산을 관리하라고 하며 앞으로 매년 500파운드씩 주겠다고 약속하지만, 그 돈이 누구의 돈인지는 밝히지 않는다).

97) whiles you was a minor : 자네가 미성년자였을 동안 / whiles : [고어] while

98) All the truth of my position came flashing on me : 내가 처한 상황의 진상이 섬광처럼 다가왔다.

99) was borne down by them : 그것들에 압도당하였다. / bear down : (적을) 압도하다, (반대편을) 꺾어 누르다

100) Put it : 표준 어법에는 어긋나지만, '이렇게 이야기하지요'의 의미로 쓰였다.

be Jaggers — put it as he had come over sea to Portsmouth[101], and had landed there, and had wanted to come on to you. 'However, you have found me out,' you says just now. Well! However, did I find you out? Why,[102] I wrote from Portsmouth to a person in London for particulars of your address. That person's name? Why, Wemmick."

I could not have spoken one word, though it had been to save my life. I stood, with a hand on the chair-back and a hand on my breast, where I seemed to be suffocating[103] — I stood so, looking wildly at him, until I grasped at the chair, when the room began to surge and turn. He caught me, drew me to the sofa, put me up against the cushions, and bent on one knee before me: bringing the face that I now well remembered, and that I shuddered at, very near to mine.

"Yes, Pip, dear boy, I've made a gentleman on you! It's me wot[104] has done it! I swore that time, sure[105] as ever I earned a guinea, that guinea should go to you. swore arterwards, sure as ever I spec'lated[106] and got rich, you should get rich. I lived rough, that you should live smooth[107]; I worked hard that you should be above work[108]. What odds,[109] dear boy? Do I tell it, fur you to feel a obligation? Not a bit. I tell it, fur you to know as that there hunted dunghill dog[110] wot you kep life in[111] got his head so high[112] that he could make a gentleman — and, Pip, you're him!"

The abhorrence in which I held the man, the dread I had of him, the repugnance with which I shrank from him, could not have been exceeded if[113] he had been some terrible beast. "Look' ee here[114], Pip. I'm your second father. You're my son — more to me nor[115] any son. I've put away[116] money, only for you to spend. When I was a hired-out[117] shepherd in a solitary hut, not seeing no faces but faces of sheep till I half forgot wot men's and women's faces wos like[118], I see yourn[119]. I drops my knife many a time in that hut when I was a eating my dinner or my supper, and I says, 'Here's the boy again, a looking at me whiles I eats and drinks!' I see you there a many times, as plain as ever I see you on them misty marshes[120]. 'Lord strike me dead[121]!' I

---

101) Portsmouth : 영국의 남부에 있는 항구로 대서양 항해의 중심이 된 도시이자 군항. Dickens의 출생지이다.
102) Why : 흠, 아, 글쎄
103) where I seemed to be suffocating : 나는 가슴이 확 막히는 것 같았다.
104) wot : what, 문법적으로는 who(또는 that)가 정확한 표현이다.
105) sure : surely
106) spec'late : speculate(투기를 하다, 요행수를 노리다)
107) that you should live smooth : so that you should live smoothly(자네가 평탄히 살 수 있도록)
108) that you should be above work : 자네가 일을 하지 않아도 되도록
109) What odds? : What's odds?, 무슨 차이가 있겠냐고?
110) hunted dunghill dog : 쫓기는 똥개. 작품의 도입부에서 Pip이 음식과 줄을 가져왔을 때, Magwitch는 추격자가 없는지 물으며 협박한다. "You'd be but a fierce young hound indeed, if at your time of life you could help to hunt a wretched warmint, hunt as near death and dunghill as this poor wretched warmint is!" (Chapter 3)
111) wot you kep life in : whom you kept life in(자네가 목숨을 유지하게 해준)
112) got his head so high : 형편이 무척 좋아졌다 / hold one's head high : 거만한 태도를 취하다
113) if : even if
114) Look'ee here : Look thee here = Look you here(이봐, 조심해.)
115) nor : [방언] than
116) put away : save
117) hired-out : hired(고용된)
118) wot men's and women's faces wos like : what men's and women's faces were like(사람들 얼굴이 어떻게 생겼는지)
119) yourn : [방언] yours, your face
120) as plain as ever I see you on them misty marshes : 안개 낀 늪지대에서 당신을 보았던 때와 같이 확실하게
121) Lord strike me dead ~ but : ~이라면 내 목을 내놓겠다

says each time — and I goes out in the open air to say it under the open heavens — 'but wot, if I gets liberty and money, I'll make that boy a gentleman!' And I done it. Why, look at you, dear boy! Look at these here lodgings o'yourn[122], fit for a lord! A lord? Ah! You shall show money with lords for wagers, and beat' em![123]"

In his heat and triumph[124], and in his knowledge that I had been nearly fainting, he did not remark on my reception of all this. It was the one grain of relief I had.[125]

"Look'ee here!" he went on, taking my watch out of my pocket, and turning towards him a ring on my finger, while I recoiled from his touch as if he had been a snake, "a gold 'un and a beauty: that's a gentleman's, I hope! A diamond all set round with rubies; that's a gentleman's, I hope! Look at your linen[126]; fine and beautiful! Look at your clothes; better ain't to be got![127] And your books too," turning his eyes round the room, "mounting up, on their shelves, by hundreds![128] And you read 'em; don't you? I see you'd been a reading of 'em when I come in. Ha, ha, ha! You shall read 'em to me, dear boy! And if they're in foreign languages wot I don't understand, I shall be just as proud as if I did[129]."

Again he took both my hands and put them to his lips, while my blood ran cold within me.

"Don't you mind talking, Pip," said he, after again drawing his sleeve over his eyes and forehead, as the click came in his throat which I well remembered[130] — and he was all the more horrible to me that he was so much in earnest; "you can't do better nor keep quiet, dear boy. You ain't looked slowly forward to this as I have[131]; you wosn't prepared for this, as I wos. But didn't you never think it might be me?"

"O no, no, no," I returned, "Never, never!"

"Well, you see it wos me, and single-handed[132]. Never a soul in it but my own self and Mr. Jaggers."

"Was there no one else?" I asked.

"No," said he, with a glance of surprise: "who else should there be? And, dear boy, how good looking you have growed! There's bright eyes[133] somewheres — eh? Isn't there bright eyes somewheres, wot you love the thoughts on?"

O Estella, Estella![134]

---

122) lodgings o'yourn : lodgings of yours(너의 거처)
123) You shall show money with lords for wagers, and beat' em! : 돈에 대해선 귀족들하고 내기를 해도 이길 테니!
124) In his heat and triumph : 흥분과 승리감으로 인해
125) It was the one grain of relief I had : 그것이 나에게는 한 가닥 위안이 되었다.
126) linen : 린넨(셔츠, 속옷, 시트 따위를 가리키는 말)
127) better ain't to be got! : 이보다 더 좋은 건 구할 수 없겠구나! / ain't : isn't
128) mounting up, on their shelves, by hundreds! : 수백 권이나 선반 위에 쌓여 있구나!
129) as if I did : as if I understood(마치 내가 그것을 이해하는 것과 마찬가지로)
130) the click came in his throat which I well remembered : 그의 목구멍에서는 내가 잘 기억하고 있는 '딸각' 하는 소리가 났다(Pip은 이전에 탈옥한 죄수에게 음식과 줄을 가져다주었을 때 이것과 같은 소리를 들은 적이 있었다).
131) You ain't looked slowly forward to this as I have : 이 일을 나처럼 천천히 기대하지도 않았겠지.
132) single-handed : 혼자의 힘으로
133) bright eyes : '애인, 연인' 등을 가리키는 당시의 속어로 추측된다.
134) O Estella, Estella! : 나중에 밝혀지지만 Estella는 Magwitch의 친딸이다.

"They shall be yourn, dear boy, if money can buy 'em. Not that a gentleman like you, so well set up as you, can't win 'em off of his own game; but money shall back[135] you! Let me finish wot I was a telling you, dear boy. From that there hut and that there hiring-out, I got money left me by my master (which died, and had been the same as me[136]), and got my liberty and went for myself[137]. In every single thing I went for, I went for you. 'Lord strike a blight upon it,' I says, wotever it was I went for, 'if it ain't for him!' It all prospered wonderful. As I giv' you to understand[138] just now, I'm famous for it. It was the money left me, and the gains of the first few year wot I sent home to Mr Jaggers — all for you — when he first come arter you, agreeable to my letter[139]."

O, that he had never come![140] That he had left me at the forge — far from contented, yet, by comparison happy[141]!

"And then, dear boy, it was a recompense[142] to me, look'ee here, to know in secret that I was making a gentleman. The blood horses[143] of them colonists might fling up the dust over me as I was walking; what do I say? I says to myself, 'I'm making a better gentleman nor ever you'll be!' When one of 'em says to another, 'He was a convict, a few year ago, and is a ignorant common[144] fellow now, for all he's lucky,' what do I say? I says to myself, 'If I ain't a gentleman, nor yet ain't got no learning, I'm the owner of such[145]. All on you[146] owns stock and land; which on you owns a brought-up London gentleman?' This was I kep myself a going. And this way I held steady afore my mind that I would for certain come one day and see my boy, and make myself known to him, on his own ground."

He laid his hand on my shoulder. I shuddered at the thought that for anything I knew[147], his hand might be stained with blood.

"It warn't easy, Pip, for me to leave them parts[148], nor yet it warn't safe. But I held to it, and the harder it was, the stronger I held, for I was determined, and my mind firm made up. At last I done it. Dear boy, I done it!"

I tried to collect my thoughts[149], but I was stunned. Throughout, I had seemed to myself to attend more to the wind and the rain than to him; even now, I could not separate his voice from those voices[150], though those were loud and his was silent.

---

135) back : support, aid(돕다)
136) had been the same as me : 나와 같은 과거가 있었던(자신과 똑같은 죄수 출신이었다는 의미이다)
137) went for myself : 나 자신을 위해 (스스로) 일했다.
138) giv' you to understand : give somebody to understand(~에게 ~을 알리다)
139) agreeable to my letter : 내 편지(내용)에 따라
140) O, that he had never come! : 아, 그가 오지 않았더라면!
141) far from contented, yet, by comparison happy: 만족스럽지는 않겠지만, 상대적으로는 행복했을 텐데
142) recompense : reward, compensation(보상)
143) The blood horses : 순종의 말
144) common : 비천한, 품위 없는
145) such : such a gentleman
146) All on you : All of you
147) for anything I knew : 내가 아는 바로는
148) them parts : the parts, the districts(그 지방, 그곳)
149) collect my thoughts : 생각을 모으다, 생각을 정리하다
150) those voices : those voices of the wind and the rain

"Where will you put me?" he asked, presently. "I must be put somewheres, dear boy."

"To sleep?" said I.

"Yes. And to sleep long and sound[151])," he answered; "for I've been sea-tossed and sea-washed, months and months."

"My friend and companion," said I, rising from the sofa, "is absent; you must have[152]) his room."

"He won't come back to-morrow; will he?"

"No," said I, answering almost mechanically, in spite of my utmost efforts; "not tomorrow."

"Because, look' ee here, dear boy," he said, dropping his voice, and laying a long finger[153]) on my breast in an impressive manner, "caution is necessary."

"How do you mean? Caution?"

"By G ─, it's Death![154])"

"What's death?"

"I was sent for life[155]). It's death to come back. There's been overmuch coming back of late years[156]), and I should of a certainty[157]) be hanged if took."

Nothing was needed but this; the wretched man, after loading wretched me with his gold and silver chains for years, had risked his life to come to me, and I held it there in my keeping![158]) If I had loved him instead of abhorring him; if I had been attracted to him by the strongest admiration and affection, instead of shrinking from him with the strongest repugnance, it could have been no worse.[159]) On the contrary, it would have been better, for his preservation[160]) would then have naturally and tenderly addressed my heart.

My first care was to close the shutters[161]), so that no light might be seen from without, and then to close and make fast the doors.[162]) While I did so, he stood at the table drinking rum and eating biscuit; and when I saw him thus engaged, I saw my convict on the marshes at his meal again. It almost seemed to me as if he must stoop down presently, to file at his leg.

When I had gone into Herbert's room, and had shut off any other communication between it and the staircase than through the room in which our conversation had been held, I asked him if he would go to bed? He said yes, but asked me for some of my "gentleman's linen" to put on in the morning. I brought it out, and laid it ready for him, and my blood again ran cold[163]) when he again

---

151) sound : 잠이 깊이 든 / sound (deep) sleep : 숙면
152) have : 사용하다
153) a long finger : 가운데 손가락, 중지
154) By G ─, it's Death! : 아, 사형이지! / By G ─ : By God(가벼운 맹세 또는 감탄). '유형수는 귀국할 시 사형'이라는 이 대목은 당시의 역사적 사실과 정확하게는 일치하지 않는다는 지적이 있다.
155) I was sent for life : 나는 종신 유형수였다. / life sentence : 종신형, 무기징역
156) There's been overmuch coming back of late years : 최근 몇 년 동안에 몰래 돌아오는 자들이 너무나 많아져서
157) of a certainty : 틀림없이, 분명히
158) I held it there in my keeping! : 그의 목숨이 나의 손 안에 있다니!
159) it could have been no worse : (~할지라도) 상황이 더 이상 나빠질 수 없었다. 최악의 상황이었다.
160) his preservation : 그를 보호하는 일
161) the shutters : 덧창
162) make fast the doors : 문을 단단히 잠그다
163) my blood again ran cold : 다시 섬뜩한 느낌이 들었다.

took me by both hands to give me good night.

I got away from him, without knowing how I did it, and mended the fire[164] in the room where we had been together, and sat down by it, afraid to go to bed. For an hour or more, I remained too stunned to think; and it was not until I began to think that I began fully to know how wrecked I was, and how the ship in which I had sailed was gone to pieces.

Miss Havisham's intentions towards me, all a mere dream; Estella not designed for me[165]; I only suffered in Satis House[166] as a convenience[167], a sting for the greedy relations[168], a model with a mechanical heart to practise on when no other practice was at hand; those were the first smarts[169] I had. But, sharpest and deepest pain of all — it was for the convict,[170] guilty of I knew not what[171] crimes, and liable to[172] be taken out of those rooms where I sat thinking, and hanged at the Old Bailey door[173], that I had deserted Joe.

I would not have gone back to Joe now, I would not have gone back to Biddy now, for any consideration[174]: simply, I suppose, because my sense of my own worthless conduct to them[175] was greater than every consideration. No wisdom on earth could have given me the comfort that I should have derived from their simplicity and fidelity; but I could never, never, undo what I had done.

In every rage of wind and rush of rain,[176] I heard pursuers. Twice, I could have sworn there was a knocking and whispering at the outer door. With these fears upon me, I began either to imagine or recall that I had had mysterious warnings of this man's approach. That, for weeks gone by, I had passed faces in the streets which I had thought like his. That, these likenesses[177] had grown more numerous, as he, coming over the sea, had drawn nearer. That, his wicked spirit had somehow sent these messengers to mine, and that now on this stormy night he was as good as his word[178], and with me.

Crowding up[179] with these reflections came the reflection that I had seen him with my childish eyes to be a desperately[180] violent man; that I had heard that other convict reiterate that he had tried to murder him; that I had seen him down in the ditch tearing and fighting like a wild beast. Out of such remembrances I brought into the light of fire, a half-formed terror that it might not be

---

164) mended the fire : 꺼져가는 불을 되살렸다, 나무를 넣어 불을 지폈다
165) Estella not designed for me : Estella는 내 짝으로 정해 놓은 것이 아니었다.
166) Satis House : Miss Havisham이 살던 저택의 이름
167) as a convenience : 하나의 편리한 도구로
168) a sting for the greedy relations : 탐욕스러운 친척들을 위한 독침(Miss Havisham에게는 그녀의 재산 상속을 노리는 친척들이 있었다)
169) smart : 아픔, 고통
170) it was for the convict : 바로 이 죄수 때문이었다(단락 마지막의 that과 함께 강조 구문을 형성한다. 이하 세 개의 구는 convict를 수식한다).
171) I knew not what : 알 수 없는, 알지 못하는
172) liable to : ~을 면하기 어려운, ~할지도 모르는
173) the Old Bailey door : the Old Bailey는 the Old Bailey Street에 있는 런던 중앙형사법원(Central Criminal Court)의 속칭
174) for any consideration : 아무리 생각해 보아도 / consideration : 고려해야 할 문제
175) my sense of my own worthless conduct to them : 내가 그들에게 가치 없게 행동했다는 의식(특히, Joe가 Pip을 보려고 런던으로 찾아왔을 때 한창 '신사'생활에 겉멋이 들어 있던 Pip은 매형의 촌스러운 용모와 행동 때문에 그를 서먹서먹하게 대하였다)
176) In every rage of wind and rush of rain : 몰아치는 바람과 쏟아지는 빗속 모든 곳에서
177) these likenesses : 이 (사람과) 닮은 얼굴들, 비슷하게 생긴 사람들
178) was as good as his word : 약속을 지켰다
179) crowd up : 마구 들이밀다, 밀어닥치다
180) desperately : [구어] 몹시, 지독하게

safe to be shut up there with him in the dead of the wild solitary night[181]. This dilated until it filled the room, and impelled me to take a candle and go in and look at my dreadful burden.

   He had rolled a handkerchief round his head, and his face was set[182] and lowering[183] in his sleep. But he was asleep, and quietly too, though he had a pistol lying on the pillow. Assured of this, I softly removed the key to the outside of his door, and turned it on him before I again sat down by the fire. Gradually I slipped from the chair and lay on the floor. When I awoke, without having parted in my sleep with the perception of my wretchedness,[184] the clocks of the Eastward churches were striking five, the candles were wasted out, the fire was dead, and the wind and rain intensified the thick black darkness.

THIS IS THE END OF THE SECOND STAGE OF PIP'S EXPECTATIONS.

---

181) in the dead of the wild solitary night : 이 거칠고 외로운 밤의 한가운데에서 / dead : 한창(~하는 중), 죽은듯한 고요함
182) set : 움직이지 않는, 이를 악문
183) lowering : 기분이 안 좋은, 찌푸린
184) without having parted in my sleep with the perception of my wretchedness : 잠을 자면서도 내가 처한 비참한 처지에 대한 생각을 떨쳐내지 못하고

George Eliot
– 「Silas Marner : The Weaver of Raveloe」

제 **5** 장

「*Silas Marner*」는 18세기 후반부터 19세기 초를 배경으로 George Eliot가 어린 시절에 보았던 "린넨 직조공"을 그리고 있다. 이 작품에 대한 접근은 도덕적 관점과 사회적 관점으로 볼 수 있다. 주인공 Marner가 잃었던 인간애를 찾으며, 인간의 사랑이 금보다 더 귀하다고 깨닫는 결론, 그리고 착한 Marner는 보상받고 Godfrey는 벌을 받는다는 인과응보식 해석이 도덕적 관점의 해석이다. 또한 개인과 사회의 유기적 관계, 이를테면 사회에서 소외되었던 Marner가 Raveloe 사회에 흡수되는 과정이 작품에서 강조된다.

출제 경향 및 수험 대책

래블로(Raveloe)라는 시골과 랜턴 야드(Lantern Yeard)라는 도시가 대조되고, 이 대조 이외에도 고립된 개인과 사회, 상류 지배층과 하층 민중의 계급적 대조가 어우러진 작품이다. Marner가 공동체와의 관계를 회복하고 공동체에 동화되는 과정을 중시하므로 이러한 대조의 관계를 작품의 해석과 연관시켜 볼 필요가 있다.

제 1 절 작가의 생애

조지 엘리어트(1819~1880, 본명은 Mary Ann Evans이고 필명으로 George Eliot를 사용하였다)는 영문학 사상 유래 없이 소설 장르가 융성했던 19세기뿐만 아니라 현대에 이르기까지 영문학에서 확고한 위치를 차지하는 작가이다. 그녀는 1819년 11월 22일 영국 워릭셔(Warwickshire)주의 너니턴(Nuneaton)에 위치한 아버리(Arbury) 사우스팜(South Farm)에서 태어났다.

조지 엘리어트의 아버지는 뉴디게이트(Newdigate)가(家)의 아버리홀의 사유지(Arbury Hall Estate)의 관리자 Robert Evans이며, 재혼 상대인 어머니는 지역 방앗간의 소유주(mill-owner)의 딸 Christiana Pearson이다. 그녀는 초등학교에서 기숙사 생활을 하면서 교육을 받았고, 중학교 시절에는 이탈리아어와 프랑스어를 배웠다. 학교 선생님인 Maris Lewis의 영향으로 조지 엘리어트는 청교도에 대한 열정도 깊어갔다. 그녀가 17세이던 1836년에 어머니가 돌아가시고, 1841년에 그녀와 그녀의 아버지는 코번트리(Conventry)로 이사했다. 이곳에서 그녀는 급진 사상을 전파하던 Charles Bray와 그의 매부인 Charles Christian Hennell을 만나 새로운 종교적·정치적인 이념과 과학적 사고를 접하게 되었다. 특히 그녀는 Hennell의 저서인 『*An Inquiry Concerning the Origin of Christianity*』(1838)를 읽고 그동안 그녀가 회의감을 갖고 있던 편협하고 극단적인 종교적인 신념을 버리고 불가지론(agnostic)적인 경향을 띠게 되었다. 1849년, 자신과 함께 살던 그녀의 아버지가 그녀에게 연 수입 100파운드만을 남기고 세상을 떠나자 생활고를 겪게 된 그녀는 런던에서 자유기고가로 활동을 시작했다. 그러던 중 그녀와 내연의 관계였던 George Henry Lewes가 죽자 그녀는 비탄에 빠져 더 이상 글을 쓰지 않았다. 그 후 그녀는 1880년에 그녀의 재산을 관리하던 은행가인 John Cross와 정식으로 결혼했으나 같은 해 12월에 사망하고 말았다.

『*Adam Bede*』(1859)는 3권으로 이루어진 Eliot의 첫 장편 소설로서 가상의 전원마을을 배경으로 네 주인공의 사랑이야기를 다룬다. 이 작품은 깊은 인간적인 동정과 엄격한 도덕적 판단이 결합된 내용에 시골풍의 분위기가 풍기는 사실주의 작품이다. 「*The Mill on the Floss*」(1860)는 가상의 작은 마을 근처의 플로스 강변에 물방앗간을 배경으로 작품이 전개된다. 「*Silas Marner: the Weaver of Raveloe*」(1861)는 고향에서 친구에게 배신당한 주인공이 신 (God)과 인간에 대한 믿음을 잃고 고독하게 혼자 살던 중, 우연히 다가온 Eppie라는 여자아이를 키우게 되면서 그 아이를 통하여 다시 인간에 대한 사랑을 되찾게 되는 이야기를 그린 작품이다. 「*Middlemarch*」(1871~1872)는 'Middlemarch'라는 지역에 사는 여러 계층의 사람들, 즉 상점주인, 노동자, 농부, 제조업자, 목수 등 평범한 사람들의 일상을 유머(humour)와 애수(pathos)를 이용하여 사실적으로 묘사한 걸작이다. 이와 같이 George Eliot의 작품들은 전통적인 영국의 농촌 공동체 생활을 주로 다루었으며, 그 속에서 살아가는 소박한 인물들의 심리를 사실주의적으로 심도 있게 묘사하였다.

> **더 알아두기**
>
> **George Eliot의 주요작품**
> * 「*Adam Bede*」(1859)
> 3권으로 이루어진 George Eliot의 첫 장편소설로서 깊은 인간적인 동정과 엄격한 도덕적 판단이 결합된 내용으로 구성된 작품이다. 전반적으로 시골풍의 분위기가 풍기는 사실주의 작품이다.
>
> * 「*Silas Marner: the Weaver of Raveloe*」(1861)
> 고향에서 친구에게 배신당한 주인공이 신(God)과 인간에 대한 믿음을 잃고 고독하게 혼자 살던 중에 우연히 다가온 Eppie라는 여자아이를 키우게 되고 그 아이를 통하여 다시 인간에 대한 사랑을 되찾게 되는 이야기를 그린 작품이다.
>
> * 「*Middlemarch*」(1871~1872)
> 'Milddlemarch'라는 지역에 사는 여러 계층의 사람들 즉 상점주인, 노동자, 농부, 제조업자, 목수 등 평범한 사람들의 일상을 유머와 애수를 이용하여 사실적으로 묘사한 작품이다.

제 2 절 작품 세계

직조공(weaver)인 Silas Marner는 친구 William Dane과 약혼녀 Sarah의 배신으로 도둑이라는 누명을 쓰고 영국 북부 지방의 고향인 Lantern Yard를 떠나 영국 중부(Midlands)에 위치한 시골 마을 Raveloe로 이주한다. 옷감을 짜고 그것을 팔아 번 돈을 모으는 것이 Marner의 유일한 낙이다. 그러나 그 돈을 몽땅 도둑맞고 실의에 빠진 Marner가 여자아이 Eppie를 키우게 되면서 신과 인간에 대한 믿음을 회복하는 이야기를 그리고 있다. 사회로부터 추방당한 고립된 영혼이 어린아이의 순수한 마음과 교류를 통해 절망을 딛고 인간사회로 복귀하는, 인간이라는 존재로서의 순수한 사랑에 대한 중요성을 강조한 작품이다.

1 배경

이 작품의 배경이 되는 Raveloe는 전통적인 귀족 사회에서 현대 사회로 진입하는 사회적 변동의 시기로 맞추어져 있다. 작가도 '구식 농촌 생활의 이야기'라고 말하고 있듯이 Raveloe라는 전통적 지역사회는 나폴레옹, 산업사회의 에너지와 청교도적인 열광이라는 시대사조와는 거리가 먼, 비교적 외부의 영향을 받지 않는 조용한 세계이다.

한편, Raveloe 마을의 Rainbow 술집에 자주 모여드는 사람들로는 자기 자랑하기를 좋아하는 수의사 Mr. Dowlas, 술집 주인 Mr. Snell, 이 마을의 전설적 내력을 잘 알고 있다는 양복점 주인이자 교구 서기인 Mr. Macey, 바퀴수선공 Mr. Winthrop과 그의 지혜롭고 다정한 부인 Dolly Winthrop 등이 있으며, 환경에 순응하며 소박하고 평범한 생활을 즐기는 그들의 낙관적인 인생 태도를 작가는 사랑과 공감으로 묘사하고 있다.

2 변화

Silas Marner의 삶의 전부였던 Lantern Yard에서의 배반은 그를 무신론자로 만든다. 낯선 지역인 Raveloe로 이주한 그는 자신의 존재에 대한 감각도 상실하고 거미처럼 순전히 충동에 의해서 옷감을 짜는 '벌레'가 된다. 그러나 이러한 생활에서 그에게 몇 가지 변화가 일어난다.

(1) 첫 번째 변화

Marner가 심장병과 몸이 붓는 병으로 고통 받는 Sally Oates를 보고 동정심이 생기면서 약초에 대한 지식을 토대로 그녀의 병을 치료하는 것이다. 약초를 다루는 그의 모습은 마을 사람들에게 두렵고도 신비한 모습으로 보여 사람들의 의심을 사기도 한다. 그러나 Marner의 행위는 인간 이하로 격하된 Marner의 마음속에 사랑이 존재한다는 증거이며, 그가 Raveloe에 온 이후 처음으로 벌레 같은 존재에서 벗어날 수 있는 가능성을 보여주는 사건이다.

(2) 두 번째 변화

금화 도난 사건은 마을 사람들이 Marner의 고통에 공감하고 그의 집을 방문하기 시작하도록 하는 계기가 된다. 이후로 Marner는 마을 공동체의 일원이 된다.

(3) 마지막 변화

마지막으로 Eppie를 얻게 되는 사건은 Marner와 이웃 사람들과의 교류가 더욱 활발해지는 결정적인 사건이다. Eppie는 Godfrey와 그의 숨겨 놓은 아내 Molly Farren의 딸이다. Molly는 Godfrey의 냉대에 대한 저항으로 자신의 신분을 밝히기 위하여 망년회가 열리고 있는 Cass가(家)에 딸을 데리고 가다가 아편을 흡입하고 눈 위에 쓰러져 동사한다. Eppie는 Marner의 집에서 나오는 불빛을 따라 그의 집으로 들어가 화덕 앞에서 잠이 든다. 새해 전야(New Year's Eve)에 집으로 돌아온 Marner는 희미한 시력 때문에 Eppie의 황금빛 머리를 자신이 도난당한 황금으로 착각하지만, 딱딱한 감촉의 금화 대신 부드럽고 따뜻한 머리털이 그의 손에 닿는다. 이렇게 Eppie의 머리를 만지는 Marner의 행위는 금화의 딱딱함과 머리의 부드러움을 대조시키며, 그의 삶을 소생시키고 황금으로부터 해방시킴을 상징한다.

3 인과응보 중요 ★★

Molly는 Godfrey의 법적 아내이지만 그의 숨겨놓은 아내의 역할로 한정되어 있다. 그녀는 긴 검은 머리에 야윈 젊은 여인으로, 누더기 옷을 입은 떠돌이 같은데, 결혼반지는 끼고 있었다는 Mr. Kimble의 외모 묘사 외에는 그녀의 실생활이나 내면생활에 대한 묘사는 찾을 수 없다. Godfrey는 Molly의 죽은 얼굴에 단 한 번의 시선을 던졌을 뿐인데, 16년간 그의 마음속에 아로새겨져 있었다는 것은 그의 일생 동안 Molly가 그의 양심의 가책으로 남아 고통을 주었다는 것이다. 이것은 그가 Molly를 남성의 성적 권력과 경제적 권력의 희생물로 만들어 인간의 시야로부터 소리 없이 사라지게 만든 죄의 대가로, 이는 죽음에 버금가는 형벌이다. Godfrey는 Molly가 죽은 후 합법적으로 Nancy와 결혼하지만 Nancy와 아이를 갖지 못한다. 한편 악하고 부도덕한 Dunstan Cass는 Marner의 돈을 훔쳐 달아나다가 채석장(stone-pits)의 물웅덩이에 빠져 죽는다.

4 사회 비판

(1) 가부장적 사회와 제도에 대한 비판

생부라면 법적 아버지가 될 요구와 권리를 당연하다고 여기는 영국 사회의 가부장적 구조와, 전통적 권위로 정당화하는 권리 및 특권제도를 비판하며 고정된 법보다 도덕적 법이 우선되어야 함을 소설에서 드러낸다.

① Godfrey는 친부의 권리를 내세워 양부인 Marner에게서 Eppie를 요구한다.

② Marner는 생부 Godfrey가 Eppie를 버렸기 때문에 이제는 아무런 권리가 없다고 주장하지만 Nancy는 혈연관계가 있는 생부의 권리가 그렇지 않은 양부의 권리보다 우세하다고 주장한다.

③ Eppie가 양부와 생부, 노동계급 생활과 상류계급 생활, 노동자의 아내와 귀부인 사이의 어려운 선택을 쉽게 할 수 있었던 것은 양부에 대한 사랑이 다른 이성적인 논리보다 우세했기 때문으로 볼 수 있다.

(2) 작가의 관점 중요 ★

① 결국 Eppie는 신데렐라가 되기를 거부하고 사랑하는 양부 곁에 남아 자신이 원하는 남자와 결혼하고 노동하는 충족된 삶을 살겠다는 도덕적 선택을 한다.

② Eppie의 태도는 유기적인 사회적 결속이 이기적인 권리와 그에 대한 윤리에 집착하는 상류계급보다는 노동계급에서 형성되고 있음을 암시한다.

5 선함과 사랑

(1) Lantern Yard

Marner는 과거에 대한 진실을 찾고 싶어 Eppie를 데리고 그의 고향 Lantern Yard로 향한다. 그러나 그곳에는 그가 기대했던 빛과 질서 대신 암흑과 파괴만이 있을 뿐이다. Lantern Yard라는 말이 상징 하듯 한때는 빛이었던 이곳은 암흑 속으로 사라졌고 산업화로 인해 교회의 자리에 공장이 흉한 모습으 로 서 있다.

(2) 자신의 내부에 있는 타인에 대한 사랑의 빛

Marner가 믿어야 할 것은 자신의 내부에 있는 타인에 대한 사랑의 빛이다. Marner가 Eppie를 친자식 처럼 사랑하게 되었을 때, 그는 충분한 빛을 갖게 된 것이다. Marner는 그가 겪은 고통을 통하여 다른 사람들과 자기 자신 속에 선(善)이 있다는 것을 확신하게 되고 그것이 바로 그의 사랑과 믿음의 근본 이 되는 것이다. 이 소설은 "오 아버지, 얼마나 우리 집이 좋아요! 우리보다 더 행복한 사람이 있을 것 같지 않아요."(O father, what a pretty home ours is! I think nobody could be happier than we are.)라는 사랑과 기쁨으로 가득한 Eppie의 말로 끝난다. 우울하고 음침하게 시작한 Silas Marner 는 이처럼 행복하고 환하게 끝난다.

제 3 절 줄거리

영국 중부의 공업도시 Lantern Yard에 사는 직조공 Silas Marner는 친구 William Dane의 배반으로 교회 의 돈을 훔쳤다는 누명을 쓰게 되어 그곳을 떠났다. 작은 농촌 마을 Raveloe로 이주한 Marner는 휴일도 없이 아마포를 짜면서 15년간 고립된 생활을 한다. 그의 유일한 위안은 리넨(아마포)을 짜면서 벌어들인 금화를 혼자 밤마다 세어보는 일이다. 이처럼 외롭게 살던 그에게 큰 변화가 일어난다. 그가 아끼던 금화를 도난당하고 느닷없는 일 때문에 Eppie를 양녀로 맡게 된 것이다. 그러나 그는 금화 대신 금발의 어린아이 를 받아들여 아버지 노릇을 하게 되면서 행복을 되찾는다. 그는 Eppie를 통해 이웃들, 즉 Raveloe의 마을 공동체와 관계를 맺음으로써 인간에 대한 신뢰와 사랑, 공동체와 관계를 회복하는 셈이다.

한편, 마을 지주의 아들인 Godfrey는 술집여자인 Molly Farren과 비밀 결혼한 사실을 두고 전전긍긍해 한다. 이 사실을 아버지께 말하겠다고 협박하는 동생과 사람들에게 진상을 폭로하려는 Molly로 인해 고 민하던 차에 갑자기 동생이 행방불명되고, Molly는 길에서 얼어 죽어 버린다. 그리고 그는 덕분에 평소 흠모하던 상류층 여성인 Nancy와 결혼한다. Nancy와 결혼한 뒤 그는 자식을 가질 수 없고, 16년 전 행방 불명되었던 동생 Dunstan의 유해가 스톤피츠 채석장 옆 물웅덩이에서 발견되면서 Marner의 금화를 훔친 범인이 동생이었던 것으로 드러난다. Godfrey는 이를 자신의 죄에 대한 징벌로 받아들이고 과거에 저지 른 죄를 숨길 수 없다는 인과응보를 깨닫는다. 이러한 깨달음으로 뒤늦게나마 그는 아내에게 Eppie가 친 딸이라고 밝히고 과거의 죄를 뉘우치기 위해 Marner의 집에 찾아가지만, Eppie를 딸로 인정하고 자기 집에 들이려는 제의를 거절당한다. Godfrey는 Marner 외에 다른 아버지를 상상할 수 없다는 Eppie의 단호한 말을 듣고, 과거에 Eppie를 인정하지 않았던 그 죄는 부유함이나 지위 그 무엇으로도 보상할 수 없음을 깨닫는다.

제 4 절 작품의 주제

1 인과응보

(1) 인과응보의 법칙을 믿지 않는 인물들

Dustan Cass는 타고난 행운을 믿고, Godfrey는 끈기 있게 자신의 운명의 귀추를 기다리지만, 두 인물 모두 인과응보를 믿지 않는다.

(2) 인과응보의 법칙을 믿는 인물들

Dolly Winthrop은 지상에서의 선행은 보상받는다고 믿는다. Silas Marner 역시 Dolly와 같은 생각을 가지지만, 교회의 돈을 훔쳤다는 누명을 쓰고 자신의 결백을 증명하기 위해 교회의 사람들이 제안한 제비뽑기 신점에 참여하는데 그 결과가 유죄로 판명나자 교회에서 파문당하고 이에 절망하여 세상을 포기하게 된다.

2 종교의 문제

(1) 기독교라는 종교 하에 Silas Marner는 엄격한 믿음을, Dolly Winthrop은 이교도적인 성격의 믿음을 제시한다.

(2) 편협한 청교도들이 살고 있는 Lantern Yard와 따뜻한 인정을 베풀며 살아가는 성공회 사람들의 Raveloe를 대조적으로 부각시키고 있다.

3 가족 간의 사랑, 변화, 인간소외

(1) 가족 간의 사랑

Godfrey는 Silas가 금을 잃은 가난한 상황에서 Eppie에게 행복을 보장해 줄 수 없다는 편견을 가지고 Eppie를 데리고 가려고 하지만, Eppie는 친부인 Godfrey를 거절하고 Silas 옆에 남는다. 이러한 Eppie의 행동은 Godfrey가 감수해야 할 인과응보의 고통인 측면도 있지만, 경제적인 어려움과 애정이 공존할 수 있다는 깨달음을 준다.

(2) 변화

모든 변화는 수많은 작은 요소에 의해서 이루어진다. 따라서 평범한 인간은 모든 변화를 통제할 수도 감지할 수도 없다.

(3) 인간소외

한 개인이 신에 대한 믿음을 상실했을 때, 그 개인은 사회의 공동체로부터 소외된다. 본 소설은 개인이 자신을 소외시킨 공동체 사회로 다시 진입하는 과정을 묘사한다.

제5절 등장인물

1 Silas Marner 중요 ★

단순하고 본능적이며, 깊이 있는 교육을 받지 못하였으나 상상력이 풍부하고 자연에 대한 경외심이 있는 노동자 계급의 주인공이다. 39세 정도의 직조공으로, 원래 살던 마을 Lantern Yard 교회에서 신앙심을 인정받던 청년이었으나, 누명을 쓰게 된 후 신(God)에 대한 불신과 인간에 대한 실망감을 돈으로 보상받고자 일에만 집중한다. 그러나 잃어버렸던 신에 대한 믿음과 인간에 대한 애정을 되찾는 인물이다. 베틀 짜는 일을 매일 하느라 허리가 휘었고 늙어 보이며, 가끔 발작을 일으키는 질병을 갖고 있다.

2 Eppie

Silas Marner가 입양하는 금발 머리의 여자아이이다. 고립된 삶을 살아가는 Marner를 외부 세계와 연결시키고, 타인들과 조화롭게 살아갈 수 있도록 하는 역할을 한다. 후에 평범한 노동자 청년인 Aaron Winthrop과 결혼한다.

3 Godfrey Cass

Silas Marner와는 정반대의 인간상을 가진 인물이다. 젊고 멋있으며, 부유하고 매력적이다. Marner가 억울한 누명을 쓸 때에도 자신이 저지른 죗값을 교묘히 피한다. 그가 악한인지 또는 비극적 주인공인지는 보는 시각에 따라 달라진다.

4 Dustan Cass

Godfrey의 동생으로, 숨겨둔 여자와 딸이 있는 형의 약점을 이용하여 형에게 돈을 뜯어내는 악한 인물이다.

5 Squire Cass

Raveloe 마을에서 가장 재력 있고 존경받는 인물이지만, 알고 보면 자신의 아들들에 대한 사랑보다 재산에 더 많은 관심을 갖는 이기적이고 자기중심적인 사람이다. Red House의 소유주이다.

6 Nancy Lammeter

Godfrey Cass가 결혼하고 싶어하는 여인이지만, 숨겨둔 아내 Molly 때문에 Godfrey가 청혼을 미루는 여인이다. 결국 둘은 결혼하게 되지만 Nancy는 입양 문제를 거부하는 등 자신이 정한 엄격한 도덕률에 갇힌 인물이다. 그녀가 높은 도덕성의 본보기인지, 아니면 엄격한 원칙에만 지배되는 성격을 가진 여인인지는 보는 시각에 따라서 달라진다.

7 Priscilla Lammeter

Nancy Lammeter보다 다섯 살 많은 언니로, 스스로가 못생겼다고 여기지만, 쾌활하고 명랑하다. 평생 독신으로 살아가기를 고집하는 인물이다.

8 Dolly Winthrop

비록 많이 배우지는 못했지만 Raveloe에서 인간이 지켜야 할 가치관을 대변하는 인물이다. 모든 인물에게 다정하며 덕목을 베푼다.

9 Aaron Winthrop

Dolly Winthrop의 아들이자 Eppie의 결혼 상대이다.

10 Molly Farren

Godfrey Cass의 숨겨진 아내이자 Eppie의 친모이다. 한때 미모의 여성이었지만 아편과 술 중독으로 동사한다.

11 그 외의 인물들

(1) William Dane

Lantern Yard에서 Silas Marner를 모함한 친구이다.

(2) Sarah

Silas Marner의 약혼녀였지만 Marner가 도둑으로 몰린 후 William Dane과 결혼한다.

(3) Sally Oates

구두 수선공의 아내이다. 심장병과 부기에 고통받지만 Marner가 약초로 치료해 준다.

(4) Mr. Macey

양복점 주인이자 교구 서기이다.

(5) Jem Rodney

Marner가 발작을 일으키는 순간을 목격하는 인물이다. Marner는 자신의 금화를 훔친 도둑으로 Jem을 의심한다.

(6) Mr. Kimble

의사 자격증은 없지만 아버지의 직업을 물려받아 Raveloe 마을의 의사로 활동한다.

제 6 절 작품의 구조(Plot)와 시점 및 기법

1 구조

총 2부로 구성(1부 : 1~15장, 2부 : 16~22장)되어 있고, 각 부의 시차는 16년이다.

(1) 1부(1~15장)

Silas Marner는 신과 사람에 대한 불신의 감정을 갖고 엄격한 청교도의 분위기가 장악하던 Lantern Yard를 떠나 인간애가 살아있는 성공회 마을인 Raveloe에 정착한다. 리넨을 짜서 번 돈을 저축하는 낙으로 살아가다 생명처럼 여기던 귀중한 돈을 도둑맞은 후 실의에 빠진다. 어느 날, 집으로 Eppie라는 소녀가 찾아오면서 Marner는 따뜻한 인간미를 되찾는다.

(2) 2부(16~22장)

10여 년이 지난 후, 돈을 훔쳐간 범인의 정체와 성인이 된 소녀 Eppie의 부모가 누구인지 밝혀진다.

2 시점과 기법

(1) 시점

3인칭 전지적 작가시점으로 소설이 전개된다. 그러나 때때로 작가의 도덕적 중요성에 대한 설교가 등장한다.

(2) 문체

정확하고 엄선된 어휘의 강건체로 쓰여 있다. 문장이 늘어지고 추상적이며 특색 없는 어휘가 쓰이기도 한다.

(3) 다양한 상징 중요 ★★

다양한 상징이 사용되고 있다. Silas Marner는 거미에 비유되고, Eppie는 나무처럼 자란다고 표현되어 있다. 말(horse)은 귀족의 등장을 알리고, Silas Marner의 금색 동전(guinea)은 Eppie의 금발(gold)과 함께 둘 다 소중한 존재임을 나타낸다. 빛과 어둠의 대조도 찾을 수 있다. Silas Marner의 베틀(loom)은 계속 움직이지만 어느 곳으로도 이동하지 않는 물건으로, Marner의 끊임없는 노동과 변함없는 성격을 상징한다.

제 7 절 Text

Part 1

Chapter 1

In the days when the spinning-wheels hummed[1] busily in the farmhouses — and even great ladies, clothed in silk and thread-lace, had their toy spinning-wheels of polished[2] oak — there might be seen in districts far away among the lanes, or deep in the bosom of the hills, certain pallid undersized men, who, by the side of the brawny country-folk looked like the remnants of a disinherited race. The shepherd's dog barked fiercely when one of these alien-looking men appeared on the upland, dark against the early winter sunset; for what dog likes a figure bent under a heavy bag? — and these pale men rarely stirred abroad without that mysterious burden. The shepherd himself, though he had good reason to believe that the bag held nothing but flaxen thread, or else the long rolls of strong linen[3] spun from that thread, was not quite sure that this trade of weaving, indispensable though it was, could be carried on entirely without the help of the Evil One. In that far-off time superstition clung easily round every person or thing that was at all unwonted, or even intermittent and occasional merely, like the visits of the peddler[4] or the knife-grinder. No one knew where wandering men had their homes or their origin; and how was a man to be explained unless you at least knew somebody who knew his father and mother? To the peasants of old times, the world outside their own direct experience was a region of vagueness and mystery; to their untravelled thought a state of wandering was a conception as dim as the winter life of the swallows that came back with the spring; and even a settler, if he came from distant parts, hardly ever ceased to be viewed with a remnant of distrust, which would have prevented any surprise if a long course of inoffensive[5] conduct on his part had ended in the commission of a crime; especially if he had any reputation for knowledge, or showed any skill in handicraft. All cleverness, whether in the rapid use of that difficult instrument the tongue, or in some other art unfamiliar to villagers[6], was in itself suspicious; honest folk, born and bred in a visible manner, were mostly not overwise or clever — at least, not beyond such a matter as knowing the signs of the weather; and the process by which rapidity and dexterity of any kind were acquired[7] was so wholly hidden that they partook of the nature of conjuring. In this way it came to pass that those scattered linen weavers — emigrants from the town into the country-were to the last regarded as[8] aliens by their rustic neighbours, and usually contracted the eccentric habits which belong to a state of loneliness.

---

1) hum : (기계 등이) 윙윙거리다
2) polished : 광택 나는, 연마된
3) linen : 리넨(아마사)
4) peddler : 행상인(이후 Raveloe에서 Silas Marner의 돈이 없어졌을 때 가장 먼저 의심받는 사람은 마을에 이따금씩 찾아오는 행상인이다)
5) inoffensive : 해가 없는, 악의가 없는
6) villager : 마을 사람, 시골 사람
7) acquired : 획득한, 습득한
8) regard A as B : A를 B로 생각(간주)하다

In the early years of this century such a linen weaver[9], named Silas Marner, worked at his vocation in a stone cottage that stood among the nutty hedgerows near the village of Raveloe, and not far from the edge of a deserted[10] stone pit. The questionable sound of Silas's loom[11], so unlike the natural cheerful trotting of the winnowing machine, or the simpler rhythm of the flail, had a half-fearful fascination for the Raveloe boys, who would often leave off their nutting or bird's-nesting to peep in at the window of the stone cottage, counterbalancing a certain awe at the mysterious action of the loom by a pleasant sense of scornful superiority, drawn from the mockery of its alternating noises, along with[12] the bent, treadmill attitude of the weaver. But sometimes it happened that Marner, pausing to adjust an irregularity in his thread, became aware of the small scoundrels, and, though chary of his time, he liked their intrusion so ill that he would descend from his loom, and opening the door would fix on them a gaze that was always enough to make them take to their legs in terror. For how was it possible to believe that those large brown protuberant eyes in Silas Marner's pale face really saw nothing very distinctly that was not close to them, and not rather that their dreadful stare could dart cramp, or rickets, or a wry mouth at any boy who happened to be in the rear? They had perhaps heard their fathers and mothers hint that Silas Marner could cure folks' rheumatism if he had a mind, and add, still more darkly, that if you could only speak the devil fair enough, he might save you the cost of the doctor. Such strange lingering echoes of the old demon-worship might perhaps even now be caught by the diligent listener among the gray-haired peasantry; for the rude mind with difficulty associates the ideas of power and benignity. A shadowy[13] conception of power that by much persuasion can be induced to refrain from inflicting harm is the shape most easily taken by the sense of the Invisible in the minds of men who have always been pressed close by primitive wants, and to whom a life of hard toil has never been illuminated by any enthusiastic religious faith. To them pain and mishap[14] present a far wider range of possibilities than gladness and enjoyment; their imagination is almost barren of the images that feed desire and hope, but is all overgrown by recollections that are a perpetual pasture to fear. "Is there anything you can fancy that you would like to eat?" I once said to an old labouring man who was in his last illness, and who had refused all the food his wife had offered him. "No," he answered, "I've never been used to nothing but common victual[15], and I can't eat that." Experience had bred no fancies in him that could raise the phantasm[16] of appetite.

And Raveloe was a village where many of the old echoes lingered, undrowned by new voices. Not that it was one of those barren parishes[17] lying on the outskirts of civilization — inhabited by meagre sheep and thinly scattered shepherds; on the contrary, it lay in the rich central plain of what

---

9) linen weaver : 직조공
10) deserted : 사람이 살지 않는
11) loom : 베틀, 직기(Silas Marner의 loom은 작품에서 중요한 상징으로 나타난다)
12) along with : ~와 함께, 같이
13) shadowy : 어슴푸레한, 환상의
14) mishap : 사고, 재난, 불상사
15) victual : 음식물, 양식
16) phantasm : 환영, 허깨비
17) barren parishes : 메마른(불모의) 교구, 지역 행정구

we are pleased to call Merry England, and held farms which, speaking from a spiritual point of view[18], paid highly desirable tithes. But it was nestled in a snug well-wooded hollow, quite an hour's journey on horseback from any turnpike, where it was never reached by the vibrations of the coach-horn, or of public opinion. It was an important-looking village, with a fine old church and large churchyard in the heart of it, and two or three large brick-and-stone homesteads, with well-walled orchards and ornamental weathercocks, standing close upon the road, and lifting more imposing fronts than the rectory, which peeped from among the trees on the other side of the churchyard — a village which showed at once the summits of its social life, and told the practised eye that there was no great park and manor house in the vicinity, but that there were several chiefs in Raveloe who could farm badly quite at their ease, drawing enough money from their bad farming, in those wartimes, to live in a rollicking fashion, and keep a jolly Christmas, Whitsun, and Easter tide.

It was fifteen years since Silas Marner had first come to Raveloe; he was then simply a pallid young man, with prominent, shortsighted brown eyes, whose appearance would have had nothing strange for people of average culture and experience, but for the villagers near whom he had come to settle it had mysterious peculiarities which corresponded with[19] the exceptional nature of his occupation, and his advent from an unknown region called "North'ard." So had his way of life: — He invited no comer to step across his door-sill, and he never strolled into the village to drink a pint at the Rainbow, or to gossip[20] at the wheelwright's: He sought no man or woman save for the purposes of his calling, or in order to supply himself with the necessaries; and it was soon clear to the Raveloe lasses that he would never urge one of them to accept him against her will quite as if he had heard them declare that they would never marry a dead man come to life again. This view of Marner's personality was not without another ground than his pale face and unexampled eyes; for Jem Rodney, the mole-catcher[21], averred[22] that, one evening as he was returning homeward, he saw Silas Marner leaning against a stile with a heavy bag on his back, instead of resting the bag on the stile as a man in his senses would have done; and that, on coming up to him he saw that Marner's eyes were set like a dead man's, and he spoke to him, and shook him, and his limbs were stiff and his hands clutched[23] the bag as if they'd been made of iron; but just as he had made up his mind that the weaver was dead, he came all right again, like, as you may say, in the winking of an eye, and said, "Good-night," and walked off. All this Jem swore he had seen, more by token that it was the very day he had been mole-catching on Squire Cass's land down by the old saw pit. Some said Marner must have been in a "fit[24]," a word which seemed to explain things otherwise incredible; but the argumentative Mr. Macey, clerk of the parish, shook his head,

---

18) speaking from a spiritual point of view : 영적인 시점으로 이야기하다.
19) correspond with : 일치하다, 교신하다
20) gossip : 잡담하다
21) mole-catcher : 두더지 사냥꾼, 밀렵꾼
22) aver : 사실이라고 단언하다, 증언하다
23) clutch : 움켜쥠
24) fit : 발작

and asked if anybody was ever known to go off in a fit and not fall down. A fit was a stroke, wasn't it? and it was in the nature of a stroke to partly take away the use of a man's limbs and throw him on the parish, if he'd got no children to look to. No, no; it was no stroke that would let a man stand on his legs, like a horse between the shafts and then walk off[25] as soon as you can say "Gee!" But there might be such a thing as a man's soul being loose from his body, and going out and in, like a bird out of its nest and back; and that was how folks got overwise, for they went to school in this shell-less state to those who could teach them more than their neighbours could learn with their five senses and the parson. And where did Master Marner get his knowledge of herbs from — and charms too, if he liked to give them away? Jem Rodney's story was no more than what might have been expected by anybody who had seen how Marner had cured Sally Oates, and made her sleep like a baby, when her heart had been beating enough to burst her body, for two months and more, while she had been under the doctor's care. He might cure more folks if he would; but he was worth speaking fair, if it was only to keep him from doing you a mischief.

It was partly to this vague fear that Marner was indebted for protecting him from the persecution that his singularities might have drawn upon him, but still more to the fact that, the old linen weaver in the neighbouring parish of Tarley being dead, his handicraft made him a highly welcome settler to the richer housewives of the district, and even to the more provident cottagers, who had their little stock of yarn[26] at the year's end. And their sense of his usefulness would have counteracted[27] any repugnance or suspicion which was not confirmed by a deficiency in the quality or the tale of the cloth he wove for them. And the years had rolled on without producing any change in the impressions of the neighbours concerning Marner, except the change from novelty to habit. At the end of fifteen years the Raveloe men said just the same things about Silas Marner as at the beginning. They did not say them quite so often, but they believed them much more strongly when they did say them. There was only one important addition which the years had brought; it was that Master Marner had laid by a fine sight of money somewhere, and that he could buy up "bigger men" than himself.

But while opinion concerning him had remained nearly stationary[28], and his daily habits had presented scarcely any visible change, Marner's inward life had been a history and a metamorphosis[29], as that of every fervid nature must be when it has fled or been condemned to solitude. His life, before he came to Raveloe, had been filled with the movement, the mental activity, and the close fellowship which in that day as in this marked the life of an artisan early incorporated in a narrow religious sect, where the poorest layman has the chance of distinguishing himself by gifts of speech, and has at the very least the weight of a silent voter in the government of his community. Marner was highly thought of in that little hidden world known to itself as the church assembling in Lantern

---

25) walk off : 떠나다, 퇴장하다
26) yarn : 방적사
27) counteract : 거스르다, 방해하다, 중화하다
28) nearly stationary : 거의 움직이지 않는
29) metamorphosis : 변형, 변질

Yard. He was believed to be a young man of exemplary life and ardent faith; and a peculiar interest had been centred in him ever since he had fallen at a prayer-meeting into a mysterious rigidity and suspension of consciousness which, lasting for an hour or more, had been mistaken for death. To have sought a medical explanation for this phenomenon[30] would have been held by Silas himself, as well as by his minister and fellow-members, a wilful self-exclusion from the spiritual significance that might lie therein. Silas was evidently a brother selected for a peculiar discipline; and though the effort to interpret this discipline was discouraged by the absence on his part of any spiritual vision during his outward trance, yet it was believed by himself and others that its effect was seen in an accession of light and fervour[31]. A less truthful man than he might have been tempted into the subsequent creation of a vision in the form of resurgent memory; a less sane man might have believed in such a creation. But Silas was both sane and honest, though, as with many honest and fervent men, culture had not defined any channels for his sense of mystery, and so it spread itself over the proper pathway of inquiry and knowledge. He had inherited from his mother some acquaintance with medicinal herbs and their preparation — a little store of wisdom which she had imparted to him as a solemn bequest[32] — but of late years he had had doubts about the lawfulness of applying this knowledge, believing that herbs could have no efficacy without prayer, and that prayer might suffice[33] without herbs; so that the inherited delight to wander through the fields in search of foxglove[34] and dandelion[35] and coltsfoot[36] began to wear to him the character of a temptation.

Among the members of his church there was one young man, a little older than himself, with whom he had long lived in such close friendship that it was the custom of their Lantern Yard brethren[37] to call them David and Jonathan. The real name of the friend was William Dane, and he, too, was regarded as a shining instance of youthful piety, though somewhat given to over-severity towards weaker brethren, and to be so dazzled by his own light as to hold himself wiser than his teachers. But whatever blemishes others might discern in William, to his friend's mind he was faultless; for Marner had one of those impressible self-doubting natures which, at an inexperienced age admire imperativeness and lean on contradiction. The expression of trusting simplicity in Marner's face, heightened by that absence of special observation, that defenceless, deer-like gaze which belongs to large prominent eyes, was strongly contrasted by the self-complacent suppression of inward triumph that lurked in[38] the narrow slanting eyes and compressed lips of William Dane. One of the most frequent topics of conversation between the two friends was assurance of salvation. Silas confessed that he could never arrive at anything higher than hope

---

30) phenomenon : 현상, 사상, 사건
31) fervour : 열렬, 열정
32) bequest : 유산, 유증
33) suffice : 만족시키다, 충분하다
34) foxglove : 디기탈리스(18세기 이래 서양의학에서는 심장 질환을 위한 약으로 사용했다)
35) dandelion : 민들레
36) coltsfoot : (식물) 머위
37) brethren : (남성의) 같은 교인들
38) lurk in : 숨다, 잠복하다

mingled with fear, and listened with longing wonder when William declared that he had possessed unshaken assurance ever since, in the period of his conversion, he had dreamed that he saw the words "calling and election sure" standing by themselves on a white page in the open Bible. Such colloquies have occupied many a pair of pale-faced weavers, whose unnurtured souls have been like young winged things, fluttering forsaken in the twilight.

It had seemed to the unsuspecting Silas that the friendship had suffered no chill even from his formation of another attachment of a closer kind. For some months he had been engaged to a young servant-woman, waiting only for a little increase to their mutual savings in order to their marriage; and it was a great delight to him that Sarah did not object to William's occasional presence in their Sunday interviews. It was at this point in their history that Silas's cataleptic fit[39] occurred during the prayer-meeting[40]; and amidst the various queries and expressions of interest addressed to him by his fellow-members, William's suggestion alone jarred with[41] the general sympathy towards a brother thus singled out for special dealings. He observed that to him this trance looked more like a visitation of Satan than a proof of divine favour, and exhorted his friend to see that he hid no accursed thing within his soul. Silas, feeling bound to accept rebuke and admonition as a brotherly office, felt no resentment but only pain at his friend's doubts concerning him; and to this was soon added some anxiety at the perception that Sarah's manner towards him began to exhibit a strange fluctuation[42] between an effort at an increased manifestation of regard and involuntary signs of shrinking and dislike. He asked her if she wished to break off[43] their engagement; but she denied this. Their engagement was known to the church, and had been recognised in the prayer-meetings; it could not be broken off without strict investigation, and Sarah could render no reason that would be sanctioned by the feeling of the community. At this time the senior deacon[44] was taken dangerously ill, and, being a childless widower[45], he was tended night and day by some of the younger brethren or sisters. Silas frequently took his turn in the night-watching with William, the one relieving the other at two in the morning. The old man, contrary to expectation, seemed to be on the way to recovery, when one night Silas, sitting up by his bedside, observed that his usual audible breathing had ceased. The candle was burning low, and he had to lift it to see the patient's face distinctly. Examination convinced him that the deacon was dead — had been dead some time, for the limbs were rigid. Silas asked himself if he had been asleep, and looked at the clock. It was already four in the morning. How was it that William had not come? In much anxiety he went to seek for help, and soon there were several friends assembled in the house, the minister among them, while Silas went away to his work, wishing he could have met William, to know the reason of his non-appearance. But at six o'clock, as he was thinking of going to seek his friend, William came,

---

39) cataleptic fit : 강직증(彊直症)의 발작
40) prayer-meeting : 기도회
41) jar with : 차이가 나다
42) fluctuation : 변동, 파동
43) break off : 갈라지다, 중단하다
44) deacon : (교회) 집사
45) widower : 홀아비

and with him the minister. They came to summon him to Lantern Yard, to meet the church members there; and to his inquiry concerning the cause of the summons the only reply was, "You will hear." Nothing further was said until Silas was seated in the vestry, in front of the minister, with the eyes of those who to him represented God's people fixed solemnly upon him. Then the minister, taking out a pocket-knife, showed it to Silas, and asked him if he knew where he had left that knife. Silas said he did not know that he had left it anywhere out of his own pocket — but he was trembling at this strange interrogation. He was then exhorted not to hide his sin, but to confess and repent. The knife had been found in the bureau by the departed deacon's bedside — found in the place where the little bag of church money had lain, which the minister himself had seen the day before. Some hand had removed that bag; and whose hand could it be, if not that of the man to whom the knife belonged? For some time Silas was mute with astonishment[46]; then he said, "God will clear me[47]: I know nothing about the knife being there, or the money being gone. Search me and my dwelling; you will find nothing but three pound five of my own savings, which William Dane knows I have had these six months." At this William groaned[48], but the minister said, "The proof is heavy against you, brother Marner. The money was taken in the night last past, and no man was with our departed brother but you, for William Dane declares to us that he was hindered by sudden sickness from going to take his place as usual[49], and you yourself said that he had not come; and, moreover, you neglected[50] the dead body."

"I must have slept," said Silas. Then after a pause he added, "Or I must have had another visitation like that which you have all seen me under, so that the thief must have come and gone while I was not in the body, but out of the body. But I say again, search me and my dwelling, for I have been nowhere else."

The search was made, and it ended in William Dane's finding the well-known bag, empty, tucked behind the chest of drawers in Silas's chamber[51]! On this William exhorted his friend to confess, and not to hide his sin any longer. Silas turned a look of keen reproach on him, and said, "William, for nine years that we have gone in and out together, have you ever known me tell a lie? But God will clear me."

"Brother," said William, "how do I know what you may have done in the secret chambers of your heart, to give Satan an advantage over you?"

Silas was still looking at his friend. Suddenly a deep flush came over his face, and he was about to speak impetuously[52], when he seemed checked again by some inward shock, that sent the flush back and made him tremble. But at last he spoke feebly, looking at William.

"I remember now — the knife wasn't in my pocket."

---

46) For some time Silas was mute with astonishment : Silas는 경악하여 잠시 말을 잃었다.
47) God will clear me : 하나님이 나의 결백을 증명해 주실 거요.
48) groan : (고통, 비탄 등으로 인한) 신음, 끙끙대는 소리
49) as usual : 여느 때처럼
50) neglected : 경시하다, 무시하다
51) chamber : room(방, 특히 침실)
52) impetuously : 충동적으로, 성급하게, 격렬하게

William said, "I know nothing of what you mean." The other persons present, however, began to inquire where Silas meant to say that the knife was, but he would give no further explanation. He only said, "I am sore stricken; I can say nothing. God will clear me."

On their return to the vestry[53] there was further deliberation. Any resort to legal measures for ascertaining the culprit[54] was contrary to the principles of the church in Lantern Yard, according to which prosecution[55] was forbidden to Christians, even had the case held less scandal to the community. But the members were bound to take other measures for finding out the truth, and they resolved on praying and drawing lots[56]. This resolution can be a ground of surprise only to those who are unacquainted with that obscure religious life which has gone on in the alleys of our towns. Silas knelt with his brethren, relying on his own innocence being certified by immediate divine interference, but feeling that there was sorrow and mourning behind for him even then — that his trust in man had been cruelly bruised. The lots declared that Silas Marner was guilty. He was solemnly suspended from church membership, and called upon to render up the stolen money; only on confession, as the sign of repentance, could he be received once more within the folds of the church. Marner listened in silence. At last, when everyone rose to depart, he went towards William Dane and said, in a voice shaken by agitation:

"The last time I remember using my knife was when I took it out to cut a strap for you. I don't remember putting it in my pocket again. You stole the money, and you have woven a plot to lay the sin at my door. But you may prosper, for all that. There is no just God that governs the earth righteously, but a God of lies, that bears witness against the innocent."

There was a general shudder at this blasphemy.

William said meekly, "I leave our brethren to judge whether this is the voice of Satan or not. I can do nothing but pray for you, Silas."

Poor Marner went out with that despair in his soul that shaken trust in God and man which is little short of madness to a loving nature. In the bitterness of his wounded spirit he said to himself, "She will cast me off[57] too." And he reflected that, if she did not believe the testimony[58] against him, her whole faith must be upset as his was. To people accustomed to[59] reason about the forms in which their religious feeling has incorporated itself, it is difficult to enter into that simple, untaught[60] state of mind in which the form and the feeling have never been severed by an act of reflection. We are apt to think it inevitable that a man in Marner's position should have begun to question the validity of an appeal to the divine judgment by drawing lots; but to him this would have been an effort of independent thought such as he had never known, and he must have made

---

53) vestry : (교회의) 제의실
54) culprit : 범인, 죄인, 피고인
55) prosecution : 기소, 고발, 수행
56) lots : 제비뽑기, 추첨
57) cast off : 벗어던지다, 포기하다(여기서 She는 Silas Marner의 약혼녀 Sarah를 지칭한다)
58) testimony : 증언
59) accustomed to : ~에 익숙해진, 길들여진
60) untaught : 배우지 않고 (자연스럽게) 터득한

the effort at a moment when all his energies were turned into[61] the anguish of disappointed faith. If there is an angel who records the sorrows of men as well as[62] their sins, he knows how many and deep are the sorrows that spring from false ideas for which no man is culpable[63].

Marner went home, and for a whole day sat alone, stunned by despair, without any impulse to go to Sarah and attempt to win her belief in his innocence. The second day he took refuge from benumbing[64] unbelief by getting into his loom and working away as usual; and before many hours were past, the minister and one of the deacons came to him with the message from Sarah that she held her engagement to him at an end. Silas received the message mutely, and then turned away from the messenger to work at his loom again. In little more than a month from that time Sarah was married to William Dane; and not long afterwards it was known to the brethren in Lantern Yard that Silas Marner had departed from the town.

Chapter 2

Even people whose lives have been made various by learning sometimes find it hard to keep a fast hold on their habitual views of life, on their faith in the Invisible, nay[65], on the sense that their past joys and sorrows are a real experience, when they are suddenly transported to a new land, where the beings around them know nothing of their history, and share none of their ideas where their mother earth shows another lap, and human life has other forms than those on which their souls have been nourished. Minds that have been unhinged from their old faith and love have perhaps sought this Lethean[66] influence of exile, in which the past becomes dreamy because its symbols have all vanished, and the present too is dreamy because it is linked with no memories. But even their experience may hardly enable them thoroughly to imagine what was the effect on a simple weaver like Silas Marner when he left his own country and people, and came to settle in Raveloe. Nothing could be more unlike his native town, set within sight of the widespread hillsides, than this low, wooded region, where he felt hidden even from the heavens by the screening trees and hedgerows[67]. There was nothing here, when he rose in the deep morning quiet and looked out on the dewy brambles and rank tufted grass, that seemed to have any relation with that life centring in Lantern Yard, which had once been to him the altar place of high dispensations. The whitewashed walls; the little pews where well-known figures entered with a subdued rustling, and where first one well-known voice and then another, pitched in a peculiar key of petition, uttered phrases at once occult and familiar, like the amulet worn on the heart; the pulpit[68] where the minister delivered

---

61) turn into : ~으로 변하다
62) as well as : 마찬가지로
63) culpable : 과실 있는, 비난할 만한
64) benumbing : 무감각하게 하는, 얼게 하는
65) nay : 아니, 글쎄
66) Lethean : 망각의 강의, 과거를 잊게 하는
67) hedgerow : 생 울타리
68) pulpit : (교회의) 설교단

unquestioned doctrine, and swayed to and fro, and handled the book in a long accustomed manner; the very pauses between the couplets of the hymn as it was given out, and the recurrent swell of voices in song: these things had been the channel of divine influences to Marner; they were the fostering home of his religious emotions — they were Christianity and God's kingdom upon earth. A weaver who finds hard words in his hymnbook knows nothing of abstractions[69] as the little child knows nothing of parental love, but only knows one face and one lap towards which it stretches its arm for refuge[70] and nurture[71].

And what could be more unlike that Lantern Yard world than the world in Raveloe? — orchard[72] looking lazy with neglected plenty; the large church in the wide churchyard, which men gazed at[73] lounging at their own doors in service time; the purple-faced[74] farmers jogging along the lanes[75] or turning in at the Rainbow; homesteads, where men supped heavily and slept in the light of the evening hearth, and where women seemed to be laying up a stock of linen for the life to come. There were no lips in Raveloe from which a word could fall that would stir Silas Marner's benumbed faith to a sense of pain. In the early ages of the world, we know, it was believed that each territory was inhabited and ruled by its own divinities, so that a man could cross the bordering heights and be out of the reach of his native gods, whose presence was confined to the streams and the groves and the hills among which he had lived from his birth. And poor Silas was vaguely conscious of something not unlike the feeling of primitive men, when they fled thus in fear or in sullenness from the face of an unpropitious[76] deity[77]. It seemed to him that the Power he had vainly trusted in among the streets and at the prayer-meetings was very far away from this land in which he had taken refuge, where men lived in careless abundance, knowing and needing nothing of that trust which, for him, had been turned to bitterness. The little light he possessed spread its beams so narrowly that frustrated belief was a curtain broad enough to create for him the blackness of night.

His first movement after the shock had been to work in his loom; and he went on with this unremittingly, never asking himself why, now he was come to Raveloe, he worked far on into the night to finish the tale of Mrs. Osgood's table-linen sooner than she expected, without contemplating beforehand[78] the money she would put into his hand for the work. He seemed to weave, like the spider, from pure impulse, without reflection. Every man's work, pursued steadily, tends in this way to become an end in itself, and so to bridge over the loveless chasms of his life. Silas's hand satisfied itself with throwing the shuttle, and his eye with seeing the little squares in the cloth

---

69) abstraction : 추상 작용, 추상적 개념
70) refuge : 피난(처)
71) nurture : 양육, 양성
72) orchard : 과수원
73) gaze at : 뚫어지게 보다, 응시하다
74) the purple-faced : 자줏빛의 얼굴을 한
75) along the lanes : 좁은 길을 따라서
76) unpropitious : 불길한, 불운한
77) deity : 신
78) beforehand : 미리, 벌써부터

complete themselves under his effort. Then there were the calls of hunger; and Silas in his solitude had to provide his own breakfast, dinner, and supper, to fetch his own water from the well, and put his own kettle on the fire; and all these immediate promptings helped, along with the weaving, to reduce his life to the unquestioning activity of a spinning insect. He hated the thought of the past; there was nothing that called out his love and fellowship toward the strangers he had come amongst; and the future was all dark, for there was no Unseen Love that cared for him.

Thought was arrested by utter bewilderment[79], now its old narrow pathway was closed, and affection seemed to have died under the bruise[80] that had fallen on its keenest nerves.

But at last Mrs. Osgood's table linen was finished, and Silas was paid in gold. His earnings in his native town, where he worked for a wholesale dealer, had been after a lower rate; he had been paid weekly, and of his weekly earnings a large proportion had gone to objects of piety[81] and charity. Now, for the first time in his life, he had five bright guineas put into his hand. No man expected a share of them, and he loved no man that he should offer him a share. But what were the guineas to him who saw no vista beyond countless days of weaving? It was needless for him to ask that, for it was pleasant to him to feel them in his palm, and look at their bright faces, which were all his own; it was another element of life, like the weaving and the satisfaction of hunger, subsisting quite aloof from the life of belief and love from which he had been cut off. The weaver's hand had known the touch of hard-won money even before the palm had grown to its full breadth: for twenty years, mysterious money had stood to him as the symbol of earthly good, and the immediate object of toil. He had seemed to love it little in the years when every penny had its purpose for him; for he loved the purpose then. But now, when all purpose was gone, that habit of looking towards the money and grasping it with a sense of fulfilled effort made a loam that was deep enough for the seeds of desire; and as Silas walked homeward across the fields in the twilight, he drew out the money and thought it was brighter in the gathering gloom.

About this time an incident happened which seemed to open a possibility of some fellowship with his neighbours. One day, taking a pair of shoes to be mended, he saw the cobbler's[82] wife seated by the fire, suffering from the terrible symptoms of heart disease and dropsy[83], which he had witnessed as the precursors of his mother's death. He felt a rush of pity at the mingled sight and remembrance, and, recalling the relief his mother had found from a simple preparation of foxglove, he promised Sally Oates to bring her something that would ease her, since the doctor did her no good. In this office of charity Silas felt, for the first time since he had come to Raveloe, a sense of unity between his past and present life, which might have been the beginning of his rescue from the insectlike existence into which his nature had shrunk. But Sally Oates's disease had raised her into a personage of much interest and importance among the neighbours, and the fact of her having

---

79) utter bewilderment : 착잡한 마음으로
80) bruise : 타박상, 멍
81) piety : 신앙심
82) cobbler : 구두 수선공
83) dropsy : 수종, 부기

found relief from drinking Silas Marner's "stuff" became a matter of general discourse. When Doctor Kimble gave physic, it was natural that it should have an effect; but when a weaver, who came from nobody knew where, worked wonders with a bottle of brown waters, the occult character of the process was evident. Such a sort of thing had not been known since the Wise Woman[84] at Tarley died; and she had charms as well as "stuff"; everybody went to her when their children had fits. Silas Marner must be a person of the same sort, for how did he know what would bring back[85] Sally Oates's breath, if he didn't know a fine sight more than that? The Wise Woman had words that she muttered to herself, so that you couldn't hear what they were; and if she tied a bit of red thread round the child's toe the while, it would keep off the water in the head. There were women in Raveloe, at that present time, who had worn one of the Wise Woman's little bags round their necks, and in consequence, had never had an idiot child, as Ann Coulter had. Silas Marner could very likely do as much and more; and now it was all clear how he should have come from unknown parts, and be so "comical-looking[86]." But Sally Oates must mind and not tell the doctor, for he would be sure to set his face against Marner. He was always angry about the Wise Woman, and used to threaten those who went to her that they should have none of his help any more.

Silas now found himself and his cottage suddenly beset by mothers who wanted him to charm away the whooping-cough, or bring back the milk, and by men who wanted stuff against the rheumatics or the knots in the hands; and, to secure themselves against a refusal, the applicants brought silver in their palms. Silas might have driven a profitable trade in charms as well as in his small list of drugs; but money on this condition was no temptation to him. He had never known an impulse towards falsity, and he drove one after another away with[87] growing irritation, for the news of him as a wise man had spread even to Tarley, and it was long before people ceased to take long walks for the sake of asking his aid. But the hope in his wisdom was at length changed into dread, for no one believed him when he said he knew no charms and could work no cures, and every man and woman who had an accident or a new attack after applying to him set the misfortune down to Master Marner's ill will and irritated glances. Thus it came to pass that his movement of pity towards Sally Oates, which had given him a transient sense of brotherhood, heightened the repulsion[88] between him and his neighbours, and made his isolation more complete.

Gradually the guineas, the crowns, and the half-crowns grew to a heap, and Marner drew less and less for his own wants, trying to solve the problem of keeping himself strong enough to work sixteen hours a day on as small an outlay[89] as possible. Have not men, shut up in solitary imprisonment, found an interest in marking the moments by straight strokes of a certain length on the wall, until the growth of the sum of[90] straight strokes, arranged in triangles, has become a

---

84) Wise Woman : 여자 주술사
85) bring back : 되돌리다, 다시 데려오다
86) comical-looking : 우스꽝스러운 외모(외양)
87) away with : 가버리게 하다
88) repulsion : 반감, 증오
89) outlay : 지출, 소비
90) sum of : 합계, 총합

mastering purpose? Do we not wile away moments of inanity[91] or fatigued waiting by repeating some trivial movement or sound, until the repetition has bred a want, which is incipient habit? That will help us to understand how the love of accumulating money grows an absorbing passion in men whose imaginations, even in the very beginning of their hoard, showed them no purpose beyond it. Marner wanted the heaps of ten to grow into a square, and then into a larger square; and every added guinea, while it was itself a satisfaction, bred a new desire. In this strange world, made a hopeless riddle to him, he might, if he had had a less intense nature, have sat weaving, weaving — looking towards the end of his pattern, or towards the end of his web, till he forgot the riddle, and everything else but his immediate sensations; but the money had come to mark off his weaving into periods, and the money not only grew, but it remained with him. He began to think it was conscious of him, as his loom was; and he would on no account have exchanged those coins, which had become his familiars, for other coins with unknown faces. He handled them, he counted them, till their form and colour were like the satisfaction of a thirst to him; but it was only in the night, when his work was done, that he drew them out to enjoy their companionship. He had taken up some bricks in his floor underneath his loom, and here he had made a hole in which he set the iron pot that contained his guineas and silver coins, covering the bricks with sand whenever he replaced them. Not that the idea of being robbed presented itself often or strongly to his mind: hoarding[92] was common in country districts in those days. There were old labourers in the parish of Raveloe who were known to have their savings by them, probably inside their flock-beds; but their rustic neighbours, though not all of them as honest as their ancestors in the days of King Alfred, had not imaginations bold enough to lay a plan of burglary. How could they have spent the money in their own village without betraying themselves? They would be obliged to "run away" — a course as dark and dubious as a balloon journey.

So, year after year, Silas Marner had lived in this solitude[93], his guineas rising in the iron pot, and his life narrowing and hardening itself more and more into a mere pulsation of desire and satisfaction that had no relation to any other being. His life had reduced itself to the mere functions of weaving and hoarding, without any contemplation of an end towards which the functions tended. The same sort of process has perhaps been undergone by wiser men, when they have been cut off from faith and love — only, instead of a loom and a heap of guineas, they have had some erudite[94] research, some ingenious project, or some well — knit theory. Strangely Marner's face and figure shrank and bent themselves into a constant mechanical relation to the objects of his life, so that he produced the same sort of impression as a handle or a crooked tube, which has no meaning standing apart. The prominent eyes that used to look trusting and dreamy, now looked as if they had been made to see only one kind of thing that was very small, like tiny grain, for which they hunted

---

91) inanity : 공허, 어리석음
92) hoard : 비축하다, 저장하다
93) solitude : 고독, 황량한 곳
94) erudite : 학식 있는

everywhere; and he was so withered95) and yellow that, although he was not yet forty, the children always called him "Old Master Marner."

Yet even in this stage of withering a little incident happened which showed that the sap of affection was not all gone. It was one of his daily tasks to fetch his water from a well a couple of fields off, and for this purpose, ever since he came to Raveloe, he had had a brown earthenware pot, which he held as his most precious utensil among the very few conveniences he had granted himself. It had been his companion for twelve years, always standing on the same spot, always lending its handle to him in the early morning, so that its form had an expression for him of willing helpfulness, and the impress of its handle on his palm gave a satisfaction mingled with that of having the fresh clear water. One day as he was returning from the well he stumbled against the step of the stile, and his brown pot, falling with force against the stones that overarched the ditch below him, was broken in three pieces. Silas picked up96) the pieces and carried them home with grief in his heart. The brown pot could never be of use to him any more, but he stuck the bits together and propped the ruin in its old place for a memorial.

This is the history of Silas Marner until the fifteenth year after he came to Raveloe. The livelong day he sat in his loom, his ear filled with its monotony, his eyes bent close down on the slow growth of sameness in the brownish web, his muscles moving with such even repetition97) that their pause seemed almost as much a constraint as the holding of his breath. But at night came his revelry: at night he closed his shutters, and made fast his doors, and drew out his gold. Long ago the heap of coins98) had become too large for the iron pot to hold them, and he had made for them two thick leather bags, which wasted no room in their resting place, but lent themselves flexibly to every corner. How the guineas shone as they came pouring out of the dark leather mouths! The silver bore no large proportion in amount to the gold, because the long pieces of linen which formed his chief work were always partly paid for in gold, and out of the silver he supplied his own bodily wants, choosing always the shillings and sixpences to spend in this way. He loved the guineas best, but he would not change the silver — the crowns and half-crowns99) that were his own earnings, begotten100) by his labour; he loved them all. He spread them out in heaps and bathed his hands in them; then he counted them and set them up in regular piles, and felt their rounded outline between his thumb and fingers, and thought fondly of the guineas that were only half-earned by the work in his loom, as if they had been unborn children — thought of the guineas that were coming slowly through the coming years, through all his life, which spread far away before him, the end quite hidden by countless days of weaving. No wonder his thoughts were still with his loom and his money when he made his journeys through the fields and the lanes to fetch and carry home his work, so that his steps never wandered to the hedge banks and the lane side in search of the once

95) withered : 시든, 말라빠진
96) pick up : 주워 올리다, 태우다
97) repetition : 되풀이, 반복
98) the heap of coins : 동전이 쌓인 더미
99) half-crowns : 반 크라운(crown과 half-crown은 은색이지만 guinea는 금색이다)
100) beget : (자식을) 보다·얻다, (어떠한 것을) 생기게 하다

familiar herbs. These too belonged to the past, from which his life had shrunk away, like a rivulet[101] that has sunk far down from the grassy fringe of its old breadth into a little shivering thread[102], that cuts a groove[103] for itself in the barren sand.

But about the Christmas of that fifteenth year a second great change came over[104] Marner's life, and his history became blent[105] in a singular manner with the life of his neighbours.

Chapter 3

The greatest man in Raveloe was Squire Cass, who lived in the large red house with the handsome flight of stone steps in front and the high stables behind it, nearly opposite the church. He was only one among several landed parishioners, but he alone was honoured with the title of Squire: for though Mr. Osgood's family was also understood to be of timeless origin — the Raveloe imagination having never ventured[106] back to that fearful blank when there were no Osgoods — still, he merely owned the farm he occupied; whereas Squire Cass had a tenant or two who complained of the game to him quite as if he had been a lord.

It was still that glorious war time which was felt to be a peculiar favour of Providence towards the landed interest, and the fall of prices had not yet come to carry the race of small squires and yeomen[107] down that road to ruin for which extravagant habits and bad husbandry were plentifully anointing their wheels. I am speaking now in relation to Raveloe and the parishes that resembled it; for our old-fashioned country life had many different aspects, as all life must have when it is spread over a various surface, and breathed on variously by multitudinous[108] currents, from the winds of heaven to the thoughts of men, which are forever moving and crossing each other with incalculable results. Raveloe lay low among the bushy trees and the rutted lanes, aloof from the currents of industrial energy and Puritan earnestness. The rich ate and drank freely, and accepting gout[109] and apoplexy[110] as things that ran mysteriously in respectable families, and the poor thought that the rich were entirely in the right of it to lead a jolly life; besides, their feasting caused a multiplication of orts[111], which were the heirlooms[112] of the poor. Betty Jane scented the boiling of Squire Cass's hams, but her longing was arrested by the unctuous liquor in which they were boiled; and when the seasons brought round the great merrymakings[113], they were regarded on all

---

101) rivulet : 시내, 개울
102) a little shivering thread : 약하게 떨리는 실
103) groove : 홈, 자국
104) come over : 멀리서 오다, ~에게 일어나다
105) blent : (blend의 과거분사) 섞다, 섞이다
106) venture : 위험에 내맡기다, 과감히 나아가다
107) yeoman : 자유농민, 자작농
108) multitudinous : 다수의, 무수한, 여러 항목으로 된
109) gout : 통풍
110) apoplexy : 중풍, 뇌졸중
111) ort : [고어, 방언] 먹다 남은 음식
112) heirloom : (집안의) 가보
113) merrymaking : (노래하고 웃고 술 마시며) 떠들썩하게 놀기

hands as a fine thing for the poor. For the Raveloe feasts were like the rounds of beef and the barrels of ale[114] — they were on a large scale, and lasted a good while, especially in the winter time. When ladies had packed up their best gowns and top knots in bandboxes, and had incurred the risk of fording streams on pillions with the precious burden in rainy or snowy weather, when there was no knowing[115] how high the water would rise, it was not to be supposed that[116] they looked forward to[117] a brief pleasure. On this ground it was always contrived in the dark seasons, when there was little work to be done[118] and the hours were long, that several neighbours should keep open house in succession[119]. When Squire Cass's standing dishes[120] diminished in plenty[121] and freshness, his guests had nothing to do but to walk a little higher up the village to Mr. Osgood's, at the Orchards, and they found hams and chines uncut, pork pies with the scent of the fire in them, spun butter in all its freshness — everything, in fact, that appetites at leisure could desire, in perhaps greater perfection though not in greater abundance than at Squire Cass's.

For the Squire's wife had died long ago, and the Red House was without that presence of the wife and mother which is the fountain of wholesome love and fear in parlour and kitchen; and this helped to account not only for there being more profusion than finished excellence in the holiday provisions, but also for the frequency with which the proud Squire condescended[122] to preside in the parlour of the Rainbow rather than under the shadow of his own dark wainscot; perhaps, also, for the fact that his sons had turned out rather ill. Raveloe was not a place where moral censure was severe, but it was thought a weakness in the Squire that he had kept all his sons at home in idleness; and though some licence was to be allowed to young men whose fathers could afford it, people shook their heads at the courses of the second son, Dunstan, commonly called Dunsey Cass, whose taste for swopping and betting might turn out[123] to be a sowing[124] of something worse than wild oats. To be sure, the neighbours said, it was no matter what became of Dunsey — a spiteful[125], jeering fellow, who seemed to enjoy his drink the more when other people went dry-always provided that his doings did not bring trouble on a family like Squire Cass's, with a monument in the church and tankards older than King George. But it would be a thousand pities if Mr. Godfrey, the eldest, a fine, open-faced[126], good-natured young man who was to come into the land some day, should take to going along the same road as his brother, as he had seemed to do of late. If he went on in that way, he would lose Miss Nancy Lammeter; for it was well known that she had looked very

---

114) ale : 에일 맥주(본래 lager beer보다 쓰고 맛이 독하며 현재 영국에서는 beer의 동의어로 쓰고 있다)
115) there is no knowing ~ : ~를 전혀 알 길이 없다
116) be supposed that : 간주되다, 생각되다
117) look forward to ~ : ~를 기대하다
118) to be done : 끝내야 할 것, 해야 할 것
119) in succession : 잇달아, 계속하여
120) standing dish : 주식, 늘 똑같은 요리
121) in plenty : 많이
122) condescend : 자기를 낮추다, 지조를 버리고 ~하다
123) turn out : find out(판명되다, 등불을 끄다)
124) sow : (씨를) 뿌리다, 심다
125) spiteful : 악의적인, 악질적
126) open-faced : 순진한 얼굴을 한

shyly on him ever since last Whitsuntide[127] twelvemonth, when there was so much talk about his being away from home days and days together. There was something wrong, more than common — that was quite clear; for Mr. Godfrey didn't look half so fresh-coloured and open as he used to do. At one time everybody was saying, What a handsome couple he and Miss Nancy Lammeter would make! and if she could come to be mistress at the Red House there would be a fine change, for the Lammeters had been brought up in that way that they never suffered a pinch of salt to be wasted, and yet everybody in their household[128] had of the best, according to his place. Such a daughter-in-law[129] would be a saving to the old Squire, if[130] she never brought a penny[131] to her fortune; for it was to be feared that, notwithstanding his incomings, there were more holes in his pocket than the one where he put his own hand in. But if Mr. Godfrey didn't turn over a new leaf[132], he might say "good-bye" to Miss Nancy Lammeter.

It was the once hopeful Godfrey who was standing, with his hands in his side pockets and his back to the fire, in the dark wainscoted parlour, one late November afternoon in that fifteenth year of Silas Marner's life at Raveloe. The fading gray light fell dimly on the walls, decorated with guns, whips, and foxes' brushes; on coats and hats flung on the chairs, on tankards sending forth a scent of flat ale, and on a half-choked fire, with pipes propped up in the chimney-corners: signs of a domestic life destitute of any hallowing charm, with which the look of gloomy vexation on Godfrey's blond face was in sad accordance. He seemed to be waiting and listening for someone's approach, and presently the sound of a heavy step, with an accompanying whistle, was heard across the large, empty entrance-hall.

The door opened, and a thickset, heavy-looking young man entered, with the flushed face and the gratuitously elated bearing which mark the first stage of intoxication. It was Dunsey, and at the sight of him Godfrey's face parted with some of its gloom to take on the more active expression of hatred[133]. The handsome brown spaniel that lay on the hearth retreated under the chair in the chimney corner.

"Well, Master Godfrey, what do you want with me?" said Dunsey, in a mocking tone. "You're my elders and betters, you know; I was obliged to come when you sent for me."

"Why, this is what I want — and just shake yourself sober[134] and listen, will you?" said Godfrey savagely[135]. He had himself been drinking more than was good for him, trying to turn his gloom into uncalculating anger. "I want to tell you I must hand over[136] that rent of Fowler's to the Squire, or else tell him I gave it you; for he's threatening to distrain[137] for it, and it'll all be out soon,

---

127) Whitsuntide : 성령 강림절 주간(Whitsunday로부터 1주간, 특히 첫 3일간)
128) household : 가족
129) daughter-in-law : 며느리
130) if : even if
131) penny : 1페니, 영국의 화폐단위
132) turn over a new leaf : 마음을 고쳐먹다, 새사람이 되다
133) hatred : 증오, 미움
134) sober : 술 취하지 않은, 맑은 정신의
135) savage : 잔인한, 무례한
136) hand over : 넘기다, 인도하다, 양도하다
137) distrain : 차압하다, 압류하다

whether I tell him or not. He said just now, before he went out, he should send word to Cox to distrain if Fowler didn't come and pay up his arrears this week. The Squire's short o' cash, and in no humour to stand any nonsense[138]; and you know what he threatened if ever he found you making away with his money again. So see and get the money, and pretty quickly, will you?"

"Oh!" said Dunsey sneeringly[139], coming nearer to his brother and looking in his face. "Suppose, now, you get the money yourself, and save me the trouble, eh? Since you was so kind as to hand it over to me, you'll not refuse me the kindness to pay it back for me; it was your brotherly love made you do it, you know."

Godfrey bit his lips and clenched his fist. "Don't come near me with that look, else I'll knock you down."

"Oh no, you won't," said Dunsey, turning away on his heel, however. "Because I'm such a good-natured brother, you know. I might get you turned out of house and home and cut off with a shilling any day. I might tell the Squire how his handsome son was married to that nice young woman Molly Farren, and was very unhappy because he couldn't live with his drunken wife, and I should slip into your place as comfortable as could be. But, you see, I don't do it ─ I'm so easy and good-natured. You'll take any trouble for me. You'll get the hundred pounds for me ─ I know you will."

"How can I get the money?" said Godfrey, quivering[140], "I haven't a shilling[141] to bless myself with. And it's a lie that you'd slip into my place; you'd get yourself turned out too, that's all. For if you begin telling tales, I'll follow. Bob's my father's favourite; you know that very well. He'd only think himself well rid of you."

"Never mind," said Dunsey, nodding his head sideways as he looked out of the window. "It 'ud be very pleasant to me to go in your company; you're such a handsome brother, and we've always been so fond of quarrelling with one another, I shouldn't know what to do without you. But you'd like better for us both to stay at home together; I know you would. So you'll manage to[142] get that little sum o' money, and I'll bid you good-bye, though I'm sorry to part."

Dunstan was moving off[143]; but Godfrey rushed after him and seized him by the arm, saying with an oath[144]:

"I tell you I have no money; I can get no money."

"Borrow of[145] old Kimble."

"I tell you he won't lend me any more, and I shan't[146] ask him."

"Well, then, sell Wildfire[147]."

---

138) in no humour to stand any nonsense : 어떤 허튼 소리도 참아낼 기분이 아니다
139) sneeringly : 비꼬며, 조롱하며
140) quivering : 진동하는, 떠는
141) shilling : 실링, 영국의 은화
142) manage to : 그럭저럭 해내다
143) move off : 떠나다
144) oath : 맹세, 선서
145) borrow of : 빌리다
146) shan't : shall not의 단축형
147) Wildfire : 여기선 Godfrey의 말 이름이다.

"Yes, that's easy talking. I must have the money directly."

"Well, you've only got to ride him to the hunt tomorrow. There'll be Bryce and Keating there, for sure. You'll get more bids than one."

"I daresay, and get back home at eight o'clock, splashed up to the chin. I'm going to Mrs. Osgood's birthday dance."

"Oho!" said Dunsey, turning his head on one side, and trying to speak in a small mincing treble. "And there's sweet Miss Nancy coming; and we shall dance with her, and promise never to be naughty again, and be taken into favour, and — "

"Hold your tongue about Miss Nancy, you fool," said Godfrey, turning red, "else I'll throttle you."

"What for?" said Dunsey, still in an artificial tone, but taking a whip from the table and beating the butt end of it on his palm. "You've a very good chance. I'd advise you to creep up[148] her sleeve again; it 'ud be saving time, if Molly should happen to take a drop too much laudanum[149] someday, and make a widower of you. Miss Nancy wouldn't mind being a second, if she didn't know it. And you've got a good-natured brother, who'll keep your secret well, because you'll be so very obliging to him."

"I tell you what it is," said Godfrey, quivering and pale again: "my patience is pretty near at an end. If you'd a little more sharpness in you, you might know that you may urge[150] a man a bit too far, and make one leap as easy as another. I don't know but what it is so now. I may as well tell the Squire everything myself. I should get you off my back, if I got nothing else. And after all, he'll know sometime. She's been threatening to come herself and tell him. So don't flatter[151] yourself that your secrecy's worth any price you choose to ask. You drain me of money till I have got nothing to pacify her with, and she'll do as she threatens some day. It's all one. I'll tell my father everything myself, and you may go to the devil."

Dunsey perceived that he had overshot his mark, and that there was a point at which even the hesitating Godfrey might be driven into decision. But he said with an air of unconcern.

"As you please; but I'll have a draught of ale first." And ringing the bell, he threw himself across two chairs, and began to rap the window-seat with the handle of his whip.

Godfrey stood, still with his back to the fire, uneasily moving his fingers among the contents of his side pockets and looking at the floor. That big muscular frame of his held plenty of animal courage, but helped him to no decision when the dangers to be braved were such as could neither be knocked down nor throttled. His natural irresolution and moral cowardice were exaggerated[152] by a position in which dreaded consequences seemed to press equally on all sides, and his irritation had no sooner provoked him to defy Dunstan and anticipate all possible betrayals, than the miseries he must bring on himself by such a step seemed more unendurable to him than the present evil.

---

148) creep up : (소매를) 올리다
149) laudanum : 아편으로 만든 식물
150) urge : 몰아대다, 재촉하다
151) flatter : 아첨하다
152) exaggerated : 과장된

The results of confession were not contingent, they were certain; whereas betrayal was not certain. From the near vision of that certainty he fell back on suspense and vacillation[153]) with a sense of repose. The disinherited son of a small squire[154]), equally disinclined to dig and to beg, was almost as helpless as an uprooted tree which, by the favour of earth and sky, has grown to a handsome bulk[155]) on the spot where it first shot upward. Perhaps it would have been possible to think of digging with some cheerfulness if Nancy Lammeter were to be won on those terms; but since he must irrevocably[156]) lose her as well as the inheritance, and must break every tie but the one that degraded him and left him without motive for trying to recover his better self, he could imagine no future for himself on the other side of confession[157]) but that of "listing for a soldier" ─ the most desperate step, short of suicide, in the eyes of respectable families. No! he would rather trust to casualties than to his own resolve ─ rather go on sitting at the feast and sipping the wine he loved, though with the sword[158]) hanging over him and terror in his heart, than rush away into the cold darkness where there was no pleasure left. The utmost concession[159]) to Dunstan about the horse began to seem easy, compared with the fulfillment of his own threat. But his pride would not let him recommence the conversation otherwise than by continuing the quarrel. Dunstan was waiting for this, and took his ale in shorter draughts than usual.

"It's just like you," Godfrey burst out[160]) in a bitter tone, "to talk about my selling Wildfire in that cool way ─ the last thing I've got to call my own, and the best bit of horse-flesh I ever had in my life. And if you'd got a spark of pride in you, you'd be ashamed to see the stables emptied and everybody sneering about it. But it's my belief you'd sell yourself, if it was only for the pleasure of making somebody feel he'd got a bad bargain."

"Ay, ay," said Dunstan, very placably, "you do me justice, I see. You know I'm a jewel for 'ticing people into bargains. For which reason I advise you to let me sell Wildfire. I'd ride him to the hunt tomorrow for you with pleasure. I shouldn't look so handsome as you in the saddle, but it's the horse they'll bid for and not the rider."

"Yes, I dare say ─ trust my horse to you!"

"As you please," said Dunstan, rapping the windowseat again with an air of great unconcern. "It's you have got to pay Fowler's money; it's none of my business. You received the money from him when you went to Bramcote, and you told the Squire it wasn't paid. I'd nothing to do with that; you chose to be so obliging as to give it me, that was all. If you don't want to pay the money, let it alone; it' s all one to me. But I was willing to[161]) accommodate you by undertaking to sell the horse, seeing it's not convenient to you to go so far tomorrow."

---

153) vacillation : 동요, 흔들림
154) small squire : 시골의 대지주
155) bulk : 거체, 거대한 것
156) irrevocable : 되돌릴 수 없는
157) confession : 자백
158) sword : 검, 칼
159) concession : 양보
160) burst out : 갑자기 말을 하다
161) be willing to do something : 기꺼이 ~할 것이다

Godfrey was silent for some moments. He would have liked to spring on Dunstan, wrench[162] the whip from his hand, and flog him to within an inch of his life, and no bodily fear could have deterred him; but he was mastered by another sort of fear, which was fed by feelings stronger even than his resentment. When he spoke again it was in a half-conciliatory tone[163].

"Well, you mean no nonsense about the horse, eh? You'll sell him all fair, and hand over the money? If you don't, you know, everything'll go to smash[164], for I've got nothing else to trust to. And you'll have less pleasure in pulling the horse over my head when your own skull's[165] to be broken too."

"Ay, ay[166]," said Dunstan, rising; "all right. I thought you'd come round[167]. I'm the fellow to bring old Bryce up to the scratch. I'll get you a hundred and twenty for him, if I get you a penny."

"But it'll perhaps rain cats and dogs tomorrow, as it did yesterday, and then you can't go," said Godfrey, hardly knowing whether he wished for that obstacle or not.

"Not it," said Dunstan; "I'm always lucky in my weather. It might rain if you wanted to go yourself. You never hold trumps, you know; I always do. You've got the beauty, you see, and I've got the luck, so you must keep me by you for your crooked sixpence[168]; you'll never get along without me."

"Confound you, hold your tongue!" said Godfrey impetuously. "And take care to keep sober tomorrow, else you'll get pitched on your head coming home, and Wildfire might be the worse for it."

"Make your tender heart easy," said Dunstan, opening the door. "You never knew me see double when I'd got a bargain to make; it'ud spoil the fun. Besides, whenever I fall, I'm warranted to fall on my legs."

With that Dunstan slammed the door behind him, and left Godfrey to that bitter rumination on his personal circumstances which was now unbroken from day to day save by the excitement of sporting, drinking, card-playing, or the rarer and less oblivious pleasure of seeing Miss Nancy Lammeter. The subtle and varied pains springing from the higher sensibility that accompanies higher culture are perhaps less pitiable than that dreary absence of impersonal enjoyment and consolation which leaves ruder minds to the perpetual[169] urgent companionship[170] of their own griefs and discontents. The lives of those rural forefathers[171], whom we are apt to think very prosaic[172] figures — men whose only work was to ride round their land, getting heavier and heavier in their

162) wrench : 비틀다
163) in a half-conciliatory tone : 반은 달래는 톤으로
164) go to smash : 파산하다, 산산이 부서지다
165) skull : 두개골, 해골, 머리
166) Ay : 긍정, 찬성, 네
167) come around : (노여움, 고통이) 가라앉다, 의식을 회복하다
168) sixpence : 하찮은 일, 6펜스
169) perpetual : 영속하는, 끊임없는
170) companionship : 교우, 교제
171) rural forefather : 시골의 조상(선조)
172) prosaic : 무미건조한, 지루한

saddles[173]), and who passed the rest of their days in the half-listless gratification of senses dulled by monotony — had a certain pathos in them nevertheless. Calamities came to them too, and their early errors carried hard consequences. Perhaps the love of some sweet maiden, the image of purity, order, and calm, had opened their eyes to the vision of a life in which the days would not seem too long, even without rioting; but the maiden was lost, and the vision passed away[174]), and then what was left to them, especially when they had become too heavy for the hunt, or for carrying a gun over the furrows, but to drink and get merry, or to drink and get angry, so that they might be independent of variety, and say over again with eager emphasis the things they had said already any time that twelve month? Assuredly amongst those flushed and dull-eyed men there were some whom — thanks to their native human kindness, even riot could never drive into brutality: men who, when their cheeks were fresh, had felt the keen point of sorrow or remorse, had been pierced by the reeds they leaned on, or had lightly put their limbs in fetters from which no struggle could loose them; and under these sad circumstances, common to us all, their thoughts could find no resting place outside the ever-trodden round of their own petty history.

That, at least, was the condition of Godfrey Cass in this six-and-twentieth year of his life. A movement of compunction[175]), helped by those small indefinable influences which every personal relation exerts on a pliant nature, had urged him into a secret marriage, which was a blight on[176]) his life. It was an ugly story of low passion, delusion[177]), and waking from delusion, which needs not to be dragged from the privacy of Godfrey's bitter memory. He had long known that the delusion was partly due to a trap laid for him by Dunstan, who saw in his brother's degrading marriage the means of gratifying at once his jealous hate and his cupidity. And if Godfrey could have felt himself simply a victim, the iron bit that destiny had put into his mouth would have chafed him less intolerably. If the curses he muttered half aloud when he was alone had had no other object than Dunstan's diabolical cunning, he might have shrunk less from the consequences of avowal. But he had something else to curse — his own vicious folly, which now seemed as mad and unaccountable to him as almost all our follies and vices do when their promptings have long passed away. For four years he had thought of Nancy Lammeter, and wooed her with tacit patient worship, as the woman who made him think of the future with joy. She would be his wife, and would make home lovely to him, as his father's home had never been; and it would be easy, when she was always near, to shake off those foolish habits that were no pleasures, but only a feverish way of annulling[178]) vacancy. Godfrey's was an essentially domestic nature, bred up in a home where the hearth had no smiles, and where the daily habits were not chastised by the presence of household order. His easy disposition made him fall in unresistingly with the family courses, but the need of some tender permanent affection, the longing for some influence that would make the good he

---

173) in the saddle : 말을 타고, 재직(재임)하고, 권력을 잡고
174) pass away : 사라지다
175) compunction : 양심의 가책
176) blight on : ~에 어두운 그림자를 드리우다, 망치다
177) delusion : 현혹
178) annul : (법률, 규정 등을) 무효로 하다

preferred easy to pursue, caused the neatness, purity, and liberal orderliness of the Lammeter household, sunned by the smile of Nancy, to seem like those fresh, bright hours of the morning, when temptations go to sleep, and leave the ear open to the voice of the good angel, inviting to industry, sobriety, and peace. And yet the hope of this paradise had not been enough to save him from a course which shut him out of it forever. Instead of keeping fast hold of the strong silken rope by which Nancy would have drawn him safe to the green banks where it was easy to step firmly, he had let himself be dragged back into mud and slime, in which it was useless to struggle. He had made ties for himself which robbed him of all wholesome motive and were a constant exasperation.

Still, there was one position worse than the present: it was the position he would be in when the ugly secret was disclosed; and the desire that continually triumphed over every other was that of warding off the evil day, when he would have to bear the consequences of his father's violent resentment for the wound inflicted on his family pride — would have, perhaps, to turn his back on that hereditary ease and dignity[179] which, after all, was a sort of[180] reason for living, and would carry with him the certainty that he was banished forever from[181] the sight and esteem of Nancy Lammeter. The longer the interval, the more chance there was of deliverance from some, at least, of the hateful consequences to which he had sold himself; the more opportunities remained for him to snatch[182] the strange gratification[183] of seeing Nancy, and gathering some faint indications of her lingering regard. Towards this gratification he was impelled, fitfully, every now and then, after having passed weeks in which he had avoided her as the far-off bright-winged prize that only made him spring forward and find his chain all the more galling. One of those fits of yearning was on him now, and it would have been strong enough to have persuaded him to trust Wildfire to Dunstan rather than disappoint the yearning, even if he had not had another reason for his disinclination towards the morrow's[184] hunt. That other reason was the fact that the morning's meet was near Batherley, the market-town where the unhappy woman lived whose image became more odious[185] to him every day; and to his thought the whole vicinage[186] was haunted by her. The yoke a man creates for himself by wrong-doing will breed hate in the kindliest nature; and the good-humoured, affectionate-hearted[187] Godfrey Cass was fast becoming a bitter man, visited by cruel wishes, that seemed to enter and depart and enter again, like demons who had found in him a ready-garnished home.

What was he to do this evening to pass the time? He might as well go to the Rainbow and hear the talk about the cock-fighting[188]; everybody was there, and what else was there to be done? —

---

179) dignity : 존엄, 위엄
180) a sort of ~ : 일종의 ~
181) be banished from : 추방되다, 내쫓기다
182) snatch : 와락 붙잡다, 잡아채다
183) gratification : 만족감, 희열
184) morrow : 아침, 다음날
185) odious : 밉살스러운, 불쾌한
186) vicinage : 근처, 주변, 이웃 사람들
187) affectionate-hearted : 마음이 따뜻한
188) cock-fighting : 닭싸움

though, for his own part, he did not care a button for cock-fighting. Snuff, the brown spaniel[189], who had placed herself in front of him, and had been watching him for some time, now jumped up in impatience for the expected caress. But Godfrey thrust her away without looking at her, and left the room, followed humbly[190] by the unresenting Snuff — perhaps because she saw no other career open to her.

---

189) spaniel : 스패니얼(귀가 축 처지고 털이 긴 개)
190) humbly : 겸손하게, 초라하게

제6장 Thomas Hardy - 「*Tess of the d'Urbervilles*」

본 소설은 비극적 힘과 도덕적 진지성을 지닌 위대한 소설이라는 평도 받았으나, 주로 공격의 대상이 되었다. 즉, 순결을 잃은 여성을 옹호하며 주인공으로 다루었기 때문에 저급하며 사악한 소설로 평가받았다. 이 소설은 남성 중심 이데올로기에 대한 Thomas Hardy의 정면도전이다. Tess의 사랑과 좌절의 과정은 성 이데올로기가 얼마나 부당한 것인가를 보여준다.

출제 경향 및 수험 대책

Thomas Hardy의 작품을 제대로 읽기 위해서는 19세기 말 영국 남부의 도셋(Dorset) 지방의 특징을 살펴볼 필요가 있다. 하디는 영구불변한 전원풍의 농촌을 다룬 것이 아니라 19세기 중반에서 말기에 이르기까지 영국 남부 농촌 삶의 변화과정을 실감나게 다루고 있기 때문이다. 그의 소설은 한정된 배경에도 불구하고 인간의 삶을 지배하는 거대한 욕망의 구도와 당대의 핵심적 변화들을 담고 있기 때문에 리얼리즘의 소설의 관점에서 분석해야 한다.

제1절 작가의 생애

소설가이자 시인인 토마스 하디(Thomas Hardy, 1840~1928)는 영국 남부의 도셋(Dorset)주 도체스터(Dorchester)에서 건축업자인 아버지와 라틴어와 프랑스의 로망스에 관심 많은 어머니 사이에서 4남매 중 장남으로 태어났다. 그의 대부분의 작품들은 그의 고향 도셋(Dorset)과 작품에서 웨식스(Wessex)로 나타나는 그 주변 지역을 배경으로 하고 있다.

Hardy는 도체스터에 위치한 남학교에서 라틴어를 배우고 학업에 충실했지만, 16세가 되던 해에 대학교육을 받을 형편이 안 되어 건축가의 도제가 되었고, 교회 건축을 공부하며 소설을 집필하기 시작하였다. 그는 22세 때인 1862년에 런던으로 가서 건축가인 Arthur Blomfield의 조수가 되었으며, 이때부터 전원생활을 동경하는 시(詩)를 집필하기 시작하였다. 이 시기에 그는 King's College London에 다니며 프랑스어를 배우기도 하였다. 특히 이 시절 그는 Shakespeare의 작품과 오페라, 연극을 즐기고, Charles Darwin, Herbert Spencer, J. S. Mill 등의 작품을 탐독하면서 그의 문학관이라고 할 수 있는 숙명론(fatalism)을 키워나갔다.

1867년 Hardy는 건강이 나빠져 고향으로 돌아가게 되었다. 그 후 그는 자신이 집필했던 원고들이 번번이 출판사에서 거절당하자 실의에 빠져 집필 활동을 그만두려고도 하였으나, 애인인 Emma Gifford의 격려로 다시 집필을 하면서 작가로서의 입지를 굳히게 되었고, 1874년에 그녀와 결혼했다. 1912년에 그녀가 갑자기 사망하자 심한 정신적 충격에 빠졌다. 아내가 죽은 이듬해에 아내를 처음 만났던 콘월(Cornwall)로 순례여행을 떠났고 이때의 비통한 심정, 시간과 변화, 회한, 추억, 외로움 등에 대한 자신의 감정과 느낌들을 시(*Poems of 1912~1913*)로 출간하였다. 그 후, Hardy는 1914년에 자신의 비서인 Florence Emily Dugdale과 재혼하였다.

그는 1927년 12월에 늑막염을 앓게 되어 그 이듬해인 1928년 1월에 사망하였다. 그의 장례에 관해 그의 가족들과 친구들은 Stinford에 있는 그의 첫 번째 부인 Emma의 옆자리에 묻히길 바랐지만, 그의 유언 집행자는 웨스트민스터 사원에 있는 Poet's Corner에 묻히길 원하였다. 그래서 그의 심장(heart)은 Emma 옆에 묻히게 되었고, 그의 유골은 Poet's Corner에 있는 Charles Dickens의 무덤 옆에 묻히게 되었다.

> **!** **더 알아두기** **Q**
>
> **Thomas Hardy의 주요작품**
> • 「*Far from the Madding Crowd*」(1847)
> • 「*The Return of the Native*」(1878)
> • 「*The Mayor of Casterbridge: The Life and Death of a Character*」(1886)
> • 「*The Woodlanders*」(1887)
> • 『*Wessex Tales*』(1888) - 단편집
> • 「*Tess of the d'Urbervilles: A Pure Woman Faithfully Presented*」(1891)
> • 「*Jude the Obscure*」(1895)
> 이 외에도 많은 시와 희곡 및 단편을 남겼다.

제 2 절 작품 세계

1 Wessex Novels 중요 ★★★

Hardy는 자신이 태어난 고향인 황량하고 척박한 Dorset 지방을 Wessex로 이름 지었다. Wessex를 배경으로 하여 쓴 그의 소설을 일컬어 'Wessex Novels'라고 한다. 'Wessex Novels'에는 그의 인생관이라고 할 수 있는 'Immanent Will'(내재 의지)이 작품의 중심을 이룬다고 할 수 있다.

2 Immanent Will(내재 의지) 중요 ★★★

우주의 어떤 힘이 인간의 생활을 통제하고 지배한다는 사상이다. 「*The Return of the Native*」는 Wessex라는 가상의 황야 공간인 에그돈 히스(Egdon Heath)를 배경으로 한 소설로 자신의 고향인 그 황야를 고수하려는 주인공 Clym과, Egdon Heath 황야를 벗어나려 하는 Eustacia의 횡포를 그린 작품이다. 소설에서 Egdon Heath는 'Immanent Will'로 작용하여 등장인물들을 무력화시킨다. 또한 'Immanent Will'은 「*Tess of the d'Urbervilles*」(1891)에서는 순결한 여인인 Tess가 태어날 때부터 죽음을 맞이할 때까지 피할 수 없는 어떤 거대한 운명적 힘(Immanent Will)에 의하여 숙명적으로 희생당하고 만다는 내용을 다루고 있다.

3 하디(Hardy)의 '인간'

(1) 고독하고 무력한 인간

하디의 소설은 황량하게 펼쳐진 대지 위에 홀로 서 있는 인물을 통하여 독자에게 대자연 속에서의 인간의 고독감과 무력감을 전달한다. 하디가 보기에 인간은 대자연 속에서 단지 하찮은 존재에 불과하며, 자신의 의지나 선택과는 무관하게 대자연의 섭리에 따라 생존할 수 있다고 보았다. 그는 인간을 자연 가운데 놓음으로써 구체화되고 개별화된 등장인물을 넘어 보편적이고 일반적인 인간을 표현한다. 하디는 인간의 삶과 행위에 있어서 가장 근원적이고 본질적인 문제에 주목하는데, 그가 표현하는 소설에서의 인물들은 지적으로나 문화적으로 세련되거나 복잡성과 모호성 등을 지닌 인간의 모습들보다는 인간의 가장 기본적인 모습들을 담고 있다. 따라서 그가 표현하는 소설의 인물들은 단순한 직업을 갖으며, 소박한 욕구를 삶의 방식에 초점을 맞추어 소설을 전개한다. 이러한 전개에서 하디는 인간과 운명의 싸움을 강력하게 제시하여 독자에게 뚜렷한 인상을 남긴다.

(2) 자연주의적 소설 [중요] ★

하디는 주어진 환경이나 운명에 의해 희생당하는 인물을 소설에서 묘사한다. 그의 소설은 전체적으로 침울하고 비관적인 분위기를 풍긴다. 소설에서 묘사하는 이러한 분위기는 당대의 빅토리아조가 20세기로 넘어가는 혼란의 시대였고, 그 가운데 충돌하는 기존의 사회와 새로운 변화의 분위기 간의 갈등이 반영되었다고 볼 수 있다.

4 리얼리즘 소설

(1) 당대 영국 농촌의 현실

리얼리즘 소설의 측면에서 이 소설은 전근대적이고 가부장적인 농촌 공동체가 근대적 자본주의로 변화하는 과정과 이 결과로 인하여 발생하는 시대적 상황을 배경으로 한다. 주인공 Tess는 농촌 중간층 계급 출신으로서, 결혼을 통해 신분 상승을 하지 않는 한 노동자가 되거나 대도시로 이주해 도시의 빈민이 될 수밖에 없는 상황이다. 그녀는 가족을 위해 할 수 없이 Alec의 정부로 팔려가다시피 한다. Tess와 그녀 가족의 운명을 통해 Hardy는 당시 농촌 사회에서 계급의 격차가 얼마나 심하고 개인의 계급이 불안정하며, 이것이 한 개인의 운명에 얼마나 큰 영향력을 주는지 보여준다.

(2) 사회적 관습과 편견

「Tess of the d'Urbervilles」는 출판되자마자 부도덕한 책이라고 비난받으며 사회적 물의를 빚었다. 결혼하지 않은 여성이 아이를 낳고, 결혼 후에는 다른 남자의 정부가 된 Tess는 당시 사회의 관점에서 볼 때 사람을 죽인 죄 이외에도 두 번(결혼하지 않은 여성이 아이를 낳고, 결혼 후에는 다른 남자의 정부가 된 것)이나 죄를 지은 여인이다. 그러나 Hardy는 그녀를 비난하기보다는 그녀를 동정하고 나중에는 '순결한 여인'(A Pure Woman Faithfully Presented)이라는 소설의 부제(副題)까지 달아놓았다. 이러한 Hardy의 행위는 빅토리아조의 여성에 대한 통념을 뒤집은 것이었다. Tess의 모든 고난과 불행은 Angel이 그녀를 버리는 것으로부터 출발한다. 이 소설에서 Angel은 파괴적이고 비인간적인 힘의 상징이라고 볼 수 있다. Angel은 자기모순과 분열을 보인다. Tess는 스스로를 죄인으로 여긴다. 이들은 내면화된 사회적 규범이 그들의 마음속에 자리 잡고 있다,

5 진화론적 관점

비평가들 중 비관론의 입장을 취하는 사람들은 Hardy가 청년시절부터 심취했던 진화론이 이 작품의 구조와 성격에 영향을 미치고 있다고 말한다. 진화론의 주요 이론을 작품에서 찾아볼 수 있는 부분들은 다음과 같다.

(1) 유전과 성격

진화론에서는 유전이야말로 자연계의 고유 성질이라고 말한다. Tess는 부모 양쪽으로부터뿐만 아니라 먼 조상으로부터의 그녀의 성격과 행동이 많은 영향을 받았다. 그녀는 아버지 쪽으로부터 무기력하고 쇠퇴한 혈통을 이어받았지만, 과거 귀족 가문에 대한 자존심과 공격성 및 폭력성을 이어받았다. 이는 그녀가 플린트콤 애쉬(Flintcomb-Ash)에 다시 나타난 Alec이 Angel을 야유하며 슬그머니 자신의 몸을 만지려할 때 장갑을 벗어 그의 얼굴을 후려치는 장면, 신혼여행을 간 웰브릿지(Well bridge) 농가에 걸려 있는 그녀 조상의 생김새가 그녀에게도 나타난다는 Angel의 말, Tess가 Alec을 살해하고 Angel을 찾아왔을 때 Angel이 그녀가 저지른 과격한 일탈 행동은 혹시 조상에게서 물려받은 피 때문이 아닌가를 자문하는 장면 등 곳곳에서 찾을 수 있다. 한편, 어머니로부터 아름다운 외모를 물려받았고 이것이 Alec과 Angel로 하여금 그녀에게 한 눈에 반하게 만드는데, 어머니 쪽의 운명론적 수동성(fatal passivity)은 Tess로 하여금 Alec과 Angel의 접근과 유혹에 쉽게 넘어가게 하고 그들의 박해를 참고 견디게 한다. 그녀의 장점과 단점, 나아가 기쁨과 고통을 가져오는 행위의 모든 것이 과거로부터 물려받은 유전에서 비롯된다는 것이다.

(2) 유전의 고리

유전의 관점에서는 개별자가 아니라 종(species)이 중요하며, 개체는 끊임없이 복제하고 반복하기 때문에 개별적인 고리는 무의미하고 독자성이 없다. Tess는 Angel에게 다음과 같이 말한다. "저도 길게 늘어선 줄의 한 고리에 불과하다는 사실을 굳이 배워서 뭐하겠어요. … 제일 좋은 것은 우리의 천성이나 과거의 행위도 수천, 수만 번 반복된다는 사실을 잊어버리는 것이에요. …" 소설의 마지막 부분에서 Tess는 죽기 전 Angel이 Liza-Lu와 결혼하길 권한다. Tess의 형질(trait)이 동생 Liza-Lu를 통하여 이어지길 바라는 그녀의 소망은 유전의 관점에서 볼 때 타당한 결말이라고 할 수 있다.

(3) 적자생존

종(species)이나 개체와 마찬가지로 개별적인 가족(family)도 생명력의 수명을 지니고 있는데, 이것은 그 가계가 주변 환경에 얼마나 잘 적응하는가 하는 적자생존에 달려 있다. Tess의 조상이 생명력이 다하여 몰락했다는 것은 d'Urberville가(家)의 후손인 Tess 역시 몰락할 운명에 처해 있다는 것을 암

시한다. Tess와 그녀의 집안, 나아가 이 집안이 속한 농촌 중간층의 몰락 역시 변화하는 역사현실에 적응하지 못하였기 때문에 이미 소멸했거나 작품 속에서 쇠퇴를 걷고 있다.

(4) 자연법칙

개체보다 종(species)을 중심으로 진화하는 자연계의 법칙에서 볼 때 개체가 겪는 행복과 불행은 아무런 의미를 갖지 못하며, 개체들이 보이는 다양한 형질이나 성격 또한 적자생존이라는 자연의 법칙 앞에서는 무력하다. Talbothays 농장에서 같이 일하는 처녀들도 각자 나름대로의 매력을 지녔지만 Angel을 사로잡지 못하여 경쟁에서 밀려나게 되고, Tess만이 Angel이 보기에 마치 여신처럼 하나의 전형적인 형태로 나타난 여성으로 여긴다. 이처럼 「Tess of the d'Urbervilles」는 잔인하고 엄격한 결정론이 지배하며 철저한 염세적 비전으로 채워진 소설이라고 볼 수 있다.

6 비극적 관점

진화론의 관점만으로는 「Tess of the d'Urbervilles」가 독자에게 주는 특유의 감동을 설명하지 못한다. 소설의 결말에서 "'정의'가 이루어졌다. 아이스킬로스의 표현을 빌리자면 '신들의 제왕'(절대자)은 테스에 대한 장난을 끝냈다."('Justice' was done, and the President of the Immortals, in Aeschylean phrase, had ended his sport with Tess.)는 Hardy의 비극적 세계관을 나타낸다. Hardy는 이 소설에서 당시 흔했던 농락당하고 버림받은 시골 처녀의 이야기를 비극의 차원으로 끌어올리는 데 성공하였다. Tess는 비록 현실에서는 수많은 패배와 좌절을 겪지만 정신적인 힘으로 다른 등장인물들을 압도하고 지배하는 인상을 준다. 그녀는 강한 자존심과 인내력, 생명력과 숭고한 심성을 지닌 여인으로, Hardy가 그린 여성 중 가장 긍정적인 인물이며 이상적 여인상이다.

(1) Tess와 주변 인물들의 비교

Tess의 삶의 원칙은 사랑의 절대성이고, Angel과의 사랑이 이루어지는 것이 그녀의 유일한 희망인 것으로 볼 때, Tess는 가장 기본적이며 소박하고 정당한 것을 요구하는 의식과 정신을 지니고 있음을 알 수 있다. 즉, 인간의 본성을 바탕으로 한 자연의 법칙과 질서를 대변하는 인물이다. 그러나 Alec과 Angel은 인위적이고 억압적인 사회의 법칙을 상징한다. Alec은 물질적인 위력과 육체적인 힘으로 그녀를 유린한다. Angel은 Tess의 꿈을 좌절시키고 사회의 제도와 관습, 도덕률을 상징한다. 이러한 두 사람의 근본적 허구성과 부분화된 왜곡은 Tess의 진가를 알아볼 수 없게 만들고 그녀와 진정한 사랑을 할 능력이 없음을 보여준다.

(2) Tess의 성격적 비극성

어머니나 주변의 다른 처녀들처럼 Tess의 수동성은 Alec에게 유혹될 때와 Angel에게 버림받았을 때 그녀의 불행을 가중시킨다. 그러나 그녀는 동시에 강렬한 자존심과 독자성도 지닌 여성이다. 이를테면, 한밤중에 동생들과 함께 죽어가는 자신의 아기에게 유아세례를 주는 장면이나 Flintcomb Ash에서 힘겹게 살면서도 Angel의 부모에게 도움을 청하기를 꺼려하는 모습, Alec의 정부가 되기를 거부하고 그를 떠나는 그녀의 행동들은 그녀의 독립적이고 성격을 드러낸다. Angel에게 버림받은 뒤에도 그를 기다리면서 Alec의 유혹을 물리치고, Angel이 돌아왔을 때 Alec을 살해하면서까지 Angel과의 사랑을 성취하려는 모습에서 보이는 Tess의 결단력이 주변 인물들의 운명론적 수동성과 그녀를 구별하게 한다.

(3) 강인한 생명력과 인내력

작품 속에서 Tess는 Alec, Angel 그리고 다시 Alec에게 세 번의 정신적 죽음을 당하지만, 세 번 모두 부활한다. 적대적인 외부의 힘에 의하여 그녀는 매번 희생되면서도 끈질긴 인내심과 Angel에 대한 변치 않는 사랑으로 그의 마음을 변하게 하고 Alec을 처단하여 최후의 승자가 된다. 그녀가 Alec을 살해하는 것은 Angel에 대한 신격화된 사랑의 필연적 결과라고 볼 수 있다. Tess의 삶은 희생양에서 비극적 주인공으로 변모하는 과정이지만, 그 과정에서 그녀 특유의 강인한 생명력과 인내가 돋보인다.

제 3 절 줄거리

가난한 행상인인 John Durbeyfield는 자신이 사실 고대 귀족 가문인 d'Urbervilles의 후손이라는 사실을 듣고 의기양양해진다. 한편 그의 딸 Tess Durbeyfield는 May Day dance에 합류해 Angel과 눈길을 주고받지만, 술에 취한 그의 아버지가 소란을 피우며 값비싼 마차를 타고 집에 가는 모습을 보고 창피해 하며 서둘러 집에 간다.

John과 Joan Durbeyfield는 가난한 그들의 상황 때문에 Tess를 d'Urberville가(家)와 친해지길 바라며 보낸다. 그곳에서 Tess는 Alec d'Urberville의 제안으로 어쩔 수 없이 새들을 돌보는 일을 한다. Durbeyfield 가(家)와 d'Urberville가(家)는 사실 아무런 관련이 없으며 d'Urberville가(家)는 고리대금업을 하면서 벌어들인 돈으로 족보를 산 집안이다. 4개월간 d'Urberville가(家)에서 일하던 Tess는 어느 날 밤 Chase 숲에서 Alec에게 겁탈을 당한다. 그리고 임신하여 아이를 낳는데, Sorrow라는 이름으로 그녀가 세례를 주지만 아기는 곧 죽는다.

아기를 묻어주고 일 년간 집에서 은둔하던 Tess는 Talbothays 낙농장에서 젖소의 우유 짜는 일을 맡는다. Talbothays에서 Tess는 행복한 날들을 보낸다. 함께 우유 짜는 동료 여성들인 Izz, Retty, Marian과 친해졌고, May Day dance에서 마주쳤던 Angel Clare와 재회하여 둘은 사랑에 빠진다. Tess는 Angel의 청혼을 받아들이지만 자신의 과거에 대한 양심의 가책을 느끼고 그의 침실 아래 자신의 과거에 대한 고백을 적은 메모를 남겨둔다. 그러나 그 메모는 카펫 아래로 들어가고 Angel은 그 메모를 보지 못한다. 결혼식 첫날밤 Angel과 Tess는 서로의 과거를 털어놓게 되는데, Tess는 Angel이 런던에서 한 연상의 여성과 가졌던 정사(情事)를 용서하지만, Angel은 Tess의 Alec과의 과거를 용서하지 않고 자신이 먼저 찾아오기 전까지 자신을 찾지 말라고 하며 배를 타고 브라질로 떠난다.

Tess는 열악한 환경 속에 농장에서 일을 하며 Angel을 그리워하다가, 우연히 Alec이 설교하는 것을 듣는다. Alec은 Angel의 아버지 Clare 목사의 복음으로 개심자(convert)가 된 것이다. Tess에게 또 다시 욕정을 느낀 Alec은 종교적 태도를 버리고 Tess에게 결혼하자는 제안을 한다. 하지만 Tess는 이를 거절하고, 어머니가 위독하다는 소식을 듣고 집으로 간다. 어머니는 회복하지만 아버지가 급작스럽게 사망하자 남은 가족들은 집에서 쫓겨나고, 그 기회에 Alec은 Tess의 가족을 도와주겠다는 제안을 하지만 거절당한다. 한편, Angel은 아내 Tess를 용서하기로 마음먹고 브라질에서 돌아오지만, Tess는 이미 Alec과 재결합하였다. Alec의 주장과 반대로 Angel이 돌아왔고, 자신과 재결합하길 원하자 Tess는 Alec을 살해한다. Herons 집주인이 Alec의 시체를 발견하고 신고하지만, Tess는 이미 Angel과 도망간 후였다. 그들은 며칠간 빈 집을 떠돌며 여행하다가 스톤헨지(Stonehenge)에 도착하고 Tess는 잠에 든다. 동이 트자 Tess는 수색대에 의해 발각돼 투옥된다. Angel과 Liza-Lu는 Tess가 처형당했다는 표시인 검은색 깃발이 감옥에서 게양되는 것을 목격한다.

제 4 절 작품의 주제

1 비극적 역설(Tragic paradox) 중요 ★★

무력한 인간이 고통과 인내를 통하여 어떻게 위엄과 숭고함에 다다를 수 있는지를 보여준다. 자신이 의도하는 삶의 원칙에 충실하며 이를 위해 목숨과도 맞바꾼다. Tess는 희생양이 아니라 오히려 고전비극의 주인공들처럼 스스로의 파멸을 분명히 인식하고 선택한다. 따라서 Tess는 법의 집행자들이 나타났을 때 움츠리지 않고 기꺼이 죽을 각오가 되어있다. Tess는 삶에서 자신의 가능성을 남김없이 소진하고 쓰러짐으로써 그녀의 죽음은 패배인 동시에 승리이며, 파멸인 동시에 성취이자 절망 가운데 환희라고 할 수 있다.

2 사회적 인습에 도전

Tess는 엄격한 도덕률 및 종교적 교리에 과감하게 도전하는 인물이다. 새로운 가치와 옛 가치 간의 갈등에 노출된 비극적인 인간상을 드러낸다. 또한 성(sex)에 대한 빅토리아 시대의 모순과 남녀관계를 폭로한다. 순결한 여인을 물질이나 혈통의 희생물로 삼는 부당한 사회적 인습을 고발한다.

제 5 절 등장인물

1 Tess Durbeyfield

Durbeyfield가(家)의 3남 4녀 중 장녀로, 모순된 감정과 행동을 가진 여인이다. 씩씩하고 독립적인가하면 수줍고 쉽게 희생당하는 성품의 소유자이자, 신구(New & Old)의 사회질서, 독립심과 의타심, 정신력과 정열이 혼재되어 존재하는 인간상이다. Alec에게 순결을 빼앗긴 Tess는 새로운 삶을 용감하게 개척해나가려 하지만 사회의 인습과 제도라는 잔혹한 운명 앞에서 또 다시 굴복당하고 만다.

2 Angel Clare

타인의 잘못에는 완고하고 엄격하지만 자신의 잘못에 대해서는 관대한 위선적인 성격의 소유자이자, 도덕적 관습과 이상을 쫓아가는 복합적인 성격의 소유자이다. 과거의 폐습과 인습으로부터 과감히 탈피하여 진보적인 사상을 주장하지만, 여성의 순결에 대해서만은 보수적인 엄격함을 보인다. 불가피하게 Alec과의 과거를 고백하는 Tess를 용서하지 않는 인물이다.

3 Alec d'Urberville

자아도취적인 인물이며, 자신의 목적달성을 위해서는 타인의 약점도 이용하는 이기적인 인간이다. Tess의 생명력과 강인한 삶의 의지를 조롱하는 냉혹한 내재적인 의지(Immanent Will)의 대변자로, 그녀에게 불행한 운명을 부여하는 역할을 한다.

4 John(Jack) Durbeyfield

Durbeyfield가(家) Tess의 아버지이다. 비록 몰락했지만 과거에는 자신이 귀족의 가문이었다는 이야기를 듣고 허영심에 사로잡혀 무책임한 생각을 가진 채 살아가는 우유부단한 성격의 인물이며, 술을 자주 마신다.

5 Joan Durbeyfield

Durbeyfield가(家) Tess의 어머니이다. 아름다운 외모를 Tess에게 물려주었을 만큼 그녀 자신도 아름다운 외모를 가졌지만, 돈 많은 신사에게 Tess를 결혼시켜야겠다는 생각에만 사로잡힌 무지한 인물이다.

6 Eliza-Louisa Durbeyfield(Liza-Lu)

Durbeyfield의 둘째 딸, 즉 Tess의 바로 아래 동생이다. Tess보다 4살 어리고 Liza-Lu로 불린다. Tess는 Angel에게 Liza-Lu를 부탁하고 그녀와 결혼하길 권유한다.

7 기타 인물들

(1) Abraham Durbeyfield

Tess보다 7살 어린 Durbeyfield가(家)의 장남이자 셋째

(2) Hope, Modesty

Abraham보다 어린 Tess의 여동생들. 그 밑으로 두 남동생이 또 있다.

(3) Marian, Izz Huett, Retty Priddle

Talbothays Dairy에서 일하는 처녀들이자 Tess의 친구들

제 6 절 작품의 구조(Plot)와 시점 및 기법

1 구조

7장의 대국면(Phases)과 59개의 Chapter로 구성되어 있다.

(1) The Maiden(처녀, Ch. 1~11)

Tess의 어머니는 사냥터 숲 끝에 있는 Trantridge 마을 Slopes에 살고 있는 d'Urberville 가문이 진짜 귀족이라고 생각한다. 그러나 이 d'Urberville 가문은 고리대금업으로 번 돈으로 d'Urberville 가문을 사고 귀족행세를 하는 것이었다. 이러한 사실을 모르는 Tess의 어머니는 부와 명예를 얻기 위해 Tess를 그 집으로 시집보내고 싶어 한다. Tess는 아버지가 기르던 말 Prince가 죽자, 어려운 집안의 형편 때문에 d'Urberville가(家)에 방문하는 데 응한다. d'Urberville가(家)에서 일하게 된 17세의 Tess는 시장에 다녀오던 길에 d'Urberville가(家)의 아들인 23살 Alec에게 순결을 잃게 된다.

(2) Maiden No More(더 이상 처녀가 아닌, Ch. 12~15)

Tess는 Alec의 아이까지 낳게 되지만, 그 아기는 일주일 후 죽고 만다. Tess는 아이에게 Sorrow라는 세례명을 주고 직접 교회 묘지 한 쪽에 묻는다.

(3) The Rally(회복, Ch. 16~24)

Marlott 마을에서 소문으로 심적 고통을 겪던 Tess는 마을을 떠나 Talbothays Dairy(낙농장)에서 일자리를 구하고 삶을 회복할 길을 찾으려 한다. 그러던 중 농업 기술을 배우고 있던 실습생이며 귀족인 26살의 Angel과 사랑에 빠지고 Tess는 인생의 가장 행복한 시간을 보낸다.

(4) The Consequence(결과, Ch. 25~34)

Tess는 부모님 댁에 갔다 온 Angel로부터 청혼을 받는다. 그를 사랑하지만 Alec과의 과거 때문에 Angel의 청혼을 거절하다가 승낙한다. 둘은 새해 전야에 결혼하고 Talbothays Dairy를 떠난다.

(5) The Woman Pays(여인의 대가, Ch. 35~44)

Tess와 Angel의 결혼생활은 첫날밤에 끝나고 만다. 서로의 지난 과오를 고백하고 용서를 받자는 Angel의 제안에 Tess는 Alec과의 과거를 솔직하게 모두 털어놓는다. 그러나 Angel은 Tess의 과오가 더 크다며 그녀의 과거를 받아들이지 않고, 자신의 아내가 "죽었다"고 말한다("Dead! dead! dead!"). Angel은 어느 정도의 돈을 Tess에게 남기고 그녀를 떠나 브라질로 간다. Tess는 Flintcomb-Ash 지역 농장에서 Marian과 Izz와 함께 일한다.

(6) The Convert(개심자, Ch. 45~52)

목사인 Angel의 아버지 Mr. Clare가 한 설교에 감화되어 마음을 고쳐먹게 되었다며 Tess 앞에 다시 나타난 Alec은 여전히 아름다운 Tess에게 욕망을 느끼고는 Angel이 다시 그녀에게 돌아오는 일은 없을 것이라며 집요하게 자신과의 재결합을 요구한다.

(7) Fulfillment(성취, Ch. 53~59)

Alec의 주장과는 달리 Angel이 Tess를 다시 찾아오자, 이미 Alec의 여인이 된 Tess는 Alec에게 자신을 두 번이나 속인 남자라고 비난하고는 Alec을 살해한다. 그리고 자신도 형장의 이슬로 사라진다.

2 시점

전지적 작가 시점이다.

3 기법

(1) Wessex 소설

Hardy는 자신이 태어난 고향인 황량하고 척박한 Dorset 지방을 Wessex로 명명하고, 이를 배경으로 하여 그가 쓴 소설을 'Wessex Novels'라 부른다. Hardy에게 Wessex는 소우주(microcosm)이다.

(2) 내재 의지(Immanent Will) 중요 ★

Wessex 소설의 중심 사상으로 인간의 의지가 선하든 악하든 간에 우주에 내재하는 어떤 냉혹한 힘은 인간의 운명을 좌지우지하여 인간의 의지를 무력화시키고 만다는 Hardy의 인생관이다.

(3) 장소에 대한 상징

Tess의 고향인 Marlott은 어머니의 뱃속처럼 온화하고 따뜻한 곳이다. Angel을 만난 Talbothays는 비옥한 곳으로 묘사되고 절망 속에서 Angel을 기다린 곳은 황량한 황무지이다.

(4) 어조와 분위기

진실과 도덕성을 제시하기 위하여 멜로드라마풍의 가벼운 어조를 먼저 사용하다가 무거운 어조가 등장한다. 타인의 욕망으로 인하여 고통스러운 삶을 살게 되고 결국은 가혹한 형벌을 받게 되는 처참하고 비극적인 분위기이다. 민담이나 전설, 고전 그리스의 비극풍 등 다양한 서사적 기법으로 전개된다.

제 7 절 Text

Chapter 1

On an evening in the latter part of May a middle-aged man was walking homeward from Shaston to the village of Marlott[1]), in the adjoining Vale of Blakemore or Blackmoor. The pair of legs that carried him were rickety, and there was a bias in his gait[2]) which inclined him somewhat to the left of a straight line. He occasionally gave a smart nod, as if in confirmation of some opinion[3]), though he was not thinking of anything in particular. An empty egg basket was slung upon his arm, the nap of his hat was ruffled, a patch being quite worn away at its brim where his thumb came in taking it off[4]). Presently he was met by an elderly parson astride on[5]) a gray mare, who, as he rode, hummed a wandering tune.

"Good night t'ee," said the man with the basket.

"Good night, Sir John," said the parson.

The pedestrian, after another pace or two, halted, and turned round.

"Now, sir, begging your pardon; we met last market-day on this road about this time, and I zaid[6])

---

1) Shaston, Marlatt : 영국의 남부 지역 Dorset에 있는 마을들의 이름. 19세기 초에 백작의 이름을 따서 Shaston은 Shaftesbury로 개칭하였다. Marlatt 역시 지금의 Marnhull의 옛 이름이다.

2) gait : 걸음걸이

3) as if in confirmation of some opinion : 마치 어떤 생각에 수긍이라도 하는 것처럼(= as if he were in confirmation of some opinion)

4) taking it off : 모자를 벗을 때(take off : ~을 벗다, 목적어가 대명사일 때는 반드시 사이에 있어야 한다)

5) astride on : ~에 걸터앉은(= sitting astride)

6) zaid : said

'Good night', and you made reply 'Good night, Sir John', as now."

"I did," said the parson.

"And once before that near a month ago."

"I may have."

"I did," said the parson.

"And once before that - near a month ago."

"I may have."

"Then what might your meaning be in calling me 'Sir John' these different times, when I be plain Jack Durbeyfield, the haggler[7]?" — The parson rode a step or two nearer. "It was only my whim," he said; and, after a moment's hesitation: "It was on account of[8] a discovery I made some little time ago, whilst[9] I was hunting up[10] pedigrees for the new county history. I am Parson Tringham, the antiquary, of Stagfoot Lane. Don't you really know, Durbeyfield, that you are the lineal representative of the ancient and knightly family of the d'Urbervilles, who derived their descent from Sir Pagan d'Urberville, that renowned knight who came from Normandy with William the Conqueror, as appears by Battle Abbey Roll[11]?"

"Never heard it before, sir!"

"Well it's true. Throw up your chin a moment, so that I may catch the profile of your face better. Yes, that's the d'Urberville nose and chin — a little debased. Your ancestor was one of the twelve knights who assisted the Lord of Estremavilla in Normandy in his conquest of Glamorganshire[12]. Branches of your family held manors over all this part of England; their names appear in the Pipe Rolls[13] in the time of King Stephen. In the reign of King John one of them was rich enough to give a manor to the Knights Hospitallers[14]; and in Edward the Second's time your forefather Brian was summoned to Westminster to attend the great Council there. You declined a little in Oliver Cromwell's time, but to no serious extent, and in Charles the Second's reign you were made Knights of the Royal Oak[15] for your loyalty. Aye, there have been generations of Sir Johns among you, and if knighthood were hereditary, like a baronetcy[16], as it practically was in old times, when men were knighted from father to son, you would be Sir, John now."

"Ye don't say so!"

"In short," concluded the parson, decisively smacking his leg with his switch, "there's hardly such another family in England."

---

7) haggler : 떠돌이 장사꾼(= peddler, huckster)
8) on account of : because of
9) whilst : while의 영국적 표현
10) hunt up : ~을 조사하다
11) Battle Abbey Roll : 노르만인의 영국 정복 당시 정복왕 윌리엄이 영국 땅에 처음 상륙하여 Hastings 근처에 지은 수도원 Battle Abbey 내에 기념비로 세워졌거나 부착된 윌리엄의 동반자들의 기념 목록
12) Glamorganshire : Glamorganshire 주는 Glam organ의 비옥한 계곡과 그림 같은 Gower 반도를 위시하여 폐허가 된 성곽들로 유명한 지역이다.
13) the Pipe Rolls : 국고(national treasury) 연보
14) the Knights Hospitallers : 제1회 십자군에 종사하였던 상이용사의 구호를 목적으로 설립된 원호 기사단
15) Knights of the Royal Oak : 떡갈나무 기사(영국의 찰스 2세가 1651년 Worcester 전쟁에서 피하여 달아날 때 잠시 몸을 숨겨 목숨을 건진 떡갈나무에서 명칭을 딴 일련의 기사 호칭)
16) baronetcy : 준남작의 지위

"Daze my eyes, and isn't there?" said Durbeyfield. "And here have I been knocking about[17], year after year, from pillar to post[18], as if I was no more than the commonest feller in the parish... And how long hev[19] this news about me been knowed, Pa'son Tringham?"

The clergyman explained that, as far as he was aware, it had quite died out of knowledge, and could hardly be said to be known at all. His own investigations had begun on a day in the preceding spring when, having been engaged in tracing the vicissitudes of the d'Urberville family, he had observed Durbeyfield's name on his waggon, and had thereupon been led to make inquiries about his father and grandfather till he had no doubt on the subject.

"At first I resolved not to disturb you with such a useless piece of information," said he. "However, our impulses are too strong for our judgment sometimes. I thought you might perhaps know something of it all the while."

"Well, I have heard once or twice, tis true, that my family had seen better days afore[20] they came to Blackmoor. But I took no notice o't, thinking it to mean that we had once kept two horses where we now keep only one. I've got a wold[21] silver spoon, and a wold graven seal at home, too; but, Lord, what's a spoon and seal? ... And to think that I and these noble d'Urbervilles were one flesh[22] all the time. 'Twas said that my gr't-grandfer had secrets, and didn't care to talk of where he came from ... And where do we raise our smoke[23], now, parson, if I may make so bold; I mean, where do we d'Urbervilles live?"

"You don't live anywhere. You are extinct as a county family."

"That's bad."

"Yes — what the mendacious family chronicles[24] call extinct in the male line — that is, gone down — gone under."

"Then where do we lie?"

"At Kingsbere-sub-Greenhill[25]: rows and rows of you in your vaults[26], with your effigies under Purbeck-marble[27] canopies."

"And where be our family mansions and estates?"

"You haven't any."

"Oh? No lands neither?"

"None; though you once had 'em in abundance[28], as I said, for your family consisted of numerous branches. In this county there was a seat of yours at Kingsbere, and another at Sherton,

---

17) knock about(or around) : [구어] 방황하다, 헤매다
18) from pillar to post : 여기저기에, (비유적) 이리저리 궁지에 몰려서
19) hev : have or has의 사투리
20) afore : before의 옛말
21) wold : 낡은(= old). 지방의 발음을 재현하려는 시도이다.
22) flesh : 혈육
23) raise one's smoke : 살다(= live)
24) family chronicles : 족보
25) Kingsbere-sub-Greenhill : Bere Heath의 최북방 교외 Dorchester에서 동쪽으로 약 10마일쯤 되는 Bere Regis라는 마을
26) vault : 납골당
27) Purbeck-marble : Dorset의 남동쪽에 있는 Purbeck island에서 파낸 질이 좋은 석회석
28) in abundance : 많이

and another at Milipond, and another at Lullstead, and another at Well bridge."

"And shall we ever come into our own again?"

"Ah — that I can't tell!"

"And what had I better do about it, sir?" asked Durbeyfield, after a pause.

"Oh — nothing, nothing; except chasten yourself with the thought of "how are the mighty fallen"[29]. It is a fact of some interest to the local historian and genealogist[30], nothing more. There are several families among the cottagers of this county of almost equal lustre. Good night."

"But you'll turn back and have a quart of beer wi' me on the strength o't, Pa'son Tringham? There's a very pretty brew in tap at The Pure Drop[31] — though, to be sure, not so good as at Rolliver's[32]."

"No, thank you — not this evening, Durbeyfield. You've had enough already." Concluding thus the parson rode on his way, with doubts as to his discretion in retailing this curious bit of lore.

When he was gone Durbeyfield walked a few steps in a profound reverie, and then sat down upon the grassy bank by the roadside, depositing his basket before him. In a few minutes a youth appeared in the distance, walking in the same direction as that which had been pursued by Durbeyfield. The latter, on seeing him, held up his hand, and the lad quickened his pace and came near.

"Boy, take up that basket! I want' ee to go on an errand[33] for me."

The lath — like stripling frowned. "Who be you, then, John Durbeyfield, to order me about and call me 'boy'? You know my name as well as I know yours!"

"Do you, do you? That's the secret — that's the secret! Now obey my orders, and take the message I'm going to charge 'ee wi' — .Well, Fred, I don't mind telling you that the secret is that I'm one of a noble race — it has been just found out by me this present afternoon P. M." And as he made the announcement, Durbeyfield, declining from his sitting position, luxuriously stretched himself out upon the bank among the daisies.

The lad stood before Durbeyfield, and contemplated his length from crown to toe[34].

"Sir John d'Urberville — that's who I am," continued the prostrate man. "That is if knights were baronets — which they be. Tis recorded in history all about me. Dost know of such a place, lad, as Kingsbere-sub-Greenhill?"

"Ees. I've been there to Greenhill Fair."

"Well, under the church of that city there lie — "

"'Tisn't a city, the place I mean; leastwise 'twaddn[35]' when I was there — 'twas a little one-eyed, blinking sort o' place,"

---

29) how are the mighty fallen : (Samuel 1:25 에서 인용) 이 소설 54장의 제목이기도 하다.
30) genealogist : 혈통 연구가
31) The Pure Drop : Marlott에 있는 술집 이름
32) Rolliver's : 롤리버네 술집
33) go on an errand : 심부름가다
34) from crown to toe : 머리끝에서 발끝까지
35) twaddn : it was not

"Never you mind the place, boy, that's not the question before us. Under the church of that there parish lie my ancestors — hundreds of 'em — in coats of mail and jewels, in gr't lead coffins weighing tons and tons. There's not a man in the county o' South-Wessex that's got grander and nobler skillentons in his family than I."

"Oh?"

"Now take up that basket, and goo[36] on to Marlott, and when you've come to The Pure Drop Inn, tell 'em to send a horse and carriage to me immediately, to carry me home[37]. And in the bottom o' the carriage they be to put a noggin[38] o' rum in a small bottle, and chalk it up to my account. And when you've done that goo on to my house with the basket, and tell my wife to put away that washing, because she needn't finish it, and wait till I come hwome, as I've news to tell her."

As the lad stood in a dubious attitude, Durbeyfield put his hand in his pocket, and produced a shilling, one of the chronically few that he possessed.

"Here's for your labour, lad."

This made a difference in the young man's estimate of the position.

"Yes, Sir John. Thank 'ee. Anything else I can do for 'ee, Sir John?"

"Tell 'em at hwome that I should like for supper — well, lamb's fry if they can get it; and if they can't, black-pot[39]; and if they can't get that, well, chitterlings[40] will do."

"Yes, Sir John."

The boy took up the basket, and as he set out the notes of a brass band[41] were heard from the direction of the village.

"What's that?" said Durbeyfield. "Not on account o' I?"

"'Tis the women's club-walking, Sir John. Why, your da'ter[42] is one o' the members."

"To be sure — I'd quite forgot it in my thoughts of greater things! Well, vamp[43] on to Marlott, will ye, and order that carriage, and maybe I'll drive round and inspect the club."

The lad departed, and Durbeyfield lay waiting on the grass and daisies in the evening sun. Not a soul passed that way for a long while, and the faint notes of the band were the only human sounds audible within the rim of blue hills.

---

36) goo : 'go'
37) hwome : home
38) noggin : 조그만 맥주잔
39) black-pot : 기름과 씬 고기 등으로 만든 스튜
40) chitterlings : 내장
41) the notes of a brass band : 관악대의 음악소리
42) your da'ter : your daughter
43) vamp : 가다

Chapter 2

The village of Marlott lay amid the north-eastern undulations of the beautiful Vale of Blakemore[44] or Blackmoor aforesaid, an engirdled and secluded region, for the most part untrodden as yet by tourist or landscape-painter, though within a four hours' journey from London.

It is a vale whose acquaintance is best made by[45] viewing it from the summits of the hills that surround it — except perhaps during the droughts of summer. An unguided ramble into its recesses in bad weather is apt to[46] engender dissatisfaction with its narrow, tortuous, and miry ways.

This fertile and sheltered tract of country, in which the fields are never brown and the springs never dry, is bounded on the south by the bold chalk ridge that embraces the prominences of Hambledon Hill, Bulbarrow, Nettlecombe-Tout, Dogbury, High Stoy, and Bubb Down. The traveller from the coast, who, after plodding northward for a score of miles over calcareous[47] downs and corn-lands, suddenly reaches the verge of one of these escarpments[48], is surprised and delighted to behold, extended like a map beneath him, a country differing absolutely from that which he has passed through. Behind him the hills are open, the sun blazes down upon fields so large as to give an unenclosed character to the landscape[49], the lanes are white, the hedges low and plashed, the atmosphere colourless. Here, in the valley, the world seems to be constructed upon a smaller and more delicate scale; the fields are mere paddocks[50], so reduced that[51] from this height their hedgerows appear a network of dark green threads overspreading the paler green of the grass. The atmosphere beneath is languorous, and is so tinged with azure[52] that what artists call[53] the middle distance partakes also of that hue, while the horizon beyond is of the deepest ultramarine. Arable lands arc few and limited; with but slight exceptions the prospect is a broad rich mass of grass and trees, mantling minor hills and dales within the major. Such is the Vale of Blackmoor.

The district is of historic, no less than[54] of topographical[55] interest. The Vale was known in former times as the Forest of White Hart, from a curious legend of King Henry III's reign[56], in which the killing[57] by a certain Thomas de la Lynd of a beautiful white hart[58] which the king had run down and spared, was made the occasion of a heavy fine. In those days, and till comparatively recent times, the country was densely wooded. Even now, traces of its earlier condition are to be

---

44) Vale of Blakemore : Sturminster Newton을 향해 Sherbone에서 남쪽으로 흐르는 넓은 계곡
45) acquaintance is best made by : ~로 잘 알려져 있다
46) be apt to : ~하기 쉽다
47) calcareous : 석회질을 함유한
48) escarpment : 급경사면
49) the sun ~ the landscape : 태양이 너무도 강렬하게 눈부신 빛을 들판에 내리찍고 있어 꽉 막힌 인상을 주지 않았다.
50) paddock : 작은 들판
51) so reduced that : 너무나 작아서
52) azure : 하늘색
53) what artists call : 소위 예술가들이 말하는
54) no less than : ~뿐만 아니라(as well as)
55) topographical : 지형상의, 지형학의
56) Henry III's reign : 헨리 3세의 재위 기간(1216~1272)
57) the killing : 뒤의 of a beautiful white hart와 연결
58) hart : 수사슴

found in the old oak copses and irregular belts of timber[59] that yet survive upon its slopes, and the hollow-trunked trees that shade so many of its pastures.

The forests have departed, but some old customs of their shades remain. Many, however, linger only in a metamorphosed or disguised form. The May-Day dance[60], for instance, was to be discerned on the afternoon under notice, in the guise of the club revel, or 'club-walking,' as it was there called.

It was an interesting event to the younger inhabitants of Marlott, though its real interest was not observed by the participators in the ceremony. Its singularity lay less in the retention of a custom of walking in procession and dancing on each anniversary than in the members being solely women. In men's clubs such celebrations were, though expiring, less uncommon; but either the natural shyness of the softer sex[61], or a sarcastic attitude on the part of male relatives had denuded[62] such women's clubs as remained (if any other did) of this their glory and consummation. The club of Marlott alone lived to uphold[63] the local Cerealia[64]. It had walked for hundreds of years, if not as benefit-club[65], as votive sisterhood of some sort; and it walked still.

The banded ones were all dressed in white gowns — a gay survival from Old Style days, when cheerfulness and May-time were synonyms — days before the habit of taking long views had reduced emotions to a monotonous average. Their first exhibition of themselves was in a processional march of two and two round the parish. Ideal and real clashed slightly as the sun lit up their figures against the green hedges and creeper-laced house-fronts; for, though the whole troop wore white garments, no two whites were among them. Some approached pure blanching; some had a bluish pallor; some worn by the older characters (which had possibly lain by folded for many a year) inclined to a cadaverous tint, and to a Georgian style[66].

In addition to the distinction of a white frock, every woman and girl carried in her right hand a peeled willow wand, and in her left a bunch of white flowers. The peeling of the former, and the selection of the latter, had been an operation of personal care.

There were a few middle-aged and even elderly women in the train, their silver-wiry hair and wrinkled faces, scourged by time and trouble[67], having almost a grotesque, certainly a pathetic, appearance in such a jaunty situation. In a true view, perhaps, there was more to be gathered and told of each anxious and experienced one, to whom the years were drawing nigh when she should say, "I have no pleasure in them"[68], than of her juvenile comrades. But let the elder be passed over here for those under whose bodices the life throbbed quick and warm.

---

59) irregular belts of timber : 드문드문 있는 산림지대
60) The May-Day dance : 5월 1일 May Queen에게 화관을 씌우고 May pole을 세워 놓고 그 주위를 돌면서 춤을 추는 축제
61) softer sex : 여성
62) had denuded : 뒤의 of this와 연결된다.
63) uphold : ~을 지켜나가다
64) Cerealia : 풍년제
65) benefit-club : 질병이나 노후에 대비하기 위한 회원들의 상호부조 모임
66) Georgian style : Georgian I~IV까지, 즉 1714~1830년까지의 시대에 유명해진 양식
67) scourged by time and trouble : 세파에 시달린
68) I have no pleasure in them : 전도서 12장 1절 참고

The young girls formed, indeed, the majority of the band, and their heads of luxuriant hair reflected in the sunshine every tone of gold, and black, and brown. Some had beautiful eyes, others a beautiful nose, others a beautiful mouth and figure: few, if any[69], had all. A difficulty of arranging their lips in this crude exposure to public scrutiny, an inability to balance their heads, and to dissociate self-consciousness from their features[70], was apparent in them, and showed that they were genuine country girls, unaccustomed to many eyes.

And as each and all of them were warmed without by the sun, so each had a private little sun for her soul to bask in; some dream, some affection, some hobby, at least some remote and distant hope which, though perhaps starving to nothing[71], still lived on, as hopes will[72]. Thus they were all cheerful, and many of them merry.

They came round by The Pure Drop Inn, and were turning out of the high road to pass through a wicket-gate into the meadows, when one of the women said —

"The Lord-a-Lord![73] Why, Tess Durbeyfield, if there isn't[74] thy father riding hwome in a carriage!"

A young member of the band turned her head at the exclamation. She was a fine and handsome girl — not handsomer than some others, possibly — but her mobile peony mouth[75] and large innocent eyes added eloquence to colour and shape. She wore a red ribbon in her hair, and was the only one of the white company who could boast of such a pronounced adornment. As she looked round Durbeyfield was seen moving along the road in a chaise belonging to The Pure Drop, driven by a frizzle-headed brawny damsel with her gown-sleeves rolled above her elbows. This was the cheerful servant of that establishment, who, in her part of factotum[76], turned groom and ostler at times. Durbeyfield, leaning back, and with his eyes closed luxuriously, was waving his hand above his head, and singing in a slow recitative —

"I've-got-a-gr't-family-vault-at-Kingsbere-and knighted-forefathers-in-lead-coffins-there![77]"

The clubbists tittered, except the girl called Tess — in whom a slow heat seemed to rise at the sense that her father was making himself foolish in their eyes.

"He's tired, that's all," she said hastily, "and he has got a lift home, because our own horse has to rest to-day."

"Bless thy simplicity, Tess," said her companions. "He's got his market-nitch[78]. Haw-haw!"

"Look here; I won't walk another inch with you, if you say any jokes about him!" Tess cried,

---

69) if any : ～이 있다 해도
70) to dissociate self-consciousness from their features : 얼굴에 수줍은 티를 나타내지 않다.
71) starving to nothing : 희망이 충족되지 않아 점점 줄어들어 결국 사라져 버린다는 뜻
72) as hopes will : 희망이란 그러기 마련인데
73) The Lord-a-Lord : 감탄어조
74) if there isn't : '혹시 ～ 아니야'의 뜻으로 여기서는 놀람의 어조
75) peony mouth : 모란꽃 같은 입
76) factotum : 잡역부
77) I've-got ~ in-lead-coffins-there! : "킹즈비어에 가면 위대한 가문의 묘지가 있지. 기사였던 조상들이 납관 속에 누워 계시네!"라고 Tess의 아버지가 술에 취해 부르는 노래
78) market-nitch : 장터에서 마시는 술

and the colour upon her cheeks spread over her face and neck. In a moment her eyes grew moist, and her glance drooped to the ground. Perceiving that they had really pained her they said no more, and order again prevailed. Tess's pride would not allow her to turn her head again, to learn what her father's meaning was, if he had any; and thus she moved on with the whole body to the enclosure where there was to be dancing on the green. By the time the spot was reached she had recovered her equanimity, and tapped her neighbour with her wand and talked as usual.

Tess Durbeyfield at this time of her life was a mere vessel of emotion untinctured by experience. The dialect was on her tongue to some extent, despite the village school: the characteristic intonation of that dialect for this district being the voicing approximately rendered by the syllable UR, probably as rich an utterance as any to be found in human speech. The pouted-up deep red mouth to which this syllable was native had hardly as yet settled into its definite shape, and her lower lip had a way of thrusting the middle of her top one upward, when they closed together after a word.

Phases of her childhood lurked in her aspect still. As she walked along to-day, for all[79] her bouncing handsome womanliness, you could sometimes see her twelfth year in her cheeks, or her ninth sparkling from her eyes; and even her fifth would flit over the curves of her mouth now and then.

Yet few knew, and still fewer considered this. A small minority, mainly strangers, would look long at her in casually passing by, and grow momentarily fascinated by her freshness, and wonder if they would ever see her again: but to almost everybody she was a fine and picturesque country girl, and no more.

Nothing was seen or heard further of Durbeyfield in his triumphal chariot under the conduct of the ostleress[80], and the club having entered the allotted space, dancing began. As there were no men in the company the girls danced at first with each other, but when the hour for the close of labour drew on, the masculine inhabitants of the village, together with other idlers and pedestrians, gathered round the spot, and appeared inclined to negotiate for a partner.

Among these on-lookers were three Young men of a superior class, carrying small knapsacks strapped to their shoulders, and stout sticks in their hands. Their general likeness to each other, and their consecutive ages, would almost have suggested that they might be, what in fact they were, brothers. The eldest wore the white tie, high waistcoat, and thin-brimmed hat of the regulation curate[81]; the second was the normal undergraduate; the appearance of the third and youngest would hardly have been sufficient to characterize him; there was an uncribbed, uncabined[82] aspect in his eyes and attire, implying that he had hardly as yet found the entrance to his professional groove[83]. That he was a desultory tentative student of something and everything might only have been predicted of him.

---

79) for all : ~임에도 불구하고
80) ostleress : hostler(마부)의 여성형
81) the regulation curate : 목사보
82) an uncribbed, uncabined : 자유롭고 속박되지 않은 기색
83) found ~ professional groove : 직업을 갖게 되면 시야가 좁아지고 어떠한 틀에 박히는 것을 의미

These three brethren told casual acquaintance that they were spending their Whitsun[84] holidays in a walking tour through the Vale of Blackmoor, their course being south-westerly from the town of Shaston on the north-east.

They leant over the gate by the highway, and inquired as to the meaning of the dance and the white-frocked maids. The two elder of the brothers were plainly not intending to linger more than a moment but the spectacle of a bevy of girls dancing without male partners seemed to amuse the third, and make him in no hurry to move on. He unstrapped his knapsack, put it, with his stick, on the hedge-bank, and opened the gate.

"What are you going to do, Angel?" asked the eldest.

"I am inclined to go and have a fling[85] with them. Why not all of us — just for a minute or two — it will not detain us long?"

"No — no; nonsense!" said the first. "Dancing in public with a troop of country hoydens[86] — Suppose we should be seen! Come along, or it will be dark before we get to Stourcastle, and there's no place we can sleep at nearer than that; besides, we must get through another chapter of A Counterblast to Agnosticism[87] before we turn in, now I have taken the trouble to bring the book."

"All right — I'll overtake you and Cuthbert in five minutes; don't stop; I give my word that I will,[88] Felix."

The two elder reluctantly left him and walked on taking their brother's knapsack to relieve him in following[89], and the youngest entered the field.

"This is a thousand pities," he said gallantly, to two or three of the girls nearest him, as soon as there was a pause in the dance.

"Where are your partners, my dears?"

"They've not left off work[90] yet," answered one of the boldest.

"They'll be here by and by[91]. Till then, will you be one, sir?"

"Certainly. But what's one among so many!"

"Better than none.[92] Tis melancholy work facing and footing it[93] to one of your own sort, and no clipsing and colling[94] at all. Now, pick and choose."

"Ssh-don't be so for'ard[95]!" said a shyer girl.

The young man, thus invited, glanced them over, and attempted some discrimination; but, as the group were all so new to him, he could not very well exercise it. He took almost the first that came

---

84) Whitsun : Whitsun은 Whitsunday를 가리키며, Easter(부활절) 이후 7번째 일요일과 그 전후의 날들
85) have a fling : 격렬한 춤을 추다
86) hoydens : 말괄량이들
87) A Counterblast to Agnosticism : 불가지론에 대한 반박
88) I give my word that ~ : that 이하의 약속을 하다
89) to relieve him in following : 나중에 따라올 때 수월하게 해주려고
90) leave off work : 하던 일을 걷어치우다
91) by and by : 이윽고, 얼마 안가서(= before long)
92) Better than none : 없는 것보다는 낫다
93) facing and footing it : 얼굴을 맞대고 추다
94) clipsing and colling : 서로 껴안다(= hugging and embracing)
95) for'ard : 건방진(= forward)

to hand, which was not the speaker, as she had expected; nor did it happen to be Tess Durbeyfield. Pedigree, ancestral skeletons, monumental record, the d'Urberville lineaments, did not help Tess in her life's battle as yet, even to the extent of attracting to her a dancing-partner over the heads of the commonest peasantry. So much for Norman blood unaided by Victorian lucre.[96]

The name of the eclipsing girl[97], whatever it was, has not been handed down; but she was envied by all as the first who enjoyed the luxury of a masculine partner that evening. Yet such was the force of example that the village young men, who had not hastened to enter the gate while no intruder was in the way, now dropped in quickly, and soon the couples became leavened with[98] rustic youth to a marked extent, till at length the plainest woman in the club was no longer compelled to foot it on the masculine side of the figure[99].

The church clock struck, when suddenly the student said that he must leave — he had been forgetting himself — he had to join his companions. As he fell out of the dance his eyes lighted on Tess Durbeyfield, whose own large orbs wore, to tell the truth, the faintest aspect of reproach that he had not chosen her. He, too, was sorry then that, owing to her backwardness, he had not observed her; and with that in his mind he left the pasture.

On account of his long delay he started in a flying-run down the lane westward, and had soon passed the hollow and mounted the next rise. He had not yet overtaken his brothers, but he paused to get breath, and looked back. He could see the white figures of the girls in the green enclosure whirling about as they had whirled when he was among them. They seemed to have quite forgotten him already.

All of them, except, perhaps, one. This white shape stood apart by the hedge alone. From her position he knew it to be the pretty maiden with whom he had not danced. Trifling as the matter was, he yet instinctively felt that she was hurt by his oversight[100]. He wished that he had asked her; he wished that he had inquired her name. She was so modest, so expressive, she had looked so soft in her thin white gown that he felt he had acted stupidly.

However, it could not be helped, and turning, and bending himself to a rapid walk, he dismissed the subject from his mind.

Chapter 3

As for Tess Durbeyfield, she did not so easily dislodge the incident from her consideration[101]. She had no spirit to dance again for a long time, though she might have had plenty of partners;

---

96) So much ~ by Victorian lucre : 빅토리아 시대의 부유함으로 도움을 받지 못하는 노르만 시대의 혈통은 고작해야 이 정도일 뿐이었다. 즉, Tess가 노르만 귀족의 후손이지만 지금은 가난하게 살기 때문에 빛이 나지 않는다는 의미 / lucre : 이익, 금전, 부
97) eclipsing girl : 친구들을 무색하게 하는 여자
98) became leavened with : ~이 침투하여 섞였다
99) figure : 댄스에서 선회운동을 하는 한 가지
100) oversight : 실수(Angel이 Tess에게 춤을 권유하지 않았던 것)
101) dislodge ~ from her consideration : ~을 잊어버리고 생각하지 않다

but, ah! they did not speak so nicely as the strange young man had done. It was not till the rays of the sun had absorbed the young stranger's retreating figure on the hill that[102] she shook off her temporary sadness and answered her would-be partner[103] in the affirmative[104].

She remained with her comrades till dusk, and participated with a certain zest in the dancing; though, being heart-whole as yet, she enjoyed treading a measure purely for its own sake; little divining when she saw 'the soft torments, the bitter sweets, the pleasing pains, and the agreeable distresses'[105] of those girls who had been wooed and won, what she herself was capable of in that kind. The struggles and wrangles of the lads for her hand in a jig[106] were an amusement to her — no more; and when they became fierce she rebuked them.

She might have stayed[107] even later, but the incident of her father's odd appearance and manner returned upon the girl's mind[108] to make her anxious, and wondering what had become of him she dropped away from the dancers and bent her steps towards the end of the village at which the parental cottage lay.

While yet many score yards off, other rhythmic sounds than those she had quitted[109] became audible to her; sounds that she knew well — so well. They were a regular series of thumpings from the interior of the house, occasioned by the violent rocking of a cradle upon a stone floor, to which movement a feminine voice kept time[110] by singing, in a vigorous gallopade[111], the favourite ditty[112] of 'The Spotted Cow'[113] —

I saw her lie do'— own in yon' — der green gro'-ove;

Come, love!' and I'll tell' you where!'

The cradle-rocking and the song would cease simultaneously for a moment, and an exclamation at highest vocal pitch would take the place of the melody.

"God bless thy diment eyes! And thy waxen cheeks! And thy cherry mouth! And thy Cubit's thighs! And every bit o'thy blessed body!"

After this invocation the rocking and the singing would recommence, and 'the Spotted Cow' proceed as before. So matters stood[114] when Tess opened the door, and paused upon the mat within it surveying the scene.

The interior, in spite of the melody, struck upon the girl's senses with an unspeakable dreariness.

---

102) It was not till ~ that : ~하고서야 비로소 that 이하의 사실을 하였다
103) would-be partner : 춤 상대가 되고 싶어 하는 사람
104) answered in the affirmative : 동의하였다
105) the soft torments, the bitter sweets, the pleasing pains, and the agreeable distresses : 구애를 받고 마음을 허락한 여자들에게서 일어나는 복잡 미묘한 감정
106) jig : 경쾌하고 동작이 빠른 춤의 일종
107) might have stayed : 머무를 수도 있었다
108) returned upon the girl's mind : ~이 머리에 떠오르다
109) those she had quitted : 그녀가 뒤로 하고 온 소리, 즉 악대의 음악소리
110) keep time : 장단을 맞추다
111) gallopade : 헝가리에서 기원한 빠르고 경쾌한 댄스곡
112) ditty : 민요, 짧막한 노래
113) The Spotted Cow : '점박이암소'라는 민요
114) So matters stood : 상황이 이러했다

From the holiday gaieties of the field — the white gowns, the nosegays[115], the willow-wands, the whirling movements on the green, the flash of gentle sentiment towards the stranger — to the yellow melancholy of this one-candled spectacle, what a step![116] Besides the jar of contrast[117] there came to her a chill self-reproach that she had not returned sooner, to help her mother in these domesticities, instead of indulging herself out-of-doors.

There stood her mother amid the group of children, as Tess had left her, hanging over the Monday washing-tub, which had now, as always, lingered on to the end of the week[118]. Out of that tub had come the day before — Tess felt it with a dreadful sting of remorse — the very white frock upon her back which she had so carelessly greened[119] about the skirt on the damping grass — which had been wrung up and ironed by her mother's own hands.

As usual, Mrs Durbeyfield was balanced on one foot beside the tub, the other being engaged in the aforesaid business of rocking her youngest child. The cradle-rockers had done hard duty for so many years, under the weight of so many children, on that flagstone floor[120] that they were worn nearly flat, in consequence of which a huge jerk accompanied each swing of the cot[121], flinging the baby from side to side like a weaver's shuttle, as Mrs Durbeyfield, excited by her song, trod the rocker with all the spring that was left in her after a long day's seething in the suds[122].

Nick-knock, nick-knock, went the cradle; the candle-flame stretched itself tall, and began jigging up and down; the water dribbled from the matron's elbows, and the song galloped on to the end of the verse, Mrs. Durbeyfield regarding her daughter the while. Even now, when burdened with a young family, Joan Durbeyfield was a passionate lover of tune. No ditty floated into Blackmoor Vale from the outer world but Tess's mother caught up its notation in a week.

There still faintly beamed from the woman's features something of the freshness, and even the prettiness, of her youth; rendering it probable that the personal charms which Tess could boast of were in main part her mother's gift, and therefore unknightly[123], unhistorical.

"I'll rock the cradle for 'ee, mother," said the daughter gently. "or I'll take off my best frock and help you wring up? I thought you had finished long ago."

Her mother bore Tess no ill-will for leaving the house-work to her single-handed efforts for so long; indeed, Joan seldom up-braided her thereon at any time, feeling but slightly the lack of Tess's assistance whilst her instinctive plan for relieving herself of her labours lay in postponing them[124]. To-night, however, she was even in a blither mood than usual. There was a dreaminess, a preoccupation, an exaltation, in the maternal look which the girl could not understand.

---

115) nosegay : 꽃다발
116) what a step! : 얼마나 판이한가!
117) jar of contrast : 뚜렷한 대조에서 오는 충격
118) lingered on to the end of the week : 우물쭈물하다 주말까지 갔다
119) green : 풀물이 들다
120) flagstone floor : 판석을 깐 바닥
121) cot : 간이침대
122) seething in the suds : 빨래하는 일
123) unknightly : (Tess의 조상이) 기사와는 관계가 없는
124) her instinctive plan for ~ in postponing them : 그녀가 힘든 일을 면하고 싶을 때 세우는 본능적인 계획은 그것을 뒤로 미루는 데 있었다.

"Well, I'm glad you've come," her mother said, as soon as the last note had passed out of her. "I want to go and fetch your father; but what's more'n that[125], I want to tell 'ee what have happened. Y'll be fess[126] enough, my poppet,[127] when th'st[128] know!" (Mrs. Durbeyfield habitually spoke the dialect; her daughter, who had passed the Sixth Standard in the National School[129] under a London-trained mistress, spoke two languages; the dialect at home, more or less; ordinary English abroad and to persons of quality.)

"Since I've been away?" Tess asked.

"Ay!"

"Had it anything to do with father's making such a mommet[130] of himself in thik[131] carriage this afternoon? Why did'er?[132] I felt inclined to sink into the ground with shame!"

"That wer[133] all a part of the larry! We've been found to be the greatest gentlefolk in the whole county — reaching all back long before Oliver Grumble's time - to the days of the Pagan Turks — with monuments, and vaults, and crests, and scutcheons, and the Lord knows what all. In Saint Charles's days we was made Knights o' the Royal Oak, our real name being d'Urberville!... Don't that make your bosom plim? 'Twas on this account that your father rode home in the vlee; not because he'd been drinking, as people supposed."

"I m glad of that. Will it do us any good, mother?"

"O yes! 'Tis thoughted that great things may come o't. No doubt a mampus of volk of our own rank will be down here in their carriages as soon as 'tis known. Your father learnt it on his way hwome from Shaston, and he has been telling me the whole pedigree of the matter."

"Where is father now?" asked Tess suddenly.

Her mother gave irrelevant information by way of answer: "He called to see the doctor to-day in Shaston. It is not consumption at all, it seems. It is fat round his heart, 'a[134] says. There, it is like this." Joan Durbeyfield, as she spoke, curved a sodden thumb and forefinger to the shape of the letter C, and used the other forefinger as a pointer. "At the present moment," he says to your father, "your heart is enclosed all round there, and all round there; this space is still open," 'a says. "As soon as it do meet, so," " — Mrs Durbeyfield closed her fingers into a circle complete — " off you will go like a shadder[135], Mr Durbeyfield," 'a says. "You mid[136] last ten years; you mid go off in ten months, or ten days."

---

125) what's more'n that : 그보다 더 중요한 일은(= what's more than that)
126) fess : 자랑스러운(= proud)
127) my poppet : 애칭. 내 귀여운 딸아(= puppet)
128) th'st : thou dost(= you do)
129) Sixth Standard in the National School : 1811년 가난한 아이들의 교육을 위해서 국립 학교가 설립되었는데 여기서 Standard는 아이들의 학력을 나타내는 기준
130) mommet : 우쭐한 행동
131) thik : the, this, that
132) Why did'er? : 왜 그런 짓을 하셨을까?(= Why did he do it?)
133) That wer : That were
134) 'a : 그(= he)
135) shadder : 그늘
136) mid : might

Tess looked alarmed. Her father possibly to go behind the eternal cloud so soon, notwithstanding this sudden greatness!

"But where is father?" she asked again.

Her mother put on a deprecating look. "Now don't you be bursting out angry! The poor man — he felt so rafted[137] after his uplifting by the pa' son's news — that he went up to Rolliver's half an hour ago. He do want to get up his strength[138] for his journey tomorrow with that load of beehives, which must be delivered, family or no[139]. He'll have to start shortly after twelve to-night, as the distance is so long."

"Get up his strength!" said Tess impetuously, the tears welling to her eyes. "O my God! Go to a public house to get up his strength! And you as well agreed as he, mother!"

Her rebuke and her mood seemed to fill the whole room, and to impart a cowed look to the furniture, and candle, and children playing about, and to her mother's face.

"No," said the latter touchily, "I be not agreed. I have been waiting for 'ee to bide[140] and keep house while I go to fetch him."

"I'll go."

"O no, Tess. You see, it would be no use."

Tess did not expostulate. She knew what her mother's objection meant. Mrs Durbeyfield's jacket and bonnet were already hanging slily upon a chair by her side, in readiness for this contemplated jaunt[141], the reason for which the matron deplored more than its necessity.

"And take the *Compleat Fortune-Teller*[142] to the outhouse," Joan continued, rapidly wiping her hands, and donning the garments.

The Compleat Fortune-Teller was an old thick volume, which lay on a table at her elbow, so worn by pocketing that the margins had reached the edge of the type. Tess took it up, and her mother started.

This going to hunt up her shiftless husband at the inn was one of Mrs Durbeyfield's still extant enjoyments in the muck and muddle[143] of rearing children. To discover him at Rolliver's, to sit there for an hour or two by his side and dismiss all thought and care of the children during the interval, made her happy. A sort of halo, an occidental glow, came over life then. Troubles and other realities took on themselves a metaphysical impalpability[144], sinking to mere mental phenomena for serene contemplation, and no longer stood as pressing concretions which chafed body and soul. The youngsters, not immediately within sight, seemed rather bright and desirable appurtenances than otherwise; the incidents of daily life were not without humorousness and jollity in their aspect there.

---

137) feel so rafted : 마음이 산란해 지다
138) get up one's strength : 원기를 북돋다
139) family or no : 가문이 어떻든지 간에
140) bide : 머물다(= stay)
141) jaunt : 소풍
142) the Compleat Fortune-Teller : 여기선 책 이름이다 / compleat = complete / fortune-teller : 점쟁이
143) muck and muddle : 성가시고 너절한 일
144) metaphysical impalpability : 형이상학적 불가사의

She felt a little as she had used to feel when she sat by her now wedded husband in the same spot during his wooing, shutting her eyes to his defects of character, and regarding him only in his ideal presentation as lover.

Tess, being left alone with the younger children, went first to the outhouse with the fortune-telling book, and stuffed it into the thatch. A curious fetishistic fear[145] of this grimy volume on the part of her mother prevented her ever allowing it to stay in the house all night, and hither it was brought back whenever it had been consulted. Between the mother, with her fast-perishing lumber of superstitions, folk-lore, dialect, and orally transmitted ballads, and the daughter, with her trained National teachings and Standard knowledge under an infinitely Revised Code[146], there was a gap of two hundred years as ordinarily understood. When they were together the Jacobean and the Victorian ages[147] were juxtaposed.

Returning along the garden path, Tess mused on what the mother could have wished to ascertain from the book on this particular day. She guessed the recent ancestral discovery to bear upon it[148], but did not divine that it solely concerned herself. Dismissing this, however, she busied herself with sprinkling the linen dried during the daytime, in company with her nine-year-old brother Abraham, and her sister Eliza-Louisa of twelve and a half, called "Liza-Lu," the youngest ones being put to bed. There was an interval of four years and more between Tess and the next of the family, the two who had filled the gap having died in their infancy, and this lent her a deputy-maternal attitude[149] when she was alone with her juniors. Next in juvenility to Abraham came two more girls, Hope and Modesty; then a boy of three, and then the baby, who had just completed his first year.

All these young souls were passengers in the Durbeyfield ship — entirely dependent on the judgment of the two Durbeyfield adults for their pleasures, their necessities, their health, even their existence. If the heads of the Durbeyfield household chose to sail into difficulty, disaster, starvation, disease, degradation, death, thither were these half-dozen little captives under hatches compelled to sail with them — six helpless creatures, who had never been asked if they wished for life on any terms[150], much less if they wished for it on such hard conditions as were involved in being of the shiftless house of Durbeyfield. Some people would like to know whence the poet whose philosophy is in these days deemed as profound and trustworthy as his song is breezy and pure, gets his authority for speaking of 'Nature's holy plan'[151].

It grew later, and neither father nor mother reappeared. Tess looked out of the door, and took a mental journey through Marlott. The village was shutting its eyes[152]. Candles and lamps were

---

145) fetishistic fear : 미신적인 공포심
146) Revised Code : 1862년과 1867년 두 차례에 걸쳐 개정된 (초등)교육 개선에 관한 법령이다.
147) the Jacobean and the Victorian ages : James 1세(1603~1625)와 Victoria 여왕(1837~1901) 시대에는 약 200년의 간격이 있다. 그만큼 교육을 받은 Tess와 미신을 믿는 어머니 Joan 사이에 간격이 있다는 의미이다.
148) bear upon it : 그것과 관련이 있다(여기서 it은 점책으로 운수를 점친 사람을 가리킨다)
149) deputy-maternal attitude : 어머니 대신 어머니 노릇을 하는 태도
150) on any terms : 어떠한 조건으로든
151) Nature's holy plan : 자연의 성스러운 계획
152) shutting its eyes : 등불이 하나 둘 꺼져가는 모습

being put out everywhere: she could inwardly behold the extinguisher[153] and the extended hand.

Her mother's fetching simply meant one more to fetch. Tess began to perceive that a man in indifferent health, who proposed to start on a journey before one in the morning, ought not to be at an inn at this late hour celebrating his ancient blood.

"Abraham," she said to her little brother, "do you put on your hat — you bain't[154] afraid? — and go up to Rolliver's, and see what has gone wi' father and mother[155]." The boy jumped promptly from his seat, and opened the door, and the night swallowed him up. Half an hour passed yet again; neither man, woman, nor child returned. Abraham, like his parents, seemed to have been limed and caught by the ensnaring inn.

"I must go myself," she said.

'Liza-Lu then went to bed, and Tess, locking them all in, started on her way up the dark and crooked lane or street not made for hasty progress; a street laid out before inches of land had value, and when one-handed clocks sufficiently subdivided the day[156].

---

153) extinguisher : 불을 끄는 사람
154) bain't : be not이나 are not의 뜻
155) what has gone wi' father and mother : 아버지와 어머니에게 무슨 일이 생겼는지(여기에서 wi'는 with이다)
156) when ~ subdivided the day : 시계 바늘 하나로 하루의 시간을 충분히 나누던 때, 즉 몇 시인지만 알면 되고 분초는 따질 줄 모르던 시대

실전예상문제

01 「*Oliver Twist*」는 Charles Dickens 의 소설이다.

제 2 장 **Jane Austen –** 「*Pride and Prejudice*」

01 다음 중 Jane Austen의 작품이 <u>아닌</u> 것은?

① 「*Mansfield Park*」
② 「*Sense and Sensibility*」
③ 「*Oliver Twist*」
④ 「*Emma*」

02 Jane Austen은 6편의 장편소설을 집필하였는데, 모두 젊은 여성의 결혼에 관한 이야기이다.

02 Jane Austen의 작품 세계에 대한 설명으로 옳지 <u>않은</u> 것은?

① 동 시대의 사람들을 위하여 글을 썼던 Austen은 자신을 의식하게 되는 배경이나 시사적인 사건의 언급을 피했다.
② Jane Austen의 소설 속에는 당시 유행하던 고딕적인 요소가 반영되어 있다.
③ Jane Austen의 여섯 편의 장편소설 중 세 개만 결혼에 관한 이야기들이다.
④ Jane Austen 소설의 중심인물들은 주로 젠트리(Gentry) 계급에 속한다.

정답 (01 ③ 02 ③)

03 「*Pride and Prejudice*」의 주제로 옳지 <u>않은</u> 것은?

① 개인이 사회에 편입되어 공동체와 조화를 이루는 과정을 다룬다.
② 특정한 종류의 인간관계를 제시한다.
③ 인간관계에서의 예법(good manners)의 중요성을 강조하지만 그것이 과도할 때에는 조소를 던진다.
④ 결혼 상대의 선택이 중심 주제이다.

03 이 소설에서는 부부나 형제자매, 친구 등과 같은 다양한 종류의 인간관계를 보여준다.

04 「*Pride and Prejudice*」에서 Elizabeth가 청혼을 거절한 상대는 누구인가?

① Mr. Collins and Mr. Darcy
② Mr. Collins and Mr. Bingley
③ Mr. Darcy and Mr. Bingley
④ Mr. Darcy and Wickham

04 Elizabeth가 청혼을 거절한 상대는 Mr. Collins와 Mr. Darcy이다. Mr. Bingley는 Jane에게 청혼하여 결혼하고 Wickham은 돈을 쫓는 난봉꾼이다.

05 「*Pride and Prejudice*」에서 Mr. Collins와 결혼하는 상대는?

① Charlotte Lucas
② Georgianna Darcy
③ Miss Bingley
④ Jane Bennet

05 Georgianna Darcy는 Mr. Darcy의 동생이다. Miss Bingley는 Mr. Darcy와 결혼을 원하지만 실패한다. Jane Bennet은 Mr. Bingley와 결혼한다.

정답 03 ② 04 ① 05 ①

06 Jane과 Bingley는 비슷한 성격을 가진 서로에게 끌려 결혼한다.

07 Catherine Earnshaw는 Emily Brontë의 「*Wuthering Heights*」에 등장하는 인물이다.

08 Lady Catherine de Bourgh는 Darcy의 이모로 남의 일에 참견하기 좋아하는 인물이다.

정답 06 ③ 07 ④ 08 ①

06 「*Pride and Prejudice*」에 등장하는 인물들과 그들의 결혼에 대한 설명으로 틀린 것은?

① Lydia와 Wickham : 성급한 열정에 의한 결혼
② Charlotte와 Collins : 경제적 현실에 의한 결혼
③ Jane과 Bingley : 부모님의 정략에 의한 결혼
④ Elizabeth와 Darcy : 대조적인 성격으로 서로를 보완하는 결혼

07 Jane Austen의 소설에서 등장인물에 해당하지 <u>않는</u> 인물은?

① Caroline Bingley
② Fitzwilliam Darcy
③ Catherine Bennet
④ Catherine Earnshaw

08 「*Pride and Prejudice*」에서 Mr. Darcy의 청혼을 Elizabeth가 거절하도록 이끈 인물은?

① Lady Catherine de Bourgh
② Mrs. Gardner
③ Mr. Bennet
④ Jane Bennet

09 Jane Austen의 소설에 대한 설명으로 <u>틀린</u> 것은?

① 남녀들은 결혼을 통해 성숙한 개인으로서의 운명을 성취하게 됨과 동시에 그들의 합쳐진 에너지와 지성으로 좀 더 나은 사회를 만드는 데 기여한다.

② 저택이나 토지의 운명은 그 소유주의 도덕적인 역량과 사회적 책임감과 밀접한 관련성을 가진다.

③ 낭만주의적 영웅과 악당이 등장하여 대조를 이룬다.

④ 도덕성과 좋은 예법이 중요시되며, 풍자되는 인물들이 나타난다.

09 Jane Austen 소설의 등장인물들은 현실적이고 평범한 인물들이다.

10 Jane Austen 소설에 관한 설명으로 <u>옳지 않은</u> 것은?

① 연장자들의 안 좋은 영향을 견뎌낸 젊은 인물들은 더 나은 인물이 된다.

② 계층 간의 갈등을 통해 사회는 더 나은 방향으로 개선된다.

③ 결혼은 사회의 근본이 되는 공적인 요소이다.

④ 개인의 올바른 행동양식이 올바른 사회를 만들게 된다.

10 계층 간의 갈등은 Austen 소설의 소재가 아니다.

11 「*Pride and Prejudice*」에서 여주인공인 Elizabeth에 관한 설명으로 <u>옳지 않은</u> 것은?

① Bennet 가문의 두 번째 딸로 소설의 여자 주인공이다.

② 자존심과 진실한 자아를 가지고 사물에 대한 정확한 판단력과 지성을 지니고 있다.

③ 낙천적이고 사교적인 성격의 소유자이다.

④ 지나친 지성과 판단력으로 편견을 불러일으키기도 한다.

11 낙천적이고 사교적인 성격의 소유자는 Mr. Bingley이다.

정답   09 ③   10 ②   11 ③

checkpoint 해설 & 정답

12 Emily Brontë의 「*Wuthering Heights*」에 대한 설명이다.

12 Jane Austen의 작품에 대한 설명이 <u>아닌</u> 것은?

① 특정한 어떤 유파의 작가군에 속하지 않는다.

② Jane Austen의 작품은 신고전주의와 낭만주의 사이에 있다.

③ 문체는 18세기 중엽 문예 전성기의 시인과 산문 작가들의 문체에 훨씬 가깝다.

④ 빅토리아조에 속한 작품이라기보다는 Blake이나 Keats의 시 정신과 맥이 닿아있는 낭만주의적 작품이다.

정답 12 ④

제 3 장   Emily Brontë – 「*Wuthering Heights*」

01 Emily Brontë의 필명은 무엇인가?

① Emily Kant

② Ellis Bell

③ Eden Marve

④ Maria Brontë

01 Emily Brontë의 필명은 Ellis Bell 이다.

02 「*Wuthering Heights*」가 출판된 연도는?

① 1845년

② 1846년

③ 1864년

④ 1847년

02 「*Wuthering Heights*」는 1847년에 초판본이 출판되었다.

03 「*Wuthering Heights*」에 대한 설명으로 옳지 <u>않은</u> 것은?

① 산업 사회의 문제점을 직접적으로 드러내고 있다.

② 남녀 간의 못다 한 사랑 이야기를 다룬다.

③ Heathcliff는 자신을 학대하고 무시한 사람들에게 복수를 행한다.

④ 로맨스와 리얼리즘 소설의 중간에 위치하고 있다.

03 이 소설은 산업 사회의 문제점을 직접적으로 드러내고 있지는 않다. Emily Brontë는 산업 사회와 동떨어진 황야에서 살았던 작가였다. 이러한 그녀의 소설에는 산업 사회의 혼란상이 직접적으로 드러나 있지는 않다.

정답 01 ② 02 ④ 03 ①

checkpoint 해설 & 정답

04 Mr. Earnshaw는 여행 중에 길에서 어린 고아인 Heathcliff를 만나 그를 집으로 데려온다. 그리고 자신의 딸 Catherine과 아들 Hindley와 함께 아들로 키운다.

04 「*Wuthering Heights*」에서 Heathcliff는 Mr. and Mrs. Earnshaw와 어떤 관계인가?

① Mr. and Mrs. Earnshaw의 조카이다.
② Mr. and Mrs. Earnshaw의 아들이다.
③ Mr. and Mrs. Earnshaw의 영지에서 발견되었다.
④ Mr. Earnshaw가 여행 중에 발견하여 집으로 데려온 고아이다.

05 이 작품의 주제는 Heathcliff의 복수와 반역, 경제적인 소외와 사회 계급문제, 남녀 간의 사랑, 그리고 Wuthering Heights와 Thrushcross Grange의 대조적인 삶의 방식이다.

05 「*Wuthering Heights*」의 주제로 볼 수 <u>없는</u> 것은?

① 복수
② 대조적인 삶의 방식
③ 사회 계급문제
④ 여성의 독립적인 삶

06 「*Wuthering Heights*」에서 인물상은 크게 두 가지의 성격으로 구분할 수 있다. Wuthering Heights형(型) 인물은 강인하고 정열적이며 격렬한 인간형인 반면에 Thrushcross Grange형(型) 인물은 수동적이고 교양적이며 조용한 인간형이다.

06 「*Wuthering Heights*」의 특징이 <u>아닌</u> 것은?

① 이중 구조로 되어 있다.
② 두 명의 화자가 있으며, Nelly(Ellen) Dean은 중심 화자이다.
③ Wuthering Heights에 거주하는 인물들은 교양적인 반면, Thrushcross Grange에 거주하는 인물들은 정열적이고 격렬하다.
④ 작가의 자기 반영적인 테크닉을 볼 수 있다.

정답 04 ④ 05 ④ 06 ③

07 「*Wuthering Heights*」에서 Frame-narrator에 해당하는 인물은?

① Catherine Earnshaw
② Heathcliff
③ Mr. Earnshaw
④ Mr. Lockwood

08 다음은 「*Wuthering Heights*」의 일부분이다. 이 장면에서 밑줄 친 "I"는 누구인가?

> "Let me in - let me in!"
> "Who are you?" I asked, struggling, meanwhile, to disengage myself.
> "Catherine Linton," it replied, shiveringly (why did I think of *Linton?* I had read Earnshaw twenty times for Linton). "I'm come home, I'd lost my way on the moor!"

① Heathcliff
② Mr. Earnshaw
③ Mr. Lockwood
④ Nelly Dean

09 다음 중 「*Wuthering Heights*」의 특징과 거리가 <u>먼</u> 것은?

① 역사소설
② 로맨스
③ 빅토리아조 소설
④ 고딕소설

07 「*Wuthering Heights*」에는 두 명의 서술자, Mr. Lockwood와 Nelly Dean (Ellen)이 있으며 도시와 사람들을 피해 한적한 지방(Yorkshire)에 있는 Thrushcross Grange에 머물기로 한 Mr. Lockwood는 Wuthering Height와 Thrushcross Grange에서 오랫동안 지낸 가정부 Nelly Dean의 이야기를 들으며 소설의 전체적인 내용을 서술하는 Frame-narrator이다.

08 집주인인 Heathcliff를 보러 Wuthering Heights에 방문한 Mr. Lockwood는 눈보라 때문에 Thrushcross Grange에 돌아가지 못하고 Wuthering Heights에 하루를 머무르게 된다. 그곳에서 Catherine Earnshaw(Linton)의 일기를 읽다가 잠이 드는데, 창문에 나타난 Catherine의 유령은 황무지에서 길을 잃고 20년 동안 기다렸다고 말한다. Heathcliff는 Catherine의 유령을 찾아 황급히 뛰어나간다. 이 장면은 초자연적 요소를 포함하는 「*Wuthering Heights*」의 고딕 소설적인 요소를 잘 드러낸다.

09 「*Wuthering Heights*」는 고딕 로맨스 소설로, 낭만주의적 속성과 빅토리아조 소설 속성을 모두 담고 있으며 로맨스와 리얼리즘 중간쯤에 위치하고 있다고 할 수 있다. 그러나 이 소설을 역사소설로 분류하기엔 어려움이 있다.

정답 07 ④　08 ③　09 ①

10　Edgar Linton과 결혼 후에도 Heathcliff를 잊지 못하는 Catherine의 이중적인 태도는 Heathcliff와 Edgar Linton의 갈등을 더욱 크게 야기시킨다. 나아가 양쪽 집안을 혼돈으로 빠트리는 결과를 낳는다. Catherine은 Heathcliff와 황야를 맨발로 헤매는가 하면, 귀부인의 모습도 보여주는 두 가지의 속성을 공유한 여주인공이다.

10　「*Wuthering Heights*」에서 Catherine에 대한 설명으로 옳지 <u>않은</u> 것은?

① Hindley의 여동생이다.
② 신분상의 장벽을 이유로 Edgar Linton과 결혼한다.
③ Linton과 결혼 후부터는 귀부인의 모습으로 변화하여 살아간다.
④ 결혼 후에도 Heathcliff를 잊지 못하고 이중적인 태도를 지닌다.

11　두 명의 서술자는 정상적이고 관습적인 평범한 시각으로 독자에게 내용을 전달한다.

11　「*Wuthering Heights*」의 구조에 대한 설명으로 옳지 <u>않은</u> 것은?

① 두 명의 서술자가 등장한다.
② 극단으로 치닫고자 하는 본능과 그 본능을 억압하고자 하는 또 다른 본능의 갈등관계를 상징한다.
③ 두 명의 서술자는 격정적이고 폭풍 같은 시각으로 독자에게 내용을 전달한다.
④ 두 명의 화자를 통해 Wuthering Heights에서 벌어지는 믿기 힘든 일들을 독자들이 믿을 수 있게 하는 가교의 역할을 한다.

12　① Mr. Lockwood는 Wuthering Heights에 숨겨진 의문을 풀기 위해 Nelly Dean(Ellen)에게 질문을 하여 답변하게 하는 형식의 서술구조를 가진다.
② Mr. Lockwood는 Wuthering Heights에 세를 들어 살고 있다.
③ Nelly Dean(Ellen)은 Catherine이 Edgar Linton과 결혼하자 그녀를 보살피기 위해 Thrushcross Grange로 거처를 옮긴다.

12　「*Wuthering Heights*」에서 서술자들에 관한 설명으로 옳은 것은?

① Mr. Lockwood는 Wuthering Heights에 숨겨진 의문을 풀기 위해 직접 조사를 한다.
② Mr. Lockwood는 Wuthering Heights를 구매하려고 한다.
③ Nelly Dean(Ellen)은 Catherine이 Edgar Linton과 결혼한 후, Wuthering Heights에 남아 가족들을 보필한다.
④ Nelly Dean(Ellen)은 포근한 모성애와 포용력으로 다른 등장인물 간의 갈등을 조율한다.

정답　10 ③　11 ③　12 ④

13 「*Wuthering Heights*」에서 Young Catherine은 누구의 딸인가?

① Catherine and Edgar Linton

② Mr. and Mrs. Linton

③ Hindley and Francis Earnshaw

④ Catherine and Heathcliff

13 Young Catherine은 Catherine과 Edgar Linton의 딸이다. Linton 가문의 재산까지 손에 넣으려는 Heathcliff에 의하여 그의 아들인 Linton Heathcliff와 강제로 결혼하게 된다. Linton Heathcliff가 죽고 미망인이 된 그녀는 Wuthering Heights에서 Heathcliff, Hareton Earnshaw와 함께 살게 된다. Heathcliff의 사망 후에는 Hareton Earnshaw와 결혼한다.

14 「*Wuthering Heights*」에서 Isabella Linton은 누구와 사랑에 빠져 결혼하는가?

① Heathcliff

② Edgar

③ Lockwood

④ Hareton

14 Isabella Linton은 Edgar Linton의 여동생이다. Heathcliff의 유혹으로 그와 결혼한다. 그러나 그가 자신의 집안에 복수를 하기 위해 자신과 결혼했다는 것을 알고 집을 나간 후 아들인 Linton Heathcliff가 12살 되던 해에 죽는다.

15 「*Wuthering Heights*」의 시대적 배경에 대한 설명으로 옳지 않은 것은?

① 빅토리아조에 속한 작품이라기보다는 낭만주의적 작품이라 할 수 있다.

② 소설이 출판되던 당시엔 불유쾌하고 악마적이라는 비판을 받아 판매가 거의 되지 않았다.

③ 훗날 Thomas Hardy, D. H. Lawrence, Joseph Conrad로 명맥이 이어진다.

④ 빅토리아조의 사회적 틀에 맞지 않는 독특한 소설이다.

15 당시엔 불유쾌하고 악마적이라는 비판을 받은 것은 사실이나 책은 매우 많이 판매되었다.

정답 13 ① 14 ① 15 ②

제 **4** 장 Charles Dickens – 「*Great Expectations*」

01 「*Adam Bede*」는 3권으로 이루어진 George Eliot의 첫 장편소설로서 인간적인 동정과 엄격한 도덕적 판단이 결합된 내용에 시골풍의 분위기가 풍기는 사실주의 작품이다.

01 다음 중 찰스 디킨스의 작품이 <u>아닌</u> 것은?

① 「*Adam Bede*」
② 「*Oliver Twist*」
③ 「*Bleak House*」
④ 「*Little Dorrit*」

02 이 작품에서는 열심히 노력한 대가로 얻은 돈은 결코 비난받지 않는다는 노동의 가치를 하나의 주제로 내세우고 있으나, 농업의 중요성과는 관계가 없다.

02 「*Great Expectations*」의 주제로 볼 수 <u>없는</u> 것은?

① 유산
② 노동의 가치
③ 농업의 중요성
④ 인간의 유대관계

03 유산 문제는 「*Little Dorrit*」에서도 볼 수 있듯이 디킨스의 소설에서 고정적으로 등장하는 주제이다. 「*Great Expectations*」에서 작가는 재산이 없다가 갑자기 생기면 사람이 어떻게 변하는가를 관찰한 후 마지막에는 재산을 다시 빼앗고 돈이 없는 상태에서 인간적 의미를 찾도록 한다.
① 프랑스 혁명은 「*A Tale of Two Cities*」의 주제이다.
③ 귀신 이야기는 「*A Christmas Carol*」의 주제이다.
④ 남녀 간의 삼각관계는 디킨스의 소설에 고정적으로 등장하는 주제가 아니다.

03 찰스 디킨스의 소설에 고정적으로 등장하는 주제는?

① 프랑스 혁명
② 유산문제
③ 귀신 이야기
④ 남녀 간의 삼각관계

정답 (01 ① 02 ③ 03 ②)

04 「*Great Expectations*」의 등장인물 중 다음 설명에 해당하는 인물은?

> Pip이 정신적인 구심점이라면 이 사람은 도덕적 실천의 구심점이라고 할 수 있다. 천성이 선량한 인물로, 비록 신분은 대장장이지만 내면에는 진정한 신사만이 가질 수 있는 온화한 심성이 넘쳐흐르고 있다.

① Abel Magwitch
② Herbert Pocket
③ Miss Havisham
④ Joseph Gargery

04 Joseph Gargery는 Pip의 매형으로 Pip이 정신적인 구심점이라면 Joseph Gargery는 도덕적 실천적인 구심점이라고 할 수 있다. Pip은 선량해지고자 애를 쓰지만 Joseph Gargery는 천성이 선량하다. 그는 영원한 Pip의 보호자로서 촌스럽다며 자신을 멀리하고 떠난 Pip이 런던에서 Magwitch와 Estella, 그리고 빚과 열병으로 고생하며 인생의 고비에 서 있었을 때, 그에게 다가가 보살펴주며 진정한 참모습을 지닌 인간상으로 다가간다. 이렇게 Joseph Gargery는 Pip에게 위대하고 진실한 인간상을 보여주고 비로소 Pip은 '위대한 유산'을 물려받게 되는 것이다.

05 「*Great Expectations*」에서 Pip에게 돈을 줌으로써 그를 런던에서 신사 수업을 받을 수 있도록 한 인물은?

① Miss Havisham
② Estella
③ Joe Gregory
④ Magwitch

05 Pip은 갑자기 익명으로 자신에게 보내어진 돈이 생기자 Miss Havisham이 자신에게 막대한 재산을 물려줬다고 생각했으나 사실은 Magwitch가 자신이 도망칠 때 먹을 것을 가져다 준 보답으로 Pip에게 보낸 것이었다.

06 「*Great Expectations*」에 대한 설명으로 옳지 않은 것은?

① 주인공 Pip은 작가의 목소리를 대변하는 인물이다.
② 총 2부(Volume)로 구성되어 있다.
③ 1인칭 화자의 시점이다.
④ 우스꽝스러운 과장법, 풍자, 중후한 어조, 비극적인 엄숙한 어조 등이 많이 쓰인다.

06 이 작품은 총 3부(Volume)로 구성되어 있다. 1부는 Pip의 소년시절에 소년의 눈으로 보고 있기 때문에 환상과 비논리가 섞여 있다. 2부는 런던에서 Pip의 청년시절 개안과 변모의 과정이 이루어지며 사회 풍자와 경제적 문제 등이 등장한다. 3부에서는 Pip이 사회의 적극적인 참여자가 되고 탐정 소설과 같은 장면이 많이 나온다.

정답 (04 ④   05 ④   06 ②)

07 디킨스의 작품들은 대부분 3인칭 시점을 사용하지만, 자전적 소설인 「*David Copperfield*」와 「*Great Expectations*」에는 1인칭 시점이 사용된다.

07 다음 중 찰스 디킨스의 작품 세계와 관련이 <u>없는</u> 것은?

① 사회 비판 및 항거의 분위기가 작품 속에 흐른다.
② 빈곤과 가난한 사람들의 투쟁을 묘사한다.
③ 대부분 1인칭 화자의 시점이 사용된다.
④ 영국 산업 사회와 열악한 노동 조건을 다룬다.

08 Miss Havisham의 저택인 Satis House에서 Estella를 처음 만난 Pip은 그녀를 사랑하게 된다. Estella는 Pip의 사회적 신분이 비천하다는 이유로 수치감을 그에게 안겨주지만 Pip은 계속 그녀에게 그의 진실한 사랑을 보인다.

08 「*Great Expectations*」에서 Pip이 신사가 되어 런던에 가서 멋지게 살아보려는 욕심이 생기게 만드는 촉매제가 되는 인물은 누구인가?

① Estella
② Compeyson
③ Magwitch
④ Pumblechook

09 인과응보는 George Eliot의 「*Silas Marner*」의 주제이다.

09 「*Great Expectations*」에 대한 설명으로 거리가 먼 것은?

① 당시에 만연했던 물질 만능주의를 고발한 작품이다.
② 식민지 유배의 문제와 식민지적 배경을 다룬다.
③ 인과응보의 주제를 내포한다.
④ 신사의 본질의 주제를 다룬다.

정답 07 ③ 08 ① 09 ③

10 다음 중 「*Great Expectations*」에 등장하지 <u>않는</u> 인물은?

① Bentley Drummle

② Herbert Pocket

③ George Wickham

④ Wemmick

11 Charles Dickens에 관한 설명으로 옳지 <u>않은</u> 것은?

① 아버지는 호인이었으나 금전관념이 희박하였다.

② 어린 시절에는 학교에 어렵지 않게 다닐 정도로 매우 부유하였다.

③ 어린 디킨스가 노동계층으로 전락하여 느끼는 좌절감은 「*David Copperfield*」에 나타나있다.

④ 여러 신문사에 글을 기고하면서 소설의 인기로 많은 돈을 벌게 되었다.

12 Charles Dickens 작품의 특징으로 옳은 것은?

① 이성보다 감성, 형식보다 내용을 중시한 낭만주의로 시작하였다.

② 현실을 객관적으로 직시하지 못하였다.

③ 신흥 귀족 계급의 일상생활을 묘사하였다.

④ 산업제도에서 생겨난 빈민굴의 빈자와 비참한 삶을 비관적이라는 신념으로 묘사하였다.

13 서술자의 자기 연민은 자전적 소설
    인「*David Copperfield*」에서 나타
    난다.

13 「*Great Expectations*」에 관한 설명으로 옳지 <u>않은</u> 것은?

① Pip의 위대한 유산은 따뜻하고 진정성 있는 인간이었다.

② 식민지 시대에 쓰인 작품인 만큼 식민지에 대한 견해에 한계
가 있다.

③ 돈의 이면에는 범죄와 음모 같은 짙은 어둠이 깔려있다.

④ 서술자의 자기 연민이나 근거 없는 편견이 강하다.

정답 13 ④

제 5 장   George Eliot – 「*Silas Marner : The Weaver of Raveloe*」

01 「*Silas Marner*」에서 주인공인 Silas Marner에 대한 설명으로 옳지 **않은** 것은?

① 단순하고 본능적이며 심도 깊은 교육을 받지 못한 인물이다.
② Lantern Yard에서도 돈만 밝히는 벌레 같은 삶을 살았다.
③ 새로 이사 간 마을에서 어떤 사건을 계기로 신에 대한 믿음과 애정을 되찾았다.
④ 상상력이 풍부하고 자연에 대해 존중하는 근로자층 계급의 주인공이다.

01 Lantern Yard의 교회에서 신앙심을 인정받던 청년이었으나 누명을 쓰게 된 후 신에 대한 불신과 인간에 대한 실망감을 돈으로 보상받으려 했다.

02 George Eliot에 대한 설명으로 옳지 **않은** 것은?

① 영국 남부 외진 마을에서 태어났다.
② 작품들은 사실주의적으로 심도 있게 묘사하였다.
③ 「*Adam Bede*」는 3권으로 이루어진 첫 장편소설이다.
④ 가명으로 작품을 썼다.

02 George Eliot은 영국 동부의 농장에서 태어났다.

03 다음 설명에서 괄호 안에 들어갈 용어를 순서대로 바르게 짝지은 것은?

> George Eliot의 작품들은 전통적인 영국의 (ⓐ) 생활을 주로 다루었으며, 그 속에서 살아가는 소박한 인물들의 심리를 유머와 애수를 사용하여 (ⓑ)적으로 심도 있게 묘사하였다.

	ⓐ	ⓑ
①	도시	초현실주의
②	농촌 공동체	사실주의
③	도시	사실주의
④	농촌 공동체	초현실주의

03 George Eliot의 작품들은 시골생활을 배경으로 평범한 주인공들의 삶과 애환, 일상을 유머와 애수를 담아 사실적으로 묘사하고 있다.

정답 01 ② 02 ① 03 ②

04 「*Silas Marner*」는 변화, 인간 소외, 과거의 중요성, 인과응보의 관계 외에도 인간적인 사랑, 종교의 문제, 계급사회의 문제, 근로의 중요성 등을 주제로 하고 있다.

05 이 작품에서는 다양한 상징이 쓰이고 있다. 예를 들어 Silas Marner는 곤충에 비유되고 Eppie는 나무처럼 자란다고 표현하고 있다.

06 Godfrey Cass는 젊고 멋있으며, 부유하고 매력적이다. 또한 Silas Marner가 억울한 누명을 쓸 때에도 본인은 죗값을 교묘히 피해간다.

04 다음 중 「*Silas Marner*」의 주제로 옳지 <u>않은</u> 것은?

① 변화
② 인간 소외
③ 미래의 중요성
④ 인과응보의 관계

05 다음 중 「*Silas Marner*」의 특징이 <u>아닌</u> 것은?

① 총 2부로 구성되어 있고 각 부의 시차는 16년이다.
② 상징은 쓰이지 않았다.
③ 3인칭 전지적 작가 시점이다.
④ 강건체를 사용하고 있다.

06 「*Silas Marner*」에서 Silas Marner와 정반대 인간상을 가진 인물은?

① Squire Cass
② Nancy Lammeter
③ Eppie
④ Godfrey Cass

정답 04 ③ 05 ② 06 ④

07 George Eliot에 대한 설명으로 옳지 <u>않은</u> 것은?

① 어린 시절에 그녀의 종교인 청교도에 대한 열정이 깊었다.
② Hendel의 저서를 읽은 후 편협하고 극단적인 종교적 신념을 버리고 불가지론적 성향을 띠게 된다.
③ 대부분 산업 사회의 폐해에 관한 작품을 썼다.
④ 생활고로 인해 자유기고가 활동을 시작했다.

07 George Eliot은 대부분 전통적인 영국의 농촌 공동체 생활을 작품에서 다루었다.

08 「Silas Marner」에 관한 설명으로 옳지 <u>않은</u> 것은?

① 주인공 Silas Marner는 Lantern Yard에서의 배반으로 무신론자가 되었다.
② Raveloe에 이사를 온 후부터 마을 공동체 사람들과 친밀한 유대관계를 맺었다.
③ 금화 도난 사건을 통해 Silas Marner는 마을 공동체의 일원이 되었다.
④ Eppie는 친딸이 아니다.

08 Raveloe에 이사를 온 후, 자신의 존재에 대한 감각을 상실하고 순전히 거미처럼 충동에 의해 옷감을 짜는 벌레처럼 생활하였다.

09 「Silas Marner」에 대한 설명으로 옳지 <u>않은</u> 것은?

① Eppie의 선택은 유기적인 사회적 결속은 상류계급보다 노동계급에서 형성되고 있음을 암시한다.
② Silas Marner가 믿어야 할 것은 자신의 내부에 있는 타인에 대한 사랑의 빛이었다.
③ 다시 돌아간 Lantern Yard는 이름의 상징처럼 빛과 질서가 가득했다.
④ 자신 속의 선함을 확신하는 것은 사랑과 믿음의 근본이 된다.

09 다시 돌아간 Lantern Yard는 암흑 속으로 사라져 공장과 감옥만 흉물처럼 남아 있었다.

정답 07 ③ 08 ② 09 ③

10 Dustan Cass는 타고난 행운을 믿었고, Godfrey Cass가 끈기 있게 자신의 운명의 귀추를 기다렸다.

10 「*Silas Marner*」의 등장인물에 대한 설명으로 옳지 <u>않은</u> 것은?

① Dunstan Cass는 끈기 있게 자신의 운명의 귀추를 기다렸다.
② Dolly Winthrop은 지상에서의 선행은 보상받는다고 믿었다.
③ Squire Cass는 마을에서 가장 존경받는 인물이지만 이기적이고 자기중심적인 면도 가지고 있다.
④ Nancy Lammeter는 자신이 정한 엄격한 도덕률에 매여 살고 있다.

11 「*Little Dorrit*」은 Charles Dickens의 작품이다.
① 「*Middlemarch*」(1871~1872)는 'Middlemarch'라는 지역에 사는 여러 계층의 사람들, 즉 상점주인, 노동자, 농부, 제조업자, 목수 등 평범한 사람들의 일상을 유머와 애수를 이용하여 사실적으로 묘사한 작품이다.
② 「*Adam Bede*」(1859)는 3권으로 이루어진 Eliot의 첫 장편소설로 인간적인 동정과 엄격한 도덕적 판단이 결합된 내용에 시골풍의 분위기가 풍기는 사실주의 작품이다.
③ 「*Silas Marner*」(1861)는 고향에서 친구에게 배신당한 주인공이 신(God)과 인간에 대한 믿음을 잃고 고독하게 혼자 살던 중, 우연히 다가온 Eppie라는 여자아이를 키우게 되면서 그 아이를 통하여 다시 인간에 대한 사랑을 되찾게 되는 이야기를 그린 작품이다.

11 George Eliot의 작품에 해당하지 <u>않는</u> 것은?

① 「*Middlemarch*」
② 「*Adam Bede*」
③ 「*Silas Marner*」
④ 「*Little Dorrit*」

정답 10 ① 11 ④

12 「*Silas Marner*」의 등장인물에 대한 설명으로 옳지 <u>않은</u> 것은?

① Silas Marner : Raveloe에서 일하는 직조공이다.
② Eppie : 금발의 여자아이다.
③ Dunstan Cass : 악한 심성을 가진 인물이다.
④ Squire Cass : 젊고 멋있으며, 부유하고 매력적이다.

13 George Eliot의 작품 중 누명을 쓰게 된 후 신에 대한 불신과 인간에 대한 실망감을 돈으로 보상받으려고 하는 인물은 누구인가?

① Adam Bede
② Silas Marner
③ Dunstan Cass
④ Godfrey Cass

14 다음 설명에서 괄호 안에 들어갈 용어를 알맞게 짝지은 것은?

> George Eliot은 「*Silas Marner*」에서 편협한 청교도들(캘빈주의자들)이 살고 있는 (ⓐ)(와)과 따뜻한 인정을 베풀며 살아가는 성공회 사람들이 사는 (ⓑ)(을)를 대조적으로 표현하고 있다.

	ⓐ	ⓑ
①	Raveloe	Lantern Yard
②	Lantern Yard	Raveloe
③	Longbourn	Meryton
④	Meryton	Longbourn

12 Squire Cass는 Godfrey와 Dunstan의 아버지로 마을에서 존경받는 인물이지만 알고 보면 자신의 아들들에 대한 사랑보다 재산에 더 많은 관심을 갖는 이기적이고 자기중심적인 사람이다.

13 Silas Marner는 Lantern Yard에서 교회의 돈을 훔쳤다는 누명을 쓰게 된 후 신에 대한 불신과 인간에 대한 실망감을 돈으로 보상받으려 한다. 그는 Eppie를 만나기 전까지 Raveloe에서 직조공으로 일만 하며 15년간 고독한 생활을 한다.

14 Silas Marner는 신과 사람에 대한 불신의 감정을 갖고 엄격한 청교도 분위기가 장악하던 마을 Lantern Yard를 떠나 인간애가 살아있는 성공회 마을인 Raveloe에 정착한다. Longbourn과 Meryton은 「*Pride and Prejudice*」에서 등장하는 가상의 마을이다.

정답 12 ④ 13 ② 14 ②

15 Eppie가 어머니 Molly와 함께 Cass 가(家)로 가던 중 Molly는 아편을 마시고 동사하게 된다. 홀로 남은 Eppie는 불빛을 따라 Marner의 집으로 가서 잠이 든다. 집으로 돌아온 Marner는 희미한 시력 때문에 Eppie의 황금빛 머리를 자신이 도난당한 황금으로 착각하지만 딱딱한 감촉의 금화 대신 부드럽고 따뜻한 머리털이 그의 손에 닿는다. 이렇게 Eppie의 머리를 만지는 Silas Marner의 행위는 금화의 딱딱함과 머리의 부드러움을 대조시키며 그를 삶으로 소생시키고 황금으로부터 해방시킴을 상징한다.

15 「*Silas Marner*」에서 Silas Marner가 집착했던 황금에서 벗어나는 계기를 주는 인물은 누구인가?

① Godfrey Cass

② William Dane

③ Dolly Winthrop

④ Eppie

정답 15 ④

제 6 장　Thomas Hardy – 「*Tess of the d'Urbervilles*」

01 Thomas Hardy의 작품 세계에 대한 설명으로 옳지 <u>않은</u> 것은?

① 극히 제한된 소수의 인물들 간의 긴밀하게 연관된 삶의 방식에 초점을 맞추고 있다.

② 인간의 삶과 행위에 있어서 가장 근원적이고 본질적인 문제에만 주목한다.

③ 자연주의적이고 비극적이다.

④ 등장인물은 구체화되고 개별화된 개인을 대변한다.

01 Hardy는 그의 작품에서 인간을 자연 가운데 놓음으로써 등장인물로 하여금 구체화되고 개별화된 개인을 넘어 보편적이고 일반화된 인간을 대변하도록 한다.

02 Thomas Hardy의 자연주의적 소설에 대한 설명으로 옳은 것은?

① 비극적인 소설의 결말이지만 미래지향적인 해결책을 제시한다.

② 주어진 환경이나 운명을 개척하는 인물을 묘사한다.

③ 전체적으로 소설이 밝고 따뜻하다.

④ 과도기의 빅토리아조의 혼란의 시대를 반영하듯이 갈등을 지닌 시대적 분위기를 반영한 갈등하는 두 세력을 내보인다.

02 ① 비극적인 소설의 결말이 보여주듯이 미래지향적인 해결책을 제시하지 않는다.
② 주어진 환경이나 운명에 희생당하는 인물을 묘사한다.
③ 전체적으로 소설이 침울하고 비관적인 분위기이다.

03 「*Tess of the d'Urbervilles*」에 대한 설명으로 옳지 <u>않은</u> 것은?

① Wessex를 배경으로 한다.

② 내재 의지가 중심 사상을 이루고 있다.

③ Angel을 만난 Talhothays는 황량한 황무지이다.

④ 멜로드라마풍의 가벼운 어조를 먼저 사용하다가 뒤이어 무거운 어조가 등장한다.

03 Talbothays는 비옥한 곳이다.

정답　01 ④　02 ④　03 ③

04 새로운 가치와 옛 가치 간의 갈등에 노출된 비극적인 인간상을 묘사했으며, 갈등을 해결하려는 작가의 시도는 찾아볼 수 없다.

04 「*Tess of the d'Urbervilles*」의 주제에 대한 설명으로 옳지 <u>않은</u> 것은?

① 엄격한 도덕률 및 종교적 교리에 과감하게 도전했다.
② 새로운 가치와 옛 가치 간의 갈등을 조화롭게 해결하려 했다.
③ 성에 대한 빅토리아 시대의 허위와 남녀관계에 대해 조명했다.
④ 순결한 여인을 재물과 혈통의 희생물로 삼는 부당한 사회적 인습을 고발했다.

05 어머니 쪽의 숙명론적 수동성(fatal passivity)은 Tess로 하여금 Alec과 Angel의 접근과 유혹에 쉽게 넘어가게 하고 그들의 박해를 견디도록 만든다.

05 진화론적 관점에서 보았을 때 「*Tess of the d'Urbervilles*」에서 Tess가 Alec과 Angel의 접근과 유혹에 쉽게 넘어가게 되는 이유는?

① 아름다운 외모
② 사회적 계급
③ 순응성과 수동성
④ 사랑에 쉽게 빠짐

06 Tess의 삶의 유일한 희망은 Angel과의 사랑이 이루어지는 것이다.

06 「*Tess of the d'Urbervilles*」에서 등장인물과 그에 대한 설명이 올바르지 <u>않은</u> 것은?

① Angel : 정신적으로 Tess를 고문한다.
② Tess : 유일한 희망은 Alec과의 사랑이 이루어지는 것이다.
③ Alec : 육체적으로 그녀를 유린한다.
④ Angel : 사회의 제도와 관습, 도덕률을 상징한다.

정답 04 ② 05 ③ 06 ②

07 「*Tess of the d'Urbervilles*」에서 Tess의 생명력과 강인한 삶의 의지를 조롱하는 냉혹한 내재적인 의지(Immanent Will)의 대변자로, 그녀에게 불행한 운명을 부여하는 역할을 하는 인물은?

① Alec d'Urbervilles
② Angel Clare
③ John Durbeyfield
④ Joan Durbeyfield

07 Alec d'Urbervilles는 자아도취적인 인물이며 자신의 목적 달성을 위해서는 타인의 약점도 이용하는 이기적이고 단순한 인간형이다. Tess의 생명력과 강인한 삶의 의지를 조롱하는 냉혹한 내재적인 의지(Immanent Will)의 대변자로 그녀에게 불행한 운명을 부여하는 역할을 한다.
② Angel은 Tess가 사랑하는 인물이다.
③·④ John Durbeyfield와 Joan Durbeyfield는 Tess의 부모님이다.

08 Angel이 Tess의 과거를 알고 실망과 분노로 떠난 곳은?

① 미국
② 브라질
③ 이탈리아
④ 아르헨티나

08 결혼 첫날밤에 서로의 지난 과오를 고백하고 용서를 받자는 Angel의 제안에 Tess는 Alec과의 과거를 솔직하게 모두 털어놓는다. 그러나 Angel은 Tess의 과오가 더 크다며 그녀의 과거를 받아들이지 않고, Tess를 떠나 브라질로 가버린다.

09 「*Tess of the d'Urbervilles*」에서 Tess의 성격으로 옳지 않은 것은?

① 강인한 생명력
② 수동성
③ 인내력
④ 비관적인 사고방식

09 Tess는 비록 외부의 환경적 힘에 의하여 희생이 되는 인물이지만 인내심과 Angel에 대한 변치 않는 사랑으로 마침내 Angel의 마음을 변하게 한다.

정답 07 ① 08 ② 09 ④

10 Alec과 Angel은 그들의 편협하고 왜곡된 가치관으로 Tess의 진면모를 알아볼 수 없고, 그녀와 진정한 사랑을 주고받을 능력이 없다.

10 「*Tess of the d'Urbervilles*」에서 Tess에 관한 설명으로 옳지 <u>않은</u> 것은?

① 작가의 이상적인 여성상이었다.
② 건강한 의식과 정신을 지니고 있다.
③ 진정한 사랑을 주고받을 능력이 없다.
④ 인간의 본성을 바탕으로 한 자연의 법칙과 질서를 대변한다.

정답 10 ③

제 **2** 편

—

19세기
미국소설

www.sdedu.co.kr

제 1 장 19세기 미국소설의 개관

제 1 절 19세기 미국소설

1 로맨스

초기의 미국작가들은 영국의 소설을 모방하여 작품을 썼지만 점점 독자적인 길을 감에 따라 영국소설과 달리 로맨스(romance)가 소설의 중요한 요소가 되었다. 로맨스는 구체적인 현실에 바탕을 둔 복잡한 인간관계를 나타내는 엄격한 의미에서의 소설(novel)이 아니라 중세문학에서처럼 현실을 구체적으로 표현하지 않으며 추상적으로 자유롭게 나타내는 서사(narrative)를 의미한다. 로맨스는 소설에서와는 달리 사회적인 인간관계 속에서 벌어지는 인물의 특성보다 신비로움 속에서 전개되는 액션을 중요시한다. 로맨스의 인물들은 현실적이지 못하고 이상적이다. 이러한 특징 때문에 미국소설은 실제적인 삶과 관계가 있는 도덕적 상상력이 부족하다. 그럼에도 로맨스는 독특한 소설 미학과 보편적인 진실, 존재론적 문제를 탐색하는 노력을 담고 있다.

2 영국소설과의 차이점

미국소설은 분명히 영국소설과는 다르다. 초기의 미국작가들은 영국의 소설을 모방해서 작품을 썼지만 점점 독자적인 길을 걷게 되었다. 그 결과 미국소설은 영국소설과 달리 로맨스(romance)가 소설의 중요한 요소가 되었다. 로맨스의 인물들은 현실적이지 못하고 이상적인 형태를 띠고 있다. 이러한 경향 때문에 미국소설은 Balzac와 George Eliot의 소설에서 나타나는 실제적인 삶과 연관된 도덕성과 같은 요소들이 부족한 것으로 나타난다. 그러나 미국소설의 로맨스적인 요소는 미국소설만이 지닌 독특한 소설 미학과 보편적인 진실을 담고 있다. 예를 들면, 탁월한 미국소설가들은 Henry James가 말한 '극단적인 상황에 대한 정열'과 Brockden Brown이 언급한 '지적인 에너지', Melville이 말한 '어둠 속의 어둠', '궁극적인 문제에 대한 순수한 회의', '액션과 의미 사이의 대담하고 예리한 변증법' 등과 같은 심오한 문제를 탐색하는 자세를 보여준다. 이러한 특징들은 미국소설을 로맨스가 지닌 비현실적이거나 이상적인 도피주의와 환상, 감상주의에 한정시키지 않고, 지적이고 도덕적인 사상과 관계있는 심리적인 영역의 탐색까지 이르게 한다.

미국소설은 영국소설의 모방에서부터 시작되었지만 영국소설이 나타내는 조화와 중용의 길을 걷기보다는 독자적인 면모를 보이게 된다. 그 이유는 유럽에서 신대륙으로 건너온 미국 사람들의 복잡한 경험과 그에서 비롯한 독특한 의식 때문이다. 미국작가들의 이러한 독특함은 역사적인 사실에서 그 이유를 찾을 수 있다.

미국소설이 로맨스적인 요소를 가지게 된 것은 Richard Chase가 지적한 바와 같이 미국소설가들이 지니게 된 다음과 같은 현실 때문이라고 할 수 있다.

(1) 전통적으로 볼 때, 초기의 미국소설가들은 영국소설을 모방하면서 작품을 쓰기 시작하였지만 소설 속에 담아야만 하는 미국적인 경험 때문에 조화와 중용의 길을 선택하는 영국소설과는 달리, 상호 모순되는 극단적인 길을 택해야 했다. 이것은 역사적인 경험과 관계가 있다.

(2) 신대륙에 상륙한 미국인들과 그들의 후예들은 처음에는 청교도주의, 그 후 서부의 개척, 그리고 이어서 나타나게 된 민주주의 제도 때문에 고독한 인간의 위치에 있었다.

(3) Yvor Winters와 다른 몇몇의 비평가들이 지적한 바와 같이 뉴잉글랜드 청교도주의가 가진 특징이 Hawthorne이나 Melville 같은 작가들에게 강렬한 영향력을 주었을 뿐 아니라, 미국인들의 의식에도 깊이 뿌리내렸다. 즉, 뉴잉글랜드의 청교도주의는 문학적인 상상력에 의하여 '선택받은 자와 저주받은 자', '빛과 어둠', '선과 악'이라는 이분법적인 결과를 가져오게 해서 미국작가들에게도 이러한 감성을 심어주었다. 따라서 미국작가들의 상상력은 구원이나 타협보다는 뉴잉글랜드의 청교도처럼 선과 악의 갈등으로 이루어진 소외 및 무질서에 관심을 기울였다. 미국소설에 지배적으로 나타나고 있는 빛과 어둠에 대한 상징적인 근원이 여기에서 비롯되었다고 보면, 이에 대한 미국작가들의 감수성은 남북전쟁 이후 흑인과 백인이 싸워온 경험 때문에 더욱 확대되었다고 볼 수 있다.

(4) 미국작가들은 구세계(the Old World)와 신세계(the New World)에 동시에 귀속하려는 의지를 가지고 있었다.

3 대표 작가들

(1) Charles Brockden Brown(1771~1810)

미국소설의 시작은 Charles Brockden Brown에 의하여 이루어졌다고 한다. 그의 소설들은 스타일과 어조, 주제 면에서 제한된 모습을 나타내지만, 앞에서 언급한 미국소설의 일반적인 특징을 두드러지게 보여준다. 그의 소설은 미국적인 로맨스의 중요한 특징인 멜로드라마적인 요소가 생생하게 나타난다. 미국문학사에서 Brown은 멜로드라마를 소설에 진지하게 사용한 최초의 작가로서 다음 세대의 로맨스 소설 작가들에게 중요한 영향을 미쳤다.

1798년부터 1801년 사이에 그는 「*Wieland*」, 「*Ormond*」, 「*Edgar Huntly*」, 「*Arthur Mervyn*」, 「*Clara Howard*」, 「*Jane Talbot*」 등 6권의 소설을 집필하였다. 이 소설들 중 「*Wieland*」가 가장 대표적인 작품으로 평가받는데, 아름다움과 공포로 가득 찬 이 소설은 지적인 면도 상당히 지니고 있다. 그러나 이 작품은 그의 다른 소설들처럼 작품의 구성에 있어 통일성이 없다. 자극적이고 불규칙하기 때문에 훌륭한 소설이라고 보기는 어렵다. 「*Wieland*」가 가진 결함은 그가 처음 쓰려고 했던 고딕(Gothic) 소설과도 관련이 있다. 그러나 James Fenimore Cooper와 Nathaniel Hawthorne이 Charles Brockden

Brown의 소설에서 나타나는 강한 리얼리즘에 대해 열광할 정도로 이 작품은 아름다움과 공포의 분위기를 잘 살린 작품이다.

(2) Washington Irving(1783~1859)

Washington Irving은 소설을 쓰지는 않았지만, 미국문학을 개척한 존재라고 할 수 있다. 그는 영국소설가인 Goldsmith와 영국의 수필가 Addison을 모방하면서 글을 쓰기 시작하였다. 그의 감상적인 수필에서는 인생을 바라보는 즐거움과 생동감이 담겨있다. 그의 글은 미국적인 쾌활함과 당시 유행한 낭만적인 영국수필의 향수가 더해진다. 이러한 그의 특징은 수필, 인물 묘사, 단편소설 등으로 구성된 그의 대표적인 작품 「*The Sketch Book*」(1819~1820)에서 볼 수 있다. 이 작품에서 작가는 책에서 배운 지식과 실제 삶에서 얻은 경험을 결합하여 어린 시절의 회상을 생생한 관찰의 기법으로 표현한다. 이 책은 주제의 연속성이나 중심적인 의도가 없고 통일성도 없다. 그러나 작품에서 느껴지는 친근함은 보편적이면서도 매력을 지닌다.

(3) James Fenimore Cooper(1789~1851)

Charles Brockden Brown처럼 미국문학의 전통을 세우는 데 큰 영향을 끼친 작가이다. 그는 미국의 깊은 숲 속에 사는 인디언들의 다양한 생활을 그리는 데 성공한 최초의 미국작가이다. Cooper의 소설을 보통 '가죽 스타킹 이야기'라고 부르는데, 「*The Pioneers*」(1823), 「*The Last of Mohicans*」(1826), 「*The Prairie*」(1827), 「*The Pathfinder*」(1840), 「*The Dearslayer*」(1841)의 순서로 총 5권으로 되어 있으며, 주인공 Natty Bumpo의 일대기이다. Natty Bumpo는 미개척지의 거주자로서 황야의 소박한 철학자이자 명사수이며, 민주주의의 이상을 인격화한 인물이다. Natty는 작가의 소년시절 때 자신의 기억 속에 남은 몇 명의 실제 인물을 대상으로 만든 가공의 인물로서, 미국의 도덕적 이상을 낭만적인 유형으로 구현하고 있다. 미국 내에서는 Cooper의 소설의 가치에 대하여 다양한 의견이 있었지만, 해외에서는 그의 소설이 독창적인 미국의 고전으로 평가되고 있다. 한편, Cooper는 작중인물의 묘사나 성격에 있어서 만족스럽지 못하다. 또한 그의 소설은 앞에서 언급했듯이 통일성이 없고, 파편적인 양상을 보인다.

(4) Edgar Allan Poe(1809~1849)

미국소설은 Edgar Allan Poe와 Nathaniel Hawthorne에 이르러서 주제와 기법 면에서 독창적이고 세련된 예술로 자리 잡게 된다. 이 두 작가들은 탁월한 문학이론과 예술기법으로 미국문학 예술의 확고한 기반을 닦아 놓았다. Edgar Allan Poe는 장편소설은 집필하지 않았지만, 단편소설의 이론과 실제에 있어서 개척자로서 업적을 쌓았다. 그가 집필한 단편의 특징은 이야기의 효과, 말의 경제성과 직접성, 그리고 절정의 순간에 초점을 둔 액션과 처음부터 끝까지 통제된 무드, 구체성을 통하여 있을 법하지 않은 일들을 있을 법한 것으로 만드는 기법 등과 영국의 낭만주의 시가 지닌 감각적 인상주의 등을 들 수 있다.

(5) Nathaniel Hawthorne(1804~1864)

Hawthorne은 미국문학의 르네상스를 일으킨 최고의 예술가였다. Poe가 설명한 바에 의하면, 소설은 시와는 달리 그 궁극적인 목적으로 아름다움보다는 진리를 추구해야 하고, 통일된 스타일과 어조를 기초로 통일된 효과와 제한된 깊이를 가져야 하는데, Hawthorne의 작품들이 바로 그러한 것이었다. Hawthorne의 소설의 소재는 캘빈주의를 신봉하는 뉴잉글랜드 조상들의 윤리적인 인생관인데, 그 이야기는 항상 교훈에 따른 우화로 되어 있다. 그러나 이러한 소재에 대한 Hawthorne의 태도는 초연하고 비판적이며 회의적이다. 그의 많은 작품들의 중심 주제는 신학적인 문제로서의 죄악이 아닌, 초기 미국에 온 이주민의 생활에 죄의식이 영향을 끼친 그들의 심리에 관한 것이다. 이러한 Hawthorne의 태도는 그의 고향인 세일럼의 역사와 그곳에 이주한 청교도들의 생활에 대한 관찰에서 시작되었다고 볼 수 있다. 그는 청교도들이 초기 이민자들에게 말하는 죄를 무서운 현실로 보았고, 이것이 그로 하여금 인간에게 연민을 갖게 했다. Hawthorne은 상징주의와 도덕적 우화의 형식을 그의 소설에 취하는데, 그의 대표적인 단편 "*Young Goodman Brown*"에서 볼 수 있듯이 작품의 구성은 Edgar Allan Poe의 단편만큼 단단하지 못하고 느슨한 면을 보인다. 그러나 그의 작품들은 Edgar Allan Poe의 작품들과는 달리 도덕적인 진지함과 상징적인 깊이를 더해주어 후대의 작가들에게 많은 영향과 도움을 주었다.

(6) Herman Melville(1819~1891)

Nathaniel Hawthorne과 함께 미국소설의 르네상스를 불러일으킨 작가이다. Melville의 상상력은 Nathaniel Hawthorne처럼 비이성적이고 모순된 경험을 깊이 인식하는 데서 연유한다. 그러나 Herman Melville과 Nathaniel Hawthorne은 소설에서 같은 주제를 다루지 않는다. Melville은 진실과 믿음 사이에서 일어나는 궁극적인 딜레마를 그의 소설에 표현한다. 그는 Nathaniel Hawthorne과 다르게 초연하고 명상적, 회의적 관점에 정착하지 못하였고, 그가 믿을 수 있는 철학적이며 종교적인 통합도 발견할 수 없었다. 따라서 이성과 예술의 진실이 합쳐진 어떠한 진실을 향하여 그의 상상 속의 방랑자가 되었다. 이러한 그의 문학적 특징은 그가 Nathaniel Hawthorne처럼 인간의 내면세계를 탐색하려는 시도에서 비롯된 것이지만, 무엇보다도 그의 개인적 경험과 연결 지을 수 있다. 그가 19세 때 가정으로부터의 억압과 감정의 갈등에서 벗어나고자 반항아가 되어 「*Moby-Dick*」의 Ishmael처럼 배를 탄 경험과 깊은 관계가 있다. Melville의 초기 작품들인 「*Typee*」(1846), 「*Omoo*」(1847), 「*Mardi*」(1849), 「*Redburn*」(1849), 「*White-Jacket*」(1850), 「*Moby-Dick*」(1850)의 주인공들은 공통적으로 진실을 찾아 헤매고 있다.

(7) Henry James(1848~1916)

Henry James는 새로운 소설 쓰기의 방법을 창안하기보다는 전통적으로 존재했던 것을 다듬는 데에 탁월한 재능을 보였다. 그는 Nathaniel Hawthorne으로부터 도덕적이고 윤리적인 문제를 다룬 스토리를 물려받아서 그 자신을 '탁월한 양심을 지닌 역사가'로 만들 때까지 그것을 세련되게 만드는 일을 반복했다. 또한 그는 Edgar Allan Poe의 집중력과 단일성을 선택했지만, 고딕적인 장치와 선정적인 주제는 버리고 경험을 바탕으로 그 방법을 각각의 상황에 적용시켰다. 특히 Henry James는 자신의 소설에서 전지적 관점의 서술이 아닌 제한적인 시점을 실험하였다. 그는 끊임없이 소설 기법을 창안하려고 했다.

(8) Sherwood Anderson(1876~1941)

Sherwood Anderson은 20세기의 목소리를 가지고 자유롭게 실현 가능한 깨달음의 삶을 억압하는 빅토리아니즘, 중산층의 억압, 청교도적 위선, 인간의 편협함 등에 저항하는 글을 집필함으로써 미국적인 특징을 보였다. 대표작으로는 「*Winesburg Ohio*」(1919)와 「*The Triumph of the Egg*」(1921)가 있다. 그는 인생에 대한 묘사와 억압된 욕망의 고통, 파멸하는 인물, 그리고 고통받는 자들에 대한 여러 시선 등을 소설에 담고 있다. 그의 작품들은 플롯이 없다. 그의 스타일은 무미건조하고 전개방식은 극적이기보다는 서술적이다. 「*Winesburg Ohio*」에서 Winesburg 사람들은 말할 수 없는 개인적인 어떤 것에 사로잡힌 사람들이고 굉장히 무서운 표정을 짓고 있다. 억압받는 그들의 감정은 독자의 시선을 이끌고 동정을 일으킨다.

(9) Ernest Hemingway(1899~1961)

Scott Fitzgerald, Thomas Wolf 등과 거의 같은 시대에 태어나 파리에서 문학 수업을 하고 돌아온 Hemingway는 「*In Our Time*」(1924), 「*The Sun Also Rises*」(1926), 「*Farewell to Alms*」(1929), 「*For Whom the Bell Tolls*」(1940), 「*The Old Man and the Sea*」(1952) 등과 같은 작품을 발표함으로써 실존적인 문학세계를 보였다. Hemingway의 특징인 간결한 문제와 객관성, 그리고 철학적인 허무주의 및 금욕주의적인 규범이 가져다준 커다란 영향력에 대한 논의가 중요하다. Hemingway는 강인한 정신을 가진 말수가 적고 젊은 금욕주의자들은 물론, 형이상학적이거나 또는 '속임수를 쓰는' 것에 대한 혐오감을 보여주었다.

(10) William Faulkner(1897~1962)

Hemingway와 동시대에 존재한 위대한 작가이자 노벨문학상 수상자인 William Faulkner는 의식의 흐름 기법을 사용하여 「*The Sound and the Fury*」(1929), 「*Light in August*」(1932), 「*Absalom, Absalom*」(1936) 등을 집필함으로써 소설에 또 다른 특색을 부여하였다. Faulkner는 남부적 특징인 신고딕 유파(neo-Gothic School)의 아버지이다. 즉, 왜곡이 그의 매체이고 그로테스크(grotesque)한 것이 그의 인물이다. 그는 극적인 효과를 위하여 그의 소설에 고딕적인 요소를 포함시킨다. 그의 왜곡과 폭력성 등은 그의 소설의 배경의 중심에 놓여 있다. Faulkner의 소설의 세계에서 흑인 노예에 대한 원죄는 모든 사람을 혼란스럽게 할 뿐 아니라 양심의 가책을 느끼게 한다. 그의 작품 전체가 남북전쟁 이후의 남부의 몰락과 타락을 그리지만 그의 의도는 충격이나 파급효과가 아니라, 계시의 성격을 띠고 있다고 볼 수 있다. 또한 그가 제시한 주제의 범위 역시 이전에 금지되었던 인간 행위의 영역과 더불어 무의식의 영역에까지 확대된다.

Edgar Alan Poe
- 「*The Black Cat*」

1인칭 시점에서 서술되는 과거 회상 방식의 단편소설이다. 화자인 '나'의 불안정한 심리상태가 잘 서술되어
단원 개요 있고, 고양이를 등장시켜 긴장감과 공포감을 잘 조성하고 있다.

> **출제 경향 및 수험 대책** 📋
>
> 이 소설 속에서 화자는 이 이야기가 가정 속에서 벌어진 일임을 강조한다. 소설 속의 집은 그 어느 곳보다도 공포의
> 공간이 된다. 우리가 일반적으로 알고 있는 집이라는 공간을 기이하고 새로운 공간으로 설정하면서 독자로 하여금 더
> 큰 기묘함과 공포감을 느끼게 하는 Poe의 작품 전개를 염두에 두고 읽어보자.

제 1 절   작가의 생애

1 성장 과정

Edgar A. Poe는 1809년 1월 9일 보스턴 유랑 극단 배우인 Elizabeth Arnold Hopkins와 David Poe,
Jr.의 둘째 아들로 태어났다. 평소에도 술에 취한 채 무대 위를 오르던 아버지 David는 Poe가 2살이 되기
전이자 여동생 Rosalie가 태어난 직후인 1810년 12월에 가출했다. 홀로 아이들을 키우려 무리하게 무대
일을 하던 어머니 Elizabeth마저 1811년 12월에 결핵으로 사망하고 고아가 된 Poe와 그의 형제들은 뿔뿔
이 흩어지게 되어 형인 Henry는 할아버지 댁에, 누이동생 Rosalie는 William Mackenzie 부인에게 맡겨
졌다. Poe는 Richmond에서 담배상을 하던 부유한 사업가인 John Allan의 서자로 들어가게 되었다. 그는
일생 동안 친어머니 초상화를 간직하면서도 자신의 초라한 가족사를 숨기고 싶어 했다. Poe는 자신의 사
업을 물려받기를 원하는 양부를 피해 Boston으로 도망간다. 이 일을 계기로 양부 John Allan과 Poe의
갈등은 더욱 커졌고, 양부가 Poe에게 한 푼의 유산도 물려주지 않을 정도까지 이르렀다.

Poe는 일찍이 사립학교에서 Shakespeare나 Walter Scott 등의 고전을 접할 수 있었다. 런던에서 양부의
손에 이끌려 다닌 기숙학교의 경험은 Poe의 문학세계에 풍부한 소재를 제공하게 된다. 「*William Wilson*」
(1840)는 그가 다닌 기숙학교 시절을 배경으로 한 것이다.

「*Ligeia*」(1838), 「*The Fall of the House of the Usher*」(1839)에서 등장하는 영국의 고대 유럽풍 대저택
이나 대성당들도 Poe의 이러한 경험이 배경이 되었다고 할 수 있다. 결국 그의 작품에 배어 있는 고전에
대한 식견이나 이국적 정서, 유럽풍의 분위기는 양부가 제공한 재정적 풍요로움과 교육 그리고 다양한 경
험에 바탕을 둔 것이었다.

2 청년시절

12세 정도 되었을 무렵 Poe는 주로 사랑의 서정시를 써서 소녀들에게 바치곤 했다. 15세에 친구의 어머니이자 「To Helen」(1831)의 원천인 동정심 많은 Jane Stith Standard에게서 이상적인 어머니 상을 발견하고 부인을 사랑하게 된다. 1824년 Jane 부인이 갑작스럽게 죽자 Poe는 극심한 우울증에 시달리다가 자신을 위로하던 이웃소녀 Sarah Elmira Royster와 사랑에 빠지기도 하였다. 1826년 Virginia 대학에 진학한 Poe가 음주와 도박에 빠져 빚이 2,000달러에 이르자 양부는 Poe를 강제로 중퇴시킨다. 고향에 돌아온 Poe는 이상적인 어머니 상이던 Jane 부인의 사망과 양부와의 불화, 결혼까지 약속했던 Elmira에게서 버림받은 절망감을 극복하지 못하고, Richmond를 떠나 자신이 태어난 Boston으로 간다. Boston에서 점원이나 신문사 등의 일을 하던 Poe는 40페이지 분량의 첫 시집인 『Tamerlane and Other Poems』(1827)를 출판했으나 세상의 이목을 끌지는 못했다. 현재 이 작품은 초기 미국 인쇄물의 희귀본으로 알려져 있다.

일정한 수입이 없어 가난했던 Poe는 한 달 반 정도의 보스턴 생활을 청산하고 Edgar A. Perry라는 가명으로 육군에 입대했다. 복무할 당시 Cape Cod 해변에서 배가 난파당할 뻔한 경험은 훗날 「Ms. Found in a Bottle」(1833)과 「The Narrative of Arthur Gordon Pym」(1838)의 소재가 된다. 군 주둔지였던 Sullivan 섬에서 자연 과학 서적을 읽고 동식물을 관찰한 경험은 16년 후 「The Golden-Bug」(1843)로 작품화된다. 그러나 군대에 잘 적응하고 스스로도 만족하였음에도 군 생활이 집필에 지장을 준다고 생각하여 제대한다. 양부와는 달리 Poe를 끔찍이 사랑하던 양모 Frances Allan이 1829년 2월에 오랜 지병으로 사망한다. 그의 삶에서 반복된 어머니의 상실은 Poe에게 깊은 심리적 외상을 남긴다. 어린 아내 Virginia에게 보였던 병적인 집착이나 아름다운 여성의 죽음을 작품 주제로 반복해 사용한 것은 그의 정신적 외상의 표현으로 볼 수 있다.

3 작가로서의 삶

1831년은 Poe의 문학 경력에 있어 새로운 도약의 기회가 된 시기였다. 미국 독서 대중의 취향이 낭만 시에서 유머러스하고 풍자적인 산문으로 변해가자 Poe는 6월에 「Metzengerstein」을 비롯하여 다섯 편의 코믹 단편을 Philadelphia Saturday Courier의 단편소설 모집에 응모하였고, 1832년 다섯 편 모두가 출판되었다. 1833년에는 「Ms. Found in a Bottle」이 Baltimore Saturday Visitor 현상 공모에 당선되어 50달러의 상금을 받았고, 1834년에는 리치먼드의 The Southern Literary Messenger에 그의 첫 번째 공포 소설 「Berenice」를 발표하였다. 작가로서의 경력을 인정받은 Poe는 The Southern Literary Messenger의 편집인이 되어 단편과 시, 서평 등을 발표하면서 작가의 길을 열어갔다.

Poe는 1837년 이후부터 8년간 작가로서 가장 왕성한 창작 시기를 보내게 되는데, 이 기간 동안 그의 유명한 공포 소설 대부분을 집필하였다. 1835년 「Morella」를, 1838년에는 「Ligeia」를, 1839년에는 「The Fall of the House of the Usher」와 「William Wilson」을 연달아 발표하였다. Poe는 당시 문호인 Washington Irving, James Fenimore Cooper, Henry Wadsworth Longfellow 등과 친분을 쌓는 등 미국 최고의 잡지 편집인으로서의 위치를 굳혔으며, 1841년에는 「The Murders in the Rue Morgue」를 발표함으로써 추리 소설이라는 새로운 장르를 열었다.

그러나 1842년 아내 Virginia의 결핵 발병은 Poe를 또 다시 절망의 늪으로 빠뜨렸다. 낙담한 Poe는 불안 감 때문에 술을 더욱 자주 마셨고 잡지사 일에 점점 소홀해졌다. 결국 편집장 자리에서 쫓겨난 Poe는 생활 고와 Virginia의 병세 악화로 절망감에 시달렸으나, 그 가운데서도 1843년 「The Tell-Tale Heart」 같은 병적이고 잔인하기 짝이 없는 살인 이야기들을 발표하는가 하면 Dupin을 주인공으로 한 추리 소설을 잇달 아 내놓았다. 이처럼 삶의 고통과 절망은 Poe를 파괴시키는 요인인 동시에 그의 창작력을 불타게 하는 촉진제이기도 했다. 1845년 그의 시 「The Raven」은 당대 엄청난 주목을 받았다. 1847년 1월 30일 아내 Virginia가 죽은 후 Poe는 극심한 우울증과 술로 지냈지만 비평문과 산문시 「Eureka : A Prose Poem」 (1848)을 발표하고 순회강연도 하는 등 작가 활동을 중단하지는 않았다. 1849년 Poe는 세간에 알려진 바 와는 달리 비교적 평온한 나날을 보내고 있었다. 강연과 시 암송공연을 지속했으며 친구들을 방문하기도 하였다. 리치먼드에서는 2개월 정도 체류했었는데 전 연인 Sarah Elmira Royster를 만나기 위한 것이었다. 그곳에서 완성된 시가 그의 마지막 시 「Annabel Lee」이다. 1849년 9월 26일 그는 10월 17일에 결혼식을 올리기로 약속했던 Royster를 뒤로한 채 비교적 건강한 상태로 리치먼드를 떠나 뉴욕으로 향하였다. 그러 나 Poe는 뉴욕으로 가지 않고 도중에 볼티모어(Baltimore)로 갔는데 그 이유는 알려지지 않았다. 당시 볼 티모어에서는 주 의원과 국회의원 선거 때문에 거리가 온통 선거 운동으로 북적거리던 때였다. Poe는 투 표장 근처의 술집에서 얼마 떨어지지 않은 길 위에서 의식을 거의 잃은 채로 발견되었고, 바로 병원 (Washington Medical College)으로 옮겨졌으나 1849년 10월 7일 40세의 나이로 숨을 거두고 말았다.

> 🔔 **더 알아두기** 🔍
>
> **Edgar Alan Poe의 주요작품**
> • 단편소설
> - 「The Black Cat」(1843)
> - 「The Fall of the House of Usher」(1839)
> - 「The Gold-Bug」(1848)
> - 「Ligeia」(1838)
> - 「The Murder in the Rue Morgue」(1841)
> - 「The Purloined Letter」(1844)
> - 「The Tell-Tale Heart」(1843)
>
> • 시
> - 「Annabel Lee」(1849) : 아름다운 여성(Virginia)의 죽음을 담은 시
> - 「To Helen」(1841) : Jane Stanard를 기리기 위한 시
> - 「The Raven」(1845)
>
> • 소설
> 「The Narrative of Arthur Gordon Pym of Nantucket」(1838)

제 2 절 작품 세계

1 Poe에 대한 견해

1880년 J. H. Ingram이 『*Edgar Allan Poe : His Life, Letters, and Opinions*』를 발간하여 긍정적인 면모를 밝히기 전까지 Poe는 주로 사악한 천재나 그런 칭호에는 역부족인 무뢰한으로 알려졌다. T. S. Eliot은 '조잡한 날림의 글쓰기'라고 혹평했고 Yvor Winters는 '몽매주의'라고 비판했다. 그러나 보들레르나 말라르메 같은 프랑스의 상징주의 시인들과 Arthur H, Quinn, Allen Tate 같은 비평가들은 Poe에 대해 호의적으로 평가했다.

오늘날 Poe를 가리켜 추리 소설(detective fiction)의 개척자, 미국문학사에 단편소설 장르를 확립한 작가, 프랑스 상징주의 시인들을 열광시킨 시인, 전 세계적으로 인정받은 최초의 미국작가로 자리매김하는 데는 아무런 이견이 없을 것이다. 특히 Poe는 "창작이 실패한다면 그것은 이론이 불완전하기 때문이다."라고 하면서 창작과 이론의 일치를 주창한 문학이론가로서 20세기 신비평의 단초를 마련하였다. 그러므로 Poe의 문학이론을 살펴볼 필요가 있다.

2 Poe의 문학이론

(1) 정서이론(Affective theory) 중요 ★★

Poe의 문학이론은 기본적으로 정서이론(affective theory)에 초점이 맞추어져 있다. 문학이론을 모방이론(imitative theory), 표현이론(expressive theory), 정서이론(affective theory)으로 분류한다면, Poe는 모방이론이 문제 삼는 재현의 대상이나 표현이론이 초점을 맞추는 작가의 감정적 표출보다는 독자에게 미치는 정서적인 효과에 주목한다. 즉, 작가는 독자에게 단일하면서도 전적인, 심리적·영적 효과를 불러일으키는 데 목적을 두어야 한다는 것이다. Poe는 이러한 정서적 효과의 극대화라는 목적을 위해 주제나 플롯, 문체나 길이 등 다른 요소들을 전부 종속시키는 유기적 문학이론을 주창하였다. 이 이론은 시와 단편 두 영역에 다 해당된다. Poe가 독자에게 미치는 정서적 효과에 이토록 열중한 것은 문학의 목적을 진리가 아니라 쾌락이라고 보았기 때문이다. 「*Letters to B*」(1836)에서 Poe는 "시의 직접적인 목적이 진리가 아니라 쾌락이란 점에서 시는 과학적인 작품과 반대된다."(A Poem, in my opinion, is opposed to a work of science by having, for its immediate object, pleasure, not truth.)라고 말하고 있다. Nathaniel Hawthorne의 작품 『*Twice-Told Tales*』의 1842년 서평에서 "모든 소설의 창작 목적은 쾌락이다."(for nothing but the pleasure itself of composition.)라고 밝히고 있다.

(2) 인위적인 창작의 범주를 설정

시와 소설의 궁극적 목적인 쾌락이 강렬하고도 순수한 영혼의 고양에서 비롯된다고 보는 Poe는 그 순간의 포착을 위해 작품의 길이를 제한하고 소재를 규정하며, 언어의 사용을 제어하는 고도로 인위적인 창작 범주를 설정한다. 예를 들면, 강렬한 흥분 상태는 일시적일 수밖에 없으므로 시의 경우에는

100줄 정도의 길이가 적당하고, 소설의 경우에는 앉은 자리에서 독파할 수 있는 30분이나 한두 시간 정도의 분량이 적당하다고 보았다. 적당한 길이는 사건의 단일화와 언어 사용의 간결함을 요구하는데, 다시 말하자면 적당한 길이의 간결한 산문이나 시가 단일성을 획득함으로써 독자에게 강렬한 인상을 줄 수 있다는 것이다. Poe 자신도 「The Valley of Unrest」(1831)와 같은 시를 집필할 때, 1831년에는 46행이던 것을 그 후 14여 년이 지나 27행으로 축소시키는 등 계속적인 수정으로 시 언어를 강렬하게 하였다. 『Twice-Told Tales』의 서평에서 "창작과정 중에는 미리 의도한 효과를 나타내지 못할 단어는 단 한 단어도 사용해서는 안 된다."라고 말한 것에서도 나타나듯이 그는 작품의 단일성 획득을 위해 치밀한 언어 사용에 주목하였다. 또한 소재 선정에 있어서도 독자의 즐거운 감정을 환기시킬 수 있기 위해서는 문학적 독창성이 요구되며, 독창성은 곧 진귀함에 있으므로 진귀함을 추구해야 한다고 보았다. Poe가 시가 갖추어야 할 최고의 미덕을 음악성이라고 정의하며 두운, 각운, 압운과 각 절의 반복 등 리듬감을 살리기 위한 정교한 시적 장치를 고집한 것 역시 독자에게 미칠 미적 효과에 주목하였기 때문이다. 이와 같이 Poe는 시와 단편 각 장르의 소재와 언어 선정, 그리고 분량 등의 문학 구성요소들을 오직 독자의 정서적 효과라는 목적을 향해 집중시키고 있다. 이것은 독자 반응을 의식한 작가의 자기 반성적인 창작 태도를 일깨웠다는 점에서 시대를 앞서 갔다고 할 수 있다. Poe가 독자 반응의 효과와 더불어 미학과 도덕의 결합을 고집한 기존의 미국적인 사고에서 벗어나 **시 자체를 위한 시, 예술 자체를 위한 예술을 주창한 것** 또한 프랑스 상징주의 미학의 전형이 되었을 뿐 아니라, 작품 위주의 비평을 핵심으로 하는 20세기 신비평 미학의 시조가 되었다. 물론 Poe의 이론이 지나치게 기교 중심적이고 협소한 면이 없진 않으며, 실제 비평에서도 그는 자주 경쟁자들의 글을 표절로 공격하고 조롱함으로써 자기중심적인 태도에서 벗어나지 못한 모습을 보이기도 했다. 그러나 F. O. Mattiessen 이나 Robert Regan의 견해처럼 이론과 실제의 엄격한 일치를 주장함으로써 비평을 이론적으로 과학화하고, 포괄적이고 보편적인 미학이론의 본질을 통찰했다는 점에 Poe의 위대성이 있다.

제 3 절 줄거리

곧 처형당할 운명인 화자(narrator)는 자신의 집에서 일어난 사건을 기록한다. 어릴 때부터 동물을 좋아하던 화자는 자신과 비슷한 성향을 가진 아내와 함께 여러 반려 동물을 키운다. 화자는 기르는 동물 중에서 Pluto라는 검은 고양이를 가장 아낀다. 화자는 날이 갈수록 폭음, 절제, 분노 및 폭력에 빠진다. 하루는 Pluto가 자신을 피한다는 생각이 들었고 화가 난 화자는 Pluto를 잡는다. Pluto가 자신의 손을 물자 화자는 Pluto의 눈 하나를 도려낸다. 다음날 약간의 후회를 느끼긴 하지만 마침내 '도착성'(perverseness)을 드러내는 화자는 Pluto의 목에 올가미를 걸어 정원 나무에 매단다. 그날 밤, 집에 화재가 일어나 모든 벽이 무너져 내리지만 화자의 침대 쪽 벽만 무너져 내리지 않았고 기괴하게도 목에 밧줄이 감겨있는 고양이 상(像)이 나타난다. 집이 불에 타버린 화자는 전 재산을 잃고 낡은 집으로 이사한다.

시간이 흐른 뒤, 화자는 술통 위에서 발견한 Pluto와 닮은 검은 고양이가 자신을 따르자 주인이 없다는 걸 알고 집에 데려온다. 그 고양이는 배 쪽에 흰색 털이 있다는 점을 제외하고는 Pluto와 비슷한데, Pluto와 같이 눈이 하나밖에 없다. 고양이는 집에 잘 적응하지만, 화자는 자신이 예상한 바와는 정반대로 그 고양이에 대해 증오심과 성가심을 느낀다. 고양이는 끈질기게 화자를 따라다니고, 화자는 고양이를 죽이고 싶은 충동을 느낀다. 고양이를 죽이려는 성질을 참던 중에 화자는 아내와 함께 지하실에 내려가려다가 고양이 때문에 넘어질 뻔하자 도끼를 꺼내어 든다. 그리고 오히려 고양이를 내려치려는 것을 말리는 아내를 죽이게 된다. 화자는 아내의 시체를 어떻게 처리할지 궁리하던 중 아내의 시체를 지하실 벽에 넣고 벽을 발라버리는 방법을 선택한다.

경찰들이 가택 수사를 여러 차례 하지만 화자의 아내의 시신을 발견하지 못하고, 화자는 점점 태연하고 자신만만해진다. 허세와 승리감에 찬 그는 넌지시 벽이 튼튼하다고 말하며 아내의 시신을 넣었던 벽을 지팡이로 두들긴다. 이때 벽 안에서 고양이의 울음소리가 나자 경찰들은 벽을 허물고 그곳에서 부패된 화자 아내의 시신과 그 머리 위에서 울음소리를 내던 빨간 입과, 불같이 영롱한 눈을 가진 고양이를 발견한다. 그 결과 화자는 교수대에서 처형당할 운명을 마주하게 된다.

제 4 절 　작품의 주제 중요★★

- 억압된 분노의 폭발
- 도착증(perverseness)의 발현
  인간으로서의 본능이나 감정 또는 도덕성의 이상으로 인하여 사회에서 일그러진 행동을 드러냄
- 광기, 알코올 중독, 인간의 어두운 내면
- 선악의 양면성을 가지고 있는 주인공의 불안정한 감수성 표출
- 주인공이 악에 눈뜨는 과정을 자연스럽게 전개
- 단순한 가정 비극(domestic tragedy)을 주제로 보는 견해도 있음

제 5 절 　등장인물

1 화자(Narrator)

도착적인 성격을 가진 인물로, 자기 내부의 악을 타인에게 전가함으로써 오히려 이상 심리로 접어들고 있음을 객관적으로 드러내고 있다. 이야기를 할 때도 끔찍한 이야기의 원인을 자신의 개인적인 감정 탓이라고 하지 않고, 보다 보편적인 인간의 본성인 '도착심리'(perverseness)와 '삐뚤어지려는 충동'(the spirit of perverseness)의 탓이라고 함으로써 자신의 행동을 보다 보편적인 것으로 돌리려 한다. 이는 자기 내부의 악을 타인에게 전가하려는 의도이다.

2 화자의 아내

순박하고 착한 성품의 인물이며, 고양이에 대한 애정에서 볼 수 있듯 동물들을 아낀다.

3 고양이(Pluto)

본래 선(善)도 악(惡)도 아니었으나, 화자의 감정이 변하고 그의 악마성이 드러남에 따라 이름 그대로 그리스-로마 신화에 나오는 명부(冥府)의 왕 Pluton(Hades)이 되어 복수의 화신으로 변한다.

제 6 절 작품의 구조(Plot)와 시점 및 기법

1 구조

"The Black Cat"은 '삐뚤어짐'(perverseness)에 관한 단순한 이야기가 아니라 악에 탐닉하는 화자에 관한 이야기인 동시에 자신의 행동에서 도덕성에 대한 의미를 거부하는 주인공의 심리에 관한 이야기이다. 형식적인 측면에서 볼 경우 이 작품은 두 부분으로 나누어진다.

(1) 첫 부분은 처음부터 화재가 발생해서 집이 타는 부분까지인데, 이 부분에서는 화재에 대한 화자의 언급을 통하여 화자의 도덕의식의 붕괴를 상징적으로 나타내고 있다.

(2) 두 번째는 Pluto를 닮은 고양이를 데려오는 장면부터 결말까지이다. 이 부분에서는 고양이에 대한 증오가 살인으로 연결된다.

2 시점

1인칭 제한적 시점이다.

3 기법

(1) 상징

고양이의 빨간 입술은 죽은 부인의 미적 아름다움을 대신한다. 고양이의 영롱한 눈은 주인공의 양심을 괴롭히는 눈이며, 검은 고양이는 양심의 가책에서 오는 고민과 공포를 상징한다.

(2) 분위기

① 배경

배경을 불탄 집과 지하실로 설정하여 암울한 분위기를 조성하였다. 이처럼 격리된 장소는 관심과 시각의 집중적인 효과를 유발한다.

② 문체

㉠ 암울한 분위기를 조성하기 위하여 무거운 저음의 't', 'd'의 철자가 있는 어휘들을 사용하였다 (예 terrified, tortured, destroyed 등).

㉡ 대문자, 이탤릭체, 느낌표를 사용하였다.

제 7 절 Text

For the most wild, yet most homely narrative which I am about to pen, I neither expect nor solicit belief[1]. Mad indeed would I be to expect it, in a case where my very senses reject their own evidence. Yet, mad am I not — and very surely do I not dream. But tomorrow I die, and today I would unburthen my soul. My immediate purpose is to place before the world, plainly, succinctly, and without comment, a series of mere household events. In their consequences, these events have terrified — have tortured — have destroyed me. Yet I will not attempt to expound them. To me, they have presented little but horror — to many they will seem less terrible than barroques[2]. Here after, perhaps, some intellect may be found which will reduce my phantasm[3] to the commonplace — some intellect more calm, more logical, and far less excitable than my own, which will perceive, in the circumstances I detail with awe, nothing more than an ordinary succession of very natural causes and effects.

From my infancy I was noted for[4] the docility and humanity of my disposition. My tenderness of heart was even so conspicuous as to make me the jest of my companions. I was especially fond of animals, and was indulged by my parents with a great variety of pets. With these I spent most of my time, and never was so happy as when feeding and caressing them. This peculiarity of character grew with my growth, and, in my manhood, I derived from it one of my principal sources of pleasure. To those who have cherished an affection for a faithful and sagacious dog, I need hardly be at the trouble of explaining[5] the nature or the intensity of the gratification thus derivable.[6] There is something in the unselfish and self-sacrificing love of a brute, which goes directly to the heart

---

1) neither expect nor solicit belief   믿어주기를 기대하지도 간청하지도 않는다.
2) barroques : 기괴한 것(= grotesques)
3) phantasm : 환상, 환영
4) be noted for : ~으로 주목받다
5) be at the trouble of -ing : 귀찮게도 ~하다
6) derivable : 파생할 수 있는

of him who has had frequent occasion to test the paltry[7] friendship and gossamer[8] fidelity of mere Man.

I married early, and was happy to find in my wife a disposition not uncongenial with my own. Observing my partiality for domestic pets, she lost no opportunity[9] of procuring those of the most agreeable kind. We had birds, gold fish, a fine dog, rabbits, a small monkey, and a cat.

This latter was a remarkably large and beautiful animal, entirely black, and sagacious to an astonishing degree[10]. In speaking of his intelligence, my wife, who at heart was not a little[11] tinctured with superstition, made frequent allusion to the ancient popular notion, which regarded all black cats as witches in disguise[12]. Not that she was ever serious upon this point — and I mention the matter at all for no better reason than that it happens, just now, to be remembered.[13]

Pluto[14] — this was the cat's name — was my favorite pet and playmate. I alone fed him, and he attended me wherever I went about the house. It was even with difficulty that I could prevent him from following me through the streets.

Our friendship lasted, in this manner, for several years, during which my general temperament and character — through the instrumentality of the Fiend Intemperance[15] — had (I blush to confess it) experienced a radical alteration for the worse[16]. I grew, day by day, more moody, more irritable, more regardless of the feelings of others. I suffered myself to use intemperate language to my wife. At length, I even offered her personal violence. My pets, of course, were made to feel the change in my disposition. I not only neglected, but ill-used them. For Pluto, however, I still retained sufficient regard to restrain me from maltreating him, as I made no scruple of[17] maltreating the rabbits, the monkey, or even the dog, when by accident, or through affection, they came in my way. But my disease grew upon me — for what disease is like Alcohol![18] — and at length even Pluto, who was now becoming old, and consequently somewhat peevish — even Pluto began to experience the effects of my ill temper.

One night, returning home, much intoxicated, from one of my haunts about town[19], I fancied that the cat avoided my presence. I seized him; when, in his fright at my violence, he inflicted a slight wound upon my hand with his teeth. The fury of a demon instantly possessed me. I knew myself no longer. My original soul seemed, at once, to take its flight from my body; and a more than

---

7) paltry : 가치 없는, 하찮은

8) gossamer : 가냘픈, 얄팍한

9) lost no opportunity : ~할 기회를 놓친 적이 없었다

10) sagacious to an astonishing degree : 놀라울 정도로 영리하다.

11) not a little : 상당히, 꽤 많이

12) witches in disguise : 변장한 마녀

13) Not that she was ever ~ to be remembered : 그녀가 이 점에 대해 진지했다고 해서가 아니라 내가 이 문제를 언급하는 이유는 단지 지금 우연히도 기억이 났기 때문이다.

14) Pluto : '플루토'라는 고양이 이름은 로마신화에 나오는 명부의 신 Pluton(그리스 신화의 하데스)과 연관 지을 수 있다.

15) Fiend Intemperance : 무절제란 이름의 악마

16) a radical alteration for the worse : 더 나쁜 방향으로의 급격한 변화

17) made no scruple of : 조금도 주저하지 않았다.

18) for what disease is like Alcohol! : 알코올 중독 같은 병이 또 어디 있단 말인가!

19) one of my haunts about town : 마을 근처 내가 자주 가는 술집 중의 하나

fiendish malevolence, gin-nurtured, thrilled every fibre of my frame. I took from my waistcoat —
pocket a pen — knife, opened it, grasped the poor beast by the throat, and deliberately cut one of
its eyes from the socket! I blush, I burn, I shudder, while I pen the damnable atrocity.

When reason returned with the morning — when I had slept off[20] the fumes of the night's
debauch[21] — I experienced a sentiment half of horror, half of remorse, for the crime of which I
had been guilty; but it was, at best, a feeble and equivocal feeling, and the soul remained untouched.
I again plunged into excess, and soon drowned in wine all memory of the deed.

In the meantime the cat slowly recovered. The socket of the lost eye presented, it is true, a
frightful appearance, but he no longer appeared to suffer any pain. He went about the house as usual,
but, as might be expected, fled in extreme terror at my approach. I had so much of my old heart[22]
left, as to be at first grieved by this evident dislike on the part of a creature which had once so
loved me. But this feeling soon gave place to[23] irritation. And then came, as if to my final and
irrevocable overthrow, the spirit of PERVERSENESS. Of this spirit philosophy takes no account.[24]
Yet I am not more sure that my soul lives, than[25] I am sure that perverseness is one of the primitive
impulses of the human heart — one of the indivisible primary faculties, or sentiments, which give
direction to the character of Man. Who has not, a hundred times, found himself committing a vile
or a silly action, for no other reason than[26] because he knows he should not? Have we not a
perpetual inclination, in the teeth of[27] our best judgment, to violate that which is Law, merely
because we understand it to be such? This spirit of perverseness, I say, came to my final overthrow.
It was this unfathomable longing of the soul to vex itself — to offer violence to its own nature —
to do wrong for the wrong's sake only[28] — that urged me to continue and finally to consummate
the injury I had inflicted upon the unoffending brute. One morning, in cold blood[29], I slipped a
noose[30] about its neck and hung it to the limb of a tree; — hung it with the tears streaming from
my eyes, and with the bitterest remorse at my heart; — hung it because I knew that it had loved
me, and because I felt it had given me no reason of offence; — hung it because I knew that in
so doing I was committing a sin a deadly sin that would so jeopardize my immortal soul as to place
it — if such a thing were possible — even beyond the reach of the infinite mercy of the Most
Merciful and Most Terrible God.

On the night of the day on which this cruel deed was done, I was aroused from sleep by the
cry of fire. The curtains of my bed were in flames. The whole house was blazing. It was with great

---

20) slept off : 잠으로써 제거하다
21) debauch : 난봉, 폭음
22) my old heart : 옛 정
23) gave place to : ~에 자리를 양보하다
24) take no account of : ~을 무시하다
25) not more … than ~ : ~보다 더 …하진 않는다
26) no other reason than : 다름 아닌 ~한 이유로
27) in the teeth of : ~임에도 불구하고(= in spite of)
28) for the wrong's sake only : 오로지 잘못된 것을 하기 위해서
29) in cold blood : 냉혹하게, 무자비하게
30) noose : 올가미

difficulty that my wife, a servant, and myself, made our escape from the conflagration. The destruction was complete. My entire worldly wealth was swallowed up, and I resigned myself thenceforward to[31] despair.

I am above the weakness of[32] seeking to establish a sequence of cause and effect, between the disaster and the atrocity. But I am detailing a chain of facts — and wish not to leave even a possible link imperfect. On the day succeeding the fire, I visited the ruins. The walls, with one exception, had fallen in. This exception was found in a compartment wall, not very thick, which stood about the middle of the house, and against which had rested the head of my bed. The plastering had here, in great measure, resisted the action of the fire — a fact which I attributed to its having been recently spread. About this wall a dense crowd were collected, and many persons seemed to be examining a particular portion of it with very minute and eager attention. The words "strange!" "singular!" and other similar expressions, excited my curiosity. I approached and saw, as if graven in bas-relief[33] upon the white surface, the figure of a gigantic cat. The impression was given with an accuracy truly marvellous. There was a rope about the animal's neck.

When I first beheld this apparition — for I could scarcely regard it as less[34] — my wonder and my terror were extreme. But at length reflection came to my aid. The cat, I remembered, had been hung in a garden adjacent to the house. Upon the alarm of fire, this garden had been immediately filled by the crowd by some one of whom the animal must have been cut from the tree and thrown, through an open window, into my chamber. This had probably been done with the view of arousing me from sleep. The falling of other walls had compressed the victim of my cruelty into the substance of the freshly-spread plaster; the lime[35] of which, with the flames, and the ammonia from the carcass, had then accomplished the portraiture as I saw it.

Although I thus readily accounted to my reason, if not altogether to my conscience, for the startling fact just detailed, it did not the less fail to[36] make a deep impression upon my fancy. For months I could not rid myself of the phantasm of the cat; and, during this period, there came back into my spirit a half-sentiment that seemed, but was not, remorse. I went so far as to regret the loss of the animal, and to look about me, among the vile haunts which I now habitually frequented, for another pet of the same species, and of somewhat similar appearance, with which to supply its place.

One night as I sat, half stupified, in a den of more than infamy, my attention was suddenly drawn to some black object, reposing upon the head of one of the immense hogsheads[37] of Gin, or of Rum, which constituted the chief furniture of the apartment. I had been looking steadily at the top of this hogshead for some minutes, and what now caused me surprise was the fact that I had not sooner perceived the object thereupon. I approached it, and touched it with my hand. It was a black

---

31) resign oneself to : 운명이라고 체념하다, 운명을 체념하다
32) am above the weakness of : ～을 좋아하지 않는다
33) as if graven in bas-relief : 마치 얕은 돌에 새겨진 것처럼
34) beheld this apparition – for I could scarcely regard it as less : 그 광경[기괴한 현상]을 바라보았다. 그것이 아니라고는 생각되지 않기 때문에
35) lime : 석회
36) it did not the less fail to : ～하는 것이 결코 덜하지 않았다, 상당히 깊은 인상을 남겼다
37) hogsheads : 큰 통 / gin과 rum은 술 이름

cat — a very large one — fully as large as Pluto, and closely resembling him in every respect but one. Pluto had not a white hair upon any portion of his body; but this cat had a large, although indefinite splotch of white, covering nearly the whole region of the breast.

Upon my touching him, he immediately arose, purred loudly, rubbed against my hand, and appeared delighted with my notice. This, then, was the very creature of which I was in search. I at once offered to purchase it of the landlord; but this person made no claim to[38] it — knew nothing of it — had never seen it before.

I continued my caresses, and, when I prepared to go home, the animal evinced a disposition to accompany me. I permitted it to do so; occasionally stooping and patting it as I proceeded. When it reached the house it domesticated itself at once, and became immediately a great favorite with my wife.

For my own part, I soon found a dislike to it — arising within me. This was just the reverse of what I had anticipated; but I know not how or why it was — its evident fondness for myself rather disgusted and annoyed. By slow degrees, these feelings of disgust and annoyance rose into[39] the bitterness of hatred. I avoided the creature; a certain sense of shame, and the remembrance of my former deed of cruelty, preventing me from physically abusing it. I did not, for some weeks, strike, or otherwise violently ill use it; but gradually — very gradually — I came to look upon it with unutterable loathing, and to flee silently from its odious presence, as from the breath of a pestilence.

What added, no doubt, to[40] my hatred of the beast, was the discovery, on the morning after I brought it home, that, like Pluto, it also had been deprived of one of its eyes. This circumstance, however, only endeared it to my wife,[41] who, as I have already said, possessed, in a high degree, that humanity of feeling which had once been my distinguishing trait, and the source of many of my simplest and purest pleasures.

With my aversion to this cat, however, its partiality for myself seemed to increase. It followed my footsteps with a pertinacity which it would be difficult to make the reader comprehend. Whenever I sat, it would crouch beneath my chair, or spring upon my knees, covering me with its loathsome caresses. If I arose to walk it would get between my feet and thus nearly throw me down, or, fastening its long and sharp claws in my dress, clamber[42], in this manner, to my breast. At such times, although I longed to destroy it with a blow, I was yet withheld from[43] so doing, partly by a memory of my former crime, but chiefly — let me confess it at once — by absolute dread of the beast.

This dread was not exactly a dread of physical evil — and yet I should be at a loss how otherwise to define it. I am almost ashamed to own[44] — yes, even in this felon's cell, I am almost ashamed

---

38) made no claim to : ~에 대해 소유권을 주장하지 않았다
39) rose into : 높아져서 ~이 되다
40) What added to : ~을 증가시킨 것은
41) This circumstance, however, only endeared it to my wife : 그러나 이 상황으로 인해 그 놈은 아내에게 더욱 사랑받을 뿐이었다.
42) clamber : 기어오르다
43) was withheld from : ~을 하지 못하다, 자제하다
44) own : 고백하다

to own — that the terror and horror with which the animal inspired me, had been heightened by one of the merest chimeras[45] it would be possible to conceive. My wife had called my attention, more than once, to the character of the mark of white hair, of which I have spoken, and which constituted the sole visible difference between the strange beast and the one I had destroyed. The reader will remember that this mark, although large, had been originally very indefinite; but, by slow degrees — degrees nearly imperceptible[46], and which for a long time my Reason struggled to reject as fanciful — it had, at length, assumed a rigorous distinctness of outline. It was now the representation of an object that I shudder to name — and for this, above all, I loathed, and dreaded, and would have rid myself of the monster had I dared[47] — it was now, I say, the image of a hideous — of a ghastly thing — of the GALLOWS![48] — oh, mournful and terrible engine of Horror and of Crime — of Agony and of Death!

And now was I indeed wretched beyond the wretchedness of mere Humanity. And a brute beast — whose fellow I had contemptuously destroyed — a brute beast to work out for me — for me a man, fashioned in the image of the High God — so much of insufferable wo! Alas! neither by day nor by night knew I the blessing of Rest any more![49] During the former[50] the creature left me no moment alone; and, in the latter[51] I started, hourly, from dreams of unutterable fear, to find the hot breath of the thing upon my face, and its vast weight — an incarnate Night — Mare that I had no power to shake off — incumbent eternally upon my heart!

Beneath the pressure of torments such as these, the feeble remnant of the good within me succumbed. Evil thoughts became my sole intimates — the darkest and most evil of thoughts. The moodiness of my usual temper increased to hatred of all things and of all mankind; while, from the sudden, frequent, and ungovernable outbursts of a fury to which I now blindly abandoned myself, my uncomplaining wife, alas! was the most usual and the most patient of sufferers.

One day she accompanied me, upon some household errand, into the cellar of the old building which our poverty compelled us to inhabit. The cat followed me down the steep stairs, and, nearly throwing me headlong, exasperated me to madness. Uplifting an axe, and forgetting, in my wrath, the childish dread which had hitherto stayed my hand[52], I aimed a blow at the animal which, of course, would have proved instantly fatal had it descended as I wished. But this blow was arrested by the hand of my wife. Goaded, by the interference, into a rage more than demoniacal[53], I withdrew my arm from her grasp and buried the axe in her brain. She fell dead upon the spot, without a groan.

---

45) chimeras : 망상, 괴물
46) degrees nearly imperceptible : 거의 알아차릴 수 없을 정도로
47) would have rid myself of the monster had I dared : 감히 할 수만 있었다면 나는 그 괴물을 없애버렸을 것이다.
48) gallows : 교수대
49) neither by day ∼ any more! : 밤이고 낮이고 나는 휴식의 은혜를 입을 수가 없었다!(쉴 수가 없었다)
50) the former : by day
51) the latter : by night
52) stay my hand : 억누르다, 억제하다
53) demoniacal : 악마 같은(= demoniac)

This hideous murder accomplished, I set myself[54] forthwith[55], and with entire deliberation[56], to the task of concealing the body. I knew that I could not remove it from the house, either by day or by night, without the risk of being observed by the neighbors. Many projects entered my mind. At one period I thought of cutting the corpse into minute fragments, and destroying them by fire. At another, I resolved to dig a grave for it in the floor of the cellar. Again, I deliberated about casting it in the well in the yard — about packing it in a box, as if merchandize, with the usual arrangements, and so getting a porter to take it from the house. Finally I hit upon[57] what I considered a far better expedient[58] than either of these. I determined to wall it up in the cellar — as the monks of the middle ages are recorded to have walled up their victims.

For a purpose such as this the cellar was well adapted. Its walls were loosely constructed, and had lately been plastered throughout with a rough plaster, which the dampness of the atmosphere had prevented from hardening. Moreover, in one of the walls was a projection[59], caused by a false chimney, or fireplace, that had been filled up, and made to resemble the rest of the cellar. I made no doubt that I could readily displace the bricks at this point, insert the corpse, and wall the whole up as before, so that no eye could detect any thing suspicious.

And in this calculation I was not deceived. By means of a crow-bar I easily dislodged the bricks, and, having carefully deposited the body against the inner wall, I propped it in that position, while, with little trouble, I relaid the whole structure as it originally stood. Having procured mortar, sand, and hair, with every possible precaution, I prepared a plaster which could not be distinguished from the old, and with this I very carefully went over the new brick-work. When I had finished, I felt satisfied that all was right. The wall did not present the slightest appearance of having been disturbed. The rubbish on the floor was picked up with the minutest care. I looked around triumphantly, and said to myself — "Here at least, then, my labor has not been in vain."

My next step was to look for the beast which had been the cause of so much wretchedness; for I had, at length, firmly resolved to put it to death[60]. Had I been able to meet with it, at the moment, there could have been no doubt of its fate; but it appeared that the crafty animal had been alarmed at[61] the violence of my previous anger, and forebore to present itself in my present mood. It is impossible to describe, or to imagine, the deep, the blissful sense of relief which the absence of the detested creature occasioned[62] in my bosom. It did not make its appearance during the night — and thus for one night at least, since its introduction into the house, I soundly and tranquilly slept; aye, slept even with the burden of murder upon my soul!

The second and the third day passed, and still my tormentor came not. Once again I breathed as

---

54) set oneself to : 헌신적으로 ~하다, ~하고자 노력하다
55) forthwith : 즉시
56) with entire deliberation : 아주 신중히
57) hit upon : 생각이 탁 떠오르다
58) expedient : 편리한
59) projection : 돌출된 부분, 앞으로 튀어나온 부분
60) put to death : 사형에 처하다
61) been alarmed at : 놀라다
62) occasioned : 일으키다, 유발하다

a freeman. The monster, in terror, had fled the premises forever! I should behold it no more! My happiness was supreme! The guilt of my dark deed disturbed me but little. Some few inquiries had been made, but these had been readily answered. Even a search had been instituted — but of course nothing was to be discovered. I looked upon my future felicity as secured.

Upon the fourth day of the assassination, a party of the police came, very unexpectedly, into the house, and proceeded again to make rigorous investigation of the premises. Secure, however, in the inscrutability[63] of my place of concealment, I felt no embarrassment whatever[64]. The officers bade me accompany them in their search. They left no nook or corner unexplored. At length, for the third or fourth time, they descended into the cellar. I quivered not in a muscle. My heart beat calmly as that of one who slumbers in innocence. I walked the cellar from end to end. I folded my arms upon my bosom, and roamed easily to and fro. The police were thoroughly satisfied and prepared to depart. The glee at my heart was too strong to be restrained. I burned to say[65] if but one word, by way of triumph[66], and to render doubly sure their assurance of my guiltlessness.

"Gentlemen," I said at last, as the party ascended the steps, "I delight to have allayed your suspicions. I wish you all health, and a little more courtesy. By the bye, gentlemen, this — this is a very well constructed house." [In the rabid[67] desire to say something easily, I scarcely knew what I uttered at all.] — "I may say an excellently well constructed house. These walls — are you going, gentlemen? — these walls are solidly put together;" and here, through the mere phrenzy[68] of bravado[69], I rapped heavily, with a cane which I held in my hand, upon that very portion of the brick-work behind which stood the corpse of the wife of my bosom.

But may God shield and deliver me from the fangs of the Arch-Fiend[70]! No sooner had the reverberation of my blows sunk into silence, than I was answered by a voice from within the tomb! — by a cry, at first muffled and broken, like the sobbing of a child, and then quickly swelling into one long, loud, and continuous scream, utterly anomalous and inhuman — a howl — a wailing shriek, half of horror and half of triumph, such as might have arisen only out of hell, conjointly from the throats of the damned[71] in their agony and of the demons that exult in the damnation.

Of my own thoughts it is folly to speak. Swooning, I staggered to the opposite wall. For one instant the party upon the stairs remained motionless, through extremity of terror and of awe. In the next, a dozen stout arms[72] were toiling[73] at the wall. It fell bodily. The corpse, already greatly decayed and clotted with gore, stood erect before the eyes of the spectators. Upon its head, with

---

63) inscrutability : 수색할 수 없음
64) no ~ whatever : 어떠한 ~도
65) burned to say : 말하고 싶어 가슴이 탔다
66) by way of triumph : 승리를 위해서
67) rabid : 광적인, 극단적인
68) phrenzy : frenzy(광분, 광란)
69) bravado : 허세
70) Arch-Fiend : 대악마, 사탄
71) the damned : 죄를 지어 지옥에 떨어진 자
72) a dozen stout arms : 여러 튼튼한 팔들(조사 나온 경찰들의 팔을 의미)
73) toil : 힘들게 일하다

red extended mouth and solitary eye of fire[74]), sat the hideous beast whose craft[75]) had seduced me into murder, and whose informing voice had consigned[76]) me to the hangman. I had walled the monster up within the tomb.

74) eye of fire : 불타는 듯한 눈
75) craft : 계략
76) consign : 이끌다, 데려가다, 인도하다(= deliver)

제 3 장

Nathaniel Hawthorne
- 「*The Scarlet Letter*」

📖 **단원개요**

「*The Scarlet Letter*」는 Hester가 딸 Pearl을 안고 처형대에 선 시점부터 Dimmesdale의 임종 직전의 고백까지인 1642~1649년까지의 시기에 해당한다. Nathaniel Hawthorne은 소설의 첫머리에서부터 청교도 사회의 한복판에 감옥과 무덤의 이미지를 심어 그 사회와 이상에 어두운 그림자를 드리운다. 그는 엄격한 청교도 규율과 구성원들의 자발적 복종 아래 민중의 활력이 억제되는 상황을 효과적으로 드러낸다.

📋 **출제 경향 및 수험 대책**

「*The Scarlet Letter*」에서 숲은 Hester의 공간이자 밝게 묘사되는 장소이다. 청교도 사회에서와는 달리 숲에서의 Hester가 보여주는 인간적 가치에 대한 작가의 옹호에 주목할 필요가 있다. 작가는 청교도 사회 특유의 억압성으로 개인들의 내면에 증오가 자라고 고립이 심화되는 현상을 보여준다. 낡은 이상에서 머문 채 개인의 삶의 파괴과정에 대해 호손은 어느 정도 비판을 가하고 있다. 작가의 이러한 관점에 근거하여 작품을 분석할 필요가 있다.

제 1 절 작가의 생애

1 유년기

Nathaniel Hawthorne(1804~1864)은 1804년 7월 4일 미국 독립기념일에 매사추세츠(Massachusetts)주 세일럼(Salem)에서 Nathaniel Hathorne(호손 가문의 원래 성씨에는 w자가 없었다)과 Elizabeth Manning의 3남매 중 둘째 아들이자 장남으로 태어났다. 그의 조상 중에 John Hathorne이라는 사람은 1692년의 악명 높은 세일럼 마녀 재판의 세 명의 판사 중 한 명이었다. Hawthorne은 이것을 가문의 수치로 여겼을 뿐 아니라 이로 인한 죄의식에 강박적으로 사로잡혔다. 그가 자신의 성(姓)에 w자를 삽입하여 바꾼 것도 이와 무관해 보이지 않는다. Hawthorne은 네 살 때 황열(yellow fever)로 선장이었던 아버지를 여의었고, 어릴 때 학교에서 공놀이를 하다가 발을 다친 적이 있었는데, 그 후 1년 동안 계속 집에서 칩거 생활을 했다. 그는 집에서 상당히 많은 책을 읽었는데, Edmund Spenser의 「*The Faerie Queene*」, John Bunyan의 「*The Pilgrim's Progress*」 등을 즐겨 읽었다.

2 청년기

1821년에 Hawthorne은 삼촌의 권유로 메인(Maine)주의 브런즈윅(Brunswick)에 위치한 Bowdoin College에 입학했는데, 그곳에서 그는 그의 인생에 중대한 영향을 미치게 될 친구들을 만났다. Horatio Bridge와 Franklin Pierce(미국 제14대 대통령) 등과는 아주 절친한 사이였고, H. W. Longfellow와는 별로 친하지는 않았지만 동기생이었다. Hawthorne은 Bowdoin College를 졸업(1825)한 후 1837년까지 12년 동안 세일럼에 있는 모친의 집에 와서 무직인 상태로 독서와 창작 수습에만 전념하였다. 이때도 Hawthorne은 어렸을 때와 마찬가지로 주로 고독과 명상, 독서를 하며 생활했는데, 그러다 보니 그의 예민한 감수성과 회의적인 성격으로 인하여 인간의 내면에 더욱더 깊은 관심을 갖게 된 것은 지극히 당연한 것이었다. 그는 인간 본성에 존재하는 신성을 믿으면서도 죄악 역시 인간에게 함께 도사리고 있다고 보았다. 따라서 Hawthorne은 그의 많은 단편소설들과 일련의 로맨스들에서 죄인들의 우화와 지성, 감정의 갈등을 통하여 어느 사회에나 있는 인간 심리와 인간 고뇌에 대한 예리한 인식을 보여주었다.

3 작품 활동과 사회 활동

Hawthorne은 1828년에 그의 첫 소설인 「Fanshawe」를 자비를 들여 익명으로 출간하였다. 그러나 그는 이 작품이 마음에 들지 않아 책이 출간된 즉시 모두 회수하여 파기해 버렸다. 이후 Hawthorne은 한동안 단편소설의 창작에만 힘을 기울였다. 1830년 『Salem Gazette』에 처음으로 「The Hollow of the Three Hills」를 게재한 이래, 1839년까지 약 10년간 신문과 잡지, 특히 『The Token』에 단편 등 총 22편을 모두 익명으로 게재하였다.

1837년에 Hawthorne은 당시까지 발표한 단편소설 36편 가운데 18편을 한데 묶어 『Twice-Told Tales』라는 단편집을 자신의 본명으로 내놓았으며, 이 단편집이 호평을 받으면서 작가로서 세상에 알려지는 계기가 되었다. 1846년에 두 번째 단편집 『Mosses from an Old Manse』(『낡은 목사관의 이끼』)를 출간하였다. 여기에 실린 첫 작품인 「The Old Manse」는 그의 자전적 에세이이며, 이 밖에도 「Young Goodman Brown」, 「The Birth-mark」, 「Rappaccini's Daughter」 등이 수록되어 있다. 또한 1852년에 발표한 단편집 『The Snow-Image, and Other Twice-Told Tales』에는 1832년에 발표한 「The Wives of the Dead」, 「My Kinsman, Major Molineux」, 1850년의 「The Great Stone Face」(큰바위 얼굴)와 「Ethan Brand」 등이 함께 실렸다.

Hawthorne은 한때 초현실주의적 유토피아 공동체(이후엔 공산주의적 공동체) 체험에 참여하기도 하였는데, 그는 1841년 4월에 브룩 농장(Brook Farm)이라는 실험 농장의 일원으로 동참하였다가 10월에 탈퇴하였다. 그가 그 농장에 참가한 동기는 사상적인 이유보다는 그의 약혼자인 Sophia Peabody와의 결혼을 위한 재정적인 안정을 위한 것으로 알려져 있다. 그는 1842년에 Sophia와 결혼한 후 매사추세츠주 콩코드(Concord)의 목사관(The Old Manse)으로 이사하였다. 여기에서 Hawthorne은 Ralph Waldo Emerson, Henry David Thoreau, Margaret Fuller, Ellery Channing 등과 친분을 쌓을 수 있었다. 1850년에 그는 가족(아내와 세 명의 자녀들)과 함께 매사추세츠주 버크셔(Berkshire) Lenox로 이사했는데, 이곳과 멀지 않은 피츠필드(Pittsfield)에 살고 있던 Herman Melville과도 친교를 나누었다.

Hawthorne은 이처럼 저명한 문호들과 활발한 교제를 했을 뿐 아니라 정치계에도 깊이 관여하였다. 그의 공직 생활은 세관(Custom House)과 인연이 많았다. 그는 오랜 시간 동안 세관에서 일을 하였으나, 1948년 11월 대통령 선거에서 휘그(Whig)당이 승리를 차지하고, 다음 해 휘그당의 Zachary Taylor가 대통령에 취임한 후, 민주 당원(Democratic Party)이었던 Hawthorne은 일종의 정치적인 보복을 당하게 되면서 세관에서 해고되었다. Hawthorne은 「The Custom-House」(1849)에서 당시 자신의 비참한 심정을 정치에 대한 회의와 함께 적나라하게 토로하였다. 세관 일을 그만둔 Hawthorne은 곧 「*The Scarlet Letter : A Romance*」를 쓰기 시작했다. 「*The Scarlet Letter : A Romance*」(1850)는 미국 최초로 대량 생산된 책 중 하나였고, 초판 2,500부가 권당 75센트에 팔리면서 그의 명성은 올라가기 시작하였다. 이 여세를 몰아 Hawthorne은 「*The House of the Seven Gables : A Romance*」(『일곱 박공의 집』)를 출간하여 6,500부를 팔았다. 1852년에는 자신의 브룩농장 체험을 바탕으로 집필한 「*The Blithedale Romance*」를 내놓아 6월에 초판 5,000부, 7월에 재판 2,350부를 발간하였다.

1853년에 Hawthorne은 대통령에 취임한 민주당 Franklin Pierce에 의해 영국의 리버풀(Liverpool) 영사에 임명되었다. Hawthorne의 사후에 출판된 1853~1856년의 영국 체재 기간 중의 기록인 『*The English Notebooks*』(1870)는 영국의 삶에 대한 관찰이 상세히 기록된 에세이 모음집이다. 영국의 영사직을 사임한 Hawthorne은 1857~1859년에 로마와 플로렌스에서 생활하고, 1860년 미국으로 귀국하여 다시 콩코드에 정착한 뒤 집필을 시작했다.

1860년 Hawthorne은 그의 마지막 소설인 「*The Marble Faun : Or, The Romance of Monte Beni*」를 미국과 영국에서 출간하였다. 영국에서는 「*Transformation, or The Romance of Monte Beni*」라는 제목으로 한 달 먼저 나왔는데, 이 제목은 출판사가 붙인 것이었다. 이 작품은 우화적·목가적·고딕적·로맨스적 요소를 지녔으며, 영국과 미국 모두에서 호평을 받았다.

1864년에 Hawthorne의 건강은 극도로 나빠졌다. 가까운 친지들은 그에게 요양을 하라고 권하였고, Hawthorne은 5월 11일 Pierce와 함께 뉴햄프셔(New Hampshire)로 요양을 나섰다가 5월 19일, 플리머스(Plymouth)에서 자던 중 세상을 떠났다. 5월 23일 Hawthorne은 콩코드의 한 묘지에 안장되었다.

🔔 더 알아두기 🔍

Nathaniel Hawthorne의 주요작품

- 소설
  - 「*Fanshawe*」(1828)
  - 「*The Scarlet Letter : A Romance*」(1850)
  - 「*The House of the Seven Gables : A Romance*」(1851)
  - 「*The Blithedale Romance*」(1852)

- 단편집
  - 『*Twice-Told Tales*』(1837)
  - 『*Mosses from an Old Manse*』(1846)

- 단편
  - 「*Young Goodman Brown*」(1835)
  - 「*Ethan Brand*」(1850)
  - 「*The Great Stone Face*」(1850)
  - 「*The Birth-Mark*」(1843)

제 2 절   작품 세계

1   시대적 배경과 개요

19세기 초 미국 낭만주의 소설의 대표 작가인 Nathaniel Hawthorne의 집안은 독실한 청교도 신자들로 이루어져 있었다. 따라서 그는 청교도의 사상과 생활태도에 깊은 관심을 가지고 많은 작품을 썼는데, Hawthorne은 선조들의 죄와 죄의식, 응보, 반청교도주의(anti-Puritanism)적 주제를 다룬다.

Hawthorne은 낭만주의자적 계보를 따르면서도 인간의 어두운 내면, 무의식, 본성 속에 내재한 죄와 악의 문제 등을 집요하게 탐구하였다. 그는 상징, 알레고리, 환상적 묘사 등과 같은 독창적인 형식을 단편들에 도입함으로써 영국소설의 관습을 따르고 있던 당시 미국소설에 신선함을 불어넣었다.

그의 작품은 교훈적 경향이 강하면서도 상징주의에 의한 철학적, 종교적, 심리적으로 의미심장한 세계가 전개되는 정교한 면이 공존한다. 「The Scarlet Letter」의 시대적 배경은 17세기 중엽 매사추세츠만 식민지 (Massachusetts Bay Colony) 보스턴(Boston)이다. 1600년대의 뉴잉글랜드(New England)는 청교도적인 가치를 최고로 여기던 시기였다. 이 시대에는 여성의 간통을 금기시하였는데, 이는 봉건적이고 가부장적인 지배체제를 유지하기 위한 것이었다. 또한 아내를 남편의 전유물로 묶어 두려는 의도도 있었으며, 혈통의 순수성을 보존하려는 측면도 적지 않았다고 한다. 그러나 아이러니한 것은 당시 남성의 간통에 대해서는 관대하였다는 점이다. 결국 주홍 글자의 형벌은 여성을 단죄하기 위한 도구였다.

2   작품의 중요성 중요 ★★★

「The Scarlet Letter」는 간통죄로 괴로워하다 결국 죄를 고백하고 죽는 Dimmesdale 목사를 통해 당시의 엄격한 청교도 사회와 죄인의 고독한 심리를 잘 나타내는 작품이다. 청교도 사회의 비정함과 형식에 치우친 신앙의 타락, 그로 인한 인간 사회의 비극, 죄의식으로 얼룩진 인간 영혼의 어두운 심리가 매우 음울하게 그려져 있다.

Hester는 키가 크고 우아한 용모를 지닌 여성으로, 숱 많은 검은 머리칼과 튀어나온 이마, 검은 눈동자가 무척이나 인상적이다. 그녀는 바느질로 생계를 꾸려나가면서도 풍요롭고 아름답고 호화로운 것을 좋아하는 본성을 발휘한다. 그리고 가슴에 달린 주홍 글자는 오히려 그녀에게 자신감을 갖게 해 타인의 감추어진 죄에 감응하는 능력까지 보이게 된다. 나아가 고통받는 사람들에게 구원의 손길을 뻗치고, 공동 사회의 모범적인 여성으로 떠받들어진다. '여성의 강인함'을 몸에 익힌 Hester의 주홍 글자 A는 '유능한'(Able)의 A로까지 해석되게 한다. 작품에서 남성 주인공은 정신을 대표하는 Dimmesdale과 지성을 대표하는 Chillingworth로 구분되며, 처음부터 끝까지 서로를 파멸시킨다. 이들과는 대조적으로, Hester는 미국 대지에 뿌리내린 강인한 여성의 원형(原型)이 되고 있다. 「The Scarlet Letter」가 단순히 이들의 삼각관계의 이야기를 넘어서 여전히 사람들에게 감동을 안겨주는 이유도 여기에 있다.

이 작품은 1640년대 보스턴 식민지 사회에서 일어난 일들을 소재로 하여 청교도가 지배하는 식민지 사회에서 억압되는 인간의 모습을 19세기 시대정신을 통해 비판하고 있다. Hawthorne은 유토피아적 신세계를 건설하려는 청교도들의 불완전성을 파헤쳤다. 그는 이 작품에서 크게 세 가지 형태의 죄, 즉 Hester의 세상에 드러난 죄, Dimmesdale의 숨겨진 죄, 그리고 Chillingworth의 용서받지 못할 죄(악, 앙심, 복수, 오만의 죄)를 다루고 있다. 동시에 Chillingworth의 타락과 죽음, 파멸을 통해 에덴동산이 상징하는 이상주의의 꿈이 얼마나 위험하고 실현 불가능한 것인가를 보여준다.

Hawthorne은 Hester와 Dimmesdale을 처음부터 죄를 범한 불완전한 인간으로 묘사하면서 이들을 통해 죄를 범한 인간, 즉 불완전한 인간이 바로 참된 미국인의 모습임을 암시하고 동시에 기계 문명 속에서 '정원의 신화'를 꿈꾸고 있는 동시대의 미국인들을 통렬히 비난하고 있다. Hawthorne은 그의 작품들을 통해 도덕적 진실성을 밝히고자 했던 것으로 보인다. 비록 그의 문학세계가 죄악으로 인해 야기된 고립과 비극이라는 인간사의 어두운 내면에 중점을 두기는 했지만, 오히려 Hawthorne 문학의 진정한 의의는 죄를 통한 구원의 완성에 있다고 볼 수 있다.

3 Scarlet Letter(주홍 글자) 'A'의 의미 종요★★★

Hawthorne이 이 소설에서 제시하는 가장 중요한 상징은 주홍 글자(scarlet letter) 'A'이다. 이 글자의 의미는 5장에서부터 나타난다. 세상 사람들의 시선 속에서 감옥의 문을 통해 사회로 나온 Hester는 예전과는 다르게 변한 모습으로 살아간다. Hester는 지역 사회를 위해 봉사하며 자선 사업까지 한다. 이처럼 그녀는 법률이 자신에게 덧씌운 주홍 글자의 운명을 회피하려 하지 않고 담담하게 받아들인다. Hester는 병간호를 하고 가난한 사람들을 위해 바느질도 하면서 도움을 필요로 하는 사람들을 헌신적으로 돕고 살아간다. 13장에서는 주홍 글자와 관련하여 완전히 변모한 Hester의 모습을 보다 구체적으로 볼 수 있는데, 그녀가 근심 걱정이 가득한 집에 찾아오면 근심이 사라지고, 새로운 빛이 비칠 때에는 그녀도 사라지는 것이다. 자연스럽게 사람들은 그녀가 달고 있는 주홍 글자 'A'를 원래의 뜻으로 받아들이기를 거부하게 된다.

주홍 글자 'A'는 다양한 의미로 해석된다.
(1) 먼저 성스럽게 변모한 Hester의 모습을 보여주는 'Angel'을 가리킨다.

(2) 'A'는 알파벳의 첫 글자로서 'Adam'의 원죄를 함축적으로 의미할 수 있다. 실제로 청교도들은 아담의 원죄에 온 인류가 동참하고 있다고 믿었다.

(3) Dimmesdale의 이름인 'Arthur'의 첫 글자일 수 있다.

(4) Hester의 능력을 함축하는 'Able'을 의미할 수도 있다. 보스턴 시민들 사이에서 Hester의 가슴에 달린 'A'가 원래 의미했던 'Adultery'(간통 또는 'Adultress', 간통을 범한 여자)에 대한 기억은 점차 희미해져 간다.

(5) Hester의 주홍 글자는 마지막 24장에서 다시 'angel and apostle'(천사와 사도)를 상징한다. 주홍 글자 'A'는 마침내 사회의 유대와 지속의 대행자를 의미한다.

4 Scaffold(교수대)

소설의 화자는 2장에서 Hester와 그녀의 딸 Pearl을 인상적으로 소개한 후 이 둘을 보스턴 장터에 세워진 교수대 위에 올려놓는다. 작품의 중요한 배경 중 하나인 신생 도시 보스턴의 장터는 오랜 세월을 거치면서 검게 변색된 음울한 감옥과 위압적인 교수대에 의해 압도된다. 특히 Hester가 서 있는 교수대는 소설 전체를 지배하는 중요한 이미지인데, 일종의 조망대에 해당하는 교수대는 2장, 12장, 23장에서 반복적으로 나타나서 작품의 구조를 균형 있게 유지시키는 역할을 할 뿐만 아니라 작품의 주제와 관련하여 매우 중요한 상징으로 부각된다.

5 Forest(숲) 중요 ★★

Hawthorne은 운명의 힘이 Hester에게 작용하는 광경을 보여주기 위해 효과적으로 자연을 이용하고 있다. 예를 들면, Hester가 Dimmesdale 목사를 은밀히 만나는 장소이자 마녀로 여겨지는 Mistress Hibbins의 안식처인 '숲'은 단순한 배경의 기능을 넘어선다. 과연 숲은 악마의 영역인가, 아니면 자연스런 사랑의 보금자리인가? 16장에서 Hester는 Dimmesdale을 만날 수 있을지도 모른다는 기대를 품고 숲속으로 산책을 간다. Pearl은 마냥 즐거워하면서 뛰어다닌다. 두 모녀가 걸어가는 오솔길 양옆에는 원시림이 빽빽이 들어차 있다. 숲의 음산한 분위기에 어울리게 모녀의 대화는 악마 이야기로 이어지는데, Pearl은 간통이라는 죄악의 결과물답게 엄마의 옷자락을 잡고서 반은 진지하고 반은 장난스런 눈빛으로 악마 이야기를 해달라고 조른다. 실제로 당시에 악마는 숲속에서 종종 만날 수 있는 형상으로 여겨졌다.

당시의 청교도들에게 있어서 보스턴과 매사추세츠만의 식민지는 하느님이 없는 영역으로 간주되었으며, 신대륙의 미개척지는 무질서의 원천이자 악마의 마지막 본거지로 여겨졌다. 왜냐하면 그 속에서 인간의 가장 원시적인 감정과 개인의 의지가 하느님의 권위나 보편적인 윤리의 개념에 구속당하지 않은 채로 자유로운 표현을 찾을 수 있다고 보았기 때문이다. 즉, 숲은 악마와 인간이 공존하는 원시의 영역이라고 할 수 있다.

제3절 줄거리

청교도의 식민지인 보스턴 형무소로부터 Hester Prynne는 사람들의 구경거리가 되기 위해 시장 한가운데 마련된 교수대 위로 끌려 나온다. 그녀의 품안에는 생후 3개월 된 갓난아기가 안겨 있었고, 가슴에는 간통죄를 저지른 여성임을 나타내는 'A'(Adultery, Adulteress)라는 주홍 글자가 새겨져 있다. 늙은 의사와 결혼한 그녀는 남편보다 2년 정도 먼저 미국으로 건너와 살고 있었고, 남편이 없는 동안 Pearl이라는 사생아를 낳게 된 것이다. 그녀는 그 벌로 평생 가슴에 'A'라는 글자를 달고 살도록 선고받는다. Bellingham 총독과 늙은 목사 John Wilson, 그리고 젊은 성직자 Arthur Dimmesdale의 힐문에도 불구하고 그녀는 불륜의 상대가 누구인지 말하지 않는다. 군중 속에서 미국 원주민과 함께 있던 의사 Chillingworth는 Hester에게 자신이 그녀의 정식 남편임을 밝히지 못하게 한다. Hester는 변두리에 있는 오두막에 살면서 바느질 일로 생계를 꾸려 나가고, 3살 난 Pearl은 그녀의 손에서 친구도 없이 자유분방하게 길러진다. 옥스퍼드를 졸업하고 성직자가 된 수재 Dimmesdale은 채찍질과 단식, 철야 등과 같은 지나친 고행으로 뼈만 앙상하게 남게 되고, 그의 건강 상담을 맡은 Chillingworth와 공동생활에 들어간다. Dimmesdale의 설교는 날이 갈수록 사람들에게서 큰 인기를 얻게 된다. 어느 날 밤, Chillingworth는 마음의 병을 고백하려 하지 않는 Dimmesdale의 가슴에서 주홍 글자를 발견한다.

7년의 세월이 흐른 어느 5월의 늦은 밤, Dimmesdale은 Governor Winthrop의 임종을 지키고 집으로 돌아가는 Hester와 Pearl을 불러 세워 놓고 셋이서 손을 잡고 교수대 위에 올라가 죄를 고백하자고 한다. 그의 고뇌를 누구보다 잘 알고 있는 Hester는 전 남편에게 그를 용서해주도록 애원하지만, 복수의 화신이 된 남편 Chillingworth에게 거절당하고, 숲에서 Dimmesdale과 만나 전남편이 Chillingworth임을 밝힌다. 영국이나 유럽으로 Dimmesdale과 도망칠 것을 계획하고 있던 Hester는 새 총독이 부임하여 떠들썩하게 축하연이 벌어진 거리로 나오고, 때마침 선임 연설을 하고 있는 Dimmesdale의 목소리가 교회로부터 흘러 나온다. 그 뒤 Dimmesdale은 Hester와 Pearl을 불러 교수대로 올라가더니, 수많은 청중들 앞에서 가슴을 헤치고 자신의 죄를 고백한 뒤 그 자리에서 죽는다.

마지막 장은 Dimmesdale의 고백에 대한 후일담으로 구성되며, 복수의 대상인 Dimmesdale이 사라지자 Chillingworth도 곧 죽고, 자신의 전 재산을 Pearl에게 남긴다. 결과적으로 부자가 된 Pearl은 유럽에서 결혼하고, Hester는 보스턴으로 돌아와 다시 주홍 글자를 달고 살아가며 힘들어 하는 여성들을 위로한다. Hester가 죽었을 때 그녀는 Dimmesdale 옆에 묻히고, 그들의 비석에는 "검은 언덕 위에 붉은 글자 A가 빛난다."(ON A FIELD, SABLE, THE LETTER A GULES)라고 새겨진다.

제 4 절 작품의 주제 중요 ★★

- 죄와 복수, 가슴과 머리의 대립, 인간의 나약함과 슬픔의 문제를 다루고 있다.
- 죄가 개인 및 사회에 미치는 영향력에 관해 고찰한다.
- 사회가 요구하는 규범에 반하여 자기완성과 사랑을 쟁취하는 인간이 과연 정당한지에 대한 문제를 다루면서 개인과 사회의 갈등을 보여준다.
- 은밀한 죄와 그로 인한 Dimmesdale의 심한 정신적 갈등으로 마침내 자신의 죄를 고백하고 구원받는 내용을 전개하면서 전형적인 영혼 구원의 과정을 보여준다.
- Hawthorne의 인본주의 사상과 Dimmesdale의 구원, Hester의 도덕적 발전과 윤리 문제에 대한 유기적 상관관계를 다루고 있다.

제 5 절 등장인물

1 Hester Prynne

작품의 여주인공이다. 고향인 영국에서 나이 차이가 많이 나는 Chillingworth와 결혼한 후, 암스테르담 (Amsterdam)에서 그의 제안으로 먼저 보스턴으로 이주하지만, 그의 도착이 불확실한 때에 Dimmesdale 목사와 간통하여 Pearl을 낳게 되었고, 주홍 글자 'A'를 가슴에 달고 살아가는 불행하고 불가사의한 성품의 소유자이다.

그러나 그녀는 사랑과 자유를 쟁취한 용기 있는 여성을 대변한다. 간통죄를 저지른 죄인이기는 하나 악(惡)함이 두드러지는 죄인이 아닌 자신이 저지른 죄로 인하여 선행을 하게 되는 여성이다. 페미니즘(feminism)의 시초로도 볼 수 있는데, 남성 중심적이고 억압적인 가부장 사회에서 여성 해방의 모습을 보여준다.

2 Arthur Dimmesdale

Hester와 간통이라는 죄를 짓고도 그 사실을 감추고 목사로 살아가는 위선적인 인물이다. 하지만 결국 심한 정신적 고통을 겪고, 자신의 죄를 하느님 앞에 뉘우쳐 영혼을 구원받는다.

3 Roger Chillingworth

Hester의 남편이다. 북미 원주민 부락에 인질로 잡혀 있으면서 야생 식물을 사용한 특별한 의료법을 터득하여, 보스턴에서 준의사(準醫師, physician)로 인정받는다. Hester와 Dimmesdale 사이의 불륜을 알아차리고는 복수심을 불태운다. 그는 거머리(leech)로 비유되며, 악을 상징한다.

4 Pearl

Hester의 딸이다. 감수성과 통찰력이 뛰어난 아이로, Hester에게 가슴에 박힌 'A'의 의미에 대해 질문하고 Dimmesdale에 관해 묻는다. Pearl의 존재는 죄악의 결과이기 때문에 악마의 자식이라고도 불렸지만 결국은 주변 인물들에게 진주(pearl)이자 보물과 같은 역할을 한다.

5 Governor Bellingham

나이 많고 부유한 보스턴 지역 총독이다. 전통적인 영국 귀족과 유사하다.

6 Mistress Hibbins

Bellingham 총독(Governor)의 누이 동생이다. 마녀라는 소리를 듣지만 실제로는 진보적 여성에 가깝다.

7 Reverend Mr. John Wilson

나이 많은 청교도 목사이다. 엄격하고 가혹하며 작품 초반에 Governor Bellingham, Arthur Dimmesdale 와 함께 Hester를 심문하는 인물이다.

8 Narrator

익명의 서술자(작가)는 폐허가 된 세일럼 세관(Salem Custom House)의 다락방에서 세관감정관인 Jonathan Pue가 썼던 200년 전 Hester Prynne에 관한 글을 발견한다. 청교도 조상들과 미국 역사에 관심을 가지고 있는 그는 이 내용을 바탕으로 글(로맨스)을 쓰기로 한다.

제 6 절 작품의 구조(Plot)와 시점 및 기법

1 구성

(1) 낮과 밤의 장면이 교차하며 진실과 거짓의 상황이 번갈아 일어난다.

(2) Scaffold Scene과 Forest Scene이 교차되며 극적 반전이 일어난다(가장 중요한 장면).

(3) 치밀한 작품 구성과 주제의 통일성, 소재의 엄격한 선택에 따른 내용의 간결함과 격렬함, 등장인물의 제한 등 여러 가지 특징이 훌륭하게 나타나 있다.

(4) Hester의 가슴 위의 주홍 글자, Chillingworth가 섬뜩한 눈초리로 항상 주시하는 Dimmesdale 목사의 가슴에 새겨진 고뇌의 상징적인 글자, 이들의 죄의 결실이라고 할 수 있는 Pearl, 그리고 밤하늘에 퍼지는 환상적인 주홍 글자 'A', Hester와 Dimmesdale의 묘비에 새겨진 어둠보다도 음산한 주홍 글자 'A', 이 모두가 작품을 압도한다. 이러한 주제적 조화의 효과는 작품의 구성상 작품 배경과 주요 인물들이 밀접한 상관관계로 표현되면서 더욱 강조된다. 이 작품의 가장 중요한 배경인 교수대는 2장, 12장, 23장에서 세 번 등장하며, 이 세 장면은 주요 등장인물들이 모두 한자리에 모이면서 'A'가 나타내는 상징적인 주제와 배경, 주요 인물과 작품구성 등이 유기적인 관계를 이루고 있다.

① 1부(1~8장) : 청교도 사회와 Hester에 대한 묘사
② 2부(9~2장) : Chillingworth의 복수
③ 3부(13~20장) : Hester의 참모습과 숲속 산책에 대한 내용
④ 4부(21~24장) : Dimmesdale의 고백과 결말

2 시점

3인칭 전지적 작가 시점

3 기법과 이미지, 문체와 어조 중요 ★★

「*The Scarlet Letter*」는 미국문학사에서 최초의 상징주의(Symbolism) 소설이다. 주요 상징으로는 다음과 같은 것들이 있다.

(1) 'A' : Adultery, Adulteress, Angel, Apostle, Able, Adam의 원죄, Dimmesdale의 이름인 Arthur의 첫 글자

(2) Scaffold(교수대) : Public Notice(공시), Puritanism(청교도주의)

(3) Market-Place(시장) : 법과 종교가 지배하는 문명과 공개성

(4) Forest(숲) : 어둡고 비밀스러움을 대변, 자연과 초자연

(5) Prison(교도소) & Cemetery(묘지) : Puritan(청교도)

(6) Wild rose-bush(야생 장미) : Hester의 열정과 자유, 낭만주의, 반(反)청교도주의

(7) Meteor(유성) : 'A'의 형태로 밤하늘에 보이는 유성은 Dimmesdale에겐 Adultery, 마을 사람들에겐 Angel의 의미로 각기 다르게 해석된다.

(8) Hester : 자연, 공개적 참회

(9) Chillingworth : 악(Evil), 거머리(leech)

(10) Dimmesdale : 위선, 은밀한 죄

(11) Pearl : Elf-child(요정 같은 아이), 진주, 보물

제 7 절 Text

Chapter 1. The Prison Door

A throng of bearded men, in sad-coloured garments and gray steeple-crowned[1] hats, intermixed[2] with women, some wearing hoods, and others bareheaded, was assembled in front of a wooden edifice[3], the door of which was heavily timbered with oak, and studded with[4] iron spikes.

The founders of a new colony, whatever Utopia of human virtue and happiness they might originally project, have invariably recognised it among their earliest practical necessities to allot a portion of[5] the virgin soil as a cemetery, and another portion as the site of a prison. In accordance with this rule, it may safely be assumed that the forefathers of Boston had built the first prison-house somewhere in the vicinity[6] of Cornhill, almost as seasonably as they marked out the first burial-ground, on Isaac Johnson's lot, and round about his grave, which subsequently became the nucleus of all the congregated sepulchres[7] in the old churchyard of King's Chapel. Certain it is that, some fifteen or twenty years after the settlement of the town, the wooden jail was already marked with weather-stains[8] and other indications of age, which gave a yet darker aspect to its beetle-browed and gloomy front. The rust on the ponderous[9] iron-work of its oaken door looked

---

1) steeple-crowned : (모자 따위의) 꼭대기가 뾰족한
2) intermix : 섞다, 섞이다
3) edifice : a building(건축물)
4) be studded with : ~이 점점이 박혀 있다
5) a portion of : ~의 일부분
6) vicinity : 근처, 부근
7) sepulchre : 무덤
8) weather-stains : 비바람에 의한 변색
9) ponderous : 대단히 무거운, 크고 무거운

more antique than anything else in the New World. Like all that pertains to[10] crime, it seemed never to have known a youthful era. Before this ugly edifice, and between it and the wheel-track of the street, was a grass-plot, much overgrown with burdock, pig-weed, apple-peru, and such unsightly vegetation[11], which evidently found something congenial in the soil that had so early borne the black flower of civilised society, a prison. But on one side of the portal, and rooted almost at the threshold, was a wild rose-bush, covered, in this month of June, with its delicate gems, which might be imagined to offer their fragrance and fragile[12] beauty to the prisoner as he went in, and to the condemned criminal as he came forth to his doom, in token that the deep heart of Nature could pity and be kind to him.

This rose-bush, by a strange chance, has been kept alive in history; but whether it had merely survived out of the stern old wilderness, so long after[13] the fall of the gigantic pines and oaks that originally overshadowed it, or whether, as there is fair authority for believing, it had sprung up[14] under the footsteps of the sainted Ann Hutchinson as she entered the prison-door, we shall not take upon us to determine. Finding it so directly on the threshold of our narrative, which is now about to issue from that inauspicious[15] portal, we could hardly do otherwise than pluck one of its flowers, and present it to the reader. It may serve, let us hope, to symbolize some sweet moral blossom that may be found along the track, or relieve the darkening close of a tale of human frailty and sorrow.

Chapter 2. The Market-Place

The grass-plot before the jail, in Prison Lane, on a certain summer morning, not less than[16] two centuries ago, was occupied by[17] a pretty large number of the inhabitants of Boston, all with their eyes intently fastened on the iron-clamped oaken door[18]. Amongst any other population, or at a later period in the history of New England, the grim rigidity that petrified the bearded physiognomies of these good people would have augured some awful business in hand. It could have betokened nothing short of the anticipated execution of some noted culprit, on whom the sentence of a legal tribunal had but confirmed the verdict[19] of public sentiment. But, in that early severity of the Puritan character, an inference of this kind could not so indubitably be drawn. It might be that a sluggish bond-servant, or an undutiful child, whom his parents had given over to the civil authority, was to be corrected at the whipping-post[20]. It might be that an Antinomian, a Quaker, or other

---

10) pertain to : 속하다, 부속하다, 적합하다, 관련하다
11) vegetation : plants(식물, 초목)
12) fragile : 허약한, 부서지기 쉬운. 여기에서는 '부드러운'의 의미
13) so long after : 매우 오랜 후까지
14) spring up : 나오다, 싹이 트다
15) inauspicious : with signs of failure(불길한)
16) not less than : 적어도, 즉, 여기에서는 적어도 2세기 전을 의미
17) be occupied by : ~에 의해 점령당하다
18) with eyes intently fastened on … : …을 뚫어지게 지켜보다
19) verdict : the decision of a jury(판결)
20) whipping-post : 태형을 위한 기둥

heterodox religionist, was to be scourged[21] out of the town, or an idle and vagrant[22] Indian, whom the white man's fire-water had made riotous about the streets, was to be driven with stripes into the shadow of the forest. It might be, too, that a witch, like old Mistress Bibbins, the bitter-tempered[23] widow of the magistrate[24], was to die upon the gallows[25]. In either case[26], there was very much the same solemnity of demeanour on the part of the spectators, as befitted[27] a people among whom religion and law were almost identical, and in whose character both were so thoroughly interfused, that the mildest and severest acts of public discipline were alike made venerable and awful. Meagre[28], indeed, and cold, was the sympathy that a transgressor might look for, from such bystanders[29], at the scaffold. On the other hand, a penalty which, in our days, would infer a degree of mocking[30] infamy and ridicule, might then be invested with almost as stern a dignity as the punishment of death itself. It was a circumstance to be noted on the summer morning when our story begins its course, that the women, of whom there were several in the crowd, appeared to take a peculiar interest in whatever penal infliction might be expected to ensue[31]. The age had not so much refinement, that any sense of impropriety restrained the wearers of petticoat and farthingale from stepping forth into the public ways, and wedging their not unsubstantial persons, if occasion were, into the throng[32] nearest to the scaffold at an execution. Morally, as well as materially, there was a coarser fibre[33] in those wives and maidens of old English birth and breeding than in their fair descendants, separated from them by a series of six or seven generations; for, throughout that chain of ancestry, every successive mother has transmitted to her child a fainter bloom, a more delicate and briefer beauty, and a slighter physical frame, if not a character of less force and solidity than her own. The women who were now standing about the prison-door stood within less than half a century of the period when the man-like Elizabeth[34] had been the not altogether unsuitable representative of the sex. They were her countrywomen; and the beef and ale of their native land, with a moral diet not a whit more refined[35], entered largely into their composition. The bright morning sun, therefore, shone on broad shoulders and well-developed busts, and on round and ruddy cheeks, that had ripened[36] in the far-off island, and had hardly yet grown paler or thinner in the atmosphere of New England. There was, moreover, a boldness and

---

21) scourge : 채찍으로 때리다, 징벌하다
22) vagrant : wandering(방랑하는)
23) bitter-tempered : 고약한 기질의
24) magistrate : 치안 판사
25) gallows : 교수대
26) In either case : 어느 쪽의 경우에도
27) as befitted : ~에 걸맞게, ~에 어울리게
28) Meagre : poor or scanty(빈약한, 부족한)
29) bystander : looker-on(방관자, 구경꾼)
30) mock : to laugh at, ridicule(조롱하다)
31) ensue : to come after, follow(후에 일어나다)
32) throng : a crowd, multitude(군중, 떼)
33) fibre : 성질, 본질
34) Elizabeth : 영국의 여왕 엘리자베스 1세(1558~1603)
35) refine : to become fine, polished, or cultivated(세련되다, 우아하게 하다)
36) ripen : 익다, 성숙하다

rotundity[37] of speech among these matrons[38], as most of them seemed to be, that would startle us at the present day, whether in respect to its purport or its volume of tone.

"Good wives," said a hard-featured dame of fifty, "I'll tell ye a piece of my mind[39]. It would be greatly for the public behoof[40], if we women, being of mature[41] age and Church members in good repute, should have the handling of such malefactresses[42] as this Hester Prynne. What think ye, gossips? If the hussy stood up for judgment before us five, that are now here in a knot together, would she come off[43] with such a sentence as the worshipful magistrates have awarded? Marry, I trow not![44]"

"People say," said another, "that the Reverend Master Dimmesdale, her godly pastor, takes it very grievously to heart that such a scandal should have come upon his congregation."

"The magistrates are God-fearing gentlemen, but merciful overmuch — that is a truth," added a third autumnal matron. "At the very least[45], they should have put the brand of a hot iron on Hester Prynne's forehead. Madame Hester would have winced at[46] that, I warrant me.[47] But she — the naughty baggage — little will she care what they put upon the bodice of her gown! Why, look you, she may cover it with a brooch, or such — like heathenish adornment, and so walk the streets as brave as ever!"

"Ah, but," interposed, more softly, a young wife, holding a child by the hand, "let her cover the mark as she will, the pang[48] of it will be always in her heart."

"What do we talk of marks and brands, whether on the bodice of her gown or the flesh of her forehead?" cried another female, the ugliest as well as the most pitiless of these self-constituted judges. "This woman has brought shame upon us all, and ought to[49] die. Is there not law for it? Truly there is, both in the Scripture and the statute-book. Then let the magistrates, who have made it of no effect, thank themselves if their own wives and daughters go astray[50]!"

"Mercy on us, goodwife!" exclaimed a man in the crowd, "is there no virtue in woman, save what springs from a wholesome fear of the gallows? That is the hardest word[51] yet! Hush now, gossips! for the lock is turning in the prison-door, and here comes Mistress Prynne herself."

The door of the jail being flung open[52] from, within, there appeared, in the first place, like a

---

37) rotundity : (목소리가) 우렁찬
38) matron : an older married woman(나이 지긋한 부인)
39) a piece of one's mind : 솔직한 의견, 비난
40) behoof : 이익
41) mature : 성숙한
42) malefactress : (여자) 악인, 범죄자 cf) malefactor : (남자) 악인
43) come off : 떼어내다, 성공하다
44) Marry, I trow not! : 흥, 어림도 없지!
45) At the very least : 최소한, 하다못해, 적어도
46) wince at : 움찔하다, ~에 움츠리다
47) I warrant me : (삽입구로) 틀림없이, 확실히
48) pang : 격통, 마음의 괴로움
49) ought to : 마땅히 ~해야만 한다
50) astray : 길을 잃고, 못된 길에 빠져
51) hardest word : 심한 말, 악담
52) fling open : (문을) 활짝 열다, 거칠게 열다

black shadow emerging into sunshine, the grim[53] and gristly presence of the town-beadle, with a sword by his side, and his staff of office in his hand. This personage prefigured and represented in his aspect the whole dismal severity[54] of the Puritanic code of law, which it was his business to administer in its final and closest application to the offender. Stretching forth the official staff in his left hand, he laid his right upon the shoulder of a young woman, whom he thus drew forward, until, on the threshold of the prison-door, she repelled[55] him, by an action marked with natural dignity and force of character, and stepped into[56] the open air as if[57] by her own free will[58]. She bore in her arms a child, a baby of some three months old, who winked and turned aside its little face from the too vivid light of day; because its existence, heretofore[59], had brought it acquaintance only with the gray twilight of a dungeon[60], or other darksome apartment of the prison.

When the young woman — the mother of this child — stood fully revealed[61] before the crowd, it seemed to[62] be her first impulse[63] to clasp the infant closely to her bosom; not so much by an impulse of motherly affection, as that she might thereby conceal a certain token[64], which was wrought[65] or fastened[66] into her dress. In a moment, however, wisely judging that one token of her shame would but poorly serve to hide another, she took the baby on her arm, and with a burning blush, and yet a haughty smile, and a glance that would not be abashed, looked around at her townspeople and neighbours. On the breast of her gown, in fine red cloth, surrounded with an elaborate[67] embroidery[68] and fantastic flourishes of gold thread, appeared the letter A It was so artistically done, and with so much fertility and gorgeous luxuriance of fancy, that it had all the effect of a last and fitting decoration to the apparel which she wore; and which was of a splendour in accordance with[69] the taste of the age, but greatly beyond what was allowed by the sumptuary[70] regulations of the colony.

The young woman was tall, with a figure of perfect elegance on a large scale. She had dark and abundant hair, so glossy that it threw off the sunshine with a gleam; and a face which, besides being beautiful from regularity of feature and richness of complexion[71], had the impressiveness belonging

---

53) grim : severe, stern(엄한, 엄격한)
54) severity : 엄격, 엄정
55) repel : 쫓아버리다, 거부하다
56) step into : 걸어 들어오다
57) as if : 마치 ~처럼
58) free will : 자유의지
59) heretofore : 지금까지, 이전에는
60) dungeon : (성 안의) 지하 감옥
61) reveal : show(보이다, 나타나다)
62) it seemed to : to 이하처럼 보였다
63) impulse : 충동
64) token : mark(표, 증거, 상징)
65) wrought : 수놓은, 꾸민
66) fasten : 단단히 고정시키다, 매달리다
67) elaborate : full of detail(정교한, 애써서 만든)
68) embroidery : 수, 자수, 수예품
69) in accordance with : ~와 일치하여, ~에 따라서
70) sumptuary : 사치를 단속하는
71) complexion : aspect(안색, 외관, 양상)

to a marked brow and deep black eyes. She was ladylike, too, after the manner of the feminine gentility of those days; characterised by a certain state and dignity, rather than by the delicate, evanescent[72], and indescribable[73] grace which is now recognised as its indication. And never had Hester Prynne appeared more ladylike, in the antique interpretation of the term, than as she issued from the prison. Those who had before known[74] her, and had expected to behold her dimmed and obscured by a disastrous cloud, were astonished, and even startled, to perceive[75] how her beauty shone out, and made a halo[76] of the misfortune and ignominy[77] in which she was enveloped. It may be true that, to a sensitive observer, there was something exquisitely painful in it. Her attire[78], which, indeed, she had wrought for the occasion in prison, and had modelled much after her own fancy, seemed to express the attitude of her spirit, the desperate recklessness of her mood, by its wild and picturesque[79] peculiarity[80]. But the point which drew all eyes, and, as it were[81], transfigured the wearer — so that both men and women who had been familiarly acquainted with Hester Prynne were now impressed as if they beheld her for the first time — was that SCARLET LETTER, so fantastically embroidered and illuminated upon her bosom. It had the effect of a spell, taking her out of the ordinary relations with humanity, and enclosing her in a sphere[82] by herself.

"She hath good skill at her needle, that's certain," remarked one of her female spectators; "but did ever a woman, before this brazen[83] hussy, contrive such a way of[84] showing it? Why, gossips,[85] what is it but to laugh in the faces of our godly magistrates, and make a pride out of[86] what they, worthy gentlemen, meant for a punishment?"

"It were well," muttered the most iron-visaged of the old dames, "if we stripped Madame Hester's rich gown off her dainty shoulders; and as for the red letter which she hath stitched so curiously, I'll bestow[87] a rag of mine own rheumatic flannel to make a fitter one!"

"Oh, peace, neighbours-peace!" whispered their youngest companion; "do not let her hear you! Not a stitch in that embroidered letter but she has felt it in her heart."

The grim[88] beadle[89] now made a gesture with his staff.

---

72) evanescent : 곧 사라지는
73) indescribable : 형용하기 어려운, 설명하기 힘든
74) had known : (과거완료) 쭉 알아왔었다
75) perceive : 지각하다, 터득하다
76) halo : 후광, 광휘
77) ignominy : disgrace(수치, 불명예)
78) attire : 의복, 복장
79) picturesque : 그림 같은, 개성이 강한
80) peculiarity : 특성, 특색, 독자성
81) as it were : that is to say(즉)
82) sphere : 영역, 범위, 본분
83) brazen : bold(뻔뻔스러운)
84) such a way of : 저런 식으로
85) Why, gossips : 제기랄
86) make pride out of : ~로 자존심을 내다
87) bestow : 수여하다, 이용하다
88) grim : 엄숙한
89) beadle : 교구 관리

"Make way, good people — make way, in the King's name!" cried he. "Open a passage[90]); and I promise ye, Mistress Prynne shall be set where man, woman, and child may have a fair sight of her brave apparel from this time till an hour past meridian[91]). A blessing on the righteous colony of the Massachusetts, where iniquity[92]) is dragged out into the sunshine! Come along, Madame Hester, and show your scarlet letter in the marketplace!"

A lane was forthwith[93]) opened through the crowd of spectators. Preceded by the beadle, and attended by an irregular procession of sternbrowed men and unkindl-visaged[94]) women, Hester Prynne set forth towards the place appointed for her punishment. A crowd of eager and curious school-boys, understanding little of the matter in hand, except that it gave them a half-holiday, ran before her progress, turning their heads continually to stare into her face and at the winking baby in her arms, and at the ignominious letter on her breast. It was no great distance, in those days[95]), from the prison-door to the market-place.[96]) Measured by the prisoner's experience, however, it might be reckoned[97]) a journey of some length; for, haughty as her demeanour was, she perchance[98]) underwent an agony from every footstep of those that thronged to see her, as if her heart had been flung into the street for them all to spurn[99]) and trample[100]) upon. In our nature, however, there is a provision[101]), alike marvellous and merciful, that the sufferer should never know the intensity[102]) of what he endures by its present torture, but chiefly by the pang that rankles after it. With almost a serene[103]) deportment, therefore, Hester Prynne passed through this portion of her ordeal[104]), and came to a sort of scaffold at the western extremity of the market-place. It stood nearly beneath the eaves[105]) of Boston's earliest church, and appeared to be a fixture there.

In fact, this scaffold constituted a portion of a penal machine, which now, for two or three generations past, has been merely historical and traditiony among us, but was held, in the old time, to be as effectual[106]) an agent in the promotion[107]) of good citizenship as ever was the guillotine among the terrorists of France. It was, in short[108]), the platform of the pillory[109]); and above it rose

---

90) Open a passage : 길을 비켜라.
91) meridian : 자오선, 정오
92) iniquity : 부정(행위), 죄(unfairness, injustice)
93) forthwith : 곧, 즉시(at once, immediately, instantly)
94) visaged : 얼굴이 ~한, ~한 생김새의
95) in those days : 그 당시에는
96) from the prison-door to the market-place : 옥문에서 장터까지
97) reckon : 계산하다, 평가하다
98) perchance : by chance, perhaps(우연히, 아마)
99) spurn : drive away(쫓아내다, 퇴짜 놓다)
100) trample : 짓밟다, 밟아 뭉개다
101) provision : 대책, 설비, 단서
102) intensity : strength(강도, 세기)
103) serene : calm(맑게 갠, 잔잔한)
104) ordeal : 시련, 괴로운 체험
105) eaves : 처마
106) effectual : effective(효과적인)
107) promotion : furtherance(촉진, 승진)
108) in short : in brief, to make a long story to short, in a few words(간단히 말하면)
109) pillory : 칼(형틀)

the framework of that instrument of discipline, so fashioned as to confine the human head in its tight grasp, and thus hold it up to the public gaze. The very ideal of ignominy was embodied and made manifest in this contrivance[110] of wood and iron. There can be no outrage[111], methinks, against our common nature — whatever be the delinquencies of the individual — no outrage more flagrant than[112] to forbid the culprit[113] to hide his face for shame[114]; as it was the essence of this punishment to do. In Hester Prynne's instance, however, as not unfrequently in other cases,[115] her sentence bore that she should stand a certain time upon the platform, but without undergoing that gripe about the neck and confinement of the head, the proneness to which was the most devilish[116] characteristic of this ugly engine. Knowing well her part, she ascended a flight of wooden steps, and was thus displayed to the surrounding multitude, at about the height of a man's shoulders above the street.

Had there been a Papist[117] among the crowd of Puritans, he might have seen in this beautiful woman, so picturesque in her attire and mien, and with the infant at her bosom, an object to remind him of the image of Divine Maternity, which so many illustrious painters have vied with[118] one another to represent: something which should remind him, indeed, but only by contrast, of that sacred image of sinless motherhood, whose Infant was to redeem[119] the world. Here, there was the taint of deepest sin in the most sacred quality of human life, working such effect, that the world was only the darker for this woman's beauty, and the more lost for the infant that she had borne.

The scene was not without a mixture of awe[120], such as must always invest the spectacle of guilt and shame in a fellow-creature, before society shall have grown corrupt enough to smile, instead of shuddering at it. The witnesses of Hester Prynne's disgrace had not yet passed beyond their simplicity. They were stern[121] enough to look upon her death, had that been the sentence, without a murmur at its severity, but had none of the heartlessness of another social state, which would find only a theme for jest[122] in an exhibition like the present. Even had there been a disposition to turn the matter into ridicule, it must have been repressed[123] and overpowered by the solemn presence of men no less dignified than[124] the governor, and several of his counsellors, a judge, a general, and the ministers of the town, all of whom sat or stood in a balcony of the meeting-house, looking down upon the platform. When such personages could constitute a part of the spectacle, without

---

110) contrivance : 고안물, 장치
111) outrage : 잔악 행위
112) no outrage more flagrant than ~ : ~만큼 극악한 잔악 행위는 없다
113) culprit : offender, the accused(죄인)
114) for shame : 창피해서, 부끄러워서
115) as not unfrequently in other cases : 다른 경우에도 흔히 그런 것처럼
116) devilish : extreme(악마 같은, 흉악한, 극단적인)
117) papist : 가톨릭 신자
118) vie with : ~와 다투다, 겨루다, 경쟁하다
119) redeem : rescue(되사다, 다시 찾다, 구원하다)
120) awe : reverence, veneration, dread(두려움, 경외)
121) stern : severe, rigorous, strict(엄중한, 근엄한)
122) a theme for jest : 농담의 주제
123) repress : control, suppress, restrain, check(억제하다, 억압하다)
124) no less ~ than : even(~에 못지않게, ~만큼)

risking the majesty or reverence of rank and office, it was safely to be inferred[125] that the infliction[126] of a legal sentence would have an earnest and effectual meaning. Accordingly, the crowd was sombre[127] and grave. The unhappy culprit, sustained herself as best a woman might, under the heavy weight of a thousand unrelenting[128] eyes, all fastened upon her, and concentrated at her bosom. It was almost intolerable to be borne. Of an impulsive and passionate nature, she had fortified herself to encounter the stings and venomous[129] stabs of public contumely[130], wreaking itself in every variety of insult; but there was a quality so much more terrible in the solemn mood of the popular mind, that she longed[131] rather to behold all those rigid[132] countenances contorted[133] with scornful merriment, and herself the object. Had a roar of laughter burst from the multitude — each man, each woman, each little shrill — voiced child contributing their individual parts — Hester Prynne might have repaid them all with a bitter and disdainful[134] smile. But, under the leaden infliction which it was her doom to endure, she felt, at moments, as if she must needs shriek out with the full power of her lungs, and cast herself from the scaffold down upon the ground, or else go mad at once[135].

Yet there were intervals when the whole scene, in which she was the most conspicuous[136] object, seemed to vanish from her eyes, or, at least, glimmered indistinctly before them, like a mass of imperfectly shaped and spectra[137] images. Her mind, and especially her memory, was preternaturally active, and kept bringing up other scenes than this roughly-hewn[138] street of a little town, on the edge of the Western wilderness: other faces than were lowering upon her from beneath the brims[139] of those steeple-crowned hats. Reminiscences the most trifling and immaterial, passages of infancy and school-days, sports, childish quarrels, and the little domestic traits[140] of her maiden years, came swarming[141] back upon her, intermingled with recollections of whatever was gravest in her subsequent[142] life; one picture precisely as vivid as another; as if all were of similar importance, or all alike a play. Possibly, it was an instinctive device of her spirit to relieve itself, by the exhibition of these phantasmagoric[143] forms, from the cruel weight and hardness of the reality.

---

125) infer : reason, guess, suppose(추론하다)
126) infliction : (고통, 벌 등을) 주기
127) sombre : 우울한, 암담한
128) unrelenting : callous, cruel, pitiless(냉혹한, 무자비한, 잔인한)
129) venomous : 독액을 분비하는, 악의에 찬, 독이 있는
130) contumely : 모욕, 굴욕
131) long : 사모하다, 갈망하다
132) rigid : stiff, strict(굳은, 단단한)
133) contort : deform(뒤틀다, 찌그러뜨리다)
134) disdainful : haughty, proud(거만한, 경멸적인)
135) go mad at once : 즉시 미쳐버리다
136) conspicuous : noticeable(똑똑히 보이는)
137) spectral : 무시무시한, 공허한, 기괴한
138) hewn : 베어서 대충 모양을 다듬은, 잘라낸
139) brim : (그릇의) 가장자리, (모자의) 테, 차양
140) trait : (마음, 성격, 습관 등의) 특색, 특성
141) swarm : 가득 차다
142) subsequent : 뒤의, 다음의
143) phantasmagoric : 허깨비 같은, 변화무쌍한

Be that as it might, the scaffold of the pillory was a point of view that revealed to Hester Prynne the entire track along which she had been treading, since her happy infancy. Standing on that miserable eminence[144], she saw again her native village, in Old England, and her paternal home: a decayed house of gray stone, with a poverty-stricken[145] aspect, but retaining a half-obliterated shield of arms over the portal, in token of[146] antique gentility. She saw her father's face, with its bold brow, and reverend white beard, that flowed over the old-fashioned Elizabethan ruff; her mother's, too, with the look of heedful and anxious love which it always wore in her remembrance, and which, even since her death, had so often laid the impediment[147] of a gentle remonstrance in her daughter's pathway. She saw her own face, glowing with girlish beauty, and illuminating all the interior of the dusky mirror in which she had been wont to gaze at it. There she beheld another countenance, of a man well stricken in years, a pale, thin, scholar-like visage, with eyes dim and bleared by the lamp-light that had served them to pore over[148] many ponderous books. Yet those same bleared optics had a strange, penetrating[149] power, when it was their owner's purpose to read the human soul. This figure of the study and the cloister[150], as Hester Prynne's womanly fancy failed not to recall, was slightly deformed[151], with the left shoulder a trifle higher than the right. Next rose before her, in memory's picture-gallery, the intricate and narrow thoroughfares, the tall gray houses, the huge cathedrals, and the public edifices, ancient in date and quaint in architecture, of a Continental city; where a new life had awaited her, still in connection with the misshapen scholar: a new life, but feeding itself on time-worn materials, like a tuft[152] of green moss on a crumbling[153] wall. Lastly, in lieu of[154] these shifting scenes, came back the rude market-place of the Puritan settlement, with all the townspeople assembled, and levelling their stern regards at Hester Prynne — yes, at herself — who stood on the scaffold[155] of the pillory, an infant on her arm, and the letter A, in scarlet, fantastically embroidered with gold thread, upon her bosom!

Could it be true? She clutched the child so fiercely to her breast that it sent forth a cry[156]; she turned her eyes downward at the scarlet letter, and even touched it with her finger, to assure herself[157] that the infant and the shame were real. Yes! — these were her realities — all else had vanished[158]!

---

144) eminence : 고귀, 명성
145) poverty-stricken : 가난에 시달리는
146) in token of : ~의 표시로, ~의 증거로
147) impediment : obstacle(방해, 장애물)
148) pore over : 자세히 보다, 탐독하다
149) penetrating : piercing
150) cloister : 수도(수녀)원 생활
151) deform : 변형시키다
152) tuft : (깃털, 머리털, 실 등의) 다발, (쿠션, 커튼 등의) 장식
153) crumble : to break or fall into small parts
154) in lieu of : ~ instead of(~ 대신에)
155) scaffold : 처형대, 교수대
156) it sent forth a cry : The baby sent forth a cry
157) assure : (재귀용법) ~이라고 확신하고 있다
158) vanish : disappear

Chapter 3. The Recognition

From this intense consciousness of being the object of severe and universal observation, the wearer of the scarlet letter was at length relieved, by discerning, on the outskirts of the crowd, a figure which irresistibly took possession of[159] her thoughts. An Indian, in his native garb, was standing there; but the red men[160] were not so infrequent visitors of the English settlements that one of them would have attracted any notice from Hester Prynne, at such a time; much less[161] would he have excluded all other objects and ideas from her mind. By the Indian's side, and evidently sustaining a companionship with him, stood a white man, clad in a strange disarray[162] of civilised and savage costume.

He was small in stature, with a furrowed visage[163], which, as yet, could hardly be termed aged. There was a remarkable intelligence in his features, as of a person who had so cultivated his mental part that it could not fail to mould the physical to itself and become manifest by unmistakable tokens[164]. Although, by a seemingly careless arrangement of his heterogeneous[165] garb, he had endeavoured to conceal or abate the peculiarity, it was sufficiently evident to Hester Prynne that one of this man's shoulders rose higher than the other. Again, at the first instant of perceiving that thin visage, and the slight deformity of the figure, she pressed her infant to her bosom, with so convulsive a force that the poor babe uttered another cry of pain, But the mother did not seem to hear it.

At his arrival in the market-place, and some time before she saw him, the stranger had bent his eyes on Hester Prynne. It was carelessly at first, like a man chiefly accustomed to look inward, and to whom external matters are of little value and import, unless they bear relation to something within his mind. Very soon, however, his look became keen and penetrative[166]. A writhing horror twisted itself across his features, like a snake gliding swiftly over them, and making one little pause, with all its wreathed[167] intervolutions[168] in open sight. His face darkened with some powerful emotion, which, nevertheless, he so instantaneously[169] controlled by an effort of his will, that, save[170] at a single moment, its expression might have passed for calmness. After a brief space, the convulsion[171] grew almost imperceptible[172], and finally subsided into the depths of his nature. When he found the eyes of Hester Prynne fastened on his own, and saw that she appeared to recognise him, he

---

159) take possession of : ～을 손에 넣다, ～을 점유(점령)하다
160) red man : Red Indian(아메리칸 인디언)
161) much less : (부정문 다음에 써서) 하물며(더구나) ～이 아니다
162) disarray : 단정하지 못한 복장
163) visage : 얼굴의 생김새
164) by unmistakable tokens : manifest를 강조하는 말
165) heterogeneous : 이종(이질)의
166) penetrative : 침투하는, 날카로운
167) writhe : 몸부림치다, 괴로워하다
168) intervolution : intervolve(서로 얽히게 하다)의 명사형
169) instantaneously : 순간적으로
170) save : but, except
171) convulsion : violent agitation(격동)
172) imperceptible : 지각할 수 없는, 눈에 보이지 않는

slowly and calmly raised his finger, made a gesture with it in the air, and laid it on his lips.

Then touching the shoulder of a townsman who stood next to him, he addressed him, in a formal and courteous manner:

"I pray you, good sir," said he, "who is this woman? — and wherefore[173] is she here set up to public shame?"

"You must needs[174] be a stranger in this region, friend," answered the townsman looking curiously at the questioner and his savage companion, "else you would surely have heard of Mistress Hester Prynne and her evil doings. She hath raised a great scandal, I promise you, in godly Master Dimmesdale's church."

"You say truly," replied the other; "I am a stranger, and have been a wanderer, sorely against my will[175]. I have met with grievous mishaps by sea and land, and have been long held in bonds among the heathen-folk[176] to the southward; and am now brought hither by this Indian, to be redeemed[177] out of my captivity[178]. Will it please you, therefore, to tell me of Hester Prynne's — have I her name rightly? — of this woman's offences, and what has brought her to yonder scaffold?"

"Truly, friend; and methinks[179] it must gladden your heart, after your troubles and sojourn[180] where iniquity is searched out, and punished in the sight of rulers and people, as here in our godly New England. Yonder woman, sir, you must know, was the wife of a certain learned man, English by birth, but who had long dwelt in Amsterdam, whence, some good time agone, he was minded to cross over and cast in his lot with us of the Massachusetts. To this purpose, he sent his wife before him, remaining himself to look after some necessary affairs. Marry, good sir, in some two years, or less, that the woman has been a dweller here in Boston, no tidings have come of this learned gentleman, Master Prynne; and his young wife, look you, being left to her own misguidance — "

"Ah! — aha! — I conceive you," said the stranger, with a bitter smile. "So learned a man as you speak of[181] should have learned this too in his books. And who, by your favour, sir, may be the father of yonder babe[182] — it is some three or four months old, I should judge — which Mistress Prynne is holding in her arms?"

"Of a truth, friend, that matter remaineth a riddle; and the Daniel who shall expound it is yet a-wanting," answered the townsman. "Madame Hester absolutely refuseth to speak, and the magistrates have laid their heads together in vain. Peradventure the guilty one stands looking on at this sad spectacle, unknown of man, and forgetting that God sees him."

---

173) wherefore : why(왜, 무엇 때문에)
174) must needs : 틀림없이 ~일 것이다
175) against my will : 나의 의지와는 반대로
176) heathen-folk : 이교도
177) redeem : 도로 찾다, 구해내다
178) out of captivity : 포로에서 석방되어
179) methinks : it seems to me(~라고 생각되다)
180) sojourn : stay(체류, 체재)
181) So ~ speak of : 당신이 말하는 것과 같이 그렇게 학식이 많은 사람
182) babe : baby

"The learned man," observed the stranger, with another smile, "should come himself to look into the mystery."

"It behoves[183] him well, if he be still in life," ponded the townsman. "Now, good sir, our Massachusetts magistracy, bethinking themselves that[184] this woman is youthful and fair, and doubtless was strongly tempted to her fall, and that, moreover, as is most likely, her husband may be at the bottom of the sea, they have not been bold to put in force the extremity of our righteous law against her. The penalty thereof[185] is death. But in their great mercy and tenderness of heart they have doomed Mistress Prynne to stand only a space of three hours on the platform of the pillory, and then and thereafter, for the remainder of her natural life, to wear a mark of shame upon her bosom."

"A wise sentence!" remarked the stranger, gravely bowing his head. "Thus she will be a living sermon against sin, until the ignominious[186] letter be engraved upon her tombstone. It irks[187] me, nevertheless, that the partner of her iniquity should not, at least, stand on the scaffold by her side. But he will be known! — he will be known! — he will be known!"

He bowed courteously to the communicative townsman, and, whispering a few words to his Indian attendant, they both made their way[188] through the crowd.

While this passed, Hester Prynne had been standing on her pedestal, still with a fixed gaze towards the stranger — so fixed a gaze that, at moments of intense absorption, all other objects in the visible world seemed to vanish, leaving only him and her. Such an interview, perhaps, would have been more terrible than even to meet him as she now did, with the hot midday sun burning down upon her face, and lighting up its shame; with the scarlet token of infamy[189] on her breast; with the sin-born infant in her arms; with a whole people, drawn forth as to a festival, staring at the features that should have been seen only in the quiet gleam of the fireside, in the happy shadow of a home, or beneath a matronly[190] veil at church. Dreadful as it was,[191] she was conscious of a shelter in the presence of these thousand witnesses. It was better to stand thus, with so many betwixt[192] him and her, than to greet him face to face — they two alone. She fled for refuge, as it were, to the public exposure, and dreaded the moment when its protection should be withdrawn from her. Involved in these thoughts[193], she scarcely heard a voice behind her until it had repeated her name more than once, in a loud and solemn tone, audible to[194] the whole multitude.

"Hearken[195] unto me, Hester Prynne!" said the voice.

---

183) behoove : be necessary or fitting for(~함이 온당하다)
184) bethink oneself that ~ : ~라는 생각이 나다
185) penalty thereof : 그것에 대한 처벌
186) ignominious : 불명예스러운
187) irk : 괴롭히다, 짜증나게 하다
188) make one's way : 나아가다
189) infamy : 불명예
190) matronly : dignified(품위 있는)
191) Dreadful ~ was : Though it was dreadful
192) betwixt : between
193) Involved ~ thoughts : as she was involved in these thoughts
194) audible to : ~에게 들리게
195) hearken : listen

It has already been noticed that directly over the platform on which Hester Prynne stood was a kind of balcony, or open gallery, appended[196] to the meeting-house. It was the place whence proclamations were wont to be made, amidst an assemblage[197] of the magistracy, with all the ceremonial that attended such public observances in those days. Here, to witness the scene which we are describing, sat Governor Bellingham himself, with four sergeants about his chair, bearing halberds[198], as a guard of honour. He wore a dark feather in his hat, a border of embroidery on his cloak, and a black velvet tunic beneath — a gentleman advanced in years, with a hard experience written in his wrinkles. He was not ill-fitted to be the head and representative of a community which owed its origin and progress, and its present state of development, not to the impulses of youth, but to the stern and tempered energies of manhood and the sombre sagacity[199] of age; accomplishing so much, precisely because it imagined and hoped so little. The other eminent characters by whom the chief ruler was surrounded were distinguished by a dignity of mien[200], belonging to a period when the forms of authority were felt to possess the sacredness[201] of Divine institutions. They were, doubtless, good men, just and sage. But, out of the whole human family, it would not have been easy to select the same number of wise and virtuous persons, who should be less capable of sitting in judgment on an erring woman's heart, and disentangling its mesh[202] of good and evil, than the sages of rigid aspect towards whom Hester Prynne now turned her face. She seemed conscious, indeed, that whatever sympathy she might expect lay in the larger and warmer heart of the multitude; for, as she lifted her eyes towards the balcony, the unhappy woman grew pale, and trembled.

The voice which had called her attention was that of the reverend and famous John Wilson, the eldest clergyman of Boston, a great scholar, like most of his contemporaries in the profession, and withal[203] a man of kind and genial spirit. This last attribute, however, had been less carefully developed than his intellectual gifts, and was, in truth,[204] rather a matter of shame than self-congratulation[205] with him. There he stood, with a border of grizzled locks[206] beneath his skull-cap[207], while his gray eyes, accustomed to[208] the shaded light of his study, were winking, like those of Hester's infant, in the unadulterated[209] sunshine. He looked like the darkly engraved portraits which we see prefixed to old volumes of sermons, and had no more right than one of those portraits would have to step forth, as

---

196) append : add(덧붙이다, 첨부하다)
197) assemblage : 사람들의 모임, 회합
198) halberd : 미늘창(15~16세기에 쓰이던 창과 도끼 겸용의 무기)
199) sagacity : 약삭빠름, 영리함
200) mien : 몸가짐, 태도
201) sacredness : 신성함
202) mesh : 그물, 망사
203) withal : with
204) in truth : truly(실은, 실제로)
205) self-congratulation : 마음속의 기쁨, 자축
206) grizzled locks : 회색빛 머리카락
207) skull-cap : 주로 실내에서 노인이 쓰는 벨벳 두건
208) accustomed to : ~에 익숙해 있는
209) unadulterated : 다른 것을 섞지 않은

he now did, and meddle with[210] a question of human guilt, passion, and anguish.

"Hester Prynne," said the clergyman, "I have striven with my young brother here, under whose preaching of the Word you have been privileged to sit" — here Mr. Wilson laid his hand on the shoulder of a pale young man beside him — "I have sought. I say, to persuade this godly youth, that he should deal with you, here in the face of Heaven and before these wise and upright rulers, and in hearing of all the people, as touching the vileness[211] and blackness of your sin. Knowing your natural temper better than I, he could the better judge what arguments to use, whether of tenderness or terror, such as might prevail over[212] your hardness and obstinacy[213], insomuch that[214] you should no longer hide the name of him who tempted you to this grievous fall. But he opposes to me — with a young man's over-softness, albeit[215] wise beyond his years — that it were wronging the very nature of woman to force her to lay open her heart's secrets in such broad daylight, and in presence of so great a multitude. Truly, as I sought to convince him, the shame lay in the commission of the sin[216], and not in the showing of it forth. What say you to it, once again, brother Dimmesdale? Must it be thou, or I, that shall deal with this poor sinner's soul?"

There was a murmur among the dignified and reverend occupants of the balcony; and Governor Bellingham gave expression to its purport[217], speaking in an authoritative voice, although tempered with respect towards the youthful clergyman whom he addressed.

"Good Master Dimmesdale," said he, "the responsibility of this woman's soul lies greatly with you. It behoves you, therefore, to exhort her to repentance and to confession, as a proof and consequence thereof."

The directness of this appeal drew the eyes of the whole crowd upon the Reverend Mr. Dimmesdale — a young clergyman who had come from one of the great English universities, bringing all the learning of the age into our wild forest-land. His eloquence and religious fervor[218] had already given the earnest of high eminence in his profession. He was a person of very striking aspect, with a white, lofty, and impending brow, large, brown, melancholy eyes, and a mouth which, unless when he forcibly compressed[219] it, was apt to be tremulous[220], expressing both nervous sensibility and a vast power of self-restraint[221]. Notwithstanding[222] his high native gifts and scholar — like attainments, there was an air about this young minister — an apprehensive, a startled, a

---

210) meddle with : 간섭하다, 참견하다
211) vileness : 타락, 비열
212) prevail over : 이기다, 극복하다
213) obstinacy : 고집
214) insomuch that : to such a degree that(~의 정도까지, ~만큼)
215) albeit : even though(~에도 불구하고)
216) commission of the sin : 죄를 저지름
217) purport : meaning(의미, 취지)
218) fervor : 열정
219) compress : 압축하다
220) tremulous : trembling(떠는, 전율하는)
221) self-restraint : 절제, 자제
222) notwithstanding : in spite of

half-frightened look — as of a being who felt himself quite astray, and at a loss in the pathway of human existence[223], and could only be at ease in some seclusion[224] of his own. Therefore, so far as his duties would permit, he trod in the shadowy by paths, and thus kept himself simple and childlike, coming forth, when occasion was, with a freshness, and fragrance, and dewy purity of thought, which, as many people said, affected them like the speech of an angel.

Such was the young man whom the Reverend Mr. Wilson and the Governor had introduced so openly to the public notice, bidding him speak. in the hearing of all men, to that mystery of a woman's soul, so sacred even in its pollution. The trying nature of his position drove the blood from his cheek, and made his lips tremulous.

"Speak to the woman, my brother," said Mr. Wilson. "It is of moment to her soul, and, therefore, as the worshipful Governor says, momentous[225] to thine own, in whose charge hers is. Exhort[226] her to confess the truth!"

The Reverend Mr. Dimmesdale bent his head, in silent prayer, as it seemed, and then came forward.

"Hester Prynne," said he, leaning over the balcony, and looking down steadfastly into her eyes, "thou hearest what this good man says, and seest the accountability[227] under which I labour. If thou feel est it to be for thy soul's peace, and that thy earthly punishment will thereby be made more effectual to salvation[228], I charge[229] thee to speak out the name of thy fellow-sinner and fellow-sufferer! Be not silent from any mistaken pity and tenderness for him; for, believe me, Hester, though he were to step down from a high place, and stand there beside thee, on thy pedestal[230] of shame, yet better were it so than to hide a guilty heart through life. What can thy silence do for him, except it tempt him — yea, compel him, as it were — to add hypocrisy[231] to sin? Heaven hath granted thee an open ignominy, that thereby thou mayst work out an open triumph over the evil within thee and the sorrow without. Take heed how thou deniest to him — who, perchance, hath not the courage to grasp it for himself — the bitter, but wholesome cup that is now presented to thy lips!"

The young pastor's voice was tremulously sweet, rich, deep, and broken. The feeling that it so evidently manifested, rather than the direct purport of the words, caused it to vibrate within all hearts, and brought the listeners into one accord[232] of sympathy. Even the poor baby at Hester's bosom was affected by the same influence, for it directed its hitherto vacant gaze towards Mr. Dimmesdale, and held up its little arms with a half-pleased, half-plaintive[233] murmur. So powerful

---

223) pathway of human existence : 인생이라는 좁은 길
224) seclusion : secluded place(세상과 동떨어진 곳, 외딴 곳)
225) momentous : 중대한
226) exhort : 열심히 당부하다, 권하다
227) accountability : 책임
228) salvation : 구원, 구제
229) charge : command(명령하다)
230) pedestal : 흉상 따위를 올려놓는 대좌
231) hypocrisy : 위선
232) one accord : 일치, 한결같음
233) plaintive : 애처로운, 가련한

seemed the minister's appeal, that the people could not believe but that Hester Prynne would speak out the guilty name, or else that the guilty one himself, in whatever high or lowly place he stood, would be drawn forth by an inward and inevitable necessity[234], and compelled to ascend the scaffold.

Hester shook her head.

"Woman, transgress[235] not beyond the limits of Heaven's mercy!" cried the Reverend Mr. Wilson, more harshly than before. "That little babe hath been gifted with a voice, to second and confirm the counsel which thou hast heard. Speak out the name! That, and thy repentance, may avail[236] to take the scarlet letter off thy breast."

"Never!" replied Hester Prynne, looking, not at Mr. Wilson, but into the deep and troubled eyes of the younger clergyman. "It is too deeply branded. Ye cannot take it off. And would that I might endure his agony as well as mine[237]!"

"Speak, woman!" said another voice, coldly and sternly, proceeding from the crowd about the scaffold. "Speak; and give your child a father!"

"I will not speak!" answered Hester, turning pale as death, but responding to this voice, which she too surely recognised. "And my child must seek a heavenly Father; she shall never know an earthly one[238]!"

"She will not speak!" murmured Mr. Dimmesdale, who, leaning over the balcony, with his hand upon his heart, had awaited the result of his appeal. He now drew back, with a long respiration[239]. "Wondrous strength and generosity of a woman's heart! She will not speak!"

Discerning the impracticable[240] state of the poor culprit's[241] mind, the elder clergyman, who had carefully prepared himself for the occasion, addressed to the multitude a discourse on sin[242], in all its branches, but with continual reference to[243] the ignominious letter. So forcibly did he dwell upon this symbol, for the hour or more during which his periods were rolling over the people's heads, that it assumed new terrors in their imagination, and seemed to derive its scarlet hue from the flames of the infernal[244] pit[245]. Hester Prynne, meanwhile, kept her place upon the pedestal of shame[246], with glazed eyes, and an air of weary indifference. She had borne that morning all that nature could endure; and as her temperament was not of the order that escapes from too intense suffering by a

---

234) necessity : 필연적인 필요성
235) transgress : 한도를 넘다, 지나치다, 죄를 짓다
236) avail : ~에 도움이 되다, 효력이 있다
237) mine : my agony
238) one : father를 받는 대명사
239) with a long respiration : 길게 숨을 쉬면서
240) impracticable : 다루기 어려운, 고집 센
241) culprit : offender(죄인)
242) discourse on sin : 죄에 관한 이야기
243) with continual reference to ~ : ~에 대해 계속 언급하면서
244) infernal : 지옥의
245) pit : 지옥, 움푹한 곳
246) shame : 수치, 치욕

swoon[247]), her spirit could only shelter itself beneath a stony crust of insensibility[248]), while the faculties of animal life remained entire. In this state, the voice of the preacher thundered remorselessly[249]), but unavailingly[250]), upon her ears. The infant, during the latter portion of her ordeal, pierced the air with its wailings and screams; she strove to hush[251]) it mechanically, but seemed scarcely to sympathise with its trouble. With the same hard demeanour[252]), she was led back to prison, and vanished from the public gaze within its iron-clamped[253]) portal. It was whispered by those who peered after her that the scarlet letter threw a lurid[254]) gleam along the dark passage-way of the interior.

---

247) swoon : 기절, 졸도
248) a stony crust of insensibility : 무감각이라는 돌처럼 단단한 껍질
249) remorselessly : 무자비하게, 무정하게
250) unavailingly : 효과 없이, 무익하게
251) hush : 조용하게 하다, 입 다물게 하다
252) demeanour : 행실, 품행, 태도
253) iron-clamped : 쇠못 따위로 조인
254) lurid : 이글이글 타는, 타는 듯이 붉은

제 **4** 장 Herman Melville
– 「*Billy Budd, Sailor*」

순진무구함과 사악함이 벌이는 한편의 드라마와도 같다. 사회에 의하여 순수함이 망가지고 사회가 유지되기 위하여 이루어지는 거짓을 여실히 보여주는 소설이다.

출제 경향 및 수험 대책

Billy Budd가 순수함을 상징하는 반면 Edward Fairfax Vere(Captain Vere)는 질서 있는 현실을 유지하기 위하여 절대적인 진실과 가치보다는 차선을 선택할 수밖에 없는 인간상을 나타낸다. 각 등장인물들이 지닌 특성을 알 필요가 있다.

제 1 절 작가의 생애

1 개관

호손과 더불어 '미국 르네상스'(American Renaissance)라 불리는 시기의 대표적 작가로 꼽히는 허먼 멜빌 (Herman Melville, 1819~1891)은 미국문학사에서 깊고 굵은 족적을 남긴 위대한 소설가이다. 오늘날 Nathaniel Hawthorne과 더불어 19세기 American Renaissance의 위대한 작가로 평가받는 Herman Melville(1819~1891)은 그의 동시대 독자들에게는 그의 이색적인 체험을 박진감 있게 형상화시킬 수 있는 뛰어난 상상력의 소유자였음에도 불구하고, 괴팍스러운 자신만의 세계를 고집하여 독자들의 외면을 자초한 작가로 기억되었다. 10여 년 간의 짧은 작가생활 중에 그는 아홉 권의 장편소설과 한 권의 단편집을 발표하는 창작열을 보였다. 그의 작가로서의 삶은 내면적으로는 자신의 독특한 세계를 일구어나간 뜨거운 열정의 표현이었지만, 외면적으로는 독자들로부터 점점 고립되었다. 당시에 가장 많은 독자층을 가졌던 여행기 장르의 초기 작품들로 얻은 명성을 그는 작품이 출간될 때마다 조금씩 잃었다. 그러다 급기야 생전의 마지막 산문 작품이 된 「*The Confidence-Man : His Masquerade*」(1857)에 이르렀을 때는 책을 출판해 줄 출판사도 찾기 어려울 정도였다. 이러한 절망적인 상황은 그로 하여금 38세라는 젊은 나이에 소설 집필을 단념하게 만들었고, 그가 죽은 지 30년이 지난 후 그의 대작 「*Moby-Dick : or, The Whale*」(1851)의 재발견으로 그 명성이 기적적으로 부활될 때까지 그는 세상에서 잊혀졌다.

2 생애

Melville은 1819년 뉴욕(New York City)에서 태어났으며, 친가와 외가 쪽 선조들이 모두 미국 독립전쟁에서 큰 활약을 했던 Melville가(家)와 Gransevoort가(家)이다. 이러한 유서 깊은 가문의 후손으로서 그의 유년시절은 유복한 편이었다. 그러나 1832년 직물 수입상이던 아버지 Allan Melville이 사업실패 끝에 갑자스럽게 사망하고 큰 빚을 남기면서 그의 삶은 시련의 연속이었다. 그는 다니던 학교도 중퇴하고 은행의 서기, 농장 일꾼, 측량 기술자로 전전하며 집안을 도왔으나, 어려운 생활고로 스무 살이 되던 해에 뉴욕과 영국의 리버풀(Liverpool)을 왕래하는 상선 St. Lawrence의 선원으로 취직하였고, 그의 소설의 무대가 될 바다로 첫 발을 내딛었다.

Melville은 리버풀에서 돌아온 후에도 여러 직업을 전전하였으나 집안 형편이 나아지지 않자, 1840년에 태평양으로 출어하는 고래잡이 배 Acushnet에 승선하여 3년 10개월의 여정을 떠난다. 고래잡이배의 선상 생활이 너무 힘들어 배가 남태평양의 마르키즈 섬(Marquesas Islands)에 도착하였을 때 Melville은 동료 선원과 함께 배를 버리고 탈주한다. Melville은 식인종으로 알려진 타이피족(Tai Pi)과 함께 1개월 정도 지낸 뒤, 인근에 있는 타히티섬(Tahiti)으로 가서 잠시 자유로운 삶을 가졌다. 1842년 겨울 다시 고래잡이 배 Charles & Henry에 승선하여 이듬해 5월 하와이(Hawaii)에 도착한다. 호놀룰루(Honolulu)에서 상점 점원 일을 하며 잠시 머물던 Melville은 본국으로 귀환하는 미국 해군 전함인 미 합중국호에 자원입대하여 1844년 10월 오랜 방랑생활을 마감하고 마침내 집으로 돌아간다. Melville의 남태평양에서의 여정은 언어와 관습, 제도와 사고방식이 다른 낯선 문화를 접하여 지식을 넓히고 세계를 보는 눈을 기른 작가 수업의 길이라고 할 수 있다. 그는 낯선 이방의 문화를 경험하며 자신의 감수성을 한층 예리하게 갈고 닦는 동시에 낯선 세계와의 대비를 통하여 자신이 떠나온 사회를 보다 냉철한 시선으로 이해할 수 있는 비판적 안목을 길렀다.

Melville이 고향을 떠나 있는 동안 그의 집안은 많이 안정되고 경제적 형편도 나아졌다. 특히 바로 위의 형 Gansevoort가 정계에 입문하여 민주당의 James K. Polk 대통령 당선에 큰 역할을 하고 있었는데, 그를 통해 Melville은 당시의 정치적 현실을 가까이서 관찰할 기회를 갖게 된다. 그의 작품이 당대의 중요한 정치적 이슈에 대한 깊은 관심과 비판적 성찰을 담고 있는 것은 바로 이와 같은 가족적 배경과도 관련이 있다.

3 작품 활동

Melville은 그의 체험담을 재미있어 하는 친지들의 권유로 글을 쓰기 시작하여 1846년 첫 작품인 「*Typee : A Peep at Polynesian Life*」(1846)를 발표하고, 이에 대한 호평에 힘입어 다음 해에는 「*Omoo : A Narrative of Adventures in the South Seas*」(1847)를 발표한다. 여행기로 출판된 두 작품의 대중적인 성공에도 불구하고 Melville은 복음주의 선교 활동에 대한 과격한 비판을 삭제하라는 보수적인 기독교 단체의 압력으로 수정판을 내야 했다. 자신이 집필의 목표로 삼았던 '탈색된 진실'의 추구가 사회적인 압력으로 훼손되는 것을 지켜본 Melville은 세 번째 작품을 쓰면서 변신을 꾀하여 '사실의 이야기'(narrative of facts)가 아니라 모험담과 철학적·종교적·문학적 한담, 알레고리와 풍자가 교차하는 독특한 양식을 지닌 「*Mardi : and a Voyage Thither*」(1849)를 발표한다. 여러모로 원숙기를 특징짓는 주제와 기법을 선보이는 작품이지만 Mardi에 대한 독자들의 반응은 기대와는 달리 냉담하였다. 인세 수입에 의존하고 있던 Melville은 다시 대중적 취향에 맞는 이야기를 쓰기로 작정하고 약 10주 만에 「*Redburn : His First Voyage*」(1849)를, 이어서 미국 해군(US Navy)에 입대하여 하와이에서 보스턴까지의 선상 체험을 다룬

「*White-Jacket : or, The World in a Man-of-War*」(1850)를 완성한다. 급하게 쓰였음에도 불구하고 두 작품은 다면적이고 생동하는 인물의 창조, 또한 일상적인 사물과 사건을 암시적으로 묘사하는 작가의 한층 원숙해진 기량이 드러나 있어 훗날의 「*Moby-Dick*」을 예감하게 한다. 1849년 잠시 영국을 방문하고 돌아온 Melville은 그 다음 해에 대작 「*Moby-Dick*」의 집필을 시작한다. 집필 도중 알게 된 Hawthorne의 영향 속에서 여러 차례의 개작을 거쳐 1851년 발간된 「Moby−Dick」은 고래와 고래잡이에 대한 많은 사실적 정보를 제공하는 동시에 삶의 총체적 진실을 현시하는 Melville 특유의 소설 세계를 보여준다. 「*Moby-Dick*」은 출간 초기에는 꽤 호의적인 반응을 얻었으나 시간이 흐를수록 부정적인 평이 늘어나고 판매 실적도 급감하였다. 이를 만회하기 위하여 중산층 여성 독자를 겨냥해서 쓴 「*Pierre : or The Ambiguities*」(1852)는 근친상간과 같은 금기적인 주제를 담고 있고, 당대 독서대중의 취향을 야유하는 체제 전복적인 소설이다. 「*Pierre*」의 출판 이후 이어진 Melville의 삶은 소설 속의 작가 Pierre의 경우처럼 독자의 상실, 그로 인한 좌절감, 소외감, 작가적 신념의 상실이 특징이다. 그 후 몇 년 동안 Melville은 여러 잡지에 「*Bartleby, the Scrivener*」(1853), 「*Benito Cereno*」(1855)를 포함한 중단편소설을 연재하며 지냈다. 1857년 Melville은 남북전쟁 전의 미국의 세태를 신랄하게 풍자한 「*The Confidence-Man*」을 발표하였으나 출판사의 파산과 함께 작품은 잊힌다. 더 이상 그의 책을 출판해 줄 출판사도, 그를 반가워하는 독자도 발견할 수 없음을 알게 된 Melville은 글쓰기를 그만두고 순회강연을 다니다가 1866년부터 뉴욕의 세관에 취직하여 1885년 퇴임할 때까지 다녔다. 소설 집필을 그만둔 Melville은 시를 쓰기 시작하였다. 그의 시는 남북전쟁을 소재로 한 시집 『*Battle-Pieces and Aspects of the War*』(1866), 유럽 문명의 세속화를 다룬 장시 「*Clarel : A Poem and Pilgrimage in the Holy Land*」(1876), 「*John Marr and Other Sailors*」(1888)와 「*Timoleon*」(1891)이 있다. 이후 1891년 Melville은 1886년부터 집필을 시작한 「*Billy Budd, Sailor*」 (1924)를 유작으로 남기고 세상을 떠났다.

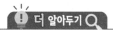

Herman Melville의 주요작품
- 「*Typee : A Peep at Polynesian Life*」(1846)
- 「*Moby-Dick or, The Whale*」(1851)
- 「*Batleby, the Scrivener*」(1853)
- 「*Benito Cereno*」(1855)
- 「*The Confidence-Man : His Masquerade*」(1857)
- 「*Billy Budd, Sailor (An Inside Narrative)*」(1924) [사후 출판]

제 2 절   작품 세계

1 Melville의 소설

(1) Melville에게 있어서 소설은 무엇보다 진실을 발견하고 그것을 사람들에게 전달하는 도구이다.

(2) 그는 소설의 집필이 '진실을 말하는 위대한 기예'라고 정의한다.

2 있는 그대로의 진실 [중요] ★★

Melville에게 진실이란 많은 사람들이 생각하는 것처럼 현상을 초월하는 어떤 보편적이고 절대적인 이념을 의미하는 것은 아니었다. 그는 사람들이 보편적이고 영원하다고 말하는 진실이 사실은 역사적이고 문화적인 조건에 매여 있는 도구적인 이데올로기(Ideologie)일 수 있음을 인식한 몇 안 되는 사람 중의 하나였다. Melville은 사람들이 말하는 진실이 위장된 이데올로기인 것을 폭로하는 것에서 자신의 진실을 발견하고는 자신이 찾고자 하는 진실을 '탈색된 진실'(unvarnished truth)이라고 불렀다.

제 3 절   줄거리

William(Billy) Budd는 Rights-of Man이라는 상선의 선원이었지만, 영국 해군에 강제로 징집되어 H. M. S. Bellipotent 전함에 배치된 순진한 해병이다. 그런데 선임 위병 하사관 Claggart가 자신과는 반대의 심성을 가진 Billy를 질투하여 그가 선상 반란(mutiny)의 음모를 꾸몄다고 누명을 씌워 Vere 함장에게 보고한다. 함장은 두 사람을 불러 대면시키고 사건을 해결하려고 하는데, Claggart의 거짓말에 당황한 Billy는 말을 더듬게 되고 분노와 답답함에 주먹으로 Claggart의 머리를 가격해 의도치 않게 죽게 만든다. Vere는 Billy의 무고함을 알고는 있으나 어쩔 수 없이 군대라는 집단의 안정을 유지하기 위하여 이 사건을 하극상으로 다루고 결국 Billy를 교수형에 처한다. Vere는 "하느님의 천사에게 맞아 죽은 거야! 그러나 그 천사는 목이 매달려야 해!"(Struck dead by an angel of God! Yet the angel must hang!)라는 논리에 따라 군법 회의를 소집하고 판결을 내린다. 다음 날 아침 Billy는 마지막으로 "Vere 함장님께 하느님의 가호가 있기를!"(Good bless Captain Vere!)이라는 말을 남기고 주변인들의 동정심과 연민을 받으며 처형당한다. Billy가 처형 직전 자신을 위한 기도가 아니라 Vere 함장을 연민의 시선으로 바라보며 기도하는 이 장면은 공정하지 못한 삶과 모순으로 뒤엉킨 사회와 선과 악이 대립하면서 양면적이고 부조리한 인간의 삶을 향한 연민의 표현이다.

제 4 절　작품의 주제 중요 ★★

- 순진무구함과 사악함이 벌이는 드라마

  타락하기 전의 아담(Adam) 또는 그리스도(Christ)의 속성과 연관된 Billy Budd와 마치 뱀과 같이 사악한 사탄(Satan)인 Claggart
- 아이러니적인 비극의 본성
- 법과 인간 품성의 관계(법은 가장 순진한 품성을 지닌 인간에게 교수형을 집행한다)
- 신(God)의 법과 인간의 법에 관한 문제
- 대립적인 가치관에 대한 문제
- 결정 및 결심의 어려움(재판관으로서의 인간적 고뇌)
- 자비(Mercy)와 정의(Justice)의 실현
- 개인의 사례와 공익(公益)[individual case and the larger social good]

제 5 절　등장인물

1 William(Billy) Budd(The Handsome Sailor)

the Rights-of-Man이라는 상선에서 대영 제국의 74포전함(seventy-four) H. M. S. Bellipotent의 앞돛대 망루병(foretopman)으로 강제 징집된 고아 출신의 21살 흑인 미남 해병이다. 그는 교육받지 못한 브리스톨(Bristol) 출신이지만 다른 선원들에게 항상 모범이 될 만큼 죄 없고 순진무구한 청년이다. 그러나 타고난 악인인 선임 위병 하사관 John Claggart로부터 반란을 일으키려 한다는 누명을 쓰고 이에 이성을 잃을 정도로 분노하여 일격에 그를 사망에 이르게 한다. Billy는 군법 회의에서 자신에게 자비심을 베푼 Vere 함장을 축복하며 교수형을 당한다. 선(善)한 본성을 타고난 인물이다.

2 Edward Fairfax Vere(Captain Vere)

H. M. S. Bellipotent의 함장이며 대령(captain)이다. '별' 같은 비어(Starry Vere)라는 칭호를 갖고 있는 그는 인간적인 정(情)과 지성(知性)을 겸비한 공정한 지휘관이다. 재판관들은 Billy가 은밀히 공모되고 있던 반란과는 전혀 관련이 없으며, Claggart를 살인하려는 의도는 없었다는 것을 인정한다. 그러나 세상사에 철저했던 Vere는 반란의 가능성을 잠재우기 위해 함장의 권한을 행사하여 군법 회의(drumhead court-martial)를 소집한 후, Billy의 살인 동기를 배제하고 결과로써만 살인 사건을 판단해야 한다는 치밀한 논리를 역설하며, 재판관들이 오로지 군법에 따라 공정한 판결을 내려야 한다고 주장한다.

3 John Claggart

H. M. S. Bellipotent에서 경찰서장과 같은 임무를 수행하는 선임 위병 하사관이다. 미남이지만 악마 (Satan)와 같은 인물로, Billy와는 달리 교활한 눈빛을 지니고 있으며 Vere와 같이 지성(知性)을 가지고 있다는 점에서 학문적으로는 거의 무지한 Billy와 뚜렷한 차이를 보인다. 그러나 악한 본성을 타고난 그는 자신과는 달리 악한 경험 없이 인생을 살아가는 Billy의 순수함, 인기 및 외모를 질투한다. 이러한 이유로 그는 Billy에게 반란을 일으키려 한다는 누명을 씌움으로써 그를 파멸시키려 하지만 오히려 Billy에게 일격을 당하고는 죽고 만다.

4 기타 인물들

(1) Captain Graveling

Rights-of-Man의 선장

(2) Lieutenant Radcliffe

Billy를 Bellipotent로 강제 징집하는 대위(중위)

(3) Narrator

50년 전 리버풀(Liverpool)에서 Billy를 목격한 이야기를 서술하는 화자

제 6 절 작품의 구조(Plot)와 시점 및 기법

(1) 시점

3인칭 화자의 시점. 그러나 때때로 등장인물의 마음속을 넘나들기도 한다.

(2) 구조

① 산만하고 균형을 잃은 구성으로 총 30장으로 구성되어 있으며, 각 장의 길이가 제멋대로이다. 어조도 강건체에서 만연체로 계속 바뀐다. 그러나 이러한 형식이 인생의 본질과 인생의 모순을 잘 표현한다고 볼 수 있다.

② 마지막 30장은 Billy에 대한 시 "BILLY IN THE DARBLES"(족쇄 찬 빌리)로 끝난다.

(3) 전개

① **모략 단계** : Billy에 대한 Claggart의 모략
② **살인 단계** : Billy Budd가 Claggart를 살해
③ **재판 과정 단계** : Billy가 교수형을 선고받음
④ **교수형 집행 단계** : Billy Budd의 운명

(4) 상징과 이미지 종요 ★★

종교적 상징과 알레고리가 가득한 비극적인 비전(vision)

① **William(Billy) Budd** : 타락하기 전의 아담(Adam)과 그리스도(Christ)의 속성을 지닌 인물로 순진성의 상징이다. 21살의 어린나이로 Baby Budd라는 별명도 가지고 있다.
② **Captain Vere** : 균형을 중시하는 인간형. 질서 있는 현실을 위하여 적대적인 진실과 가치보다는 차선책을 택하는 사려 깊고 고뇌할 줄 아는 인간상을 대변한다.
③ **Claggart** : 악마(Satan)의 속성을 지닌 인물로 악의 상징이다.

제 7 절 Text

Chapter 1

In the time before steamships[1], or then more frequently than now, a stroller along the docks of any considerable seaport would occasionally have his attention arrested by[2] a group of bronzed mariners, man-of-war's[3] men or merchant-sailors in holiday attire ashore on liberty. In certain instances they would flank, or, like a body-guard quite surround some superior figure of their own class, moving along with them like Aldebaran among the lesser lights of his constellation. That signal object was the "Handsome Sailor" of the less prosaic time alike of the military and merchant navies. With no perceptible trace of the vainglorious about him, rather with the off-hand unaffectedness of natural regality, he seemed to accept the spontaneous homage of his shipmates. A somewhat remarkable instance recurs to me. In Liverpool, now half a century ago, I saw under the shadow of the great dingy[4] street-wall of Prince's Dock (an obstruction long since removed) a common sailor, so intensely black that he must needs have been a native African of the unadulterate blood of Ham. A symmetric figure much above the average height. The two ends of

---

1) steamship : (대형) 기선
2) arrested by ∼ : ∼에 의해 잡히다
3) man-of-war : 군함(현재는 warship이 일반적임)
4) dingy : 거무죽죽한

a gay silk handkerchief thrown loose about the neck danced upon the displayed ebony of his chest; in his ears were big hoops of gold, and a Highland bonnet with a tartan band set off his shapely head.

It was a hot noon in July; and his face, lustrous with perspiration, beamed with barbaric good humor. In jovial sallies right and left, his white teeth flashing into view, he rollicked[5] along, the centre of a company of his shipmates. These were made up of such an assortment of tribes and complexions as would have well fitted them to be marched up by Anacharsis Cloots before the bar of the first French Assembly as Representatives of the Human Race. At each spontaneous tribute rendered by the wayfarers to this black pagod of a fellow — the tribute of a pause and stare, and less frequent an exclamation[6], — the motley retinue showed that they took that sort of pride in the evoker of it which the Assyrian priests doubtless showed for their grand sculptured Bull when the faithful prostrated themselves.

To return. If in some cases a bit of a nautical[7] Murat in setting forth his person ashore, the Handsome Sailor of the period in question evinced nothing of the dandified Billy-be-Damn, an amusing character all but extinct now, but occasionally to be encountered, and in a form yet more amusing than the original, at the tiller of the boats on the tempestuous Erie Canal[8] or, more likely, vaporing in the groggeries[9] along the towpath. Invariably a proficient in his perilous calling, he was also more or less of a mighty boxer or wrestler. It was strength and beauty. Tales of his prowess[10] were recited. Ashore he was the champion; afloat the spokesman; on every suitable occasion always foremost. Close-reefing top-sails in a gale, there he was, astride the weather yard-arm-end, foot in the Flemish horse as "stirrup," both hands tugging at the "earring" as at a bridle, in very much the attitude of young Alexander curbing the fiery Bucephalus. A superb figure, tossed up as by the horns of Taurus against the thunderous sky, cheerily hallooing to the strenuous file along the spar.

The moral nature was seldom[11] out of keeping with the physical make. Indeed, except as toned by the former, the comeliness and power, always attractive in masculine conjunction, hardly could have drawn the sort of honest homage the Handsome Sailor in some examples received from his less gifted associates.

Such a cynosure[12], at least in aspect, and something such too in nature, though with important variations made apparent as the story proceeds, was welkin-eyed[13] Billy Budd, or Baby Budd, as more familiarly under circumstances hereafter to be given he at last came to be called, aged twenty-one, a foretopman[14] of the British fleet toward the close of the last decade of the eighteenth

---

5) rollick : 흥겹게 뛰놀다, 야단치다
6) exclamation : 외침, 절규, 감탄
7) nautical : 항해상의
8) Erie Canal : 이리 운하(미국 뉴욕 주 버팔로와 올버니를 연결하는 운하)
9) groggery : 술집
10) prowess : 기량, (특히 전장에서의) 용기, 무용
11) seldom : 드물게, 좀처럼 ~ 않는
12) cynosure : 주목의 대상, 관심의 초점
13) welkin eyed : 하늘(welkin)의 눈을 가진
14) foretopman : 앞 돛대 망루 선원

century. It was not very long prior to the time of the narration that follows that he had entered the King's Service, having been impressed on the Narrow Seas from a homeward-bound English merchantman into a seventy-four outward-bound[15], H.M.S.[16] *Bellipotent;* which ship, as was not unusual in those hurried days, having been obliged to put to sea short of her proper complement of men. Plump upon Billy at first sight in the gangway[17] the boarding officer Lieutenant Ratcliffe pounced, even before the merchantman's crew was formally mustered on the quarter-deck for his deliberate inspection. And him only he elected. For whether it was because the other men when ranged before him showed to ill advantage after Billy, or whether he had some scruples in view of the merchantman being rather short-handed[18], however it might be, the officer contented himself with his first spontaneous choice. To the surprise of the ship's company, though much to the Lieutenant's satisfaction, Billy made no demur[19]. But, indeed, any demur would have been as idle as the protest of a goldfinch popped into a cage.

Noting this uncomplaining acquiescence[20], all but cheerful one might say, the shipmates turned a surprised glance of silent reproach at the sailor. The Shipmaster was one of those worthy mortals found in every vocation, even the humbler ones — the sort of person whom everybody agrees in calling "a respectable man." And nor so strange to report as it may appear to be — though a ploughman of the troubled waters, lifelong contending with the intractable elements, there was nothing this honest soul at heart loved better than simple peace and quiet. For the rest, he was fifty or thereabouts[21], a little inclined to corpulence, a prepossessing face, unwhiskered, and of an agreeable color — a rather full face, humanely intelligent in expression. On a fair day with a fair wind and all going well, a certain musical chime in his voice seemed to be the veritable unobstructed outcome of the innermost man. He had much prudence, much conscientiousness[22], and there were occasions when these virtues were the cause of overmuch disquietude in him. On a passage, so long as his craft was in any proximity to land, no sleep for Captain Graveling. He took to heart those serious responsibilities not so heavily borne by some shipmasters.

Now while Billy Budd was down in the forecastle getting his kit together, the *Bellipotent*'s lieutenant, burly[23] and bluff, nowise disconcerted by Captain Graveling's omitting to proffer the customary hospitalities on an occasion so unwelcome to him, an omission simply caused by preoccupation of thought, unceremoniously invited himself into the cabin, and also to a flask from the spirit-locker, a receptacle which his experienced eye instantly discovered. In fact he was one of those sea-dogs in whom all the hardship and peril[24] of naval life in the great prolonged wars of

---

15) outward-bound : 외국행의, 외항의
16) H. M. S. : 영국군함. His(Her) Majesty's Service(Ship)
17) gangway : 현문(배의 현측에 있는 출입구)
18) short-handed : 일손이 모자라다
19) demur : 이의, 반대
20) acquiescence : 묵종, 본의 아닌 동의
21) thereabouts : 그 부근에, 그 무렵에, 대략
22) conscientiousness : 양심
23) burly : (몸이) 억센, 건장한
24) peril : 위험, 위태

his time never impaired the natural instinct for sensuous enjoyment. His duty he always faithfully did; but duty is sometimes a dry obligation, arid he was for irrigating its aridity, whensoever possible, with a fertilizing decoction of strong waters. For the cabin's proprietor there was nothing left but to play the part of the enforced host with whatever grace and alacrity were practicable. As necessary adjuncts25) to the flask, he silently placed tumbler and water-jug26) before the irrepressible guest. But excusing himself from partaking just then, he dismally watched the unembarrassed officer deliberately diluting his grog a little, then tossing it off in three swallows, pushing the empty tumbler away, yet not so far as to be beyond easy reach, at the same time settling himself in his seat and smacking his lips with high satisfaction, looking straight at the host.

These proceedings27) over, the master broke the silence; and there lurked a rueful reproach in the tone of his voice: "Lieutenant, you are going to take my best man from me, the jewel of 'em."

"Yes, I know," rejoined the other, immediately drawing back the tumbler preliminary to a replenishing; "Yes, I know. Sorry."

"Beg pardon28), but you don't understand, Lieutenant. See here now. Before I shipped that young fellow, my forecastle was a rat-pit of quarrels. It was black times, I tell you, aboard the Rights here. I was worried to that degree my pipe had no comfort for me. But Billy came; and it was like a Catholic priest striking peace in an Irish shindy. Not that he preached to them or said or did anything in particular; but a virtue went out of him, sugaring the sour ones. They took to him like hornets to treacle; all but the buffer of the gang, the big shaggy chap with the fire-red whiskers. He indeed out of envy, perhaps, of the newcomer, and thinking such a 'sweet and pleasant fellow,' as he mockingly designated him to the others, could hardly have the spirit of a gamecock, must needs bestir himself in trying to get up an ugly row with him. Billy forebore with him and reasoned with him in a pleasant way — he is something like myself, Lieutenant, to whom aught like a quarrel is hateful — but nothing served. So, in the second dogwatch one day the Red Whiskers in presence of the others, under pretence of showing Billy just whence a sirloin steak was cut — for the fellow had once been a butcher29) — insultingly gave him a dig under the ribs. Quick as lightning Billy let fly his arm. I dare say he never meant to do quite as much as he did, but anyhow he gave the burly fool a terrible drubbing. It took about half a minute, I should think. And, lord bless you, the lubber was astonished at the celerity. And will you believe it, Lieutenant, the Red Whiskers now really loves Billy — loves him, or is the biggest hypocrite30) that ever I heard of. But they all love him. Some of 'em do his washing, darn his old trousers for him; the carpenter is at odd times making a pretty little chest of drawers for him. Anybody will do anything for Billy Budd; and it's the happy family here. But now, Lieutenant, if that young fellow goes — I know how it will be

---

25) adjunct : 부가물, 부속물
26) water-jug : 주전자, 항아리(주로 물을 긷거나 술을 담는 데 쓰는 그릇)
27) proceeding : 행위, 행동
28) Beg pardon : I beg your pardon(죄송합니다, 실례지만).
29) butcher : 도살자, 잔인한 살인자
30) hypocrite : 위선자, 겉으로 착한 체하는 사람

aboard the Rights. Not again very soon shall I, coming up[31] from dinner, lean over the capstan smoking a quiet pipe — no, not very soon again, I think. Ay, Lieutenant, you are going to take away the jewel of 'em; you are going to take away my peacemaker!" And with that the good soul had really some ado[32] in checking a rising sob.

"Well," said the lieutenant who had listened with amused interest to all this, and now was waxing merry with his tipple; "Well, blessed are the peacemakers, especially the fighting peacemakers! And such are the seventy-four beauties some of which you see poking their noses out of the port-holes of yonder war-ship lying-to for me," pointing through the cabin window at the *Bellipotent*. "But courage! Don't look so downhearted[33], man. Why, I pledge you in advance the royal approbation. Rest assured that His Majesty will be delighted to know that in a time when his hard tack is not sought for by sailors with such avidity as should be; a time also when some shipmasters privily resent the borrowing from them a tar or two for the service; His Majesty, I say, will be delighted to learn that one shipmaster at least cheerfully surrenders to the King, the flower of his flock, a sailor who with equal loyalty makes no dissent. — But where's my beauty? Ah," looking through the cabin's open door, "here he comes; and, by Jove — lugging along his chest-Apollo with his portmanteau! — My man," stepping out[34] to him, "you can't take that big box aboard a war-ship. The boxes there are mostly shot-boxes. Put your duds in a bag, lad. Boot and saddle for the cavalryman, bag and hammock for the man-of-war's man."

The transfer from chest to bag was made. And, after seeing his man into the cutter[35] and then following him down, the lieutenant pushed off from the Rights-of-Man[36]. That was the merchant-ship's name; though by her master and crew abbreviated in sailor fashion into the Rights. The hard-headed[37] Dundee owner was a staunch admirer of Thomas Paine whose book in rejoinder to Burke's arraignment of the French Revolution had then been published for some time and had gone everywhere. In christening his vessel after the title of Paine's volume, the man of Dundee was something like his contemporary shipowner, Stephen Girard of Philadelphia, whose sympathies, alike with his native land and its liberal philosophers, he evinced by naming his ships after Voltaire, Diderot, and so forth.

But now, when the boat swept under the merchantman's stern, and officer and oarsmen were noting — some bitterly and others with a grin, — the name emblazoned there; just then it was that the new recruit jumped up from the bow where the coxswain had directed him to sit, and waving his hat to his silent shipmates sorrowfully looking over at him from the taffrail, bade the lads a genial good-bye. Then, making a salutation[38] as to the ship herself, "And good-bye to you too, old

---

31) coming up : 오르다, 떠오르다, 도착하다
32) ado : 야단법석, 소동, 고생
33) downhearted : 낙담한
34) step out : 나가다, 걸음을 빨리하다, 서두르다
35) cutter : 커터형 범선(군함에 딸린 소형 배)
36) Rights-of-Man : Rights-of-Man이라는 배 이름은 Thomas Paine의 저서 『Rights of Man』(1791)에서 따온 이름이다.
37) hard-headed : cool-headed(냉철한)
38) make a salutation : 경례를 하다

Rights-of-Man." "Down, Sir!" roared the Lieutenant, instantly assuming all the rigour[39] of his rank[40], though with difficulty repressing a smile.

To be sure, Billy's action was a terrible breach of naval decorum. But in that decorum he had never been instructed; in consideration of which the Lieutenant would hardly have been so energetic in reproof but for the concluding farewell to the ship. This he rather took as meant to convey a covert sally on the new recruit's part, a sly slur at impressment in general, and that of himself in especial. And yet, more likely, if satire it was in effect, it was hardly so by intention, for Billy, tho' happily endowed with the gayety of high health, youth, and a free heart, was yet by no means of a satirical turn. The will to it and the sinister dexterity were alike wanting. To deal in double meanings and insinuations of any sort was quite foreign to his nature.

As to his enforced enlistment, that he seemed to take pretty much as he was wont to take any vicissitude of weather. Like the animals, though no philosopher, he was, without knowing it, practically a fatalist[41]. And, it may be, that he rather liked this adventurous turn in his affairs, which promised an opening into novel scenes and martial excitements.

Aboard the *Bellipotent* our merchant-sailor was forthwith rated as an able-seaman and assigned to the starboard watch of the fore-top. He was soon at home in the service, not at all disliked for his unpretentious good looks and a sort of genial happy-go-lucky air. No merrier man in his mess: in marked contrast to certain other individuals included like himself among the impressed[42] portion of the ship's company; for these when not actively employed were sometimes, and more particularly in the last dogwatch when the drawing near of twilight induced revery[43], apt to fall into a saddish mood which in some partook of sullenness. But they were not so young as our foretopman, and no few of them must have known a hearth[44] of some sort; others may have had wives and children left, too probably, in uncertain circumstances, and hardly any but must have had acknowledged kith and kin, while for Billy, as will shortly be seen, his entire family was practically invested in himself.

Chapter 2

Though our new-made foretopman was well received in the top and on the gun decks[45], hardly here was he that cynosure he had previously been among those minor ship's companies of the merchant marine, with which companies only had he hitherto consorted.

He was young; and despite his all but fully developed frame, in aspect looked even younger than he really was, owing to a lingering adolescent expression in the as yet smooth face, all but feminine

---

39) rigour : rigor(엄함, 엄격)
40) rank : 군대의 계급
41) fatalist : 운명론자
42) impress : 징병하다
43) revery : reverie(백일몽, 공상, 환상)
44) hearth : (단란한) 가정
45) gun deck : (해군) 포열갑판

in purity of natural complexion, but where, thanks to his seagoing, the lily was quite suppressed and the rose had some ado visibly to flush through the tan.

To one essentially such a novice in the complexities of factitious life, the abrupt transition from his former and simpler sphere to the ampler and more knowing world of a great war-ship; this might well have abashed him had there been any conceit or vanity in his composition. Among her miscellaneous multitude, the *Bellipotent* mustered[46] several individuals who, however inferior in grade, were of no common natural stamp, sailors more signally susceptive of that air which continuous martial discipline and repeated presence in battle can in some degree impart even to the average man. As the Handsome Sailor, Billy Budd's position aboard the seventy-four was something analogous to that of a rustic beauty transplanted from the provinces and brought into competition with the highborn dames of the court. But this change of circumstances he scarce noted. As little did he observe that something about him provoked[47] an ambiguous smile in one or two harder faces among the blue-jackets. Nor less unaware was he of the peculiar favorable effect his person and demeanor had upon the more intelligent gentlemen of the quarter-deck. Nor could this well have been otherwise. Cast in a mold peculiar to the finest physical examples of those Englishmen in whom the Saxon strain would seem not at all to partake of any Norman or other admixture, he showed in face that humane look of reposeful good nature which the Greek sculptor in some instances gave to his heroic strong man, Hercules[48]. But this again was subtly modified by another and pervasive quality. The ear, small and shapely, the arch of the foot, the curve in mouth and nostril, even the indurated hand dyed to the orange-tawny of the toucan's bill, a hand telling alike of the halyards and tar-bucket; but, above all, something in the mobile expression, and every chance attitude and movement, something suggestive of a mother eminently favored by Love and the Graces; all this strangely indicated a lineage in direct contradiction to his lot. The mysteriousness here became less mysterious through a matter-of-fact[49] elicited[50] when Billy, at the capstan, was being formally mustered into the service. Asked by the officer, a small brisk little gentleman, as it chanced among other questions, his place of birth, he replied, "Please, Sir, I don't know."

"Don't know where you were born? — Who was your father?"

"God knows, Sir."

Struck by the straightforward simplicity of these replies, the officer next asked, "Do you know anything about your beginning?"

"No, Sir. But I have heard that I was found in a pretty silk-lined basket hanging one morning from the knockers[51] of a good man's door in Bristol."

"Found say you? Well," throwing back his head and looking up and down the new recruit; "Well, it turns out to have been a pretty good find. Hope they'll find some more like you, my man; the

---

46) muster : 소집하다, (용기 등을) 분발시키다
47) provoke : 화나게 하다, (감정, 욕망 등을) 불러일으키다
48) Hercules : 헤라클레스(그리스 신화에 나오는 Zeus의 아들로 힘센 영웅)
49) matter-of-fact : 사실의, 평범한
50) elicited : (진리 등을) 도출하다, 이끌어내다
51) knocker : 문 두드리는 사람

fleet sadly needs them."

Yes, Billy Budd was a foundling[52], a presumable by-blow, and, evidently, no ignoble one. Noble descent was as evident in him as in a blood horse.

For the rest, with little or no sharpness of faculty or any trace of the wisdom of the serpent, nor yet quite a dove, he possessed that kind and degree of intelligence going along with the unconventional rectitude of a sound human creature, one to whom not yet has been proffered[53] the questionable apple of knowledge[54]. He was illiterate; he could not read, but he could sing, and like the illiterate nightingale was sometimes the composer of his own song.

Of self-consciousness[55] he seemed to have little or none, or about as much as we may reasonably impute to a dog of Saint Bernard's breed.

Habitually living with the elements and knowing little more of the land than as a beach, or, rather, that portion of the terraqueous globe providentially set apart for dance-houses, doxies and tapsters, in short what sailors call a "fiddlers'-green," his simple nature remained unsophisticated[56] by those moral obliquities which are not in every case incompatible with that manufacturable thing known as respectability. But are sailors, frequenters of "fiddlers'-greens," without vices? No; but less often than with landsmen do their vices, so called, partake of crookedness of heart, seeming less to proceed from viciousness than exuberance of vitality after long constraint; frank manifestations in accordance with natural law. By his original constitution aided by the cooperating influences of his lot, Billy in many respects was little more than a sort of upright barbarian, much such perhaps as Adam presumably might have been ere the urbane Serpent wriggled himself into his company.

And here be it submitted that apparently going to corroborate the doctrine of man's Fall, a doctrine now popularly ignored, it is observable that where certain virtues pristine[57] and unadulterate peculiarly characterize anybody in the external uniform of civilization, they will upon scrutiny seem not to be derived from custom or convention, but rather to be out of keeping with these, as if indeed exceptionally transmitted from a period prior to Cain's city and citified man. The character marked by such qualities has to an unvitiated taste an untampered — with flavor like that of berries, while the man thoroughly civilized, even in a fair specimen of the breed, has to the same moral palate a questionable smack[58] as of a compounded wine. To any stray inheritor of these primitive qualities found, like Caspar Hauser, wandering dazed in any Christian capital of our time, the good-natured poet's famous invocation, near two thousand years ago, of the good rustic out of his latitude in the Rome of the Cesars, still appropriately holds:

"Honest and poor, faithful in word and thought, What has thee[59], Fabian, to the city brought?"

---

52) foundling : 업둥이
53) proffer : 권하다, 내밀다
54) apple of knowledge : 선악과(fruit of the tree of knowledge of good and evil)
55) self-consciousness : 자각
56) unsophisticated : 순박한, 순진한
57) pristine : 본래의, 소박한, 청순한, 자연 그대로의
58) smack : 입맛을 다시다
59) thee : thou의 목적격 [고어] 너(를)에게

Though our Handsome Sailor had as much of masculine beauty[60] as one can expect anywhere to see; nevertheless, like the beautiful woman in one of Hawthorne's minor tales, there was just one thing amiss in him. No visible blemish, indeed, as with the lady; no, but an occasional liability to a vocal defect. Though in the hour of elemental uproar[61] or peril he was everything that a sailor should be, yet under sudden provocation of strong heart-feeling, his voice otherwise singularly musical, as if expressive of the harmony within, was apt to develop an organic hesitancy, in fact, more or less of a stutter[62] or even worse. In this particular Billy was a striking instance that the arch interferer, the envious marplot[63] of Eden, still has more or less[64] to do with every human consignment to this planet of Earth. In every case, one way or another he is sure to slip in his little card, as much as to remind us — I too have a hand here.

The avowal of such an imperfection[65] in the Handsome Sailor should be evidence not alone that he is not presented as a conventional hero, but also that the story in which he is the main figure is no romance.

Chapter 3

At the time of Billy Budd's arbitrary[66] enlistment[67] into the *Bellipotent* that ship was on her way to join the Mediterranean fleet. No long time clapsed[68] before the junction was effected. As one of that fleet the seventy-four participated in its movements, though at times, on account of her superior sailing qualities, in the absence of frigates[69], despatched on separate duty as a scout and at times on less temporary service. But with all this the story has little concernment, restricted as it is to the inner life of one particular ship and the career of an individual sailor.

It was the summer of 1797. In the April of that year had occurred the commotion[70] at Spithead followed in May by a second and yet more serious outbreak in the fleet at the Nore. The latter is known, and without exaggeration in the epithet, as the Great Mutiny[71]. It was indeed a demonstration more menacing to England than the contemporary manifestoes and conquering and proselyting armies of the French Directory.

To the British Empire the Nore Mutiny was what a strike in the fire-brigade would be to London threatened by general arson. In a crisis when the kingdom might well have anticipated the famous

---

60) masculine beauty : 남성미
61) uproar : 소란, 소동, 떠들어대는 소리
62) stutter : 말을 더듬다
63) marplot : 쓸데없이 참견하여 계획을 망쳐놓는 사람
64) more or less : 다소, 어느 정도, 대체로
65) imperfection : 결함, 불완전(상태)
66) arbitrary : 임의의, 제멋대로의
67) enlistment : 모병, 입대
68) elapse : (시간이) 경과하다, 지나다
69) frigate : 호위함
70) commotion : 동요, 소요, 폭동
71) mutiny : (특히 군인선원들의) 반란, 폭동. Spithead Mutiny와 Nore Mutiny는 1797년에 발생한 영국 해군 선원들의 대규모 반란이다.

signal that some years later published along the naval line of battle what it was that upon occasion England expected of Englishmen; that was the time when at the mast-heads of the three-deckers and seventy-fours moored in her own roadstead — a fleet, the right arm of a Power then all but the sole free conservative one of the Old World — the blue-jackets, to be numbered by thousands, ran up with huzzas the British colors with the union and cross wiped out; by that cancellation transmuting the flag of founded law and freedom defined, into the enemy's red meteor of unbridled and unbounded revolt. Reasonable discontent growing out of practical grievances in the fleet had been ignited into irrational combustion, as by live cinders blown across the Channel from France in flames.

The event converted into irony for a time those spirited strains of Dibdin — as a song-writer no mean auxiliary to the English Government at the European conjuncture — strains celebrating, among other things, the patriotic[72] devotion of the British tar[73]):

"And as for my life, 'tis[74] the King's!"

Such an episode in the Island's grand naval story her naval historians naturally abridge; one of them (William James) candidly acknowledging that fain would he pass it over did not "impartiality forbid fastidiousness." And yet his mention is less a narration than a reference, having to do hardly at all with details. Nor are these readily to be found in the ᵒlibraries. Like some other events in every age befalling states everywhere, including America, the Great Mutiny was of such character that national pride along with views of policy would fain shade it off into the historical background. Such events cannot be ignored, but there is a considerate way of historically treating them. If a well-constituted individual refrains from blazoning aught amiss or calamitous in his family, a nation in the like circumstance may without reproach be equally discreet[75].

Though after parleyings[76] between Government and the ringleaders, and concessions by the former as to some glaring abuses, the first uprising — that at Spithead with difficulty was put down, or matters for the time pacified; yet at the Nore the unforeseen renewal of insurrection on a yet larger scale, and emphasized in the conferences that ensued by demands deemed by the authorities not only inadmissible but aggressively insolent, indicated — if the Red Flag did not sufficiently do so — what was the spirit animating the men. Final suppression, however, there was; but only made possible perhaps by the unswerving loyalty of the marine corps and voluntary resumption of loyalty among influential sections of the crews.

To some extent the Nore Mutiny may be regarded as analogous[77] to the distempering irruption of contagious fever[78] in a frame constitutionally sound, and which anon throws it off[79].

---

72) patriotic : 애국의, 애국심이 강한
73) British tar : 영국의 선원
74) 'tis : It is의 단축형
75) discreet : 사려 깊은, 신중한
76) parley : 협상
77) analogous : 유사한, 닮은
78) contagious fever : 전염성의 열병
79) throw off : 관계를 끊다, 내던지다

At all events, of these thousands of mutineers were some of the tars who not so very long afterwards — whether wholly prompted thereto[80] by patriotism, or pugnacious instinct, or by both, — helped to win a coronet for Nelson at the Nile, and the naval crown of crowns for him at Trafalgar. To the mutineers those battles, and especially Trafalgar, were a plenary absolution and a grand one. For all that goes to make up scenic[81] naval[82] display, and heroic magnificence in arms[83], those battles, especially Trafalgar[84], stand unmatched in human annals.

---

80) thereto : 그것에, 거기에
81) scenic : 경치가 아름다운, 극적인, 생생한
82) naval : 해군의, 군함의(에 의한)
83) in arms : 무장을 하고
84) Trafalgar : (Battle of Trafalgar) 트라팔가 해전. Horatio Nelson 제독이 1805년 스페인과 프랑스 연합 함대를 격파

Mark Twain
- 「The Adventures of Huckleberry Finn」

제 **5** 장

이 작품은 가장 미국적인 작품의 표본으로 평가된다. 우선 교육받지 못한 미국 남부의 가난한 백인 소년의 사투리를 문학 언어로 사용한 점이 파격적이다. 이 작품의 힘은 바로 이 언어의 힘에 있으며 그 언어의 다양성은 미국문학의 민주적 혁명에 비견된다. Mark Twain은 점잖은 전통에서는 문학어로 고려 대상이 되지 않던 토속어를 거침없이 표현하면서 미국문학의 고유한 가치를 형성해낸다.

출제 경향 및 수험 대책

이 작품의 주제는 미국 정체성의 진단서이다. 노예제도와 남북전쟁으로 이어지는 미국의 역사, 속물적 감상주의와 봉건적 신분질서의 잔재를 통하여 Mark Twain이 어떻게 미국의 도덕성을 표현하는지를 중점적으로 볼 필요가 있다.

제 1 절 작가의 생애

1 생애

마크 트웨인(Mark Twain, 본명 Samuel Langhorne Clemens, 1835~1910)은 미국의 셰익스피어, 미국문학의 링컨으로 일컬어지며 예술성과 대중성을 겸비한 국민작가로 사랑받아 왔다. 미국에서 Twain이 확보한 위상은 아마도 그가 남북전쟁이 끝나고 산업화가 진행되는 19세기 말의 미국인들의 삶과 문화적인 특성을 새로운 땅과 새로운 사회에 걸맞은 새로운 목소리로 국내뿐 아니라 국외에도 널리 보여준 역할을 해낸 작가이기 때문이다. Twain은 미국 중서부 미주리(Missouri)주 플로리다(Florida)에서 John Marshall Clemens와 Jane Lampton의 일곱 자녀 중 여섯 번째 아이로 태어났다. 그는 미시시피 강(Mississippi River 서쪽의 소도시인 한니발(Hannibal)에서 그의 어린 시절을 보냈다. 19세기 중엽 미국문학의 르네상스기에 활동한 작가들 대부분이 동부에서 태어나고 동부에서 집필 활동을 한 점과 이 시기 미국의 문화적인 이질성 등을 볼 때, 19세기 작가로서 지방 출신이라는 사실에서 그의 문학적 특징이 크다.

변호사이자 판사였던 그의 부친 John Marshall Clemens는 이곳저곳으로 이사를 다니며 돈을 벌기 위해 여러 일에 손을 댔으나 성공을 하지 못했고 자식들에게도 안정적인 교육을 제공하지 못하였다. 1847년 아버지가 사망한 직후부터 Twain은 생계를 위하여 견습 기자, 인쇄공 등의 생활을 하며 1859년에 미시시피 강의 증기선의 수로 안내원 자격증을 땄다. 그가 증기선의 파일럿이 되어 강을 오르내리며 강물의 흐름을 통해 자연을 읽는 법을 배우고 다양한 체험을 한 사람들과 만난 것 등은 작가로서 그의 이력에 많은 영향을 주었다.

1861년 남북전쟁이 발발하면서 증기선 운항이 어려워지자 그는 파일럿을 그만두고 약 2주간 남부 연합군(Confederate militia)으로 전쟁에 참전하였는데, 당시 그가 경험한 심리적 충격과 감정은 「The Private History of a Campaign that Failed」(1885)에 고백의 형태로 드러난다. 전쟁터를 벗어난 후 Twain은 금광을 찾아 나선 형 Orion의 요청으로 네바다(Nevada)로 향한다. Clemens 형제는 광산을 찾는 것에는 실패했지만 그곳에 남아서 생계를 위해 잡지와 신문에 글을 썼다.

1862년 그는 Territorial Enterprise의 기자가 되었고 이때부터 필명으로 Mark Twain을 사용하기 시작하였다. Twain은 「The Celebrated Jumping Frog of Calaveras County」(1865)가 대중적인 인기를 얻음으로써 본격적으로 작가의 길에 접어들게 되었다. 이 작품 이후의 주요 작품들은 서부에서 그가 경험한 것들을 그의 상상력의 주요한 원천으로 삼았고 서부 언어는 이후의 작품에도 지속적인 영향을 주었다.

2 변화의 시기

Twain이 서부 생활을 청산하고 뉴욕(New York)주로 이주한 1867년은 그의 이력에 중요한 변화를 가져온 시기이다. 그는 샌프란시스코(San Francisco) Alta California의 특파원이 되어 뉴욕으로 가게 되는데, 이곳에서 그는 도약의 발판을 마련한다. 아내 Olivia Langdon은 뉴욕 주의 탄광 소유주인 아버지와 박애주의자인 어머니 사이에서 엘리트 교육을 받은 여성이었다. 그녀는 Twain이 남서부의 조야한 문화적 색채를 여전히 가지고 있고, 동부에서는 작가로서의 명성도 없었던 상황에서 Twain에게 부와 명예를 제공할 수 있었던 것은 분명하다. 이때부터 그는 남서부적인 유산을 버리고 동부 문화에 빠르게 적응하면서 북부의 담론을 내세우기 시작하였고, 1869년과 1870년에 들어서면서부터 공식적으로 남부를 공격하기 시작한다. 미국의 역사상 남부인과 북부인이라는 정체성이 가장 극명하게 대립되던 시기에 남부인에서 북부인으로 편입되는 일은 단순히 지리상의 이주만을 의미하는 것이 아니다. 이는 자신의 내부에 자리 잡고 있는 남부적인 가치관과 사회적·정치적인 입장의 변화까지 수반되는 훨씬 복합적인 문제였다. Twain의 처가는 진보적인 동부의 명문가로서, 열렬한 노예 제도의 폐지를 주장했던 장인은 남북전쟁 전에 이미 도망친 노예들을 숨겨주는가 하면 노예 해방 운동가들을 집에 초대하고 자유를 얻은 흑인의 교육비도 지원했으며, Frederic Douglass와 같은 흑인들을 집에 머물도록 했다. Twain은 처가를 비롯한 진보적인 동부 분위기의 영향을 받아 가치관도 변했겠지만, 동부에서 성공한 작가로서 살아남으려 했던 한 개인의 이기적인 생존 욕구도 강했던 것으로 보인다. 그가 코네티컷(Connecticut)주의 하트포드(Hartford)로 이사하고 처가의 재정적인 도움을 받아 지은 화려한 대저택은 세속적인 성공에 대한 Twain의 욕망을 상징적으로 보여준다.

3 문학 활동

Twain은 1870년대와 1880년대 초반에 많은 걸작을 낳았다. 여행기 「The Innocents Abroad, or The New Pilgrim's Progress」(1869)와 「Roughing It」(1872)을 시작으로 「The Gilded Age : A Tale of Today」(1873)(Charles Dudley Warner와 공저), 「The Adventures of Tom Sawyer」(1876), 「The Prince and the Pauper」(1881), 「Life on the Mississippi」(1883), 「The Adventures of Huckleberry Finn」(1884)에 이르기까지의 작품들을 출간한 Twain은 유머를 담은 사회비평을 하면서 미국적인 소재를 미국적인 언어와 서사 형식으로 완성시킨 훌륭한 작가로서 명성을 쌓아나갔다.

1890년 그는 사업에 실패하고 이듬해에 유럽으로 떠나 그곳에서 여러 작품을 썼지만 「*A Connecticut Yankee in King Arthur's Court*」(1889)와 「*Pudd'nhead Wilson*」(1894)을 제외하고는 대중적인 인기를 얻거나 예술적인 성취도가 높은 작품을 쓰지는 못하였다. 그 후 귀국하여 빚을 갚기 위해 세계 일주 강연 여행을 떠났고, 결국 4년 만인 1898년에야 빚을 모두 청산할 수 있었다.

Twain은 1900년 열렬한 미국인들의 환영 속에 귀국하여 시사 문제에 대해 적극적인 발언을 하는 한편 활발한 창작활동을 하였고, 예일대학(Yale)에서 명예 석사 학위와 문학 박사 학위를, 미주리대학교 (University of Missouri)에서 명예 법학 박사 학위를, 옥스퍼드대학(Oxford)에서 명예 문학 박사 학위 (Dr. Litt.)를 받았다. 그는 1910년, 75세를 일기로 세상을 떠났다.

> **❗ 더 알아두기 🔍**
>
> **Mark Twain의 주요작품**
> - 「*The Gilded Age : A Tale of Today*」(1873)
> - 「*The Adventures of Tom Sawyer*」(1876)
> - 「*Life on the Mississippi*」(1883)
> - 「*The Adventures of Huckleberry Finn*」(1884)
> - 「*A Connecticut Yankee in King Arthur's Court*」(1889)

제 2 절 작품 세계

1 작품의 배경

독립 전쟁을 치르고 영국으로부터 독립하여 독립국으로서의 주체성을 확립한 미국은 독자적인 미국문학의 존재를 절실하게 필요로 하게 되었다. 이러한 문화적 욕구는 다른 작가들의 작품 활동으로 어느 정도 충족되고 있었다. 따라서 대중들의 문학에 대한 관심도는 점점 높아지게 되었는데 이때 나온 작품이 바로 「*The Adventures of Huckleberry Finn*」이다. 이 작품은 Mississippi 3부작 중 마지막 작품으로 당시 미국사회가 가지고 있던 모순과 문제점을 비판하고 있다. 작품이 출판된 1884년 미국에서는 이미 노예제가 폐지(1865)됐지만, 「*The Adventures of Huckleberry Finn*」의 배경은 노예제가 존재하던 남북전쟁 이전을 배경으로 한다.

2 작품의 특징 중요 ★★★

(1) 한 고아 소년이 자신의 체험담을 말하는 이야기 문학의 형식으로 주인공이 일상에서 일어난 사건을 기술한다.

(2) 주인공 Huck은 미국인들이 진정으로 추구하는 이상적인 인간상이라고 할 수 있다. 그는 **문명에 찌들지 않은 원초적 모습**을 지니고 불평등이나 허위, 물질에 대한 집착, 사기 등으로 가득한 어른들의 가식적인 세계에서 오염되지 않은 'Child of Nature'의 모습이다. 그는 자유와 정의를 추구하고 인간에게 부여되는 거룩한 정신이 오염되는 것을 거부하며 외적인 환경에 도전하며 나아가는 모습을 보여준다.

(3) 「*The Adventures of Tom Sawyer*」(1876)와 「*The Adventures of Huckleberry Finn*」(1885)을 비교하자면 「*The Adventures of Huckleberry Finn*」은 「*The Adventures of Tom Sawyer*」를 출판한 직후 집필을 시작하여 약 7~8년에 걸쳐 완성한 작품이지만 작품에서 드러나는 세계관과 분위기에서 뚜렷한 차이가 있다. St. Petersburg는 「*The Adventures of Tom Sawyer*」가 아늑하고 평화로운 반면, 「*The Adventures of Huckleberry Finn*」은 고독감을 느끼게 하고 죽음을 연상하게 하는 어두운 곳으로 묘사된다고 하였다.

(4) 작가는 작품의 언어에 있어서 독자들과 다른 계층의 인물을 그리면서 그들의 사투리와 속어로 작품을 전개한다.

(5) **악한 소설(picaresque novel)**

① picaresque novel은 스페인어의 'picaro'(건달, 재미있는 무뢰한)에서 유래하였는데, 건달의 이야기를 다루면서 상류층의 이상주의적 문학에 맞서는 하류층을 등장시킨다. 이들은 기존의 관습에 대립하는 태도를 취한다. 부도덕한 현실사회에 맞서 재치 있고 임기응변과 가벼운 탈선을 하면서 사회적인 모험담의 특징을 지닌 소설장르이다.

② 주인공 Huck은 미국 사회의 하류층 백인태생으로 술주정뱅이 아버지만 있을 뿐이다. Huck은 교양이나 관습과는 거리가 멀고 함부로 담배를 피우며 학교를 결석하는 불량소년이다. 그러나 그는 신선하고 현실적이며 생동감 있는 성격을 지닌 인물이다. 물질주의 사회에 끌려가는 인물이기보다는 사회와 문화에 격리되었지만 보다 깊은 진실을 찾는 인물이기도 하다.

제 3 절 줄거리

미주리주 세인트피터즈버그(St. Petersburg)의 술주정뱅이 Pap Finn의 아들인 주인공 Huck은 Widow Douglas 댁에 입양되어 Miss Watson과 Widow Douglas에 의해 교양인으로 교육을 받는 중에, Huck이 돈을 벌었다는 소문을 듣고 나타난 아버지에게 유괴된다. 아버지로 인해 오두막에 갇힌 Huck은 술에 만취한 아버지의 폭력에 생명의 위협을 느끼고, 우연히 발견한 카누를 타고 도망칠 계획을 한다.

Huck은 오두막에 돼지 피를 뿌려놓고 자신의 피로 꾸며서 강도들에 의해 자신이 죽임을 당한 것처럼 만들어 놓은 후 카누를 타고 미시시피 강에 있는 잭슨 섬(Jackson's Island)에 숨어 지내며 자유를 만끽한다. 삼일 뒤 Huck은 잭슨 섬에서 우연히 루이지애나(Louisiana)주 뉴올리언스(New Orleans)로 팔려 갈까봐 도망쳐 나온 Miss Watson의 흑인 노예 Jim을 만난다. 이 둘은 함께 홍수에 떠내려 온 뗏목을 타고 Mississippi 강을 따라 자유를 찾아 떠난다. 두 사람은 뗏목을 타고 여행하면서 사기꾼들과 여러 사람들을 만나고 다양한 사건에 휘말리기도 한다. Jim이 사기꾼들에 의해 아칸소(Arkansas)주 Phelps의 농장에 팔려가자 Huck은 Jim을 찾으러 나선다. Phelps의 농장이 Tom Sawyer의 이모 Aunt Sally와 Uncle Phelps의 집인 것을 알게 된 Huck은 자신이 Tom인 척 한다. 마침 친척집에 온 Tom은 자신을 이복형제 Sid로 행세를 하고, 둘은 Jim의 탈출을 돕기로 한다. Huck과 Tom은 헛간에 묶여있는 Jim을 풀어주고 함께 강으로 도망가는데, Tom은 이때 마을 농부들에 의해 다리에 총알을 맞는다. Huck은 의사를 부르러 가고 Jim은 Tom을 간호한다. 세인트피터즈버그에서 파이크스빌(Pikesville)에 위치한 Aunt Sally의 집에 온 Aunt Polly로 인하여 Huck와 Tom의 본래 정체가 밝혀지고, Tom은 두 달 전 죽은 Miss Watson이 이미 Jim을 해방시켜 준다는 유언을 남겼다는 소식을 밝힌다. Tom은 Huck과 자신이 맞은 총알을 자랑스러워하고 새로운 모험을 위해 광야(Indian Territory, 현재 오클라호마주)로 떠나겠다는 결심을 하며 소설은 끝난다.

제 4 절 작품의 주제

1 성장소설(Bildungsroman)

13살 정도의 백인 소년 Huck이 성인(成人)으로 성장하는 과정을 다루고 있다. Huck은 다양한 모험과 경험을 통해 Miss Watson이 가르치는 것이나 남부 사회의 가치관과는 달리 자신만의 도덕관념과 가치관을 성립하며, 독자적인 논리와 양심에 따라 행동한다. 처음에는 도망친 노예 Jim을 도와주는 것이 그의 주인인 Miss Watson에게 손해를 끼친다는 딜레마를 가졌으나, Huck만이 자신의 유일한 친구이자 약속을 지키는 백인이라는 Jim의 말에 그를 팔아넘기지 않고 Jim을 자신과 동등한 인간으로 대하며 도와준다.

2 19세기 미국 남부에 대한 풍자

노예 제도와 인종 차별(racism) 등 19세기의 미국 남부 사회에 관한 풍자가 나타난다.

3 자유에 대한 갈망과 인간성의 회복 중요 ★★

문명, 위선, 허위, 인습 및 속박으로부터 벗어나 자유와 인간성을 주제로 다룬다. Huck은 자신을 교양인으로 만들려 하는 Widow Douglas로부터 벗어나려 하고, 자신을 학대하는 아버지로부터도 달아나려 한다. 그와 함께 모험하는 Jim 또한 노예 신분에서 벗어나 진정한 자유를 얻고자 한다.

제 5 절 등장인물

1 Huckleberry Finn(Huck)

주인공이자 Tom Sawyer의 가장 친한 친구이다. 교회와 문명의 가르침보다 미신을 믿고, 숲속에서 담배 피우는 것을 더 좋아하며 어느 누구로부터 제약받는 것을 싫어하고 혼자 사는 것을 더 좋아하는 아이다. 교양을 갖춘 인간으로 만들고 싶어 하는 어른들과 문명사회에 적응을 못하고 결국 자연인(自然人)으로 돌아간다.

2 Jim

단순한 성격에 두려움도 많지만 인간에 대한 온정을 지닌 흑인 노예이다. Huck이 아버지 Pap Finn으로부터 도망치던 날, 그도 Miss Watson으로부터 도망쳐 나와 Huck의 살인자라는 의심을 받고 도망친 노예로 현상금이 걸린다. 그는 Huck과 함께 미시시피 강을 따라 내려가며 모험을 하다가, 마침내 Miss Watson의 유언에 따라 자유의 몸이 된다.

3 Tom Sawyer

Tom은 Huck과 무슨 일이든 함께 하지만 차이점도 가지고 있다. Huck은 독서를 싫어하고 어른의 세계로 진입하기를 거부하는 비문명적 성격이며 집도 없이 살아가는 자유인이지만, Tom은 독서에 따른 상식도 많고 상상력과 꿈이 많은 낭만적인 성격이다. Tom은 사회에 순응하고자 하는 의지를 가지고 있다.

4 Judge Thatcher

술주정뱅이 아버지 Pap으로부터 Huck을 보호하고 Huck의 재산도 관리하는 전형적인 아버지의 이미지를 담고 있는 인물이다.

5 Aunt Sally(Phelps)

Tom의 작은 이모로, 선한 인품의 소유자이다. Tom에게 가지고 있는 애정만큼이나 Huck에게도 애정을 쏟으며 둘을 교양인으로 만들고 싶어 한다. 그러나 노예 제도나 인종 차별에 대해선 무지하다. Silas Phelps의 부인이다.

6 Aunt Polly

Tom의 큰 이모이다. 세인트피터즈버그에서 Aunt Sally의 집으로 직접 찾아온다.

7 Widow Douglas

Miss Watson의 언니로서 미망인이다. Huck을 보호하면서 교양인으로 만들고 싶어 한다.

8 Miss Watson

Widow Douglas의 동생으로, 평생 미혼으로 지내며 Widow Douglas와 함께 산다. Jim의 주인이지만 유서로 Jim을 노예의 신분에서 해방시켜 준다.

9 The dauphin and the duke

프랑스 루이 16세 황태자와 영국 공작(duke)이라고 자칭하는 백인 사기꾼들이다. Huck, Jim과 함께 미시시피 강을 따라 모험하지만, 그들은 마을에서 저급하고 짧은 셰익스피어 공연을 하며 마을 사람들의 돈을 갈취하고, Jim이 도망친 노예인 점을 간파한 후 그를 팔아넘긴다. 사기꾼인 것이 들통 나 마을 사람들에게 온몸에 타르(tar)와 깃털 세례를 받는다.

제 6 절 　작품의 구조(Plot)와 시점 및 기법

1 시점

1인칭 제한적 시점으로 처음부터 주인공인 Huck에 의해 이야기가 전개된다.

2 어법

(1) 1인칭 시점의 효과

주인공 Huck의 1인칭 시점으로 전개되는 본 작품은 사회비평적인 서술을 자연스럽게 느껴지도록 한다. 작가는 주요 등장인물들이 사투리와 일상 언어, 그리고 반어적인 어법을 사용하게 하였는데 이 점과 관련하여 Ernest Hemingway는 모든 미국문학의 원류는 Mark Twain이라고도 언급하였다. 그 이유는 「*The Adventures of Huckleberry Finn*」에서 Huck이 교육과 문명을 거부하는 화자이고 고백적인 자서전 형식의 글쓰기를 통해 전통적인 사고에 도전하는 미국의 신세계에 적합한, 새롭게 열린 사고의 길을 열었기 때문이다.

(2) 반어법과 해학, 개척정신 중요 ★

반어법과 해학으로 미국의 가장 심각하고 예민한 사회 문제인 인종 차별을 과감히 풍자하면서도 미국 고유의 정서인 유머로 미국 문화의 토대를 다시 생각하게 한다.
흑인을 주인공의 동반자이자 분신으로 세우고, 문학 작품에 흑인 방언을 사용한 저자의 개척 정신도 돋보인다.

3 대조적 상징

작품의 배경을 강(Mississippi River), 섬(Jackson's Island), 마을 등으로 변화시킨다. 강은 사회적·문명적 위선과 기만으로부터 벗어난 자유, 섬(Jackson's Island)은 자유와 위험, 속박이 혼재된 중간지대, 마을은 문명과 속박을 상징하면서 대조적인 상징의 기법을 보여준다.

4 우화와 상징

(1) 신(神)과 인간에 대한 알레고리

미시시피 강은 신성(神性)이며 아름다움과 함께 공포도 느끼게 한다. 미시시피 강은 Jim에게 노예제가 없는 주(state)인 오하이오(Ohio)로 가는 자유를 상징하고, Huck에게는 사회적 관습과 법, 문명으로부터 벗어나는 자유를 의미한다.

(2) 선(善)과 악(惡)에 관한 알레고리

Huck은 작은 마을의 소년으로서 접해보지 못했던 사회의 악을 모험을 통해 겪는다.

제 7 절 Text

Chapter 1

    YOU don't know about me[1] without you have read[2] a book by the name of The Adventures of Tom Sawyer; but that ain't no matter[3]. That book was made by Mr. Mark Twain, and he told the truth, mainly. There was things which he stretched[4], but mainly he told the truth. That is nothing. I never seen anybody[5] but lied[6] one time or another, without it was Aunt Polly, or the widow, or maybe Mary[7] — Aunt Polly — Tom's Aunt Polly, she is — and Mary, and the Widow Douglas is all told about in that book, which is mostly a true book, with some stretchers, as I said before.

    Now the way that the book winds up[8] is this: Tom and me found the money that the robbers hid in the cave, and it made us rich. We got six thousand dollars apiece — all gold. It was an awful sight[9] of money when it was piled up. Well, Judge Thatcher he took it and put it out at interest, and it fetched us a dollar a day apiece all the year round — more than a body could tell what to do with. The Widow Douglas she took me for her son, and allowed she would sivilize[10] me; but it was rough living in the house all the time, considering how dismal regular and decent the widow was in all her ways; and so when I couldn't stand it no longer I lit out. I got into my old rags and my sugar-hogshead again, and was free and satisfied[11]. But Tom Sawyer he hunted me up and said he was going to start a band of robbers, and I might join if I would go back to the widow and be respectable. So I went back.

    The widow she cried over me, and called me a poor lost lamb, and she called me a lot of other names, too, but she never meant no harm by it. She put me in them new clothes again, and I couldn't do nothing but sweat and sweat, and feel all cramped up. Well, then, the old thing commenced again. The widow rung a bell for supper, and you had to come to time[12]. When you got to the table you couldn't go right to eating, but you had to wait for the widow to tuck down[13] her head and grumble a little over the victuals, though there warn't really anything the matter with them, — that is, nothing only everything was cooked by itself[14]. In a barrel of odds and ends[15]

---

1) me : Huckleberry Finn
2) without you have read ~ : 전치사 without을 접속사로 잘못 사용한 말투. without you having read ~(= unless you have read ~)
3) that ain't no matter : 이 작품에서는 이중 부정의 형태가 계속 나오는데 이는 긍정이 아니라 부정을 의미하는 비속한 말투이다.
4) stretch : exaggerate(과장하다)
5) I ~ anybody : I have never seen anybody
6) but lied : who did not lie(여기서 but은 유사관계대명사)
7) Mary : Mary는 Aunt Polly의 딸이자 Tom의 사촌이다.
8) wind up: 마무리 짓다
9) a sight : a lot(= a large quantity)
10) sivilize : civilize
11) I ~ satisfied : 난 옛 누더기를 입고 설탕 통에 들어가고 나서야 만족스럽고 자유로웠다.
12) come to time : come right away
13) tuck down : 숙이다
14) nothing ~ itself : nothing wrong except that everything ~ itself
15) odds and ends : 잡스러운 것, 섞인 것

it is different; things get mixed up, and the juice kind of swaps[16] around, and the things go better.

After supper she got out her book and learned me about Moses and the Bulrushers[17], and I was in a sweat to find out all about him; but by and by she let it out that Moses had been dead a considerable long time; so then I didn't care no more about him, because I don't take no stock in dead people.

Pretty soon I wanted to smoke, and asked the widow to let me. But she wouldn't. She said it was a mean practice and wasn't clean, and I must try to not do it any more. That is just the way with some people. They get down on a thing when they don't know nothing about it. Here she was a bothering about Moses, which was no kin to her, and no use to anybody, being gone, you see, yet finding a power of fault with me for doing a thing that had some good in it. And she took snuff[18], too; of course that was all right, because she done it herself.

Her sister, Miss Watson, a tolerable slim old maid, with goggles on, had just come to live with her, and took a set at me now with a spelling-book. She worked me middling hard for about an hour, and then the widow made her ease up[19]. I couldn't stood it much longer. Then for an hour it was deadly dull, and I was fidgety[20]. Miss Watson would say, "Don't put your feet up there, Huckleberry;" and "Don't scrunch up like that, Huckleberry — set up straight;" and pretty soon she would say, "Don't gap and stretch like that, Huckleberry — why don't you try to behave?" Then she told me all about the bad place[21], and I said I wished I was there. She got mad then, but I didn't mean no harm. All I wanted was to go somewheres; all I wanted was a change, I warn't particular. She said it was wicked to say what I said; said she wouldn't say it for the whole world; she was going to live so as to[22] go to the good place[23]. Well, I couldn't see no advantage in going where she was going, so I made up my mind I wouldn't try for it. But I never said so, because it would only make trouble, and wouldn't do no good.

Now she had got a start, and she went on and told me all about the good place. She said all a body would have to do there was to go around all day long with a harp and sing, forever and ever[24]. So I didn't think much of it. But I never said so. I asked her if she reckoned Tom Sawyer would go there, and she said not by a considerable sight[25]. I was glad about that, because I wanted him and me to be together.

Miss Watson she kept pecking at me, and it got tiresome and lonesome. By and by they fetched the niggers[26] in and had prayers, and then everybody was off to bed. I went up to my room with

---

16) swap : exchange
17) Moses and the Bulrushers : Widow Douglas는 자신이 Huck을 양자로 삼아서 기르게 된 것을 파라오의 공주가 갈대 바구니 속에 실린 채 나일 강에 버려진 아기 모세를 구하였던 것(Exodus 2 :1~10)에 비유하였다.
18) snuff : 코담배
19) ease up : relieve from pressure(= ease off, 여유를 가지다, 완화되다)
20) fidgety : (지루하거나 초조해서) 가만히 못 있는
21) the bad place : 지옥
22) so as to : in order to
23) the good place : 천국
24) forever and ever : 영원히(여기에서는 약간 비꼬는 투로 사용)
25) not by a considerable sight : by no means(결코 ~이 아닌)
26) niggers : negroes(흑인들)

a piece of candle, and put it on the table. Then I set down[27] in a chair by the window and tried to think of something cheerful, but it warn't no use. I felt so lonesome I most wished I was dead. The stars were shining, and the leaves rustled in the woods ever so mournful[28]; and I heard an owl, away off, who-whooing[29] about somebody that was dead, and a whippowill[30] and a dog crying about somebody that was going to die; and the wind was trying to whisper something to me, and I couldn't make out what it was, and so it made the cold shivers run over me. Then away out in the woods I heard that kind of a sound that a ghost makes when it wants to tell about something that's on its mind and can't make itself understood, and so can't rest easy in its grave, and has to go about that way every night grieving. I got so down-hearted[31] and scared I did wish I had some company. Pretty soon a spider went crawling up my shoulder, and I flipped it off and it lit in the candle; and before I could budge it was all shriveled up. I didn't need anybody to tell me that was an awful bad sign and would fetch me some bad luck, so I was scared and most shook the clothes off of[32] me. I got up and turned around in my tracks[33] three times and crossed my breast[34] every time; and then I tied up a little lock of my hair with a thread to keep witches away. But I hadn't no confidence. You do that when you've lost a horse-shoe that you've found, instead of nailing it up over the door, but I hadn't ever heard anybody say it was any way to keep off bad luck when you'd killed a spider.

I set down again, a shaking all over, and got out my pipe for a smoke; for the house was all as still as death now, and so the widow wouldn't know. Well, after a long time I heard the clock away off in the town go boom[35] — boom — boom — twelve licks[36]; and all still again — stiller than ever. Pretty soon I heard a twig snap[37] down in the dark amongst the trees — something was a stirring. I set still and listened. Directly I could just barely hear a "me-yow! me-yow!"[38] down there. That was good! Says I[39], me-yow! me-yow!" as soft as I could, and then I put out[40] the light and scrambled out of the window on to the shed. Then I slipped down to the ground and crawled in amongst the trees, and, sure enough, there was Tom Sawyer waiting for me.

---

27) I set down : I sat down
28) mournful : 슬픔에 잠긴, 슬픔을 나타내는
29) who-whooing : hooting(부엉이의 울음소리), 본문에서 부엉이는 흉조이다.
30) whippowill : whippoorwill(쏙독새), 이 새가 울면 사람이 죽거나 불운이 닥치는 징조라는 미국의 미신이 있다.
31) down-hearted : 기가 죽은, 낙담한
32) off of : from
33) in one's tracks : where one stands; on the spot(제자리에서)
34) cross my breast : 내 가슴에 십자가를 긋다
35) go boom : 붕 하고 소리가 나다
36) twelve licks : twelve strokes(12시를 치다)
37) snap : break suddenly off(갑자기 무너지다, 꺾이다)
38) me-yow : mew or miaow(고양이의 울음소리)
39) Says I : I say[= said] (일인칭의 전달동사에 's'를 붙이는 것은 비문법적이고 비속한 말투로 이 작품에서 때때로 과거의 의미로 쓰인다)
40) put out : 끄다

Chapter 2

WE went tiptoeing along a path amongst the trees back towards the end of the widow's garden, stooping down[41] so as the branches[42] wouldn't scrape our heads. When we was passing by the kitchen I fell over a root and made a noise. We scrouched down and laid still.[43] Miss Watson's big nigger, named Jim[44], was setting[45] in the kitchen door; we could see him pretty clear, because there was a light behind him. He got up and stretched his neck out about a minute, listening. Then he says:

"Who dah?"[46]

He listened some more; then he come tiptoeing down and stood right between us; we could a touched him, nearly. Well, likely it was minutes and minutes that there warn't a sound, and we all there so close together. There was a place on my ankle that got to itching, but I dasn't scratch[47] it; and then my ear begun to itch; and next my back, right between my shoulders. Seemed like I'd die if I couldn't scratch. Well, I've noticed that thing plenty times since. If you are with the quality[48], or at a funeral, or trying to go to sleep when you ain't sleepy — if you are anywheres where it won't do for you to scratch, why you will itch all over in upwards of a thousand places. Pretty soon Jim says:

"Say, who is you? Whar is you?[49] Dog my cats ef[50] I didn' hear sumf'n[51]. Well, I know what I's gwyne to do[52]: I's gwyne to set down here and listen tell I hears it agin[53]."

So he set down on the ground betwixt[54] me and Tom. He leaned his back up against a tree, and stretched his legs out till one of them most touched one of mine. My nose begun to itch. It itched till the tears come into my eyes. But I dasn't[55] scratch. Then it begun to itch on the inside. Next I got to itching underneath. I didn't know how I was going to set still. This miserableness went on as much as six or seven minutes; but it seemed a sight longer than that. I was itching in eleven different places now. I reckoned I couldn't stand it more'n a minute longer, but I set my teeth hard and got ready to try. Just then Jim begun to breathe heavy; next he begun to snore — and then I was pretty soon comfortable again.

Tom he made a sign to me — kind of a little noise with his mouth — and we went creeping

---

41) stoop down : 웅크리다
42) so as the branches ∼ : (as는 that을 잘못 사용한 말투) so that the branches ∼
43) laid still : lay still
44) Jim : Nigger Jim은 Mark Twain이 어린 시절 Florida에 있는 외갓집에서 만난 Uncle an'l이라는 흑인의 이미지이다.
45) was setting : was sitting
46) Who dah? : Who is there?
47) dasn't scratch : dared not scratch(감히 긁을 수 없었다)
48) the quality : person of quality
49) whar is you? : who are you? / what is you? / where are you?
50) Dog my cats ef ∼ : [강한 긍정의 형식] blamed me if ∼(∼라면 사람이 아니다)
51) sumf'n : something
52) what I's gwyne to do : what I am going to do
53) agin : again
54) betwixt : between
55) dasn't : dared not

away on our hands and knees[56]. When we was ten foot off[57] Tom whispered to me, and wanted to tie Jim to the tree for fun. But I said no; he might wake and make a disturbance, and then they'd find out I warn't in[58]. Then Tom said he hadn't got candles enough, and he would slip in the kitchen and get some more. I didn't want him to try. I said Jim might wake up and come. But Tom wanted to resk[59] it; so we slid in there and got three candles, and Tom laid five cents on the table for pay. Then we got out, and I was in a sweat[60] to get away; but nothing would do Tom but he must crawl to where Jim was, on his hands and knees, and play something on him. I waited, and it seemed a good while, everything was so still and lonesome.

As soon as Tom was back we cut[61] along the path, around the garden fence, and by and by fetched up[62] on the steep top of the hill the other side of the house. Tom said he slipped Jim's hat off[63] of his head and hung it on a limb[64] right over him, and Jim stirred a little, but he didn't wake. Afterwards Jim said the witches bewitched him and put him in a trance[65], and rode him all over the State, and then set him under the trees again, and hung his hat on a limb to show who done it. And next time Jim told it he said they rode him down to New Orleans; and, after that, every time he told it he spread it more and more, till by and by he said they rode him all over the world, and tired him most to death, and his back[66] was all over saddle-boils[67]. Jim was monstrous proud[68] about it, and he got so he wouldn't hardly notice the other niggers. Niggers would come miles to hear Jim tell about it, and he was more looked up to than any nigger in that country. Strange niggers would stand with their mouths open and look him all over, same as if[69] he was a wonder. Niggers is always talking about witches in the dark by the kitchen fire; but whenever one was talking and letting on[70] to know all about such things, Jim would happen in and say, "Hm! What you know 'bout witches?" and that nigger was corked up[71] and had to take a back seat[72]. Jim always kept that five-center piece round his neck with a string, and said it was a charm the devil give to him with his own hands, and told him he could cure anybody with it and fetch witches whenever he wanted to just by saying something to it; but he never told what it was he said to it. Niggers would come from all around there and give Jim anything hey had, just for a sight

---

56) on our hands and knees : on all fours(네 발로)
57) was ten foot off : were ten feet off(10피트 정도 갔을 때)
58) I warn't in : I wasn't in the house
59) resk : risk(모험을 하다)
60) be in a sweat : be very anxious
61) cut : skiff off ; make off with alertness(급히 떠나다, 달아나다)
62) by and by fetched up : at last reached; stopped at last(마침내 ∼에 다다랐다, 멈추었다)
63) slip ∼ off of … : ∼을 …에서 슬쩍 벗기다
64) limb : 나뭇가지
65) be in a trance : 정신이 딴 데 팔려 있다, 최면 상태에 있다
66) his back : his ass(그의 엉덩이), 그의 허리
67) saddle-boil : (말 따위에 오래 앉아 있음으로써 생기는) 종기, 부스럼
68) be monstrous proud : be mighty proud(대단히 자랑하다)
69) same as if ∼ : just as if ∼(바로 마치 ∼인 듯)
70) let on : pretend(∼인 척하다)
71) cork up : silence forcefully(입을 틀어막아 버리다)
72) take a back seat : 뒤로 물러서다

of that five-center piece; but they wouldn't touch it, because the devil had had his hands on it. Jim was most ruined for a servant, because he got so stuck up[73] on account of[74] having seen the devil and been rode by witches.

Well, when Tom and me got to the edge of the hill-top we looked away down into the village and could see three or four lights twinkling, where there was sick folks, maybe; and the stars over us was sparkling ever so fine; and down by the village was the river, a whole mile broad, and awful still and grand. We went down the hill and found Jo Harper and Ben Rogers, and two or three more of the boys, hid in the old tanyard[75]. So we unhitched[76] a skiff[77] and pulled down the river two mile and a half, to the big scar[78] on the hillside, and went ashore.

We went to a clump of bushes, and Tom made everybody swear to keep the secret, and then showed them a hole in the hill, right in the thickest part of the bushes. Then we lit the candles, and crawled in on our hands and knees. We went about two hundred yards, and then the cave opened up. Tom poked about[79] amongst the passages, and pretty soon ducked under a wall where you wouldn't a noticed that there was a hole. We went along a narrow place and got into a kind of room, all damp and sweaty and cold, and there we stopped. Tom says:

"Now, we'll start this band of robbers and call it Tom Sawyer's Gang. Everybody that wants to join has got to take an oath, and write his name in blood."

Everybody was willing. So Tom got out a sheet of paper that he had wrote the oath on, and read it. It swore every boy to stick to the band, and never tell any of the secrets; and if anybody done anything to any boy in the band, whichever boy was ordered to kill that person and his family must do it, and he mustn't eat and he mustn't sleep till he had killed them and hacked[80] a cross in their breasts, which was the sign of the band. And nobody that didn't belong to the band could use that mark, and if he did he must be sued; and if he done it again he must be killed. And if anybody that belonged to the band told the secrets, he must have his throat cut, and then have his carcass[81] burnt up and the ashes scattered all around, and his name blotted off[82] of the list with blood and never mentioned again by the gang, but have a curse put on it and be forgot forever.

Everybody said it was a real beautiful oath, and asked Tom if he got it out of his own head. He said, some of it, but the rest was out of pirate-books[83] and robber-books, and every gang that was high-toned[84] had it.

---

73) got so stuck up : became very conceited or arrogant(굉장히 잘난 체했다)
74) on account of : because of
75) tanyard : 무두질 공장
76) unhitch : unfasten(풀다, 끄르다)
77) skiff : a flat-bottomed open boat(밑이 납작하고 뚜껑이 달리지 않은 배)
78) the big scar : 큰 낭떠러지
79) poke about : 이곳저곳을 찾아다니다
80) hack : 마구 자르다, 난도질하다
81) carcass : 시체
82) blot off : 뭉개어 지우다, 더럽게 해버리다
83) pirate-book : 해적에 관한 책
84) high-toned : stylish(멋진, 고상한)

Some thought it would be good to kill the families of boys that told the secrets. Tom said it was a good idea, so he took a pencil and wrote it in. Then Ben Rogers says:

"Here's Huck Finn, he hain't got no family[85]; what you going to do 'bout him?"

"Well, hain't he got a father?" says Tom Sawyer.

"Yes, he' s got a father, but you can't never find him these days. He used to lay drunk with the hogs in the tanyard, but he hain't been seen in these parts for a year or more."

They talked it over, and they was going to rule me out, because they said every boy must have a family or somebody to kill, or else it wouldn't be fair and square[86] for the others. Well, nobody could think of anything to do — everybody was stumped, and set still. I was most ready to cry; but all at once I thought of a way, and so I offered them Miss Watson - they could kill her. Everybody said:

"Oh, she'll do[87]. That's all right. Huck can come in."

Then they all stuck a pin in their fingers to get blood to sign with, and I made my mark on the paper.

"Now," says Ben Rogers, "what's the line of business of this Gang?"

"Nothing only robbery and murder," Tom said.

"But who are we going to rob? — houses, or cattle, or — "

"Stuff[88] stealing cattle and such things ain't robbery; it's burglary," says Tom Sawyer. "We ain't burglars. That ain't no sort of style.[89] We are highwaymen[90]. We stop stages and carriages on the road, with masks on, and kill the people and take their watches and money."

"Must we always kill the people?"

"Oh, certainly. It's best. Some authorities think different, but mostly it's considered best to kill them — except some that you bring to the cave here, and keep them till they're ransomed[91]."

"Ransomed? What's that?"

"I don't know. But that's what they do. I've seen it in books; and so of course that's what we've got to do."

"But how can we do it if we don't know what it is?"

"Why blame it all[92], we've got to do it. Don't I tell you it's in the books? Do you want to go to doing different from what' s in the books, and get things all muddled up[93] ?"

"Oh, that's all very fine to say, Tom Sawyer, but how in the nation[94] are these fellows going to be ransomed if we don't know how to do it to them? — that's the thing I want to get at. Now, what do you reckon it is?"

---

85) he hain't got no family : he has no family(= he has not got any family)
86) be fair and square : 맞다, 일치하다
87) she'll do : she serves right(그녀면 충분하다)
88) stuff! : nonsense!(말도 안 돼!)
89) That ~ style : 밤 도둑질은 멋이 없어.
90) highwaymen : 노상강도들
91) ransom : 몸값을 받아내다, 배상을 받고 석방하다
92) Why blame it all : Why confound it all(제기랄!)
93) muddle up : 뒤섞다, 혼란시키다, 엉망진창을 만들다
94) how in the nation : how on earth ~(도대체 어떻게 ~) / nation은 강조의 부사어구로 damnation의 완곡어로 사용된다.

"Well, I don't know. But per'aps[95] if we keep them till they're ransomed, it means that we keep them till they're dead."

"Now, that's something like. That'll answer. Why couldn't you said that before? We'll keep them till they're ransomed to death; and a bothersome lot they'll be, too — eating up everything, and always trying to get loose."

"How you talk[96], Ben Rogers. How can they get loose when there's a guard over them, ready to shoot them down if they move a peg[97]?"

"A guard! Well, that is good. So somebody's got to set up all night[98] and never get any sleep, just so as to watch them. I think that's foolishness. Why can't a body take a club and ransom them as soon as they get here?"

"Because it ain't in the books so — that's why. Now, Ben Rogers, do you want to do things regular, or don't you? — that's the idea. Don't you reckon that the people that made the books knows what's the correct thing to do? Do you reckon you can learn 'em anything? Not by a good deal.[99] No, sir, we'll just go on and ransom them in the regular way."

"All right. I don't mind; but I say it's a fool way, anyhow. Say, do we kill the women, too?"

"Well, Ben Rogers, if I was as ignorant[100] as you I wouldn't let on. Kill the women? No; nobody ever saw anything in the books like that. You fetch them to the cave, and you're always as polite as pie[101] to them; and by and by they fall in love with you, and never want to go home any more."

"Well, if that's the way I'm agreed, but I don't take no stock in it. Mighty[102] soon we'll have the cave so cluttered up with women, and fellows waiting to be ransomed, that there won't be no place for the robbers. But go ahead, I ain't got nothing to say."

Little Tommy Barnes was asleep now, and when they waked him up he was scared, and cried, and said he wanted to go home to his ma[103], and didn't want to be a robber any more.

So they all made fun of[104] him, and called him crybaby[105], and that made him mad, and he said he would go straight and tell all the secrets. But Tom give him five cents to keep quiet, and said we would all go home and meet next week, and rob somebody and kill some people.

Ben Rogers said he couldn't get out much[106], only Sundays, and so he wanted to begin next Sunday; but all the boys said it would be wicked to do it on Sunday, and that settled the thing. They agreed to get together and fix a day[107] as soon as they could, and then we elected Tom

---

95) per'aps : perhaps
96) How you talk : 설마
97) move a peg : 조금이라도 움직이다
98) set up all night : sit up all night(불침번을 서다)
99) Not by a good deal : Not by a long sight(전혀 그럴 수 없는 일이지)
100) ignorant : 무식한
101) as polite as pie : very polite
102) mighty : very, quite(대단히, 매우)
103) his ma : his mother
104) make fun of : ~을 놀리다, 비웃다
105) crybaby : 울보
106) get out much : 자주 밖으로 나오다
107) fix a day : 어떤 날을 정하다

Sawyer first captain and Jo Harper second captain of the Gang, and so started home.

I clumb[108]) up the shed and crept into my window just before day was breaking. My new clothes was all greased[109]) up and clayey[110]), and I was dog-tired[111]).

Chapter 3

WELL, I got a good going-over[112]) in the morning from old Miss Watson on account of my clothes; but the widow she didn't scold, but only cleaned off the grease and clay, and looked so sorry that I thought I would behave awhile if I could. Then Miss Watson she took me in the closet and prayed, but nothing come of it. She told me to pray every day, and whatever I asked for I would get it[113]). But it warn't so. I tried it. Once I got a fish-line, but no hooks[114]). It warn't any good to me without hooks. I tried for the hooks three or four times, but somehow I couldn't make it work. By and by, one day, I asked Miss Watson to try for me, but she said I was a fool. She never told me why, and I couldn't make it out no way.

I set down one time back in the woods, and had a long think about it. I says to myself, if a body can get anything they pray for, why don't Deacon Winn get back the money he lost on pork? Why can't the widow get back her silver snuffbox that was stole? Why can't Miss Watson fat up?[115]) No, says I to myself, there ain't nothing in it. I went and told the widow about it, and she said the thing a body could get by praying for it was "spiritual gifts." This was too many for me,[116]) but she told me what she meant — I must help other people, and do everything I could for other people, and look out for them all the time, and never think about myself. This was including Miss Watson, as I took it. I went out in the woods and turned it over in my mind[117]) a long time, but I couldn't see no advantage about it — except for the other people; so at last I reckoned I wouldn't worry about it any more, but just let it go. Sometimes the widow would take me one side and talk about Providence in a way to make a body's mouth water[118]); but maybe next day Miss Watson would take hold and knock it all down again. I judged I could see that there was two Providences, and a poor chap[119]) would stand considerable show with the widow's Providence, but if Miss Watson's got him there warn't no help for him any more. I thought it all out, and reckoned I would

---

108) dumb : climbed(올라갔다)
109) grease : 기름으로 더럽히다
110) clayey : 진흙투성이의
111) dog-tired : 몹시 지친
112) going-over : 조사, 검사
113) whatever ~ it : 여기에서 it은 whatever I asked for를 의미하며 중복되어 사용되었다.
114) hook : 낚싯바늘
115) Why can't Miss Watson fat up? : Miss Watson이 'a tolerable slim old maid'임을 알 수 있다.
116) This was too many for me : This was too much for me to understand
117) turn something in one's mind : 어떤 것에 대하여 숙고하다
118) talk about ~ mouth water : 구약의 요엘 3장 18절에 나오는 "and in that day the mountains shall drip sweet wine, and the hills shall flow with milk …"라는 구절에 비유하여 한 말
119) chap : 놈, 녀석

belong to the widow's if he wanted me, though I couldn't make out how he was a-going[120] to be any better off[121] then than what he was before, seeing I was so ignorant, and so kind of low-down[122] and ornery[123]).

Pap he hadn't been seen for more than a year, and that was comfortable for me; I didn't want to see him no more. He used to always whale[124] me when he was sober[125] and could get his hands on me; though I used to take to the woods most of the time when he was around. Well, about this time he was found in the river drownded, about twelve mile above town, so people said. They judged it was him, anyway; said this drownded man was just his size, and was ragged, and had uncommon long hair, which was all like pap; but they couldn't make nothing out of[126] the face, because it had been in the water so long it warn't much like a face at all. They said he was floating on his back in the water. They took him and buried him on the bank. But I warn't comfortable long, because I happened to think of something. I knowed mighty well that a drownded man don't float on his back, but on his face. So I knowed, then, that this warn't pap, but a woman dressed up in a man's clothes. So I was uncomfortable again. I judged the old man would turn up again by and by, though I wished he wouldn't.

We played robber now and then[127] about a month, and then I resigned[128]. All the boys did. We hadn't robbed nobody, hadn't killed any people, but only just pretended. We used to hop[129] out of the woods and go charging down on hog-drivers and women in carts taking garden stuff to market, but we never hived[130] any of them. Tom Sawyer called the hogs "ingots,"[131] and he called the turnips and stuff "julery,"[132] and we would go to the cave and powwow[133] over what we had done, and how many people we had killed and marked. But I couldn't see no profit in it. One time Tom sent a boy to run about town with a blazing[134] stick, which he called a slogan (which was the sign for the Gang to get together), and then he said he had got secret news by his spies that next day a whole parcel[135] of Spanish merchants and rich A-rabs[136] was going to camp in Cave Hollow with two hundred elephants, and six hundred camels, and over a thousand "sumter"[137]

---

120) a-going : going에 붙는 'a-'는 의미 없는 접사로 Huck의 사투리적인 말투를 나타낸다.
121) be better off : 형편이 더 좋아지다, 나아지다
122) low-down : 천한, 야비한
123) ornery : mean(비천한)
124) whale : 때리다
125) sober : 취하지 않은, 온전한, 제정신의
126) can not make nothing out of ~ : ~을 전혀 분간할 수 없다
127) now and then : sometimes, once in a while(때때로, 이따금)
128) resign : 그만두다, 사임하다
129) hop : 뛰어다니다, 깡충 뛰다
130) hive : [속어] 빼앗다, 분리시키다
131) ingot : bar of gold or silver(금덩어리나 은덩어리)
132) julery : jewelry(보석류)
133) powwow : discuss, confer(의논하다, 토론하다)
134) blazing : 불이 환하게 타는, 불이 붙은
135) parcel : company(한 떼)
136) A-rabs : Arabs
137) sumter : sumpter(짐 나르는 짐승)

mules[138]), all loaded down with di'monds[139]), and they didn't have only a guard of four hundred soldiers, and so we would lay in ambuscade[140]), as he called it, and kill the lot and scoop the things. He said we must slick up[141]) our swords and guns, and get ready. He never could go after even a turnip-cart but he must have the swords and guns all scoured up[142]) for it, though they was only lath[143]) and broomsticks, and you might scour at them till you rotted, and then they warn't worth a mouthful of ashes more than what they was before. I didn't believe we could lick[144]) such a crowd of Spaniards and A-rabs, but I wanted to see the camels and elephants, so I was on hand next day, Saturday, in the ambuscade; and when we got the word we rushed out of the woods and down the hill. But there warn't no Spaniards and A-rabs, and there warn't no camels nor no elephants[145]). It warn't anything but a Sunday-school picnic, and only a primer-class at that. We busted it up, and chased the children up the hollow; but we never got anything but some doughnuts and jam, though Ben Rogers got a rag doll, and Jo Harper got a hymn-book and a tract[146]); and then the teacher charged in, and made us drop everything and cut. I didn't see no di'monds, and I told Tom Sawyer so. He said there was loads of them there, anyway; and he said there was A-rabs there, too, and elephants and things. I said, why couldn't we see them, then? He said if I warn't so ignorant, but had read a book called *Don Quixote*[147]), I would know without asking. He said it was all done by enchantment[148]). He said there was hundreds of soldiers there, and elephants and treasure, and so on, but we had enemies which he called magicians; and they had turned the whole thing into an infant Sunday-school, just out of spite. I said, all right; then the thing for us to do was to go for[149]) the magicians. Tom Sawyer said I was a numskull[150]).

"Why," said he, "a magician could call up a lot of genies[151]), and they would hash you up[152]) like nothing before you could say Jack Robinson. They are as tall as a tree and as big around as a church."

"Well," I says, "s'pose[153]) we got some genies to help us — can't we lick the other crowd then?"

"How you going to get them?"

"I don't know. How do they get them?"

---

138) mule : 노새
139) di'monds : diamonds
140) ambuscade : ambush(매복, 기습)
141) slick up : put things in trim(가지런히 하다, 정리해 놓다, 닦다)
142) scour up : rub up(문질러 닦다, 윤이 나게 하다)
143) lath : 얇은 나뭇조각
144) lick : defeat, beat(이기다, 패배시키다)
145) there ~ elephants : there were neither camels nor elephants
146) tract : 손에 들고 다니기 쉽게 만든 종교적인 내용을 담은 휴대용 책자
147) Don Quixote : 『돈키호테』, 1605년에 출판된 세르반테스(Cervantes)의 소설
148) enchantment : 마법, 요술, 마력
149) go for : attack
150) numskull : numbskull(멍청이)
151) genie : 정령, 요정
152) hash up : 꼼짝 못하게 만들다, 굴복시키다
153) s'pose : suppose(= it)

"Why, they rub an old tin lamp or an iron ring,[154] and then the genies come tearing in, with the thunder and lightning a-ripping around and the smoke a-rolling, and everything they're told to do they up and do it. They don't think nothing of pulling a shot-tower[155] up by the roots, and belting a Sunday-school superintendent over the head with it — or any other man."

"Who makes them tear around so?"

"Why, whoever rubs the lamp or the ring. They belong to whoever rubs the lamp or the ring, and they've got to do whatever he says. If he tells them to build a palace forty miles long out of di'monds, and fill it full of chewing-gum, or whatever you want, and fetch an emperor's daughter from China for you to marry, they've got to do it — and they've got to do it before sun-up next morning, too. And more: they've got to waltz that palace around over the country wherever you want it, you understand."

"Well," says I, "I think they are a pack of flatheads[156] for not keeping the palace themselves 'stead of[157] fooling them away[158] like that. And what's more — if I was one of them I would see a man in Jericho before I would drop my business and come to him for the rubbing of an old tin lamp."

"How you talk, Huck Finn. Why, you'd have to come when he rubbed it, whether you wanted to or not."

"What! and I as high as a tree and as big as a church? All right, then; I would come; but I lay I'd make that man climb the highest tree there was in the country."

"Shucks,[159] it ain't no use to talk to you, Huck Finn. You don't seem to know anything, somehow — perfect saphead[160]."

I thought all this over for two or three days, and then I reckoned I would see if there was anything in it. I got an old tin lamp and an iron ring, and went out in the woods and rubbed and rubbed till I sweat like an Injun[161], calculating[162] to build a palace and sell it; but it warn't no use, none of the genies come. So then I judged that all that stuff was only just one of Tom Sawyer's lies. I reckoned he believed in the A-rabs and the elephants, but as for me I think different. It had all the marks of a Sunday-school.

---

154) Why ～ ring : "Aladdin or the Wonderful Lamp" 또는 Arabian Nights에서 "The Fisherman and the Genie"의 내용과 유사하다.
155) a shot-tower : 탄환 제조탑(총알을 만들 때 사용하는 높은 탑으로, 끓는 납을 물속으로 떨어뜨린 다음 식혀서 총탄으로 사용하였다)
156) flatheads : 얼간이들, 멍청이들
157) 'stead of : instead of
158) fool away : 헛되이 소비하다, 보내다
159) Shucks : 쳇! 아채(불쾌나 후회 등의 소리)
160) saphead : 바보, 얼간이
161) like an Injun : like an Indian
162) calculate : 기대하다, 예측하다

제 6 장 Henry James
– 「*Washington Square*」, 「*The Real Thing*」

「*Washington Square*」는 3인칭 전지적 작가시점으로 소설의 전반부와 후반부의 약간을 제외한 대부분이 주인공 Catherine과 Townsend의 관계에 얽힌 대화로 이루어져 있다. 적은 수의 등장인물로 구성되어 있으며 내성적이지만 자아의식이 강한 여성이 자유의지를 추구하는 과정을 그린다.
「*The Real thing*」에서는 진정한 예술은 실재가 아닌 허구를 통하여 사실을 재현한다는 아이러니를 보여준다.

출제 경향 및 수험 대책 🗐

「*Washington Square*」는 타인의 자유를 유린하려는 자(Dr. Sloper)와 자신의 자유를 지키려는 자(Catherine Sloper) 간의 심리적 갈등, 타인의 인생을 간섭하는 행위가 어떠한 결과를 만들어내는지, 그리고 등장인물들 간의 긴장감의 요소를 알아볼 필요가 있다.
「*The Real thing*」에서는 예술가의 도덕적 딜레마를 소재로 하여 예술은 사실(Reality)의 있는 그대로의 반영이 아니라 변형임을 강조하고 있음에 주목해야 한다.

제 1 절 작가의 생애

Henry James는 1843년 4월 15일에 뉴욕에서 태어났다. 그가 생후 6개월쯤 Henry의 아버지는 가족을 이끌고 유럽여행으로 2년 동안 영국과 프랑스에 머무른다. 여기에서 그의 아버지가 무서운 환각에 사로잡히기 시작하고, 겨우 두 살인 Henry도 그와 비슷한 상황에 부딪혔다. 이것은 그의 일생에 있어 첫 번째의 고통스러운 기억이 되었다. 소년 Henry는 많은 유명 인사들을 만났다. Ralph Waldo Emerson은 수시로 찾아오는 아버지의 친구였으며, Washington Irving과 Winfield Scott, William Makepeace Thackeray를 포함하여 외국에서 오는 손님이 많았다.

1855년 제네바(Geneva)의 학교에 입학한 Henry는 곧 학교생활에 실망하게 되고, Henry의 가족은 파리(Paris)를 거쳐 런던(London)으로 향한다. 그러나 1856년 여름, 가족은 또다시 파리로 건너가고, 아이들은 그곳에서 가정교사의 교육을 받으며 명승지를 찾아다녔다. 이후 아버지는 1858년 가족을 이끌고 미국으로 돌아가 로드아일랜드(Rhode Island)주 뉴포트(Newport)에 자리 잡았다. 이곳에서 15살의 Henry는 화가인 John La Farge와 훗날 비평가이자 번역가가 된 Thomas Sergeant Perry와 친구가 되었다. Henry는 이러한 친구들과의 교류로 화실과 친숙해져 그의 소설에는 그림에 관한 내용이 많이 나오게 된다. Perry는 Henry가 작가가 되고 싶다는 열의에 가득 차 있는 것을 알고 연극과 소설을 번역하도록 권유했다.

1861년 봄, 남북전쟁이 일어나 뉴잉글랜드(New England)의 많은 젊은이들이 한꺼번에 자원하여 전쟁에 참여했으나, 화재로 인하여 부상을 당했던 Henry는 그 부상과 후유증으로 북군에 참가하지 않았다. Henry는 1862년에 하버드 법과대학에 입학하였으나 그는 이곳에서 단편 「*A Tragedy of Error*」(1864)를 『*Continental Monthly*』에 익명으로 발표하였다.

Henry James는 1869년 처음으로 혼자 유럽여행을 떠날 때까지 아직 많은 책을 내놓지는 못하였으나 계속해서 단편소설과 평문을 『*The Nation*』에 발표하였다. 이 무렵 그는 런던으로 건너가 Minny Temple의 권유로 William Morris, Dante Gabriel Rossetti, John Ruskin, 그리고 George Eliot을 만났다. 그해 5월 Henry는 로마(Rome)에 가는데, 이곳에서 Minny는 1870년 24세의 나이로 폐결핵으로 인해 사망하고 만다. 그녀의 죽음은 훗날 Henry가 '우리 청춘의 종언'(the end of our youth)이라고 회상했듯 그에게 매우 중요한 사건이었다.

뉴잉글랜드(New England)의 고향으로 돌아온 Henry는 작가로서의 수련과정을 계속하였다. 『*Atlantic Monthly*』에 첫 번째 장편소설인 「*Watch and Ward*」(1871)를 연재하면서 외국에 나가 있는 미국인의 이야기를 다룬 이른바 'International Theme'(국제 주제)을 개발하기 시작하였다. 미국의 여러 잡지에 글을 쓰면서 Henry는 다시 로마로 돌아갔다. 여기서 그는 승마를 취미로 삼아 여러 미국 여인들과 함께 시골길에서 말달리기를 즐겼다. 이들 가운데 그에게 특별히 영향을 미친 Elizabeth Boott는 Henry의 초기 걸작인 「*The Portrait of a Lady*」(1881)의 여주인공으로 등장한다.

고국에서 살아야 한다는 의무감에 미국으로 귀국한 Henry는 최초의 장편소설 「*Roderick Hudson*」(1875)을 뉴욕에서 탈고하였으나 그는 유럽에 대한 그리움을 떨칠 수 없었다. 그리하여 22살의 청년 Henry는 1875년 파리에 정착하여 『*Atlantic Monthly*』로부터 선불로 원고료를 받고, 『*New York Tribune*』으로부터 여행기 집필의 사례금도 받아 여유롭게 영국여행을 한다. 이때부터 Henry James는 작가로서 명성을 떨치기 시작하였다. 이 무렵 파리에서 Henry가 세계적인 대작가의 한 사람으로 존경하던 Ivan Turgenev를 만난다. 그는 Henry를 프랑스의 선구적인 작가들에게 소개시켜주었고, Henry는 많은 문인들과 친분을 쌓지만 결국 그들이 문학의 한계와 도덕보다 문체를 선호하는 것에 실망한다. 파리에서의 문학적인 교류에도 불구하고 자신이 영원한 이방인이라는 것을 깨달은 Henry는 1876년 미련 없이 다시 영국으로 건너간다. 영국에서 그는 보다 더 지체 높은 인사들과 교제하게 된다.

1882년 1월 초에 그가 워싱턴(Washington D. C.)을 방문했을 때 어머니의 병세가 위독해져 돌아가셨고, 5월에 런던으로 돌아왔다가 귀국하던 중 대서양을 횡단하고 있던 뉴욕행 여객선에서 그의 아버지의 죽음을 맞이한다. 1883년 Henry가 유럽으로 돌아왔을 때 또다시 죽음이 그에게 충격을 주었다. 동생 Wilkinson이 죽고 그가 존경하던 Turgenev도 죽었다. 이때부터 다음 해에 걸쳐 런던의 Macmillan Company는 그의 14권짜리의 전집을 출판하였다.

1885년 고국과의 인연이 끊어졌다고 생각한 Henry는 켄싱턴(Kensington)의 4층 건물에 장기 임대계약을 했다. 그 해에 「*The Bostonians*」(1885~1886)와 「*The Princess Casamassima*」(1885~1886)가 출판되었다. 이때에 Henry는 「*The Art of Fiction*」(1884)에서 의식적으로 도덕적인 목적을 가지고 작품을 써야 한다는 Walter Besent의 주장에 반대의 글을 남기기도 하였다.

Henry가 연극에 손을 대게 된 것은 1890년 배우 Edward Compton이 Henry에게 「*The American*」(1876~1877)의 각색을 제안하고 250파운드를 선불로 주었기 때문이다. 이 연극은 겨우 70일간 상연되어 돈을 벌지는 못하였고, Henry는 여전히 연극에서 성공하기를 바라며 1893년 「*Guy Domville*」을 집필하였으나 1895년까지 이것은 공연되지 못하였다. 1895년 Henry는 「*Guy Domville*」을 결국 공연하게 되었으나 이 연극은 실패작이었다. 몇몇 평론가의 호평에도 불구하고 겨우 한 달 만에 연극은 막을 내렸다. 「*Guy Domville*」의 비참한 실패 후에 Henry는 자괴적인 상황에 빠져들고 심한 상처를 입어 끝없이 의기소침해지고 말았다.

그는 런던 교외에 보금자리를 가져야겠다고 생각하여 플레이든(Playden)의 역사적인 분위기를 선택하지만 여름에 라이(Rye) 근처로 이사한다. 그곳이 바로 램 하우스(Lamb House)인데, 그는 다음 해에 그 집을 사서 여생을 이곳에서 보냈다.

20세기로 들어서며 Henry는 자신이 살고 있는 지역의 친숙한 인사가 되었다. 자전거를 타고 시골길을 달리는 모습이 자주 목격되었으며 많은 문학 동호인들과의 교제도 빈번하였다. 그의 후기 3대 걸작인 「The Wings of the Dove」(1902)와 「The Golden Bowl」(1904), 「The Ambassadors」(1903)도 이 시기에 쓰였다. 또한 「The Beast in the Jungle」(1903)도 이때에 쓰인 단편소설이다.

1904년 8월, 20년 만에 미국을 다시 찾은 Henry는 신문의 호평을 받는 인물이 되어 미국의 학술원 American Academy of Arts and Letters 회원으로서 여러 곳에서 강연을 하여 여행 경비를 벌기도 했다. 제1차 세계대전이 일어날 때 Henry의 램 하우스 집이 해변에 위치하고 있었기 때문에 그는 끊임없는 감시에 시달려야 했고, 외출 시에는 경찰에 신고해야만 했다. 그것이 그에게는 매우 성가신 일이어서 1915년 7월 28일, 그는 조지 5세 (King George V)에게 선서를 하고 영국 시민이 되기로 결정한다. 전쟁에 시달리는 사람들을 열심히 도와주던 그는 1915년 12월 2일 칼라인 맨션(Carlyle Mansion)의 집에서 뇌출혈로 쓰러진다. 수상이 된 Edward Marsh가 Henry에게 공로훈장을 수여하자고 제안하여 다음 해 1월 1일에 칙명을 받아 병상의 Henry에게 훈장이 수여되었다. 의식을 회복한 Henry는 "수줍은 내 얼굴을 보이지 않게 불을 꺼주시오."라고 말했다고 전해진다. 얼마간의 시간이 지나자 다시 정신이 혼미해진 Henry는 1916년 2월 2일 저녁까지 삶을 이어 갔다. 그가 죽은 후 웨스트민스터 사원(Westminster Abbey)에 시신을 안치하자는 말이 나왔으나, 그의 아내와 딸 Peggy에 의해서 첼시(Chelsea)의 교회에서 장례식이 마련되었고 본인의 희망대로 화장을 한 후 유골을 미국으로 가져갔다.

Henry James의 작가로서의 명성은 당시에 그렇게 높지 않았다. 그러나 제2차 세계대전으로 세상이 둘로 갈라진 뒤, 복잡한 현대 생활에 대한 그의 감각이 복잡하고 깊이 있는 것으로 재음미되기 시작하였다. Henry James의 강력한 비전이 인식되면서 그는 최고의 작가 위치를 얻게 되었다.

> **더 알아두기**
>
> **Henry James의 주요작품**
> - 「Roderick Hudson」(1875)
> - 「The American」(1877)
> - 「Daisy Miller」(1878)
> - 「Washington Square」(1880)
> - 「The Portrait of a Lady」(1881)
> - 「The Bostonians」(1886)
> - 「What Maisie Knew」(1897)
> - 「The Turn of Screw」(1898)
> - 「The Wings of the Dove」(1902)
> - 「The Ambassadors」(1903)
> - 「The Golden Bowl」(1904)

제 **2** 절 **작품 세계**

1 Henry James의 소설

Henry James는 반세기가 넘는 동안 작품 활동을 하며 소설·연극·평론·서평·기행문·전기 등 다양한 문학 작품을 내놓았다. 그는 비평가들에 의해 흔히 구분되는 초기·중기·후기의 발전과정에서 136편의 장·단편소설과 300여 편의 문학 에세이를 집필하였다. 그중 가장 큰 성공을 거둔 것은 소설분야이다. Henry James는 소설의 형식과 주제에 대한 실험과 개발을 멈추지 않았다. 그는 새로운 소설 쓰기의 기법에 대하여 강조하였다. 그는 객관적 시점, 장면의 극화, 원근법, 포괄과 배제, 책략과 이완, 구성과 동기 등과 같은 소설의 미학에 특히 관심을 기울이며 실천함으로써 현대 소설 기법의 발전에 많은 공헌을 했다. 그러나 그의 미학적 이론은 그의 자유로운 상상의 흐름을 억제하고, 서술 기교는 스토리를 장황하게 하여 내용이 형식에 희생되었다는 비난을 듣기도 한다. Henry James의 문장은 다소 장황하고 간접적이며 암시적이어서 그의 작품을 난해하고 애매하게 만들었다. 그의 이러한 기교적인 문장은 작품의 진의를 이해하기 어렵게 하는 면이 있다.

2 작품의 특징 중요 ★★★

(1) 심리적 사실주의(Psychological Realism)

Henry James는 소설의 플롯에서 나타나는 외부적인 현상보다는 인물들의 의식세계 속에 나타나는 심리상태나 정서에 더 중점을 두는 '심리적 사실주의' 기법을 창시한 현대소설의 선구자이다. 그는 인간 행동의 외면세계만을 단순히 묘사하는 데 중점을 두었던 초기의 사실주의(realism)에서 벗어나 작중인물들의 행동이 유발되는 내면의 심리세계를 분석하고 전개하는 데 역점을 두는 '의식의 흐름'(stream of consciousness) 기법을 개척했다.

(2) 국제적인 주제(International theme)와 도덕성

그의 소설에는 지배적인 두 가지 주제가 있다. 하나는 미국과 유럽, 그리고 미국인과 유럽인 사이의 복잡하고 미묘한 관계를 대비시키는 국제 주제이며, 다른 하나는 이 국제 주제와 깊은 관련성을 가진 도덕성에 대한 주제이다.

그가 소설에서 표현하는 도덕성은 일반적인 도덕성의 결핍이나 부정 같은 악의 요소만이 아니라 국제 상황에 처한 미국인의 도덕적 갈등을 제시하는 Henry James 소설 특유의 주제이다. 국제적인 주제는 단순한 풍습과 성격의 대조 효과에 머물지 않았다. 국제 상황의 대조 효과와 도덕적 갈등이 그의 소설에 중점적으로 표현된다. 이러한 소재와 주제는 그의 초기 소설부터 후기 소설에 이르기까지 그 발전 과정을 이해하는 데 큰 역할을 한다. 그러나 이 두 가지 주제는 오랫동안 비평가들에게 논란의 대상이 되어 왔는데, Henry James 소설에서 나타난 도덕의 부재, 도덕률의 불일치, 또는 작가의 도덕의식과 도덕적 통찰력의 부족이 비평가들에 의하여 자주 거론되는 문제이다. 실제로 그는 작품 속에서 확연한 흑백판정에 의한 도덕 교훈의 제시를 거부하고 그의 지론이라고 할 수 있는 '무의식적인 도덕성'을 작품 속에 교묘히 넣는 고도의 소설기법을 사용하고 있다. 즉, 그는 등장인물들의 행위를 자기 자신의 기준과 취향에 따라 설명하거나 비평하지 않는다. 인물들에게 자신의 견해를 강요하지 않고 도덕적 중립의 태도를 고수하기 때문에 그의 작가적 의도에 대한 애매함의 문제까지 제기되어 논란을 거듭하게 되었다.

3 작품의 발전 과정

(1) 초기(1871~1879)

영국과 프랑스의 사실주의 전통을 이어 프랑스의 중편소설(nouvelle)을 즐겨 사용하면서도 국제적 비극을 많이 취급하였다. 일종의 아름다운 서정시로 불리는 「*Daisy Miller*」가 그 대표적인 작품으로서 미국인의 애독서가 되었고, 인기를 끌었던 「*The Portrait of a Lady*」와 같은 작품에서는 미국의 도덕적 우월성을 강조하고 있다. 통속적인 장편소설인 「*Roderick Hudson*」과 「*The American*」에서도 국제 간의 비극을 그리고 있다.

(2) 중기(1891~1900)

작품 활동 중기에 접어든 Henry James는 초기에 이룩한 명성을 유지하기 위해 여러 자료를 수집하고 국제적 관계의 화제를 이용하여 「*The Princess Casamassima*」(1885~1886)와 같은 사회연구의 작품을 쓰는가 하면 문예와 미술 등 심미주의적인 작품인 「*The Spoils of Poynton*」(1897), 「*The Tragic Muse*」(1889~1890)를 발표하였다. 그러나 불행하게도 이 시기에 5년에 걸쳐 시도한 극작 활동의 실패는 그를 주로 단편소설 집필에 치중하게 했고, 다른 한편으로는 그의 소설에 극적 요소, 대칭 구조 등의 기법적인 발전을 가져다주었다. 이 무렵부터 그의 문장이 너무 까다롭고 어려워져 난해한 작가로 규정되기도 했지만 「*The Altar of the Dead*」(1895)와 같은 작품에서 볼 수 있는 그의 수려한 문체는 매혹적이다.

(3) 후기(1900~1916)

Henry James는 후기에 이르러 다시 초기의 국제 주제로 돌아가면서 인물의 일거수일투족에 심리적 해부를 시도하고 자신의 작품을 형이상학적인 심리소설로 상향시켰다. 그는 자신이 밝혀 온 문학이론과 자기가 지니고 있는 작가적인 장점과 재능을 살려 예술가로서의 참모습을 보이기 시작했다. 즉, 등장인물 가운데 한 사람을 선택하여 그 중심인물의 눈을 통해 사건의 핵심에 접근하고 진상을 여실하게 묘사하며 비판하도록 하였다. 이것을 Henry는 '저술상의 중심'(a compositional center) 또는 '예리한 중심적 의식'(an acute central consciousness)라고 칭했다. 이런 이유로 그의 후기의 3대 걸작인 「*The Wings of the Dove*」와 「*The Golden Bowl*」, 「*The Ambassadors*」는 그의 작가적 실체를 규명함에 있어서 반드시 읽어야 할 작품들이다.

제 **3** 절 「*Washington Square*」

1 줄거리

이 작품의 주인공인 Catherine Sloper는 뉴욕에서 의사로서 성공한 아버지인 Dr. Sloper의 외동딸이지만, 그녀의 어머니는 그녀가 태어난 지 일주일 만에 세상을 떠나고 만다. Catherine은 그녀의 어머니와는 달리 건강하게는 자랐지만, 그녀의 아버지가 바라는 지적이고 분별력 있는 처녀로는 자라지 못한다. 아버지는 딸이 착한 사람이 되기보다는 영리한 사람이 되기를 기대했다. 다른 사람들에게 딸 자랑을 하는 즐거움도 누리고 싶었지만 자신의 자존심을 충족시키지 못하고 우유부단하게 자라는 딸에 대해 별다른 기대를 하지 않으면서 지냈다. 시간이 흘러 어느덧 스물한 살의 숙녀가 된 Catherine은 자신의 사촌 여동생의 약혼 연회에서, 타고난 말솜씨를 가지고 있으며 조각상 같이 잘생긴 왕자와 같은 용모를 지닌 데다 영리하기까지 한 Morris Townsend라는 청년과 만나게 된다. 순진한 Catherine은 첫눈에 그에게 마음을 빼앗겨 버리지만, 그녀의 아버지는 Morris가 볼품없는 자신의 딸을 진심으로 사랑하기보다는 자신이 죽은 후에 딸이 물려받을 유산을 목적으로 결혼을 하려는 온전치 못한 사람으로 그를 판단한다. 하지만 Catherine은 아버지의 반대를 무릅쓰고 Washington Square로 Morris의 방문을 계속 허용한다. 급기야 둘이 약혼식까지 치르자, Dr. Sloper는 두 사람을 떼어 놓기 위해 딸과 함께 유럽으로 여행을 떠난다. 심지어 그는 여행이 끝나갈 무렵 알프스(Alps) 산맥 근처에서 딸에게 겁을 주면서까지 Morris와의 결혼을 포기할 것을 설득하지만 Morris에 대한 Catherine의 애정은 식지 않는다. 유럽에서 돌아와 Morris와 결혼하기만을 고대하던 Catherine은 Morris에게 배신을 당한다. 그는 Catherine이 여행 중 자신과의 결혼을 아버지에게 설득시키지 못했음을 알고 유산 상속의 희망이 사라지자 미련 없이 그녀를 떠나버린 것이다.

Morris의 배신 후 Catherine은 영원히 지울 수 없는 마음의 상처를 지닌 채 살아간다. 그녀는 그 후 몇 번 결혼을 할 기회를 가졌지만 모두 거절하고 독신으로 늙어간다. 세월이 흘러 Dr. Sloper가 예순 여덟이 되던 해에 그는 자신의 딸이 계속 결혼하지 않고 독신으로 늙어가는 이유가 Morris를 잊지 못해서라고 생각하고 자신이 죽은 후에도 Morris와 결혼하지 말 것을 딸에게 간곡히 부탁한다. 그러나 이미 중년의 나이가 된 Catherine은 이제 어느 누구도 그녀의 마음을 좌지우지하지 못할 정도로 자신의 중심을 지니고 있었고 동시에 자신의 아버지에 대한 존경심과 두려움도 없어졌기 때문에 그녀는 아버지의 제안을 단호히 거절한다. Dr. Sloper는 일흔이 되던 해에 앓던 병으로 사망하는데, 유언장에 딸에게 줄 상속분을 대폭 줄여놓는다. 그렇게 그가 죽은 후 몇 해가 지난 어느 초가을 예전처럼 반듯하지는 않지만 대머리에 광택이 나는 턱수염을 기르고 나타난 Morris가 갑자기 Catherine에게 다시 구혼한다. 그러나 Catherine이 그에게 이제 와서 불필요한 행동을 하고 있다고 말하고 Morris는 조용히 물러난다.

2 작품의 주제

(1) 타인의 인생을 간섭하는 행위는 필연적으로 가해자와 희생자를 만들어냄

(2) 자유의지의 추구에 따르는 파문과 궁극적인 승리

(3) 타인의 자유를 유린하려는 재(Dr. Sloper)와 자신의 자유를 지키려는 재(Catherine Sloper) 간의 심리적 갈등

(4) 옳지 못한 이성관(異性觀) 제시

진정한 사랑만이 행복하고 축복받는 결혼에 이를 수 있는 것이다.

3 등장인물

(1) Catherine Sloper

Dr. Austin Sloper의 외동딸로 내성적이지만 자아의식이 강한 여성이다. 결혼 적령기에 자신의 큰 고모인 Mrs. Almond의 집에서 열린 그녀의 딸 Marian의 약혼식 자리에서 젊고 똑똑한데다가 수려한 외모를 겸비한 청년 Morris를 만난다. 그러나 아버지의 방해와 청년의 변심으로 Morris와 결혼에 이르지 못한다. 자아를 회복하고 어머니의 유산으로 자선사업을 하며 아버지의 죽음 후에는 Washington Square의 빈집을 작은 고모인 Mrs. Penniman과 지키며 살아간다.

(2) Dr. Austin Sloper

뉴욕의 존경받는 의사이다. 돈 많은 아내와 사별한 후 외동딸 Catherine을 키우며 살아간다. 부녀간의 따뜻한 정보다는 냉철한 관찰자이자 지배자로 딸에게 군림하며 자신의 가치관을 자식에게 강요한다.

(3) Morris Townsend

키가 크고 미남이며 언변이 뛰어나지만 인성이나 직업에 있어서는 부족한 인물이다. 우아한 옷차림으로 치장한 순진한 Catherine에게 결혼을 목적으로 접근하지만 그녀가 아버지와의 유럽 여행 동안 부친을 설득하는 데 실패했다는 사실을 알고 유산 상속의 희망이 없어지자 미련 없이 그녀를 떠난다. Morris의 배신은 Catherine에게 지울 수 없는 상처가 된다. 40대의 나이가 되어 다시 나타나 청혼을 하지만 Catherine에게 거절당한다.

(4) Catherine Harrington(Mrs. Sloper)

Dr. Austin Sloper의 아내이다. 첫째 아들은 세 살 때 죽고, 그 후 딸인 Catherine을 낳지만 그녀를 낳은 지 일주일 만에 많은 유산을 남기고 젊은 나이에 갑자기 사망한다.

(5) Mrs. (Elizabeth) Almond

Dr. Sloper의 큰 여동생이자 Catherine Sloper의 큰 고모이다.

(6) Mrs. (Lavinia) Penniman

Dr. Sloper의 작은 여동생이자 Catherine Sloper의 작은 고모이다. 가난한 목사인 남편과 사별한 후

궁핍하게 살아가던 중 조카인 Catherine의 교육을 맡겠다는 명목으로 오빠인 Dr. Sloper의 집인 Washington Square에 살게 된다. Catherine을 지적이고 영리하게 길러야 한다는 Dr. Sloper의 주장과 달리 선량하게 기르는 것이 우선이라고 주장한다.

4 작품의 구조(Plot)와 시점 및 기법

(1) 구조와 시점

본 작품은 3인칭 전지적 작가시점이다. 총 35장으로 소설의 전반부와 후반부의 약간을 제외한 대부분이 주인공 Catherine과 Townsend의 관계에 얽힌 대화로 이루어져 있어 다소 지루함을 준다.

(2) 기법

① 상징

㉠ 작품에서 칼은 희생 또는 살해를 상징한다.

[예]

- 19장 : "Don't you wish also by chance to murder your child?"
- 24장 : "We have fattened the sheep for him before he kills it!"
- 30장 : "Dear Morris, you are killing me!"

㉡ 집은 신분, 명예, 지위를 상징한다.

[예]

- 3장 : "This structure, and many of its neighbours, which it exactly resembles, ... remain to this day very solid and honourable dwellings."
- 14장 : Mrs. Montgomery's "magnified babyhouse"
- 16장 : "the closed portal of happiness"/ "a devilish comfortable house"

② 기법

멜로드라마(Melodrama)와 같은 플롯과 인물 구성이라고 볼 수 있다. 특히 아버지가 딸과 구혼자의 결혼을 방해하는 장면은 심리적 갈등을 중심으로 서술되고 있다.

5 Text

Chapter 1

DURING a portion[1] of the first half of the present century, and more particularly during the latter part of it, there flourished[2] and practised in the city of New York a physician who enjoyed perhaps

---

1) portion : 일부, 몫
2) flourish : 번성하다, 번창하다

an exceptional share of the consideration which, in the United States, has always been bestowed upon[3] distinguished members of the medical profession. This profession in America has constantly[4] been held in honor, and more successfully than elsewhere has put forward a claim to the epithet of 'liberal.' In a country in which, to play a social part, you must either earn your income or make believe that you earn it, the healing art has appeared in a high degree to combine two recognized sources of credit. It belongs to the realm of the practical, which in the United States is a great recommendation; and it is touched by the light of science — a merit appreciated in a community in which the love of knowledge has not always been accompanied by leisure and opportunity.

It was an element in Doctor Sloper's reputation[5] that his learning and his skill were very evenly balanced; he was what you might call a scholarly doctor, and yet there was nothing abstract in his remedies — he always ordered you to take something. Though he was felt to be extremely thorough, he was not uncomfortably theoretic; and if he sometimes explained matters rather more minutely than might seem of use to the patient, he never went so far (like some practitioners one had heard of) as to trust to the explanation alone, but always left behind him an inscrutable prescription. There were some doctors that left the prescription without offering any explanation at all; and he did not belong to that class either, which was after all the most vulgar. It will be seen that I am describing a clever man: and this is really the reason why Doctor Sloper had become a local celebrity.

At the time at which we are chiefly concerned with him he was some fifty years of age, and his popularity was at its height. He was very witty, and he passed in the best society of New York for a man of the world — which, indeed, he was, in a very sufficient[6] degree. I hasten to add, to anticipate possible misconception, that he was not the least of a charlatan[7]. He was a thoroughly honest man — honest in a degree of which he had perhaps lacked the opportunity to give the complete measure; and, putting aside the great goo[i-nature of the circle in which he practised, which was rather fond of boasting that it possessed the 'brightest' doctor in the country, he daily justified his claim to the talents attributed to him by the popular voice. He was an observer, even a philosopher, and to be bright was so natural to him, and (as the popular voice said) came so easily, that he never aimed at mere effect, and had none of the little tricks and pretensions of second-rate reputations. It must be confessed that fortune had favored him, and that he had found the path to prosperity very soft to his tread. He had married, at the age of twenty-seven, for love, a very charming girl, Miss Catherine Harrington, of New York, who, in addition to her charms, had brought him a solid dowry[8]. Mrs. Sloper was amiable[9], graceful, accomplished, elegant, and in 1820 she had been one of the pretty girls of the small but promising[10] capital[11] which clustered about the

---

3) bestow upon : (시간, 생각 등을) 바치다, 사용하다
4) constantly : 항상, 계속해서
5) reputation : 명성
6) sufficient : 충분한
7) charlatan : 돌팔이, 사기꾼
8) dowry : (신부의) 지참금
9) amiable : 쾌활한, 상냥한
10) promising : 전도유망한
11) capital : 자본가

Battery and overlooked the Bay, and of which the uppermost boundary was indicated by the grassy waysides of Canal Street. Even at the age of twenty-seven Austin Sloper had made his mark sufficiently to mitigate[12] the anomaly of his having been chosen among a dozen suitors[13] by a young woman of high fashion, who had ten thousand dollars of income and the most charming eyes in the island of Manhattan. These eyes, and some of their accompaniments, were for about five years a source of extreme satisfaction to the young physician, who was both a devoted and a very happy husband.

The fact of his having married a rich woman made no difference in the line he had traced for himself, and he cultivated his profession with as definite a purpose as if[14] he still had no other resources than his fraction of the modest patrimony which, on his father's death, he had shared with his brothers and sisters. This purpose had not been preponderantly to make money — it had been rather to learn something and to do something. To learn something interesting, and to do something useful — this was, roughly speaking, the programme he had sketched, and of which the accident of his wife having an income appeared to him in no degree to modify the validity. He was fond of his practice, and of exercising a skill of which he was agreeably conscious, and it was so patent a truth that if he were not a doctor there was nothing else he could be, that a doctor he persisted in being, in the best possible conditions. Of course his easy domestic situation saved him a good deal of drudgery, and his wife's affiliation to the 'best people' brought him a good many of those patients whose symptoms are, if not more interesting in themselves than those of the lower orders, at least more consistently displayed. He desired experience, and in the course of twenty years he got a great deal. It must be added that it came to him in some forms which, whatever might have been their intrinsic value, made it the reverse of welcome. His first child, a little boy of extraordinary promise, as the Doctor, who was not addicted to easy enthusiasm[15], firmly believed[16], died at three years of age, in spite of everything that the mother's tenderness and the father's science could invent to save him. Two years later Mrs Sloper gave birth to a second infant — an infant of a sex which rendered the poor child, to the Doctor's sense, an inadequate[17] substitute for his lamented[18] first-born, of whom he had promised himself to make an admirable man. The little girl was a disappointment; but this was not the worst. A week after her birth the young mother, who, as the phrase is, had been doing well, suddenly betrayed alarming symptoms, and before another week had elapsed Austin Sloper was a widower.

For a man whose trade[19] was to keep people alive he had certainly done poorly in his own family; and a bright doctor who within three years loses his wife and his little boy should perhaps

---

12) mitigate : 완화하다, 누그러뜨리다
13) suitor : 소송인, 구혼자
14) as if : 마치 ~이었던 것처럼(가정법 과거완료)
15) enthusiasm : 열광, 열의, 열중, 열중시키는 것
16) firmly believed : 확고하게 믿는
17) inadequate : 불충분한, 부족한
18) lamented : 애석한, 애도를 받는
19) trade : 직업

be prepared to see either his skill or his affection impugned. Our friend, however, escaped criticism; that is, he escaped all criticism but his own, which was much the most competent and most formidable. He walked under the weight of this very private censure for the rest of his days, and bore forever the scars of a castigation[20] to which the strongest hand he knew had treated him on the night that followed his wife's death. The world, which, as I have said, appreciated him, pitied him too much to be ironical; his misfortune made him more interesting, and even helped him to be the fashion. It was observed that even medical families cannot escape the more insidious forms of disease, and that, after all, Doctor Sloper had lost other patients beside the two I have mentioned; which constituted an honorable precedent[21]. His little girl remained to him; and though she was not what he had desired, he proposed to himself to make the best of her. He had on hand a stock of unexpended authority, by which the child, in its early years, profited largely. She had been named, as a matter of course, after her poor mother, and even in her most diminutive babyhood[22] the Doctor never called her anything but Catherine. She grew up a very robust and healthy child, and her father, as he looked at her, often said to himself that, such as she was, he at least need have no fear of losing her. I say 'such as she was,' because, to tell the truth[23] — But this is a truth of which I will defer the telling.

Chapter 2

WHEN the child was about ten years old, he invited his sister, Mrs. Penniman, to come and stay with him. The Miss Slopers had been but two in number, and both of them had married early in life. The younger, Mrs. Almond by name, was the wife of a prosperous, merchant and the mother of a blooming family. She bloomed herself, indeed, and was a comely[24], comfortable, reasonable woman, and a favorite with her clever brother, who, in the matter of women, even when they were nearly related to him, was a man of distinct preferences. He preferred Mrs Almond to his sister Lavinia, who had married a poor clergyman[25], of a sickly constitution[26] and a flowery style of eloquence[27], and then, at the age of thirty-three, had been left a widow — without children, without fortune — with nothing but the memory of Mr. Penniman's flowers of speech, a certain vague aroma of which hovered about[28] her own conversation. Nevertheless, he had offered her a home under his own roof, which Lavinia accepted with the alacrity[29] of a woman who had spent the ten years of

---

20) castigation : 징계, 혹평
21) precedent : 종례, 관례
22) babyhood : 유년기
23) to tell the truth : 사실을 말하자면
24) comely : (여자가) 얼굴이 잘생긴, 미모의
25) clergyman : 성직자
26) constitution : 체질, 체격, 설립
27) flowery style of eloquence : 현란한 화술
28) hover about : 공중을 맴돌다, 배회하다
29) alacrity : 민첩함, 활발함

her married life in the town of Poughkeepsie. The Doctor had not proposed to Mrs. Penniman to come and live with him indefinitely; he had suggested that she should make an asylum[30] of his house while she looked about for unfurnished[31] lodgings. It is uncertain whether Mrs. Penniman ever instituted a search for unfurnished lodgings, but it is beyond dispute that she never found them. She settled herself with her brother and never went away, and, when Catherine was twenty years old, her Aunt Lavinia was still one of the most striking features of her immediate *entourage*[32]. Mrs. Penniman's own account of the matter was that she had remained to take charge of her niece's education. She had given this account, at least, to every one but the Doctor, who never asked for explanations which he could entertain himself any day with inventing. Mrs. Penniman, moreover, though she had a good deal of a certain sort of artificial assurance, shrunk, for indefinable reasons, from presenting herself to her brother as a fountain of instruction. She had not a high sense of humor, but she had enough to prevent her from making this mistake; and her brother, on his side, had enough to excuse her, in her situation, for laying him under contribution during a considerable part of a lifetime. He therefore assented tacitly to the proposition which Mrs. Penniman had tacitly laid down, that it was of importance that the poor motherless girl should have a brilliant woman near her. His assent could only be tacit[33], for he had never been dazzled by his sister's intellectual lustre[34]. Save when he fell in love with Catherine Harrington, he had never been dazzled, indeed, by any feminine characteristics whatever; and though he was to a certain extent what is called a ladies' doctor, his private opinion of the more complicated sex was not exalted. He regarded[35] its complications as more curious than edifying, and he had an idea of the beauty of reason, which was, on the whole[36], meagerly gratified by what he observed in his female patients. His wife had been a reasonable woman, but she was a bright exception; among several things that he was sure of, this was perhaps the principal. Such a conviction, of course, did little either to mitigate[37] or to abbreviate his widowhood; and it set a limit to his recognition, at the best, of Catherine's possibilities and of Mrs. Penniman's ministrations[38]. He nevertheless, at the end of six months, accepted his sister's permanent presence[39] as an accomplished fact, and as Catherine grew older, perceived that[40] there were in effect good reasons why she should have a companion of her own imperfect sex. He was extremely polite to Lavinia, scrupulously[41], formally polite; and she had never seen him in anger but once in her life, when he lost his temper in a theological discussion with her late husband. With her he never discussed theology nor, indeed, discussed anything; he

---

30) asylum : 피난지
31) unfurnished : (가구 등이) 갖추어지지 않은
32) entourage : 측근
33) tacit : 암묵적인, 무언의
34) lustre(luster) : 빛
35) regard A as B : A를 B로 간주하다
36) on the whole : 대체적으로
37) mitigate : 완화하다, 누그러뜨리다
38) ministration : 목사의 직무, 봉사, 돌보기
39) presence : 존재, 실존
40) perceive that ~ : ~할 것임을 알다
41) scrupulously : 양심적인, 꼼꼼한, 세심한

contented himself with making known, very distinctly, in the form of a lucid ultimatum, his wishes with regard to Catherine.

Once, when the girl was about twelve years old, he had said to her 'Try and make a clever woman of her, Lavinia; I should like her to be a clever woman.'

Mrs. Penniman, at this, looked thoughtful a moment. "My dear Austin," she then inquired, "do you think it is better to be clever than to be good?"

"Good for what?" asked the Doctor. "You are good for nothing[42] unless you are clever."

From this assertion Mrs. Penniman saw no reason to dissent; she possibly reflected that her own great use in the world was owing to her aptitude for many things.

"Of course I wish Catherine to be good," the Doctor said next day; "but she won't be any the less virtuous[43] for not being a fool. I am not afraid of her being wicked; she will never have the salt of malice in her character. She is 'as good as good bread,' as the French say; but six years hence[44] I don't want to have to compare her to good bread-and-butter."

"Are you afraid she will be insipid? My dear brother, it is I who supply the butter; so you needn't fear!" said Mrs. Penniman, who had taken in hand the child's 'accomplishments,' overlooking her at the piano, where Catherine displayed a certain talent, and going with her to the dancing-class, where it must be confessed that she made but a modest figure.

Mrs. Penniman was a tall, thin, fair, rather faded woman, with a perfectly amiable disposition, a high standard of gentility, a taste for light literature, and a certain foolish indirectness and obliquity of character. She was romantic; she was sentimental; she had a passion for little secrets and mysteries — a very innocent passion, for her secrets had hitherto[45] always been as unpractical as addled[46] eggs. She was not absolutely veracious; but this defect was of no great consequence, for she had never had anything to conceal. She would have liked to have a lover, and to correspond with him under an assumed name, in letters left at a shop. I am bound to say that her imagination never carried the intimacy further than this. Mrs. Penniman had never had a lover, but her brother, who was very shrewd, understood her turn of mind. "When Catherine is about seventeen," he said to himself, "Lavinia will try and persuade her that some young man with a mustache is in love with her. It will be quite untrue; no young man, with a mustache or without, will ever be in love with Catherine. But Lavinia will take it up, and talk to her about it; perhaps even, if her taste for clandestine operations doesn't prevail with her, she will talk to me about it. Catherine won't see it, and won't believe it, fortunately for her peace of mind; poor Catherine isn't romantic."

She was a healthy, well-grown child, without a trace of her mother's beauty. She was not ugly; she had simply a plain, dull, gentle countenance[47]. The most that had ever been said for her was that she had a 'nice' face; and, though she was an heiress, no one had ever thought of regarding

---

42) for nothing : 부질없는
43) virtuous : 덕이 높은
44) six years hence : 앞으로 6년 후에
45) hitherto : 지금까지(는)
46) addled : 상한, 부패한
47) countenance : 표정, 안색

her as a belle. Her father's opinion of her moral purity was abundantly justified; she was excellently, imperturbably good; affectionate, docile, obedient, and much addicted to speaking the truth. In her younger years she was a good deal of a romp, and, though it is an awkward confession to make about one's heroine, I must add that she was something of a glutton[48]. She never, that I know of, stole raisins out of the pantry; but she devoted her pocket-money to the purchase of cream-cakes. As regards this, however, a critical attitude would be inconsistent with a candid reference to the early annals of any biographer[49]. Catherine was decidedly not clever; she was not quick with her book, nor, indeed, with anything else. She was not abnormally deficient, and she mustered[50] learning enough to acquit herself respectably in conversation with her contemporaries — among whom it must be avowed[51], however, that she occupied a secondary place. It is well known that in New York it is possible for a young girl to occupy a primary one. Catherine, who was extremely modest, had no desire to shine, and on most social occasions, as they are called, you would have found her lurking in the background. She was extremely fond of her father, and very much afraid of him; she thought him the cleverest and handsomest and most celebrated of men. The poor girl found her account so completely in the exercise of her affections that the little tremor[52] of fear that mixed itself with her filial[53] passion gave the thing an extra relish rather than blunted its edge. Her deepest desire was to please him, and her conception of happiness was to know that she had succeeded in pleasing him. She had never succeeded beyond a certain point.

Though, on the whole, he was very kind to her, she was perfectly aware of this, and to go beyond the point in question seemed to her really something to live for. What she could not know, of course, was that she disappointed him, though on three or four occasions the Doctor had been almost frank about it. She grew up peacefully and prosperously; but at the age of eighteen Mrs. Penniman had not made a clever woman of her. Doctor Sloper would have liked to be proud of his daughter; but there was nothing to be proud of in poor Catherine. There was nothing, of course, to be ashamed of; but this was not enough for the Doctor, who was a proud man, and would have enjoyed being able to think of his daughter as an unusual girl. There would have been a fitness in her being pretty and graceful, intelligent and distinguished for her mother had been the most charming woman of her little day — and as regards her father, of course he knew his own value. He had moments of irritation at having produced a commonplace child, and he even went so far at times as to take a certain satisfaction in the thought that his wife had not lived to find her out. He was naturally slow in making this discovery himself, and it was not till Catherine had become a young lady grown that he regarded the matter as settled. He gave her the benefit of a great many doubts; he was in no haste to conclude. Mrs. Penniman frequently assured him that his daughter had a delightful nature; but he knew how to interpret this assurance. It meant, to his sense, that Catherine was not wise

---

48) glutton : 대식가
49) biographer : 전기 작가
50) muster : (용기를) 불러일으키다, 소집하다, 집합하다
51) avowed : 공공연한
52) tremor : 떨림, 전율
53) filial : 자식으로서의

enough to discover that her aunt was a goose — a limitation of mind that could not fail to be agreeable to Mrs. Penniman. Both she and her brother, however, exaggerated[54] the young girl's limitations; for Catherine, though she was very fond of her aunt, and conscious of the gratitude she owed her, regarded her without a particle of that gentle dread which gave its stamp to her admiration of her father. To her mind there was nothing of the infinite about Mrs. Penniman; Catherine saw her all at once, as it were[55], and was not dazzled by the apparition; whereas her father's great faculties seemed, as they stretched away, to lose themselves in a sort of luminous vagueness, which indicated, not that they stopped, but that Catherine's own mind ceased to follow them.

It must not be supposed that Doctor Sloper visited his disappointment upon the poor girl, or ever let her suspect that she had played him a trick. On the contrary, for fear of being unjust to her, he did his duty with exemplary zeal, and recognized that she was a faithful and affectionate child. Besides, he was a philosopher: he smoked a good many cigars over his disappointment, and in the fullness of time he got used to it. He satisfied himself that he had expected nothing, though, indeed, with a certain oddity of reasoning. "I expect nothing," he said to himself; "so that, if she gives me a surprise, it will be all clear gain. If she doesn't, it will be no loss." This was about the time Catherine had reached her eighteenth year; so that it will be seen her father had not been precipitate. At this time she seemed not only incapable of giving surprises; it was almost a question whether she could have received one — she was so quiet and irresponsive. People who expressed themselves roughly called her stolid[56]. But she was irresponsive because she was shy, uncomfortably, painfully shy[57]. This was not always understood, and she sometimes produced an impression of insensibility. In reality, she was the softest creature in the world.

Chapter 3

As a child she had promised to be tall; but when she was sixteen she ceased to grow, and her stature, like most other points in her composition, was not unusual. She was strong, however, and properly made, and, fortunately, her health was excellent. It had been noted that the Doctor was a philosopher, but I would not have answered for his philosophy if the poor girl had proved a sickly and suffering person. Her appearance of health constituted her principal claim to beauty; and her clear, fresh complexion, in which white and red were very equally distributed, was, indeed, an excellent thing to see. Her eye was small and quiet, her features were rather thick, her tresses[58] brown and smooth. A dull, plain girl she was called by rigorous critics — a quiet, lady-like girl, by those of the more imaginative sort; but by neither class was she very elaborately discussed. When

---

54) exaggerate : 과장하다
55) as it were : 말하자면, 마치
56) stolid : 둔감한
57) painfully shy : 지독하게 수줍은
58) tresses : 긴 머리

it had been duly impressed upon her that she was a young lady — it was a good while before she could believe it — she suddenly developed a lively taste for dress: a lively taste is quite the expression to use. I feel as if I ought to write it very small, her judgment in this matter was by no means[59] infallible; it was liable to confusions and embarrassments. Her great indulgence of it was really the desire of a rather inarticulate nature to manifest itself; she sought to be eloquent in her garments, and to make up for[60] her diffidence[61] of speech by a fine frankness of costume. But if she expressed herself in her clothes, it is certain that people were not to blame for not thinking her a witty person. It must be added that, though she had the expectation of a fortune — Doctor Sloper for a long time had been making twenty thousand dollars a year by his profession, and laying aside[62] the half of it — the amount of money at her disposal was not greater than the allowance made to many poorer girls. In those days, in New York, there were still a few altar-fires flickering in the temple of Republican simplicity, and Doctor Sloper would have been glad to see his daughter present herself, with a classic grace, as a priestess of this mild faith. It made him fairly grimace, in private, to think that a child of his should be both ugly and overdressed. For himself, he was fond of the good things of life, and he made a considerable use of them; but he had a dread of vulgarity, and even a theory that it was increasing in the society that surrounded him. Moreover, the standard of luxury in the United States thirty years ago was carried by no means so high as at present[63], and Catherine's clever father took the old-fashioned view of the education of young persons. He had no particular theory on the subject; it had scarcely as yet[64] become a necessity of self-defence to have a collection of theories. It simply appeared to him proper and reasonable that a well-bred young woman should not carry half her fortune on her back. Catherine's back was a broad one, and would have carried a good deal; but to the weight of the paternal displeasure she never ventured to expose it, and our heroine was twenty years old before she treated herself, for evening wear, to a red satin[65] gowns trimmed with gold fringe[66]; though this was an article which, for many years, she had coveted in secret. It made her look, when she sported it, like a woman of thirty; but oddly enough, in spite of her taste for fine clothes, she had not a grain of coquetry, and her anxiety when she put them on was as to whether they, and not she, would look well. It is a point on which history has not been explicit, but the assumption is warrantable; it was in the royal raiment just mentioned that she presented herself at a little entertainment given by her aunt, Mrs. Almond. The girl was at this time in her twenty-first year, and Mrs. Almond's party was the beginning of something very important.

Some three or four years before this, Doctor Sloper had moved his household gods up town, as

---

59) by no means : never(결코)
60) make up for : 만회하다
61) diffidence : 자신이 없음, 수줍음
62) lay aside : 저축하다
63) at present : presently(곧, 당장)
64) as yet : 지금으로서는
65) satin : 새틴, 공단
66) fringe : (숄이나 스카프 따위에 다는) 장식

they say in New York. He had been living ever since his marriage in an edifice of red brick, with granite copings and an enormous fan-light over the door, standing in a street within five minutes' walk of the City Hall which saw its best days (from the social point of view) about 1820. After this, the tide of fashion began to set steadily northward, as, indeed, in New York, thanks to the narrow channel in which it flows, it is obliged to do, and the great hum of traffic rolled farther to the right and left of Broadway. By the time the Doctor changed his residence, the murmur of trade had become a mighty uproar, which was music in the ears of all good citizens interested in the commercial development, as they delighted to call it, of their fortunate isle. Doctor Sloper's interest in this phenomenon was only indirect — though, seeing that, as the years went on, half of his patients came to[67] be overworked men of business, it might have been more immediate — and when most of his neighbors' dwellings (also ornamented with granite copings and large fan-lights) had been converted into offices, warehouses, and shipping agencies, and otherwise applied to the base uses of commerce, he determined to look out for a quieter home. The ideal of quiet and of genteel retirement, in 1835, was found in Washington Square, where the Doctor built himself a handsome, modern, wide-fronted house, with a big balcony before the drawing-room windows, and a flight[68] of white marble steps ascending to a portal which was also faced with white marble. This structure, and many of its neighbors, which it exactly resembled, were supposed, forty years ago, to embody the last results of architectural science, and they remain to this day very solid and honorable dwellings. In front of them was the square, containing a considerable quantity of inexpensive vegetation, enclosed by a wooden paling, which increased its rural and accessible appearance; and round the corner was the more august precinct of the Fifth Avenue, taking its origin at this point with a spacious and confident air[69] which already marked it for high destinies. I know not whether it is owing to the tenderness of early associations, but this portion of New York appears to many persons the most delectable[70]. It has a kind of established repose which is not of frequent occurrence in other quarters of the long, shrill city; it has a riper, richer, more honorable look than any of the upper ramifications of the great longitudinal thoroughfare — the look of having had something of a social history. It was here, as you might have been informed on good authority, that you had come into[71] a world which appeared to offer a variety of sources of interest; it was here that your grandmother lived, in venerable solitude, and dispensed a hospitality which commended itself alike to the infant imagination and the infant palate; it was here that you took your first walks abroad, following the nursery-maid with unequal step, and sniffing up the strange odor of the ailanthus[72] — trees which at that time formed the principal umbrage of the Square, and diffused an aroma that you were not yet critical enough to dislike as it deserved; it was here, finally, that your first school, kept by a broad-bosomed, broad-based old lady with a ferule, who was always

67) came to : ~에 이르다
68) flight : 층계
69) air : 느낌, 분위기
70) delectable : 유쾌한, 즐거운, 매력이 넘치는
71) come into : ~에 들어가다, 상속하다(inherit)
72) ailanthus : 가죽나무

having tea in a blue cup, with a saucer that didn't match, enlarged the circle both of your observations and your sensations. It was here, at any rate[73], that my heroine spent many years of her life; which is my excuse for this topographical parenthesis.

Mrs. Almond lived much farther up town, in an embryonic street, with a high number — a region where the extension of the city began to assume a theoretic air, where poplars grew beside the pavement (when there was one), and mingled their shade with the steep roofs of desultory Dutch houses, and where pigs and chickens disported themselves in the gutter. These elements of rural picturesqueness have now wholly departed from New York street scenery; but they were to be found within the memory of middle-aged persons in quarters which now would blush to be reminded of them. Catherine had a great many cousins, and with her Aunt Almond's children, who ended by being nine in number, she lived on terms of considerable intimacy. When she was younger they had been rather afraid of her; she was believed, as the phrase is, to be highly educated, and a person who lived in the intimacy of their Aunt Penniman had something of reflected grandeur. Mrs. Penniman, among the little Almonds, was an object of more admiration than sympathy. Her manners were strange and formidable[74] and her mourning robes — she dressed in black for twenty years after her husband's death, and then suddenly appeared, one morning, with pink roses in her cap — were complicated in odd, unexpected places with buckles, bugles, and pins, which discouraged familiarity. She took children too hard, both for good and for evil, and had an oppressive air of expecting subtle things of them; so that going to see her was a good deal like being taken to church and made to sit in a front pew[75]. It was discovered after awhile, however, that Aunt Penniman was but an accident in Catherine's existence, and not a part of its essence, and that when the girl came to spend a Saturday with her cousins, she was available for 'follow-my-master,' and even for leap-frog. On this basis an understanding was easily arrived at, and for several years Catherine fraternized with[76] her young kinsmen. I say young kinsmen, because seven of the little Almonds were boys, and Catherine had a preference for those games which are most conveniently played in trousers[77]. By degrees, however, the little Almonds' trousers began to lengthen, and the wearers to disperse and settle themselves in life. The elder children were older than Catherine, and the boys were sent to college or placed in counting-rooms. Of the girls, one married very punctually[78], and the other as punctually became engaged. It was to celebrate this latter event that Mrs. Almond gave the little party I have mentioned. Her daughter was to marry a stout young stock broker, a boy of twenty: it was thought a very good thing.

---

73) at any rate : 여하튼
74) formidable : 어마어마한, 강력한, 무서운
75) pew : (교회의) 신도 좌석, 자리
76) fraternize with : 형제처럼 친하게 사귀다, 화목하다
77) trousers : 바지
78) punctually : 시간대로, 정각에, 엄수하여

제 4 절 「*The Real Thing*」

1 줄거리

화가인 '나'에게 어느 날 기품 있는 Monarch 부부가 찾아와 자신들을 모델로 써 달라는 부탁을 한다. '나'는 마침 '호화판 책'(*édition de luxe*에서 첫 부분인 "Rutland Ramsay")의 삽화를 요청받은 상황이었는데 Monarch 부부가 그러한 상류 사회를 다루는 삽화의 모델로 적절하다고 생각하고 그 두 사람을 모델로 써 본다. 그러나 너무 진짜 같은 이 모델들은 '나'의 상상력을 발휘할 수 없게 만들면서 훌륭한 그림의 완성을 막게 되고, 오히려 Miss Churm과 Oronte라는 직업 모델을 써서 상상력을 첨가하여 그린 경우가 더 낫기에 '나'는 그들을 모델로 쓰지 않기로 한다. Monarch 부부는 생활비를 벌기 위해 '나'의 잡일이라도 돕겠다고 하지만 '나'는 약간의 돈을 그들에게 주며 그들을 내보낸다.

2 주제 중요 ★★

(1) 진정한 예술은 허구를 통하여 사실을 재현한다는 아이러니

(2) 예술가의 도덕적 딜레마

(3) 예술은 사실(Reality)의 있는 그대로의 반영이 아니라 변형임

3 등장인물

(1) The Artist

예술가(화가)이자 서술자인 '나'는 영국에 거주하며 화실에서 잡지와 소설책 등에 실릴 삽화와 그림 작업을 위한 모델을 고용한다.

(2) The Monarchs(Mr. Monarch & Mrs. Monarch)

한때는 사정이 괜찮았으나 생활고에 시달리는 교양 있고 인물이 좋은 퇴역 소령(少領) 부부이다.

(3) Miss Churm

화실에 고용된 직업 모델로서 볼품없고 천박한 인물이지만 훌륭한 모델이다.

(4) Oronte

Mr. Monarch 대신 Mrs. Monarch가 데려온 이태리 청년이다. 새로 고용한 청년 모델로 순진한 인물이다.

(5) Jack Hawley

화가의 친구이자 비평가로 문제 해결에 조언과 함께 도움을 준다. 날카로운 비평을 아끼지 않는 인물로 화가의 조언가로 활약한다.

4 작품의 구조(Plot)와 시점 및 기법

(1) 구조

① 1장 : Monarch 부부가 '나'의 집으로 찾아와 모델로 일하고 싶다고 요청한다.
② 2장 : Miss Churm이 찾아와 작업에 들어가기 전에 소령 부부에 대한 이야기를 나눈다.
③ 3~4장 : Monarch 부부를 모델로 쓰면서 느끼게 되는 '진짜'와 '예술' 사이의 아이러니를 그리고 있다.

(2) 시점

1인칭 제한적 시점이다.

(3) 기법 중요 ★

① 아이러니(Irony)
   ㉠ 잘생기고 역할에 알맞은 진짜 모델들이 화가에게는 오히려 창작의 방해물이 되었다.
   ㉡ 퇴역한 소령 부부가 화실의 하인(下人)으로 전락하게 된다.
   ㉢ Monarch 부부는 모델로는 적합하지 않았으나 그들과의 추억이 훌륭한 문학 작품의 소재가 되었다.

5 Text

Chapter 1

When the porter's wife who used to answer the house-bell, announced "A gentleman and a lady, sir," I had, as I often had in those days — the wish being father to the thought — an immediate vision of sitters. Sitters my visitors in this case proved to be; but not in the sense I should have preferred. There was nothing at first however to indicate that they mightn't have come for a portrait. The gentleman, a man of fifty, very high and very straight, with a moustache slightly grizzled[1] and a dark grey walking-coat admirably fitted, both of which I noted professionally — I don't mean as a barber or yet as a tailor — would have struck me as a celebrity if celebrities often were striking. It was a truth of which I had for some time been conscious that a figure with a good deal of frontage was, as one might say[2], almost never a public institution. A glance at the lady helped to remind me of this paradoxical law: she also looked too distinguished to be a "personality." Moreover one would scarcely come across two variations together.

Neither of the pair immediately spoke — they only prolonged the preliminary gaze suggesting that each wished to give the other a chance. They were visibly shy; they stood there letting me take them in[3] which, as I afterwards perceived, was the most practical thing they could have done. In this way their embarrassment served their cause. I had seen people painfully reluctant to mention that they desired anything so gross as to be represented on canvas; but the scruples[4] of my new friends appeared almost insurmountable. Yet the gentleman might have said "I should like a portrait of my wife," and the lady might have said "I should like a portrait of my husband." Perhaps they weren't husband and wife — this naturally would make the matter more delicate. Perhaps they wished to be done together — in which case they ought to have brought a third person to break the news.

"We come from Mr. Rivet," the lady finally said with a dim smile that had the effect of a moist sponge passed over a "sunk" piece of painting, as well as of a vague allusion to vanished beauty. She was as tall and straight, in her degree, as her companion, and with ten years less to carry. She looked as sad as a woman could look whose face was not charged with expression; that is her tinted oval mask showed waste as an exposed surface shows friction. The hand of time had played over her freely, but to an effect of elimination. She was slim and stiff, and so well-dressed, in dark blue cloth, with lappets[5] and pockets and buttons, that it was clear she employed the same tailor as her husband. The couple had an indefinable air of prosperous thrift — they evidently got a good deal of luxury for their money. If I was to be one of their luxuries, it would behoove me to consider my terms.

"Ah, Claude Rivet recommended me?" I echoed; and I added that it was very kind of him, though I could reflect that, as he only painted landscape, this wasn't a sacrifice.

The lady looked very hard at the gentleman, and the gentleman looked round the room. Then, staring at the door a moment and stroking his moustache, he rested his pleasant eyes on me with the remark: "He said you were the right one."

"I try to be, when people want to sit."

"Yes, we should like to," said the lady anxiously.

---

1) grizzled : 회색의
2) as one might say[put] : 말하자면
3) take in : 집에 맞아들이다
4) scruples : 주저함
5) lappet : (옷 등의) 늘어진 자락

"Do you mean together?"

My visitors exchanged a glance. "If you could do anything with *me,* I suppose it would be double," the gentleman stammered.

"Oh, yes, there's naturally a higher charge for two figures than for one."

"We should like to make it pay," the husband confessed.

"That's very good of you," I returned, appreciating so unwonted[6] a sympathy — for I supposed he meant pay the artist.

A sense of strangeness seemed to dawn on the lady. "We mean for the illustrations — Mr. Rivet said you might put one in[7]."

"Put in — an illustration?" I was equally confused.

"Sketch her off, you know," said the gentleman, colouring.

It was only then that I understood the service Claude Rivet had rendered me; he had told them how I worked in black and white[8], for magazines, for storybooks, for sketches of contemporary life, and consequently had copious employment for models. These things were true, but it was not less true — I may confess it now; whether because the aspiration was to lead to everything or to nothing I leave the reader to guess — that I couldn't get the honours, to say nothing of[9] the emoluments[10], of a great painter of portraits out of my head. My "illustrations" were my pot-boilers[11]; I looked to a different branch of art — far and away the most interesting it had always seemed to me — to perpetuate my fame. There was no shame in looking to it also to make my fortune; but that fortune was by so much further from being made from the moment my visitors wished to be "done" for something. I was disappointed; for in the pictorial sense I had immediately *seen* them. I had seized their type — I had already settled what I would do with it. Something that wouldn't absolutely have pleased them, I afterwards reflected.

"Ah, you're — you're a — ?" I began as soon as I had mastered my surprise. I couldn't bring out[12] the dingy word "models" : it seemed so little to fit the case.

"We haven't had much practice," said the lady.

"We've got to *do* something, and we've thought that an artist in your line might perhaps make something of us," her husband threw off. He further mentioned that they didn't know many artists and that they had gone first, on the off chance[13] — he painted views of course, but sometimes put in figures; perhaps I remembered — to Mr. Rivet, whom they had met a few years before at a place in Norfolk where he was sketching.

"We used to sketch a little ourselves," the lady hinted.

---

6) unwonted : 보기 드문
7) put in : 임명하다
8) black and white : 펜화, 묵화
9) to say nothing of : ~은 제쳐놓고
10) emolument : 임금(돈)
11) pot-boilers : 돈벌이가 목적인 작품
12) bring out : 끄집어내다
13) off chance : 가능성이 적은

"It's very awkward, but we absolutely *must* do something," her husband went on.

"Of course we're not so *very* young," she admitted with a wan smile.

With the remark that I might as well[14] know something more about them the husband had handed me a card extracted from a neat new pocketbook-their appurtenances[15] were all of the freshest — and inscribed with the words "Major Monarch." Impressive as these words were they didn't carry my knowledge much further; but my visitor presently added: "I've left the army and we've had the misfortune to lose our money. In fact our means are dreadfully small."

"It's awfully trying — a regular strain," said Mrs. Monarch.

They evidently wished to be discreet — to take care not to swagger because they were gentlefolk. I felt them willing to recognise this as something of a drawback, at the same time that I guessed at an underlying sense — their consolation in adversity — that they had their points. They certainly had; but these advantages struck me as preponderantly social; such, for instance, as would help to make a drawing-room look well. However, a drawing-room was always, or ought to be, a picture.

In consequence of his wife's allusion to their age Major Monarch observed: "Naturally[16] it's more for the figure that we thought of going in[17]. We can still hold ourselves up[18]." On the instant I saw the figure was indeed their strong point. His "naturally" didn't sound vain, but it lighted up the question. "*She* has the best one," he continued, nodding at his wife with a pleasant after-dinner absence of circumlocution. I could only reply, as if we were in fact sitting over our wine, that this didn't prevent his own from being very good; which led him in turn to make answer: "We thought that if you ever have to do people like us we might be something like it. *She,* particularly — for a lady in a book, you know."

I was so amused by them that, to get more of it, I did my best to take their point of view; and though it was an embarrassment to find myself appraising physically, as if they were animals on hire or useful blacks, a pair whom I should have expected to meet only in one of the relations in which criticism is tacit[19], I looked at Mrs. Monarch judicially enough to be able to exclaim after a moment with conviction: "Oh, yes, a lady in a book!" She was singularly like a bad illustration.

"We'll stand up, if you like," said the Major; and he raised himself before me with a really grand air.

I could take his measure at a glance — he was six feet two and a perfect gentleman. It would have paid any club in process of formation and in want of a stamp to engage him at a salary to stand in the principal window. What struck me at once was that in coming to me they had rather missed their vocation; they could surely have been turned to better account for advertising purposes. I couldn't of course see the thing in detail, but I could see them make somebody's fortune — I don't mean their own. There was something in them for a waistcoat-maker, an hotel-keeper or a

---

14) as well : 게다가
15) appurtenances : 부속물
16) naturally : 당연히, 물론
17) go in : 시작하다
18) hold up : 보여주다
19) tacit : silent(무언의)

soap-vendor. I could imagine "We always use it" pinned on their bosoms with the greatest effect; I had a vision of the brilliancy with which they would launch a table d' hote[20].

Mrs. Monarch sat still, not from pride but from shyness, and presently her husband said to her: "Get up[21], my dear, and show how smart you are." She obeyed, but she had no need to get up show it. She walked to the end of the studio and then came back blushing, her fluttered eyes on the partner of her appeal. I was reminded of an incident I had accidentally had a glimpse of in Paris — being with a friend there, a dramatist about to produce a play, when an actress came to him to ask to be entrusted with a part. She went through her paces before him, walked up and down as Mrs. Monarch was doing. Mrs. Monarch did it quite as well, but I abstained from applauding. It was very odd to see such people apply for such poor pay. She looked as if she had ten thousand a year. Her husband had used the word that described her: she was in the London current jargon[22] essentially and typically "smart." Her figure was, in the same order of ideas, conspicuously and irreproachably "good." For a woman of her age her waist was surprisingly small; her elbow moreover had the orthodox crook. She held her head at the conventional angle, but why did she come to *me?* She ought to have tried on jackets at a big shop. I feared my visitors were not only destitute but "artistic" — which would be a great complication. When she sat down again I thanked her, observing that what a draughtsman most valued in his model was the faculty of keeping quiet.

"Oh, *she* can keep quiet," said Major Monarch. Then he added jocosely: "I've always kept her quiet."

"I'm not a nasty[23] fidget[24], am I?" It was going to wring[25] tears from me, I felt, the way she hid her head, ostrich-like, in the other broad bosom.

The owner of this expanse addressed his answer to me. "Perhaps it isn't out of place to mention — because we ought to be quite businesslike, oughtn't we? — that when I married her she was known as the Beautiful Statue."

"Oh dear!" said Mrs. Monarch ruefully.

"Of course I should want a certain amount of expression," I rejoined.

"Of course!" — and I had never heard such unanimity.

"And then I suppose you know that you'll get awfully tired."

"Oh, we never get tired!" they eagerly cried.

"Have you had any kind of practice?"

They hesitated — they looked at each other. "We've been photographed- *immensely*," said Mrs. Monarch.

"She means the fellows have asked us themselves," added the Major.

---

20) table d' hote : (호텔 등에 있는) 공동식탁
21) get up : 일어서다
22) jargon : 통어(通語), 방언
23) nasty : 더러운, 성가신
24) fidget : 안절부절못하는(침착하지 못한) 사람
25) wring : 한번 비틀기, 짜다

"I see — because you're so good-looking."

"I don't know what they thought, but they were always after us."

"We always got our photographs for nothing," smiled Mrs. Monarch.

"We might have brought some, my dear," her husband remarked.

"I'm not sure we have any left. We've given quantities away[26]," she explained to me.

"With our autographs and that sort of thing," said the Major.

"Are they to be got in the shops?" I inquired as a harmless pleasantry.

"Oh, yes, hers — they used to be."

"Not now," said Mrs. Monarch with her eyes on the floor.

Chapter 2

I could fancy the "sort of thing" they put on the presentation copies of their photographs, and I was sure they wrote a beautiful hand. It was odd how quickly I was sure of everything that concerned them. If they were now so poor as to have to earn shillings and pence they could never have had much of a margin. Their good looks had been their capital, and they had good-naturedly made the most of the career that this resource marked out[27] for them. It was in their faces, the blankness, the deep intellectual repose of the twenty years of country-house visiting[28] that had given them pleasant intonations. I could see the sunny drawing-rooms, sprinkled with periodicals she didn't read, in which Mrs. Monarch had continuously sat; I could see the wet shrubberies in which she had walked, equipped to admiration for either exercise. I could see the rich covers the Major had helped to shoot and the wonderful garments in which, late at night, he repaired[29] to the smoking-room to talk about them. I could imagine their leggings and waterproofs, their knowing tweeds[30] and rugs, their rolls of sticks and cases of tackle and neat umbrellas; and I could evoke the exact appearance of their servants and the compact variety of their luggage on platforms of country stations.

They gave small tips, but they were liked; they didn't do anything themselves, but they were welcome. They looked so well everywhere; they gratified the general relish for stature, complexion and "form." They knew it without fatuity[31] or vulgarity, and they respected themselves in consequence. They weren't superficial; they were thorough and kept themselves up — it had been their line. People with such a taste for activity had to have some line. I could feel how even in a dull house they could have been counted on for the joy of life. At present something had happened — it didn't matter what, their little income had grown less, it had grown least — and they had to

---

26) give away : 배부하다
27) mark out : 표시하다, 정하다
28) visiting : 방문, 체류
29) repair : 자주 드나들다
30) tweed : [직물] 트위드
31) fatuity : 우둔함

do something for pocket-money. Their friends could like them, I made out[32]), without liking to support them. There was something about them that represented credit — their clothes, their manners, their type; but if credit is a large empty pocket in which an occasional chink[33]) reverberates[34]), the chink at least must be audible. What they wanted of me was help to make it so. Fortunately they had no children — I soon divined that. They would also perhaps wish our relations to be kept secret: this was why it was "for the figure" — the reproduction of the face would betray them.

I liked them — I felt, quite as their friends must have done — they were so simple; and I had no objection to them if they would suit. But somehow with all their perfections I didn't easily believe in them. After all they were amateurs, and the ruling passion of my life was the detestation of the amateur. Combined with this was another perversity — an innate preference for the represented subject over the real one: the defect of the real one was so apt to be a lack of representation. I liked things that appeared; then one was sure. Whether they *were* or not was a subordinate and almost always a profitless question. There were other considerations, the first of which was that I already had two or three recruits in use, notably a young person with big feet, in alpaca[35]), from Kilburn, who for a couple of years had come to me regularly for my illustrations and with whom I was still — perhaps ignobly — satisfied. I frankly explained to my visitors how the case stood, but they had taken more precautions than I supposed. They had reasoned out their opportunity, for Claude Rivet had told them of the projected *édition de luxe* of one of the writers of our day — the rarest of the novelists — who, long neglected by the multitudinous vulgar and dearly prized by the attentive (need I mention Philip Vincent?), had had the happy fortune of seeing, late in life, the dawn and then the full light of a higher criticism; an estimate in which on the part of the public there was something really of expiation[36]). The edition preparing, planned by a publisher of taste, was practically an act of high reparation[37]); the woodcuts[38]) with which it was to be enriched were the homage of English art to one of the most independent representatives of English letters. Major and Mrs. Monarch confessed to me they had hoped I might be able to work *them* into my branch of the enterprise. They knew I was to do the first of the books, "Rutland Ramsay," but I had to make clear to them that my participation in the rest of the affair — this first book was to be a test — must depend on the satisfaction I should give. If this should be limited my employers would drop me with scarce common forms. It was therefore a crisis for me, and naturally I was making special preparations, looking about for new people, should they be necessary, and securing the best types. I admitted however that I should like to settle down[39]) to two or three

32) make out : understand(이해하다)
33) chink : 주화, 현금
34) reverberate : 울리다
35) alpaca : 남미 페루에서 나는 직물의 한 종류
36) expiation : 보상, 속죄
37) reparation : 보상, 변상
38) woodcut : 목판화
39) settle down : 착수하다

good models who would do for[40] everything.

"Should we have often — a — put on special clothes?" Mrs. Monarch timidly demanded.

"Dear, yes — that's half the business."

"And should we be expected to supply our own costumes?"

"Oh, no; I've got a lot of things. A painter's models put on — or put off — anything he likes."

"And you mean — a — the same?"

"The same?"

Mrs. Monarch looked at her husband again.

"Oh, she was just wondering," he explained, "if the costumes are in *general* use." I had to confess that they were, and I mentioned further that some of them — I had a lot of genuine greasy last — century things — had served their time, a hundred years ago, on living world-stained men and women. "We'll put on anything that fits," said the Major.

"Oh, I arrange that — they fit in the pictures."

"I'm afraid I should do better for the modern books. I'd come as you like," said Mrs. Monarch.

"She has got a lot of clothes at home: they might do for contemporary life," her husband continued.

"Oh, I can fancy scenes in which you'd be quite natural." And indeed I could see the slipshod[41] rearrangements of stale properties[42] — the stories I tried to produce pictures for without the exasperation of reading them — whose sandy tracts[43] the good lady might help to people. But I had to return to the fact that for this sort of work — the daily mechanical grind — I was already equipped: the people I was working with were fully adequate.

"We only thought we might be more like some characters," said Mrs. Monarch mildly, getting up.

Her husband also rose; he stood looking at me with a dim wistfulness that was touching in so fine a man. "Wouldn't it be rather a pull sometimes to have — a — to have — ?" He hung fire[44]; he wanted me to help him by phrasing what he meant. But I couldn't — I didn't know. So he brought it out awkwardly: "The *real* thing; a gentleman, you know, or a lady." I was quite ready to give a general assent — I admitted that there was a great deal in that. This encouraged Major Monarch to say, following up[45] his appeal with an unacted gulp[46]: "It's awfully hard — we've tried everything." The gulp was communicative; it proved too much for his wife. Before I knew it Mrs. Monarch had dropped again upon[47] a divan[48] and burst into tears. Her husband sat down beside her, holding one of her hands; whereupon she quickly dried her eyes with the other, while I felt

---

40) do for : 대역을 하다, ~의 도움이 되다
41) slipshod : 조잡한
42) properties : 각본
43) tract : 소책자, 영역, 넓이
44) hang fire : 망설이다
45) follow up : 덧붙이다
46) gulp : 꾹 참다
47) drop upon : 떨어뜨리다
48) divan : sofa(긴 의자)

embarrassed as she looked up at me. "There isn't a confounded job I haven't applied for — waited for — prayed for. You can fancy we'd be pretty bad first. Secretaryships and that sort of thing? You might as well ask for a peerage[49]). I'd be anything — I'm strong; a messenger or a coal-heaver. I'd put on a gold-laced cap and open carriage-doors in front of the haberdasher's; I'd hang about a station to carry portmanteaus; I'd be a postman. But they won't *look* at you; there are thousands as good as yourself already on the ground. *Gentlemen,* poor beggars, who've drunk their wine, who've kept their hunters!"

I was as reassuring as I know how to be, and my visitors were presently on their feet again while, for the experiment, we agreed on an hour. We were discussing it when the door opened and Miss Churm came in with a wet umbrella. Miss Churm had to take the omnibus to Maida Vale and then walk half a mile. She looked a trifle blowsy[50]) and slightly splashed. I scarcely ever saw her come in without thinking[51]) afresh how odd it was that, being so little in herself, she should yet be so much in others. She was a meagre little Miss Churm, but was such an ample heroine of romance. She was only a freckled[52]) cockney, but she could represent everything, from a fine lady to a shepherdess; she had the faculty as she might have had a fine voice or long hair. She couldn't spell and she loved beer, but she had two or three "points," and practice, and a knack[53]), and mother-wit[54]), and a whimsical sensibility, and a love of the theatre, and seven sisters, and not an ounce[55]) of respect, especially for the *h*. The first thing my visitors saw was that her umbrella was wet, and in their spotless perfection they visibly winced[56]) at it. The rain had come on since their arrival.

"I'm all in a soak; there was a mess of people in the bus. I wish you lived near a station," said Miss Churm. I requested her to get ready as quickly as possible, and she passed into the room in which she always changed her dress. But before going out she asked me what she was to get into this time.

"It's the Russian princess, don't you know?" I answered; "the one with the 'golden eyes,' in black velvet, for the long thing in the Cheapside."

"Golden eyes? I *say!*" cried Miss Churm, while my companions watched her with intensity as she withdrew. She always arranged herself, when she was late, before I could turn round[57]); and I kept my visitors a little on purpose, so that they might get an idea, from seeing her, what would be expected of themselves. I mentioned that she was quite my notion of an excellent model — she was really very clever.

---

49) peerage : 귀족 지위
50) blowsy : 덥수룩한
51) scarcely ~ without -ing : ~하면 반드시 ~하다
52) freckled : 주근깨가 있는
53) knack : 요령
54) mother-wit : 지혜, 상식
55) ounce : 조금
56) wince : 움찔하다
57) turn (a)round : 반대의 경향을 보이다

"Do you think she looks like a Russian princess?" Major Monarch asked with lurking[58] alarm.

"When I make her, yes."

"Oh, if you have to *make* her — !" he reasoned, not without point.

"That's the most you can ask. There are so many who are not makable."

"Well, now, *here's* a lady" — and with a persuasive smile he passed his arm into his wife's — "who's already made!"

"Oh, I'm not a Russian princess," Mrs. Monarch protested a little coldly. I could see she had known some and didn't like them. There at once was a complication of a kind I never had to fear with Miss Churm.

This young lady came back in black velvet — the gown was rather rusty and very low on her lean shoulders — and with a Japanese fan in her red hands. I reminded her that in the scene I was doing she had to look over[59] someone's head. "I forget whose it is; but it doesn't matter. Just look over a head."

"I'd rather look over a stove," said Miss Churm; and she took her station near the fire. She fell into position, settled herself into a tall attitude, gave a certain backward inclination to her head and a certain forward droop[60] to her fan, and looked, at least to my prejudiced sense, distinguished and charming, foreign and dangerous. We left her looking so while I went downstairs with Major and Mrs. Monarch.

"I believe I could come about as near it as that," said Mrs. Monarch.

"Oh, you think she's shabby, but you must allow for the alchemy of art."

However, they went off with an evident increase of comfort founded on their demonstrable advantage in being the real thing. I could fancy them shuddering over Miss Churm. She was very droll about them when I went back, for I told her what they wanted.

"Well, if *she* can sit I'll tyke to[61] bookkeeping[62]," said my model.

"She's very ladylike," I replied as an innocent form of aggravation.

"So much the worse for *you*. That means she can't turn round."

"She'll do for the fashionable novels."

"Oh, yes, she'll *do* for them!" my model humorously declared. "Ain't they bad enough without her?" I had often sociably denounced them to Miss Churm.

Chapter 3

It was for the elucidation of a mystery in one of these works that I first tried Mrs. Monarch. Her

---

58) lurking : 살짝 움직이는
59) look over : ~을 살펴보다
60) droop : 숙임, 수그러짐
61) tyke to : take to(~로 옮기다, ~하기 시작하다)
62) bookkeeping : 부기, 경리

husband came with her, to be useful if necessary — it was sufficiently clear that as a general thing he would prefer to come with her. At first I wondered if this were for "propriety's[63]" sake — if he were going to be jealous and meddling. The idea was too tiresome, and if it had been confirmed it would speedily have brought our acquaintance to a close. But I soon saw there was nothing in it and that if he accompanied Mrs. Monarch it was — in addition to the chance of being wanted-simply because he had nothing else to do. When they were separate his occupation was gone, and they never had been separate. I judged rightly that in their awkward situation their close union was their main comfort and that this union had no weak spot. It was a real marriage, an encouragement to the hesitating, a nut for pessimists to crack[64]. Their address was humble — I remember afterwards thinking it had been the only thing about them that was really professional — and I could fancy the lamentable lodgings in which the Major would have been left alone. He could sit there more or less grimly with his wife — he couldn't sit there anyhow without her.

He had too much tact to try and make himself agreeable when he couldn't be useful; so when I was too absorbed in my work to talk he simply sat and waited. But I liked to hear him talk — it made my work, when not interrupting it, less mechanical, less special. To listen to him was to combine the excitement of going out with the economy of staying at home. There was only one hindrance — that I seemed not to know any of the people this brilliant couple had known. I think he wondered extremely, during the term of our intercourse, whom the deuce[65] I did know. He hadn't a stray sixpence of an idea to fumble[66] for, so we didn't spit[67] it very fine; we confined ourselves to questions of leather and even of liquor — saddlers and breeches-makers and how to get excellent claret[68] cheap — and matters like "good trains" and the habits of small game[69]. His lore on these last subjects was astonishing — he managed to interweave the station-master with the ornithologist[70]. When he couldn't talk about greater things he could talk cheerfully about small, and since I couldn't accompany him into reminiscences of the fashionable world he could lower the conversation without a visible effort to my level.

So earnest a desire to please was touching in a man who could so easily have knocked one down. He looked after[71] the fire and had an opinion on the draught of the stove without my asking him, and I could see that he thought many of my arrangements not half knowing. I remember telling him that if I were only rich I'd offer him a salary to come and teach me how to live. Sometimes he gave a random sigh of which the essence might have been: "Give me even such a bare old barrack as *this,* and I'd do something with[72] it!" When I wanted to use him he came alone; which was

---

63) propriety : 예의범절
64) a hard nut to crack : 어려운 문제
65) deuce : 도대체
66) fumble : 찾아다니다
67) spit : 열변을 토해내다
68) claret : 클라레(포도주)
69) game : 사냥감, 기르고 있는 짐승 떼
70) ornithologist : 조류학자
71) look after : take care of(돌보다)
72) do with : ~을 다루다

an illustration of the superior courage of women. His wife could bear her solitary second floor, and she was in general more discreet; showing by various small reserves that she was alive to the propriety of keeping our relations markedly professional — not letting them slide[73] into sociability. She wished it to remain clear that she and the Major were employed, not cultivated, and if she approved of me as a superior, who could be kept in his place, she never thought me quite good enough for an equal.

She sat with great intensity, giving the whole of her mind to it, and was capable of remaining for an hour almost as motionless as before a photographer's lens. I could see she had been photographed often, but somehow the very habit that made her good for that purpose unfitted her for mine. At first I was extremely pleased with her ladylike air, and it was a satisfaction, on coming to follow her lines, to see how good they were and how far they could lead the pencil. But after a little skirmishing[74] I began to find her too insurmountably stiff; do what I would with it my drawing looked like a photograph or a copy of a photograph. Her figure had no variety of expression — she herself had no sense of variety. You may say that this was my business and was only a question of placing her. Yet I placed her in every conceivable position and she managed to obliterate their differences. She was always a lady certainly, and into the bargain[75] was always the same lady. She was the real thing, but always the same thing. There were moments when I rather writhed[76] under the serenity of her confidence that she *was* the real thing. All her dealings with me and all her husband's were an implication that this was lucky for *me*. Meanwhile I found myself trying to invent types that approached her own, instead of making her own transform itself — in the clever way that was not impossible for instance to poor Miss Churm. Arrange as I would and take the precautions I would, she always came out, in my pictures, too tall — landing me in the dilemma of having represented a fascinating woman as seven feet high, which (out of respect perhaps to my own very much scantier inches) was far from my idea of such a personage.

The case was worse with the Major — nothing I could do would keep him down[77], so that he became useful only for representation of brawny[78] giants. I adored variety and range, I cherished human accidents, the illustrative note; I wanted to characterise closely, and the thing in the world I most hated was the danger of being ridden[79] by a type. I had quarrelled with some of my friends about it; I had parted company with them for maintaining that one had to be, and that if the type was beautiful — witness Raphael[80] and Leonardo[81] — the servitude was only a gain. I was neither Leonardo nor Raphael — I might only be a presumptuous[82] young modern searcher; but I held that

---

73) let slide : 내버려두다
74) skirmish : 사소한 접전(싸움, 충돌)을 하다, 찾아다니다
75) into the bargain : 게다가
76) writhe : (괴로워서) 몸부림치다
77) keep down : 억누르다, 일어서지 않고 있다
78) brawny : 힘이 센, 근육이 억센
79) being ridden : 지배된, 사로잡힌
80) Raphael : 라파엘로(Raffaello Sanzio da Urbino, 1483~1520)
81) Leonardo : 레오나르도 다 빈치(Leonardo da Vinci, 1452~1519)
82) presumptuous : 무례한

everything was to be sacrificed sooner than character. When they claimed that the obsessional form could easily *be* character I retorted, perhaps superficially, "Whose?" It couldn't be everybody's — it might end in being nobody's.

After I had drawn Mrs. Monarch a dozen times I felt surer even than before that the value of such a model as Miss Churm resided precisely in the fact that she had no positive stamp, combined of course with the other fact that what she did have was a curious and inexplicable talent for imitation. Her usual appearance was like a curtain which she could draw up at request for a capital performance. This performance was simply suggestive; but it was a word to the wise — it was vivid and pretty. Sometimes even I thought it, she was plain herself, too insipidly pretty; I made it a reproach to her that the figures drawn from her were monotonously (betement[83], as we used to say) graceful. Nothing made her more angry: it was so much her pride to feel she could sit for[84] characters that had nothing in common with each other. She would accuse me at such moments of taking away her "reputytion.[85]"

It suffered a certain shrinkage, this queer quantity, from the repeated visits of my new friends. Miss Churm was greatly in demand, never in want of employment, so I had no scruple in putting her off[86] occasionally, to try them more at my ease. It was certainly amusing at first to do the real thing — it was amusing to do Major Monarch's trousers. They *were* the real thing, even if he did come out colossal. It was amusing to do his wife's back hair — it was so mathematically neat — and the particular "smart" tension of her tight stays[87]. She lent herself especially to positions in which the face was somewhat averted or blurred; she abounded in ladylike back views and *profils perdus*[88]. When she stood erect she took naturally one of the attitudes in which court painters represent queens and princesses; so that I found myself wondering whether, to draw out this accomplishment, I couldn't get the editor of the Cheapside to publish a really royal romance, "A Tale of Buckingham Palace." Sometimes, however, the real thing and the make-believe came into contact; by which I mean that Miss Churm, keeping an appointment or coming to make one on days when I had much work in hand, encountered her invidious[89] rivals. The encounter was not on their part, for they noticed her no more than if she had been the housemaid; not from intentional loftiness, but simply because as yet, professionally, they didn't know how to fraternise[90], as I could imagine they would have liked — or at least that the Major would. They couldn't talk about the omnibus — they always walked; and they didn't know what else to try — she wasn't interested in good trains or cheap claret. Besides, they must have felt — in the air[91] — that she was amused at them, secretly derisive of their ever knowing how. She wasn't a person to conceal the limits of her faith if she

---

83) betement : 바보같이, 어리석게도
84) sit for : 모델을 서다, ~을 위해 포즈를 취하다
85) reputytion : reputation(명성)
86) put off : 연기하다, 미루다
87) stays : corset(멋을 내는 속옷)
88) profil(s) perdu(s) : 비스듬하게 후방에서 그려져 눈과 코가 가려진 얼굴을 말함
89) invidious : 질투를 느끼게 하는, 불쾌한
90) fraternise : 친하게 지내다
91) in the air : (어떤) 기운이 감도는

had had a chance to show them. On the other hand Mrs. Monarch didn't think her tidy; for why else did she take pains to say to me — it was going out of the way, for Mrs. Monarch — that she didn't like dirty women?

One day when my young lady happened to be present with my other sitters — she even dropped in, when it was convenient, for a chat — I asked her to be so good as to lend a hand in getting tea, a service with which she was familiar and which was one of a class that, living as I did in my small way, with slender domestic resources, I often appealed to my models to render. They liked to lay hands on my property, to break the sitting, and sometimes the china — it made them feel Bohemian. The next time I saw Miss Churm after this incident she surprised me greatly by making a scene about it — she accused me of having wished to humiliate her. She hadn't resented the outrage at the time, but had seemed obliging[92] and amused, enjoying the comedy of asking Mrs. Monarch, who sat vague and silent, whether she would have cream and sugar, and putting an exaggerated simper into the question. She had tried intonations — as if she too wished to pass for[93] the real thing — till I was afraid my other visitors would take offence.

Oh, *they* were determined not to do this, and their touching patience was the measure of their great need. They would sit by the hour, uncomplaining, till I was ready to use them; they would come back on the chance of being wanted and would walk away cheerfully if it failed. I used to go to the door with them to see in what magnificent order they retreated. I tried to find other employment for them — I introduced them to several artists. But they didn't "take," for reasons I could appreciate, and I became rather anxiously aware that after such disappointments they fell back upon me with a heavier weight. They did me the honour to think me most their form. They weren't romantic enough for the painters, and in those days there were few serious workers in black and white. Besides, they had an eye to the great job I had mentioned to them — they had secretly set their hearts on supplying the right essence for my pictorial vindication of our fine novelist. They knew that for this undertaking I should want no costume effects, none of the frippery[94] of past ages — that it was a case in which everything would be contemporary and satirical and presumably genteel. If I could work them into it their future would be assured, for the labour would of course be long and the occupation steady.

One day Mrs. Monarch came without her husband — she explained his absence by his having had to go to the City. While she sat there in her usual relaxed majesty there came at the door a knock which I immediately recognized as the subdued appeal of a model out of work. It was followed by the entrance of a young man whom I at once saw to be a foreigner and who proved in fact an Italian acquainted with[95] no English word but my name, which he uttered in a way[96]

---

92) obliging : 정중한, 친절한
93) pass for : ~로 간주되다
94) frippery : 겉치레
95) be acquainted with : 숙지하다
96) in a way : 보기에 따라서는

that made it seem to include all others. I hadn't then visited his country, nor was I proficient in his tongue; but as he was not so meanly constituted — what Italian is? — as to depend only on that member for expression he conveyed to me, in familiar but graceful mimicry, that he was in search of exactly the employment in which the lady before me was engaged. I was not struck with him at first, and while I continued to draw I dropped few signs of interest or encouragement. He stood his ground, however — not importunately[97], but with a dumb dog-like fidelity in his eyes that amounted to innocent impudence, the manner of a devoted servant — he might have been in the house for years — unjustly suspected. Suddenly it struck me that this very attitude and expression made a picture; whereupon I told him to sit down and wait till I should be free. There was another picture in the way he obeyed me, and I observed as I worked that there were others still in the way he looked wonderingly, with his head thrown back, about a high studio. He might have been crossing himself[98] in Saint Peter's. Before I finished I said to myself, "The fellow's a bankrupt orange-monger[99], but a treasure."

When Mrs. Monarch withdrew he passed across the room like a flash to open the door for her, standing there with the rapt[100], pure gaze of the young Dante spellbound[101] by the young Beatrice. As I never insisted, in such situations, on the blankness of the British domestic, I reflected that he had the making of a servant — and I needed one, but couldn't pay him to be only that — as well as of a model; in short I resolved to adopt my bright adventurer if he would agree to officiate in the double capacity. He jumped at my offer, and in the event my rashness — for I had really known nothing about him — wasn't brought home to me. He proved a sympathetic though a desultory[102] ministrant, and had in a wonderful degree the sentiment de la pose[103]. It was uncultivated, instinctive, a part of the happy instinct that had guided him to my door and helped him to spell out my name on the card nailed to it. He had had no other introduction to me than a guess, from the shape of my high north window, seen outside, that my place was a studio and that as a studio it would contain an artist. He had wandered to England in search of fortune, like other itinerants, and had embarked, with a partner and a small green handcart, on the sale of penny ices. The ices had melted away and the partner had dissolved in their train. My young man wore tight yellow trousers with reddish stripes and his name was Oronte. He was sallow but fair[104], and when I put him into some old clothes of my own he looked like an Englishman. He was as good as Miss Churm, who could look, when requested, like an Italian.

---

97) importunately : 집요하게
98) crossing oneself : 성호(십자가)를 긋다
99) monger : 장수, 상인
100) rapt : 황홀한
101) spellbound : 매료된
102) desultory : 산만한
103) sentiment de la pose : sentiment of the pose(포즈의 정취)
104) fair : 살결이 흰

Chapter 4

I thought Mrs. Monarch's face slightly convulsed[105] when, on her coming back with her husband, she found Oronte installed. It was strange to have to recognize in a scrap of a lazzarone[106] a competitor to her magnificent Major. It was she who scented danger first, for the Major was anecdotically unconscious. But Oronte gave us tea, with a hundred eager confusions — he had never been concerned in so queer a process — and I think she thought better of me for having at last an "establishment." They saw a couple of drawings that I had made of the establishment, and Mrs. Monarch hinted that it never would have struck her he had sat for them." "Now the drawings you make from us, they look exactly like us," she reminded me, smiling in triumph; and I recognized that this was indeed just their defect. When I drew the Monarchs I couldn't anyhow get away from them — get into the character I wanted to represent; and I hadn't the least desire my model should be discoverable in my picture. Miss Churm never was, and Mrs. Monarch thought I hid her, very properly, because she was vulgar; whereas if she was lost it was only as the dead who go to heaven are lost — in the gain of an angel the more.

By this time[107] I had got a certain start with "Rutland Ramsay," the first novel in the great projected series; that is, I had produced a dozen drawings, several with the help of the Major and his wife, and I had sent them in for approval. My understanding with the publishers, as I have already hinted, had been that I was to be left to do my work, in this particular case, as I liked, with the whole book committed to me; but my connexion with the rest of the series was only contingent. There were moments when, frankly, it *was* a comfort to have the real thing under one's hand[108]; for there were characters in "Rutland Ramsay" that were very much like it. There were people presumably as erect as the Major and women of as good a fashion as Mrs. Monarch. There was a great deal of country-house life — treated, it is true, in a fine fanciful ironical generalized way — and there was a considerable implication of knickerbockers[109] and kilts[110]. There were certain things I had to settle at the outset; such things for instance as the exact appearance of the hero and the particular bloom and figure of the heroine. The author of course gave me a lead, but there was a margin for interpretation. I took the Monarchs into my confidence[111], I told them frankly what I was about, I mentioned my embarrassments and alternatives. "Oh, take *him!*" Mrs. Monarch murmured sweetly, looking at her husband; and "What could you want better than my wife?" the Major inquired with the comfortable candour that now prevailed between us.

---

105) convulse : 경련을 일으키다
106) lazzarone : 거지
107) by this time : 이때까지
108) under one's hand : 가까이에
109) knickerbockers : 낙낙한 반바지
110) kilt : 짧은 바지
111) take somebody into one's confidence : 털어놓다

I wasn't obliged to answer these remarks — I was only obliged to place my sitters. I wasn't easy in mind, and I postponed a little timidly perhaps the solving of my question. The book was a large canvas, the other figures were numerous, and I worked off at first some of the episodes in which the hero and the heroine were not concerned. When once I had set *them* up I should have to stick to them — I couldn't make my young man seven feet high in one place and five feet nine in another. I inclined on the whole to the latter measurement, though the Major more than once reminded me that *he* looked about as young as any one. It was indeed quite possible to arrange him, for the figure, so that it would have been difficult to detect his age. After the spontaneous Oronte had been with me a month, and after I had given him to understand several times over that his native exuberance would presently constitute an insurmountable barrier to our further intercourse, I waked to a sense of his heroic capacity. He was only five feet seven, but the remaining inches were latent. I tried him almost secretly at first, for I was really rather afraid of the judgment my other models would pass on[112] such a choice. If they regarded Miss Churm as little better than[113] a snare what would they think of the representation of a person so little the real thing as an Italian street-vendor of a protagonist formed by a public school?

If I went a little in fear of them it wasn't because they bullied me, because they had got an oppressive foothold, but because in their really pathetic decorum and mysteriously permanent newness they counted on me so intensely. I was therefore very glad when Jack Hawley came home: he was always of such good counsel. He painted badly himself, but there was no one like him for putting his finger on the place. He had been absent from England for a year; he had been somewhere I don't remember where — to get a fresh eye. I was in a good deal of dread of any such organ, but we were old friends; he had been away for months and a sense of emptiness was creeping into my life. I hadn't dodged a missile for a year.

He came back with a fresh eye, but with the same old black velvet blouse, and the first evening he spent in my studio we smoked cigarettes till the small hours. He had done no work himself, he had only got the eye; so the field was clear for the production of my little things. He wanted to see what I had produced for the Cheapside, but he was disappointed in the exhibition. That at least seemed the meaning of two or three comprehensive groans which, as he lounged on my big divan, his leg folded under him, looking at my latest drawings, issued from his lips with the smoke of the cigarette.

"What's the matter with you?" I asked.

"What's the matter with you?"

"Nothing save that I'm mystified."

"You are indeed. You're quite off the hinge[114]. What's the meaning of this new fad?" And he tossed me, with visible irreverence, a drawing in which I happened to have depicted both my elegant

---

112) pass on : 판단하다
113) little[no] better than : ~만큼, 마찬가지
114) off the hinge : 정신이 이상한

models. I asked if he didn't think it good, and he replied that it struck him as execrable[115], given the sort of thing I had always represented myself to him as wishing to arrive at; but I let that pass[116] — I was so anxious to see exactly what he meant. The two figures in the picture looked colossal, but I supposed this was not what he meant, inasmuch as, for aught he knew to the contrary, I might have been trying for some such effect. I maintained that I was working exactly in the same way as when he last had done me the honour to tell me I might do something some day. "Well, there's a screw loose somewhere," he answered; "wait a bit and I'll discover it." I depended upon him to do so; where else was the fresh eye? But he produced at last nothing more luminous than "I don't know — I don't like your types." This was lame for a critic who had never consented to discuss with me anything but the question of execution, the direction of strokes and the mystery of values.

"In the drawings you've been looking at I think my types are very handsome."

"Oh, they won't do!"

"I've been working with new models."

"I see you have. *They* won't do."

"Are you very sure of that?"

"Absolutely- they're stupid."

"You mean *I* am — for I ought to get round[117] that."

"You can't — with such people. Who are they?"

I told him, so far as[118] was necessary, and he concluded heartlessly: "*Ce sont des* gens *qu'il faut mettre a la porte*[119]."

"You've never seen them; they're awfully good" — I flew to their defense.

"Not seen them? Why, all this recent work of yours drops to pieces with them. It's all I want to see of them."

"No one else has said anything against it -the Cheapside people are pleased."

"Every one else is an ass, and the Cheapside people the biggest asses of all. Come, don't pretend at this time of day to have pretty illusions about the public, especially about publishers and editors. It's not for *such* animals you work — it's for those who know, *coloro che sanno*[120]; so keep straight for me if you can't keep straight for yourself. There was a certain sort of thing you used to try for — and a very good thing it was. But this twaddle[121] isn't *in* it." When I talked with Hawley later about "Rutland Ramsay" and its possible successors he declared that I must get back into my boat again or I should go to the bottom. His voice in short was the voice of warning.

I noted the warning, but I didn't turn my friends out of doors. They bored me a good deal; but the very fact that they bored me admonished me not to sacrifice them — if there was anything to

---

115) execrable : 서투른, 형편없는
116) let pass : 눈감아주다
117) get round : (문제를) 해결하다. (상대방에게 잘 해주어서) ~를 설득시키다
118) so far as : ~에 관하여
119) Ce ~ porte : (프랑스어) 해고해야 할 사람들이다.
120) coloro che sanno : (이태리어) 아는 사람들
121) twaddle : nonsense(쓸데없는 소리)

be done with them — simply to irritation. As I look back at this phase they seem to me to have pervaded my life not a little[122]. I have a vision of them as most of the time in my studio, seated against the wall on an old velvet bench to be out of the way, and resembling the while a pair of patient courtiers[123] in a royal ante-chamber[124]. I'm convinced that during the coldest weeks of the winter they held their ground because it saved them fire. Their newness was losing its gloss, and it was impossible not to feel them objects of charity. Whenever Miss Churm arrived they went away, and after I was fairly launched in "Rutland Ramsay" Miss Churm arrived pretty often. They managed to express to me tacitly that they supposed I wanted her for the low life of the book, and I let them suppose it, since they had attempted to study the work — it was lying about the studio — without discovering that it dealt only with the highest circles. They had dipped into the most brilliant of our novelists without deciphering many passages. I still took an hour from them, now and again, in spite of Jack Hawley's warning: it would be time enough to dismiss them, if dismissal should be necessary, when the rigour of the season was over. Hawley had made their acquaintance — he had met them at my fireside — and thought them a ridiculous pair. Learning that he was a painter they tried to approach him, to show him too that they were the real thing; but he looked at them, across the big room, as if they were miles away; they were a compendium[125] of everything he most objected to in the social system of his country. Such people as that[126], all convention and patent-leather, with ejaculations that stopped conversation, had no business in a studio. A studio was a place to learn to see, and how could you see through[127] a pair of feather-beds?

The main inconvenience I suffered at their hands was that at first I was shy of letting it break upon[128] them that my artful little servant had begun to sit for me for "Rutland Ramsay." They knew I had been odd enough — they were prepared by this time to allow oddity to artists to pick a foreign vagabond out of the streets when I might have had a person with whiskers and credentials; but it was some time before they learned how high I rated his accomplishments. They found him in an attitude more than once, but they never doubted I was doing him as an organ-grinder. There were several things they never guessed, and one of them was that for a striking scene in the novel, in which a footman briefly figured, it occurred to me to make use of Major Monarch as the menial. I kept putting this off, I didn't like to ask him to don[129] the livery[130] — besides the difficulty of finding a livery to fit him. At last, one day late in the winter, when I was at work on the despised Oronte, who caught one's idea on the wing, and was in the glow of feeling myself go very straight, they came in, the Major and his wife, with their society laugh about nothing (there was less and less to laugh at); came in like country — callers — they always reminded me of that — who have

---

122) not a little : much(많은)
123) courtier : (과거 왕을 보필하던) 신하
124) ante-chamber : 대기실
125) compendium : 요약, 개론
126) as that : 게다가
127) see through : 간파하다
128) break upon : 문득 입에서 나오다
129) don : (옷, 모자 따위를) 걸치다, 쓰다
130) livery : 제복

walked across the park after church and are presently persuaded to stay to luncheon. Luncheon was over, but they could stay to tea — I knew they wanted it. The fit was on me, however, and I couldn't let my ardour cool and my work wait, with the fading daylight, while my model prepared it. So I asked Mrs. Monarch if she would mind laying it out[131] — a request which for an instant brought all the blood to her face. Her eyes were on her husband's for a second, and some mute telegraphy passed between them. Their folly was over the next instant; his cheerful shrewdness put an end to it[132]. So far from pitying their wounded pride, I must add, I was moved to give it as complete a lesson as I could. They bustled about together and got out the cups and saucers[133] and made the kettle boil. I know they felt as if they were waiting on my servant, and when the tea was prepared, I said: "He'll have a cup, please — he's tired." Mrs. Monarch brought him one where he stood, and he took it from her as if he had been a gentleman at a party squeezing a crush-hat with an elbow.

Then it came over me that she had made a great effort for me — made it with a kind of nobleness — and that I owed her a compensation. Each time I saw her after this I wondered what the compensation could be. I couldn't go on doing the wrong thing to oblige them. Oh, it *was* the wrong thing, the stamp of the work for which they sat — Hawley was not the only person to say it now. I sent in a large number of the drawings I had made for "Rutland Ramsay," and I received a warning that was more to the point than Hawley's. The artistic adviser of the house for which I was working was of opinion that many of my illustrations were not what had been looked for. Most of these illustrations were the subjects in which the Monarchs had figured. Without going into the question of what had been looked for, I had to face the fact that at this rate[134] I shouldn't get the other books to do. I hurled myself in despair on Miss Churm — I put her through all her paces. I not only adopted Oronte publicly as my hero, but one morning when the Major looked in to see if I didn't require him to finish a Cheapside figure for which he had begun to sit the week before, I told him I had changed my mind- I'd do the drawing from my man. At this my visitor turned pale and stood looking at me. "Is *he* your idea of an English gentleman?" he asked.

I was disappointed, I was nervous, I wanted to get on[135] with my work; so I replied with irritation: "Oh my dear Major — I can't be ruined for *you!*"

It was a horrid speech, but he stood another moment — after which, without a word, he quitted the studio. I drew a long breath, for I said to myself that I shouldn't see him again. I hadn't told him definitely that I was in danger of having my work rejected, but I was vexed at his not having felt the catastrophe in the air, read with me the moral of our fruitless collaboration, the lesson that in the deceptive atmosphere of art even the highest respectability may fail of being plastic.

I didn't owe my friends money, but I did see them again. They reappeared together three days later, and, given[136] all the other facts, there was something tragic in that one. It was a clear proof

131) lay out : 설계하다
132) put ~ to it : 난처하게 하다
133) saucer : 찻잔, 접시
134) at this rate : 이래서는
135) get on : 서두르다
136) given : 배제하는, 빼는

제6장 Henry James – 「Washington Square」, 「The Real Thing」 **291** they could find nothing else in life to do. They had threshed the matter out[137] in a dismal conference — they had digested the bad news that they were not in for the series. If they weren't useful to me even for the Cheapside, their function seemed difficult to determine, and I could only judge at first that they had come, forgivingly, decorously, to take a last leave. This made me rejoice in secret that I had little leisure for a scene; I had placed both my other models in position together and I was pegging away[138] at a drawing from which I hoped to derive glory. It had been suggested by the passage in which Rutland Ramsay, drawing up a chair to Artemisia's piano-stool, says extraordinary things to her while she ostensibly fingers out a difficult piece of music. I had done Miss Churm at the piano before — it was an attitude in which she knew how to take on an absolutely poetic grace. I wished the two figures to "compose" together with intensity, and my little Italian had entered perfectly into my conception. The pair were vividly before me, the piano had been pulled out[139]; it was a charming show of blended youth and murmured love, which I had only to catch and keep. My visitors stood and looked at it, and I was friendly to them over my shoulder.

They made no response, but I was used to silent company and went on with my work, only a little disconcerted — even though exhilarated by the sense that *this* was at least the ideal thing — at not having got rid of[140] them after all. Presently I heard Mrs. Monarch's sweet voice beside or rather above me: "I wish her hair were a little better done." I looked up and she was staring with a strange fixedness at Miss Churm, whose back was turned to her. "Do you mind my just touching it?" she went on — a question which made me spring up for an instant as with the instinctive fear that she might do the young lady a harm. But she quieted me with a glance I shall never forget — I confess I should like to have been able to paint *that* - and went for a moment to my model. She spoke to her softly, laying a hand on her shoulder and bending over her; and as the girl, understanding, gratefully assented, she disposed her rough curls, with a few quick passes, in such a way as to make Miss Churm's head twice as charming. It was one of the most heroic personal services I've ever seen rendered. Then Mrs. Monarch turned away[141] with a low sigh and, looking about her as if for something to do, stooped to the floor with a noble humility and picked up a dirty rag[142] that had dropped out of my paint-box.

The Major meanwhile had also been looking for something to do, and, wandering to the other end of the studio, saw before him my breakfast-things neglected, unremoved. "I say, can't I be useful *here?*" he called out to me with an irrepressible quaver. I assented with a laugh that I fear was awkward, and for the next ten minutes, while I worked, I heard the light clatter[143] of china and the tinkle[144] of spoons and glass. Mrs. Monarch assisted her husband — they washed up my

---

137) thresh out : 검토하다
138) peg away : 열심히 일하다
139) pull out : 철수하다
140) get rid of : be freed of, be relieved of
141) turn away : 방향을 바꾸다
142) rag : (걸레나 행주 등으로 쓰는) 해진 천
143) clatter : 달가닥 소리
144) tinkle : 땡그랑거리는 소리

crockery[145]), they put it away[146]). They wandered off into my little scullery[147]), and I afterwards found that they had cleaned my knives and that my slender stock of plates had an unprecedented surface. When it came over me, the latent eloquence of what they were doing, I confess that my drawing was blurred for a moment — the picture swam. They had accepted their failure, but they couldn't accept their fate. They had bowed their heads in bewilderment to the perverse and cruel law in virtue of which the real thing could be so much less precious than the unreal; but they didn't want to starve. If my servants were my models, then my models might be my servants. They would reverse the parts — the others would sit for the ladies and gentlemen and they would do the work. They would still be in the studio — it was an intense dump appeal to me not to turn them out[148]). "Take us on," they wanted to say — "we'll do anything."

When all this hung before me the *afflatus*[149]) vanished — my pencil dropped from my hand; my sitting[150]) was spoiled and I got rid of my sitters, who were also evidently rather mystified and awestruck. Then, alone with the Major and his wife I had a most uncomfortable moment. He put their prayer into[151]) a single sentence: "I say, you know — just let *us* do for[152]) you, can't you?" I couldn't — it was dreadful to see them emptying my slops[153]); but I pretended I could, to oblige them, for about a week. Then I gave them a sum of money to go away, and I never saw them again. I obtained the remaining books, but my friend Hawley repeats that Major and Mrs. Monarch did me a permanent harm, got me into false ways. If it be true I'm content to have paid the price — for the memory.

---

145) crockery : 도자기류
146) put it away : 치우다
147) scullery : 식기실(食器室)
148) turn out : 해고하다, 내쫓다
149) afflatus : 영감
150) sitting : (일 등으로 인한) 소요시간, 모델 작업을 위한 정좌자세
151) put into : ~로 표현하다
152) do for : ~의 도움이 되다, ~을 대신해 살림을 돌보다
153) empty the slops : 구정물을 비워내다

Stephen Crane
- 「*The Red Badge of Courage : An Episode of the American Civil War*」

단원 개요

Stephen Crane의 「*The Red Badge of Courage*」는 환경이나 강력한 힘에 의하여 어쩔 수 없이 좌절하는 인물을 묘사하기는 하지만, 나약하고 실패하는 것만이 아니라 삶의 과정에서 끊임없이 갈등하고 치열하게 싸우는 인간적인 모습을 감동적으로 생생하게 드러내는 작품이다.

출제 경향 및 수험 대책

작가는 환경에 의하여 좌절하거나 삶을 개척하는 영웅과 같은 일방적인 묘사가 아니라 역동적으로 바뀌어가는 인간의 모습을 생생히 그려낸다. Fleming이 환경에 따라 움직이는 인물에 불과하다는 부정적인 평가나 인본주의를 터득한 성장한 인간이라는 일면적인 평가를 지양하고, 갈등하는 한 인물로서 그의 진정한 모습에 주목하여 작품을 분석할 필요가 있다.

제 1 절 작가의 생애

1 Stephen Crane의 생애

Stephen Crane(1871~1900)은 미국 뉴저지(New Jersey)의 뉴어크(Newwark)에서 목사의 14번째 아이이자 막내아들로 태어났다. 아버지인 Jonathan Townley Crane은 감리교 목사였고, 어머니인 Mary Helen Crane은 당시 기독교 여성 금주연합에서 활약하며 자식들에게 기독교인으로서 청교도적인 청빈함과 경건함을 항상 강조했다. 1880년, 아버지가 죽은 후에도 Crane의 어머니는 미국 감리교 전통의 엄숙한 분위기가 감도는 애즈베리파크(Asbery Park)로 이사했다. Crane은 어렸을 때부터 종교적인 분위기 속에 자랐지만 이러한 분위기에 답답함을 느끼고 반항하게 된다. 기존 교육제도에 반발하여 독서를 하면서 문학적인 소양을 스스로 길렀다. 그는 14세 때부터 여러 학교를 다녔지만 정식 교육과정에 관심이 없었으며 문학 과목과 야구경기에만 관심을 쏟았고, 일반 교과과목 공부에는 소홀했다.

대학시절부터 신문사를 운영하던 형의 도움으로 여러 신문사의 통신원으로 일할 수 있었고, 그곳에서 소설가로서의 글쓰기 훈련을 할 수 있었다. 그는 당시 뉴욕 주변의 빈민들에게 관심을 가졌고, 그들의 열악한 생활을 지속적으로 기사화했다. 시러큐스 대학교(Syracuse University) 시절에 발표한 「*Maggie : A Girl of the Streets*」(1893)는 이러한 청년시절에 작가로서의 훈련과 관심의 결과라 할 수 있다. 대학을 떠난 후에도 그는 뉴욕에서 하층민들과 긴 시간을 함께하려고 노력했다. 구속받는 것을 싫어하여 스스로 어디에 얽매이지 않고 자유롭게 생활했다.

그는 황량하고 위험한 미국 서부를 신문기자로서 여행하기도 하였고, 종군기자로서 그리스 터키 전쟁에 참전하기도 하였다. 종군기자의 임무가 끝난 후 주로 영국에 머물면서 유럽의 문인들과 친분을 쌓았다. Joseph Conrad와의 친교는 Crane이 인간의 심리를 인상주의적 수법으로 작품화하는 데 많은 도움을 주었다고 볼 수 있다. 1889년 미국-스페인 전쟁(Spanish-American War)에 다시 종군기자로 참전하여 전투와 관련된 짧은 스케치를 남겼다.

그는 밀린 빚을 갚고 생활비를 벌기 위해 많은 작품들을 집필하였으나, 이전의 걸작들에 비하여 문학적 긴장감이 덜하다는 평을 받았다. 영국의 옥스테드(Oxted)와 서식스(Sussex) 지방 등으로 거처를 옮기며 요양을 하면서 「The Monster」(1898) 같은 장편과 수많은 단편을 출판하였다.

Crane은 선천적으로 약한 체질임에도 불구하고 젊었을 때부터 몸을 돌보지 않아 극도로 쇠약해졌다. 1900년 6월, 29세의 젊은 나이로 사망하며 유해는 고향인 미국의 New Jersey의 가족묘지에 안치되었다.

2 작품 활동

(1) 「Maggie : A Girl on the Streets」(1893)

Crane의 첫 번째 걸작이다. Johnston Smith라는 가명을 사용하여 자비로 출판할 정도로 이 작품에 대한 인정을 받지는 못했다.

(2) 「The Red Badge of Courage」(1895)

이 작품은 출판한 지 일 년 만에 미국과 영국에서 9판까지 출판될 정도로 큰 성공을 거두었다. 일반 독자들의 예상과는 다르게 이 작품을 집필할 당시의 Crane은 전쟁에 대한 경험이 거의 없었다. 이 소설은 다른 과거의 전쟁소설과는 달리 전투상황이 전혀 밝혀지지 않은 남북전쟁의 작은 전투에서, 싸움보다는 도망갈 궁리나 하고 심적인 두려움에 떨고 있는 군인들의 내적 심리상태의 묘사에 집중하였다. 이러한 작품의 특징은 인간의 불안한 내부 심리에 관심을 갖기 시작한 세기말 독자들을 매료시켰다.

(3) 「The Open Boat」(1898)

뉴욕에서 한 창녀를 도와주려다가 경찰과 갈등을 겪은 Crane은 어려움을 피하기 위하여 잠시 Florida로 이동하고 여기서 죽을 때까지 생을 함께한 Cora Taylor를 만나게 된다. 안정된 삶을 거부하고, 새롭고 어려운 곳을 찾아다니며 어려운 사람들의 삶에 뛰어들기 좋아했던 Crane은 종군기자가 되기 위하여 미국에서 Cuba로 떠나는 Commodore라는 배에 탑승했으나 Cuba로 가는 도중 험한 파도를 만나 난파하고, 거의 이틀 동안 조난당했다가 구사일생으로 구출된다. 이때의 생생한 경험이 훗날 생사를 넘나드는 난파선에서 형제애의 중요성을 강조한 「The Open Boat」의 바탕이 된다.

> **더 알아두기**
>
> **Stephen Crane의 주요작품**
> • 「Maggie : A Girl on the Streets」(1893)
> • 「The Red Badge of Courage」(1895)
> • 「The Open Boat」(1898)

제 2 절 작품 세계

1 주인공의 심리

(1) 「*Maggie : A Girl on the Streets*」(1893)의 Maggie

뉴욕이라는 도시 환경 속에서 좌절하고 마는 인간의 외적인 모습을 묘사한 작품이다. 객관적인 묘사로 의지가 약한 주인공을 표현한다.

(2) 「*The Red Badge of Courage*」(1895)의 주인공 Henry Fleming

일반 전쟁소설에 흔히 등장하는 주인공의 모습과는 다르다. 즉, 자신보다 전우를 먼저 생각하고 전투가 일어나면 앞장서서 싸우며 의리 있고 용감한 모습의 주인공이 아니다. Fleming은 실제로 전투가 벌어졌을 때에도 역할이 별로 없다. 한없이 나약하며 작은 일에도 쉽게 동요하는 병사이다. 이 작품은 전투라는 극한 상황 속에서 흔들리는 인간의 심리, 가령 실제 전투가 벌어졌을 경우에 싸워야 하는지 도망가야 하는지를 갈등하는 모습 등이 생생하게 묘사되면서 인간이 내적으로 얼마나 약한 존재인지를 드러낸다.

2 작품에 대한 평가

(1) 성장소설로 볼 수 있는가?

Fleming이 실제 전투를 경험해가면서 어른으로 성장하였는가는 비평가들의 지속적인 논쟁거리이다. 전투의 여러 과정을 거치며 동료인 Jim Conklin의 희생적이고 장렬한 죽음을 접하면서 Fleming은 도덕적으로 성장할 뿐만 아니라 종교적으로도 새롭게 태어났다는 견해가 있다. 그러나 Fleming은 총탄이 오고가는 위험한 실제 전투에서 본능적으로 싸울 수밖에 없는 대다수 군인들 중의 한명일 뿐이라고 보는 견해도 있다.

(2) 다양한 해석의 가능성

독자들에게 확정된 메시지를 직접적으로 전달하지 않는 Crane의 작품 특징 때문에 다양한 해석이 가능하다. Crane은 허무주의를 표방하는 미국 자연주의 작가이다. 그는 성장하는 주인공을 묘사함으로써 거친 환경 앞에 무조건적인 나약한 모습이 아니라 인간이 긍정적으로 성숙할 수 있는 모습을 독자들에게 대안으로 제시한다. James Tuttleton, William Dillingham 같은 비평가들은 현대를 사는 우리의 모습과 Fleming이 서로 다를 바 없다고 주장한다. 문학적 긴장감을 불러일으키는 Fleming의 섬세한 심리변화를 통해 Crane의 묘사가 예술적으로 어떤 효과를 주는지를 살펴보는 것이 주인공의 삶의 양면성을 이해하는 데 매우 중요하다.

3 심리묘사 종요 ★★

(1) Crane은 처음부터 끝까지 주인공의 심리묘사를 통해 인간의 나약한 모습을 표현한다. Fleming은 자신의 미래가 불확실하기 때문에 불안해한다. 그는 입대 전에 기대했던 장엄하기까지 한 "그리스 시대의 전투"(Greeklike struggle)를 머릿속으로 그리며 마음의 평정심을 찾는다. 이러한 묘사는 Fleming이 실제보다 자신이 만들어놓은 비현실적인 모습에 마음이 이끌림을 보여준다. 헛된 상상을 하면서 마음의 평화를 얻기도 하지만, 때로는 두려움에 사로잡혀 심한 동요도 보여준다. 그는 현재의 두려움 때문에 사소한 것에 강한 집착을 보이며 어색한 행동을 한다.

(2) 외적인 환경에 수동적으로 반응하며 본능에 따라 반응하는 동물 같은 모습은 전형적인 자연주의 작품에 등장하는 인물에게서 볼 수 있는 특징이다. Fleming은 총포소리가 전장에 울려 퍼지면서 실제로 전투가 시작되자 두려움에 사로잡혀 어느 것에도 집중하지 못한다. 전투가 계속 진행되면서 죽음의 실체가 실제로 자신에게 다가옴을 느낀 Fleming은 군인으로서의 자신을 생각하지 못하고 총을 버리고 숲으로 도망친다. 첫 전투 직후 Fleming이 가졌던 자기만족은 환상에 불과하다는 것을 보여준다.

(3) 자연주의 철학 – 우연이 때때로 인간의 삶을 지배

두려움에 떨면서 도망쳤던 Fleming은 아군 부상병 무리에 운 좋게 합류하면서 그의 운명이 바뀐다. 아군이 휘두른 총에 이마에 상처(the red badge of courage)를 입는데, 이 상처가 Fleming을 영웅으로 만들면서 다음 전투부터 적 앞에서 마치 동물처럼 본능적으로 미친 듯이 용감하게 싸운다. 이 과정을 통해 Fleming은 누구보다도 용감한 영웅이 된다. 그는 과거의 자신의 비겁한 모습을 반성하고 주위의 동료를 생각하며 전투에서 몸을 던져 열심히 싸운다. 남을 배려하며 자신을 희생하는 Fleming의 행동은 주변사람들이 그를 위대한 영웅으로 여기게 한다. 그리고 Fleming 자신도 스스로 어른(man)이 되었다고 믿는다.

4 문학적 긴장

외부로 드러나는 주인공의 행동묘사와 내적인 심리묘사를 통해 작품 내내 문학적 긴장이 지속된다. 환경에 좌절되는 희생자이거나 자신의 삶을 스스로 개척해서 완전한 승리를 쟁취하는 긍정적인 영웅의 모습 등과 같은 일방적인 묘사로 주인공을 표현하지 않는다. 이 작품은 끊임없이 긴장을 야기시키면서 갈등하고 변화하는 실제 인간의 모습을 생생하게 묘사한다. 작가는 Fleming을 단순히 환경과 유전의 힘에 따라 움직이는 자연주의적 인물로 묘사하기도 하지만, 반면에 진정으로 인본주의를 터득한 성숙한 인물로 변화하는 인물로도 그리면서 갈등하는 인간의 진정한 모습을 부각시킨다.

제 3 절 줄거리

키다리 Jim Conklin과 늘 시끄러운 Wilson은 군부대가 이동할 것이라는 소문을 놓고 격렬하게 논쟁을 벌인다. 계속되는 반복 훈련에 지쳐 실제 전투를 체험하기를 간절히 원하는 Henry Fleming은 고참들의 논쟁을 경청하면서 막상 총탄이 퍼붓기 시작하면 자신은 놀라서 도망치지나 않을까 하는 생각을 한다. Wilson과 Conklin은 다 같이 싸운다면 꿋꿋이 버티며 싸울 것이라고 말하고 Fleming은 그들의 대답에 고마워하고 안심한다.

Fleming은 농촌 출신의 청년으로 '그리스 시대의 전투'(Greeklike struggle) 장면을 꿈꾸며 군대 생활을 동경했다. 처음에 그의 어머니는 그의 참전을 만류했지만 아들이 농촌 생활에 싫증을 내자 옷가지를 꾸려 주며 잘 처신하라고 충고했다. 결국 Fleming은 남북전쟁의 북군(the Union)에 합류한다.

어느 흐린 날 아침, Fleming은 부대가 이동할 예정이라고 듣는다. 그는 지루하고 의미 없는 행군보다는 죽는 것이 낫다고 생각한다. 그리고 장군들이 바보가 아닐까라는 생각도 한다. 갑자기 전투가 시작되지만 Fleming이 하는 일은 다른 동료들과 함께 땅바닥에 엎드려 적의 동정을 살피는 일이 전부이다. 주위 몇몇 동료는 부상을 입지만 Fleming은 무엇이 진행되는지, 전투의 목표가 무엇인지를 알지 못한다. 적군의 공격이 시작되자 Fleming은 이제까지의 혼란스러운 생각을 잊고 계속해서 소총만 쏘아댄다. 공격이 끝나고 총소리가 멈춘 후에도 머리 위의 하늘이 여전히 푸르른 것이 Fleming에게는 이상하게 느껴진다. 병사들이 정신을 차리고 상처에 붕대를 감고 장비를 정리할 때 다시 적들이 기습 공격을 시작한다. 아직 준비를 갖추지 못한 데다 첫 전투로 인해 탈진한 동료들은 공포에 질려 퇴각하고 Fleming도 공포에 사로잡혀 같이 뛴다.

공포에 질린 퇴각이 끝났을 때 도주하던 병사들은 아군이 이기고 적군이 패배했다는 사실을 알게 된다. 이에 Fleming은 죄책감을 느껴 자기 중대와 합류하기가 두려워 숲속으로 도망치는데, 그곳에서 다람쥐 한 마리가 그를 보고 놀라서 도망친다. Fleming은 도망치는 다람쥐를 보면서 겁쟁이의 도주가 어떤 것인가를 보여주는 것같이 느끼고, 자연이 창조한 피조물들은 위험에서 도망치고, 자신도 그 자연의 섭리에 따라 행동했다는 생각을 한다.

숲속에서 개미 떼가 꼬인 시체를 목격한 Fleming은 서둘러 후퇴하는 부상병 대열에 끼어든다. 사상자를 비롯한 부상자들은 발을 끌거나 들것에 얹혀 운반되지만 부상당한 곳이 없는 Fleming은 자신이 이 대열에 속하지 않는다고 느낀다. 그중 먼지와 피로 범벅이 된 한 병사가 Jim Conklin임을 목격한 Fleming은 자신이 도망간 사실이 발각될까봐 겁에 질린다.

Fleming은 그를 부축해 주려고 하지만 Jim은 발작을 하더니 곧 쓰러져 죽고 만다. 양심의 가책을 또 느낀 Fleming은 도주해서 자기 연대로 돌아가려고 하지만, 동료 병사들이 그를 도망자라고 비난할 것이 두렵다. 스스로를 겁쟁이라고 느끼는 Fleming은 오히려 죽어 누워 있는 영웅 같은 시체들을 부러워한다.

앞쪽에서 포탄이 꽝음을 내며 터지는 소리가 들리고, Fleming은 자기 연대의 대열에 가까이 가지만 서둘러 후퇴하는 병사들 중 한 명이 소총의 개머리판으로 Fleming의 머리를 가격해 Fleming의 머리에 상처가 난다. Fleming은 또 다른 연대에 합류하게 되는데, 그곳에서 자신이 죽을 때를 대비해 Fleming에게 편지를 맡겨둔 Wilson을 만난다. Fleming은 '전쟁의 상처'(red badge of courage)로 간주되는 자신의 머리 상처 때문에 Wilson보다 우월한 위치에 서게 된다.

다시 전투가 시작되고, Fleming은 마치 짐승처럼 미친 듯이 계속 총을 쏜다. 사격 중지 명령이 내리자 Fleming은 자신의 눈앞에 적군이 하나도 없다는 것을 목격한다. 연대 중위는 공개적으로 그를 칭찬하지만,

앞으로 모든 아군의 병사가 죽게 될 만한 전투에 Fleming과 Wilson을 포함한 그의 부대를 참여시키려고 한다. 이를 우연히 엿들은 Fleming은 인간이란 거대한 우주 속에서 어쩔 수 없는 하찮은 존재에 불과하다는 사실을 깨닫는다.

다음 전투가 시작되자마자 기수가 죽고, Fleming과 Wilson은 대신 깃발을 집어 든다. 비록 전투에서 승리는 못했지만 지휘관이 Fleming의 용맹함을 칭찬한다. 그의 부대는 또 한 번 적과의 접전을 벌이고, Fleming은 이제 베테랑 병사가 된다. 전투가 끝나자 Fleming과 Wilson은 승승장구하는 그들의 연대와 진군을 계속한다.

제 4 절 작품의 주제 중요 ★

- 용기의 본질은 무엇이며 용기는 어떻게 획득되는지에 대한 문제
- 병영생활의 지겨움과 병사들의 대화, 장교들의 오만함, 끊임없는 대포소리 등을 통하여 전쟁의 본질을 표현함
- 개인과 조직사회의 관계
- 성장소설
- 자연주의(Naturalism)적 주제
  여러 우연한 사건들이 한 청년을 영웅으로 만든다.
- 인간의 나약한 내면
- 자연(Nature)
  전쟁과 별개로 존재하며 처음에는 고요한 피난처처럼 보인다. 그러나 소설이 진행되면서 Fleming은 자연이 인간에게 무관심하다는 것을 깨닫는다.

제 5 절 등장인물

1 Henry Fleming(The Youth)

이 작품의 주인공이자 일등병이다. 고전 신화에서 나오는 영웅과 같은 환상으로 전쟁 참전을 지원한 시골 청년이다. 그의 환상은 단조로운 훈련의 반복과 실제 전투로 곧 깨어졌으나, 현실에 눈을 뜨고 본능에 따르는 동물처럼 행동한다. 전투 초기에서는 공포심에 떨면서 연대를 이탈하지만 그 다음 전투부터는 전투가 끝나도 미친 듯이 총을 쏘아대면서 동료들로부터 칭찬을 받고 마침내 전쟁의 영웅이 된다. Fleming은 그 후의 전투에서도 맹렬하게 적군과 싸우며 자신이 진정한 어른이 되었다고 생각한다.

2 Henry's mother

1장에서 등장하는 인물로, 열심히 일하는 농사꾼이다. 현실적인 감각을 터득한 인물이다.

3 Jim Conklin(The Tall Soldier)

큰 키의 고참병으로, 두 번째 전투에서 아군의 총에 맞아 부상을 당하고 무력하게 죽는다.

4 Wilson(The Loud Soldier or The Friend)

Henry Fleming과 절친한 동료애를 느끼는 일등병 동기이다. 처음에는 목소리만 클 뿐 나약하고 겁쟁이 같은 모습을 보이지만, 점차 전투에서 용기를 획득하면서 부상당한 Fleming을 간호할 정도의 인간적인 병사로 변한다. 이후의 전투에서는 Fleming과 함께 적군의 깃발을 빼앗는 등의 행위를 하며 Fleming과 더불어 전쟁의 영웅이 된다.

5 The Tattered Soldier

(전투로 인하여) 찢겨진 군복(tattered)을 입은 병사로서 부상으로 사망한다. 부상을 입은 상태에서 Fleming과 전투 현장에서 만나 잠시 동행하지만, Fleming은 그를 무관심하게 대하고 그의 죽음을 방관한다. Fleming이 전투 중 도망간 것에 대한 양심(consciousness), 죄책감(guilt) 및 수치심(shame)을 느끼게 하는 인물이다.

6 Lieutenant Hasbrouck

연대의 중위로, 전투의 현장에서 병사들에게 싸움을 재촉하고 명령을 내리는 것이 그의 주된 임무이다.

7 Bill Smithers

부상으로 인해 병원에 입원해 있는 병사이다.

제 6 절 작품의 구조(Plot)와 시점 및 기법

1 구조

(1) 24장의 짧은 부분들로 구성되어 있다. 각 장은 항상 Henry Fleming의 용기의 상실과 획득, 성인으로의 나아감이라는 주제를 가지고 있다.

(2) 군대의 전진과 주둔, 공격과 휴식 등을 통해 일종의 시소게임(seesaw game) 같은 구성이라고도 한다.

(3) Henry Fleming의 심리상태에 주목하면 절망과 희망의 교차적인 구성으로 볼 수 있다.

2 시점

작가는 3인칭 시점을 사용하고 있으나 Fleming의 눈에 보이고 느껴지는 대로 그리고 있다.

3 기법

(1) **인상주의적 사실주의(Impressionistic Realism)**

남북전쟁을 최초로 다룬 사실주의적 작품이며, 인상주의(impressionism)적 기법을 사용한다. Crane이 직접 전투에 참가한 적은 없다. 그러나 전투에 참가한 경험이 있었던 자신의 형으로부터 들은 군대생활을 바탕으로 실제 전투 장면을 실감나게 재현한다.

(2) **어조**

1800년대 미국에서 교육을 받지 못한 사람들의 지방 사투리가 많이 사용된다.

(3) **이미지**

동물을 사용한 이미저리(animal imagery), 종교적 심상, 색채 심상 등을 사용하여 주변 환경과 등장인물들의 심리적 변화 등을 선명하게 부각시킨다.

(4) **상징** 중요 ★

① flag(깃발) → courage(용기)
② squirrel(다람쥐), rabbit(토끼), chicken(닭) → coward(겁쟁이), fleeing(도피)
③ forest(숲) → refuge(피신), fleeing(도피)

④ war(전쟁) → boyish dream of glory(명예에 대한 소년의 꿈)

⑤ wound(상처) → courage(용기)

⑥ badge of courage(용기의 배지) → badge of shame(수치의 배지)

제 7 절   Text

Chapter 1

THE cold passed reluctantly from the earth, and the retiring fogs revealed an army stretched out[1] on the hills, resting. As the landscape changed from brown to green, the army awakened, and began to tremble with eagerness at the noise of rumors. It cast its eyes upon the roads, which were growing from long troughs of liquid mud to proper thoroughfares. A river, amber-tinted[2] in the shadow of its banks, purled at the army's feet; and at night, when the stream had become of a sorrowful blackness, one could see across it the red, eye-like gleam of hostile camp-fires set in the low brows of distant hills.

Once a certain tall soldier developed virtues[3] and went resolutely to wash a shirt. He came flying back from a brook waving his garment bannerlike. He was swelled with a tale he had heard from a reliable friend, who had heard it from a truthful cavalryman, who had heard it from his trustworthy brother, one of the orderlies at division headquarters. He adopted the important air of a herald in red and gold.

"We're goin't'[4] move t'morrah — sure," he said pompously to a group in the company street. "We're goin' 'way up the river, cut across, an' come around in behint 'em.

To his attentive audience he drew a loud and elaborate plan of a very brilliant campaign. When he had finished, the blue-clothed men[5] scattered[6] into small arguing groups between the rows of squat brown huts. A negro teamster who had been dancing upon a cracker box with the hilarious encouragement of two score soldiers was deserted. He sat mournfully down. Smoke drifted lazily from a multitude of quaint chimneys.

"It's a lie! that's all it is — a thunderin' lie!" said another private loudly. His smooth face was flushed, and his hands were thrust[7] sulkily into his trousers' pockets. He took the matter as an

---

1) stretched out : 뻗어 있는, 펼쳐진
2) amber-tinted : 호박색으로 물든
3) virtue : 덕, 미덕, 장점
4) goin't' : going to
5) blue-clothed men : 푸른 옷을 입은 사람들(the Union, 남북전쟁의 북군)
6) scatter : (뿔뿔이) 흩어지다, 흩뿌리다
7) thrust: 밀다, 밀치다, 쑤셔 넣다

affront[8]) to him. "I don't believe the derned old army's ever going to move. We're set. I've got ready to move eight times in the last two weeks, and we ain't moved yet."

The tall soldier felt called upon[9]) to defend the truth of a rumor he himself had introduced. He and the loud one came near to fighting over it.

A corporal[10]) began to swear before the assemblage. He had just put a costly board floor in his house, he said. During the early spring he had refrained from[11]) adding extensively to the comfort of his environment because he had felt that the army might start on the march at any moment. Of late,[12]) however, he had been impressed that they were in a sort of eternal camp.

Many of the men engaged in a spirited debate. One outlined in a peculiarly lucid manner all the plans of the commanding general. He was opposed by men who advocated that there were other plans of campaign. They clamored at each other, numbers making futile bids for the popular attention. Meanwhile, the soldier who had fetched the rumor bustled about with much importance. He was continually assailed by questions.

"What's up, Jim?"

"Th' army's goin' t' move."

"Ah, what yeh talkin' about? How yeh[13]) know it is?"

"Well, yeh kin b'lieve me er not, jest as yeh like[14]). I don't care a hang."

There was much food for thought[15]) in the manner in which he replied. He came near to convincing them by disdaining to produce proofs. They grew much excited over[16]) it.

There was a youthful private who listened with eager ears to the words of the tall soldier and to the varied comments of his comrades[17]). After receiving a fill of discussions concerning marches and attacks, he went to his hut and crawled[18]) through an intricate hole that served it as a door. He wished to be alone with some new thoughts that had lately come to him.

He lay down on a wide bunk that stretched across the end of the room. In the other end[19]), cracker boxes were made to serve as furniture. They were grouped about the fireplace. A picture from an illustrated weekly was upon the log walls[20]), and three rifles were paralleled on pegs. Equipments hung on handy projections, and some tin dishes lay upon a small pile of firewood. A folded tent was serving as a roof. The sunlight, without, beating upon it, made it glow a light yellow shade. A small window shot an oblique square of whiter light upon the cluttered floor. The smoke from

8) affront : 모욕
9) call upon : 요청하다, 부탁하다, 방문하다
10) corporal : 고참병(상등병), 최하위 하사관
11) refrain from : 그만두다, 삼가다
12) Of late : 최근에
13) yeh : you
14) yeh kin b'lieve me er not, jest as yeh like : you can believe me or not, just as you like
15) food for thought : 생각할 것
16) excited over : 흥분하다, 격하다
17) comrades : 동료, 전우
18) crawl : 기다, 포복하다
19) In the other end : (방의) 다른 한쪽 끝에는
20) log wall : 통나무 벽

the fire at times neglected the clay chimney and wreathed into the room, and this flimsy[21] chimney of clay and sticks made endless threats to set ablaze the whole establishment.

The youth was in a little trance of astonishment. So they were at last going to fight. On the morrow, perhaps, there would be a battle, and he would be in it. For a time he was obliged to labor to make himself believe. He could not accept with assurance an omen that he was about to mingle in one of those great affairs of the earth.

He had, of course, dreamed of battles all his life — of vague and bloody conflicts that had thrilled him with their sweep and fire. In visions he had seen himself in many struggles. He had imagined peoples secure in the shadow of his eagle-eyed prowess[22]. But awake he had regarded battles as crimson blotches on the pages of the past. He had put them as things of the bygone[23] with his thought — images of heavy crowns and high castles. There was a portion of the world's history which he had regarded as the time of wars, but it, he thought, had been long gone over the horizon and had disappeared forever.

From his home his youthful eyes had looked upon[24] the war in his own country with distrust. It must be some sort of a play affair. He had long despaired of witnessing a Greeklike struggle. Such would be no more, he had said. Men were better, or more timid. Secular and religious education had effaced[25] the throat-grappling instinct, or else firm finance held in check the passions.

He had burned several times to enlist. Tales of great movements shook the land. They might not be distinctly Homeric[26], but there seemed to be much glory in them. He had read of marches, sieges[27], conflicts[28], and he had longed to[29] see it all. His busy mind had drawn for him large pictures extravagant in color, lurid with breathless deeds.

But his mother had discouraged him. She had affected to look with some contempt upon the quality of his war ardor and patriotism. She could calmly seat herself and with no apparent difficulty give him many hundreds of reasons why he was of vastly more importance on the farm than on the field of battle. She had had certain ways of expression that told him that her statements on the subject came from a deep conviction. Moreover, on her side, was his belief that her ethical motive in the argument was impregnable.

At last, however, he had made firm rebellion against this yellow light thrown upon the color of his ambitions. The newspapers, the gossip of the village, his own picturings, had aroused him to an uncheckable degree. They were in truth fighting finely down there. Almost every day the newspapers printed accounts of a decisive victory.

One night, as he lay in bed, the winds had carried to him the clangoring of the church bell as

---

21) flimsy : (피륙, 종이 등이) 얇은, 연약한
22) prowess : 용맹
23) bygone : 과거의, 지난
24) look upon : ~로 간주하다
25) effaced : 지우다, 삭제하다
26) Homeric : 호머(고대 그리스의 서사시인, Iliad와 Odyssey의 저자)식의, 호머풍의, 웅대한
27) siege : 포위공격
28) conflict : 투쟁, 전투
29) long to : 애타게 바라다, 열망하다

some enthusiast jerked the rope frantically to tell the twisted news of a great battle. This voice of the people rejoicing in the night had made him shiver in a prolonged[30] ecstasy of excitement. Later, he had gone down to his mother's room and had spoken thus: "Ma, I'm going to enlist."

"Henry, don't you be a fool," his mother had replied. She had then covered her face with the quilt. There was an end to the matter for that night.

Nevertheless, the next morning he had gone to a town that was near his mother's farm and had enlisted in a company that was forming there. When he had returned home his mother was milking[31] the brindle cow[32]. Four others stood waiting. "Ma, I've enlisted," he had said to her diffidently. There was a short silence. "The Lord's will be done[33], Henry," she had finally replied, and had then continued to milk the brindle cow.

When he had stood in the doorway with his soldier's clothes on his back, and with the light of excitement and expectancy[34] in his eyes almost defeating the glow of regret for the home bonds, he had seen two tears leaving their trails on his mother's scarred cheeks.

Still, she had disappointed him by saying nothing whatever about returning with his shield or on it. He had privately primed himself for a beautiful scene. He had prepared certain sentences which he thought could be used with touching effect. But her words destroyed his plans. She had doggedly peeled potatoes and addressed him as follows: "You watch out, Henry, an' take good care of yerself in this here fighting business — you watch out, an' take good care of yerself. Don't go a-thinkin' you can lick the hull rebel army at the start, because yeh can't. Yer jest one little feller[35] amongst a hull lot of others, and yeh've got to keep quiet an' do what they tell yeh. I know how you are, Henry.

"I've knet yeh eight pair of socks, Henry, and I've put in all yer best shirts, because I want my boy to be jest as warm and comf'able as anybody in the army. Whenever they get holes in 'em, I want yeh to send 'em right — away back to me, so's I kin dern 'em.

"An' all us be careful an' choose yer comp'ny[36]. There's lots of bad men in the army, Henry. The army makes 'em wild, and they like nothing better than the job of' leading off a young feller like you, as ain't never been away from home much and has allus had a mother, an' a-learning 'em to drink and swear. Keep clear of them folks, Henry. I don't want yeh to ever do anything, Henry, that yeh would be 'shamed to let me know about. Jest think as if I was a-watchin' yeh. If yeh keep that in yer mind allus, I guess yeh'll come out about right.

"Yeh must allus remember yer father, too, child, an' remember he never drunk a drop of licker[37] in his life, and seldom swore a cross oath."

---

30) prolonged : 오래 끄는, 장기의
31) milk : 우유를 짜내다
32) brindle cow : 얼룩무늬 소
33) The Lord's will be done : 주님의 뜻대로 될 것이다.
34) expectancy : 기대
35) feller : 녀석, 나무꾼
36) an' choose yer comp'ny : and choose your company / company : 중대, 동료
37) drop of licker : drop of liquor

"I don't know what else to tell yeh, Henry, excepting that yeh must never do no shirking, child, on my account. If so be a time comes when yeh have to be kilt or do a mean[38] thing, why, Henry, don't think of anything 'cept[39] what's right, because there's many a woman has to bear up 'ginst[40] sech[41] things these times, and the Lord'll take keer of[42] us all."

"Don't forget about the socks and the shirts, child; and I've put a cup of blackberry jam with yer bundle, because I know yeh like it above all things. Good-by[43], Henry. Watch out, and be a good boy."

He had, of course, been impatient under the ordeal of this speech. It had not been quite what he expected, and he had borne it with an air of irritation. He departed feeling vague relief.

Still, when he had looked back from the gate, he had seen his mother kneeling among the potato parings. Her brown face, upraised, was stained with tears, and her spare form was quivering. He bowed his head and went on, feeling suddenly ashamed of his purposes.

From his home he had gone to the seminary to bid adieu to many schoolmates. They had thronged about him with wonder and admiration. He had felt the gulf now between them and had swelled with[44] calm pride. He and some of his fellows who had donned blue were quite overwhelmed with privileges for all of one afternoon, and it had been a very delicious thing. They had strutted.

A certain light-haired girl had made vivacious fun at his martial spirit, but there was another and darker girl whom he had gazed at steadfastly, and he thought she grew demure and sad at sight of his blue and brass. As he had walked down the path between the rows of oaks, he had turned his head and detected her at a window watching his departure. As he perceived her, she had immediately begun to stare up through the high tree branches at the sky. He had seen a good deal of flurry and haste in her movement as she changed her attitude. He often thought of it.

On the way to Washington his spirit had soared[45]. The regiment was fed and caressed at station after station until the youth had believed that he must be a hero. There was a lavish expenditure of bread and cold meats, coffee, and pickles and cheese. As he basked in[46] the smiles of the girls and was patted and complimented by the old men, he had felt growing within him the strength to do mighty deeds[47] of arms.

After complicated journeyings with many pauses, there had come months of monotonous life in a camp. He had had the belief that real war was a series of death struggles with small time in between for sleep and meals; but since his regiment[48] had come to the field the army had done

---

38) mean : 비열한, 더러운, 짓궂은
39) 'cept : except
40) bear up 'ginst : bear up against(훌륭히 견디다)
41) sech : such
42) take keer of : take care of
43) Good-by : Good-bye
44) swell with : 증가시키다, 늘리다, 의기양양하게 하다
45) soar : (비행기 등이) 날아오르다, (희망, 기운 등이) 솟구치다
46) bask in : 햇볕을 찍다, (은혜 등을) 입다
47) deed : 행위, 업적
48) regiment : (군사) 연대

little but sit still and try to keep warm.

He was brought then gradually back to his old ideas. Greeklike struggles would be no more. Men were better, or more timid. Secular and religious education had effaced the throat-grappling instinct, or else firm finance held in check the passions.

He had grown to regard himself merely as a part of a vast blue demonstration[49]. His province was to look out, as far as he could, for his personal comfort. For recreation he could twiddle his thumbs and speculate on the thoughts which must agitate[50] the minds of the generals. Also, he was drilled[51] and drilled and reviewed, and drilled and drilled and reviewed.

The only foes he had seen were some pickets along the river bank. They were a sun-tanned, philosophical lot, who sometimes shot reflectively at the blue pickets. When reproached for[52] this afterward, they usually expressed sorrow, and swore by their gods that the guns had exploded without their permission. The youth, on guard duty one night, conversed across the stream with one of them. He was a slightly ragged man, who spat skillfully between his shoes and possessed a great fund of bland and infantile assurance. The youth liked him personally.

"Yank," the other had informed him, "yer a right dum good feller." This sentiment, floating to him upon the still air, had made him temporarily regret war.

Various veterans had told him tales. Some talked of gray, bewhiskered[53] hordes who were advancing with relentless curses and chewing tobacco with unspeakable valor; tremendous bodies of fierce soldiery who were sweeping along like the Huns. Others spoke of tattered and eternally[54] hungry men who fired despondent powders. "They'll charge through hell's fire an' brimstone t' git a holt on a haversack[55], an' sech stomachs ain't a-lastin' long," he was told. From the stories, the youth imagined the red, live bones sticking out through slits in the faded uniforms.

Still, he could not put a whole faith in veterans' tales, for recruits were their prey.

They talked much of smoke, fire, and blood, but he could not tell how much might be lies. They persistently[56] yelled "Fresh fish!" at him, and were in no wise to be trusted.

However, he perceived now that it did not greatly matter what kind of soldiers he was going to fight, so long as[57] they fought, which fact no one disputed. There was a more serious problem. He lay in his bunk pondering upon it. He tried to mathematically prove to himself that he would not run from a battle.

Previously he had never felt obliged to wrestle too seriously with this question. In his life he had taken certain things for granted, never challenging his belief in ultimate success, and bothering little about means and roads. But here he was confronted with a thing of moment. It had suddenly

---

49) blue demonstration : (남북전쟁 시의) 북군(北軍)의 양동작전
50) agitate : 흔들다, 선동하다, 교란하다
51) drill : 훈련시키다
52) reproach for : 꾸짖다, 비난하다
53) bewhiskered : 구레나룻을 기른
54) eternally : 영원히, 끊임없이
55) haversack : (군인, 여행자가 어깨에 비스듬히 메는) 가방, 숄더백
56) persistently : 끈덕지게, 고집스레
57) so long as : ~하는 동안은, ~하는 한은

appeared to him that perhaps in a battle he might run. He was forced to admit that as far as[58] war was concerned he knew nothing of himself.

A sufficient time before he would have allowed the problem to kick its heels at the outer portals of his mind, but now he felt compelled to give serious attention to it.

A little panic-fear grew in his mind. As his imagination went forward to a fight, he saw hideous possibilities. He contemplated the lurking menaces of the future, and failed in an effort to see himself standing stoutly in the midst of them. He recalled his visions of broken-bladed glory, but in the shadow of the impending tumult he suspected them to be impossible pictures.

He sprang from[59] the bunk and began to pace nervously to and fro. "Good Lord, what's th' matter with me?" he said aloud.

He felt that in this crisis his laws of life were useless. Whatever he had learned of himself was here of no avail. He was an unknown quantity. He saw that he would again be obliged to experiment as he had in early youth. He must accumulate information of himself, and meanwhile[60] he resolved to remain close upon his guard lest those qualities of which he knew nothing should everlastingly disgrace him. "Good Lord!" he repeated in dismay[61].

After a time the tall soldier slid dexterously[62] through the hole. The loud private followed. They were wrangling[63].

"That's all right," said the tall soldier as he entered. He waved his hand expressively. "You can believe me or not, jest as you like. All you got to do is to sit down and wait as quiet as you can. Then pretty soon you'll find out I was right."

His comrade[64] grunted stubbornly. For a moment he seemed to be searching for a formidable reply. Finally he said: "Well, you don't know everything in the world, do you?"

"Didn't say I knew everything in the world," retorted the other sharply. He began to stow various articles snugly into his knapsack.

The youth, pausing in his nervous walk, looked down at the busy figure. "Going to be a battle, sure, is there, Jim?" he asked.

"Of course there is," replied the tall soldier. "Of course there is. You jest wait 'til tomorrow, and you'll see one of the biggest battles ever was. You jest wait."

"Thunder!" said the youth.

"Oh, you'll see fighting this time, my boy, what'll be regular out — and — out fighting," added the tall soldier, with the air of a man who is about to exhibit a battle for the benefit of his friends.

"Huh!" said the loud one from a corner.

"Well," remarked the youth, "like as not this story'll turn out jest like them others did."

---

58) as far as ~ : ~까지
59) spring from : 벌떡 일어나다
60) meanwhile : 그동안
61) dismay : 당황, 어찌할 바를 모름, 낙담
62) dexterously : 민첩하게
63) wrangle : 말다툼하다, 언쟁을 벌이다
64) comrade : 동료, 전우

"Not much it won't," replied the tall soldier, exasperated[65]. "Not much it won't. Didn't the cavalry all start this morning?" He glared about him. No one denied his statement. "The cavalry[66] started this morning," he continued. "They say there ain't hardly any cavalry left in camp. They're going to Richmond, or some place, while we fight all the Johnnies[67]. It's some dodge like that. The regiment's got orders, too. A feller what seen 'em go to headquarters told me a little while ago. And they're raising blazes all over camp — anybody can see that."

"Shucks![68]" said the loud one.

The youth remained silent for a time[69]. At last he spoke to the tall soldier. "Jim!"

"What?"

"How do you think the reg'ment'll do?"

"Oh, they'll fight all right, I guess, after they once get into it," said the other with cold judgment. He made a fine use of the third person. "There's been heaps of fun poked at 'em because they're new, of course, and all that; but they'll fight all right, I guess."

"Think any of the boys'll run?" persisted the youth.

"Oh, there may be a few of 'em run, but there's them kind in every regiment, 'specially when they first goes under fire," said the other in a tolerant way. "Of course it might happen that the hull kit-and-boodle might start and run, if some big fighting came first-off[70], and then again they might stay and fight like fun. But you can't bet on[71] nothing. Of course they ain't never been under fire yet, and it ain't likely they'll lick the hull rebel army all-to-oncet the first time; but I think they'll fight better than some, if worse than others. That's the way I figger[72]. They call the reg'ment 'Fresh fish' and everything; but the boys come of good stock, and most of 'em'll fight like sin after they oncet git shootin'," he added, with a mighty emphasis on the last four words.

"Oh, you think you know — " began the loud soldier with scorn[73].

The other turned savagely upon him. They had a rapid altercation[74], in which they fastened upon each other various strange epithets[75].

The youth at last interrupted them. "Did you ever think you might run yourself, Jim?" he asked. On concluding the sentence he laughed as if[76] he had meant to aim a joke. The loud soldier also giggled.

The tall private waved his hand. "Well," said he profoundly, "I've thought it might get too hot for Jim Conklin in some of them scrimmages[77], and if a whole lot of boys started and run, why,

---

65) exasperated : 격분하여
66) cavalry : 기병대, 기갑부대
67) Johnnies : Johnny Reb[남북전쟁에서 남측 군인들(Confederate)], cf) 북측 군인들은 Billy Yank라고 불린다.
68) shucks! : 이런, 쳇!, 제기랄!
69) for a time : 당분간(은), 잠시
70) first-off : 우선, 첫째로
71) bet on : ~에 대해 내기를 걸다, (돈 등을) 걸다
72) figger : figure(생각하다, 판단하다)
73) scorn : 경멸, 조소, 냉소
74) altercation : 언쟁, 격론
75) epithet : 별명, 호칭, 욕
76) as if : 마치 ~인 것처럼
77) scrimmage : 드잡이, 격투, 난투

I s'pose I'd start and run. And if I once started to run, I'd run like the devil, and no mistake. But if everybody was a — standing and a — fighting, why, I'd stand and fight. Be jiminey, I would. I'll bet on it."

"Huh!" said the loud one.

The youth of this tale felt gratitude for these words of his comrade. He had feared that all of the untried men possessed a great and correct confidence. He now was in a measure reassured[78].

Chapter 2

THE next morning the youth discovered that his tall comrade had been the fast-flying messenger of a mistake. There was much scoffing at the latter by those who had yesterday been firm adherents[79] of his views, and there was even a little sneering by men who had never believed the rumor. The tall one fought with a man from Chatfield Corners and beat him severely[80].

The youth felt, however, that his problem was in no wise lifted from him. There was, on the contrary[81], an irritating prolongation. The tale had created in him a great concern for himself. Now, with the newborn question in his mind, he was compelled to sink back into his old place as part of a blue demonstration.

For days he made ceaseless[82] calculations, but they were all wondrously unsatisfactory. He found that he could establish nothing. He finally concluded that the only way to prove himself was to go into the blaze, and then figuratively to watch his legs to discover their merits and faults. He reluctantly[83] admitted that he could not sit still and with a mental slate and pencil derive an answer. To gain it, he must have blaze, blood, and danger, even as a chemist requires this. that, and the other. So he fretted for an opportunity.

Meanwhile he continually tried to measure himself by his comrades. The tall soldier, for one, gave him some assurance. This man's serene[84] unconcern dealt him a measure of confidence, for he had known him since childhood, and from his intimate knowledge he did not see how he could be capable of anything that was beyond him, the youth. Still, he thought that his comrade might be mistaken about himself. Or, on the other hand, he might be a man heretofore doomed to peace and obscurity, but, in reality, made to shine in war.

The youth would have liked to have discovered another who suspected himself. A sympathetic comparison of mental notes would have been a joy to him.

---

78) He ~ reassured : 그는 이제 안심할 수 있는 처지가 되었다.
79) adherent : 신봉자
80) severely : 심하게, 엄하게
81) on the contrary : 그와는 반대로, 이에 반하여
82) ceaseless : 끊임없는, 부단한
83) reluctant : 마음 내키지 않는, 달갑지 않은
84) serene : 고요한, 침착한

He occasionally tried to fathom a comrade with seductive[85] sentences. He looked about to find men in the proper mood. All attempts failed to bring forth any statement which looked in any way like a confession to those doubts which he privately acknowledged in himself. He was afraid to make an open declaration of his concern, because he dreaded to place some unscrupulous confidant upon the high plane of the unconfessed from which elevation he could be derided.

In regard to his companions his mind wavered[86] between two opinions, according to his mood. Sometimes he inclined to believing them all heroes. In fact, he usually admitted in secret the superior development of the higher qualities in others. He could conceive of men going very insignificantly about the world bearing a load of courage unseen, and although he had known many of his comrades through boyhood, he began to fear that his judgment of them had been blind. Then, in other moments, he flouted these theories, and assured himself that his fellows were all privately wondering and quaking.

His emotions made him feel strange in the presence of men who talked excitedly of a prospective battle as of a drama they were about to witness, with nothing but eagerness and curiosity apparent in their faces. It was often that he suspected them to be liars.

He did not pass such thoughts without severe condemnation[87] of himself. He dinned reproaches at times. He was convicted[88] by himself of many shameful crimes against the gods of traditions.

In his great anxiety his heart was continually clamoring at what he considered the intolerable slowness of the generals. They seemed content to perch tranquilly on the river bank, and leave him bowed down by the weight of a great problem. He wanted it settled forthwith. He could not long bear such a load, he said. Sometimes his anger at the commanders reached an acute stage, and he grumbled about the camp like a veteran.

One morning, however, he found himself in the ranks of his prepared regiment. The men were whispering speculations and recounting the old rumors. In the gloom before the break of the day their uniforms glowed a deep purple hue[89]. From across the river the red eyes were still peering[90] In the eastern sky there was a yellow patch[91] like a rug laid for the feet of the coming sun; and against it, black and patternlike, loomed the gigantic[92] figure of the colonel on a gigantic horse.

From off[93] in the darkness came the trampling[94] of feet. The youth could occasionally see dark shadows that moved like monsters. The regiment stood at rest for what seemed a long time. The youth grew impatient. It was unendurable the way these affairs were managed. He wondered how long they were to be kept waiting.

---

85) seductive : 유혹적인, 매력 있는
86) waver : 흔들리다, 나부끼다
87) condemnation : 비난, 규탄
88) convict : ~에게 유죄를 선고(입증)하다
89) hue : tint(색조, 빛깔)
90) peer: 응시하다
91) patch : 헝겊조각, 단편, 파편, 넓이(area)
92) gigantic : 거대한, 거인 같은
93) from off : ~으로부터
94) trample : 내리밟다, 거칠게 대하다

As he looked all about him and pondered upon[95] the mystic gloom, he began to believe that at any moment the ominous distance might be a flare, and the rolling crashes of an engagement come to his ears. Staring once at the red eyes across the river, he conceived them to be growing larger, as the orbs of a row of dragons advancing. He turned toward the colonel and saw him lift his gigantic arm and calmly stroke his mustache.

At last he heard from along the road at the foot of the hill the clatter Of a horse's galloping hoofs. It must be the coming of orders. He bent forward, scarce breathing. The exciting clickety-click, as it grew louder and louder, seemed to be beating upon his soul. Presently a horseman with jangling[96] equipment drew rein before the colonel of the regiment. The two held a short, sharp-worded conversation. The men in the foremost ranks craned their necks.

As the horseman wheeled his animal and galloped away[97] he turned to shout over his shoulder, "Don't forget that box of cigars!" The colonel mumbled in reply. The youth wondered what a box of cigars had to do with war.

A moment later the regiment went swinging off into the darkness. It was now like one of those moving monsters wending with many feet. The air was heavy, and cold with dew. A mass of wet grass, marched upon, rustled like silk.

There was an occasional flash and glimmer of steel from the backs of all these huge crawling reptiles[98]. From the road came creakings and grumblings as some surly guns were dragged away.

The men stumbled along still muttering speculations. There was a subdued debate. Once a man fell down, and as he reached for his rifle[99] a comrade, unseeing, trod upon his hand. He of the injured fingers swore bitterly and aloud. A low, tittering laugh went among his fellows.

Presently they passed into a roadway[100] and marched forward with easy strides. A dark regiment moved before them, and from behind also came the tinkle of equipments on the bodies of marching men.

The rushing yellow of the developing day went on behind their backs. When the sunrays at last struck full and mellowingly upon the earth, the youth saw that the landscape was streaked with two long, thin, black columns[101] which disappeared on the brow of a hill in front and rearward vanished in a wood. They were like two serpents crawling from the cavern of the night.

The river was not in view. The tall soldier burst into praises of what he thought to be his powers of perception.

Some of the tall one's companions cried with emphasis that they, too, had evolved the same thing, and they congratulated themselves upon it. But there were others who said that the tall one's plan was not the true one at all. They persisted with other theories. There was a vigorous[102] discussion.

---

95) ponder upon : 묵묵히 생각하다, 숙고하다
96) jangle : 맹맹 울리다, 귀에 거슬리는 (요란한) 소리를 내다
97) galloped away : 질주해 가다
98) reptile : 파충류, 비열한 사람
99) rifle : 라이플총, 소총
100) pass into a roadway : 차도로 들어서다
101) column : 행렬, 종대
102) vigorous : 활기 있는, 원기 왕성한

The youth took no part in them. As he walked along in careless line he was engaged with his own eternal debate. He could not hinder himself from dwelling upon[103] it. He was despondent[104] and sullen, and threw shifting glances about him. He looked ahead, often expecting to hear from the advance the rattle of firing.

But the long serpents[105] crawled slowly from hill to hill without bluster of smoke. A dun-colored[106] cloud of dust floated away to the right. The sky overhead was of a fairy blue.

The youth studied the faces of his companions, ever on the watch to detect kindred emotions. He suffered disappointment. Some ardor of the air which was causing the veteran commands to move with glee — almost with song — had infected the new regiment. The men began to speak of victory as of a thing they knew. Also, the tall soldier received his vindication[107]. They were certainly going to come around[108] in behind the enemy. They expressed commiseration for that part of the army which had been left upon the river bank, felicitating[109] themselves upon being a part of a blasting[110] host.

The youth, considering himself as separated from the others, was saddened by the blithe and merry speeches that went from rank to rank. The company wags all made their best endeavors. The regiment tramped to the tune of laughter.

The blatant soldier often convulsed whole files by his biting sarcasms aimed at the tall one.

And it was not long before all the men seemed to forget their mission. Whole brigades[111] grinned in unison, and regiments laughed.

A rather fat soldier attempted to pilfer a horse from a dooryard. He planned to load his knapsack upon it. He was escaping with his prize when a young girl rushed from the house and grabbed the animal's mane. There followed a wrangle. The young girl, with pink cheeks and shining eyes, stood like a dauntless statue.

The observant regiment, standing at rest in the roadway, whooped at once, and entered whole-souled[112] upon the side of the maiden. The men became so engrossed in this affair that they entirely ceased to remember their own large war. They jeered the piratical private, and called attention to various defects in his personal appearance; and they were wildly enthusiastic in support of the young girl.

To her, from some distance, came bold advice. "Hit him with a stick."

There were crows and catcalls showered upon him when he retreated without the horse. The regiment rejoiced at his downfall. Loud and vociferous[113] congratulations were showered upon the

---

103) dwell upon : 곰곰이 생각하다, 자세히 설명하다, ~에 유의하다, 이야기를 길게 늘어놓다
104) despondent : 낙담한, 실의에 빠진
105) serpent : 뱀, 여기에서는 군대의 행렬을 의미
106) dun-colored : 회갈색의
107) vindication : 옹호, 변호
108) come around : 주변에 몰려들다
109) felicitate : 축하하다, 행운으로 생각하다
110) blasting : 폭발, (나팔 등의) 소리
111) brigade : 여단
112) whole-souled : 마음으로부터의, 성의 있는
113) vociferous : 큰소리로 외치는, 고함치는, 시끄러운

maiden, who stood panting and regarding the troops with defiance.

At nightfall the column broke into regimental pieces, and the fragments went into the fields to camp. Tents sprang up like strange plants. Camp fires, like red, peculiar blossoms, dotted the night.

The youth kept from intercourse with his companions as much as circumstances would allow him. In the evening he wandered a few paces into the gloom. From this little distance the many fires, with the black forms of men passing to and fro before the crimson[114] rays, made weird and satanic effects.

He lay down[115] in the grass. The blades[116] pressed tenderly against his cheek. The moon had been lighted and was hung in a treetop. The liquid stillness of the night enveloping him made him feel vast pity for himself. There was a caress in the soft winds; and the whole mood of the darkness, he thought, was one of sympathy for himself in his distress.

He wished, without reserve, that he was at home again making the endless rounds from the house to the barn, from the barn to the fields, from the fields to the barn, from the barn to the house. He remembered he had often cursed the brindle cow and her mates, and had sometimes flung milking stools. But, from his present point of view, there was a halo of happiness about each of their heads, and he would have sacrificed all the brass buttons on the continent to have been enabled to return to them. He told himself that he was not formed for a soldier. And he mused seriously upon the radical differences between himself and those men who were dodging implike around the fires.

As he mused thus he heard the rustle of grass, and, upon turning his head, discovered the loud soldier. He called out, "Oh, Wilson!"

The latter approached and looked down. "Why, hello, Henry; is it you? What you doing here?"

"Oh, thinking," said the youth.

The other sat down and carefully lighted his pipe. "You're getting blue[117], my boy. You're looking thundering peeked. What the dickens is wrong with you?"

"Oh, nothing," said the youth.

The loud soldier launched then into the subject of the anticipated[118] fight. "Oh, we've got 'em now!" As he spoke his boyish face was wreathed in a gleeful[119] smile, and his voice had an exultant ring. "We've got 'em now. At last, by the eternal thunders, we'll lick 'em good!

"If the truth was known," he added, more soberly, "they've licked us about every clip up to now[120]; but this time — this time — we'll lick 'em good!"

"I thought you was objecting to this march a little while ago," said the youth coldly.

---

114) crimson : 피비린내 나는, 진홍색의
115) lay down : ~에 눕다
116) blade : 잎사귀
117) get blue : 우울해지다
118) anticipated : 기대하다
119) gleeful : 매우 기뻐하는
120) up to now : 지금껏, 지금 이 시간까지

"Oh, it wasn't that," explained the other. "I don't mind marching, if there's going to be fighting at the end of it. What I hate is this getting moved here and moved there, with no good coming of it, as far as I can see, excepting sore feet and damned short rations[121])."

"Well, Jim Conklin says we'll get a plenty of fighting this time."

"He's right for once, I guess, though I can't see how it come. This time we're in for a big battle, and we've got the best end of it, certain sure. Gee rod! how we will thump 'em!"

He arose and began to pace to and fro excitedly. The thrill of his enthusiasm made him walk with an elastic step. He was sprightly, vigorous, fiery in his belief in success. He looked into[122]) the future with clear, proud eye, and he swore with the air of an old soldier.

The youth watched him for a moment in silence. When he finally spoke his voice was as bitter as dregs[123]). "Oh, you're going to do great things, I s'pose!"

The loud soldier blew a thoughtful cloud of smoke from his pipe. "Oh, I don't know," he remarked with dignity; "I don't know. I s'pose I'll do as well as the rest. I'm going to try like thunder." He evidently[124]) complimented himself upon the modesty of this statement.

"How do you know you won't run when the time comes?" asked the youth.

"Run?" said the loud one; "run? — of course not!" He laughed.

"Well," continued the youth, "lots of good-a-'nough men have thought they was going to do great things before the fight, but when the time come they skedaddled[125])."

"Oh, that's all true, I s'pose[126])," replied the other; "but I'm not going to skedaddle. The man that bets on my running will lose his money, that's all." He nodded confidently.

"Oh, shucks!" said the youth. "You ain't the bravest man in the world, are you?"

"No, I ain't," exclaimed the loud soldier indignantly[127]); "and I didn't say I was the bravest man in the world, neither. I said I was going to do my share of fighting — that's what I said. And I am, too. Who are you, anyhow? You talk as if you thought you was Napoleon Bonaparte." He glared at[128]) the youth for a moment, and then strode away.

The youth called in a savage voice after his comrade: "Well, you needn't git mad about it!" But the other continued on his way and made no reply.

He felt alone in space when his injured comrade had disappeared. His failure to discover any mite of resemblance in their view points made him more miserable than before. No one seemed to be wrestling with such a terrific personal problem. He was a mental outcast. He went slowly to his tent and stretched himself on a blanket by the side of the snoring tall soldier. In the darkness he saw visions of a thousand-tongued fear that would babble at his back and cause him to flee, while

---

121) short rations : 제한된 양식(배급량)
122) look into : ~을 들여다보다, 조사하다
123) dreg : 잔재, 찌꺼기, 하찮은 것
124) evidently : 분명히, 명백히
125) skedaddled : 달아나다, 내빼다
126) I s'pose : I suppose
127) indignantly : 분개하여
128) glare at : 도끼눈으로 보다

others were going coolly about their country's business. He admitted that he would not be able to cope with this monster. He felt that every nerve in his body would be an ear to hear the voices, while other men would remain stolid and deaf.

And as he sweated with the pain of these thoughts, he could hear low, serene[129] sentences. "I'll bid five." "Make it six." "Seven." "Seven goes."

He stared at the red, shivering reflection of a fire on the white wall of his tent until, exhausted and ill from the monotony of his suffering, he fell asleep.

Chapter 3

WHEN another night came the columns[130], changed to purple streaks, filed across two pontoon bridges. A glaring fire wine-tinted the waters of the river. Its rays, shining upon the moving masses of troops, brought forth here and there sudden gleams of silver or gold. Upon the other shore a dark and mysterious range of hills was curved against the sky. The insect voices of the night sang solemnly.

After this crossing the youth assured himself that at any moment they might be suddenly and fearfully assaulted[131] from the caves of the lowering woods. He kept his eyes watchfully upon the darkness.

But his regiment went unmolested to a camping place, and its soldiers slept the brave sleep of wearied men. In the morning they were routed out with early energy, and hustled along a narrow road that led deep into the forest.

It was during this rapid march that the regiment lost many of the marks of a new command.

The men had begun to count the miles upon their fingers, and they grew tired. "Sore feet an' damned short rations, that's all," said the loud soldier. There was perspiration[132] and grumblings[133]. After a time they began to shed[134] their knapsacks. Some tossed them unconcernedly down; others hid them carefully, asserting their plans to return for them at some convenient time. Men extricated themselves from thick shirts. Presently few carried anything but their necessary clothing, blankets, haversacks, canteens[135], and arms and ammunition. "You can now eat and shoot," said the tall soldier to the youth.

"That's all you want to do."

There was sudden change from the ponderous infantry of theory to the light and speedy infantry of practice. The regiment, relieved of a burden, received a new impetus. But there was much loss

---

129) serene : 고요한, 차분한
130) column : 행렬, 종대
131) assault : 공격하다, 습격하다
132) perspiration : 발한, (땀날 정도의) 노력
133) grumbling : 불평, 항의
134) shed : 벗어버리다
135) canteen : 수통, 휴대 식기

of valuable knapsacks, and, on the whole, very good shirts.

But the regiment was not yet veteranlike in appearance[136]. Veteran regiments in the army were likely to be very small aggregations of men. Once, when the command had first come to the field, some perambulating veterans, noting the length of their column, had accosted[137] them thus: "Hey, fellers[138], what brigade is that?" And when the men had replied that they formed a regiment and not a brigade, the older soldiers had laughed, and said, "O Gawd![139]"

Also, there was too great a similarity in the hats. The hats of a regiment should properly represent the history of headgear for a period of years. And, moreover, there were no letters of faded gold speaking from the colors. They were new and beautiful, and the color bearer habitually oiled the pole.

Presently the army again sat down to think. The odor[140] of the peaceful pines was in the men's nostrils. The sound of monotonous[141] axe blows ran through the forest, and the insects, nodding upon their perches, crooned like old women. The youth returned to his theory of a blue demonstration.

One gray dawn, however, he was kicked in the leg by the tall soldier, and then, before he was entirely awake, he found himself running down a wood road in the midst of men who were panting from the first effects of speed. His canteen banged rhythmically upon his thigh, and his haversack bobbed softly. His musket bounced a trifle from his shoulder at each stride and made his cap feel uncertain upon his head.

He could hear the men whisper jerky sentences: "Say-what's all this — about?" "What th' thunder — we — skedaddlin' this way fer?" "Billie — keep off m' feet. Yeh run — like a cow." And the loud soldier's shrill voice could be heard: "What th' devil they in sich a hurry for?"

The youth thought the damp fog of early morning moved from the rush of a great body of troops. From the distance came a sudden spatter of firing.

He was bewildered. As he ran with his comrades he strenuously tried to think, but all he knew was that if he fell down those coming behind would tread upon him. All his faculties seemed to be needed to guide him over and past obstructions. He felt carried along by a mob.

The sun spread disclosing[142] rays, and, one by one[143], regiments burst into view like armed men just born of the earth. The youth perceived that the time had come. He was about to be measured. For a moment he felt in the face of his great trial like a babe, and the flesh over his heart seemed very thin. He seized time to look about him calculatingly.

But he instantly saw that it would be impossible for him to escape from the regiment. It inclosed

---

136) veteranlike in appearance : 베테랑 같은 외모
137) accost : 말을 건네다
138) feller : fellows
139) O Gawd! : Oh, God!
140) odor : 냄새, 향기
141) monotonous : 단조로운
142) disclose : 드러내다, 노출시키다
143) one by one : 하나(한 사람)씩

him. And there were iron laws of tradition and law on four sides. He was in a moving box.

As he perceived this fact it occurred to him that he had never wished to come to the war. He had not enlisted of his free will. He had been dragged by the merciless government. And now they were taking him out to be slaughtered.

The regiment slid down a bank and wallowed across a little stream. The mournful current moved slowly on, and from the water, shaded black, some white bubble eyes looked at the men.

As they climbed the hill on the farther side artillery[144] began to boom. Here the youth forgot many things as he felt a sudden impulse of curiosity. He scrambled up[145] the bank with a speed that could not be exceeded by a bloodthirsty man.

He expected a battle scene.

There were some little fields girted and squeezed by a forest. Spread over the grass and in among the tree trunks, he could see knots and waving lines of skirmishers[146] who were running hither and thither and firing at the landscape. A dark battle line lay upon a sunstruck clearing that gleamed[147] orange color. A flag fluttered.

Other regiments floundered up the bank. The brigade was formed in line of battle, and after a pause started slowly through the woods in the rear of the receding skirmishers, who were continually melting into the scene to appear again farther on. They were always busy as bees, deeply absorbed in their little combats.

The youth tried to observe everything. He did not use care to avoid trees and branches, and his forgotten feet were constantly knocking against stones or getting entangled[148] in briers. He was aware that these battalions with their commotions were woven red and startling into the gentle fabric of softened greens and browns. It looked to be a wrong place for a battle field.

The skirmishers[149] in advance fascinated him. Their shots into thickets and at distant and prominent trees spoke to him of tragedies — hidden, mysterious, solemn.

Once the line encountered the body of a dead soldier. He lay upon his back staring at the sky. He was dressed in an awkward suit of yellowish brown. The youth could see that the soles of his shoes had been worn to the thinness of writing paper, and from a great rent in one the dead foot projected piteously. And it was as if fate had betrayed the soldier. In death it exposed to his enemies that poverty which in life he had perhaps concealed from his friends.

The ranks opened covertly to avoid the corpse. The invulnerable dead man forced a way for himself. The youth looked keenly at the ashen face. The wind raised the tawny beard. It moved as if a hand were stroking it. He vaguely desired to walk around and around the body and stare; the impulse of the living to try to read in dead eyes the answer to the Question.

144) artillery : 대포
145) scramble up : 기어오르다
146) skirmisher : [군사] 척후병(적의 상황이나 지형 따위를 정찰하고 탐색하는 병사)
147) gleam : 어슴푸레 빛나다
148) entangle : 뒤얽히게 하다, 어지럽히다
149) skirmisher : 척후병, 산병

During the march the ardor which the youth had acquired when out of view of the field rapidly faded to nothing. His curiosity was quite easily satisfied. If an intense scene had caught him with its wild swing as he came to the top of the bank, he might have gone roaring on. This advance upon Nature was too calm. He had opportunity to reflect. He had time in which to wonder about himself and to attempt[150] to probe his sensations.

Absurd ideas took hold upon him. He thought that he did not relish the landscape. It threatened him. A coldness swept over his back, and it is true that his trousers felt to him that they were no fit for his legs at all.

A house standing placidly in distant fields had to him an ominous look. The shadows of the woods were formidable[151]. He was certain that in this vista there lurked fierce-eyed[152] hosts. The swift thought came to him that the generals did not know what they were about. It was all a trap. Suddenly those close forests would bristle with rifle barrels. Ironlike brigades[153] would appear in the rear. They were all going to be sacrificed. The generals were stupids. The enemy would presently swallow the whole command. He glared about him, expecting to see the stealthy approach of his death.

He thought that he must break from the ranks and harangue[154] his comrades. They must not all be killed like pigs; and he was sure it would come to pass unless they were informed of these dangers. The generals were idiots to send them marching into a regular pen. There was but one pair of eyes in the corps. He would step forth and make a speech. Shrill and passionate words came to his lips.

The line, broken into moving fragments by the ground, went calmly on through fields and woods. The youth looked at the men nearest him, and saw, for the most part, expressions of deep interest, as if they were investigating something that had fascinated them. One or two stepped with overvaliant airs as if they were already plunged into[155] war. Others walked as upon thin ice. The greater part of the untested men appeared quiet and absorbed. They were going to look at war, the red animal-war, the blood-swollen god. And they were deeply engrossed in this march.

As he looked the youth gripped his outcry at his throat. He saw that even if the men were tottering[156] with fear they would laugh at his warning. They would jeer him, and, if practicable, pelt him with missiles. Admitting that he might be wrong, a frenzied declamation of the kind would turn him into a worm.

He assumed, then, the demeanor of one who knows that he is doomed alone to unwritten responsibilities. He lagged, with tragic glances at the sky. He was surprised presently by the young lieutenant of his company, who began heartily to beat him with a sword, calling out in a loud and

---

150) attempt : 시도하다, 기도하다
151) formidable : 무시무시한, 만만찮은
152) fierce-eyed : 사나운 눈을 한
153) Ironlike brigade : 무쇠처럼 강한 여단(군사)
154) harangue : (대중 앞에서의) 긴 연설, 비난, (장황한) 설교
155) plunge into : 던져 넣다, 뛰어들다
156) totter : 비틀비틀 걷다

insolent[157] voice: "Come, young man, get up into ranks there. No skulking[158] 'll do here." He mended his pace with suitable haste. And he hated the lieutenant, who had no appreciation of fine minds. He was a mere brute.

After a time the brigade was halted[159] in the cathedral light of a forest. The busy skirmishers were still popping. Through the aisles of the wood could be seen the floating smoke from their rifles. Sometimes it went up[160] in little balls, white and compact.

During this halt many men in the regiment began erecting tiny hills in front of them. They used stones, sticks, earth, and anything they thought might turn a bullet. Some built comparatively large ones, while others seemed content with little ones.

This procedure caused a discussion among the men. Some wished to fight like duelists[161], believing it to be correct to stand erect and be, from their feet to their foreheads, a mark. They said they scorned the devices of the cautious. But the others scoffed in reply, and pointed to the veterans on the flanks who were digging at the ground like terriers. In a short time there was quite a barricade along the regimental fronts. Directly, however, they were ordered to withdraw from that place.

This astounded the youth. He forgot his stewing over the advance movement. "Well, then, what did they march us out here for?" he demanded of the tall soldier. The latter with calm faith began a heavy explanation, although he had been compelled to leave a little protection of stones and dirt to which he had devoted much care and skill.

When the regiment was aligned in another position each man's regard for his safety caused another line of small intrenchments[162]. They ate their noon meal behind a third one. They were moved from this one also. They were marched from place to place with apparent aimlessness.

The youth had been taught that a man became another thing in a battle. He saw his salvation in such a change. Hence this waiting was an ordeal to him. He was in a fever of impatience. He considered that there was denoted a lack of[163] purpose on the part of the generals. He began to complain to the tall soldier. "I can't stand this much longer," he cried. "I don't see what good it does to make us wear out our legs for nothin'." He wished to return to camp, knowing that this affair was a blue demonstration; or else to go into a battle and discover that he had been a fool in his doubts, and was, in truth[164], a man of traditional courage. The strain of present circumstances he felt to be intolerable.

The philosophical[165] tall soldier measured a sandwich of cracker and pork and swallowed it in a nonchalant[166] manner. "Oh, I suppose we must go reconnoitering around the country jest to keep

---

157) insolent : 건방진, 오만한
158) skulk : flee(몰래 달아나다)
159) halt : (행진 중에) 정지하다
160) go up : 오르다, 올라가다, ~에 이르다, 세워지다
161) duelist : 결투자
162) intrenchment : entrenchment(참호)
163) lack of ~ : ~가 부족한, ~가 없는
164) in truth : 정말로, 실제로, 사실은
165) philosophical : 철학적인
166) nonchalant : 아랑곳하지 않는, 무관심한, 태연한

'em from getting too close, or to develop 'em, or something."

"Huh!" said the loud soldier.

"Well," cried the youth, still fidgeting, "I'd rather do anything most than go tramping[167] 'round the country all day doing no good to nobody and jest tiring ourselves out."

"So would I," said the loud soldier. "It ain't right. I tell you if anybody with any sense was a-runnin' this army it — "

"Oh, shut up!" roared the tall private. "You little fool. You little damn' cuss. You ain't had that there coat and them pants on for six months, and yet you talk as if — "

"Well, I wanta do some fighting anyway," interrupted the other. "I didn't come here to walk. I could 'ave walked to home — 'round an' 'round the barn, if I jest wanted to walk."

The tall one, red-faced, swallowed another sandwich as if taking poison in despair.

But gradually[168], as he chewed, his face became again quiet and contented. He could not rage in fierce argument in the presence of such sandwiches. During his meals he always wore an air of blissful contemplation of the food he had swallowed. His spirit seemed then to be communing with the viands.

He accepted new environment and circumstance with great coolness, eating from his haversack at every opportunity. On the march he went along with the stride of a hunter, objecting to neither gait[169] nor distance[170]. And he had not raised his voice when he had been ordered away from three little protective piles of earth and stone, each of which had been an engineering feat worthy of being made sacred to the name of his grandmother.

In the afternoon the regiment went out over the same ground it had taken in the morning. The landscape then ceased to threaten the youth. He had been close to it and become familiar with[171] it.

When, however, they began to pass into a new region, his old fears of stupidity and incompetence[172] reassailed him, but this time he doggedly let them babble. He was occupied with his problem, and in his desperation he concluded that the stupidity did not greatly matter.

Once he thought he had concluded that it would be better to get killed directly and end his troubles. Regarding death thus out of the corner of his eye, he conceived it to be nothing but rest, and he was filled with a momentary astonishment that he should have made an extraordinary commotion over the mere matter of getting killed. He would die; he would go to some place where he would be understood. It was useless to expect appreciation of his profound[173] and fine senses from such men as the lieutenant. He must look to the grave for comprehension.

---

167) tramp : 광광거리며 걷다, 터벅터벅 걷다, 짓밟다
168) gradually : 차차, 차츰, 점차로
169) gait : 걸음걸이
170) neither A nor B : A도 아니고 B도 아니다
171) familiar with ~ : ~에 익숙하다, ~에 정통하다
172) incompetence : 무능력
173) profound : 깊은, 심원한

The skirmish fire increased to a long clattering sound[174]. With it was mingled far-away cheering. A battery[175] spoke.

Directly the youth could see the skirmishers running. They were pursued by the sound of musketry fire. After a time the hot, dangerous flashes of the rifles were visible. Smoke clouds went slowly and insolently across the fields like observant phantoms. The din became crescendo, like the roar of an oncoming train.

A brigade ahead of them and on the right went into action with a rending roar. It was as if it had exploded. And thereafter it lay stretched in the distance behind a long gray wall, that one was obliged to[176] look twice at to make sure that it was smoke.

The youth, forgetting his neat plan of getting killed, gazed spellbound. His eyes grew wide and busy with the action of the scene. His mouth was a little ways open.

Of a sudden[177] he felt a heavy and sad hand laid upon his shoulder. Awakening from his trance[178] of observation he turned and beheld the loud soldier.

"It's my first and last battle, old boy," said the latter, with intense gloom. He was quite pale and his girlish lip was trembling.

"Eh?" murmured[179] the youth in great astonishment.

"It's my first and last battle, old boy," continued the loud soldier. "Something tells me — "

"What?"

"I'm a gone coon[180] this first time and — and I w — want you to take these here things to — my — folks." He ended in a quavering sob[181] of pity for himself. He handed the youth a little packet done up in a yellow envelope[182].

"Why, what the devil — [183]" began the youth again.

But the other gave him a glance as from the depths[184] of a tomb, and raised his limp hand in a prophetic[185] manner and turned away.

174) clattering sound : 달가닥달가닥(찰가닥찰가닥)하는 소리
175) battery : 포병 중대, 전지
176) oblige to ～ : ～하지 않을 수 없었다
177) (all) of a sudden : suddenly(갑자기)
178) trance : 황홀, 무아지경
179) murmur : 중얼거리다
180) a gone coon : 구제할 길이 없는 사람, 절망적인 상황
181) sob : 흐느낌
182) a little packet done up in a yellow envelope : 노란 봉투에 싸여진 꾸러미
183) what the devil ～ : what in the world ～, what on earth ～(도대체 무엇 ～)
184) depth : 깊이, 깊은 곳
185) prophetic : 예언적인

제2편 실전예상문제

제2장 Edgar Alan Poe – 「*The Black Cat*」

01 다음 중 Edgar Allan Poe의 작품이 <u>아닌</u> 것은?

① 「*Ligeia*」
② 「*The Fall of the House of the Usher*」
③ 「*The Murders in the Rue Morgue*」
④ 『*Wessex Tales*』

01 총 5편으로 이루어진 단편집인 『*Wessex Tales*』(1888)는 Thomas Hardy의 작품이다.

02 Edgar Allan Poe에 대한 설명으로 옳지 <u>않은</u> 것은?

① 시의 경우에는 100줄 정도의 길이가 적당하다고 하였다.
② 소설은 앉은 자리에서 독파할 수 있는 분량이 적당하다고 하였다.
③ 아름다운 여성의 죽음이야말로 가장 소설적인 소재라고 설정하기도 하였다.
④ 작품의 단일성 획득을 위해 치밀하게 언어 사용을 규제하였다.

02 아름다운 여성의 죽음이야말로 가장 시적인 소재라고 설정하기도 하였다.

03 Edgar Allan Poe의 문학이론과 가장 부합하는 것은?

① 정서이론
② 모방이론
③ 표현이론
④ 사실이론

03 Edgar Allan Poe는 모방이론이 문제 삼는 재현의 대상이나 표현이론이 초점을 맞추는 작가의 감정적 표출보다는 독자에게 미치는 정서적인 효과에 주목한다.

정답 (01④ 02③ 03①)

04 이 작품은 선악의 양면성을 가지고 있는 주인공의 불안정한 감수성의 표출을 보여주고 있다.

04 「*The Black Cat*」의 주제로 볼 수 <u>없는</u> 것은?

① 억압된 분노의 폭발
② 도착 성격의 발로
③ 주인공이 악에 눈뜨며 이에 침잠된 과정의 발전
④ 악한 본성만을 가지고 있는 주인공의 불안정한 감수성 표출

05 「*The Black Cat*」에서 도착 심리는 화자에 해당하며 고양이에 해당하지 않는다. 고양이 Pluto는 본래 선(善)도 악(惡)도 아니었으나 화자의 감정이 변하고 그의 악마성이 드러남에 따라 이름 그대로 그리스 로마신화에 나오는 명부의 왕 Pluto(Hades)가 되어 복수의 화신으로 변한다.

05 「*The Black Cat*」에 나타난 고양이의 상징적 의미에 해당하지 <u>않는</u> 것은?

① 고양이의 빨간 입술은 죽은 부인의 미적 아름다움을 나타낸다.
② 고양이의 꼬리는 도착 심리를 나타낸다.
③ 고양이의 영롱한 눈은 주인공의 양심을 괴롭히는 눈이다.
④ 검은 고양이는 양심의 가책에서 오는 고민과 공포를 상징한다.

06 「*Young Goodman Brown*」은 Nathaniel Hawthorne의 단편소설이다.
①·③ Poe의 시에 해당한다.
④ Poe의 단편소설이다.

06 다음 중 Edgar Allan Poe의 작품에 해당하지 <u>않는</u> 것은?

① 「*Annabel Lee*」
② 「*Young Goodman Brown*」
③ 「*To Helen*」
④ 「*The Black Cat*」

정답 04 ④ 05 ② 06 ②

07 Edgar Allan Poe에 관한 설명으로 옳지 <u>않은</u> 것은?

① 자기 파괴적이고 복잡한 성격을 지녔다.
② 여동생이 태어난 직후, 아버지가 돌아가셨다.
③ Poe의 가족은 어머니가 돌아가신 후 뿔뿔이 흩어졌다.
④ Poe와 양부는 매우 사이가 좋지 않았다.

08 「*The Black Cat*」에 관한 설명으로 옳은 것은?

① 전지적 작가 시점이다.
② 주인공은 결국엔 자신의 행동의 도덕적인 의미를 인정하게 된다.
③ 질투가 빚은 단순한 가정 비극을 주제로 보는 견해도 있다.
④ 배경은 밝은 지하실로 설정되어 있다.

09 「*The Black Cat*」에서 화자가 고양이를 죽이려 하자 이를 말리는 부인을 죽이게 되는데 이때 부인을 죽이는 데 쓰인 도구는?

① 총
② 칼
③ 화자의 손
④ 도끼

---

07 여동생 Rosalie가 태어난 직후인 1810년 12월에 아버지가 가출하였다.

08 ① 1인칭 제한적 시점이다.
② 주인공은 자신의 행동의 도덕적인 의미를 인정하지 않는다.
④ 배경은 불탄 지하실로 설정되어 있다.

09 고양이를 죽이려던 중에 화자는 아내와 함께 지하실에 내려가려다가 고양이 때문에 넘어질 뻔하자 도끼를 꺼내어 든다. 그리고 오히려 고양이를 내려치려는 것을 말리는 아내를 죽이게 된다.

정답 07 ② 08 ③ 09 ④

10 Edgar Allan Poe는 정서적 효과를 극대화하기 위해서 주제나 플롯 문체 길이 등 다른 전부를 종속시키는 유기적 문학이론이 필요하다고 주창하였으며, 순간의 포착을 위해 작품의 길이를 제한하고 소재를 규정하고 언어의 사용을 제어해야 한다고 주장했다.

10 Edgar Allan Poe의 작품 세계에 대한 설명으로 알맞지 <u>않은</u> 것은?

① 창작이 실패한다면 그것은 이론이 불완전하기 때문이라고 주장했다.

② 정서적 효과를 극대화하기 위하여 언어의 사용을 제한하지 말아야 한다.

③ 시의 목적은 쾌락이기 때문에 과학적인 작품과 반대가 된다.

④ 단일성과 간결함이 독자에게 강렬한 인상을 줄 수 있다.

정답 10 ②

제 3 장   Nathaniel Hawthorne – 「*The Scarlet Letter*」

01 Nathaniel Hawthrone에 관한 설명으로 올바르지 <u>않은</u> 것은?

① 첫 소설은 자비를 들여 익명으로 출판하였다.

② 공산주의 공동체 실험 농장에 참여하였다.

③ 「The Custom House」에서 자신의 비참한 심정을 경제에 대한 회의감으로 적나라하게 토로했다.

④ 세관을 그만두고 「The Scarlet Letter」 집필을 시작하였다.

01 「The Custom House」에서 자신의 비참한 심정을 정치에 대한 회의감으로 적나라하게 토로했다.

02 「*The Scarlet Letter*」에 등장하는 중요한 상징이 <u>아닌</u> 것은?

① Angel

② Scaffold

③ Forest

④ A Scarlet Letter

02 Angel은 The Scarlet Letter가 의미하는 것 중 하나로 성스럽게 변모한 Hester의 모습을 나타내지만 작품에 직접 등장하지는 않는다.

03 다음 중 Nathaniel Hawthrone의 자전적 에세이는?

① 「*Young Goodman Brown*」

② 「*The Birthmark*」

③ 「*Rappaccini's Daughter*」

④ 「*The Old Manse*」

03 1846년에 내놓은 두 번째 단편집 『*Mosses from an Old Manse*』에 실린 첫 작품이 「*The Old Manse*」이며 그의 자전적 에세이이다.

정답 01 ③   02 ①   03 ④

04 낭만주의적 계보를 쫓으면서도 인간의 어두운 내면, 무의식의 심리, 본성 속에 내재한 죄와 악의 문제 등을 집요하게 탐구하는 특성을 보였다.

04 Nathaniel Hawthrone의 작품 세계에 대한 설명으로 옳지 <u>않은</u> 것은?

① 낭만주의적 계보만을 쫓았다.
② 실제 삶처럼 모호함을 특징으로 가진다.
③ 그의 단편들은 상징, 알레고리, 환상적 묘사 등 독창적인 형식을 도입하였다.
④ 청교도의 사상과 생활태도에 깊은 관심을 가지고 많은 작품을 썼다.

05 「*The Scarlet Letter*」에서는 가슴과 머리의 대립관계, 은밀한 죄와 그로 인한 자신의 심한 정신적 갈등으로 인해 마침내 죄를 고백하고 구원받는 전형적인 영혼 구원의 과정이 나타난다.

05 「*The Scarlet Letter*」의 주제로 볼 수 <u>없는</u> 것은?

① 죄와 복수의 문제
② 인간의 약함과 슬픔
③ 가슴과 머리의 일치
④ 개인과 사회의 갈등

06 「*The Scarlet Letter*」는 1640년대 보스턴의 식민지 사회에서 일어난 일들을 소재로 하여 청교도가 지배하는 식민지 사회에서 억압받는 인간의 모습을 19세기의 시대정신을 통하여 비판하고 있다.

06 「*The Scarlet Letter*」에 대한 설명으로 옳지 <u>않은</u> 것은?

① Hester와 Dimmesdale은 처음부터 죄를 범한 불완전한 인간으로 묘사되었다.
② 「*The Scarlet Letter*」의 시대적 배경에서는 여성의 간통을 금기시하였다.
③ 성공회가 지배하는 식민지 사회에서 억압받는 인간의 모습을 19세기의 시대정신을 통하여 비판하고 있다.
④ Chillingworth의 타락과 죽음을 통하여 에덴동산이 상징하는 이상주의의 꿈이 얼마나 위험하고 실현 불가능한 것인가를 보여준다.

정답 (04 ① 05 ③ 06 ③)

07 「*The Scarlet Letter*」에서 'A'가 의미하는 것이 <u>아닌</u> 것은?

① Adam
② Able
③ Adult
④ Arthur

07 Adam은 원죄를 상징하고 Hester의 능력을 함축하여 Able로도 쓰이고 Dimmesdale의 이름인 Arthur의 첫 글자이기도 하다. 원래는 간통이라는 의미인 Adultery이다.

08 「*The Scarlet Letter*」에서 여주인공인 Hester Prynne에 대한 설명으로 옳지 <u>않은</u> 것은?

① 사랑과 자유를 쟁취한 용기 있는 여성이다.
② 간통을 저지른 죄인이다.
③ 페미니스트이다.
④ 지은 죄로 인하여 선행을 하게 되는, 즉 선을 행하기 위한 전 단계로 죄를 지었다.

08 페미니스트의 시초로 볼 수도 있으나 온전한 의미의 페미니스트라 할 수는 없다.

09 「*The Scarlet Letter*」에서 상징물과 그 의미가 <u>잘못</u> 연결된 것은?

① Forest – 어둡고 비밀스러움의 상징
② Market-Place – 법과 종교가 지배하는 문명이자 공개성
③ Pearl – 위선, 은밀한 죄
④ A Wild Rose – Hester의 열정과 자유

09 Pearl은 사랑과 구원을 의미한다.

정답 (07 ③ 08 ③ 09 ③)

10 익명의 화자는 폐허가 된 세일럼 세관(Salem Custom House)의 다락방에서 세관감정관인 Jonathan Pue가 200년 전에 썼던 Hester Prynne에 관한 글을 발견한다. 청교도 조상들과 미국 역사에 관심을 가지고 있는 그는 이 내용을 바탕으로 글(로맨스)을 쓰기로 한다.

10 「*The Scarlet Letter*」에서 화자는 Hester의 이야기를 어떻게 알게 되었는가?

① 나이 지긋한 친척으로부터 들었다.
② Salem Custom House의 다락방에서 200년 전에 쓰인 글을 발견하면서 알게 되었다.
③ Salem Custom House에서 일하는 한 노인으로부터 들었다.
④ 그가 꿈을 꾼 내용이다.

11 「*The Scarlet Letter*」에서는 크게 세 가지의 형태의 죄, 즉 Hester의 세상에 드러난 죄, Dimmesdale의 숨겨진 죄, Chillingworth의 용서 받지 못할 죄(순수 악, 양심, 복수, 오만의 죄)를 다루고 있다. Pearl의 존재는 죄악의 결과이기 때문에 그는 악마의 자식으로 불렸지만 악마의 죄를 상징하지는 않는다. Pearl은 결국 관련 인물들에게 진주(pearl)이자 보물과 같은 역할을 하게 된다.

11 「*The Scarlet Letter*」에 관한 설명으로 옳지 <u>않은</u> 것은?

① Chillingworth는 순수한 악, 양심과 복수의 죄를 보여준다.
② Hester는 세상에 드러난 죄를 보여준다.
③ Dimmesdale은 숨겨진 죄를 보여준다.
④ Pearl은 악마의 죄를 나타낸다.

정답 (10 ② 11 ④)

제 4 장 **Herman Melville – 「*Billy Budd, Sailor*」**

01 Herman Mellvile에 대한 설명으로 <u>틀린</u> 것은?

① 「*Moby-Dick*」의 저자이다.
② 직접 정계에 입문하여 활동하기도 하였다.
③ 활동 당시에 괴팍스러운 자신만의 세계를 고집하여 독자들의 외면을 자초하였다.
④ 여행기 장르의 작품들로 인하여 명성을 얻게 되었다.

> **01** Mellvile은 바로 위의 형이 정계에 입문하여 민주당의 James Polk 대통령 당선에 큰 역할을 하는 것을 통해 당시의 정치적 현실을 가까이서 관찰할 수 있었다.

02 다음 중 Herman Mellvile의 작품이 <u>아닌</u> 것은?

① 「*Pierre*」
② 「*Moby-Dick*」
③ 「*White Jacket*」
④ 「*Washington Square*」

> **02** 「*Washington Square*」는 Henry James의 소설이다.

03 「*Billy Budd, Sailor*」의 주제로 알맞지 <u>않은</u> 것은?

① 자비와 정의의 실현
② 법과 인간 품성의 관계
③ 대립적 가치의 수용
④ 아이러니적인 비극의 본성

> **03** 「*Billy Budd, Sailor*」의 주제는 대립적 가치에 대한 집착이다.

04 「*Billy Budd, Sailor*」에서 상징하는 바가 <u>잘못</u> 연결된 것은?

① Billy Budd – 순진성의 상징
② Captain Vere – 신의 법을 상징
③ Claggart – 악마의 속성
④ Billy Budd – 그리스도의 속성

> **04** Captain Vere는 사려 깊고 고뇌하는 인간의 법을 상징한다.

정답 01 ② 02 ④ 03 ③ 04 ②

05 「*Billy Budd, Sailor*」는 화해와 수용, 용서의 과정을 다루고 있다.

05 「*Billy Budd, Sailor*」에서 나타나지 <u>않은</u> 것은?

① 자비와 정의의 실현
② 복수의 과정
③ 결정 및 결심의 어려움
④ 신의 법과 인간의 법에 관한 문제

06 Billy Budd는 타락하기 전의 아담 또는 그리스도의 속성과 연관이 된다.

06 「*Billy Budd, Sailor*」에서 Billy Budd의 속성으로 볼 수 있는 것은?

① 모세
② 뱀
③ 아담
④ 사탄

07 친가와 외가 쪽 선조들이 모두 독립전쟁에서 큰 활약을 한 New York의 명문가에서 태어났기 때문에 아버지의 사업 실패 전까지 유년시절은 유복했다.

07 Herman Melville에 대한 설명으로 옳지 <u>않은</u> 것은?

① 초기에 여행기 장르의 작품을 썼다.
② 어려운 어린 시절을 보냈다.
③ 당대에 중요한 정치적 이슈에 대한 깊은 관심과 비평적 성찰을 담고 있다.
④ 친지들의 권유로 글쓰기를 시작했다.

정답 05 ② 06 ③ 07 ②

08 「*Billy Budd, Sailor*」에서 주인공 Billy Budd에 대한 설명으로 옳지 <u>않은</u> 것은?

① 죄 없고 순수한 21세의 고아 출신 흑인 해병이다.
② Claggart의 누명에 이성을 잃고 분노하여 그를 사망에 이르게 했다.
③ 자신을 교수형에 처한 Vere 함장을 저주하며 죽는다.
④ 선한 본성을 가졌다.

08 자신을 교수형에 처한 Vere 함장을 축복하며 죽는다.

09 「*Billy Budd, Sailor*」에서 Claggart와 Billy Budd에 대한 설명으로 옳지 <u>않은</u> 것은?

① Billy - 학문적으로 거의 무지하다.
② Billy - 뚜렷한 자의식을 가지고 있다.
③ Claggart - 악한 본성을 타고 났다.
④ Claggart - 잘생긴 외모에 지성을 겸비한 인물이다.

09 Billy는 다른 선원에게 항상 모범이 될 만큼 죄 없고 순수하며, 순진무구한 청년이다.

10 「*Billy Budd, Sailor*」에서 Claggart가 Billy Budd에게 누명을 씌우는 이유는?

① 한 여인과의 삼각관계로 인하여
② Billy가 자신보다 잘 생겼기 때문에
③ Billy가 Claggart에 대한 나쁜 소문을 퍼뜨렸기 때문에
④ 악한 경험 없이 인생을 살아가는 Billy에게 질투심을 느꼈기 때문에

10 Claggart는 악한 경험 없이 인생을 살아가는 Billy를 질투하여 그를 파멸시키려 하지만, 오히려 Billy에게 일격을 당하고 죽고 만다.

정답 08 ③ 09 ② 10 ④

11 함장은 Billy의 무고함을 알고 있었으나 어쩔 수 없이 군대라는 집단의 안정을 유지하기 위하여 이 사건을 하극상으로 다루어 Billy를 교수형에 처한다.

11 「*Billy Budd, Sailor*」에서 Captain Vere가 Billy Budd를 교수형에 처하는 이유는?

① Claggart에게 누명을 씌웠기 때문에
② Captain Vere를 위협했기 때문에
③ 반란을 꾀했기 때문에
④ 군대라는 집단의 안정을 위해서

12 작품의 어조는 강건체에서 만연체로 계속 바뀌는데 이러한 형식이야말로 인생의 본질과 인생의 모순을 나타내는 가장 적절한 구조라고 볼 수 있다.

12 「*Billy Budd, Sailor*」에 대한 설명으로 옳지 <u>않은</u> 것은?

① 각 장의 길이가 제멋대로이다.
② 통일된 어조로 작품이 진행된다.
③ 진행 단계는 총 4단계로 나누어진다.
④ 3인칭 화자의 시점이지만 종종 등장인물의 마음속을 넘나드는 경향을 보인다.

13 Billy Budd가 처음 승선한 the Rights-of-Man이라는 상선이고, 대영제국의 함대인 H. M. S. Bellipotent로 강제 징집이 되었다. Pequod와 Rachel은 「*Moby-Dick : or The Whale*」에 나오는 배 이름이다.

13 「*Billy Budd, Sailor*」에서 Billy Budd가 처음 승선한 배의 이름은?

① the Rights-of-Man
② the H. M. S. Bellipotent
③ the Pequod
④ the Rachel

정답 11 ④ 12 ② 13 ①

제5장 Mark Twain – 「*The Adventures of Huckleberry Finn*」

01 Mark Twain에 대한 설명으로 옳지 <u>않은</u> 것은?

① 「*Life of the Mississippi*」의 작가이다.

② 미국을 대표하는 작가이다.

③ Mark Twain의 본명은 Samuel Langhorne Clemens이다.

④ 북부인에서 남부인으로 편입하였다.

01 Twain은 남부인에서 북부인으로 편입하였다.

02 「*The Adventures of Huckleberry Finn*」에 대한 설명으로 옳지 <u>않은</u> 것은?

① 성장소설이다.

② 19세기의 미국 남부에 관한 풍자를 담고 있다.

③ 각 장의 이야기들은 다양하고 흥미진진하나 연속성이 단절되어 있다.

④ Mississippi 3부작 중 첫 작품이다.

02 「*The Adventures of Huckleberry Finn*」은 Mississippi 3부작 중 마지막 작품이다.

03 「*The Adventures of Huckleberry Finn*」의 주제가 <u>아닌</u> 것은?

① 자유의 확보와 인간성 회복

② 성장소설

③ 인과응보의 관계

④ 신과 인간에 대한 알레고리

03 소설의 전개상 인과관계가 존재할 수 있으나 이 작품의 주제로 보기에는 어렵다.

04 Mark Twain에 대한 설명으로 옳지 <u>않은</u> 것은?

① 남북전쟁에 참가하였다.

② 신문사의 기자가 되어 필명으로 Mark Twain을 썼다.

③ 부유한 지성인의 가정에서 태어났다.

④ Mississippi 강의 증기선 수로 안내원 자격증을 땄다.

04 Twain의 아버지는 이곳저곳으로 이사를 다니며 돈을 벌기 위해 여러 일에 손을 댔으나 성공하지 못하여 자식들에게 안정적인 교육도 시키지 못했다.

정답 01 ④ 02 ④ 03 ③ 04 ③

checkpoint   해설 & 정답

05 미망인 Douglas는 Huck을 보호하며 교양인으로 만들기 위해 노력하는 인물이다.

05 「*The Adventures of Huckleberry Finn*」의 등장인물과 그에 대한 설명으로 옳게 짝지어지지 <u>않은</u> 것은?

① Jim - 노예로 있다가 도망친 흑인 소년으로 Huck과 Tom의 일행에 합류한다.
② Douglas - Huck을 학대하여 견디지 못한 Huck이 가출하게 만든다.
③ Tom - Huck과 함께 Joe가 숨겨 두었던 보물을 찾아내어 벼락부자가 되었다.
④ Huck - 자신에 대해 이중적인 잣대를 가지고 있다.

06 Huckleberry Finn은 문명에 찌들지 않은 원초적인 모습을 지니고 있는 인물로, 어른들의 세계 즉, 불평등, 허위, 물질에 대한 집착, 사기 등으로 가득한 가식의 세계에서 오염되지 않고 문명에 찌들지 않은 자유인의 모습으로 등장한다.

06 「*The Adventures of Huckleberry Finn*」에서 Huckleberry Finn이 상징하는 것으로 옳지 <u>않은</u> 것은?

① 문명에 찌들지 않은 자유인
② 문명에 적응한 미국인
③ 미국인의 이상적인 모습
④ 무한한 발전과 가능성을 지니고 있는 순수한 미국인

07 주인공인 Huckleberry Finn은 교육과 문명을 거부하는 태도를 보인다.

07 「*The Adventures of Huckleberry Finn*」에서 쓰인 기법으로 옳지 <u>않은</u> 것은?

① 1인칭 시각으로 사회 비평적 서술을 자유롭게 느끼게 하였다.
② 주요 등장인물들은 사투리와 일상 언어, 반어적 어법을 사용한다.
③ 교육과 문명을 적극적으로 받아들이려 한다.
④ 대조적 상징을 사용한다.

정답   05 ②   06 ②   07 ③

08 「*The Adventures of Huckleberry Finn*」에서 Huck와 Jim은 뗏목을 어떻게 얻었는가?

① Huck와 Jim이 훔쳤다.

② Huck와 Jim이 만들었다.

③ 노예 상인으로부터 구입했다.

④ 홍수가 났을 때 발견했다.

08 Huck와 Jim은 홍수가 났을 때 강 근처에서 뗏목을 발견했다.

09 「*The Adventures of Huckleberry Finn*」의 장르와 거리가 먼 것은?

① picaresque(악한소설)

② bildungsroman(성장소설)

③ satire(풍자)

④ moral fable(도덕적 우화)

09 「*The Adventures of Huckleberry Finn*」은 picaresque novel(악한소설)이자 bildungsroman(성장소설)이다. 또한 노예 제도와 인종 차별(racism) 등 19세기의 미국 남부 사회에 관한 풍자가 나타난다. 「*The Adventures of Huckleberry Finn*」은 도덕적 우화(moral fable)에 해당되지 않는다.

10 「*The Adventures of Huckleberry Finn*」에서 Jim은 어떻게 노예 신분에서 해방되는가?

① Huck과 뗏목을 타서 아칸소(Arkansas)주로 탈출한다.

② Tom이 돈으로 Jim을 사서 해방시켜 준다.

③ Miss Watson이 유언으로 Jim을 해방시켜 주었다.

④ 노예제가 없는 오하이오(Ohio)주로 탈출한다.

10 Tom은 두 달 전 죽은 Miss Watson이 이미 Jim을 해방시켜 주는 유언을 남겼다는 소식을 밝힌다.

11 「*The Adventures of Huckleberry Finn*」에 등장하는 장소가 아닌 곳은?

① Boston

② Mississippi River

③ St. Petersburg

④ Jackson's Island

11 Boston은 Nathaniel Hawthorne의 「*The Scarlet Letter*」의 배경 장소로 등장한다.

정답 08 ④ 09 ④ 10 ③ 11 ①

01 「*Maggie : A Girl of the Street*」은 Stephen Crane의 작품이다.

제 **6** 장   Henry James – 「*Washington Square*」, 「*The Real Thing*」

01 다음 중 Henry James의 작품이 <u>아닌</u> 것은?

① 「*The Ambassadors*」
② 「*The Wings of the Dove*」
③ 「*Maggie : A Girl of the Street*」
④ 「*The Turns of the Screw*」

02 Henry James는 그의 첫 장편소설인 「*Watch and Ward*」를 연재하면서 외국에 나가 있는 미국인의 이야기를 다룬 국제상황을 소재로 소설을 쓰기 시작하였다.

02 Henry James가 국제상황에 대한 주제를 개발하기 시작하며 연재한 작품은?

① 「*Watch and Ward*」
② 「*The Golden Bowl*」
③ 「*The Princess Casamassima*」
④ 「*The America*」

03 Henry James는 새로운 기술적 고안의 도입을 강조하면서 객관적 시점, 장면의 극화, 원근법, 포괄과 배제, 책략과 이완, 구성과 동기 등의 소설 미학에 큰 관심을 가졌다. 그리고 그는 이를 실천함으로써 현대 소설의 기법에 많은 공헌을 하였다.

03 Henry James에 대한 설명으로 옳지 <u>않은</u> 것은?

① 기존 소설형식과 주제를 고집하였다.
② 초기, 중기, 후기의 발전과정을 보여준다.
③ 그의 문장은 작품을 난해하고 애매하게 만들었다.
④ 소설, 연극, 평론, 서평, 기행문, 전기 등 다양한 문학적 작품을 내놓았다.

정답   01 ③   02 ①   03 ①

04 Henry James의 작품 발전 형태에 대한 설명으로 옳지 <u>않은</u> 것은?

① 초기 - 프랑스의 중편소설을 즐겨 사용하면서도 국제적 비극을 많이 취급하였다.

② 중기 - 5년에 걸쳐 시도한 극작 활동의 실패는 단편소설의 집필에 집중하도록 했다.

③ 후기 - 작품을 형이하학적 평면구조에서 형이상학적인 심리소설로 상향시켰다.

④ 후기 - 사회연구의 작품도 쓰고 문예와 미술 등 심미주의적인 작품을 발표하였다.

04 중기에 해당하는 특징이다.

05 다음 중 「*Washington Square*」의 주제가 <u>아닌</u> 것은?

① 옳지 못한 이성관 제시

② 타인의 인생을 간섭하는 행위의 비인간성

③ 자유의지의 추구에 따르는 파문과 궁극적인 승리

④ 자식을 지키려는 부모와 자식의 애틋한 감정

05 「*Washington Square*」의 주제는 남의 자유를 유린하려는 자와 그것을 지키려는 자 사이의 심리적 갈등을 다루고 있다.

06 「*Washington Square*」의 등장인물에 관한 설명으로 틀린 것은?

① Dr. Sloper : 자신의 가치관을 자식에게 강요하는 인물이다.

② Townsend : Catherine을 진정으로 사랑하는 인물이다.

③ Mrs. Almond : 이성적인 성격의 소유자이다.

④ Catherine Sloper : 내성적이지만 자아의식이 강한 인물이다.

06 Townsend는 키 크고 멋진 외모에 언변도 뛰어나고 영리한 인물이다. 그는 우아한 옷차림의 Catherine에게 결혼을 목적으로 접근했으나 실패하고, 그녀의 유산 상속에 대한 희망이 사라지자 미련 없이 그녀를 떠난다.

정답 (04 ④ 05 ④ 06 ②)

07 '칼'은 희생 또는 살해를 상징하고, '집'은 신분, 명예, 지위를 상징한다.

07 「*Washington Square*」에서 '칼'이 상징하는 것은?

① 명예
② 지위
③ 희생
④ 신분

08 총 35장으로 소설의 전반부와 후반부의 약간을 제외한 대부분이 주인공 Catherine과 Townsend의 관계에 얽힌 대화로 이루어져 있어, 소설의 전반부와 후반부를 제외하면 다소 지루한 면이 있는 소설이다.

08 「*Washington Square*」의 구조적인 특징으로 옳지 <u>않은</u> 것은?

① 총 35장으로 구성되어 있다.
② 각 부의 서두에 주요 인물의 대화문을 그대로 한 대목씩 싣고 있다.
③ 소설의 전반부와 후반부를 제외하면 매우 흥미롭다.
④ 대부분은 Catherine과 Townsend의 혼인관계에 얽힌 대화이다.

09 이 작품은 처음부터 끝까지 주인공인 '나'에 의하여 이야기가 서술되고 있다.

09 다음 중 「*The Real Thing*」의 시점으로 옳은 것은?

① 3인칭 관찰자 시점
② 둘 이상의 시점
③ 전지적 작가 시점
④ 1인칭 제한적 시점

정답 07 ③ 08 ③ 09 ④

10 「*The Real Thing*」에 등장하는 인물 중 화가의 친구이자 비평가로 문제 해결에 도움은 주는 인물은 누구인가?

① Miss Churm
② Jack Hawley
③ Monarchs
④ Oronte

10 ① Miss Chum은 화실에 고용된 직업 모델로서 천박한 인물이다.
③ Monarchs는 한때는 사정이 좋았지만 현재는 경제난에 봉착한 퇴역 소령 부부이다.
④ Oronte는 새로 고용된 청년 모델로 순진하고 유연한 인물이다.

11 다음 중 「*The Real Thing*」의 주제가 <u>아닌</u> 것은?

① 예술가의 도덕적 딜레마
② 진정한 예술은 허구를 통하여 사실을 재현한다는 모순
③ 개인과 조직사회의 관계
④ 예술은 사실 그 자체의 반영이 아니라 변형

11 「*The Real Thing*」은 예술과 허구와의 관계에 대한 깊이 있는 관찰과 사고를 주제로 하고 있다.

12 「*The Real Thing*」에서 볼 수 있는 아이러니가 <u>아닌</u> 것은?

① 진정한 예술은 '진짜' 그 자체의 반영이다.
② 잘생기고 역할에 알맞은 진짜 인물이 화가에게는 오히려 방해물이 된다.
③ 모델 역할을 하던 부부가 화실의 하인으로 전락한다.
④ 모델 부부가 모델로는 적합하지 못했으나 그 추억은 훌륭한 문학 작품의 소재가 되었다.

12 「*The Real Thing*」은 예술이 사실 (Reality) 그 자체의 반영이 아니라 변형이라는 주제를 담고 있다.

정답 10 ② 11 ③ 12 ①

제 **7** 장   Stephen Crane – 「*The Red Badge of Courage : An Episode of the American Civil War*」

01 「*The Custom House*」는 Nathaniel Hawthorne의 소설이다.

01 다음 중 Stephen Crane의 작품이 <u>아닌</u> 것은?

① 「*The Open Boat*」
② 「*The Monster*」
③ 「*The Custom House*」
④ 「*Maggie : A Girl of the Street*」

02 집필 당시 Crane은 전쟁에 대한 직접적인 경험이 없었다. 전투에 참가한 경험이 있었던 자신의 형으로부터 들은 군대생활을 바탕으로 실제 전투 장면을 실감나게 재현했다.

02 Stephen Crane에 대한 설명으로 옳지 <u>않은</u> 것은?

① 전쟁에 직접 참전한 경험을 바탕으로 소설을 집필하였다.
② 스스로를 어디에 매어두지 않고 자유롭게 생활하였다.
③ 뉴욕을 배경으로 작품 활동을 하였다.
④ Johnston Smith라는 가명을 사용하기도 하였다.

03 Fleming의 심리상태로 보아 절망과 희망의 교차적인 구성으로 보기도 한다.

03 「*The Red Badge of the Courage*」의 구성에 대한 설명으로 옳지 <u>않은</u> 것은?

① 24장으로 구성되어 있다.
② 각 장은 Fleming의 용기와 상실, 획득, 성인으로 나아감의 주제를 가진다.
③ 군대의 공격과 주둔 등을 통해 일종의 Seesaw Game 같은 구성을 지닌다.
④ Fleming의 심리상태에 대한 묘사는 하지 않는다.

정답 01 ③ 02 ① 03 ④

04 「*The Red Badge of the Courage*」의 주제로 볼 수 없는 것은?

① 강한 인간의 내면
② 자연주의적 주제
③ 전쟁의 본질
④ 개인과 조직사회의 관계

04 작가는 나약한 인간의 내면을 주인공인 Fleming을 통해서 보여주고 있다.

05 「*The Red Badge of the Courage*」에 대한 설명으로 옳은 것은?

① 적절한 과장이 사회를 풍자하는 역할을 했다.
② 환상적인 비유를 사용하여 소설의 풍미를 살렸다.
③ 주인공은 등장인물과의 갈등을 통하여 평화주의자가 된다.
④ 인상주의적 사실주의 기법으로 소설이 쓰였다.

05 남북전쟁을 최초로 다룬 사실주의적 작품이다.

06 「*The Red Badge of the Courage*」에 등장하는 상징이 잘못 짝지어진 것은?

① flag – courage
② forest – fleeting
③ wound – death
④ squirrel – coward

06 wound는 courage를 상징한다.

07 「*The Red Badge of the Courage*」에서 Henry Fleming을 영웅적으로 만든 직접적 계기는?

① 우연한 사건으로 하사받은 훈장
② 전쟁의 실체에 대한 깨달음
③ 동료의 죽음
④ 우연히 생긴 이마의 상처

07 Fleming이 우연하게 이마에 상처를 입은 후로 그는 본능적으로 행동하는 동물처럼 미친 듯이 용감하게 싸운다.

정답 04 ① 05 ④ 06 ③ 07 ④

08 Fleming은 실제로 전투가 벌어졌을 때에도 역할이 별로 없을 뿐만 아니라 나약하고 쉽게 동요하는 병사였다.

09 고참병 Jim Conkiln은 'The tall soldier'로 지칭된다.

10 두려움에 떨면서 도망치던 Fleming이 아군 부상병 무리에 운 좋게 합류하게 되면서 그의 운명은 완전히 뒤바뀌는 것은 우연이 때때로 인간의 삶을 지배한다는 자연주의 철학을 드러내고 있다.

---

08 「*The Red Badge of the Courage*」에 대한 설명으로 옳지 <u>않은</u> 것은?

① 뛰어난 심리묘사가 두드러진다.
② 성장소설이다.
③ Fleming은 전형적인 영웅의 성향을 지닌 병사이다.
④ 비평가들 사이에는 Fleming이 성장했는지 또는 성장하지 않았는지에 대한 의견이 분분하다.

09 「*The Red Badge of the Courage*」에서 Jim Conkiln을 가리키는 호칭은 무엇인가?

① The tattered soldier
② The tall soldier
③ The loud soldier
④ The youth

10 「*The Red Badge of the Courage*」에서 두려움에 떨면서 도망치던 Fleming이 아군 부상병 무리에 운 좋게 합류하게 되면서 그의 운명은 완전히 바뀐다. 이것이 나타내고 있는 철학은 무엇인가?

① 자연주의
② 사실주의
③ 인상주의
④ 인본주의

정답 08 ③ 09 ② 10 ①

부록

—

최종모의고사

I wish you the best of luck

영어영문학과 2단계

최종모의고사 | 19세기 영미소설

제한시간: 50분 | 시작 ___시 ___분 – 종료 ___시 ___분

↪ 정답 및 해설 370p

01 Jane Austen에 대한 설명으로 옳지 <u>않은</u> 것은?

① 1775년 영국의 햄프셔의 Steventon에서 태어났다.
② 활발한 사회생활을 했으며 글 쓰는 것 외에도 그녀의 생을 가족에게 애정을 쏟았다.
③ 젊은 시절에는 무도회와 파티에서 많은 남성들의 관심을 받기도 하였다.
④ 27세가 될 무렵 햄프셔의 부유한 지주와 결혼하여 행복한 가정을 꾸렸다.

02 「*Pride and Prejudice*」에 관한 설명으로 옳은 것은?

① Mr. Bennet은 자진하여 딸들을 데리고 Netherfield의 무도회에 갔다.
② Darcy와 Wickham은 어렸을 때부터 친한 친구이다.
③ Elizabeth는 Pemberley에 가서 Darcy를 찾기 위해 애쓴다.
④ Darcy는 Wickham으로 인해 곤경에 빠진 Lydia를 도와준다.

03 「*Pride and Prejudice*」에 등장하는 Lady Catherine de Bourgh의 성격은 어떠한가?

① 다정하고 친절하다.
② 내성적이고 자존심이 세다.
③ 어리석고 편협하다.
④ 오만하고 자존심이 세다.

04 「*Pride and Prejudice*」에서 Bennet 가족이 사는 지역의 명칭은?

① Pemberley
② Rosings
③ Longbourn
④ Bueeows

05 「*Wuthering Heights*」의 등장인물에 관한 설명으로 틀린 것은?

① Heathcliff : 복수와 집념의 인간형으로 변한다.
② Catherine Earnshaw : 황야를 맨발로 헤매는가 하면, 귀부인의 모습도 보여준다.
③ Hindley Earnshaw : 거칠면서도 심약한 성격으로 복수의 첫 번째 희생자이다.
④ Edgar Linton : Wuthering Heights에서 계속 시중을 든다.

06 「*Wuthering Heights*」에 대한 특징으로 틀린 것은?

① 1, 2, 3세대에 걸친 이야기 구성이다.
② 절제되고 농축된 어법이 사용되었다.
③ 자연과 초자연적인 것들에 관한 이미지가 자주 나온다.
④ 작가의 자기 반영적인 테크닉이 두드러진다.

07 「*Wuthering Heights*」에서 Wuthering Heights에 거주하면서 Lockwood에게 이야기를 전달하는 인물은 누구인가?

① Joseph
② Nelly
③ Hareton
④ Heathcliff

08 「*Great Expectations*」의 주제에 관한 설명으로 틀린 것은?

① 막대한 유산 : 아이러니하게도 Pip이 기대했던 모든 것은 사라진다.

② 노동의 가치 : 열심히 노력한 대가는 결코 비난받지 않는다.

③ 돈 : 절대적으로 우월한 가치를 지닌다.

④ 선과 악 : 선악은 이분법적으로 분리될 수 없어 혼재되어 있다.

09 「*Great Expectations*」의 등장인물에 대한 설명에서 괄호 안에 들어갈 용어를 올바르게 짝지은 것은?

> (ⓐ)(은)는 결혼식 당일 아침에 사기꾼 (ⓑ)(으)로부터 사기 결혼에 휘말린 이후, 세상과 담을 쌓고 남성들을 저주하며 복수의 대상으로 삼는다. 그녀는 양녀 (ⓒ)(을)를 야비하고 어리석은 (ⓓ)(와)과 결혼하게 유도하여 Pip의 마음에 상처를 입힌다.

① ⓐ - Molly

② ⓑ - Magwitch

③ ⓒ - Estella

④ ⓓ - Compeyson

10 「*Great Expectations*」에서 Pip이 처음으로 Magwitch를 만나는 장소는?

① 감옥
② 보트
③ 무덤
④ 런던

11 「*Great Expectations*」에서 Estella는 결국 누구의 딸인가?

① Magwitch

② Miss Havisham

③ Joe Gargery

④ Pip

12 George Eliot의 소설로 고향에서 친구에게 배신당한 주인공이 신(God)과 인간에 대한 믿음을 잃고 고독하게 혼자 살던 중, 우연히 다가온 Eppie라는 여자아이를 키우게 되면서 그 아이를 통하여 다시 인간에 대한 사랑을 되찾게 되는 이야기를 그린 작품은?

① 「*Middlemarch*」
② 「*Adam Bede*」
③ 「*Silas Marner*」
④ 「*Northanger Abbey*」

13 다음 중 「*Silas Marner*」에 대한 설명으로 옳은 것은?

① Raveloe는 시대적 변화가 두드러진 곳이었다.
② 작가는 인물들의 사실적 묘사를 통해 당시의 사회상을 풍자한다.
③ Silas Marner는 Lantern Yard에서의 배반으로 인해 무신론자가 되었다.
④ 작가는 인물들의 낙관적인 인생 태도를 비판한다.

14 「*Silas Marner*」에서 비판하는 대상으로 옳지 <u>않은</u> 것은?

① 생부가 곧 법적 아버지라는 법적 구조
② 영국 사회의 가부장적 구조
③ 도덕적 법의 우위
④ 전통적 권위의 정당화

15 「*Tess of the d'Urbervilles*」의 주제로 옳지 <u>않은</u> 것은?

① 성에 대한 빅토리아 시대의 허위
② 엄격한 도덕률 및 종교적 교리에 도전한 인간상
③ 감성과 이성 사이의 대립
④ 회의주의적인 비관주의

16 「*Tess of the d'Urbervilles*」의 전개과정을 순서대로 나열한 것은?

> a. 소생
> b. 개심자
> c. 순결을 잃음
> d. 처녀
> e. 인과응보
> f. 여자의 속죄
> g. 결과

① d → c → a → g → f → b → e
② d → b → a → f → g → c → e
③ b → a → c → e → g → f → d
④ b → f → d → a → c → g → e

17 「*Tess of the d'Urbervilles*」에서 미래의 남편에게 Tess의 과거를 밝히지 말라고 Tess에게 말한 인물은 누구인가?

① Tess의 엄마
② Tess의 아버지
③ Angel
④ Alec

18 Edgar Allan Poe에 대한 평가로 적절하지 <u>않은</u> 것은?

① 추리소설을 개척했다.
② 장편소설 장르를 확립했다.
③ 프랑스 상징주의 시인들을 열광시켰다.
④ 세계적으로 인정받은 최초의 미국 작가이다.

19 「*The Black Cat*」에 대한 설명으로 **틀린** 것은?

① 소설의 배경을 뒤뜰로 설정하여 암울한 분위기를 조성하였다.

② 인간의 광기와 어두운 내면을 묘사하였다.

③ 악에 탐닉하는 화자에 관한 이야기이다.

④ 자신의 행동에서 도덕적인 의미를 인정하기 거부하는 심리에 관한 이야기이다.

20 「*The Black Cat*」에서 화자는 고양이 Pluto를 미워했다. 그는 Pluto에게 어떤 일을 저질렀는가?

① Pluto를 때렸다.

② Pluto를 밖에 버렸다.

③ Pluto의 눈 한쪽을 도려내었다.

④ Pluto를 지하실에 가두었다.

21 「*The Scarlet Letter*」에서 종종 '요정'으로 비유되는 인물은?

① Hester

② Pearl

③ Dr. Chillingworth

④ Dimmesdale

22 「*The Scarlet Letter*」에서 '거머리'로 비유되는 인물은?

① Hester

② Pearl

③ Dr. Chillingworth

④ Dimmesdale

23 「*The Scarlet Letter*」에서 다루는 죄의 형태가 올바르게 짝지어진 것은?

① 세상에 드러난 죄 – Hester Prynne
② 숨겨진 죄 – Roger Chillingworth
③ 용서받지 못할 오만의 죄 – Arthur Dimmesdale
④ 용서받지 못할 오만의 죄 – Pearl

24 「*The Scarlet Letter*」에서 글씨 'A'의 의미로 해석할 수 <u>없는</u> 것은?

① 성스럽게 변모한 Hester의 모습을 보여주는 Angel
② Adam의 원죄
③ Dimmesdale의 이름인 Arthur
④ 선악과인 Apple

25 「*Billy Budd, Sailor*」에 대한 설명으로 옳지 <u>않은</u> 것은?

① 상징이 가득한 비극적인 비전(vision)이다.
② 각 장의 길이가 비교적 균등하다.
③ 3인칭 화자의 시점이다.
④ 순진무구함과 사악함이 벌이는 내용이다.

26 「*Billy Budd, Sailor*」에서 Billy Budd의 마지막 유언은?

① God bless America!
② God save the Queen!
③ God bless Captain Vere!
④ My God, why have you forsaken me!

27 「*The Adventures of Huckleberry Finn*」에서 작가가 풍자하는 것은?

① 종교
② 편견
③ 미국사회
④ 정치

28 「*The Adventures of Huckleberry Finn*」에 등장하는 강(river)의 이름은?

① Colorado
② Mississippi
③ Missouri
④ Oklahoma

29 「*The Adventures of Huckleberry Finn*」에 대한 설명에서 괄호 안에 들어갈 용어로 알맞은 것은?

> 이 작품은 (   )의 전형도 따르고 있다. 주인공 Huck은 미국 남부사회의 무식한 백인 태생으로 교양도 없는 불량소년이다. 그러나 한편 그는 현실적인 면모도 보이며 작가의 희망을 대변하는 인물이기도하다.

① 추리소설   ② 악한소설
③ 환상소설   ④ 성장소설

30 「*The Adventures of Huckleberry Finn*」의 구성에 대한 설명으로 옳지 <u>않은</u> 것은?

① 각 장의 내용이 유기적으로 이어져 흥미를 지속시킨다.
② 첫 번째는 Huck이 자신과 Tom, Jim을 소개하는 부분이다.
③ 두 번째는 Huck과 Jim이 도망나와 자연에서의 생활을 즐기는 부분이다.
④ 세 번째는 Huck이 다시 Tom의 집으로 귀환하는 부분이다.

31 「*The Adventures of Huckleberry Finn*」 소설의 끝 부분에서 사람들에게 Jim이 자유인이 되었다고 알려주는 인물은 누구인가?

① Aunt Polly

② Tom

③ Huck

④ Pap

32 Henry James 작품의 주제에 관한 설명으로 옳지 않은 것은?

① 국제상황에 처한 미국인의 도덕적 갈등은 Henry James 소설 특유의 주제이다.

② 국제상황의 대조와 도덕적 갈등은 일종의 공식이 되었다.

③ 작가는 도덕적 중립의 태도를 고수한다.

④ 작품 속에서 지나친 도덕적 교훈의 직접적인 제시가 논란의 대상이었다.

33 「*Washington Square*」에 대한 설명으로 옳지 않은 것은?

① 각 부의 서두에 주요 인물의 대화문을 그대로 한 대목씩 싣고 있다.

② Mrs. Penniman은 비현실적인 고집을 피워 결국 무시당한다.

③ Dr. Sloper는 딸이 노처녀로 늙는 이유가 Morris 때문이라고 생각한다.

④ 국제상황 주제가 극명하게 드러나고 있다.

34 「*The Real Thing*」에 대한 설명으로 옳지 않은 것은?

① Henry James의 초현실주의 작품이다.

② 진정한 예술은 허구를 통하여 사실을 재현한다는 모순을 보여준다.

③ 예술은 사실 그 자체의 반영이 아니다.

④ 1인칭 제한적 시점이다.

35 「*The Real Thing*」의 주제로 옳은 것은?

① 예술가의 도덕적 딜레마
② 가족의 사랑
③ 용기의 본질
④ 돈과 명예

36 「*The Real Thing*」에서 소설 속의 '나'가 'Monarch' 부부를 모델로 쓴 이유는?

① 부탁을 거절할 수 없어서
② 상류사회에 대한 책의 삽화를 요청받은 상황이어서
③ 로맨스 책의 삽화를 요청받은 상황이어서
④ 직업 모델만큼 못생겨서

37 「*The Red Badge of Courage*」에 대한 설명으로 옳은 것은?

① 크게 세 부분으로 나뉜다.
② Wilson의 심리상태로 보아 절망과 희망의 교차적인 구성이다.
③ 1인칭 관찰자 시점이다.
④ 남북전쟁을 최초로 다룬 사실주의적 작품이다.

38 「*The Red Badge of Courage*」에서 상징하는 바가 올바르게 연결되지 <u>않은</u> 것은?

① flag → courage
② wound → boyish dream of glory
③ forest → refuge, fleeing
④ squirrel → coward

39 「*The Red Badge of Courage*」에서 Henry가 전투에서 퇴각할 때 숲으로 도망치면서 마주친 것은?

① 탈영병
② 나무에 기대어 앉은 채 죽은 병사
③ 나무에 매달려 죽은 병사
④ 죽은 사슴

40 「*The Red Badge of Courage*」에서 Henry가 전투의 상황에서 몰두하고 있을 때 그의 마음속에서 여러 번 떠오르는 생각은 무엇인가?

① 언제 전쟁이 끝나는가
② 나는 왜 여기에 있는가
③ 누가 나를 구해줄까
④ 집에 가고 싶다

제한시간: 50분 | 시작 ___시 ___분 – 종료 ___시 ___분

↱ 정답 및 해설 375p

01 「*Pride and Prejudice*」는 다음과 같은 문장으로 소설의 시작이 전개된다. 괄호 안에 들어갈 용어로 적절한 것은?

> '상당한 재산을 가진 독신 남성이라면 틀림없이 (   )(을)를 찾고 있을 것이다'라는 말은 보편적인 진리이다.

① 집
② 직위
③ 아내
④ 취미

02 Jane Austen의 이상적인 사회에 대해 옳은 설명을 모두 고르면?

> a. 개인의 공적인 삶과 사적인 삶은 관련이 있다.
> b. 각 저택의 운명은 소유주의 운명과 밀접히 관련이 있다.
> c. 소설 속 장소와 인물들의 관계는 관련이 있다.
> d. 소설 속 저택이나 토지는 소유주의 외적 가치의 반영이다.

① a, b
② a, c, d
③ b, d
④ a, b, c

03 「*Pride and Prejudice*」에서 Wickham이 Elizabeth에게 Darcy에 대해 편견을 갖게 한 내용은 무엇인가?

① Darcy가 결투에서 Wickham의 사촌을 죽였다.
② Darcy는 Wickham이 Darcy의 여동생과 결혼하는 것을 반대했다.
③ Darcy가 자신의 조국을 배반했다.
④ Darcy가 Wickham의 경제적 권리를 박탈했다.

04 「*Pride and Prejudice*」에서 Bennet 가족이 거주하고 있는 지역의 이름은?

① Pemberley
② London
③ Longbourn
④ Netherfield

05 다음 중 Emily Brontë의 작품기법이 <u>아닌</u> 것은?

① 자기 반영적
② 자연과 초자연물
③ 절제되고 농축된 기법
④ 다양하고 변모하는 기술 기법

06 다음 중 「*Wuthering Heights*」의 특징이 <u>아닌</u> 것은?

① 이중 구조로 되어있다.
② 작가의 자기 반영적 테크닉을 볼 수 있다.
③ 소설의 인물상은 크게 세 가지로 나뉜다.
④ 두 명의 서술자가 있다.

07 「*Wuthering Heights*」의 저자 Emily Brontë가 성장하고 생활한 지역은?

① Sussex
② Gloucestershire
③ Yorkshire
④ Warwickshire

08 「*Wuthering Heights*」에서 Catherine에 대한 설명으로 옳지 <u>않은</u> 것은?

① Hindley의 여동생이다.
② Edgar와 결혼한 후에도 Heathcliff를 잊지 못한다.
③ 소설 내내 귀부인의 속성만을 보여준다.
④ Heathcliff와의 신분차이로 Edgar를 선택한다.

09 Charles Dickens의 소설에서 고정적으로 등장하는 주제는?

① 남녀 간의 삼각관계
② 계급문제
③ 유산문제
④ 산업화문제

10 「*Great Expectations*」에서 Pip의 매형인 Joe가 Pip을 만나기 위해 London에 왔을 때 Pip의 반응은?

① 모른척한다.
② 기뻐한다.
③ 화를 낸다.
④ 당황한다.

11 「*Great Expectations*」에서 Estella와 결혼하는 인물은?

① Compeyson
② Pip
③ Herbert
④ Drummle

12 「*Great Expectations*」에서 Miss Havisham은 어떤 이유로 죽음을 맞는가?

① 말에서 떨어졌다.
② 창문에서 떨어졌다.
③ 화재로 죽었다.
④ 지병으로 죽었다.

13 「*Silas Marner*」에서 Silas는 약초의 치료방법을 어떻게 알게 되었는가?

① Lantern Yard에 있을 때 교육을 받았다.
② 그의 어머니가 그에게 가르쳐주었다.
③ 약초에 대한 책을 읽었다.
④ 약초에 대한 지식이 없었지만 아는 것처럼 행동했다.

14 「*Silas Marner*」에서 Silas가 Lantern Yard에서 교회의 돈을 훔쳤다는 누명을 쓰고도 자신의 결백을 굳이 주장하지 <u>않은</u> 이유는 무엇인가?

① 신이 그의 누명을 벗겨주실 것으로 믿었기 때문에
② 그 당시에 강직증의 병으로 투병 중이었기 때문에
③ 진실을 말하도록 허락받지 못하였기 때문에
④ 그가 실제로 돈을 훔쳤기 때문에

15 「*Silas Marner*」에서 Molly가 새해 축하 댄스에 오려고 한 이유는 무엇인가?

① 그 파티에서 그녀가 Godfrey를 만나면 그의 사랑을 얻을 것이라고 생각했다.
② 그녀는 사람들에게 자신이 Godfrey와 결혼한 사이라는 것을 알리고 싶었다.
③ 그녀는 Godfrey에게 자신이 한 말을 사과하고 싶었다.
④ 그녀는 자신의 딸을 Godfrey와 Nancy에게 입양시키고 싶었다.

16 「*Silas Marner*」에서 Godfrey가 Eppie에게 자신이 그녀의 생부라고 고백했을 때, Eppie의 태도는 어땠는가?

① Eppie는 Godfrey가 생모인 Molly를 버린 것에 분노한다.
② 생부인 Godfrey가 제안하는 부유한 삶에 고민한다.
③ Eppie는 Godfrey와 함께 살려는 마음이 없고 그의 제안을 거절한다.
④ Eppie는 비겁한 Godfrey와 결혼한 Nancy를 동정한다.

17 Thomas Hardy가 작품을 쓸 당시 농촌의 현실이 <u>아닌</u> 것은?

① 전근대적이고 가부장적인 농촌 공동체가 근대적 자본주의 영농방식으로 변화하는 상황이었다.
② 농촌 중간층 출신은 농업 노동자가 되거나 대도시의 빈민이 되곤 했다.
③ 계급의 격차와 괴리가 심각했다.
④ 개인의 계급 신분은 매우 안정적이었다.

18 「*Tess of the d'Urbervilles*」에서 Tess와 Angel이 서로 처음 만난 곳은?

① Chase 숲
② May Day Dance
③ Trantridge
④ Talbothhays 농장

19 「*Tess of the d'Urbervilles*」에서 Alec은 Flintcomb Ash에서 어떤 모습으로 Tess에게 나타나는가?

① 농부
② 설교가
③ 농장주
④ 판매원

20 「*Tess of the d'Urbervilles*」에서 Tess가 d'Urbervilles 저택에서 일을 한 이유는?

① 그녀의 귀족 신분을 얻기 위하여
② 그녀의 가족이 돈을 필요로 했기 때문에
③ 그녀가 Alec을 사랑했기 때문에
④ 그녀의 집에 머무를 수 없었기 때문에

21 「*The Black Cat*」에서 소설에 등장하는 동물들은 종종 어떤 이미지를 드러내는가?

① 천진무구함
② 가학적인 충동
③ 사랑
④ 어리석음

22 「*The Black Cat*」에서 다음 설명에 해당하는 인물은 누구인가?

> 본래 선도 악도 아니었으나 화자의 감정이 변하고 그의 악과 마성이 드러남에 따라 이름 그대로 명부의 왕이 되어 복수의 화신으로 변한다.

① 아내
② 경찰
③ 화자
④ Pluto

23 「*The Black Cat*」에 대한 다음 설명에서 괄호 안에 들어갈 적절한 용어를 순서대로 제시한 것은?

> 「*The Black Cat*」에서 고양이의 빨간 입술은 죽은 부인의 미적 (㉠)(을)를 나타낸다. 고양이의 영롱한 눈은 주인공의 (㉡)(을)를 괴롭히는 눈이며 검은 고양이는 양심의 가책에서 오는 고민과 (㉢)(을)를 상징한다.

	㉠	㉡	㉢
①	아름다움	양심	공포
②	상상	아름다움	양심
③	이미지	공포	양심
④	양심	공포	상상

24 Edgar Allan Poe의 작품에 관한 설명으로 옳지 <u>않은</u> 것은?

① 1833년 「*Ms. Found in a Bottle*」이 현상 공모에 당선되어 50달러의 상금을 받았다.
② 1834년에 발표한 「*Berenice*」는 Poe의 첫 공포 소설이다.
③ 1840년 25편의 단편을 엮어 출판한 『*Tales of the Grotesque and Arabesque*』는 판매량이 가장 높았다.
④ 1841년 「*The Murders in the Rue Morgue*」를 발표하여 추리 소설이라는 새로운 장르를 개척하였다.

25 「*The Scarlet Letter*」에서 소설의 화자가 'scarlet letter'에 대하여 쓰고자 한 이유는 무엇인가?

① 화자가 미국 역사에 흥미가 있었기 때문에
② Pearl의 손자였기 때문에
③ 그의 가족에게 감명을 주고 싶어서
④ 화자가 Hester와 친밀한 사이였기 때문에

26 「*The Scarlet Letter*」에서 Dimmesdale이 수많은 청중들 앞에서 자신의 죄를 고백하고 죽었을 때 이를 본 마을사람들의 태도는 어떠했는가?

① 사람들은 격분하고 교회에 등을 돌렸다.
② 사람들은 Dimmesdale의 이름을 교회명부에서 삭제했다.
③ 사람들은 Dimmesdale을 더욱 존경하게 되었다.
④ Dimmesdale이 죽은 후 사람들은 그를 곧 잊었다.

27 「*The Scarlet Letter*」의 구성을 순서대로 배열한 것은?

a. Dimmesdale의 구원
b. 청교도사회
c. Hester의 참모습
d. Chillingworth의 복수

① b - d - a - c
② b - d - c - a
③ a - c - b - d
④ a - c - d - b

28 「*The Scarlet Letter*」에서 Hester와 Chillingworth는 미국 Boston에 정착하기 전에 어느 지역에서 살았는가?

① 파리
② 런던
③ 암스테르담
④ 뉴욕

29 「*Billy Budd, Sailor*」에서 주인공 Billy Budd가 Bellipotent에서 불리던 별명은?

① Billy-Boy

② Bubbles

③ Baby

④ Buddy

30 「*Billy Budd, Sailor*」에서 주인공 Billy Budd가 처형되기 직전에 한 말은?

① "Vere 함장님! 당신은 죗값을 치를 겁니다."

② "상관의 명령을 따르십시오."

③ "Vere 함장님께 하느님의 가호가 있기를!"

④ "나는 결백합니다!"

31 「*Billy Budd, Sailor*」에서 Claggart는 Billy Budd에게 어떤 누명을 씌우는가?

① 화재를 일으켰다고

② 음식을 훔쳤다고

③ 적군에게 정보를 주었다고

④ 반란을 일으키려 한다고

32 「*Billy Budd, Sailor*」에서 Billy Budd가 대영 제국의 74포전함(seventy-four) H. M. S. Bellipotent 에서 맡고 있는 임무는?

① 1등 항해사

② 정비사

③ 망루병

④ 조향사

33 「*The Adventures of Huckleberry Finn*」에서 다음 설명에 해당하는 인물은 누구인가?

> 문명에 찌들지 않은 원초적인 모습을 지니고 있는 인물로 어른들의 세계, 즉 불평등, 허위, 물질에 대한 집착, 사기 등으로 가득한 가식의 세계에서 오염되지 않은 'Child of Nature'의 모습으로 등장한다.

① Tom
② Jim
③ Huck
④ Douglas

34 「*The Adventures of Huckleberry Finn*」에서 Jim과 Huck이 뗏목을 타고 Mississippi 강을 따라 떠날 때, Jim이 가려고 생각한 처음 목적지는 어디인가?

① 아칸소주 농장
② 뉴올리언즈
③ 오하이오 강
④ 세인트루이스

35 「*The Adventures of Huckleberry Finn*」의 시작 부분에서 Huck. Jim, Tom이 살고 있는 지역은 어느 곳으로 설정되어 있는가?

① 뉴올리언스
② 세인트피터즈버그
③ 세인트루이즈
④ 파이크스빌

36 「*Washington Square*」에서 Morris Townsend와 Catherine이 서로 처음 만난 장소는?

① 워싱턴 스퀘어
② 사촌 여동생의 약혼 축하 연회
③ Morris의 집
④ Catherine의 집

37 「*The Real Thing*」에 대한 설명으로 옳은 것은?

① 모델을 하던 부부는 원래 천박한 인물이다.
② 모델 역할에 적합한 부부는 모델료를 받지 않았다.
③ 모델 역할에 알맞은 진짜 인물은 모델로 적합하지 않았다.
④ 모델 부부가 적합하지 않았으나 그들을 모델로 쓸 수밖에 없었다.

38 Henry James의 소설에서 나타나는 지배적인 주제가 <u>아닌</u> 것은?

① 세대 간의 갈등
② 미국인과 유럽인의 미묘한 관계
③ 미국인의 도덕적 갈등
④ 도덕성의 결핍과 부재

39 「*The Red Badge of Courage*」에 대한 설명으로 괄호 안에 들어갈 말은?

> 「*The Red Badge of Courage*」는 (   )(을)를 최초로 다룬 사실주의적 작품이다.

① 독립전쟁
② 노예제도
③ 남북전쟁
④ 식민지

40 「*The Red Badge of Courage*」에 대한 설명으로 옳지 <u>않은</u> 것은?

① 3인칭 시점이다.
② 주인공 Fleming은 영웅주의에 대한 환상으로 입대를 자원하였다.
③ 사실주의적 서술기법을 사용한다.
④ Stephen Crane이 직접 전투에 참가하여 경험한 것을 바탕으로 썼다.

제1회

01	02	03	04	05	06	07	08	09	10
④	④	④	③	④	①	②	③	③	③
11	12	13	14	15	16	17	18	19	20
①	③	③	③	③	①	①	②	①	③
21	22	23	24	25	26	27	28	29	30
②	③	①	④	②	③	③	②	②	①
31	32	33	34	35	36	37	38	39	40
②	④	④	①	①	②	④	②	②	②

01 정답 ④

Jane Austen은 언니와 함께 평생 미혼으로 지냈다. 27세가 될 무렵 햄프셔의 부유한 지주의 청혼을 받아들인 적이 있으나, 자신이 그를 사랑하지 않음을 깨닫고 그 다음날 약혼을 취소하였다.

02 정답 ④

Darcy는 Elizabeth 모르게 Wickham을 설득하여 Lydia와 결혼식을 올릴 수 있도록 도왔고 모든 비용까지 대주었다.

03 정답 ④

Lady Catherine de Bourgh는 Darcy의 이모이자 재산이 많은 귀족이다. 권위적이고 우월 의식이 있으며, 남의 일에 참견하기를 좋아한다. 딸인 Anne de Bourgh를 Darcy와 결혼시키길 원하지만 Darcy가 오히려 신분이 낮은 Elizabeth와 결혼하려 하자 반대한다.

04 정답 ③

Bennet 가족은 Longbourn에서 살고 있다.
① Pemberley는 Darcy의 저택이다.

05 정답 ④

Edgar Linton은 Thrushcross Grange 저택의 주인으로 Isabella Linton의 오빠이자, Catherine(Cathy) Earnshow의 남편이다. Joseph과 Zillah가 Wuthering Heights 저택에서 일하던 하인들이다.

06 정답 ①

이 소설은 남녀 간의 이루지 못한 사랑에 대한 것으로, 단순히 개인적인 애정뿐만이 아니라 유산분배에 따른 경제적인 문제까지 다루고 있으며, 1, 2대에 걸친 사람들의 비극을 다루고 있다.

07 정답 ②

「*Wuthering Heights*」는 1801년경에 Lockwood 라는 한 신사가 Thrushcross Grange 저택을 빌리고 Wuthering Heights라고 불리는 저택을 방문하는 데서 시작한다. 그는 Earnshaw 가문과 Linton 두 집안의 역사를 아는 늙은 가정부 Nelly에게서 이야기를 듣는다.

08 정답 ③

돈은 이 작품에서 미묘한 가치를 지닌다. 돈은 Herbert Pocket을 돕고, Pip이 감옥에 가지 않도록 해주기도 하지만 위험한 요소를 지닌 대상이다. Charles Dickens는 돈이라는 주제를 통해 진정한 신사는 재산이 아닌 인간적인 신의를 지키고 타인에 대한 믿음을 지키며 성실하게 사는 모습을 통해 이룰 수 있는 것임을 보여주고 있다.

09 정답 ③

ⓐ는 Miss Havisham, ⓑ는 Compeyson, ⓓ는 Bentley Drummle이다. Miss Havisham은 Estella를 남성에 대한 복수의 도구로 사용하고자 한다.

10 정답 ③

Pip이 돌아가신 부모님 묘지 앞에서 울고 있을 때 두 명의 탈옥수를 만난다. 이들은 사기꾼 Compeyson과 Magwitch였다. Pip은 그들로부터 협박을 받아 그들에게 음식을 주고 사슬을 끊을 수 있는 도구를 대장간에서 훔쳐다 주었다.

11 정답 ①

Estella는 결국 Magwitch의 딸로 밝혀진다.

12 정답 ③

① 'Middlemarch'라는 지역의 상점주인, 노동자, 농부, 제조업자, 목수 등의 일상을 다룬 작품이다.
② George Eliot의 첫 장편소설이고 3권으로 이루어졌으며 깊은 인간적인 동정과 엄격한 도덕적 판단이 결합된 내용에 시골풍의 분위기가 풍기는 사실주의 작품이다.
④ Jane Austen의 작품이다.

13 정답 ③

영국 중부의 Raveloe는 비교적 외부의 영향을 받지 않는 조용한 세계였다. George Eliot은 주어진 환경에 순응하며 소박하고 평범한 생활을 즐기는 낙관적 인생 태도를 사랑과 공감으로 묘사한다.

14 정답 ③

George Eliot은 Eppie의 친부 Godfrey와 양부 Marner의 대립을 통해 당대 사회의 부조리함을 비판하고 있다. 결과적으로 고정된 법보다 도덕적 법이 우선되어야 한다는 것이다.

15 정답 ③

Thomas Hardy는 빅토리아 시대에 성에 대한 이중적 잣대의 불합리성과 엄격한 도덕, 종교적 교리에 도전했던 인간상을 작품 속에 그리고 있다. 이외에도 부당한 사회적 인습을 고발하고 있다.

16 정답 ①

총 일곱 부분으로 이루어진 「*Tess of the d'Urbervilles*」의 대국면은 '처녀, 순결을 잃음, 소생, 결과, 여자의 속죄, 개심자, 인과응보'의 순서이다.

17 정답 ①

Tess의 엄마 Joan은 Tess가 아이를 출산한 것을 비밀로 하라고 Tess에게 타이른다.

18 정답 ②

Edgar Allan Poe는 추리소설과 단편소설의 개척자로 프랑스 상징주의 시인들의 엄청난 지지를 받았다. 또한 전세계적으로 인정을 받은 최초의 미국 작가로 평가되고 있다.

19 정답 ①

Edgar Allan Poe는 소설의 배경을 불탄 지하실로 설정하여 암울한 분위기를 조성하였다. 지하실처럼 사방이 격리된 장소는 독자의 관심과 집중 효과를 유발한다.

20 정답 ③

하루는 Pluto가 자신을 피한다는 생각이 들었고 화가 난 화자는 Pluto를 잡는다. Pluto가 자신의 손을 물자 화가 난 화자는 Pluto의 눈 하나를 도려낸다.

21 정답 ②

Pearl은 소설 속에서 활기가 넘치고 제멋대로 뛰어놀다가 달아나버리는 모습들을 보여주면서 종종 '요정'으로 묘사된다.

22 정답 ③

Dr. Chillingworth는 소설 속에서 거머리로 비유된다.

23 정답 ①

세상에 드러난 죄는 주인공 Hester, 세상에 숨겨진 죄는 Arthur Dimmesdale, 용서받지 못할 오만함의 죄는 Roger Chillingworth를 통해 그려지고 있다. Pearl은 악의 씨앗으로 불리지만, 결국 보물 같은 역할을 한다.

24 정답 ④

'A'는 Hester의 능력을 함축하는 'Able'을 함축할 수도 있으며, 마지막 24장에서 다시 'angel and apostle'(천사와 사도)의 상징이 된다.

25 정답 ②

Herman Melville의 「Billy Budd, Sailor」는 산만하고 각 장의 길이가 일정하지 않다. 어조 또한 강건체에서 만연체로 계속 바뀌며, 이는 인생의 본질과 모순을 나타내는 효과를 준다.

26 정답 ③

순수하고 죄 없는 Billy Budd는 모략을 당해 억울하게 죽음을 맞지만 군법회의에서 자신에게 자비심을 베푼 Vere 함장을 축복하며 기꺼이 교수형을 당한다.

27 정답 ③

작가는 Huckleberry Finn을 통하여 문명에 찌들지 않은 원초적인 모습을 그리면서 불평등, 허위, 물질에 대한 집착, 사기 등으로 가득한 당대의 사회를 풍자한다.

28 정답 ②

Huckleberry Finn은 흑인 노예 Jim을 만난다. 이 둘은 함께 홍수에 떠내려 온 뗏목을 타고 Mississippi 강을 따라 자유를 찾아 떠난다. 두 사람은 뗏목을 타고 여행하면서 사기꾼들과 여러 사람들을 만나고 다양한 사건에 휘말리기도 한다.

29 정답 ②

악한소설(picaresque novel)은 주인공이 주로 건달이나 악한이며, 그의 행동과 범행을 중심으로 진행된다. 기사들이 등장하는 환상적인 로맨스나 상류층의 이상주의적 문학에 맞서는 하류층 문학으로, 일종의 모험담의 성격을 가진다.

30 정답 ①

Mark Twain의 「The Adventures of Huckleberry Finn」은 크게 세 부분으로 나뉜다. Huck이 자신과 Tom, Jim을 소개하는 장면, Huck과 Jim이 집과 문명을 떠나서 자연으로 돌아가는 부분, 마지막으로 Huck과 Jim이 Tom의 집으로 돌아오는 부분이다. 각각의 장 안에서 다양하고 흥미진진한 사건들이 전개되는 한편, 이야기의 연속성이 너무 단절되어 있다는 평가를 받는다.

31 정답 ②

Tom은 두 달 전 죽은 Miss Watson이 이미 Jim을 해방시켜 주는 유언을 남겼다는 소식을 밝힌다.

32 정답 ④

Henry James는 그의 지론이라고 할 수 있는 '무의식적인 도덕성'을 작품 속에 교묘히 넣는 고도의 소설기법을 사용하고 있다.

33 정답 ④

Henry James의 소설 주제는 크게 두 가지로 나뉜다. 첫 번째는 미국과 유럽, 그리고 미국인과 유럽인 사이의 복잡·미묘한 관계를 대비시킨 국제상황이라는 주제이며 다른 하나는 인간의 도덕성이다. 그러나 「Washington Square」에서는 국제상황 주제를 다루지 않았다.

34 정답 ①

「The Real Thing」의 주제는 진정한 예술은 허구를 통해 사실을 재현한다는 모순을 보여주는 작품으로, 예술인들의 도덕적 딜레마를 다루고 있다. 또한 이 작품은 작가의 사실주의 작품으로 꼽힌다.

35 정답 ①

예술은 사실 그 자체를 그대로 반영하는 것이 아니라 사실을 어느 정도 변형할 때 가능하다는 것을 주제로 다루고 있다. 이를 통해 예술가들이 처한 도덕적 딜레마를 표현한다.

36 정답 ②

화가인 '나'는 잘생기고 사교적인 'Monarch' 부부가 찾아와 자신들을 모델로 써달라고 부탁한다. 때마침 상류사회에 관한 삽화를 부탁받은 입장이라서 모델로 삼고자 '나'는 부부의 요청을 승낙한다.

37 정답 ④

이 작품은 24장의 짧은 부분들로 구성되어 있다. 주인공 Fleming의 심리상태를 묘사하면서 절망과 희망이 뒤섞인 교차적인 구성을 이루고 있다. 3인칭 서술 시점이지만 사실 Fleming의 시점이기도 하다.

38 정답 ②

Stephen Crane의 『*The Red Badge of Courage*』는 남북전쟁을 주제로 하는 최초의 전쟁소설로 다양한 상징이 사용된다. 그중 wound(상처)는 courage(용기)를 상징한다.

39 정답 ②

Fleming은 죄책감을 느껴 자기 중대와 합류하기가 두려워 숲속으로 도망치는데, 숲속에서 나무에 기대어 앉은 채 죽은 병사를 목격한다.

40 정답 ②

Henry는 전투의 상황에서 나는 왜 여기(전투 현장)에 있는지에 대한 생각을 한다.

제2회

01	02	03	04	05	06	07	08	09	10
③	④	④	③	④	③	③	③	③	④
11	12	13	14	15	16	17	18	19	20
④	③	②	①	②	③	④	②	②	②
21	22	23	24	25	26	27	28	29	30
②	④	①	③	①	③	②	③	③	③
31	32	33	34	35	36	37	38	39	40
④	③	③	③	②	②	③	①	③	④

01 정답 ③

「Pride and Prejudice」 소설의 첫 시작은 "'상당한 재산을 가진 독신 남성이라면 틀림없이 아내를 찾고 있을 것이다'라는 말은 보편적인 진리이다."라는 유명한 명대사로 시작된다.

02 정답 ④

소설 속 저택이나 토지는 소유주의 내적 가치의 반영이다.

03 정답 ④

Wickham은 자신의 경제적 권리를 Darcy가 박탈했으며 그 이유로 인하여 자신이 지금 가난한 군인에 머물러 있다고 말한다. Elizabeth는 이 말을 듣고 Darcy에 대해 더욱 안 좋은 편견을 갖게 된다.

04 정답 ③

Bennet 가족이 거주하는 지역은 Longbourn이다.
① Pemberley는 Darcy의 저택이다.
④ Netherfield는 Bingley가 이사 온 곳이다.

05 정답 ④

작가는 절제되고 농축된 서술 기법을 일관적으로 사용하였다.

06 정답 ③

본 소설의 인물은 크게 두 가지 유형으로 나뉜다. 하나는 강인하고 정열적이며 격렬한 인간형인 Wuthering Heights형이고, 다른 하나는 Thrushcross Grange형으로 수동적이고 교양적이며 조용한 인간형이다.

07 정답 ③

Emily Brontë는 Yorkshire의 작은 마을의 목사관에서 살았다. 이곳의 한쪽은 Yorkshire의 황량한 황무지이고, 다른 쪽은 교구의 무덤이 존재했는데, 바로 Emily Brontë의 문학적 상상력의 바탕이 되는 곳이라고 할 수 있다.

08 정답 ③

Heathcliff와 황야를 맨발로 헤매는 모습과 귀부인의 속성 두 가지를 모두 보여준다.

09 정답 ③

작가는 재산이 없다가 갑자기 생기면 사람이 어떻게 변하는가를 관찰한 후 인간적 의미를 찾도록 한다.

10 정답 ④

런던에서 Pip은 허영을 부리며 속물적인 인간이 되어가고, 매형인 Joe가 그를 찾아왔을 때 당황하면서 반갑게 맞이하지 않는다.

11 정답 ④

Estella는 어리석은 신사들이 모이는 '숲속의 방울새' 그룹 중에서도 가장 둔한 인물인 Drummle과 결혼한다. Drummle은 우둔하고 퉁명스러운 성격의 소유자로, Estella와 사랑이 없는 결혼을 하고 몇 년 후 죽는다.
① Compeyson은 Miss Havisham의 결혼식 날에 신부를 배반하고 나타나지 않은 남자이다. 교육을 받은 좋은 인물이지만 심성이 악한 사기꾼이다.
③ Herbert는 Miss Havisham의 조카로, Pip과 친한 친구가 된다. Pip과는 나이가 비슷한 친구로, 서로 인생의 협력자가 된다.

12 정답 ③

Miss Havisham은 Satis House에서 발생한 화재로 죽고 Satis House는 폐허가 된다.

13 정답 ②

Marner가 심장병과 몸이 붓는 병으로 고통받는 Sally Oates를 보고 동정심이 생기면서 약초에 대한 지식을 토대로 그녀의 병을 치료하는데 그의 약초에 대한 지식은 그의 어머니로부터 배운 것이었다.

14 정답 ①

Silas는 Lantern Yard 교회에서 신앙심을 인정받던 청년이었으나, 돈을 훔쳤다는 누명을 쓰고 신(God)이 자신의 누명을 벗겨주실 거라 믿지만 그의 믿음은 이루어지지 않는다. 이 사건 이후로 Silas는 신에 대한 불신과 인간에 대한 실망감을 돈으로 보상받고자 일에만 집중한다.

15 정답 ②

Molly는 사람들에게 자신이 Godfrey와 결혼한 사이라는 것을 알리고 싶어서 새해 축하 댄스에 가려 했지만 아편과 술 중독으로 길에서 얼어 죽는다.

16 정답 ③

Godfrey는 과거에 저지른 죄를 숨길 수 없다는 것을 깨닫고 뒤늦게나마 그는 아내에게 Eppie가 친딸이라고 밝히고 과거의 죄를 뉘우치려고 Marner의 집에 찾아간다. 그는 Eppie를 딸로 인정하고 자기 집에서 함께 살자고 Eppie에게 제안하지만, Eppie는 Marner 외에 다른 아버지를 상상할 수 없다며 단호히 Godfrey의 제안을 거절한다.

17 정답 ④

개인의 계급 신분이 불안정하였다.

18 정답 ②

Tess와 Angel은 May Day dance에서 서로 처음 만나 눈길을 주고받지만, 술에 취한 Tess의 아버지가 소란을 피우며 값비싼 마차를 타고 집에 가는 모습을 보고 Tess는 창피해 하며 서둘러 집에 간다.

19 정답 ②

Alec은 Angel의 아버지 Clare 목사의 복음으로 개심자(convert)가 되어 열정적인 설교가의 모습으로 변화한 듯 보인다. 그러나 그가 Tess를 본 순간 그는 종교적 태도를 버리고 Tess에게 결혼하자는 제안을 한다.

20 정답 ②

Tess의 아버지 John과 어머니 Joan Durbeyfield는 몹시 가난하여 돈이 필요했기 때문에 Tess가 d'Urberville가(家)와 친해지길 바라며 그곳에서 일을 하도록 보낸다. 그곳에서 Tess는 Alec d'Urberville의 제안으로 어쩔 수 없이 새들을 돌보는 일을 한다.

21 정답 ②

소설의 화자는 Pluto라는 고양이 외에도 새, 금붕어, 개, 토끼, 원숭이 등의 애완동물을 길렀으나 그의 분노와 폭력성으로 동물들을 학대한다. 소설에 등장하는 동물들은 화자의 가학적인 충동을 드러내는 대상이 된다.

22 정답 ④

Pluto는 고양이의 이름이자 그리스 신화의 명부(冥府)의 신의 이름으로 화자의 감정 변화로 결국 죽음에 이른다.

23 정답 ①

고양이의 빨간 입술은 죽은 부인의 아름다움을, 고양이의 눈은 주인공의 양심을 괴롭히고 공포로 전개된다.

24 정답 ③

1840년 25편의 단편을 엮어 출판한『Tales of the Grotesque and Arabesque』는 판매량도 저조하였을 뿐 아니라 비평가들의 주목도 받지 못했다.

25 정답 ①

화자는 폐허가 된 세일럼 세관(Salem Custom House)의 다락방에서 약 200년 전 세관감정관인 Jonathan Pue가 쓴 Hester Prynne에 관한 글을 발견한다. 청교도 조상들과 미국 역사에 관심을 가지고 있었던 그는 이 내용을 바탕으로 글(로맨스)을 쓰기로 한다.

26 정답 ③

Dimmesdale은 Hester와 Pearl을 불러 교수대로 올라가더니, 수많은 청중들 앞에서 가슴을 헤치고 자신의 죄를 고백한 뒤 그 자리에서 죽는다. 이 모습을 본 사람들은 그를 더욱 존경한다.

27 정답 ②

「The Scarlet Letter」는 청교도의 경직된 사회분위기에서 자신의 존재를 숨긴 채 복수를 꿈꾸는 Chillingworth와 양심의 가책으로 괴로워하는 Dimmesdale의 구원을 다루고 있다. 죄인으로 여겨지던 Hester는 결국 구원자의 모습으로 변화된다.

28 정답 ③

Hester는 고향인 영국에서 나이 차이가 많이 나는 Chillingworth와 결혼한 후, 암스테르담(Amsterdam)에서 그와 함께 살다가 그의 제안으로 먼저 보스턴으로 이주하였다,

29 정답 ③

고아 출신의 21살 흑인 미남 해병인 Billy Budd 는 교육받지 못한 브리스톨(Bristol) 출신이지만 다른 선원들에게 항상 모범이 될 만큼 죄 없고 순진무구한 청년으로서 Bellipotent에서 'Baby' 라는 별명으로 불린다.

30 정답 ③

Billy는 마지막으로 "Vere 함장님께 하느님의 가호가 있기를!"(Good bless Captain Vere!)이 라는 말을 남기고, 주변인들의 동정심과 연민을 받으며 처형당한다. Billy가 Vere 함장을 연민 의 시선으로 바라보는 이 장면은 공정하지 못한 삶과 모순으로 뒤엉킨 사회에서 부조리한 인간 의 삶을 향한 연민의 표현이다.

31 정답 ④

Claggart는 Billy를 파멸시키고자 Billy가 반란 을 일으키려 한다는 누명을 씌움으로써 그를 파 멸시키려 한다.

32 정답 ③

Billy Budd는 대영 제국의 74포전함(seventy-four) H. M. S. Bellipotent의 앞 돛대 망루병 (foretopman)으로 강제 징집된 고아 출신의 21 살 흑인 미남 해병이다.

33 정답 ③

주인공 Huck은 교육과 문명을 받아들이려 하지 않는 인물이다.

34 정답 ③

Jim이 오하이오(Ohio) 강을 가려고 한 이유는 오하이오 주가 노예제가 없는 지역이고, 그에게 는 그곳이 자유를 상징하기 때문이다.

35 정답 ②

소설의 시작 부분에서 Huck. Jim, Tom은 미주 리주 세인트피터즈버그(St. Petersburg)에서 살 고 있다.

36 정답 ②

Catherine은 자신의 사촌 여동생 Marian의 약혼 축하 연회에서 Morris Townsend를 처음 만나 게 된다.

37 정답 ③

「*The Real Thing*」은 역할에 알맞은 진짜 인물 이 화가에게는 오히려 방해물이 된다는 것을 보 여줌으로써 진정한 예술은 허구를 통하여 재현 된다는 모순을 담고 있다.

38 정답 ①

Henry James 소설의 지배적인 주제는 미국과 유럽, 그리고 미국인과 유럽인 사이의 복잡하고 미묘한 관계를 대비시키는 국제 주제이며, 이 국 제 주제와 깊은 관련성을 가진 도덕성에 대한 주제이다.

39 정답 ③

「*The Red Badge of Courage*」는 남북전쟁을 최초로 다룬 사실주의적 작품이다.

40 정답 ④

Stephen Crane이 직접 전투에 참가한 적은 없다. 그러나 전투에 참가한 경험이 있었던 자신의 형으로부터 들은 군대생활을 바탕으로 실제 전투 장면을 실감나게 재현했다.

여기서 멈출 거예요? 곁에가 바로 눈앞에 있어요.
마지막 한 걸음까지 SD에듀가 함께할게요!

독학학위제 2단계 전공기초과정인정시험 답안지(객관식)

★ 수험생은 수험번호와 응시과목 코드번호를 표기(마킹)한 후 일치여부를 반드시 확인할 것.

전공분야

성 명

수험번호

(1) 2 — — — —

(2) ① ● ③ ④

과목코드 / 응시과목

교시코드 ① ② ③ ④

응시과목			
1 ① ② ③ ④	21 ① ② ③ ④
2 ① ② ③ ④	22 ① ② ③ ④
3 ① ② ③ ④	23 ① ② ③ ④
4 ① ② ③ ④	24 ① ② ③ ④
5 ① ② ③ ④	25 ① ② ③ ④
6 ① ② ③ ④	26 ① ② ③ ④
7 ① ② ③ ④	27 ① ② ③ ④
8 ① ② ③ ④	28 ① ② ③ ④
9 ① ② ③ ④	29 ① ② ③ ④
10 ① ② ③ ④	30 ① ② ③ ④
11 ① ② ③ ④	31 ① ② ③ ④
12 ① ② ③ ④	32 ① ② ③ ④
13 ① ② ③ ④	33 ① ② ③ ④
14 ① ② ③ ④	34 ① ② ③ ④
15 ① ② ③ ④	35 ① ② ③ ④
16 ① ② ③ ④	36 ① ② ③ ④
17 ① ② ③ ④	37 ① ② ③ ④
18 ① ② ③ ④	38 ① ② ③ ④
19 ① ② ③ ④	39 ① ② ③ ④
20 ① ② ③ ④	40 ① ② ③ ④

과목코드 / 응시과목

교시코드 ① ② ③ ④

응시과목			
1 ① ② ③ ④	21 ① ② ③ ④
2 ① ② ③ ④	22 ① ② ③ ④
3 ① ② ③ ④	23 ① ② ③ ④
4 ① ② ③ ④	24 ① ② ③ ④
5 ① ② ③ ④	25 ① ② ③ ④
6 ① ② ③ ④	26 ① ② ③ ④
7 ① ② ③ ④	27 ① ② ③ ④
8 ① ② ③ ④	28 ① ② ③ ④
9 ① ② ③ ④	29 ① ② ③ ④
10 ① ② ③ ④	30 ① ② ③ ④
11 ① ② ③ ④	31 ① ② ③ ④
12 ① ② ③ ④	32 ① ② ③ ④
13 ① ② ③ ④	33 ① ② ③ ④
14 ① ② ③ ④	34 ① ② ③ ④
15 ① ② ③ ④	35 ① ② ③ ④
16 ① ② ③ ④	36 ① ② ③ ④
17 ① ② ③ ④	37 ① ② ③ ④
18 ① ② ③ ④	38 ① ② ③ ④
19 ① ② ③ ④	39 ① ② ③ ④
20 ① ② ③ ④	40 ① ② ③ ④

※ 감독관 확인란

(인)

관 리 번 호 (연번) (응시자수)

답안지 작성시 유의사항

1. 답안지는 반드시 컴퓨터용 사인펜을 사용하여 다음 예와 같이 표기할 것.
   예) 잘된표기: ● 잘못된표기: ⊗ ⊙ ○ ◑
2. 수험번호 (1)에는 아라비아 숫자로 쓰고, (2)에는 "●"와 같이 표기할 것.
3. 과목코드는 뒷면 "과목코드번호"를 보고 해당과목의 코드번호를 찾아 표기하고,
   응시과목란에는 응시과목명을 한글로 기재할 것.
4. 교시코드는 문제지 전면의 교시를 해당란에 "●"와 같이 표기할 것.
5. 한번 표기한 답은 긁거나 수정액 및 스티커 등 어떠한 방법으로도 고쳐서는
   아니되고, 고친 문항은 "0"점 처리함.

독학학위제 2단계 전공기초과정인정시험 답안지(객관식)

★ 수험생은 수험번호와 응시과목 코드번호를 표기(마킹)한 후 일치여부를 반드시 확인할 것.

컴퓨터용 사인펜만 사용

전공분야

성   명

답안지 작성시 유의사항

1. 답안지는 반드시 컴퓨터용 사인펜을 사용하여 다음 *보기*와 같이 표기할 것.
   보기 잘 된 표기: ● 잘못된 표기: ⊗ ⊗ ⊙ ⊙ ○ ◑ ●
2. 수험번호 (1)에는 아라비아 숫자로 쓰고, (2)에는 "●"와 같이 표기할 것.
3. 과목코드는 "과목코드번호"를 보고 해당과목의 코드번호를 찾아 표기하고,
   응시과목란에는 응시과목명을 한글로 기재할 것.
4. 교시코드는 문제지 전면 의 교시를 해당란에 "●"와 같이 표기할 것.
5. 한번 표기한 답은 긁거나 수정액 및 스티커 등 어떠한 방법으로도 고쳐서는
   아니되고, 고친 문항은 "0"점 처리함.

[이 답안지는 마킹연습용 모의답안지입니다.]

독학학위제 2단계 전공기초과정인정시험 답안지(객관식)

컴퓨터용 사인펜만 사용

★ 수험생은 수험번호와 응시과목 코드번호를 표기(마킹)한 후 일치여부를 반드시 확인할 것.

전공분야

성명

(1)
(2)

수 험 번 호

2							

※ 감독관 확인란

(인)

관 리 번 호

(응시자수)
(여번)

답안지 작성 시 유의사항

1. 답안지는 반드시 컴퓨터용 사인펜을 사용하여 다음 보기와 같이 표기할 것.
   보기) 잘된 표기: ● 잘못된 표기: ⊘ ⊗ ◑ ◐ ○ ●
2. 수험번호 (1)에는 아라비아 숫자로 쓰고, (2)에는 "●"와 같이 표기할 것.
3. 과목코드는 뒷면 "과목코드번호"를 보고 해당과목의 코드번호를 찾아 표기하고,
   응시과목란에는 응시과목명을 한글로 기재할 것.
4. 교시코드는 문제지 전면의 교시를 해당란에 "●"와 같이 표기할 것.
5. 한번 표기한 답은 긁거나 수정액 및 스티커 등 어떠한 방법으로도 고쳐서는
   아니되고, 고친 문항은 "0"점 처리함.

과목코드

교시코드

응시과목					응시과목				
1	①	②	③	④	21	①	②	③	④
2	①	②	③	④	22	①	②	③	④
3	①	②	③	④	23	①	②	③	④
4	①	②	③	④	24	①	②	③	④
5	①	②	③	④	25	①	②	③	④
6	①	②	③	④	26	①	②	③	④
7	①	②	③	④	27	①	②	③	④
8	①	②	③	④	28	①	②	③	④
9	①	②	③	④	29	①	②	③	④
10	①	②	③	④	30	①	②	③	④
11	①	②	③	④	31	①	②	③	④
12	①	②	③	④	32	①	②	③	④
13	①	②	③	④	33	①	②	③	④
14	①	②	③	④	34	①	②	③	④
15	①	②	③	④	35	①	②	③	④
16	①	②	③	④	36	①	②	③	④
17	①	②	③	④	37	①	②	③	④
18	①	②	③	④	38	①	②	③	④
19	①	②	③	④	39	①	②	③	④
20	①	②	③	④	40	①	②	③	④

[이 답안지는 마킹연습용 모의답안지입니다.]

절취선

독학학위제 2단계 전공기초과정인정시험 답안지(객관식)

★ 수험생은 수험번호와 응시과목 코드번호를 반드시 확인할 것.

컴퓨터용 사인펜만 사용

★ 수험생은 수험번호와 응시과목 코드번호를 표기(마킹)한 후 일치여부를 반드시 확인할 것.

전공분야

성명

수	험	번	호					

| (1) | 2 | ① ● ③ ④ |
| (2) | | |

응시과목

과목코드

교시코드

답안지 작성시 유의사항

1. 답안지는 반드시 컴퓨터용 사인펜을 사용하여 다음 보기와 같이 표기할 것.
   보기 정된 표기: ● 잘못된 표기: ⊘ ⊗ ● ⊙ ◑ ○●
2. 수험번호 (1)에는 아라비아 숫자로 쓰고, (2)에는 "●"와 같이 표기할 것.
3. 과목코드는 "응시과목"란의 해당과목의 코드번호를 찾아 표기하고,
   응시과목란에는 응시과목명을 한글로 기재할 것.
4. 교시코드는 문제지 전면의 교시를 해당란에 "●"와 같이 표기할 것.
5. 한번 표기한 답은 긁거나 수정액 및 스티커 등 어떠한 방법으로도 고쳐서는
   아니되고, 고친 문항은 "0"점 처리함.

※ 감독관 확인란

(인)

관 리 번 호

(응시자수)

(연번)

적취서

[이 답안지는 마킹연습용 모의답안지입니다.]

참고문헌

1. 김보원 · 윤미선, 『영국소설의 이해』, 한국방송통신대학교출판문화원, 2018.
2. 근대영미소설학회, 『19세기 영국소설 강의』, 민음사, 1998.
3. 근대영미소설학회, 『19세기 미국소설 강의』, 신아사, 2003.
4. 바나드 · 로버트, 김용수 옮김, 『영문학사』, 한신문화사, 1998.
5. 영미문학연구회, 『영미문학의 길잡이1-영국문학』, 창비, 2007.
6. 영미문학연구회, 『영미문학의 길잡이2-미국문학과 비평이론』, 창비, 2016.
7. 정진농 · 정해룡, 『영문학이란 무엇인가』, 한신문화사, 1999.
8. 제임스 · 캘로우 등, 박영의 등 옮김, 『미국문학개관 1, 2』, 한신문화사, 1997.

여기서 멈출 거예요? 그치가 바로 눈앞에 있어요.
마지막 한 걸음까지 SD에듀가 함께할게요!

좋은 책을 만드는 길
독자님과 함께하겠습니다.

도서나 동영상에 궁금한 점, 아쉬운 점, 만족스러운 점이
있으시다면 어떤 의견이라도 말씀해 주세요.
SD에듀는 독자님의 의견을 모아 더 좋은 책으로 보답하겠습니다.

www.sdedu.co.kr

SD에듀 독학사 영어영문학과 2단계 19세기 영미소설

초 판 발 행	2023년 01월 25일 (인쇄 2022년 10월 14일)
발 행 인	박영일
책 임 편 집	이해욱
편 저	서지윤
편 집 진 행	송영진 · 양희정
표지디자인	박종우
편집디자인	차성미 · 장성복
발 행 처	(주)시대고시기획
출 판 등 록	제10-1521호
주 소	서울시 마포구 큰우물로 75 [도화동 538 성지 B/D] 9F
전 화	1600-3600
팩 스	02-701-8823
홈 페 이 지	www.sdedu.co.kr
I S B N	979-11-383-3142-5 (13840)
정 가	25,000원

SD에듀 **독학사**

영어영문학과

왜? 독학사 영어영문학과인가?

4년제 영어영문학과 학위를 최소 시간과 비용으로 단 1년 만에 초고속 합격 가능!

1 현대인에게 필수 외국어라 할 수 있는 영어의 체계적인 **학습에 적합**

2 토익, 토플, 텝스, 新텝스, 지텔프, 플렉스 등 공무원/군무원 시험 **대체검정능력시험 준비에 유리**

3 일반 기업 및 외국계 기업, 교육계, 언론계, 출판계, 번역·통역, 관광·항공 등 다양한 분야 **취업 진출**

영어영문학과 과정별 시험과목(2~4과정)

1~2과정 교양 및 전공기초 과정은 객관식 40문제 구성
3~4과정 전공심화 및 학위취득 과정은 객관식 24문제+**주관식 4문제** 구성

2과정(전공기초)		3과정(전공심화)		4과정(학위취득)
영어학개론	>	영어발달사[근간]	>	영미문학개관[근간]
영문법		고급영문법[근간]		영어학개론[근간]
영국문학개관		미국문학개관[근간]		고급영어[근간]
중급영어		고급영어[근간]		영미소설[근간]
19세기 영미소설		20세기 영미소설[근간]		
19세기 영미시[근간]		20세기 영미시[근간]		

SD에듀 영어영문학과 학습 커리큘럼

기본이론부터 실전 문제풀이 훈련까지!
SD에듀가 제시하는 각 과정별 최적화된 커리큘럼 따라 학습해보세요.

기본이론
핵심 이론 분석으로
확실한 개념 이해
Step 01

문제풀이
실전예상문제를
통해 실전 문제에 적용
Step 02

모의고사
최종모의고사로
실전 감각 키우기
Step 03

─── 독학사 2~4과정 영어영문학과 신간 교재 ───

독학학위제 출제내용을 100% 반영한 내용과 문제로 구성된 완벽한 최신 기본서 라인업!

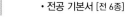

START

2과정

• 전공 기본서 [전 6종]
 – 영어학개론 /
  영문법 /
  영국문학개관 /
  중급영어 /
  19세기 영미소설 /
  19세기 영미시(근간)

• 전공 기본서 [전 6종]
 – 영어발달사(근간) /
  고급영문법(근간) /
  미국문학개관(근간) /
  고급영어(근간) /
  20세기 영미소설(근간) /
  20세기 영미시(근간)

3과정

4과정

• 전공 기본서 [전 4종]
 – 영미문학개관(근간) /
  영어학개론(근간) /
  고급영어(근간) /
  영미소설(근간)

GOAL!

※ 표지 이미지 및 구성은 변경될 수 있습니다.

➕ **독학사 전문컨설턴트가 개인별 맞춤형 학습플랜을 제공해 드립니다.** ─────

SD에듀 홈페이지 **www.sdedu.co.kr** 상담문의 **1600-3600** 평일 9~18시 · 토요일 · 공휴일 휴무

나는 이렇게 합격했다

여러분의 힘든 노력이 기억될 수 있도록
당신의 합격 스토리를 들려주세요.

합격생 인터뷰
상품권 증정

추첨을 통해
선물 증정

베스트 리뷰자 1등
아이패드 증정

베스트 리뷰자 2등
에어팟 증정

SD에듀 합격생이 전하는 합격 노하우

"기초 없는 저도 합격했어요
여러분도 가능해요."
검정고시 합격생 이*주

"불안하시다고요?
SD에듀와 나 자신을 믿으세요."
소방직 합격생 이*화

"강의를 듣다 보니
자연스럽게 합격했어요."
사회복지직 합격생 곽*수

"선생님 감사합니다.
제 인생의 최고의 선생님입니다."
G-TELP 합격생 김*진

"시험에 꼭 필요한 것만 딱딱!
SD에듀 인강 추천합니다."
물류관리사 합격생 이*환

"시작과 끝은 SD에듀와 함께!
SD에듀를 선택한 건 최고의 선택"
경비지도사 합격생 박*익

합격을 진심으로 축하드립니다!

합격수기 작성 / 인터뷰 신청

QR코드 스캔하고 ▷ ▷ ▷ ▶
이벤트 참여하여 푸짐한 경품받자!

합격의 공식 시대에듀
SD에듀